The Chrestomanci Quartet

Other Books by Diana Wynne Jones

Archer's Goon
Aunt Maria
Believing Is Seeing: Seven Stories
Castle in the Air
Changeover
The Dalemark Quartet
  Book 1: Cart and Cwidder
  Book 2: Drowned Ammet
  Book 3: The Spellcoats
  Book 4: The Crown of Dalemark
Dark Lord of Derkholm
Deep Secret
Dogsbody
Eight Days of Luke
Everard's Ride
Fire and Hemlock
Hexwood
Hidden Turnings: A Collection of Stories Through Time and Space
The Homeward Bounders
Howl's Moving Castle
Minor Arcana
The Ogre Downstairs
Power of Three
Stopping for a Spell
A Sudden Wild Magic
A Tale of Time City
The Time of the Ghost
The Tough Guide to Fantasyland
Warlock at the Wheel and Other Stories
Witch's Business
Year of the Griffin
Yes, Dear

The Chrestomanci Quartet

Charmed Life
Witch Week
The Magicians of Caprona
The Lives of Christopher Chant

DIANA WYNNE JONES

SFBC FANTASY

This is a work of fiction. All the characters and events portrayed in these novels are either fictitious or are used fictitiously.

First SFBC Fantasy printing: December 2000.

Published by arrangement with William Morrow and Company, a division of HarperCollins*Publishers*
1350 Avenue of the Americas
New York, NY 10019

Visit The SFBC at *http://www.sfbc.com*

ISBN # 0-7394-1439-9

PRINTED IN THE UNITED STATES OF AMERICA.

Contents

CHARMED LIFE

FOR CLAIRE,
NICHOLAS,
AND FRANCES

CHAPTER 1

Cat Chant admired his elder sister Gwendolen. She was a witch. He admired her and he clung to her. Great changes came about in their lives and left him no one else to cling to.

The first great change came about when their parents took them out for a day trip down the river in a paddle steamer. They set out in great style, Gwendolen and her mother in white dresses with ribbons, Cat and his father in prickly blue-serge Sunday suits. It was a hot day. The steamer was crammed with other people in holiday clothes, talking, laughing, eating whelks with thin slices of white bread and butter, while the paddleboat steam organ wheezed out popular tunes so that no one could hear themselves talk.

In fact the steamer was too crowded and too old. Something went wrong with the steering. The whole laughing, whelk-eating, Sunday-dressed crowd was swept away in the current from the dam. They hit one of the posts which were supposed to stop people being swept away, and the paddle steamer, being old, simply broke into pieces. Cat remembered the organ playing and the paddles beating the blue sky. Clouds of steam screamed from broken pipes and drowned the screams from the crowd, as every single person aboard was swept away through the dam. It was a terrible accident. The papers called it the Saucy Nancy Disaster. The ladies in their clinging skirts were quite unable to swim. The men in tight blue serge were very little better off. But Gwendolen was a witch, so she could not drown. And Cat, who flung his arms around Gwendolen when the boat hit the post, survived too. There were very few other survivors.

The whole country was shocked by it. The paddleboat company and the town of Wolvercote between them paid for the funerals. Gwendolen and Cat were given heavy black clothes at public expense, and rode behind the procession of hearses in a carriage pulled by black horses with black plumes on their heads. The other survivors rode with them. Cat looked at them and wondered if they were witches and warlocks, but he never found out. The Mayor of Wolvercote had set up a Fund for the survivors. Money poured in from all over the country. All the other survivors took their share and went away to start new lives elsewhere. Only Cat and Gwendolen were left and, since nobody could discover any of their relations, they stayed in Wolvercote.

They became celebrities for a time. Everyone was very kind. Everyone said what beautiful little orphans they were. It was true. They were both fair and pale, with blue eyes, and looked good in black. Gwendolen was very pretty, and tall for her age. Cat was small for his age. Gwendolen was very motherly to Cat, and people were touched. Cat did not mind. It made up a little for the empty, lost way he was feeling. Ladies gave him cake and toys. Town Councillors came and asked how he was getting on; and the Mayor called and patted him on the head. The Mayor explained that the money from the Fund was being put into a Trust for them until they were grown up. Meanwhile, the town would pay for their education and upbringing.

"And where would you little people like to live?" he asked kindly.

Gwendolen at once said that old Mrs. Sharp downstairs had offered to take them in. "She's been ever so kind to us," she explained. "We'd love to live with her."

Mrs. Sharp had been very kind. She was a witch too—the printed sign in her parlor window said *Certified Witch*—and interested in Gwendolen. The Mayor was a little dubious. Like all people who had no talent for witchcraft, he did not approve of those who had. He asked Cat how he felt about Gwendolen's plan. Cat did not mind. He preferred living in the house he was used to, even if it was downstairs. Since the Mayor felt that the two orphans ought to be made as happy as possible, he agreed. Gwendolen and Cat moved in with Mrs. Sharp.

Looking back on it, Cat supposed that it was from this time on that he was certain Gwendolen was a witch. He had not been sure before. When he had asked his parents, they had shaken their heads, sighed, and looked unhappy. Cat had been puzzled, because he remembered the terrible trouble there had been when Gwendolen gave him cramps. He could not see how his parents could blame Gwendolen for it unless she truly was a witch. But all that was changed now. Mrs. Sharp made no secret of it.

"You've a real talent for magic, dearie," she said, beaming at Gwendolen, "and I wouldn't be doing my duty by you if I let it go to waste.

We must see about a teacher for you right away. You could do worse than go to Mr. Nostrum next door for a start. He may be the worst necromancer in town, but he knows how to teach. He'll give you a good grounding, my love."

Mr. Nostrum's charges for teaching magic turned out to be £1 an hour for the Elementary Grades, and a guinea an hour for the Advanced Grades beyond. Rather expensive, as Mrs. Sharp said. She put on her best hat with black beads and ran around to the Town Hall to see if the Fund would pay for Gwendolen's lessons.

To her annoyance, the Mayor refused. He told Mrs. Sharp that witchcraft was not part of an ordinary education. Mrs. Sharp came back rattling the beads on her hat with irritation, and carrying a flat cardboard box the Mayor had given her, full of the odds and ends the kind ladies had cleared out of Gwendolen's parents' bedroom.

"Blind prejudice!" Mrs. Sharp said, dumping the box on the kitchen table. "If a person has a gift, they have a right to have it developed—and so I told him! But don't worry, dearie," she said, seeing that Gwendolen was looking decidedly stormy. "There's a way around everything. Mr. Nostrum would teach you for nothing, if we found the right thing to tempt him with. Let's have a look in this box. Your poor Ma and Pa may have left something that might be just the thing."

Accordingly, Mrs. Sharp turned the box out onto the table. It was a queer collection of things—letters and lace and souvenirs. Cat did not remember having seen half of them before. There was a marriage certificate, saying that Francis John Chant had married Caroline Mary Chant twelve years ago at St. Margaret's Church, Wolvercote, and a withered nosegay his mother must have carried at the wedding. Underneath that, he found some glittery earrings he had never seen his mother wear.

Mrs. Sharp's hat rattled as she bent swiftly over these. "Those are diamond earrings!" she said. "Your Ma must have had money! Now, if I took those to Mr. Nostrum—But we'd get more for them if I took them around to Mr. Larkins." Mr. Larkins kept the junk shop on the corner of the street—except that it was not always exactly junk. Among the brass fenders and chipped crockery you could find quite valuable things, and also a discreet notice saying *Exotic Supplies*—which meant that Mr. Larkins also stocked bats' wings, dried newts, and other ingredients of magic. There was no question that Mr. Larkins would be very interested in a pair of diamond earrings. Mrs. Sharp's eyes pouched up, greedy and beady, as she put out her hand to pick up the earrings.

Gwendolen put out her hand for them at the same moment. She did not say anything. Neither did Mrs. Sharp. Both their hands stood still in the air. There was a feeling of fierce invisible struggle. Then Mrs. Sharp took her hand away. "Thank you," Gwendolen said coldly, and put the earrings away in the pocket of her black dress.

"You see what I mean?" Mrs. Sharp said, making the best of it. "You have real talent, dearie!" She went back to sorting the other things in the box. She turned over an old pipe, ribbons, a spray of white heather, menus, concert tickets, and picked up a bundle of old letters. She ran her thumb down the edge of it. "Love letters," she said. "His to her." She put the bundle down without looking at it and picked up another. "Hers to him. No use." Cat, watching Mrs. Sharp's broad mauve thumb whirring down a third bundle of letters, thought that being a witch must save a great deal of time. "Business letters," said Mrs. Sharp. Her thumb paused, and went slowly back up the pile again. "Now what have we here?" she said. She untied the pink tape from around the bundle and carefully took out three letters. She unfolded them.

"Chrestomanci!" she exclaimed. And, as soon as she said it, she clapped one hand over her mouth and mumbled behind it. Her face was red. Cat could see she was surprised, frightened, and greedy, all at the same time. "Now what was *he* doing writing to your Pa?" she said, as soon as she had recovered.

"Let's see," said Gwendolen.

Mrs. Sharp spread the three letters out on the kitchen table, and Gwendolen and Cat bent over them. The first thing that struck Cat was the energy of the signature on all three:

The next thing he saw was that two of the letters were written in the same energetic writing as the signature. The first was dated twelve years ago, soon after his parents had been married. It said:

Dear Frank,

Now don't get on your high horse. I only offered because I thought it might help. I still will *help, in any way I can, if you let me know what I can do. I feel you have a claim on me.*

Yrs ever,

Chrestomanci

The second letter was shorter:

Dear Chant,
The same to you. Go to blazes.
Chrestomanci

The third letter was dated six years ago, and it was written by someone else. Chrestomanci had only signed it.

Sir,
You were warned six years ago that something like what you relate might come to pass, and you made it quite clear that you wished for no help from this quarter. We are not interested in your troubles. Nor is this a charitable institution.
Chrestomanci

"What did your Pa *say* to him?" Mrs. Sharp wondered, curious and awestruck. "Well—what do you think, dearie?"

Gwendolen held her hands spread out above the letters, rather as if she was warming them at a fire. Both her little fingers twitched. "I don't know. They feel important—especially the first one and the last one—awfully important."

"Who's Chrestomanci?" Cat asked. It was a hard name to say. He said it in pieces, trying to remember the way Mrs. Sharp had said it: KREST-OH-MAN-SEE. "Is that the right way?"

"Yes, that's right—and never you mind who he is, my love," said Mrs. Sharp. "And important's a weak word for it, dearie. I wish I knew what your Pa had *said.* Something not many people'd dare say, by the sound of it. And look what he got in return! Three genuine signatures! Mr. Nostrum would give his eyes for those, dearie. Oh, you're in luck! He'll teach you for those all right! So would any necromancer in the country."

Gleefully, Mrs. Sharp began packing the things away in the box again. "What have we here?" A little red book of matches had fallen out of the bundle of business letters. Mrs. Sharp took it up carefully and, quite as carefully, opened it. It was less than half full of flimsy cardboard matches. But three of the matches had been burnt, without being torn out of the book first. The third one along was so very burnt that Cat supposed it must have set light to the other two.

"Hm," said Mrs. Sharp. "I think you'd better keep this, dearie." She passed the little red book to Gwendolen, who put it in the pocket of her dress along with the earrings. "And what about you having this, my love?" Mrs. Sharp said to Cat, remembering that he had a claim too.

She gave him the spray of white heather. Cat wore it in his buttonhole until it fell to pieces.

Living with Mrs. Sharp, Gwendolen seemed to expand. Her hair seemed brighter gold, her eyes deeper blue, and her whole manner was glad and confident. Perhaps Cat contracted a little to make room for her—he did not know. Not that he was unhappy. Mrs. Sharp was quite as kind to him as she was to Gwendolen. Town Councillors and their wives called several times a week and patted him on the head in the parlor. They sent him and Gwendolen to the best school in Wolvercote. Cat was happy there. The only drawback was that Cat was left-handed, and schoolmasters always punished him if they caught him writing with his left hand. But they did that at all the schools Cat had been to, and he was used to it. He had dozens of friends. All the same, at the heart of everything, he felt lost and lonely. So he clung to Gwendolen, because she was the only family he had.

Gwendolen was often rather impatient with him, though usually she was too busy and happy to be downright cross. "Just leave me alone, Cat," she would say. "Or else." Then she would pack exercise books into a music case and hasten next door for a lesson with Mr. Nostrum.

Mr. Nostrum was delighted to teach Gwendolen for the letters. Mrs. Sharp gave him one every term for a year, starting with the last. "Not all at once, in case he gets greedy," she said. "And we'll give him the best last."

Gwendolen made excellent progress. Such a promising witch was she, indeed, that she skipped the First Grade Magic exam and went straight on to the Second. She took the Third and Fourth grades together just after Christmas and, by the following summer, she was starting on Advanced Magic. Mr. Nostrum regarded her as his favorite pupil—he told Mrs. Sharp so over the wall—and Gwendolen always came back from her lessons with him pleased and golden and glowing. She went to Mr. Nostrum two evenings a week, with her magic case under her arm, just as many people might go to music lessons. In fact, music lessons were what Mrs. Sharp put Gwendolen down as having, on the accounts she kept for the Town Council. Since Mr. Nostrum never got paid, except by the letters, Cat thought this was rather dishonest of Mrs. Sharp.

"I have to put something by for my old age," Mrs. Sharp told him crossly. "I don't get much for myself out of keeping you, do I? And I can't trust your sister to remember me when she's grown up and famous. Oh dear me no—I've no illusions about that!"

Cat knew Mrs. Sharp was probably right. He was a little sorry for her, for she had certainly been kind, and he knew by now that she was not a very good witch herself. The *Certified Witch* which the notice in Mrs. Sharp's parlor window claimed her to be was, in fact, the very lowest qualification. People only came to Mrs. Sharp for charms when they could not afford the three Accredited Witches farther down the street. Mrs. Sharp eked out her earnings by acting as an agent for Mr. Larkins at the junk shop. She got him Exotic Supplies—that is to say, the stranger ingredients needed for spells—from as far away as London. She was very proud of her contacts in London. "Oh yes," she often said to Gwendolen, "I've got the contacts, I have. I know those that can get me a pound of dragon's blood any time I ask, for all it's illegal. While you have me, you'll never be in need."

Perhaps, in spite of having no illusions about Gwendolen, Mrs. Sharp was really hoping to become Gwendolen's manager when Gwendolen grew up. Cat suspected she was, anyway. And he was sorry for Mrs. Sharp. He was sure that Gwendolen would cast her off like an old coat when she became famous—like Mrs. Sharp, Cat had no doubt that Gwendolen would be famous. So he said, "There's me to look after you, though." He did not fancy the idea, but he felt he ought to say it.

Mrs. Sharp was warmly grateful. As a reward, she arranged for Cat to have real music lessons. "Then that Mayor will have nothing to complain of," she said. She believed in killing two birds with one stone.

Cat started to learn the violin. He thought he was making good progress. He practiced diligently. He never could understand why the new people living upstairs always banged on the floor when he started to play. Mrs. Sharp, being tone-deaf herself, nodded and smiled while he played, and encouraged him greatly.

He was practicing away one evening when Gwendolen stormed in and shrieked a spell in his face. Cat found, to his dismay, that he was holding a large striped cat by the tail. He had its head tucked under his chin, and he was sawing at its back with the violin bow. He dropped it hurriedly. Even so, it bit him under the chin and scratched him painfully.

"What did you do that for?" he said. The cat stood in an arch, glaring at him.

"Because that's just what it sounded like!" said Gwendolen. "I couldn't stand it a moment longer. Here, pussy, pussy!" The cat did not like Gwendolen either. It scratched the hand she held out to it. Gwendolen smacked it. It ran away, with Cat in hot pursuit, shouting, "Stop it! That's my fiddle! Stop it!" But the cat escaped, and that was the end of the violin lessons.

Mrs. Sharp was very impressed with this display of talent from Gwendolen. She climbed on a chair in the yard and told Mr. Nostrum about it over the wall. From there, the story spread to every witch and necromancer in the neighborhood.

That neighborhood was full of witches. People in the same trade like to cluster together. If Cat came out of Mrs. Sharp's front door and turned right down Coven Street, he passed, besides the three *Accredited Witches*, two *Necromancy Offereds,* a *Soothsayer,* a *Diviner,* and a *Willing Warlock.* If he turned left, he passed MR. HENRY NOSTRUM A.R.C.M. *Tuition in Necromancy,* a *Fortune-Teller,* a *Sorcery For All Occasions,* a *Clairvoyant,* and lastly Mr. Larkins' shop. The air in the street, and for several streets around, was heavy with the scent of magic being done.

All these people took a great and friendly interest in Gwendolen. The story of the cat impressed them enormously. They made a great pet of the creature—naturally, it was called Fiddle. Though it remained bad-tempered, captious, and unfriendly, it never went short of food. They made an even greater pet of Gwendolen. Mr. Larkins gave her presents. The Willing Warlock, who was a muscular young man always in need of a shave, popped out of his house whenever he saw Gwendolen passing and presented her with a bull's-eye. The various witches were always looking out simple spells for her.

Gwendolen was very scornful of these spells. "Do they think I'm a baby or something? I'm *miles* beyond this stuff!" she would say, casting the latest spell aside.

Mrs. Sharp, who was glad of any aid to witchcraft, usually gathered the spell up carefully and hid it. But once or twice, Cat found the odd spell lying about. Then he could not resist trying it. He would have liked to have had just a little of Gwendolen's talent. He always hoped that he was a late developer and that, some day, a spell would work for him. But they never did—not even the one for turning brass buttons to gold, which Cat particularly fancied.

The various fortune-tellers gave Gwendolen presents too. She got an old crystal ball from the Diviner and a pack of cards from the Soothsayer. The Fortune-Teller told her fortune for her. Gwendolen came in golden and exultant from that.

"I'm going to be famous! He said I could rule the world if I go the right way about it!" she told Cat.

Though Cat had no doubt that Gwendolen would be famous, he could not see how she could rule the world, and he said so. "You'd only rule one country, even if you married the King," he objected. "And the Prince of Wales got married last year."

"There are more ways of ruling than that, stupid!" Gwendolen retorted. "Mr. Nostrum has lots of ideas for me, for a start. Mind you, there are some snags. There's a change for the worse that I have to surmount, and a dominant Dark Stranger. But when he told me I'd rule the world my fingers all twitched, so I *know* it's true!" There seemed no limit to Gwendolen's glowing confidence.

The next day, Miss Larkins the Clairvoyant called Cat into her house and offered to tell his fortune too.

CHAPTER 2

Cat was alarmed by Miss Larkins. She was the daughter of Mr. Larkins at the junk shop. She was young and pretty and fiercely red-headed. She wore the red hair piled into a bun on top of her head, from which red tendrils of hair escaped and tangled becomingly with earrings like hoops for parrots to sit on. She was a very talented clairvoyant and, until the story of the cat became known, Miss Larkins had been the pet of the neighborhood. Cat remembered that even his mother had given Miss Larkins presents.

Cat knew Miss Larkins was offering to tell his fortune out of jealousy of Gwendolen. "No. No, thank you very much," he said, backing away from Miss Larkins' little table spread with objects of divination. "It's quite all right. I don't want to know."

But Miss Larkins advanced on him and seized him by his shoulders. Cat squirmed. Miss Larkins used a scent that shrieked *VIOLETS!* at him, her earrings swung like manacles, and her corsets creaked when she was close to. "Silly boy!" Miss Larkins said, in her rich, melodious voice. "I'm not going to hurt you. I just want to *know*."

"But—but I don't," Cat said, twisting this way and that.

"Hold still," said Miss Larkins, and tried to stare deep into Cat's eyes.

Cat shut his eyes hastily. He squirmed harder than ever. He might have got loose, had not Miss Larkins abruptly gone off into some kind of trance. Cat found himself being gripped with a strength that would have surprised him even in the Willing Warlock. He opened his eyes to find Miss Larkins staring blankly at him. Her body shook, creaking her corsets like old doors swinging in the wind. "Oh, please let go!" Cat said. But Miss Larkins did not appear to hear. Cat took hold of the fingers gripping his shoulders, and tried to prise them loose. He could not move them. After that, he could only stare helplessly at Miss Larkins' blank face.

Miss Larkins opened her mouth, and quite a different voice came out. It was a man's voice, brisk and kindly. "You've taken a weight off my mind, lad," it said. It sounded pleased. "There'll be a big change coming up for you now. But you've been awfully careless—four gone already, and only five left. You must take more care. You're in danger from at least two directions, did you know?"

The voice stopped. By this time, Cat was so frightened that he dared not move. He could only wait until Miss Larkins came to herself, yawned, and let go of him in order to cover her mouth elegantly with one hand.

"There," she said, in her usual voice. "That was it. What did I say?"

Finding Miss Larkins had no idea what she had said brought Cat out in goose pimples. All he wanted to do was to run away. He dashed for the door.

Miss Larkins pursued him, seized his arms again, and shook him. "Tell me! Tell me! What did I say?" With the violence of her shaking, her red hair came down in sheets. Her corsets sounded like bending planks. She was terrifying. "What voice did I use?" she demanded.

"A—a man's voice," Cat faltered. "Sort of nice, and no nonsense about it."

Miss Larkins seemed dumbfounded. "A *man*? Not Bobby or Doddo—not a child's voice, I mean?"

"No," said Cat.

"How peculiar!" said Miss Larkins. "I never use a man. What did he say?"

Cat repeated what the voice had said. He thought he would never forget it if he lived to ninety.

It was some consolation to find that Miss Larkins was quite as puzzled by it as he was. "Well, I suppose it was a warning," she said dubiously. She also seemed disappointed. "And nothing else? Nothing about your sister?"

"No, nothing," said Cat.

"Oh well, can't be helped," Miss Larkins said discontentedly, and she let go of Cat in order to put her hair up again.

As soon as both her hands were safely occupied in pinning her bun, Cat ran. He shot out into the street, feeling very shaken.

And he was caught by two more people almost at once.

"Ah. Here is young Eric Chant now," said Mr. Nostrum, advancing down the pavement. "You are acquainted with my brother William, are you, Young Chant?"

Cat was once more caught by an arm. He tried to smile. It was not that he disliked Mr. Nostrum. It was just that Mr. Nostrum always talked in this jocular way and called him Young Chant every few words, which made it very difficult to talk to Mr. Nostrum in return. Mr. Nostrum was small and plumpish, with two wings of grizzled hair. He had a cast in his left eye too, which always stared out sideways. Cat found that added to the difficulty of talking to Mr. Nostrum. Was he looking and listening? Or was his mind elsewhere with that wandering eye?

"Yes—yes, I've met your brother," Cat reminded Mr. Nostrum. Mr. William Nostrum came to visit his brother regularly. Cat saw him almost once a month. He was quite a well-to-do wizard, with a practice in Eastbourne. Mrs. Sharp claimed that Mr. Henry Nostrum sponged on his wealthier brother, both for money and for spells that worked. Whatever the truth of that, Cat found Mr. William Nostrum even harder to talk to than his brother. He was half as large again as Mr. Henry and always wore morning dress with a huge silver watch-chain across his tubby waistcoat. Otherwise, he was the image of Mr. Henry Nostrum, except that both his eyes were out of true. Cat always wondered how Mr. William saw anything. "How do you do, sir," he said to him politely.

"Very well," said Mr. William in a deep, gloomy voice, as if the opposite was true.

Mr. Henry Nostrum glanced up at him apologetically. "The fact is, Young Chant," he explained, "we have met with a little setback. My brother is upset." He lowered his voice, and his wandering eye wandered all around Cat's right side. "It's about those letters from—You Know Who. We can find out nothing. It seems Gwendolen knows nothing. Do you, Young Chant, perchance know why your esteemed and lamented father should be acquainted with—with, let us call him, the August Personage who signed them?"

"I haven't the faintest idea, I'm afraid," said Cat.

"Could he have been some relation?" suggested Mr. Henry Nostrum. "Chant is a Good Name."

"I think it must be a bad name too," Cat answered. "We haven't any relations."

"But what of your dear mother?" persisted Mr. Nostrum, his odd eye traveling away, while his brother managed to stare gloomily at the pavement and the rooftops at once.

"You can see the poor boy knows nothing, Henry," Mr. William said. "I doubt if he would be able to tell us his dear mother's maiden name."

"Oh, I do know that," said Cat. "It's on their marriage lines. She was called Chant too."

"Odd," said Mr. Nostrum, swirling an eye at his brother.

"Odd, and peculiarly unhelpful," Mr. William agreed.

Cat wanted to get away. He felt he had taken enough strange questions to last till Christmas. "Well, if you want to know that badly," he said, "why don't you write and ask Mr.—er—Mr. Chres—"

"Hush!" said Mr. Henry Nostrum violently.

"Hum!" said his brother, almost equally violently.

"August Personage, I mean," Cat said, looking at Mr. William in alarm. Mr. William's eyes had gone right to the sides of his face. Cat was afraid he might bc going off into a trance, like Miss Larkins.

"It will serve, Henry, it will serve!" Mr. William cried out. And, with great triumph, he lifted the silver watchchain off his middle and shook it. "Then for silver!" he cried.

"I'm so glad," Cat said politely. "I have to be going now." He ran off down the street as fast as he could. When he went out that afternoon, he took care to turn right and go out of Coven Street past the Willing Warlock's house. It was rather a nuisance, since that was the long way around to where most of his friends lived, but anything was better than meeting Miss Larkins or the Nostrums again. It was almost enough to make Cat wish that school had started.

When Cat came home that evening, Gwendolen was just back from her lesson with Mr. Nostrum. She had her usual glowing, exulting look, but she was looking secretive and important too.

"That was a good idea of yours of writing to Chrestomanci," she said to Cat. "I can't think why I didn't think of it. Anyway, I just have."

"Why did you do it? Couldn't Mr. Nostrum?" Cat asked.

"It came more naturally from me," said Gwendolen. "And I suppose it doesn't matter if he gets my signature. Mr. Nostrum told me what to write."

"Why does he want to know anyway?" Cat said.

"Wouldn't you like to know!" Gwendolen said exultingly.

"No," said Cat. "I wouldn't." Since this had brought what happened that morning into his mind, which still made him almost wish the Autumn term had started, he said, "I wish the horse chestnuts were ripe."

"Horse chestnuts!" Gwendolen said, in the greatest disgust. "What a low mind you have! They won't be ready for a good six weeks."

"I know," said Cat, and for the next two days he carefully turned right every time he left the house.

They were the lovely golden days that happen when August is passing into September. Cat and his friends went out along the river. On the second day, they found a wall and climbed it. There was an orchard beyond, and here they were lucky enough to discover a tree loaded with sweet white apples—the kind that ripen early. They filled their pockets and then their hats. Then a furious gardener chased them with a rake. They ran. Cat was very happy as he carried his full, knobby hat home. Mrs. Sharp loved apples. He just hoped she would not reward him by making gingerbread men. As a rule, gingerbread men were fun. They leapt up off the plate and ran when you tried to eat them, so that when you finally caught them you felt quite justified in eating them. It was a fair fight, and some got away. But Mrs. Sharp's gingerbread men never did that. They simply lay, feebly waving their arms, and Cat never had the heart to eat them.

Cat was so busy thinking of all this that, though he noticed a four-wheel cab standing in the road as he turned the corner by the Willing Warlock's house, he paid no attention to it. He went to the side door and burst into the kitchen with his hatful of apples, shouting, "I say! Look what I've got, Mrs. Sharp!"

Mrs. Sharp was not there. Instead, standing in the middle of the kitchen, was a tall and quite extraordinarily well-dressed man.

Cat stared at him in some dismay. He was clearly a rich new Town Councillor. Nobody but those kind of people wore trousers with such pearly stripes, or coats of such beautiful velvet, or carried tall hats as shiny as their boots. The man's hair was dark. It was smooth as his hat. Cat had no doubt that this was Gwendolen's Dark Stranger, come to help her start ruling the world. And he should not have been in the kitchen at all. Visitors were always taken straight to the parlor.

"Oh, how do you do, sir. Will you come this way, sir?" he gasped.

The Dark Stranger gave him a wondering look. And well he might, Cat thought, looking around distractedly. The kitchen was in its usual mess. The range was all ash. On the table, Cat saw, to his further dismay, Mrs. Sharp had been making gingerbread men. The ingredients for the spell lay on one end of the table—all grubby newspaper packets and seedy little jars—and the gingerbread itself was strewn over the middle of the table. At the far end, the flies were gathering around the meat for lunch, which looked nearly as messy as the spell.

"Who are you?" said the Dark Stranger. "I have a feeling I should know you. What have you got in your hat?"

Cat was too busy staring around to attend properly, but he caught the last question. His pleasure returned. "Apples," he said, showing the Stranger. "Lovely sweet ones. I've been scrumping."

The Stranger looked grave. "Scrumping," he said, "is a form of stealing."

Cat knew that as well as he did. He thought it was very joyless, even for a Town Councillor, to point it out. "I know. But I bet you did it when you were my age."

The Stranger coughed slightly and changed the subject. "You haven't said yet who you are."

"Sorry. Didn't I?" said Cat. "I'm Eric Chant—only they always call me Cat."

"Then is Gwendolen Chant your sister?" the Stranger asked. He was looking more and more austere and pitying. Cat suspected that he thought Mrs. Sharp's kitchen was a den of vice.

"That's right. Won't you come this way?" Cat said, hoping to get the Stranger out of it. "It's neater through here."

"I had a letter from your sister," the Stranger said, standing where he was. "She gave me the impression you had drowned with your parents."

"You must have made a mistake," Cat said distractedly. "I didn't drown because I was holding on to Gwendolen, and she's a witch. It's cleaner through here."

"I see," said the Stranger. "I'm called Chrestomanci, by the way."

"Oh!" said Cat. This was a real crisis. He put his hat of apples down in the middle of the spell, which he very much hoped would ruin it. "Then you've got to come in the parlor at once."

"Why?" said Chrestomanci, sounding rather bewildered.

"Because," said Cat, thoroughly exasperated, "you're far too important to stay here."

"What makes you think I'm important?" Chrestomanci asked, still bewildered.

Cat was beginning to want to shake him. "You must be. You're wearing important clothes. And Mrs. Sharp said you were. She said Mr. Nostrum would give his eyes just for your three letters."

"*Has* Mr. Nostrum given his eyes for my letters?" asked Chrestomanci. "It hardly seems worth it."

"No. He just gave Gwendolen lessons for them," said Cat.

"What? For his eyes? How uncomfortable!" said Chrestomanci.

Fortunately, there were thumping footsteps just then, and Gwendolen burst in through the kitchen door, panting, golden and jubilant. "Mr. Chrestomanci?"

"Just Chrestomanci," said the Stranger. "Yes. Would you be Gwendolen?"

"Yes. Mr. Nostrum told me there was a cab here," gasped Gwendolen.

She was followed by Mrs. Sharp, nearly as breathless. The two of them took over the conversation, and Cat was thankful for it. Chrestomanci at last consented to be taken to the parlor, where Mrs. Sharp deferentially offered him a cup of tea and a plate of her weakly waving gingerbread men. Chrestomanci, Cat was interested to see, did not seem to have the heart to eat them either. He drank a cup of tea—austerely, without milk or sugar—and asked questions about how Gwendolen and Cat came to be living with Mrs. Sharp. Mrs. Sharp tried to give the impression that she looked after them for nothing, out of the goodness of her heart. She hoped Chrestomanci might be induced to pay her for their keep, as well as the Town Council.

But Gwendolen had decided to be radiantly honest. "The town pays," she said, "because everyone's so sorry about the accident." Cat was glad she had explained, even though he suspected that Gwendolen might already be casting Mrs. Sharp off like an old coat.

"Then I must go and speak to the Mayor," Chrestomanci said, and he stood up, dusting his splendid hat on his elegant sleeve. Mrs. Sharp sighed and sagged. She knew what Gwendolen was doing too. "Don't be anxious, Mrs. Sharp," said Chrestomanci. "No one wishes you to be out of pocket." Then he shook hands with Gwendolen and Cat and said, "I should have come to see you before, of course. Forgive me. Your father was so infernally rude to me, you see. I'll see you again, I hope." Then he went away in his cab, leaving Mrs. Sharp very sour, Gwendolen jubilant, and Cat nervous.

"Why are you so happy?" Cat asked Gwendolen.

"Because he was touched at our orphaned state," said Gwendolen. "He's going to adopt us. My fortune is made!"

"Don't talk such nonsense!" snapped Mrs. Sharp. "Your fortune is the same as it ever was. He may have come here in all his finery, but he said nothing and he promised nothing."

Gwendolen smiled confidently. "You didn't see the heart-wringing letter I wrote."

"Maybe. But he's not got a heart to wring," Mrs. Sharp retorted. Cat rather agreed with Mrs. Sharp—particularly as he had an uneasy feeling that, before Gwendolen and Mrs. Sharp arrived, he had somehow managed to offend Chrestomanci as badly as his father once did. He hoped Gwendolen would not realize that. He knew she would be furious with him.

But, to his astonishment, Gwendolen proved to be right. The Mayor called that afternoon and told them that Chrestomanci had arranged for Cat and Gwendolen to come and live with him as part of his own family. "And I see I needn't tell you what lucky little people you are," he said, as Gwendolen uttered a shriek of joy and hugged the dour Mrs. Sharp.

Cat felt more nervous than ever. He tugged the Mayor's sleeve. "If you please, sir, I don't understand who Chrestomanci is."

The Mayor patted him kindly on the head. "A very eminent gentleman," he said. "You'll be hobnobbing with all the crowned heads of Europe before long, my boy. What do you think of that, eh?"

Cat did not know what to think. This had told him precisely nothing, and made him more nervous than ever. He supposed Gwendolen must have written a very touching letter indeed.

So the second great change came about in Cat's life, and very dismal he feared it would be. All that next week, while they were hurrying about being bought new clothes by Councillors' wives, and while Gwendolen grew more and more excited and triumphant, Cat found he was missing Mrs. Sharp, and everyone else, even Miss Larkins, as if he had already left them. When the time came for them to get on the train, the town gave them a splendid send-off, with flags and a brass band. It upset Cat. He sat tensely on the edge of his seat, fearing he was in for a time of strangeness and maybe even misery.

Gwendolen, however, spread out her smart new dress and arranged her nice new hat becomingly, and sank elegantly back in her seat. "I did it!" she said joyously. "Cat, isn't it marvelous!"

"No," Cat said miserably. "I'm homesick already. What have you done? Why do you keep being so happy?"

"You wouldn't understand," said Gwendolen. "But I'll tell you part of it. I've got out of dead-and-alive Wolvercote at last—stupid Councillors and piffling necromancers! And Chrestomanci was bowled over by me. You saw that, didn't you?"

"I didn't notice specially," said Cat. "I mean, I saw you were being nice to him—"

"Oh, shut up, or I'll give you worse than cramps!" said Gwendolen. And, as the train at last chuffed and began to draw out of the station, Gwendolen waved her gloved hand to the brass band, up and down, just like Royalty. Cat realized she was setting out to rule the world.

CHAPTER 3

The train journey lasted about an hour, before the train puffed into Bowbridge, where they were to get out.

"It's frightfully small," Gwendolen said critically.

"Bowbridge!" shouted a porter, running along the platform. "Bowbridge. The young Chants alight here, please."

"Young Chants!" Gwendolen said disdainfully. "Can't they treat me with more respect?" All the same, the attention pleased her. Cat could see that, as she drew on her ladylike gloves, she was shaking with excitement. He cowered behind her as they got out and watched their trunks being tossed out on to the windy platform. Gwendolen marched up to the shouting porter. "*We* are the young Chants," she told him magnificently.

It fell a little flat. The porter simply beckoned and scurried away to the entrance lobby, which was windier even than the platform. Gwendolen had to hold her hat on. Here, a young man strode toward them in a billow of flapping coat.

"*We* are the young Chants," Gwendolen told him.

"Gwendolen and Eric? Pleased to meet you," said the young man. "I'm Michael Saunders. I'll be tutoring you with the other children."

"*Other* children?" Gwendolen asked him haughtily.

But Mr. Saunders was evidently one of those people who are not good at standing still. He had already darted off to see about their trunks. Gwendolen was a trifle annoyed. But when Mr. Saunders came back and led them outside into the station yard, they found a motor car waiting—long, black, and sleek. Gwendolen forgot her annoyance. She felt this was entirely fitting.

Cat wished it had been a carriage. The car jerked and thrummed and smelled of petrol. He felt sick almost at once. He felt sicker still when they left Bowbridge and thrummed along a winding country road. The only advantage he could see was that the car went very quickly. After only ten minutes, Mr. Saunders said, "Look—there's Chrestomanci Castle now. You get the best view from here."

Cat turned his sick face and Gwendolen her fresh one the way he pointed. The Castle was gray and turreted, on the opposite hill. As the road turned, they saw it had a new part, with a spread of big windows, and a flag flying above. They could see grand trees—dark, layered cedars and big elms—and glimpse lawns and flowers.

"It looks marvelous," Cat said sickly, rather surprised that Gwendolen had said nothing. He hoped the road did not wind too much in getting to the Castle.

It did not. The car flashed around a village green and between big gates. Then there was a long tree-lined avenue, with the great door of the old part of the Castle at the end of it. The car scrunched around on the gravel sweep in front of it. Gwendolen leaned forward eagerly, ready to be first one out. It was clear there would be a butler, and perhaps footmen too. She could hardly wait to make her grand entry.

But the car went on, past the gray, knobbly walls of the old Castle, and stopped at an obscure door where the new part began. It was almost a secretive door. There was a mass of rhododendron trees hiding it from both parts of the Castle.

"I'm taking you in this way," Mr. Saunders explained cheerfully, "because it's the door you'll be using mostly, and I thought it would help you find your way about if you start as you mean to go on."

Cat did not mind. He thought this door looked more homely. But Gwendolen, cheated of her grand entry, threw Mr. Saunders a seething look and wondered whether to say a most unpleasant spell at him. She decided against it. She was still wanting to give a good impression. They got out of the car and followed Mr. Saunders—whose coat had a way of billowing even when there was no wind—into a square polished passageway indoors. A most imposing lady was waiting there to meet them. She was wearing a tight purple dress and her hair was in a very tall jet-black pile. Cat thought she must be Mrs. Chrestomanci.

"This is Miss Bessemer, the housekeeper," said Mr. Saunders. "Eric and Gwendolen, Miss Bessemer. Eric's a bit car-sick, I'm afraid."

Cat had not realized his trouble was so obvious. He was embarrassed. Gwendolen, who was very annoyed to be met by a mere housekeeper, held her hand out coldly to Miss Bessemer.

Miss Bessemer shook hands like an Empress. Cat was just thinking she was the most awe-inspiring lady he had ever met when she turned to him with a very kind smile. "Poor Eric," she said. "Riding in a car bothers me ever so too. You'll be all right now you're out of the thing—but if you're not, I'll give you something for it. Come and get washed, and have a look-see at your rooms."

They followed the narrow purple triangle of her dress up some stairs, along corridors, and up more stairs. Cat had never seen anywhere so luxurious. There was carpet the whole way—a soft green carpet, like grass in the dewy morning—and the floor at the sides was polished so that it reflected the carpet and the clean white walls and the pictures hung on the walls. Everywhere was very quiet. They heard nothing the whole way, except their own feet and Miss Bessemer's purple rustle.

Miss Bessemer opened a door onto a blaze of afternoon sun. "This is your room, Gwendolen. Your bathroom opens off it."

"Thank you," said Gwendolen, and she sailed magnificently in to take possession of it. Cat peeped past Miss Bessemer and saw the room was very big, with a rich, soft Turkey carpet covering most of the floor.

Miss Bessemer said, "The Family dines early when there are no visitors so that they can eat with the children. But I expect you'd like some tea all the same. Whose room shall I have it sent to?"

"Mine, please," Gwendolen said at once.

There was a short pause before Miss Bessemer said, "Well, that's settled then, isn't it? Your room is up here, Eric."

The way was up a twisting staircase. Cat was pleased. It looked as if his room was going to be part of the old castle. And he was right. When Miss Bessemer opened the door, the room beyond was round, and the three windows showed that the wall was nearly three feet thick. Cat could not resist racing across the glowing carpet to scramble on one of the deep window seats and look out. He found he could see across the flat tops of the cedars to a great lawn like a sheet of green velvet, with flower gardens going down the hillside in steps beyond it. Then he looked around the room itself. The curved walls were whitewashed, and so was the thick fireplace. The bed had a patchwork quilt on it. There was a table, a chest-of-drawers, and a bookcase with interesting-looking books in it.

"Oh, I like this!" he said to Miss Bessemer.

"I'm afraid your bathroom is down the passage," said Miss Bessemer, as if this was a drawback. But, as Cat had never had a private bathroom before, he did not mind in the least.

As soon as Miss Bessemer had gone, he hastened along to have a look at it. To his awe, there were three sizes of red towel and a sponge as big as a melon. The bath had feet like a lion's. One corner of the room was tiled, and with red rubber curtains, for a shower. Cat could not resist experimenting. The bathroom was rather wet by the time he had finished. He went back to his room, a little damp himself. His trunk and box were there by this time, and a maid with red hair was unpacking them. She told Cat her name was Mary and wanted to know if she was putting things in the right places. She was perfectly pleasant, but Cat was very shy of her. The red hair reminded him of Miss Larkins, and he could not think what to say to her.

"Er—may I go down and have some tea?" he stammered.

"Please yourself," she said—rather coldly, Cat thought.

He ran downstairs again, feeling he might have gotten off on the wrong foot with her.

Gwendolen's trunk was standing in the middle of her room. Gwendolen herself was sitting in a very queenly way at a round table by the window, with a big pewter teapot in front of her, a plate of brown bread and butter, and a plate of biscuits.

"I told the girl I'd unpack for myself," she said. "I've got secrets in my trunk and my box. And I asked her to bring tea at once because I'm starving. And just look at it! Did you ever see anything so dull? Not even jam!"

"Perhaps the biscuits are nice," Cat said hopefully. But they were not, or not particularly.

"We shall starve, in the midst of luxury!" sighed Gwendolen.

Her room was certainly luxurious. The wallpaper seemed to be made of blue velvet. The top and bottom of the bed was upholstered like a chair, in blue velvet with buttons in it, and the blue velvet bedspread matched it exactly. The chairs were painted gold. There was a dressing table fit for a princess, with little golden drawers, gold-backed brushes, and a long oval mirror surrounded by a gilded wreath. Gwendolen admitted that she liked the dressing table, though she was not so sure about the wardrobe, which had painted garlands and maypole dancers on it.

"It's to hang clothes in, not to look at," she said. "It distracts me. But the bathroom is lovely."

The bathroom was tiled with blue and white tiles, and the bath was sunk down into the tiled floor. Over it, draped like a baby's cradle, were blue curtains for when you wanted a shower. The towels matched the tiles. Cat preferred his own bathroom, but that may have been because he had to spend rather a long time in Gwendolen's. Gwendolen locked him in it while she unpacked. Through the hiss of the shower—Gwendolen had only herself to blame that she found her bathroom thoroughly soaked afterwards—Cat heard her voice raised in annoyance at someone who had come in to take the dull tea away and caught her with her trunk open. When Gwendolen finally unlocked the bathroom door, she was still angry.

"I don't think the servants here are very civil," she said. "If that girl says one thing more, she'll find herself with a boil on her nose—even if her name is Euphemia! Though," Gwendolen added charitably, "I'm inclined to think being called Euphemia is punishment enough for anyone. You have to go and get your new suit on, Cat. She says dinner's in half an hour and we have to change for it. Did you ever hear anything so formal and unnatural!"

"I thought you were looking forward to that kind of thing," said Cat, who most certainly was not.

"You can be grand *and* natural," Gwendolen retorted. But the thought of the coming grandeur soothed her all the same. "I shall wear my blue dress with the lace collar," she said. "And I do think being called Euphemia is a heavy enough burden for anyone to bear, however rude they are."

As Cat went up his winding stair, the Castle filled with a mysterious booming. It was the first noise he had heard. It alarmed him. He learned later that it was the dressing gong, to warn the Family that they had half an hour to change in. Cat, of course, did not take nearly that time to put his suit on. So he had yet another shower. He felt damp and weak and almost washed out of existence by the time the maid who was so unfortunate in being called Euphemia came to take him and Gwendolen downstairs to the drawing room where the Family was waiting.

Gwendolen, in her pretty blue dress, sailed in confidently. Cat crept behind. The room seemed full of people. Cat had no idea how all of them came to be part of the Family. There was an old lady in lace mittens, and a small man with large eyebrows and a loud voice who was talking about stocks and shares; Mr. Saunders, whose wrists and ankles were too long for his shiny black suit; and at least two younger ladies; and at least two younger men. Cat saw Chrestomanci, quite splendid in very dark red velvet; and Chrestomanci saw Cat and Gwendolen and looked at them with a vague, perplexed smile, which made Cat quite sure that Chrestomanci had forgotten who they were.

"Oh," said Chrestomanci. "Er. This is my wife."

They were ushered in front of a plump lady with a mild face. She had a gorgeous lace dress on—Gwendolen's eyes swept up and down it with considerable awe—but otherwise she was one of the most ordinary ladies they had ever seen. She gave them a friendly smile. "Eric and Gwendolen, isn't it? You must call me Milly, my dears." This was a relief, because neither of them had any idea what they should have called her. "And now you must meet my Julia and my Roger," she said.

Two plump children came and stood beside her. They were both rather pale and had a tendency to breathe heavily. The girl wore a lace dress like her mother's, and the boy had on a blue velvet suit, but no clothes could disguise the fact that they were even more ordinary-looking than their mother. They looked politely at Gwendolen and at Cat, and all four said, "How do you do?" Then there seemed nothing else to say.

Luckily, they had not stood there long before a butler came and opened the double doors at the end of the room, and told them that dinner was served. Gwendolen looked at this butler in great indignation. "Why didn't he open the door to *us*?" she whispered to Cat as they all went in a ragged sort of procession to the dining room. "Why were we fobbed off with the housekeeper?"

Cat did not answer. He was too busy clinging to Gwendolen. They were being arranged around a long polished table, and if anyone had tried to put Cat in a chair that was not next to Gwendolen's, he thought he would have fainted from terror. Luckily, no one tried. Even so, the meal was terrifying enough. Footmen kept pushing delicious food in silver plates over Cat's left shoulder. Each time that happened, it took Cat by surprise, and he jumped and jogged the plate. He was supposed to help himself off the silver plate, and he never knew how much he was allowed to take. But the worst difficulty was that he was left-handed. The spoon and fork that he was supposed to lift the food with from the footman's plate to his own were always the wrong way around. He tried changing them over, and dropped a spoon. He tried leaving them as they were, and spilled gravy. The footman always said, "Not to worry, sir," and made him feel worse than ever.

The conversation was even more terrifying. At one end of the table, the small loud man talked endlessly of stocks and shares. At Cat's end, they talked about Art. Mr. Saunders seemed to have spent the summer traveling abroad. He had seen statues and paintings all over Europe and much admired them. He was so eager that he slapped the table as he talked. He spoke of Studios and Schools, *Quattrocento* and Dutch Interiors, until Cat's head went around. Cat looked at Mr. Saunders' thin, square-cheeked face and marveled at all the knowledge behind it. Then Milly and Chrestomanci joined in. Milly recited a string of names Cat had never heard in his life before. Chrestomanci made comments on them, as if these names were intimate friends of his. Whatever the rest of the Family was like, Cat thought, Chrestomanci was not ordinary. He had very black bright eyes, which were striking even when he was looking vague and dreamy. When he was interested—as he was about Art—the black eyes screwed up in a way that seemed to spill the brightness of them over the rest of his face. And, to Cat's dismay, the two children were equally interested. They kept up a mild chirp, as if they actually knew what their parents were talking about.

Cat felt crushingly ignorant. What with this talk, and the trouble over the suddenly appearing silver plates, and the dull biscuits he had eaten for tea, he found he had no appetite at all. He had to leave half his ice-cream pudding. He envied Gwendolen for being able to sit so calmly and scornfully, enjoying her food.

It was over at last. They were allowed to escape up to her upholstered bed with a bounce.

"What a childish trick!" she said. "They were showing off just to make us feel small. Mr. Nostrum warned me they would. It's to disguise the thinness of their souls. What an awful, dull wife! And did you ever see anyone so plain and stupid as those two children! I know I'm going to hate it here. This Castle's crushing me already."

"It may not be so bad once we get used to it," Cat said, without hope.

"It'll be worse," Gwendolen promised him. "There's something about this Castle. It's a bad influence, and a deadness. It's squashing the life and the witchcraft out of me. I can hardly breathe."

"You're imagining things," said Cat, "because you want to be back with Mrs. Sharp." And he sighed. He missed Mrs. Sharp badly.

"No, I'm not imagining it," said Gwendolen. "I should have thought it was strong enough even for you to feel. Go on, try. Can't you feel the deadness?"

Cat did not really need to try, to see what she meant. There was something strange about the Castle. He had thought it was simply that it was so quiet. But it was more than that: there was a softness to the atmosphere, a weightiness, as if everything they said or did was muffled under a great feather quilt. Normal sounds, like their two voices, seemed thin. There were no echoes to them. "Yes, it is queer," he agreed.

"It's more than queer—it's terrible," said Gwendolen. "I shall be lucky if I survive." Then she added, to Cat's surprise, "So I'm not sorry I came."

"I am," said Cat.

"Oh, you would need looking after!" said Gwendolen. "All right. There's a pack of cards on the dressing table. They're for divination, really, but if we take the trumps out we can use them to play Snap with, if you like."

CHAPTER 4

The same softness and silence were there when the red-haired Mary woke Cat the next morning and told him it was time to get up. Bright morning sunshine was flooding the curved walls of his room. Though Cat knew now that the Castle must be full of people, he could hear not a sound from any of them. Nor could he hear anything from outside the windows.

I know what it's like! Cat thought. It's like when it's snowed in the night. The idea made him feel so pleased and so warm that he went to sleep again.

"You really must get up, Eric," Mary said, shaking him. "I've run your bath, and your lessons start at nine. Make haste, or you won't have time for breakfast."

Cat got up. He had so strong a feeling that it had snowed in the night that he was quite surprised to find his room warm in the sun. He looked out of the windows, and there were green lawns and flowers, and rooks circling the green trees, as if there had been some mistake. Mary had gone. Cat was glad, because he was not at all sure he liked her, and he was afraid of missing breakfast. When he was dressed, he went along to the bathroom and let the hot water out of the bath. Then he dashed down the twisting stairs to find Gwendolen.

"Where do we go for breakfast?" he asked her anxiously.

Gwendolen was never at her best in the morning. She was sitting on her blue velvet stool in front of her garlanded mirror, crossly combing her golden hair. Combing her hair was another thing which always made her cross. "I don't know and I don't care! Shut up!" she said.

"Now that's no way to speak," said the maid called Euphemia, briskly following Cat into the room. She was rather a pretty girl, and she did not seem to find her name the burden it should have been. "We're waiting to give you breakfast along here. Come on."

Gwendolen hurled her comb down expressively and they followed Euphemia to a room just along the corridor. It was a square, airy room, with a row of big windows but, compared with the rest of the Castle, it was rather shabby. The leather chairs were battered. The grassy carpet had stains on it. None of the cupboards would shut properly. Things like clockwork trains and tennis rackets bulged out. Julia and Roger were sitting waiting at a table by the windows, in clothes as shabby as the room.

Mary, who was waiting there too, said, "And about time!" and began to work an interesting lift in a cupboard by the fireplace. There was a clank. Mary opened the lift and fetched out a large plate of bread and butter and a steaming brown jug of cocoa. She brought these over to the table and Euphemia poured each child a mug of the cocoa.

Gwendolen stared from her mug to the plate of bread. "Is this all there is?"

"What else do you want?" asked Euphemia.

Gwendolen could not find words to express what she wanted. Porridge, bacon and eggs, grapefruit, toast and kippers all occurred to her at once, and she went on staring.

"Make up your mind," Euphemia said at last. "My breakfast's waiting for me too, you know."

"Isn't there any marmalade?" said Gwendolen.

Euphemia and Mary looked at one another. "Julia and Roger are not allowed marmalade," Mary said.

"Nobody forbade *me* to have it," said Gwendolen. "Get me some marmalade at once."

Mary went to a speaking tube by the lift and, after much rumbling and another clank, a pot of marmalade arrived. Mary brought it and put it in front of Gwendolen.

"Thank you," Cat said fervently. He felt as strongly about it as Gwendolen—more, in fact, because he hated cocoa.

"Oh, no trouble, I'm sure!" Mary said, in what was certainly a sarcastic way, and the two maids went out.

For a while, nobody said anything. Then Roger said to Cat, "Pass the marmalade, please."

"You're not supposed to have it," said Gwendolen, whose temper had not improved.

"Nobody will know if I use one of your knives," Roger said placidly.

Cat passed him the marmalade and his knife too. "Why aren't you allowed it?"

Julia and Roger looked at one another in a mild, secretive way. "We're too fat," Julia said, calmly taking the knife and the marmalade after Roger had done with them. Cat was not surprised when he saw how much marmalade they had managed to pile on their bread. Marmalade stood on both slices like a sticky brown cliff.

Gwendolen looked at them with disgust, and then, rather complacently, down at her trim linen dress. The contrast was certainly striking. "Your father is such a handsome man," she said. "It must be such a disappointment to him that you're both pudgy and plain, like your mother."

The two children looked at her placidly over their cliffs of marmalade. "Oh, I wouldn't know," said Roger.

"Pudgy is comfortable," said Julia. "It must be a nuisance to look like a china doll, the way you do."

Gwendolen's blue eyes glared. She made a small sign under the edge of the table. The bread and thick marmalade whisked itself from Julia's hands and slapped itself on Julia's face, marmalade side inward. Julia gasped a little. "How dare you insult me!" said Gwendolen.

Julia peeled the bread slowly off her face and then fumbled out a handkerchief. Cat supposed she was going to wipe her face. But she let the marmalade stay where it was, trundling in blobs down her plump cheeks, and simply tied a knot in the handkerchief. She pulled the knot slowly tight, looking meaningly at Gwendolen while she did so. With the final pull, the half-full jug of cocoa shot steaming into the air. It hovered for a second, and then shot sideways to hang just above Gwendolen's head. Then it began to joggle itself into tipping position.

"Stop it!" gasped Gwendolen. She put up a hand to ward the jug off. The jug dodged her and went on tipping. Gwendolen made another sign and gasped out strange words. The jug took not the slightest notice. It went on tipping until cocoa was brimming in the very end of its spout. Gwendolen tried to lean out sideways away from it. The jug simply joggled along in the air until it was hanging over her head again.

"Shall I make it pour?" Julia asked. There was a bit of a smile under the marmalade.

"You dare!" screamed Gwendolen. "I'll tell Chrestomanci on you! I'll—oh!" She sat up straight again, and the jug followed her faithfully. Gwendolen made another grab at it, and it dodged again.

"Careful. You'll make it spill. And what a shame about your pretty dress," Roger said, watching complacently.

"Shut up, you!" Gwendolen shouted at him, leaning out the other way so that she was nearly in Cat's lap. Cat looked up nervously as the jug came and hovered over him too. It seemed to be going to pour.

But, at that moment, the door opened and Chrestomanci came in, wearing a flowered silk dressing gown. It was a red and purple dressing gown, with gold at the neck and sleeves. It made Chrestomanci look amazingly tall, amazingly thin, and astonishingly stately. He could have been an emperor, or a particularly severe bishop. He was smiling as he came in, but the smile vanished when he saw the jug.

The jug tried to vanish too. It fled back to the table at the sight of him, so quickly that cocoa slopped out of it on to Gwendolen's dress—which may or may not have been an accident. Julia and Roger both looked stricken. Julia unknotted her handkerchief as if for dear life.

"Well, I *was* coming in to say good morning," Chrestomanci said. "But I see that it isn't." He looked from the jug to Julia's marmalade-glistening cheeks. "If you two ever want to eat marmalade again," he said, "you'd better do as you're told. And the same goes for all four of you."

"I wasn't doing anything wrong," Gwendolen said, as if butter—not to speak of marmalade—would not have melted in her mouth.

"Yes, you were," said Roger.

Chrestomanci came to the end of the table and stood looking down on them, with his hands in the pockets of his noble robe. He looked so tall like that that Cat was surprised that his head was still under the ceiling. "There's one absolute rule in this Castle," he said, "which it will pay you all to remember. No witchcraft of any kind is to be practiced by children, unless Michael Saunders is here to supervise you. Have you understood, Gwendolen?"

"Yes," said Gwendolen. She gripped her lips together and clenched her hands, but she was still shaking with rage. "I refuse to keep such a silly rule!"

Chrestomanci did not seem to hear, or to notice how angry she was. He turned to Cat. "Have you understood too, Eric?"

"Me?" Cat said in surprise. "Yes, of course."

"Good," said Chrestomanci. "Now I *will* say good morning."

"Good morning, Daddy," said Julia and Roger. "Er—good morning," Cat said. Gwendolen pretended not to hear. Two could play at that game. Chrestomanci smiled and swept out of the room like a very long procession of one person.

"Telltale!" Gwendolen said to Roger, as soon as the door had shut. "And that was a dirty trick with that jug! You were both doing it, weren't you?"

Roger smiled sleepily, not in the least disturbed. "Witchcraft runs in our family," he said.

"And we've both inherited it," said Julia. "I must go and wash." She picked up three slices of bread to keep her going while she did so, and left the room, calling over her shoulder, "Tell Michael I won't be long, Roger."

"More cocoa?" Roger said politely, picking up the jug.

"Yes, please," said Cat. It never bothered him to eat or drink things that had been bewitched, and he was thirsty. He thought that if he filled his mouth with marmalade and strained the cocoa through it, he might not taste the cocoa. Gwendolen, however, was sure Roger was trying to insult her. She flounced around in her chair and stayed haughtily looking at the wall until Mr. Saunders suddenly threw open a door Cat had not noticed before and said cheerfully:

"Right, all of you. Lesson time. Come on through and see how you stand up to some grilling."

Cat hastily swallowed his cocoa-flavored marmalade. Beyond the door was a schoolroom. It was a real, genuine schoolroom, although there were only four desks in it. There was a blackboard, a globe, the pitted school floor, and the schoolroom smell. There was that kind of glass-fronted bookcase without which no schoolroom is complete, and the battered gray-green and dark blue books without which no schoolroom bookcase is complete. On the walls were big pictures of the statues Mr. Saunders had found so interesting.

Two of the desks were brown and old. Two were new and yellow with varnish. Gwendolen and Cat sat silently in the new desks. Julia hurried in, with her face shining from soap, and sat in the old desk beside Roger's, and the grilling began. Mr. Saunders strode gawkily up and down in front of the blackboard, asking keen questions. His tweed jacket billowed out from his back, just as his coat had done in the wind. Perhaps that was why the sleeves of the jacket were so much too short for Mr. Saunders' long arms. The long arm shot out, and a foot of bony wrist with a keen finger on the end of it pointed at Cat. "What part did witchcraft play in the Wars of the Roses?"

"Er," said Cat. "Ung. I'm afraid I haven't done them yet, sir."

"Gwendolen," said Mr. Saunders.

"Oh—a very big part," Gwendolen guessed airily.

"Wrong," said Mr. Saunders. "Roger."

From the grilling, it emerged that Roger and Julia had forgotten a great deal over the summer but, even so, they were well ahead of Cat in most things, and far ahead of Gwendolen in everything.

"What *did* you learn at school?" Mr. Saunders asked her, in some exasperation.

Gwendolen shrugged. "I've forgotten. It wasn't interesting. I was concentrating on witchcraft, and I intend to go on doing that, please."

"I'm afraid you can't," said Mr. Saunders.

Gwendolen stared at him, hardly able to believe she had heard him right. "What!" she almost shrieked. "But—but I'm terribly talented! I *have* to go on with it!"

"Your talents will keep," said Mr. Saunders. "You can take up witchcraft again when you've learned something else. Open your arithmetic book and do me the first four exercises. Eric, I think I'll set you going on some History. Write me an essay on the reign of King Canute." He moved on to set work for Roger and Julia.

Cat and Gwendolen opened books. Gwendolen's face was red, then white. As Mr. Saunders bent over Roger, her inkwell sailed up out of the socket in her desk and emptied itself over the back of Mr. Saunders' billowing tweed jacket. Cat bit his lip in order not to laugh. Julia watched with calm interest. Mr. Saunders did not seem to notice. The inkwell returned quietly to its socket.

"Gwendolen," said Mr. Saunders without turning around. "Get the ink jar and funnel out of the bottom of the cupboard and refill that inkwell. And fill it properly, please."

Gwendolen got up, jauntily and defiantly, found the big flask and funnel, and started to fill her inkwell. Ten minutes later, she was still pouring away. Her face was puzzled at first, then red, then white with fury again. She tried to put the flask down, and found she could not. She tried whispering a spell.

Mr. Saunders turned and looked at her.

"You're being perfectly horrible!" said Gwendolen. "Besides, I'm allowed to do witchcraft when you're here."

"No one is allowed to pour ink over their tutor," Mr. Saunders said cheerfully. "And I'd already told you that you've given up witchcraft for the time being. Keep on pouring till I tell you to stop."

Gwendolen poured ink for the next half hour, and got angrier every minute of it.

Cat was impressed. He suspected that Mr. Saunders was rather a powerful magician. Certainly, when he next looked at Mr. Saunders, there was no sign of any ink on his back. Cat looked at Mr. Saunders fairly often, to see whether it was safe to change his pen from his right to his left hand. He had been punished so often for writing left-handed that he was good at keeping an eye on his teachers. When Mr. Saunders turned his way, Cat used his right hand. It was slow and reluctant. But as soon as Mr. Saunders turned away again, Cat changed his pen over and got on like a house on fire. The main trouble was that, in order not to smudge the ink with his left hand, he had to hold the paper sideways. But he was pretty deft at flicking his book straight again whenever Mr. Saunders seemed likely to look at him.

When the half hour was over, Mr. Saunders, without turning around, told Gwendolen to stop pouring ink and do sums. Then, still without turning around, he said to Cat, "Eric, what are you doing?"

"An essay on King Canute," Cat said innocently.

Then Mr. Saunders did turn around, but by that time the paper was straight and the pen in Cat's right hand. "Which hand were you writing with?" he said. Cat was used to this. He held up his right hand with the pen in it. "It looked like both hands to me," Mr. Saunders said, and he came over and looked at the page Cat had written. "It *was* both."

"It doesn't show," Cat said miserably.

"Not much," Mr. Saunders agreed. "Does it amuse you to write with alternate hands, or something?"

"No," Cat confessed. "But I'm left-handed."

Then, as Cat had feared, Mr. Saunders flew into a towering rage. His face went red. He slammed his big, knobby hand down on Cat's desk so that Cat jumped and the inkwell jumped too, sending ink splashing over Mr. Saunders' great hand and over Cat's essay. *"Left-handed!"* he roared. "Then why the Black Gentleman don't you write with your left hand, boy?"

"They—they punish me if I do," Cat faltered, very shaken, and very perplexed to find Mr. Saunders was angry for such a peculiar reason.

"Then they deserve to be tied up in knots and roasted!" roared Mr. Saunders, "whoever *they* are! You're doing yourself untold harm by obeying them, boy! If I catch you writing with your right hand again, you'll be in really serious trouble!"

"Yes," Cat said, relieved but still very shaken. He looked mournfully at his ink-splashed essay and hoped Mr. Saunders might use a little witchcraft on that too. But Mr. Saunders took the book and tore the page right out.

"Now do it again properly!" he said, slapping the book back in front of Cat.

Cat was still writing all over again about Canute when Mary came in with a tray of milk and biscuits and a cup of coffee for Mr. Saunders. And after the milk and biscuits, Mr. Saunders told Cat and Gwendolen they were free till lunch. "Though not because of a good morning's work," he said. "Go out and get some fresh air." As they went out of the schoolroom, he turned to Roger and Julia. "Now we'll have a little witchcraft," he said. "And let's hope you haven't forgotten all that too."

Gwendolen stopped in the doorway and looked at him.

"No. Not you," Mr. Saunders said to her. "I told you."

Gwendolen whirled around and ran away, through the shabby playroom and down the corridor beyond. Cat ran after her as hard as he could, but he did not catch up with her until they came to a much grander part of the Castle, where a big marble staircase curled away, downward and the light came from an elegant dome in the roof.

"This isn't the right way," Cat panted.

"Yes it is," Gwendolen said fiercely. "I'm going to find Chrestomanci. Why should those two fat little fools learn witchcraft and not me? I've got twice their gifts. It took two of them just to levitate a jug of cocoa! So I want Chrestomanci."

By a stroke of good fortune, Chrestomanci was coming along the gallery on the other side of the staircase, behind a curly marble balustrade. He was wearing a fawn-colored suit now, instead of the imperial dressing gown, but he looked, if possible, even more elegant. By the look on his face, his thoughts were miles away. Gwendolen ran around the head of the marble staircase and stood herself in front of him. Chrestomanci blinked, and looked vaguely from her to Cat. "Was one of you wanting me?"

"Yes. Me," said Gwendolen. "Mr. Saunders won't give me witchcraft lessons, and I want you to tell him he must."

"Oh, but I can't do that," Chrestomanci said absentmindedly. "Sorry and so on."

Gwendolen stamped her foot. It made no noise to speak of, even there on the marble floor, and there was no echo. Gwendolen was forced to shout instead. "*Why not?* You must, you must, you *must!*"

Chrestomanci looked down at her in a peering, surprised way, as if he had only just seen her. "You seem to be annoyed," he said. "But I'm afraid it's unavoidable. I told Michael Saunders that he was on no account to teach either of you witchcraft."

"*You* did! Why *not?*" Gwendolen shouted.

"Because you were bound to misuse it, of course," said Chrestomanci, as if it were quite obvious. "But I'll reconsider it in a year or so, if you still want to learn." Then he smiled kindly at Gwendolen, obviously expecting her to be pleased, and drifted dreamily away down the marble stairs.

Gwendolen kicked the marble balustrade and hurt her foot. That sent her into a rage as strong as Mr. Saunders'. She danced and jumped and shrieked at the head of the stairs until Cat was quite frightened of her. She shook her fist after Chrestomanci. "I'll show you! You wait!" she screamed. But Chrestomanci had gone out of sight around the bend in the staircase and perhaps he could not hear. Even Gwendolen's loudest scream sounded thin and small.

Cat was puzzled. What *was* it about this Castle? He looked up at the dome where the light came in and thought that Gwendolen's screaming ought to have echoed around it like the dickens. Instead, it made a small, high squawking. While he waited for her to get her temper back, Cat experimentally put his fingers to his mouth and whistled as hard as he could. It made a queer, blunt noise, like a squeaky boot. It also brought the old lady with the mittens out of a door in the gallery.

"You noisy little children!" she said. "If you want to scream and whistle, you must go out in the grounds and do it there."

"Oh, come on!" Gwendolen said crossly to Cat, and the two of them ran away to the part of the Castle they were used to. After a bit of muddling around, they discovered the door they had first come in by and let themselves outside through it.

"Let's explore everywhere," said Cat. Gwendolen shrugged and said it suited her, so they set off.

Beyond the shrubbery of rhododendrons, they found themselves out on the great smooth lawn with the cedar trees. It spread across the entire front of the newer part of the Castle. On the other side of it, Cat saw the most interesting high sun-soaked old wall, with trees hanging over it. It was clearly the ruins of an even older castle. Cat set off toward it at a trot, past the big windows of the newer Castle, dragging Gwendolen with him. But, halfway there, Gwendolen stopped and stood poking at the shaved, green grass with her toe.

"Hm," she said. "Do you think this counts as in the Castle?"

"I expect so," said Cat. "Do come on. I want to explore those ruins there."

However, the first wall they came to was a low one, and the door in it led them into a very formal garden. It had broad gravel paths, running very straight, between box hedges. There were yew trees everywhere, clipped into severe pyramids, and all the flowers were yellow, in tidy clumps.

"Boring," said Cat, and led the way to the ruin wall beyond.

But once again there was a lower wall in the way, and this time they came out into an orchard. It was a very tidy orchard, in which all the trees were trained flat, to stand like hedges on either side of the winding gravel paths. They were loaded with apples, some of them quite big. After what Chrestomanci had said about scrumping, Cat did not quite dare pick one, but Gwendolen picked a big red Worcester and bit into it.

Instantly, a gardener appeared from around a corner and told them reproachfully that picking apples was forbidden.

Gwendolen threw the apple down in the path. "Take it then. There was a maggot in it anyway."

They went on, leaving the gardener staring ruefully at the bitten apple. And instead of reaching the ruins, they came to a goldfish pond, and after that to a rose garden. Here Gwendolen, as an experiment, tried picking a rose. Instantly another gardener appeared and explained respectfully that they were not allowed to pick roses. So Gwendolen threw the rose down too. Then Cat looked over his shoulder and discovered that the ruins were somehow behind them now. He turned back. But he still did not seem to reach them. It was nearly lunchtime before he suddenly turned into a steep little path between two walls and found the ruins above him, at the top of the path.

Cat pelted joyfully up the steep path. The sun-soaked wall ahead was taller than most houses, and there were trees at the top of it. When he was close enough, Cat saw that there was a giddy stone staircase jutting out of the wall, more like a stone ladder than a stair. It was so old that snapdragons and wallflowers had rooted in it, and hollyhocks had grown up against the place where the stair met the ground. Cat had to push aside a tall red hollyhock in order to put his foot on the first stair.

No sooner had he done so than yet another gardener came puffing up the steep path. "You can't go there! That's Chrestomanci's garden up there, that is!"

"Why can't we?" said Cat, deeply disappointed.

"Because it's not allowed, that's why."

Slowly and reluctantly, Cat came away. The gardener stood at the foot of the stair to make sure he went. "Bother!" Cat said.

"I'm getting rather sick of Chrestomanci forbidding things," said Gwendolen. "It's time someone taught him a lesson."

"What are you going to do?" said Cat.

"Wait and see," said Gwendolen, pressing her lips together in her stormiest way.

CHAPTER 5

Gwendolen refused to tell Cat what she was going to do. This meant that Cat had rather a melancholy time. After a wholesome lunch of turnips and boiled mutton, they had lessons again. After that, Gwendolen ran hastily away and would not let Cat come with her. Cat did not know what to do.

"Would you care to come out and play?" Roger asked.

Cat looked at him and saw that he was just being polite. "No, thank you," he said politely. He was forced to wander around the gardens on his own. There was a wood lower down, full of horse chestnuts, but they were not nearly ripe. As Cat was halfheartedly staring up into one, he saw there was a tree house in it, about halfway up. This was more like it. Cat was just about to climb up to it when he heard voices and saw Julia's skirt flutter among the leaves. So that was no good. It was Julia and Roger's private tree house, and they were in it.

Cat wandered away again. He came to the lawn, and there was Gwendolen, crouching under one of the cedars, very busy digging a small hole.

"What are you doing?" said Cat.

"Go away," said Gwendolen.

Cat went away. He was sure what Gwendolen was doing was witchcraft and had to do with teaching Chrestomanci a lesson, but it was no good asking Gwendolen when she was being this secretive. Cat had to wait. He waited through another terrifying dinner, and then through a long, long evening. Gwendolen locked herself in her room after dinner and told him to go away when he knocked.

* * *

Next morning, Cat woke up early and hurried to the nearest of his three windows. He saw at once what Gwendolen had been doing. The lawn was ruined. It was not a smooth stretch of green velvet any longer. It was a mass of molehills. As far as Cat could see in both directions, there were little green mounds, little heaps of raw earth, long lines of raw earth and long green furrows of raised grass. There must have been an army of moles at work on it all night. About a dozen gardeners were standing in a gloomy huddle, scratching their heads over it.

Cat threw on his clothes and dashed downstairs. Gwendolen was leaning out of her window in her frilly cotton nightdress, glowing with pride. "Look at that!" she said to Cat. "Isn't it marvelous! There's acres of it too. It took me hours yesterday evening to make sure it was all spoiled. That will make Chrestomanci think a bit!"

Cat was sure it would. He did not know how much a huge stretch of turf like that would cost to replace, but he suspected it was a great deal. He was afraid Gwendolen would be in really bad trouble.

But, to his astonishment, nobody so much as mentioned the lawn. Euphemia came in a minute later, but all she said was, "You'll both be late for your breakfast again." Roger and Julia said nothing at all. They silently accepted the marmalade and Cat's knife when he passed them over, but the sole thing either of them said was when Julia dropped Cat's knife and picked it up again, all fluffy. She said, "Bother!" And when Mr. Saunders called them through for lessons, the only things he talked about were what he was teaching them. Cat decided that nobody knew Gwendolen had caused the moles. They could have no idea what a strong witch she was.

There were no lessons after lunch that day. Mr. Saunders explained that they always had Wednesday afternoons off. And at lunchtime, every molehill had gone. When they looked out of the playroom window, the lawn was like a sheet of velvet again.

"I don't believe it!" Gwendolen whispered to Cat. "It must be an illusion. They're trying to make me feel small."

They went out and looked after lunch. They had to be fairly cautious about it because Mr. Saunders was taking his afternoon off in a deck chair under one of the cedars, reading a yellow paperback book which seemed to amuse him a great deal. Gwendolen sauntered out into the middle of the lawn and pretended to be admiring the Castle. She pretended to tie her bootlace and prodded the turf with her fingers.

"I don't understand it!" she said. Being a witch, she knew the close, smooth turf was no illusion. "It really is all right! How was it done?"

"They must have carted in new turf while we were having lessons," Cat suggested.

"Don't be stupid!" said Gwendolen. "New turf would all be in squares still, and this isn't."

Mr. Saunders called to them.

Gwendolen looked, for a second, more apprehensive than Cat had ever seen her. But she hid it fairly well and led the way casually over to the deck chair. Cat saw that the yellow book was in French. Fancy being able to laugh at something in French! Mr. Saunders must be a learned magician as well as a strong one.

Mr. Saunders laid the book facedown on the once-more-beautiful grass and smiled up at them. "You two went away so quickly that you never gave me time to dish you out your pocket money. Here you are." He handed them each a large silver coin. Cat stared at his. It was a crown piece—five whole shillings. He had never had so much money to spend in his life. Mr. Saunders added to his amazement by saying, "You'll get that every Wednesday. I don't know whether you're savers or spenders. What Julia and Roger usually do is to go down to the village and blow it all on sweets."

"Thank you," said Cat, "very much. Shall we go down to the village, Gwendolen?"

"We may as well," Gwendolen agreed. She was divided between a defiant desire to stay at the Castle and face whatever trouble was coming over the moles and relief at an excuse to get away. "I expect Chrestomanci will send for me as soon as he realizes it was me," she said as they walked down the avenue of trees.

"Do you think it was Mr. Saunders who put the lawn right?" Cat asked.

Gwendolen frowned. "He couldn't have. He was teaching us."

"Those gardeners," suggested Cat. "Some of them could be warlocks. They did turn up awfully quickly to forbid us things."

Gwendolen laughed scornfully. "Think of the Willing Warlock."

Cat did, a little dubiously. The Willing Warlock was not much more gifted than Mrs. Sharp. He was usually hired for heavy carrying jobs, or to make the wrong horse win at the races. "All the same," he argued, "they could be specialists—garden warlocks."

Gwendolen only laughed again.

The village was just beyond the Castle gates, at the foot of the hill where the Castle stood. It was a pretty place, around a big green. Across the green, there were shops: a beautiful bow-fronted baker's and an equally beautiful sweet shop and post office. Cat wanted to visit both, but Gwendolen stopped at a third shop, which was a junk shop. Cat did not mind going into that either. It looked interesting. But Gwendolen shook her head irritably and stopped a village boy who was loitering near it.

"I was told a Mr. Baslam lives in this village. Can you tell me where he lives?"

The boy made a face. "Him? He's no good. Down there, at the end of that alley, if you really want to know." And he stood looking at them, with the air of someone who has earned sixpence for his pains.

Neither Cat nor Gwendolen had any money beside their crown pieces. They had to go away without giving him anything. The boy shouted after them.

"Stuck-up little witch! Mingy little warlock!"

Gwendolen did not mind this in the least, but Cat was so ashamed that he wanted to go back and explain.

Mr. Baslam lived in a shabby cottage with an ill-written notice propped in one window: *Eggsotick Serplys.* Gwendolen looked at it rather pityingly as she hammered on the door with the dingy knocker. When Mr. Baslam opened his door, he proved to be a fat person in old trousers which sagged to make room for his fatness, and with red, drooping eyes like a St. Bernard's. He started to shut the door again as soon as he saw them.

"Not today, thank you," he said, and a strong smell of beer came out with the words.

"Mr. Nostrum sent me," said Gwendolen. "Mr. William Nostrum."

The door stopped shutting. "Ah," said Mr. Baslam. "Then you better both come in. This way." He led them into a poky room containing four chairs, a table, and several dozen cases of stuffed animals. There was hardly room for all the cases of stuffed animals. They stood higgledy-piggledy, one on top of another, and they were all very dusty. "Sit down then," said Mr. Baslam, rather grudgingly.

Cat sat down gently and tried not to breathe too deeply. Beside the beery smell from Mr. Baslam, there was a faint rotting smell and a smell like pickles. Cat thought that some of the stuffed animals had not been properly cured. The smell did not seem to bother Gwendolen. She sat looking like a picture of a perfect little girl. Her cream-colored dress spread crisply around her and her broad hat becomingly shaded her golden hair. She looked at Mr. Baslam with severe blue eyes.

"I think your notice is spelled wrong."

Mr. Baslam drooped his St. Bernard eyes and made gestures that were meant to be joking. "I know. I know. But I don't want to be taken serious, do I? Not on the very threshold, as it were. Now what was you wanting? Mr. William Nostrum don't tell me too much of his plans. I'm only a humble supplier."

"I want some supplies, of course," said Gwendolen.

Cat listened, rather bored, to Gwendolen bargaining for the materials of witchcraft. Mr. Baslam fumbled in the backs of stuffed animal cases and fetched out newspaper screws of this and that—newts' eyes, snakes' tongues, cardamom, hellebore, mummy, niter, seed of moly, and various resins—which probably accounted for the unpleasant smell. He wanted more for them than Gwendolen would pay. She was determined to lay out her five shillings to the best possible advantage. Mr. Baslam seemed to resent it. "Know your own mind, don't you?" he said peevishly.

"I know how much things should cost," said Gwendolen. She took her hat off, packed the little screws of newspaper carefully into its crown, and put it neatly back on her head again. "And last, I think I shall be wanting some dragon's blood," she said.

"Ooooh!" said Mr. Baslam, dolefully shaking his head so that his hanging cheeks flapped. "Dragon's blood is banned from use, young lady. You ought to know that. I don't know as I can manage you any of that."

"Mr. Nostrum—both Mr. Nostrums—told me you could get *anything,*" said Gwendolen. "They said you were the best agent they knew. And I'm not asking for dragon's blood *now*. I'm ordering some."

Mr. Baslam looked gratified at being praised by the Nostrum brothers, but he was still dubious. "It's a fearful strong charm needs dragon's blood," he said plaintively. "You won't be doing anything that strong yourself, a young lady like you, now."

"I don't know yet," said Gwendolen. "But I think I might. I'm on Advanced Magic, you know. And I want dragon's blood in case I need it."

"It'll come dear," Mr. Baslam warned her. "It's costly stuff. There's the risk to pay for, you see. I don't want the law on me."

"I can pay," said Gwendolen. "I'll pay in installments. You can take the rest of the five shillings on account."

Mr. Baslam was unable to resist this. The way he looked at the crown piece Gwendolen handed to him made Cat see vividly a long row of frothing pints of beer. "Done," said Mr. Baslam. Gwendolen smiled graciously and got up to go. Cat thankfully leapt up too. "What about you, young gentleman?" Mr. Baslam asked wheedlingly. "Aren't you going to try your hand at a bit of necromancy at all?"

"He's just my brother," said Gwendolen.

"Oh. Ah. Um. Yes," said Mr. Baslam. "He's that one, of course. Well, good day to you both. Come again, any time."

"When will you have the dragon's blood?" Gwendolen asked him on the doorstep.

Mr. Baslam thought. "Say a week?"

Gwendolen's face glowed. "How quick! I knew you were a good agent. Where do you get it from so quickly?"

"Now that would be telling, wouldn't it?" said Mr. Baslam. "It has to come from another world, but which one is a trade secret, young lady."

Gwendolen was jubilant as they went back along the alley. "A week!" she said. "That's the quickest I've ever heard. It has to be smuggled in from this other world, you know. He must have awfully good connections there."

"Or he's got some already, inside a stuffed bird," said Cat, who had not liked Mr. Baslam at all. "Whatever do you want dragon's blood for? Mrs. Sharp says it costs fifty pounds an ounce."

"Be quiet," said Gwendolen. "Oh, quick! Hurry, Cat! Get into that sweet shop. She mustn't know where I've been."

Out on the village green, a lady carrying a parasol was talking to a clergyman. She was Chrestomanci's wife. Cat and Gwendolen bundled themselves into the shop and hoped she had not seen them. There, Cat bought them a bag of toffee each. Milly was still there, so he bought some licorice too. Milly was still talking to the clergyman even then, so he bought Gwendolen a pen wiper and himself a postcard of the Castle. Milly was still there. But Cat could not think of anything else to buy, so they had to come out of the shop.

Milly beckoned to them as soon as they did. "Come and meet the dear vicar."

The vicar, who was old, with a weak and wandering look, shakily shook hands with them and said he would see them on Sunday. Then he said he really must be going now.

"And so must we," said Milly. "Come on, my dears. We'll walk back to the Castle together."

There was nothing to do but walk beside her under the shadow of her parasol, across the green and between the lodge gates. Cat was afraid she was going to ask them why they had been visiting Mr. Baslam. Gwendolen was sure she was going to ask her about the moles in the lawn. But what Milly said was, "I am glad of a chance to talk to you, my loves. I haven't had a moment to see how you were getting on. Are you all right? Are you finding it very strange?"

"A—a little," Cat admitted.

"The first few days are always the worst, anywhere," said Milly.

"I'm sure you'll soon find your way around. And don't hesitate to use the toys in the playroom if you want. They're for everyone. Private toys are in one's own room. How are you liking your rooms?"

Cat looked up at her in astonishment. She was talking as if moles and witchcraft had never existed. Milly beamed back at him. Despite her elegant ruched dress and her lacy parasol, she was a most ordinary, kind, good-natured lady. Cat liked her. He assured Milly that he liked his room, and his bathroom—particularly the shower—and explained that he had never had a bathroom to himself before.

"Oh, I'm glad. I did so hope you'd like it," said Milly. "Miss Bessemer wanted to put you next to Roger, but I thought that room was so dull—and it doesn't have a shower. Look at it some time and you'll see what I mean."

She walked on up the avenue, chattering away, and Cat found himself doing all the rest of the talking. As soon as it was clear that Milly was not going to mention either lawns or exotic supplies, Gwendolen began to despise her. She kept up a scornful silence, and left Cat to talk. After a while, Milly asked Cat what thing about the Castle he was finding strangest.

Cat answered shyly, but without hesitation, "The way everyone talks at supper."

Milly let out such a yell of despair that Cat jumped and Gwendolen was more scornful than ever. "Oh dear! Poor Eric! I've seen you looking! Isn't it awful? Michael gets these enthusiasms, and then he can talk of nothing else. It should be wearing off in a day or so, though, and then we can have reasonable talk again and make a few jokes. I like to laugh at dinner, don't you? I'm afraid nothing will stop poor Bernard talking about stocks and shares, but you mustn't take any notice of that. Nobody listens to Bernard. Do you like eclairs, by the way?"

"Yes," said Cat.

"Oh good!" said Milly. "I've ordered tea for us on the lawn, since this is your first Wednesday and I didn't want to waste this lovely weather. Isn't it funny how September's nearly always fine? If we slip through the trees here, we should be on the lawn as soon as tea is."

Sure enough, they followed Milly out of the shrubbery to find a whole cluster of deck chairs around the one where Mr. Saunders was, and footmen putting out tables and carrying trays. Most of the Family were gathering among the deck chairs. Gwendolen followed Milly and Cat over, looking nervous and defiant. She knew Chrestomanci was going to speak to her about the lawn now and, to make matters worse, she was not going to have a chance to take the exotic supplies out of her hat before he did.

But Chrestomanci was not there, though everyone else was. Milly pushed between stocks-and-shares Bernard and Julia, and past the old lady with mittens, to point her parasol sternly at Mr. Saunders. "Michael, you are absolutely forbidden to talk about Art during tea," she said, and spoiled the sternness rather by laughing.

The Family evidently felt much the same as Cat. Several of them said "Hear, hear!" and Roger said, "Can we start, Mummy?"

Cat enjoyed the tea. It was the first time he had enjoyed anything since he came to the Castle. There were paper-thin cucumber sandwiches and big squashy eclairs. Cat ate even more than Roger did. He was surrounded by cheerful, ordinary chat from the Family, with a hum of stocks and shares in the background, and the sun lay warm and peaceful on the green stretches of the lawn. Cat was glad someone had somehow restored it. He liked it better smooth. He began to think he could almost be happy at the Castle, with a little practice.

Gwendolen was nothing like so happy. The newspaper packets weighed on her head. Their smell spoiled the taste of the eclairs. And she knew she would have to wait until dinner before Chrestomanci spoke to her about the lawn.

Dinner was later that night because of the tea. Dusk was falling when they filed into the dining room. There were lighted candles all down the polished table. Cat could see them, and the rest of the room, reflected in the row of long windows facing him. It was a pleasing sight, and a useful one. Cat could see the footman coming. For once he was not taken by surprise when the man thrust a tray of little fish and pickled cabbage over his shoulder. And, as he was now forbidden to use his right hand, Cat felt quite justified in changing the serving things over. He began to feel he was settling in.

Because he had not been allowed to talk about Art at tea, Mr. Saunders was more than usually eloquent at dinner. He talked and he talked. He took Chrestomanci's attention to himself, and he talked at him. Chrestomanci seemed dreamy and good-humored. He listened and nodded. And Gwendolen grew crosser every minute. Chrestomanci said not a word about lawns, neither here nor in the drawing room beforehand. It became clearer and clearer that no one was going to mention the matter at all.

Gwendolen was furious. She wanted her powers recognized. She wanted to show Chrestomanci she was a witch to be reckoned with. So there was nothing for it but to begin on another spell. She was a little hampered by not having any ingredients to hand, but there was one thing she could do quite easily.

The dinner went on. Mr. Saunders talked on. Footmen came around with the next course. Cat looked over at the windows to see when the silver plate would come to him. And he nearly screamed.

There was a skinny white creature there. It was pressed against the dark outside of the glass, mouthing and waving. It looked like the lost ghost of a lunatic. It was weak and white and loathsome. It was draggled and slimy. Even though Cat realized almost at once that it was Gwendolen's doing, he still stared at it in horror.

Milly saw him staring. She looked herself, shuddered, and tapped Chrestomanci gently on the back of the hand with her spoon. Chrestomanci came out of his gentle dream and glanced at the window too. He gave the piteous creature a bored look, and sighed.

"And so I still think Florence is the finest of all the Italian states," said Mr. Saunders.

"People usually put in a word for Venice," said Chrestomanci. "Frazier, would you draw the curtains, please? Thank you."

"No, no. In my opinion, Venice is overrated," Mr. Saunders asserted, and he went on to explain why, while the butler drew the long orange curtains and shut the creature out of sight.

"Yes, maybe you're right. Florence has more to offer," Chrestomanci agreed. "By the way, Gwendolen, when I said the Castle, I meant of course the Castle grounds as well as indoors. Now, do carry on, Michael. Venice."

Everyone carried on, except Cat. He could imagine the creature still mouthing and fumbling at the glass behind the orange curtains. He could not eat for thinking of it.

"It's all right, stupid! I've sent it away," said Gwendolen. Her voice was sticky with rage.

CHAPTER 6

Gwendolen gave vent to her fury in her room after dinner. She jumped on her bed and threw cushions about, screaming. Cat stood prudently back against the wall waiting for her to finish. But Gwendolen did not finish until she had pledged herself to a campaign against Chrestomanci.

"I hate this place!" she bawled. "They try to cover everything up in soft, sweet niceness. I hate it, I hate it!" Her voice was muffled among the velvets of her room and swallowed up in the prevailing softness of the Castle. "Do you hear it?" Gwendolen screamed. "It's an eiderdown of hideous niceness! I wreck their lawn, so they give me tea. I conjure up a lovely apparition, and they have the curtains drawn. *Frazier, would you draw the curtains, please!* Ugh! Chrestomanci makes me sick!"

"I didn't think it was a lovely apparition," Cat said, shivering.

"Ha, ha! You didn't know I could do that, did you?" said Gwendolen. "It wasn't to frighten *you*, you idiot. It was to give Chrestomanci a shock. I hate him! He wasn't even interested."

"What did he have us to live here for, if he isn't interested in you either?" Cat wondered.

Gwendolen was rather struck by this. "I hadn't thought of that," she said. "It may be serious. Go away. I want to think about it. Anyway," she shouted, as Cat was going to the door, "he's going to *be* interested, if it's the last thing I do! I'm going to do something every day until he notices!"

Once again, Cat was mournfully on his own. Remembering what Milly had said, he went along to the playroom. But Roger and Julia were there, playing with soldiers on the stained carpet. The little tin grenadiers were marching about. Some were wheeling up cannon. Others were lying behind cushions, firing their rifles with little pinpricks of bangs. Roger and Julia turned around guiltily.

"You won't mention this, will you?" said Julia.

"Would you like to come and play too?" Roger asked politely.

"Oh, no thanks," Cat said hastily. He knew he could never join in this kind of game unless Gwendolen helped him. But he did not dare disturb Gwendolen in her present mood. And he had nothing to do. Then he remembered that Milly had obviously expected him to poke about the Castle more than he had done. So he set off to explore, feeling rather daring.

The Castle seemed strange at night. There were dim little electric lights at regular intervals. The green carpet glowed gently, and things were reflected in the polished floor and walls even more strongly than they were by day. Cat walked softly along, accompanied by several reflected ghosts of himself, until he hardly felt real. All the doors he saw were closed. Cat listened at one or two and heard nothing. He had not quite the courage to open any of them. He went on and on.

After a while he found he had somehow worked around to the older part of the Castle. Here the walls were whitewashed stone and all the windows went in nearly three feet before there was any glass. Then Cat came to a staircase which was the twin of the one that twisted up to his room, except that it twisted in the opposite direction. Cat went cautiously up it.

He was just on the last bend when a door at the top opened. A brighter square of light shone on the wall at the head of the stairs, and a shadow stood in it that could only belong to Chrestomanci. No one else's shadow could be so tall, with such a smooth head and such a lot of ruffles on its shirt front. Cat stopped.

"And let's hope the wretched girl won't try that again," Chrestomanci said, out of sight above. He sounded a good deal more alert than usual, and rather angry.

Mr. Saunders' voice, from farther away, said, "I've had about enough of her already, frankly. I suppose she'll come to her senses soon. What possessed her to give away the source of her power like that?"

"Ignorance," said Chrestomanci. "If I thought she had the least idea what she was doing, it would be the last thing she ever did in that line—or any other."

"My back was to it," said Mr. Saunders. "Which was it? Number five?"

"No. Number three, by the look of its hair. A revenant," said Chrestomanci. "For which we must be thankful." He began to come down the stairs. Cat was too scared to move. "I'll have to get the Examining

Board to revise their Elementary Magic Courses," Chrestomanci called back as he came downstairs, "to include more theory. These hedge wizards push their good pupils straight on to advanced work without any proper grounding at all." Saying this, Chrestomanci came down around the corner and saw Cat. "Oh, hello," he said. "I'd no idea you were here. Like to come up and have a look at Michael's workshop?"

Cat nodded. He did not dare do otherwise.

Chrestomanci seemed quite friendly, however, and so did Mr. Saunders when Chrestomanci ushered Cat into the room at the top of the stairs. "Hello, Eric," he said in his cheerful way. "Have a look around. Does any of this mean anything to you?"

Cat shook his head. The room was round, like his own, but larger, and it was a regular magician's workshop. That much he could see. He recognized the five-pointed star painted on the floor. The smell coming from the burning cresset hanging from the ceiling was the same smell that had hung about Coven Street, back in Wolvercote. But he had no idea of the use of the things set out on the various trestle tables. One table was crowded with torts and limbecks, some bubbling, some empty. A second was piled with books and scrolls. The third bench had signs chalked all over it and a mummified creature of some sort lying among the signs.

Cat's eyes traveled over all this, and over more books crammed into shelves around the walls, and more shelves filled with jars of ingredients—big jars, like the ones in sweet shops. He realized Mr. Saunders worked in a big way. His scudding eyes raced over some of the labels on the huge jars: *Newts' Eyes, Gum Arabic, Elixir St. John's Wort, Dragon's Blood (dried).* The last jar was almost full of dark brown powder. Cat's eyes went back to the mummified animal stretched among the signs chalked on the third table. Its feet had claws like a dog's. It looked like a large lizard. But there seemed to be wings on its back. Cat was almost sure it had once been a small dragon.

"Means nothing, eh?" said Mr. Saunders.

Cat turned around and found that Chrestomanci had gone. That made him a little easier. "This must have cost a lot," he said.

"The taxpayer pays, fortunately," said Mr. Saunders. "Would you like to learn what all this is about?"

"You mean, learn witchcraft?" Cat asked. "No. No thanks. I wouldn't be any good at it."

"Well, I had at least two other things in mind besides witchcraft," Mr. Saunders said. "But what makes you think you'd be no good?"

"Because I can't do it," Cat explained. "Spells just don't work for me."

"Are you sure you went about them in the right way?" Mr. Saunders asked. He wandered up to the mummified dragon—or whatever—and gave it an absentminded flick. To Cat's disgust, the thing twitched all over. Filmy wings jerked and spread on its back. Then it went lifeless again. The sight sent Cat backing toward the door. He was almost as alarmed as he was the time Miss Larkins suddenly spoke with a man's voice. And, come to think of it, the voice had been not so unlike Mr. Saunders'.

"I went about it every way I could think," Cat said, backing. "And I couldn't even turn buttons into gold. And that was simple."

Mr. Saunders laughed. "Perhaps you weren't greedy enough. All right. Cut along, if you want to go."

Cat fled, in great relief. As he ran through the strange corridors, he thought he ought to let Gwendolen know that Chrestomanci had, after all, been interested in her apparition, and even angry. But Gwendolen had locked her door and would not answer when he called to her.

He tried again next morning. But before he had a chance to speak to Gwendolen, Euphemia came in, carrying a letter. As Gwendolen snatched it eagerly from Euphemia, Cat recognized Mr. Nostrum's jagged writing on the envelope.

The next moment, Gwendolen was raging again. "Who did this? When did this come?" The envelope had been neatly cut open along the top.

"This morning, by the postmark," said Euphemia. "And don't look at me like that. Miss Bessemer gave it to me open."

"How *dare* she!" said Gwendolen. "How dare she read my letters! I'm going straight to Chrestomanci about this!"

"You'll regret it if you do," said Euphemia, as Gwendolen pushed past her to the door.

Gwendolen whirled around on her. "Oh, shut up, you stupid frog-faced girl!" Cat thought that was a little unfair. Euphemia, though she did have rather goggling eyes, was actually quite pretty. "Come on, Cat!" Gwendolen shouted at him, and she ran away along the corridor with her letter. Cat panted behind her and, once again, did not catch up with her until they were beside the marble staircase. "Chrestomanci!" bawled Gwendolen, thin and small and unechoing.

Chrestomanci was coming up the marble staircase in a wide, flowing dressing gown that was partly orange and partly bright pink. He looked like the Emperor of Peru.

By the suave, vague look on his face, he had not noticed Gwendolen and Cat.

Gwendolen shouted down at him. "Here, you! Come here at once!" Chrestomanci's face turned upward and his eyebrows went up. "Someone's been opening my letters," said Gwendolen. "And I don't care who it is, but I'm not having it! Do you hear?"

Cat gasped at the way she spoke. Chrestomanci seemed perplexed. "How are you not having it?" he said.

"I won't put up with it!" Gwendolen shouted at him. "In future, my letters are going to come to me closed!"

"You mean you want me to steam them open and stick them down afterward?" Chrestomanci asked doubtfully. "It's more trouble, but I'll do that if it makes you happier."

Gwendolen stared at him. "You mean *you* did it? *You* read a letter addressed to *me*?"

Chrestomanci nodded blandly. "Naturally. If someone like Henry Nostrum writes letters to you, I have to make sure he's not writing anything unsuitable. He's a very seedy person."

"He was my teacher!" Gwendolen said furiously. "You've no right to!"

"It's a pity," said Chrestomanci, "that you were taught by a hedge wizard. You'll have to unlearn such a lot. And it's a pity too that I've no right to open your letters. I hope you don't get many, or my conscience will give me no peace."

"You intend to go on?" Gwendolen said. "Then watch out. I warn you!"

"That is very considerate of you," said Chrestomanci. "I like to be warned." He came up the rest of the marble stairs and went past Gwendolen and Cat. The pink and orange dressing gown swirled, revealing a bright scarlet lining. Cat blinked.

Gwendolen stared vengefully as the dazzling dressing gown flowed away along the gallery. "Oh no, don't notice me, will you!" she said. "Make jokes. You wait! Cat, I'm so furious!"

"You were awfully rude," said Cat.

"He deserved it," said Gwendolen, and began to hurry back toward the playroom. "Opening poor Mr. Nostrum's letter! It isn't that I mind him reading it. We arranged a code, so horrid Chrestomanci will never know what it's really saying, but there *is* the signature. But it's the insult. The indignity. I'm at their mercy in this Castle. I'm all on my own in distress and I can't even stop them reading my letters. But I'll show them. You wait!"

Cat knew better than to say anything. Gwendolen slammed into the playroom, flounced down at the table, and began at last to read her letter.

"I told you so," said Euphemia, while Mary was working the lift.

Gwendolen shot her a look. "You wait too," she said, and went on reading. After a bit, she looked in the envelope again. "There's one for you too," she said to Cat, and tossed him a sheet of paper. "Mind you reply to it."

Cat took it, wondering nervously why Mr. Nostrum should write to him. But it was from Mrs. Sharp. She wrote:

Me dear Cat,

Ow are you doin then me love? I fine meself lonesum an missin you both particular you the place seems so quiete. Thourght I was lookin forwards to a bit peace but missin yer voice an wishin you was comin in, bringin appels. One thing happen an that was a gennelman come an give five poun for the ole cat that was yer fidel so I feel flush and had idear of packin you up a parsel of jinjerbredmen and mebbe bringin them to you one of these days but Mr. Nostrum sez not to. Spect your in the lap of luckshury anyhows. Love to Gwendolen. Wish you was back here Cat and the money means nothin.

Your loving,
Ellen Sharp

Cat read this with a warm, smiling, tearful feeling. He found he was missing Mrs. Sharp as much as she evidently missed him. He was so homesick he could not eat his bread, and the cocoa seemed to choke him. He did not hear one word in five that Mr. Saunders said.

"Is something the matter with you, Eric?" Mr. Saunders demanded.

As Cat dragged his mind back from Coven Street, the window blacked out. The room was suddenly pitch dark. Julia squeaked. Mr. Saunders groped his way to the switch and turned the light on. As he did so, the window became transparent again, revealing Roger grinning, Julia startled, Gwendolen sitting demurely, and Mr. Saunders with his hand on the switch looking irritably at her.

"I suppose the cause of this is outside the Castle grounds, is it?" he said.

"Outside the lodge gates," Gwendolen said smugly. "I put it there this morning." By this, Cat knew her campaign against Chrestomanci had been launched.

The window blacked out again.

"How often are we to expect this?" Mr. Saunders said in the dark.

"Twice every half hour," said Gwendolen.

"Thank you," Mr. Saunders said nastily, and he left the light on.

"Now we can see, Gwendolen, write out one hundred times, *I must keep the spirit of the laws and not the letter* and, Roger, take that grin off your face."

All that day, all the windows in the Castle blacked out regularly twice every half hour. But if Gwendolen had hoped to make Chrestomanci angry, she did not succeed. Nothing happened, except that everyone kept the lights on all the time. It was rather a nuisance, but no one seemed to mind.

Before lunch, Cat went outside onto the lawn to see what the blackouts looked like from the other side. It was rather as if two black shutters were flicking regularly across the rows of windows. They started at the top right-hand corner and flicked steadily across, along the next row from left to right, and then from right to left along the next, and so on, until they reached the bottom. Then they started at the top again. Cat had watched about half a complete performance when he found Roger beside him, watching critically with his pudgy hands in his pockets.

"Your sister must have a very tidy mind," Roger said.

"I think all witches have," said Cat. Then he was embarrassed. Of course he was talking to one—or at least to a warlock in the making.

"I don't seem to have," Roger remarked, not in the least worried. "Nor has Julia. And I don't think Michael has, really. Would you like to come and play in our tree house after lessons?"

Cat was very flattered. He was so pleased that he forgot how homesick he was. He spent a very happy evening down in the wood, helping to rebuild the roof of the tree house. He came back to the Castle when the dressing gong went, and found that the window-spell was fading. When the windows darkened, it only produced a sort of gray twilight indoors. By the following morning it was gone, and Chrestomanci had not said a word.

Gwendolen returned to the attack the next morning. She caught the baker's boy as he cycled through the lodge gates with the square front container of his bicycle piled high with loaves for the Castle. The baker's boy arrived at the kitchen looking a little dazed and saying his head felt swimmy. As a consequence, the children had to have scones for breakfast. It seemed that when the bread was cut, the most interesting things happened.

"You're giving us all a good laugh," Mary said, as she brought the scones from the lift. "I'll say that for your naughtiness, Gwendolen. Roberts thought he'd gone mad when he found he was cutting away at an old boot. So Cook cuts another, and next moment she and Nancy are trying to climb on the same chair because of all those white mice.

But it was Mr. Frazier's face that made me laugh the most, when he says 'Let me' and finds himself chipping at a stone. Then the—"

"Don't encourage her. You know what she's like," said Euphemia.

"Be careful I don't start on you," Gwendolen said sourly.

Roger found out privately from Mary what had happened to the other loaves. One had become a white rabbit, one had been an ostrich egg—which had burst tremendously all over the boot boy—and another a vast white onion. After that, Gwendolen's invention had run out and she had turned the rest into cheese. "Old bad cheese, though," Roger said, giving honor where honor was due.

It was not known whether Chrestomanci also gave honor where it was due because, once again, he said not a word to anyone.

The next day was Saturday. Gwendolen caught the farmer delivering the churn of milk the Castle used daily. The breakfast cocoa tasted horrible.

"I'm beginning to get annoyed," Julia said tartly. "Daddy may take no notice, but he drinks tea with lemon." She stared meaningly at Gwendolen. Gwendolen stared back, and there was that invisible feeling of clashing Cat had noticed when Gwendolen had wanted her mother's earrings from Mrs. Sharp. This time, however, Gwendolen did not have things all her own way. She lowered her eyes and looked peevish.

"I'm getting sick of getting up early, anyway," she said crossly.

This, from Gwendolen, simply meant she would do something later in the day in future. But Julia thought she had beaten Gwendolen, and this was a mistake.

They had lessons on Saturday morning, which annoyed Gwendolen very much. "It's monstrous," she said to Mr. Saunders. "Why do we have to be tormented like this?"

"It's the price I have to pay for my holiday on Wednesday," Mr. Saunders told her. "And, speaking of tormenting, I prefer you to bewitch something other than the milk."

"I'll remember that," Gwendolen said sweetly.

CHAPTER 7

It rained on Saturday afternoon. Gwendolen shut herself into her room and, once again, Cat did not know what to do. He wrote to Mrs. Sharp on the back of his postcard of the Castle, but that only took ten minutes, and it was too wet to go out and mail it. Cat was hanging about at the foot of his stairs, wondering what to do now, when Roger came out of the playroom and saw him.

"Oh, good," said Roger. "Julia won't play soldiers. Will you?"

"But I can't—not like you do," Cat said.

"It doesn't matter," said Roger. "Honestly."

But it did. No matter how cunningly Cat deployed his lifeless tin army, as soon as Roger's soldiers began to march, Cat's men fell over like ninepins. They fell in batches and droves and in battalions. Cat moved them furiously this way and that, grabbing them by handfuls and scooping them with the lid of the box, but he was always on the retreat. In five minutes he was reduced to three soldiers hidden behind a cushion.

"This is no good," said Roger.

"No, it isn't," Cat agreed mournfully.

"Julia," said Roger.

"What?" said Julia. She was curled in the shabbiest armchair, managing to suck a lollipop, to read a book called *In the Hands of the Lamas,* and to knit, all at the same time. Her knitting, hardly surprisingly, looked like a vest for a giraffe which had been dipped in six shades of gray dye.

"Can you make Cat's soldiers move for him?" said Roger.

"I'm reading," said Julia, around the edges of the lollipop. "It's thrilling. One of them's got lost and they think he's perished miserably."

"Be a sport," said Roger. "I'll tell you whether he did perish, if you don't."

"If you do, I'll turn your underpants to ice," Julia said amiably. "All right." Without taking her eyes off her book or the lollipop out of her mouth, she fumbled out her handkerchief and tied a knot in it. She laid the knotted handkerchief on the arm of her chair and went on knitting.

Cat's fallen soldiers picked themselves up from the floor and straightened their tin tunics. This was a great improvement, though it was still not entirely satisfactory. Cat could not tell his soldiers what to do. He had to shoo them into position with his hands. The soldiers did not seem happy. They looked up at the great flapping hands above them in the greatest consternation. Cat was sure one fainted from terror. But he got them positioned in the end—with great cunning, he thought.

The battle began. The soldiers seemed to know how to do that for themselves. Cat had a company in reserve behind a cushion and, when the battle was at its fiercest, he shooed them out to fall on Roger's right wing. Roger's right wing turned and fought. And every one of Cat's reserve turned and ran. The rest of his army saw them running away and ran too. In three seconds, they were all trying to hide in the toy cupboard, and Roger's soldiers were cutting them down in swathes.

Roger was exasperated. "Julia's soldiers *always* run away!"

"Because that's just what I would do," Julia said, putting out a knitting needle to mark her place in her book. "I can't think why all soldiers don't."

"Well, make them a bit braver," said Roger. "It's not fair on Eric."

"You only said make them move," Julia was arguing when the door opened and Gwendolen put her head in.

"I want Cat," she said.

"He's busy," said Roger.

"That doesn't matter," said Gwendolen. "I need him."

Julia stretched out a knitting needle toward Gwendolen and wrote a little cross in the air with it. The cross floated, glowing, for a second. "Out," said Julia. "Go away." Gwendolen backed away from the cross and shut the door again. It was as if she could not help herself. The expression on her face was very annoyed indeed. Julia smiled placidly and pointed her knitting needle toward Cat's soldiers. "Carry on," she said. "I've filled their hearts with courage."

When the dressing gong sounded, Cat went to find out what Gwendolen had wanted him for. Gwendolen was very busy reading a fat, new-looking book and could not spare him any attention at first. Cat tipped his head sideways and read the title of the book. *Otherworld Studies,*

Series III. While he was doing it, Gwendolen began to laugh. "Oh, I see how it works now!" she exclaimed. "It's even better than I thought! I know what to do now!" Then she lowered the book and asked Cat what he thought he was doing.

"Why did you need me?" said Cat. "Where did you get that book?"

"From the Castle library," said Gwendolen. "And I don't need you now. I was going to explain to you about Mr. Nostrum's plans, and I might even have told you about mine, but I changed my mind when you just sat there and let that fat prig Julia send me away."

"I didn't know Mr. Nostrum had any plans," Cat said. "The dressing gong's gone."

"Of course he has plans—and I heard it—why do you think I wrote to Chrestomanci?" said Gwendolen. "But it's no good trying to wheedle me. I'm not going to tell you and you're going to be sorry. And piggy-priggy Julia is going to be sorrier even sooner!"

Gwendolen revenged herself on Julia at the start of dinner. A footman was just passing a bowl of soup over Julia's shoulder when the skirt of Julia's dress turned to snakes. Julia jumped up with a shriek. Soup poured over the snakes and flew far and wide, and the footman yelled, "Lord have mercy on us!" among the sounds of the smashing soup bowl.

Then there was dead silence, except for the hissing of snakes. There were twenty of them, hanging by their tails from Julia's waistband, writhing and striking. Everyone froze, with their heads stiffly turned Julia's way. Julia stood like a statue, with her arms up out of reach of the snakes. She swallowed and said the words of a spell.

Nobody blamed her. Mr. Saunders said, "Good girl!"

Under the spell, the snakes stiffened and fanned out, so that they were standing like a ballet skirt above Julia's petticoats. Everyone could see where Julia had torn a flounce of a petticoat building the tree house and mended it in a hurry with red darning wool.

"Have you been bitten?" said Chrestomanci.

"No," said Julia. "The soup muddled them. If you don't mind, I'll go and change this dress now."

She left the room, walking very slowly and carefully, and Milly went with her. While the footmen, all rather green in the face, were clearing up the spilled soup, Chrestomanci said, "Spitefulness is one thing I won't have at the dinner table. Gwendolen, oblige me by going to the playroom. Your food will be brought to you there."

Gwendolen got up and went without a word. As Julia and Milly did not come back, the dining table seemed rather empty that evening. It was all stocks and shares from Bernard at one end, and statues again from Mr. Saunders at the other.

Cat found that Gwendolen was rather triumphant. She felt she had made an impression on Chrestomanci at last. So she returned to the attack with a will on Sunday.

On Sunday the Family dressed in its best and walked down to Morning Service at the village church. Witches are not supposed to like church. Nor are they supposed to be able to work magic there. But this never bothered Gwendolen at all. Mrs. Sharp had many times remarked on it, as showing what exceptional talents Gwendolen had. Gwendolen sat next to Cat in the Chrestomanci pew, looking the picture of demure innocence in her *broiderie anglaise* Sunday dress and hat, and found her place in her prayer book as if she were truly saintly.

The village people nudged one another and whispered about her. This rather pleased Gwendolen. She liked to be well known. She kept up the pretense of saintliness until the sermon had begun.

The vicar climbed shakily into the pulpit and gave his text in a weak, wandering voice. "For there were many in the congregation that were not sanctified." This was certainly to the point. Unfortunately, nothing else he said was. He told, in his weak, wandering voice, of weak, wandering episodes in his early life. He compared them with weak, wandering things he thought were happening in the world today. He told them they had better be sanctified or all sorts of things—which he forgot to mention—would happen, which reminded him of a weak, wandering thing his aunts used to tell him.

Mr. Saunders was asleep by this time, and so was stocks-and-shares Bernard. The old lady with mittens was nodding. One of the saints in the stained-glass windows yawned, and put up his crosier elegantly to cover his mouth. He looked around at his neighbor, who was a formidable nun. Her robes hung in severe folds, like a bundle of sticks. The bishop stretched out his stained-glass crosier and tapped the nun on the shoulder. She resented it. She marched into his window and began shaking him.

Cat saw her. He saw the colored, transparent bishop clouting the nun over the wimple, and the nun giving him as good as she got. Meanwhile, the hairy saint next to them made a dive for *his* neighbor, who was a kingly sort of saint, holding a model of the Castle. The kingly saint dropped his model and fled for protection, in a twinkle of glassy feet, behind the robes of a simpering lady saint. The hairy saint jumped gleefully up and down on the model of the Castle.

One by one, all the windows came to life. Almost every saint turned and fought the one next to him. Those who had no one to fight either hitched up their robes and did silly dances, or waved to the vicar, who rambled on without noticing. The little tiny people blowing trumpets in the corners of the windows sprang and gamboled and frisked, and pulled transparent faces at anyone who was looking. The hairy saint winkled the kingly one out from behind the simpering lady and chased him from window to window in and out of all the other fighting couples.

By this time, the whole congregation had seen. Everyone stared, or whispered, or leaned craning this way and that to watch the twinkling glass toes of the kingly saint.

There was such a disturbance that Mr. Saunders woke up, puzzled. He looked at the windows, understood, and looked sharply at Gwendolen. She sat with her eyes demurely cast down, the picture of innocence. Cat glanced at Chrestomanci. For all he could tell, Chrestomanci was attending to the vicar's every word and had not even noticed the windows. Milly was sitting on the edge of her seat, looking agitated. And the vicar still rambled on, quite unconscious of the turmoil.

The curate, however, felt he ought to put a stop to the unseemly behavior of the windows. He fetched a cross and a candle. Followed by a giggling choirboy swinging incense, he went from window to window murmuring exorcisms. Gwendolen obligingly stopped each saint in its tracks as he came to it—which meant that the kingly saint was stranded halfway across the wall. But, as soon as the curate's back was turned, he began to run again, and the free-for-all went on more riotously than before. The congregation rolled about, gasping.

Chrestomanci turned and looked at Mr. Saunders. Mr. Saunders nodded. There was a sort of flicker, which jolted Cat where he sat and, when he looked at the windows, every saint was standing stiff and glassy there, as they should be. Gwendolen's head came up indignantly. Then she shrugged. At the back of the church a great stone crusader sat up on his tomb and, with much rasping of stone, thumbed his nose at the vicar.

"Dearly beloved—" said the vicar. He saw the crusader. He stopped, confounded.

The curate hastened up and tried to exorcise the crusader. A look of irritation crossed the crusader's face. He lifted his great stone sword. But Mr. Saunders made a sharp gesture. The crusader, looking even more irritated, lowered his sword and lay down again with a thump that shook the church.

"There are some in this congregation who are certainly not sanctified," the vicar said sadly. "Let us pray."

When everyone straggled out of church, Gwendolen sauntered out among them, quite impervious to the shocked looks everyone gave her as she passed. Milly hurried after her and seized her arm. She looked most upset. "That was disgraceful, you ungodly child! I don't dare *speak* to the poor vicar. There is such a thing as going too far, you know!"

"Have I gone it?" Gwendolen asked, really interested.

"Very nearly," said Milly.

But not quite, it seemed. Chrestomanci did not say anything to Gwendolen, though he said a great deal, very soothingly, both to the vicar and to the curate.

"Why doesn't your father tell Gwendolen off?" Cat asked Roger as they walked back up the avenue. "Taking no notice of her just makes her worse."

"I don't know," said Roger. "He comes down on *us* hard enough if we use witchcraft. Perhaps he thinks she'll get tired of it. Has she told you what she's going to do tomorrow?" It was clear Roger could hardly wait.

"No. She's cross with me for playing soldiers with you," said Cat.

"Her stupid fault for thinking she owns you," said Roger. "Let's get into old clothes and build some more of the tree house."

Gwendolen was angry when Cat went off with Roger again. Maybe that was why she thought of what she did next. Or perhaps, as she said, she had other reasons. At all events, when Cat woke up on Monday morning, it was dark. It felt very early. It looked even earlier. So Cat turned over and went to sleep again.

He was astonished to find Mary shaking him a minute later. "It's twenty to nine, Eric. Get up, do!"

"But it's dark!" Cat protested. "Is it raining?"

"No," said Mary. "Your sister's been hard at it again. And where she gets the strength from, a little girl like her, beats me!"

Feeling tired and Mondayish, Cat dragged himself out of bed and found he could not see out of the windows. Each window was a dark crisscross of branches and leaves—green leaves, bluish cedar sprays, pine needles, and leaves just turning yellow and brown. One window had a rose pressed against it, and there were bunches of grapes squashed on both of the others. And behind them, it looked as if there was a mile-thick forest. "Good Lord!" he said.

"You may well look!" said Mary. "That sister of yours has fetched every tree in the grounds and stood them as close as they can get to the Castle. You wonder what she'll think of next."

The darkness made Cat weary and gloomy. He did not want to get dressed. But Mary stood over him, and made him wash too. The reason she was so dutiful, Cat suspected, was that she wanted to tell someone all about the difficulties the trees were causing. She told Cat that the yew trees from the formal garden were packed so tight by the kitchen door that the men had to hack a path for the milk to come through. There were three oak trees against the main front door, and no one could budge it. "And the apples are all underfoot among the yew trees, so it smells like a cider press in the kitchen," Mary said.

When Cat arrived wearily in the playroom, it was even darker there. In the deep greenish light, he could see that Gwendolen was, understandably, white and tired. But she looked satisfied enough.

"I don't think I like these trees," Cat whispered to her when Roger and Julia had gone through to the schoolroom. "Why couldn't you do something smaller and funnier?"

"Because I'm not a laughingstock!" Gwendolen hissed back. "And I needed to do it. I had to know how much power I could draw on."

"Quite a lot, I should think," Cat said, looking at the mass of horse-chestnut leaves pressed against the window.

Gwendolen smiled. "Better still when I've got my dragon's blood."

Cat nearly blurted out that he had seen dragon's blood in Mr. Saunders' workshop. But he stopped himself in time. He did not care for mighty works like this.

They spent another morning with the lights on, and at lunchtime, Cat, Julia, and Roger went out to have a look at the trees. They were disappointed to find that it was quite easy to get out of their private door. The rhododendrons were three feet away from it. Cat thought Gwendolen must intentionally have left them a way out, until he looked up and saw, from their bent branches and mashed leaves, that the bushes had indeed been squashed against the door earlier. It looked as if the trees were retreating.

Beyond the rhododendrons, they had to fight their way through something like a jungle. The trees were rammed so tight that, not only had twigs and leaves broken off by cartloads, but great branches had been torn away too, and fallen tangled with smashed roses, broken clematis, and mangled grapes. When the children tore themselves out on the other side of the jungle, blank daylight hit them like a hammer blow. They blinked. The gardens, the village, and even the hills beyond were bald. The only place where they could still see trees was above the old, gray, ruined wall of Chrestomanci's garden.

"It must have been a strong spell," said Roger.

"It's like a desert," said Julia. "I never thought I'd miss the trees so much!"

But halfway through the afternoon it became clear that the trees were going back to their proper places. They could see sky through the schoolroom window. A little later the trees had spread out and retreated so much that Mr. Saunders turned the light off. Shortly after that Cat and Roger noticed the ruins of the tree house, smashed to bits in the crowding, dangling-out of a chestnut tree.

"*Now* what are you staring at?" said Mr. Saunders.

"The tree house is broken," Roger said, looking moodily at Gwendolen.

"Perhaps Gwendolen would be kind enough to mend it again," Mr. Saunders suggested sarcastically.

If he was trying to goad Gwendolen into doing a kindly act, he failed. Gwendolen tossed her head. "Tree houses are stupid babyish things," she said coldly. She was very annoyed at the way the trees were retreating. "It's too bad!" she told Cat just before dinner. By that time the trees were almost back to their usual places. The only ones nearer than they should be were those on the hill opposite. The view looked smaller, somehow. "I hoped it would do for tomorrow too," Gwendolen said discontentedly. "Now I shall have to think of something else."

"Who sent them back? The garden warlocks?" Cat asked.

"I wish you wouldn't talk nonsense," said Gwendolen. "It's obvious who did it."

"You mean Mr. Saunders?" said Cat. "But couldn't the spell have been used up just pulling all the trees here?"

"You don't know a thing about it," said Gwendolen.

Cat knew he knew nothing of magic, but he found it queer all the same. The next day, when he went to see, there were no fallen twigs, torn-off branches, or squashed grapes anywhere. The yew trees in the formal garden did not seem to have been hacked at all. And though there was not a trace of an apple underfoot around the kitchen, there were boxes of firm, round apples in the courtyard. In the orchard, the apples were all either hanging on the trees or being picked and put in more boxes.

While Cat was finding this out, he had to flatten himself hastily against one of the hedgelike apple trees to make way for a galloping Jersey cow pursued by two gardeners and a farm boy. There were cows galloping in the wood when Cat went hopefully to look at the tree house. Alas, that was still a ruin. And the cows were doing their best to ruin the flowerbeds and not making much impression.

"Did you do the cows?" he asked Gwendolen.

"Yes. But it was just something to show them I'm not giving up," said Gwendolen. "I shall get my dragon's blood tomorrow and then I can do something really impressive."

CHAPTER 8

Gwendolen went down to the village to get her dragon's blood on Wednesday afternoon. She was in high glee. There were to be guests that night at the Castle and a big dinner party. Cat knew that everyone had carefully not mentioned it before, for fear Gwendolen would take advantage of it. But she had to be told on Wednesday morning because there were special arrangements for the children. They were to have their supper in the playroom, and they were supposed to keep out of the way after that.

"I'll keep out of the way, all right," Gwendolen promised. "But that won't make any difference." She chuckled about it all the way to the village.

Cat was embarrassed when they got to the village. Everyone avoided Gwendolen. Mothers dragged their children indoors and snatched babies out of her way. Gwendolen hardly noticed. She was too intent on getting to Mr. Baslam and getting her dragon's blood. Cat did not fancy Mr. Baslam, or the decaying pickle smell among his stuffed animals. He let Gwendolen go there on her own, and went to mail his postcard to Mrs. Sharp in the sweet shop. The people there were rather cool with him, even though he spent nearly two shillings on sweets, and they were positively cold in the cake shop next door. When Cat came out onto the green with his parcels, he found that children were being snatched out of his way too.

This so shamed Cat that he fled back to the Castle grounds and did not wait for Gwendolen. There he wandered moodily, eating toffees and penny buns, and wishing he was back with Mrs. Sharp. From time to time he saw Gwendolen in the distance. Sometimes she was dashing about. Sometimes she was squatting under a tree, carefully doing something. Cat did not go near her. If they were back with Mrs. Sharp, he thought, Gwendolen would not need to do whatever impressive thing she was planning. He found himself wishing she was not quite such a strong and determined witch. He tried to imagine a Gwendolen who was not a witch, but he found himself quite unable to. She just would not be Gwendolen.

Indoors, the usual silence of the Castle was not quite the same. There were tense little noises, and the thrumming feeling of people diligently busy just out of earshot. Cat knew it was going to be a big, important dinner party.

After supper, he craned out of Gwendolen's window watching the guests come up the piece of avenue he could see from there. They came in carriages and in cars, all very large and rich-looking. One carriage was drawn by six white horses and looked so impressive that Cat wondered if it might not even be the King.

"All the better," said Gwendolen. She was squatting in the middle of the carpet, beside a sheet of paper. At one end of the paper was a bowl of ingredients. At the other crawled, wriggled, or lay a horrid heap of things. Gwendolen had collected two frogs, an earthworm, several earwigs, a black beetle, a spider, and a little pile of bones. The live things were charmed and could not move off the paper.

As soon as Cat was sure that there were no more carriages arriving, Gwendolen began pounding the ingredients together in the bowl. As she pounded, she muttered things in a groaning hum, and her hair hung down and quivered over the bowl. Cat looked at the wriggling, hopping creatures and hoped that they were not going to be pounded up as ingredients too. It seemed not. Gwendolen at length sat back on her heels and said, "Now!"

She snapped her fingers over the bowl. The ingredients caught fire, all by themselves, and burned with small blue flames. "It's working!" Gwendolen said excitedly. She snatched up a twist of newspaper from beside her and carefully untwisted it. "Now for a pinch of dragon's blood." She took a pinch of the dark brown powder and sprinkled it on the flames. There was a fizzing, and a thick smell of burning. Then the flames leapt up, a foot high, blazing a furious green and purple, coloring the whole room with dancing light.

Gwendolen's face glowed in the green and purple. She rocked on her heels, chanting, chanting strings of things Cat could not understand. Then, still chanting, she leaned over and touched the spider. The spider grew. And grew. And grew more. It grew into a five-foot monster—a greasy roundness with two little eyes on the front, hanging like a hammock amid eight bent and jointed furry legs. Gwendolen pointed. The door of her room sprang open of its own accord—which made her smile exultantly—and the huge spider went silently creeping toward it, swaying on its hairy legs. It squeezed its legs inward to get through the door, and crept onward, down the passage beyond.

Gwendolen touched the other creatures, one by one. The earwigs lumbered up and off, like shiny horned cows, bright brown and glistening. The frogs rose up, as big as men, and walked flap, flop on their enormous feet, with their arms trailing like gorillas. Their mottled skin quivered, and little holes in it kept opening and shutting. The puffy place under their chins made gulping movements. The black beetle crawled on branched legs, such a big black slab that it could barely get through the door. Cat could see it, and all the others, going in a slow, silent procession down the grass-green glowing corridor.

"Where are they going?" he whispered.

Gwendolen chuckled. "I'm sending them to the dining room, of course. I don't think the guests will want much supper."

She took up a bone next, and knocked each end of it sharply on the floor. As soon as she let go of it, it floated up into the air. There was a soft clattering, and more bones came out of nowhere to join it. The green and purple flames roared and rasped. A skull arrived last of all, and a complete skeleton was dangling there in front of the flames. Gwendolen smiled with satisfaction and took up another bone.

But bones when they are bewitched have a way of remembering who they were. The dangling skeleton sighed, in a hollow, singing voice, "Poor Sarah Jane. I'm poor Sarah Jane. Let me rest."

Gwendolen waved it impatiently toward the door. It went dangling off, still sighing, and a second skeleton dangled after it, sighing, "Bob the gardener's boy. I din't mean to do it." They were followed by three more, each one singing softly and desolately of who it had been, and all five went slowly dangling after the black beetle. "Sarah Jane," Cat heard from the corridor. "I din't mean to." "I was Duke of Buckingham once."

Gwendolen took no notice of them and turned to the earthworm. It grew too. It grew into a massive pink thing as big as a sea serpent. Loops of it rose and fell and writhed all over the room. Cat was nearly sick. Its bare pink flesh had hairs on it like a pig's bristles. There were rings on it like the wrinkles around his own knuckles. Its great sightless front turned blindly this way and that until Gwendolen pointed to the door. Then it set off slowly after the skeletons, length after length of bare pink loops.

Gwendolen looked after it critically. "Not bad," she said. "I need one last touch though."

Carefully, she dropped another tiny pinch of dragon's blood on the flames. They burned with a whistling sound—brighter, sicker, yellower. Gwendolen began to chant again, waving her arms this time. After a moment, a shape seemed to be gathering in the quivering air over the flames. Whiteness was boiling, moving, forming into a miserable bent thing with a big head. Three more somethings were roiling and hardening beneath it. When the first thing flopped out of the flames onto the carpet, Gwendolen gave a gurgle of pleasure. Cat was amazed at how wicked she looked.

"Oh don't!" he said. The three other somethings flopped onto the carpet too, and he saw they were the apparition at the window and three others like it. The first was like a baby that was too small to walk—except that it *was* walking, with its big head wobbling. The next was a cripple, so twisted and cramped upon itself that it could barely hobble. The third was the apparition at the window pitiful, wrinkled, and draggled. The last had its white skin barred with blue stripes. All were weak and white and horrible. Cat shuddered all over.

"Please send them away!" he said.

Gwendolen only laughed again and waved the four apparitions toward the door.

They set off, toiling weakly. But they were only halfway there when Chrestomanci came through the door and Mr. Saunders came after him. In front of them came a shower of bones and small dead creatures, pattering onto the carpet and getting squashed under Chrestomanci's long, shiny shoes. The apparitions hesitated, gibbering. Then they fled back to the flaming bowl and vanished. The flames vanished at the same time, into thick, black, smelly smoke.

Gwendolen stared at Chrestomanci and Mr. Saunders through the smoke. Chrestomanci was magnificent in dark blue velvet, with lace ruffles at his wrists and on the front of his shirt. Mr. Saunders seemed to have made an effort to find a suit that reached to the ends of his legs and arms, but had not quite succeeded. One of his big, black patent-leather boots was unlaced, and there was a lot of shirt and wrist showing as he slowly coiled an invisible skein of something around his bony right hand. Both he and Chrestomanci looked back at Gwendolen most unpleasantly.

"You *were* warned, you know," Chrestomanci said. "Carry on, Michael."

Mr. Saunders put the invisible skein in his pocket. "Thanks," he said. "I've been itching to for a week now." He strode down on Gwendolen in a billow of black coat, yanked her to her feet, hauled her to a chair, and put her face down over his knee. There he dragged off his unlaced, big black boot and commenced spanking her with it hard and often.

While Mr. Saunders labored away, and Gwendolen screamed and squirmed and kicked, Chrestomanci marched up to Cat and boxed Cat's ears, twice on each side. Cat was so surprised that he would have fallen over, had not Chrestomanci hit the other side of his head each time and brought him upright again.

"What did you do that for?" Cat said indignantly, clutching both sides of his ringing face. "I didn't do anything."

"That's why I hit you," said Chrestomanci. "You didn't try to stop her, did you?" While Cat was gasping at the unfairness of this, he turned to the laboring Mr. Saunders. "I think that'll do now, Michael."

Mr. Saunders ceased swatting, rather regretfully. Gwendolen slid to her knees on the floor, sobbing with pain, and making screams in between her sobs at being treated like this.

Chrestomanci went over and poked at her with his shiny foot. "Stop it. Get up and behave yourself." And, when Gwendolen rose to her knees, staring piteously and looking utterly wronged, he said, "You thoroughly deserved that spanking. And, as you probably realize, Michael has taken away your witchcraft too. You're not a witch any longer. In future, you are not going to work one spell, unless you can prove to both of us that you are not going to do mischief with it. Is that clear? Now go to bed, and for goodness sake try and think about what you've been doing."

He nodded to Mr. Saunders, and they both went out, Mr. Saunders hopping because he was still putting his boot back on, and squashing the rest of the dead creatures as he hopped.

Gwendolen flopped forward on her face and drummed her toes on the carpet. "The beast! The beasts! How dare they treat me like this! I shall do a worse thing than this now, and serve you all right!"

"But you can't do things without witchcraft," Cat said. "Was what Mr. Saunders was winding up your witchcraft?"

"Go away!" Gwendolen screamed at him. "Leave me alone. You're as bad as the rest of them!" And, as Cat went to the door, leaving her drumming and sobbing, she raised her head and shouted after him, "I'm not beaten yet! You'll see!"

Not surprisingly, Cat had bad dreams that night. They were terrible dreams, full of giant earthworms and great, slimy, porous frogs. They became more and more feverish. Cat sweated and moaned and finally woke up, feeling wet and weak and rather too bony, the way you do when you have just had a bad illness or a fearsome dream. He lay for a little while feeling wretched. Then he began to feel better and fell asleep again.

When Cat woke again, it was light. He opened his eyes on the snowy silence of the Castle and was suddenly convinced that Gwendolen had done something else. He had no idea what made him so sure. He thought he was probably imagining it. If Mr. Saunders had truly taken Gwendolen's witchcraft away from her, she could not have done a thing. But he still knew she had.

He got up and padded to the windows to see what it was. But, for once, there was nothing abnormal about the view from any of them. The cedars spread above the lawn. The gardens blazed down the hill. The day was swimming in sun and mist, and not so much as a footprint marked the pearly gray-green of the grass. But Cat was still so sure that something, somewhere, was different that he got dressed and stole off downstairs to ask Gwendolen what she had done.

When Cat opened the door of her room, he could smell the sweet, charred, heavy smell that went with witchcraft. But that could have been left over from last night. The room was quite tidy. The dead creatures and the burned bowl had been cleared away. The only thing out of place was Gwendolen's box, which had been pulled out of the painted wardrobe and stood with its lid half off near her bed.

Gwendolen was a sleeping hump under the blue velvet bedspread. Cat shut the door very gently behind him, in order not to disturb her. Gwendolen heard it. She sat up in bed with a bounce and stared at him.

As soon as she did, Cat knew that whatever was wrong, it was wrong with Gwendolen herself. She had her nightdress on back to front. The ribbons which usually tied it at the back were dangling at the front. That was the only thing obviously wrong. But there was something odd about the way Gwendolen was staring at him. She was astonished, and rather frightened.

"Who are you?" she said.

"I'm Cat, of course," said Cat.

"No you're not. You're a boy," said Gwendolen. "Who are you?"

Cat realized that when witches lost their witchcraft, they also lost their memories. He saw he would have to be very patient with Gwendolen. "I'm your brother, Eric," he said patiently, and came across to the bed so that she could look at him. "Only you always call me Cat."

"My brother!" she exclaimed, in the greatest astonishment. "Well, that can't be bad. I've always wanted a brother. And I know I can't be dreaming. It was too cold in the bath, and it hurts when I pinch myself.

So would you mind telling me where I am? It's a Stately Home of some kind, isn't it?"

Cat stared at her. He began to suspect that her memory was perfectly good. It was not only the way she spoke and what she said. She was thinner than she should be. Her face was the right pretty face, with the right blue eyes, but the downright look on it was not right. The golden hair hanging over her shoulders was an inch longer than it had been last night.

"You're not Gwendolen!" he said.

"What a dreadful name!" said the girl in the bed. "I should hope not! I'm Janet Chant."

CHAPTER 9

By this time, Cat was as bewildered as the strange girl seemed to be. Chant? he thought. Chant? Has Gwendolen a twin sister she hasn't told me about? "But my name's Chant too," he said.

"Is it, now?" said Janet. She knelt up in bed and scrubbed her hands thoughtfully about in her hair, in a way Gwendolen never would have done. "Truly *Chant?* It's not that much of a common name. And you thought I was your sister? Well, I've put two and two together about a hundred times since I woke up in the bath, and I keep getting five. Where are we?"

"In Chrestomanci Castle," said Cat. "Chrestomanci had us to live here about a year after our parents died."

"There you are!" said Janet. "My Mum and Dad are alive and kicking—or they were when I said good night to them last night. Who's Chrestomanci? Could you just sketch your life history for me?"

Puzzled and uneasy, Cat described how and why he and Gwendolen had come to live in the Castle, and what Gwendolen had done then.

"You mean Gwendolen really *was* a witch!" Janet exclaimed.

Cat wished she had not said *was*. He had a growing suspicion that he would never see the real Gwendolen again. "Of course she is," he said. "Aren't you?"

"Great heavens, no!" said Janet. "Though I'm beginning to wonder if I mightn't have been, if I'd lived here all my life. Witches are quite common, are they?"

"And warlocks and necromancers," said Cat. "But wizards and magicians don't happen so often. I think Mr. Saunders is a magician."

"Medicine men, witch doctors, shamans, devils, enchanters?" Janet asked rapidly. "Hags, fakirs, sorcerers? Are they thick on the ground too?"

"Most of those are for savages," Cat explained. "Hag is rude. But we have sorcerers and enchanters. Enchanters are very strong and important. I've never met one."

"I see," said Janet. She thought for a moment and then swung herself out of bed, in a sort of scramble that was more like a boy's than a girl's, and again quite unlike the way Gwendolen would have done it. "We'd better have a hunt around," she said, "in case dear Gwendolen has been kind enough to leave a message."

"Don't call her that," Cat said desolately. "Where do you think she *is*?"

Janet looked at him and saw he was miserable. "Sorry," she said. "I won't again. But you do see I might be a bit cross with her, don't you? She seems to have dumped me here and gone off somewhere. Let's hope she has a good explanation."

"They spanked her with a boot and took away her magic," Cat said.

"Yes, you said," Janet replied, pulling open drawers in the golden dressing table. "I'm terrified of Chrestomanci already. But did they really take away her magic? How did she manage to do this, if they did?"

"I don't understand that either," Cat said, joining in the search. By now, he would have given his little finger for a word from Gwendolen—any kind of word. He felt horribly lonely. "Why were you in the bath?" he said, wondering whether to search the bathroom.

"I don't know. I just woke up there," said Janet, shaking out a tangle of hair ribbons in the bottom drawer. "I felt as if I'd been dragged through a hedge backward, and I'd no clothes on, so I was freezing."

"Why had you no clothes on?" Cat said, stirring Gwendolen's underclothes about, without success.

"I was hot in bed last night," said Janet. "So naked I came into this world. And I wandered about pinching myself—especially after I found this fabulous room. I thought I must have been turned into a princess. But there was this nightdress lying on the bed, so I put it on—"

"You've got it on back to front," said Cat.

Janet stopped scanning the things on the mantelpiece to look down at the trailing ribbons. "Have I? It won't be the only thing I'm going to get back to front, by the sound of it. Try looking in that artistic wardrobe. Then I explored outside here, and all I found was miles of long green corridor, which gave me the creeps, and stately grounds out of the windows, so I came back in here and went to bed. I hoped that when I woke up it would all have gone away. And instead there was you. Found anything?"

"No," said Cat. "But there's her box—"

"It must be in there," said Janet.

They squatted down and unpacked the box. There was not much in it. Cat knew that Gwendolen must have taken a lot of things with her to wherever she had gone. There were two books, *Elementary Spells* and *Magic for Beginners,* and some pages of notes on them. Janet looked at Gwendolen's large, round writing.

"She writes just like I do. Why did she leave these books? Because they're First Form standard and she's up to O Levels, I suppose." She put the books and notes to one side and, as she did so, the little red book of matches fell out from among them. Janet picked it up and opened it, and saw that half the matches were burned without having been torn out. "That looks suspiciously like a spell to me," she said. "What are these bundles of letters?"

"My parents' love letters, I think," said Cat.

The letters were in their envelopes still, stamped and addressed. Janet squatted with a bundle in each hand. "These stamps are penny blacks! No, it's a man's head on them. What's your King called?"

"Charles the Seventh," said Cat.

"No Georges?" Janet asked. But she saw Cat was mystified and looked back at the letters again. "Your mother and father were both called Chant, I see. Were they first cousins? Mine are. Granny didn't want them to marry, because it's supposed to be a bad thing."

"I don't know. They may have been. They looked rather alike," Cat said, and felt lonelier than ever.

Janet looked rather lonely too. She tucked the little book of matches carefully inside the pink tape that tied together the letters addressed to Miss Caroline Chant—like Gwendolen, she evidently had a tidy mind—and said, "Both tall and fair, with blue eyes? My Mum's name is Caroline too. I'm beginning to see. Come on, Gwendolen, *give*!" And saying this, Janet tossed aside the letters and, in a most untidy way, scrabbled up the remaining folders, papers, writing sets, pen wipers, and the bag with *Souvenir from Blackpool* on it. At the very bottom of the box was a large pink sheet of paper, covered all over with Gwendolen's best and roundest writing. "Ah!" said Janet, pouncing on it. "I thought so! She's got the same secretive mind as I have." And she spread the letter on the carpet so that Cat could read it too. Gwendolen had written:

Dear Replacement,

I have to leave this terrible place. Nobody understands me. Nobody notices my talents. You will soon see because you are my exact double so you will be a witch too. I have been very clever. They do not know all my resauces. I have found out how to go to another world and I am going there for good. I know I shall be Queen of it because my fortune was told and said so. There are hundreds of other worlds only some are nicer than others, they are formed when there is a big event in History like a battle or an earthquake when the result can be two or more quite diferent things. Both those things hapen but they cannot exist together so the world splits into two worlds witch start to go diferent after that. I know there must be Gwendolens in a lot of worlds but not how many. One of you will come here when I go because when I move it, will make an empty space that will suck you in. Do not greive however if your parents still live. Some other Gwendolen will move into your place and pretend to be you because we are all so clever. You can carry on here making Chrestomanci's life a misery and I shall be greatful knowing it is in good hands.

Your loving
Gwendolen Chant

PS. Burn this.
PS2. Tell Cat I am quite sorry but he must *do what Mr. Nostrum says.*

Having read this, Cat knelt wanly beside Janet, knowing he really would never see Gwendolen again. He seemed to be stuck with Janet instead. If you know a person as well as Cat knew Gwendolen, an exact double is hardly good enough. Janet was not a witch. The expressions on her face were nothing like the same. Looking at her now, Cat saw that, where Gwendolen would have been furious at being dragged into another world, Janet was looking as wan as he felt.

"I wonder how Mum and Dad are getting on with *my* Dear Replacement," she said wryly. Then she pulled herself together. "Do you mind if I don't burn this? It's the only proof I've got that I'm not Gwendolen who's suddenly gone mad and thinks she's this girl called Janet Chant. May I hide it?"

"It's your letter," said Cat.

"And your sister," said Janet. "God bless her dear little sugar-coated shining soul! Don't get me wrong, Cat. I admire your sister. She thinks big. You have to admire her! All the same, I wonder if she's thought of the clever hiding place where I'm going to put her letter. I shall feel better if she hasn't."

Janet bounced up in her un-Gwendolen-like way and took the letter over to the gilded dressing table. Cat bounced up and followed her. Janet took hold of the gold-garlanded mirror and swung it toward her on its swivels. The back was plain plywood. She dug her nails under the edge of the plywood and prised. It came free quite easily.

"I do this with my mirror at home," Janet explained. "It's a good hiding place—it's about the one place my parents never think of. Mum and Dad are dears, but they're terribly nosy. I think it's because I'm their only one. And I like to be private. I write private stories for my eyes only, and they *will* try to read them. Oh, purple-spotted dalmatians!"

She raised the wood up and showed Cat the signs painted on the red-coated back of the glass itself.

"Cabala, I think," said Cat. "It's a spell."

"So she did think of it!" said Janet. "Really, it's hell having a double. You both get the same ideas. And working on that principle," she said, sliding Gwendolen's letter between the plywood and the glass and pressing the plywood back in place, "I bet I know what the spell's for. It's so Gwendolen can have a look from time to time and see how Dear Replacement's getting on. I hope she's looking now." Janet swung the mirror back to its usual position and crossed her eyes at it, hideously. She took hold of the corners of her crossed eyes and pulled them long and Chinese, and stuck her tongue out as far as it would go. Then she pushed her nose up with one finger and twisted her mouth right around to one cheek. Cat could not help laughing. "Can't Gwendolen do this?" Janet said out of the side of her face.

"No," Cat giggled.

That was the moment when Euphemia opened the door. Janet jumped violently. She was much more nervous than Cat had realized. "I'll thank you to stop pulling faces," said Euphemia, "and get out of your nightdress, Gwendolen." She came into the room to make sure that Gwendolen did. She gave a croaking sort of shriek. Then she melted into a brown lump.

Janet's hands went over her mouth. She and Cat stared in horror as the brown lump that had been Euphemia grew smaller and smaller. When it was about three inches high, it stopped shrinking and put out large webbed feet. On these webbed feet, it crawled forward and stared at them reproachfully out of protruding yellowish eyes near the top of its head.

"Oh dear!" said Cat. It seemed that Gwendolen's last act had been to turn Euphemia into a frog.

Janet burst into tears. Cat was surprised. She had seemed so self-assured. Sobbing heavily, Janet knelt down and tenderly picked up the brown, crawling Euphemia. "You poor girl!" she wept. "I know just how you feel. Cat, what are we to do? How do you turn people back?"

"I don't know," Cat said soberly. He was suddenly burdened with huge responsibilities. Janet, in spite of the confident way she talked, clearly needed looking after. Euphemia clearly needed it even more. If it had not been for Chrestomanci, Cat would have raced off to get Mr. Saunders to help that moment. But he suddenly realized that if Chrestomanci ever found out what Gwendolen had done this time, the most terrible things would happen. Cat was quite sure of this. He discovered that he was terrified of Chrestomanci. He had been terrified of him all along, without realizing it. He knew he would have to keep both Janet and Euphemia a secret somehow.

Feeling desperate, Cat raced to the bathroom, found a damp towel, and brought it to Janet. "Put her down on this. She'll need to be wet. I'll ask Roger and Julia to turn her back. I'll tell them you won't. And for goodness sake don't tell anyone you aren't Gwendolen—please!"

Janet lowered Euphemia gently onto the towel. Euphemia scrambled around in it and continued to stare accusingly at Janet. "Don't look like that. It wasn't me," Janet said, sniffing. "Cat, we'll have to hide her. Would she be comfortable in the wardrobe?"

"She'll have to be," said Cat. "You get dressed."

A look of panic came over Janet's face. "Cat, what does Gwendolen *wear*?"

Cat thought all girls knew what girls wore. "The usual things—petticoats, stockings, dress, boots—you know."

"No, I don't," said Janet. "I always wear trousers."

Cat felt his problems mounting up. He hunted for clothes. Gwendolen seemed to have taken her best things with her, but he found her older boots, her green stockings and the garters to match, her second-best petticoats, her green cashmere dress with the smocking and—with some embarrassment—her bloomers. "There," he said.

"Does she really wear two petticoats?" said Janet.

"Yes," said Cat. "Get them on."

But Janet proved quite unable to get them on without his help. If he left her to do anything, she put it on back to front. He had to put her petticoats on her, button her up the back, tie her garters, fasten her boots, and put her dress on a second time, right way around, and tie its sash for her. When he had finished, it looked all right, but Janet had an odd air of being dressed up, rather than dressed. She looked at herself critically in the mirror. "Thanks, you're an angel. I look rather like an Edwardian child. And I feel a right Charley."

"Come on," said Cat. "Breakfast." He carried Euphemia, croaking furiously, to the wardrobe and wrapped her firmly in the towel. "Be quiet," he told her. "I'll get you changed back as soon as I can, so stop making that fuss, please!" He shut the door on her and wedged it with a page of Gwendolen's notes. Faint croaking came from behind it. Euphemia had no intention of being quiet. Cat did not really blame her.

"She's not happy in there," Janet said, weakening. "Can't she stay out in the room?"

"No," said Cat. Frog though she was, Euphemia still looked like Euphemia. He knew Mary would recognize her as soon as she set eyes on her. He took Janet's resisting elbow and towed her along to the playroom.

"Don't you two ever get up till the last minute?" said Julia. "I'm sick of waiting politely for breakfast."

"Eric's been up for hours," said Mary, hovering about. "So I don't know what you've both been up to. Oh, what's Euphemia *doing*?"

"Mary's beside herself this morning," Roger said. He winked. For a moment there were two Marys, one real and one vague and ghostly. Janet jumped. It was only the second piece of witchcraft she had seen and she did not find it easy to get used to.

"I expect it's Gwendolen's fault," said Julia, and she gave Janet one of those meaning stares.

Janet was very put-out. Cat had forgotten to warn her how much Julia had disliked Gwendolen ever since the snakes. And a meaning stare from a witch is worse than a meaning stare from an ordinary person. Julia's pushed Janet backward across the room, until Cat put himself in the way of it.

"Don't do that," he said. "She's sorry."

"Is she?" said Julia. "*Are* you?" she asked, trying to get the stare around Cat to Janet again.

"Yes, horribly sorry," Janet said fervently, not having the least idea why. "I've had a complete change of heart."

"I'll believe that when I see it," said Julia. But she left off staring in order to watch Mary bringing the usual bread, the marmalade, and the jug of cocoa.

Janet looked, sniffed the cocoa steaming from the jug, and her face fell, rather like Gwendolen's on the first day. "Oh dear. I hate cocoa," she said.

Mary rolled her eyes to the ceiling. "You and your airs and graces! You never said you hated it before."

"I—I've had a revulsion of feeling," Janet invented. "When I had my change of heart, all my taste buds changed too. I—you haven't any coffee, have you?"

"Where? Under the carpet or something?" Mary demanded. "All right. I'll ask the kitchen. I'll tell them your taste buds are revolting, shall I?"

Cat was very pleased to hear that cocoa was not compulsory after all. "Could I have coffee too?" he asked, as Mary went to the lift. "Or I prefer tea, really."

"But you waited to say so until Euphemia goes missing and leaves me all on my own!" Mary said, getting very put-upon.

"She never does anything anyway," Cat said in surprise.

Mary flounced crossly to the speaking tube and ordered a pot of coffee and a pot of tea. "For Her Highness and His Nibs," she said to it. "*He* seems to have caught it now. What wouldn't I give for a nice normal child in this place, Nancy!"

"But I *am* a nice normal child!" Janet and Cat protested in unison.

"And so are we—nice, anyhow," Julia said comfortably.

"How can you be normal?" Mary demanded as she let down the lift. "All four of you are Chants. And when was a Chant ever normal? Answer me that."

Janet looked questioningly at Cat, but Cat was as puzzled as she was. "I thought your name was Chrestomanci," he said to Roger and Julia.

"That's just Daddy's title," said Julia.

"You're some kind of cousin of ours," said Roger. "Didn't you know? I always thought that was why Daddy had you to live here."

As they started breakfast, Cat thought that this, if anything, made the situation more difficult than ever.

CHAPTER 10

Cat watched his moment and, when Mr. Saunders called them to lessons, he caught Roger's arm and whispered, "Look, Gwendolen's turned Euphemia into a frog and—"

Roger gave a great snore of laughter. Cat had to wait for him to stop.

"And she won't turn her back. Can *you*?"

Roger tried to look serious, but laughter kept breaking through. "I don't know. Probably not, unless she'll tell you what spell she used. Finding out which spell without knowing is Advanced Magic, and I'm not on that yet. Oh, how funny!" He bent over the table and yelled with laughter.

Naturally, Mr. Saunders appeared at the door, remarking that the time for telling jokes was after lessons. They had to go through to the schoolroom. Naturally, Cat found Janet had sat in his desk by mistake. He got her out as quietly as he could and sat in it himself, distractedly wondering how he could find out which spell Gwendolen had used.

It was the most uncomfortable morning Cat had ever known. He had forgotten to tell Janet that the only thing Gwendolen knew about was witchcraft. Janet, as he had rather suspected, knew a lot, about a lot of things. But it all applied to her own world. About the only subject she would have been safe in was simple arithmetic. And Mr. Saunders chose that morning to give her a History test. Cat, as he scratched away left-handed at an English essay, could see the panic growing on Janet's face.

"What do you mean, Henry the Fifth?" barked Mr. Saunders. "Richard the Second was on the throne until long after Agincourt. What was his greatest magical achievement?"

"Defeating the French," Janet guessed. Mr. Saunders looked so exasperated that she babbled, "Well, I think it was. He hampered the French with iron underwear, and the English wore wool, so they didn't stick in the mud, and probably their longbows were enchanted too. That would account for them not missing."

"Who," said Mr. Saunders, "do you imagine won the Battle of Agincourt?"

"The English," said Janet. This of course was true for her world, but the panic-stricken look on her face as she said it suggested that she suspected the opposite was true in this world. Which, of course, it was.

Mr. Saunders put his hands to his head. "No, no, no! The *French*! Don't you know *anything,* girl?"

Janet looked to be near tears. Cat was terrified. She was going to break down any second and tell Mr. Saunders she was not Gwendolen. She did not have Cat's reasons for keeping quiet. "Gwendolen never knows anything," he remarked loudly, hoping Janet would take the hint. She did. She sighed with relief and relaxed.

"I'm aware of that," said Mr. Saunders. "But somewhere, somewhere inside that marble head there must be a little cell of gray matter. So I keep looking."

Unfortunately, Janet, in her relief, became almost jolly. "Would you like to take my head apart and look?" she asked.

"Don't tempt me!" cried Mr. Saunders. He hid his eyes with one knobby hand and fended at Janet with the other. He looked so funny that Janet laughed. This was so unlike Gwendolen that Mr. Saunders lowered his hand across his nose and stared at her suspiciously over it. "What have you been up to now?"

"Nothing," Janet said guiltily.

"Hm," said Mr. Saunders, in a way which made both Cat and Janet very uncomfortable.

At last—very long last—it was time for Mary to bring the milk and biscuits, which she did, with a very portentous look. Crouched on the tray beside Mr. Saunders' cup of coffee was a large, wet-looking, brown thing. Cat's stomach seemed to leave him and take a plunge into the Castle cellars. From the look of Janet, hers was doing the same.

"What have you got there?" said Mr. Saunders.

"Gwendolen's good deed for today," Mary said grimly. "It's Euphemia. Look at its face."

Mr. Saunders bent and looked. Then he whirled around on Janet so fiercely that Janet half got out of her seat. "So that's what you were laughing about!"

"I didn't do it!" said Janet.

"Euphemia was in Gwendolen's room, shut in the wardrobe, croaking her poor head off," said Mary.

"I think this calls for Chrestomanci," Mr. Saunders said. He strode toward the door.

The door opened before he got there and Chrestomanci himself came in, cheerful and busy, with some papers in one hand. "Michael," he said, "have I caught you at the right—?" He stopped when he saw Mr. Saunders' face. "Is something wrong?"

"Will you please to look at this frog, sir," said Mary. "It was in Gwendolen's wardrobe."

Chrestomanci was wearing an exquisite gray suit with faint lilac stripes to it. He held his lilac silk cravat out of the way and bent to inspect the frog. Euphemia lifted her head and croaked at him beseechingly. There was a moment of ice-cold silence. It was a moment such as Cat hoped never to live through again. "Bless my soul!" Chrestomanci said, gently as frost freezes a window. "It's Eugenia."

"Euphemia, Daddy," said Julia.

"Euphemia," said Chrestomanci. "Of course. Now who did this?" Cat wondered how such a mild voice could send the hair pricking upright at the back of his head.

"Gwendolen, sir," said Mary.

But Chrestomanci shook his smooth black head. "No. Don't give a dog a bad name. It couldn't have been Gwendolen. Michael took her witchcraft away last night."

"Oh," said Mr. Saunders, rather red in the face. "Stupid of me!"

"So who could it have been?" Chrestomanci wondered.

There was another freezing silence. It seemed to Cat about as long as an Ice Age. During it, Julia began to smile. She drummed her fingers on her desk and looked meditatively at Janet. Janet saw her and jumped. She drew in her breath sharply. Cat panicked. He was sure Janet was going to say what Gwendolen had done. He said the only thing he could think of to stop her.

"I did it," he said loudly.

Cat could hardly bear the way they all looked at him. Julia was disgusted, Roger astonished. Mr. Saunders was fiercely angry. Mary looked at him as if he was a frog himself. But Chrestomanci was politely incredulous, and he was worst of all. "I beg your pardon, Eric," he said. "This was *you*?"

Cat stared at him with a strange misty wetness around his eyes. He thought it was due to terror. "It was a mistake," he said. "I was trying a spell. I—I didn't expect it to work. And then—and then Euphemia came in and turned into a frog. Just like that," he explained.

Chrestomanci said, "But you were told not to practice magic on your own."

"I know." Cat hung his head, without having to pretend. "But I knew it wouldn't work. Only it did, of course," he explained.

"Well, you must undo the spell at once," said Chrestomanci.

Cat swallowed. "I can't. I don't know how to."

Chrestomanci treated him to another look so polite, so scathing, and so unbelieving, that Cat would gladly have crawled under his desk had he been able to move at all. "Very well," said Chrestomanci. "Michael, perhaps you could oblige."

Mary held the tray out. Mr. Saunders took Euphemia and put her on the schoolroom table. Euphemia croaked agitatedly. "Only a minute now," Mr. Saunders said soothingly. He held his hands cupped around her. Nothing happened. Looking a little puzzled, Mr. Saunders began to mutter things. Still nothing happened. Euphemia's head bobbed anxiously above his bony fingers, and she was still a frog. Mr. Saunders went from looking puzzled to looking baffled. "This is a very strange spell," he said. "What did you use, Eric?"

"I can't remember," said Cat.

"Well, it doesn't respond to anything I can do," said Mr. Saunders. "You'll have to do it, Eric. Come over here."

Cat looked helplessly at Chrestomanci, but Chrestomanci nodded as if he thought Mr. Saunders was quite right. Cat stood up. His legs had gone thick and weak, and his stomach seemed to have taken up permanent quarters in the Castle cellars. He slunk toward the table. When Euphemia saw him coming, she showed her opinion of the matter by taking a frantic leap off the edge of the table. Mr. Saunders caught her in midair and put her back.

"What do I do?" Cat said, and his voice sounded like Euphemia croaking.

Mr. Saunders took Cat by his left wrist and planted Cat's left hand on Euphemia's clammy back. "Now take it off her," he said.

"I—I—" said Cat. He supposed he ought to pretend to try. "Stop being a frog and turn into Euphemia again," he said, and wondered miserably what they would do to him when Euphemia didn't.

But, to his astonishment, Euphemia did. The frog turned warm under his fingers and burst into growth. Cat shot a look at Mr. Saunders as the brown lump grew furiously larger and larger. He was almost sure he caught a secret smile on Mr. Saunders' face. The next second, Euphemia was sitting on the edge of the table. Her clothes were a little crumpled and brown, but there was nothing else froggish about her. "I never dreamt it was *you*!" she said to Cat. Then she put her face in her hands and cried.

Chrestomanci came up and put his arm around her. "There, there, my dear. It must have been a terrible experience. I think you need to go and lie down." And he took Euphemia out of the room.

"Phew!" said Janet.

Mary grimly handed out the milk and biscuits. Cat did not want his. His stomach had not yet come back from the cellars. Janet refused biscuits.

"I think the food here is awfully fattening," she said unwisely. Julia took that as a personal insult. Her handkerchief came out and was knotted. Janet's glass of milk slipped through her fingers and smashed on the pitted floor.

"Clean it up," said Mr. Saunders. "Then get out, you and Eric. I've had enough of both of you. Julia and Roger, get out magic textbooks, please."

Cat took Janet out into the gardens. It seemed safest there. They wandered across the lawn, both rather limp after the morning's experiences.

"Cat," said Janet, "you're going to be very annoyed with me, but it's absolutely essential that I cling to you like a limpet all the time we're awake, until I know how to behave. You saved my bacon twice this morning. I thought I was going to die when she brought in that frog. *Rigor mortis* was setting in, and then you turned her back again! I didn't realize you were a witch too—no, it's a warlock, isn't it? Or are you a wizard?"

"I'm not," said Cat. "I'm not any of those things. Mr. Saunders did it to give me a fright."

"But Julia is a witch, isn't she?" said the shrewd Janet. "What have I done to make her hate me so—or is it just general Gwendolenitis?"

Cat explained about the snakes.

"In which case I don't blame her," said Janet. "But it's hard that she's in the schoolroom at the moment brushing up her witchcraft, and here I am without a rag of a spell to defend myself with. You don't know of a handy karate teacher, do you?"

"I never heard of one," Cat said cautiously, wondering what karate might be.

"Oh well," said Janet. "Chrestomanci's a wonderfully fancy dresser, isn't he?"

Cat laughed. "Wait till you see him in a dressing gown!"

"I hardly can. It must be something! Why is he so terrifying?"

"He just is," said Cat.

"Yes," said Janet. "He just is. When he saw the frog was Euphemia and went all mild and astonished like that, it froze the goose pimples on my back. I *couldn't* have told him I wasn't Gwendolen—not even under the most refined modern tortures—and that's why I shall have to stick to you. Do you mind terribly?"

"Not at all," said Cat. But he did rather. Janet could not have been more of a burden if she had been sitting on his shoulders with her legs wrapped around his chest. And to crown it all, it seemed as if there had been no need for his false confession. He took Janet to the ruins of the tree house because he wanted something else to think about. Janet was enchanted with it. She swung herself up into the horse chestnut to look at it, and Cat felt rather as you do when someone else gets into your railway carriage. "Be careful," he called crossly.

There was a strong rending noise up in the tree. "Drat!" said Janet. "These are ridiculous clothes for climbing trees in."

"Can't you sew?" Cat called as he climbed up too.

"I despise it as female bondage," said Janet. "Yes, I can, actually. And I'm going to have to. It was both petticoats." She tested the creaking floor that was all that remained of the house and stood up on it, trailing two different colors of frill below the hem of Gwendolen's dress. "You can see into the village from here. There's a butcher's cart just turning in to the Castle drive."

Cat climbed up beside her and they watched the cart and the dappled horse pulling it.

"Don't you have cars at all?" Janet asked. "Everyone has cars in my world."

"Rich people do," said Cat. "Chrestomanci sent his to meet us off the train."

"And you have electric light," said Janet. "But everything else is old-fashioned compared with my world. I suppose people can get what they want by witchcraft. Do you have factories, or long-playing records, or high-rise buildings, or television, or airplanes at all?"

"I don't know what airplanes are," said Cat. He had no idea what most of the other things were either, and he was bored with this talk.

Janet saw he was. She looked around for a change of subject and saw clusters of big green horse chestnut cases hanging all around them at the ends of the branches. The leaves there were already singed-looking around the edges, suggesting that the chestnuts could not be far off ripe. Janet edged out along a branch and tried to reach the nearest cluster of green cases. They bobbed at the tips of her fingers, just out of reach. "Oh, dachshunds!" she said. "They look almost ripe."

"They aren't," said Cat. "But I wish they were." He took a lathe out of the wreckage of the house and slashed at the chestnut cases with it. He missed, but he must have shaken them. Eight or so dropped off the tree and went *plomp* on the ground below.

"Who says they're not ripe?" said Janet, leaning down.

Cat craned out of the tree and saw brown shiny chestnuts showing in the split green cases. "Oh, hurray!" He came down the tree like a monkey, and Janet crashed after him, with her hair full of twigs. They scooped up the chestnuts greedily—wonderful chestnuts with grain on them like the contours in a map.

"A skewer!" Janet moaned. "My kingdom for a skewer! We can thread them on my bootlaces."

"Here's a skewer," said Cat. There was one lying on the ground by his left hand. It must have fallen out of the tree house.

They drilled chestnuts furiously. They took the laces out of Gwendolen's second-best boots. They discovered the rules of the game were the same in both their worlds, and they went to the formal garden and held a battle royal there on the gravel path. As Janet firmly smashed Cat's last chestnut and yelled, "Mine! Mine's a sevener now!" Milly came around a corner past a yew tree and stood laughing at them.

"Do you know, I wouldn't have thought the chestnuts were ripe yet. But it's been a lovely summer."

Janet looked at her in consternation. She had no idea who this plump lady in the beautiful flowered silk dress could be.

"Hallo, *Milly*," said Cat. Not that this helped Janet much.

Milly smiled and opened the handbag she was carrying. "There are three things Gwendolen needs, I think. Here." She handed Janet two safety pins and a packet of bootlaces. "I always believe in being prepared."

"Th—thanks," Janet stammered. She was horribly conscious of her gaping boots, her twig-filled hair, and the two trailing strips of petticoat. She was even more confused by not knowing who Milly was.

Cat knew that. He knew by now that Janet was one of those people who are not happy unless they have an explanation for everything. So he said fulsomely to Milly, "I do think Roger and Julia are lucky, having a mother like you, Milly."

Milly beamed and Janet looked enlightened. Cat felt dishonest. He *did* think that, but he would never have dreamt of saying it but for Janet.

Having gathered that Milly was Chrestomanci's wife, Janet was quite unable to resist going on and gathering as much more information as she could. "Milly," she said, "were Cat's parents first cousins like—I mean, were they? And what relation is Cat to you?"

"That sounds like those questions they ask you to find out how clever you are," said Milly. "And I don't know the answer, Gwendolen. It's my husband's family you're related to, you see, and I don't know too much about them. We need Chrestomanci here to explain, really."

As it happened, Chrestomanci came through the doorway in the garden wall at that moment. Milly rustled up to him, beaming.

"My love, we were needing you."

Janet, who had her head down, trying to pin her petticoats, glanced up at Chrestomanci and then looked thoughtfully down at the path, as if the stones and sand there had suddenly become rather interesting.

"It's quite simple," Chrestomanci said, when Milly had explained the question. "Frank and Caroline Chant were my cousins—and first cousins to one another too, of course. When they insisted on getting married, my family made a great fuss, and my uncles cut them off without a shilling in a thoroughly old-fashioned way. It is, you see, rather a bad thing for cousins to marry when there's witchcraft in the family. Not that cutting them off made the slightest difference, of course." He smiled at Cat. He seemed thoroughly friendly. "Does that answer the question?"

Cat had an inkling of how Gwendolen had felt. It was confusing and exasperating the way Chrestomanci would seem friendly when one ought to have been in disgrace. He could not resist asking, "Is Euphemia all right?"

Then he wished he had not asked. Chrestomanci's smile snapped off like a light. "Yes. She's feeling better now. You show touching concern, Eric. I believe you were so sorry for her that you hid her in a wardrobe?"

"My love, don't be so terrifying," Milly said, hooking her arm through Chrestomanci's. "It was an accident, and it's all over now." She led him away down the path. But, just before they went out of sight behind a yew tree, Chrestomanci turned and looked over his shoulder at Cat and Janet. It was his bewildered look, but it was far from reassuring.

"Hot-cross bun-wrappers! Jiminy purple creepers!" Janet whispered. "I'm beginning to hardly dare move in this place!" She finished pinning her petticoat. When Milly and Chrestomanci had had nearly a minute in which to walk out of hearing, she said, "She's sweet—Milly—an absolute honey. But him! Cat, is it possible Chrestomanci is a rather powerful enchanter?"

"I don't think he is," said Cat. "Why?"

"Well," said Janet, "partly it's the feeling he gives—"

"I don't get a feeling," said Cat. "I'm just frightened of him."

"That's *it*," said Janet. "You're probably muddled anyhow from having lived with witches all your life. But it isn't only a feeling. Have you noticed how he always comes when people call him? He's done it twice now."

"Those were two complete accidents," said Cat. "You can't build ideas on accidents."

"He disguises it quite well, I admit," said Janet. "He comes looking as if it was something else he was doing, but—"

"Oh, do shut up! You're getting as bad as Gwendolen. She couldn't stop thinking of him for a moment," Cat said crossly.

Janet pounded her open right boot on the gravel. "I am not Gwendolen! I'm not even really *like* her! Get that into your fat head, will you!"

Cat started to laugh.

"Why are you laughing?" said Janet.

"Gwendolen always stamps when she's angry too," said Cat.

"Gah!" said Janet.

CHAPTER 11

By the time Janet had laced both her boots, Cat was sure it was lunch-time. He hurried Janet back to the private door. They had nearly reached it when a thick voice spoke among the rhododendrons.

"Young lady! Here a minute!"

Janet gave Cat an alarmed look and they both hurried for the door. It was not a pleasant voice. The rhododendrons clashed and rustled indignantly beside them. A fat old man in a dirty raincoat spilled out of them. Before they had recovered from the surprise of seeing him, he had scuttled around between them and the door, where he stood looking at them reproachfully out of drooping red eyes and breathing beer-scented breath over them.

"Hallo, Mr. Baslam," Cat said, for Janet's benefit.

"Didn't you hear me, young lady?" Mr. Baslam demanded.

Cat could see Janet was frightened of him, but she answered as coolly as Gwendolen might have done. "Yes, but I thought it was the tree speaking."

"The *tree* speaking!" said Mr. Baslam. "After all the trouble I been to for you, you take me for a tree! Three whole pints of bitter I had to buy that butcher to have him bring me in that cart of his, and I'm fair jolted to bits!"

"What do you want?" Janet said nervously.

"It's like this," said Mr. Baslam. He pulled aside his raincoat and searched slowly in the pockets of his loopy trousers.

"We have to go in for lunch," said Cat.

"All in good time, young gentleman. Here we are," said Mr. Baslam. He held his pale, grubby hand out toward Janet with two twinkling things in it. "These."

"Those are my mother's earrings!" Cat said, in surprise and for Janet's benefit. "How did you get those?"

"Your sister give them to me to pay for a little matter of some dragon's blood," said Mr. Baslam. "And I dare say it was in good faith, young lady, but they're no good to me."

"Why not?" asked Janet. "They look like—I mean, they're real diamonds."

"True enough," said Mr. Baslam. "But you never told me they was charmed, did you? They got a fearsome strong spell on them to stop them getting lost, these have. Terrible noisy spell. They was all night in the stuffed rabbit shouting out 'I belong to Caroline Chant,' and this morning I has to wrap them in a blanket before I dares take them to a man I know. And he wouldn't touch them. He said he wasn't going to risk anything shouting the name of Chant. So have them back, young lady. And you owe me fifty-five quid."

Janet swallowed. So did Cat. "I'm very sorry," Janet said. "I really had no idea. But—but I'm afraid I haven't any source of income at all. Couldn't you get the charm taken off?"

"And risk inquiries?" said Mr. Baslam. "That charm's deep in, I tell you."

"Then why aren't they shouting now?" said Cat.

"What do you think I am?" said Mr. Baslam. "Could I sit in the joints of mutton shouting out I belonged to Miss Chant? No. This man I know obliges me with a bit of a spell on account. But he says to me, he says, 'I can't only shut them up for an hour or so. That's a real strong charm. If you want it took off permanent, you'd have to take them to an enchanter. And that would cost you as much as the earrings are worth, besides getting questions asked.' Enchanters are important people, young lady. So here I sits in them bushes, scared to death the spell's going to wear off before you comes by, and now you say you've no income! No—you have them back, young lady, and hand over a little something on account instead."

Janet looked nervously at Cat. Cat sighed and felt in his pockets. All he had was half a crown. He offered it to Mr. Baslam.

Mr. Baslam backed away from it with a hurt, drooping look, like a whipped St. Bernard. "Fifty-five quid I ask for, and you offer me half a crown! Son, are you having a joke on me?"

"It's all either of us has got," said Cat, "at the moment. But we each get a crown piece every week. If we give you that, we'll have paid you back in—" He did hurried calculations. Ten shillings a week, fifty-two weeks in a year, twenty-six pounds a year. "It'll only take two years." Two years was an appalling time to be without money. Still,

Mr. Baslam had got Gwendolen her dragon's blood, and it seemed fair that he should be paid.

But Mr. Baslam looked more hurt than ever. He turned away from Cat and Janet and gazed mournfully up at the Castle walls. "You live in a placc like this, and tell me you can only get hold of ten bob a week! Don't play cruel games with me. You can lay your hands on no end of lucre if you puts your minds to it."

"But we can't, honestly," Cat protested.

"I think you should try, young gentleman," said Mr. Baslam. "I'm not unreasonable. All I'm asking is twenty quid part payment, interest of ten percent included, and the price of the shutting up spell thrown in. That should come quite easy to you."

"You know perfectly well it won't!" Janet said indignantly. "You'd better keep those earrings. Your stuffed rabbit may look pretty in them."

Mr. Baslam gave her a very whipped look. At the same time, a thin, singing noise began to come from the palm of his hand where the earrings lay. It was too faint for Cat to pick out the words, but it put paid to any notion that Mr. Baslam had been lying. Mr. Baslam's drooping look became less whipped. He looked more like a bloodhound hot on the trail. He let the earrings slide between his fat fingers and fall on the gravel.

"There they lie," he said, "if you care to stoop for them. I may remind you, young lady, that trade in dragon's blood is illicit, illegal, and banned. I've obliged you in it. You've fobbed me off. Now I'm telling you that I need twenty quid by next Wednesday. That should give you time. If I don't get it, then Chrestomanci hears of the dragon's blood Wednesday evening. And if he does, then I wouldn't be in your shoes, young lady, not for twenty-thousand quid and a diamond tiara. Have I made myself clear?"

He had, appallingly. "Suppose we give you the dragon's blood back?" Cat suggested desperately. Gwendolen had taken Mr. Baslam's dragon's blood with her, of course, but there was always that huge jar of it in Mr. Saunders' workshop.

"What would I do with dragon's blood, son?" said Mr. Baslam. "I'm not a warlock. I'm only a poor supplier, and there's no demand for dragon's blood around here. It's the money I need. Twenty quid of it, by next Wednesday, and don't forget." He gave them a bloodhound nod which flapped his eyes and his cheeks, and edged back into the rhododendrons. They heard him rustling stealthily away.

"What a nasty old man!" Janet said in a shaken whisper. "I wish I really was Gwendolen. I'd turn him into a four-headed earwig. Ugh!" She bent and scrabbled the earrings up off the gravel.

Immediately the air by the door was filled with high, singing voices. "I belong to Caroline Chant! I belong to Caroline Chant!"

"Oh dear!" said Janet. "They know."

"Give them to me," said Cat. "Quick. Someone will hear."

Janet poured the earrings into Cat's palm. The voices stopped at once. "I can't get used to all this magic," said Janet. "Cat, what am I to do? How can I pay that horrible man?"

"There must be something we can sell," said Cat. "There's a junk shop in the village. Come on. We *must* get to lunch."

They hurried up to the playroom, to find that Mary had already put plates of stew and dumplings in their places.

"Oh, look," said Janet, who needed to relieve her feelings somehow. "Nourishing fattening lunch. How nice!"

Mary glared at both of them and left the room without speaking. Julia's look was quite as unpleasant. As Janet sat down in front of her stew, Julia pulled her handkerchief out of her sleeve, already knotted, and laid it in her lap. Janet put her fork into a dumpling. It stuck there. The dumpling was a white pebble, swimming with two others in a plateful of mud.

Janet carefully laid down her fork, with the pebble impaled on it, and put her knife neatly across the mud. She was trying to control herself but, for a moment, she looked like Gwendolen at her most furious. "I was quite hungry," she said.

Julia smiled. "What a pity," she said cosily. "And you've got no witchcraft to defend yourself with, have you?" She tied another smaller knot at the end of her handkerchief. "You've got all sorts of things in your hair, Gwendolen," she said as she pulled it tight. The twigs sticking in Janet's hair writhed and began dropping on the table and over her skirt. Each one was a large, stripy caterpillar.

Janet was no more bothered by wriggly things than Gwendolen. She picked the caterpillars off and put them in a heap in front of Julia. "I've a good mind to shout for your father," she said.

"Oh, no, don't be a telltale," said Roger. "Let her be, Julia."

"Certainly not," said Julia. "She's not getting any lunch."

After the meeting with Mr. Baslam, Cat was not really very hungry. "Here," he said, and changed his plate of stew with Janet's mud. Janet started to protest. But, as soon as the plate of mud was in front of Cat, it was steaming stew again. And the looping heap of caterpillars was simply a pile of twigs.

Julia turned to Cat, not at all pleased. "Don't you interfere. You annoy me. She treats you like a slave and all you do is stick up for her."

"But I only changed the plates!" Cat said, puzzled. "Why—"

"It could have been Michael," Roger suggested.

Julia glowered at him too. "Was it you?" Roger blandly shook his head. Julia looked at him uncertainly. "If I have to go without marmalade again," she said at length, "Gwendolen's going to know about it. And I hope the stew chokes you."

Cat found it hard to concentrate on lessons that afternoon. He had to watch Janet like a hawk. Janet had decided that the only safe thing was to be totally stupid—she thought Gwendolen must have been pretty stupid anyway—and Cat knew she was overdoing it. Even Gwendolen had known the twice-times table. Cat was worried too, in case Julia started knotting that handkerchief of hers when Mr. Saunders' back was turned. Luckily, Julia did not quite dare. But Cat's main worry was how to find twenty pounds by next Wednesday. He could hardly bear to think of what might happen if he did not. The very least thing, he knew, would be Janet confessing she was not Gwendolen. He thought of Chrestomanci giving him that scathing stare and saying, "*You* went with Gwendolen to buy dragon's blood, Eric? But you knew it was illegal. And you tried to cover up by making Janet pretend to be Gwendolen? You show touching concern, Eric." The mere idea made Cat shrivel up inside. But he had nothing to sell except a pair of earrings that shouted that they belonged to someone else. If he wrote to the Mayor of Wolvercote and asked if he could have twenty pounds out of the Fund, the Mayor would only write to Chrestomanci to ask why Cat wanted it. And then Chrestomanci would stare scathingly and say, "*You* went with Gwendolen to buy dragon's blood, Eric?" It was hopeless.

"Are you feeling well, Eric?" Mr. Saunders asked several times.

"Oh, yes," Cat replied each time. He was fairly sure that having your mind in three places at once did not count as illness, much as it felt like it.

"Play soldiers?" Roger suggested after lessons.

Cat would have liked to, but he dared not leave Janet on her own. "I've got to do something," he said.

"With Gwendolen. I know," Roger said wearily. "Anyone would think you were her left leg, or something."

Cat felt hurt. The annoying thing was that he knew Janet could have done without her left leg more easily than she could have done without him. As he hurried after Janet to Gwendolen's room, he wished heartily it was really Gwendolen he was hurrying after.

Inside the room, Janet was feverishly collecting things: Gwendolen's spell books, the ornaments on the mantelpiece, the gold-backed brush and hand mirror off the dressing table, the jar on the bedside table, and half the towels from the bathroom.

"What are you doing?" said Cat.

"Finding things we can sell. Is there anything you can bear to spare from your room?" said Janet. "Don't look like that. I know it amounts to stealing, but I get so desperate when I think of that horrible Mr. Bisto going to Chrestomanci that I don't care anymore." She went to the wardrobe and rattled the clothes along the rail. "There's an awfully good coat in here."

"You'll need that on Sunday if it turns cold," Cat said drearily. "I'll go and see what I've got—only promise me to stay here until I come back."

"Sho' ting," said Janet. "I daren't move widdout you, bwana. But hurry up."

There were fewer things in Cat's room, but he collected what he could find, and added the great sponge from the bathroom. He felt like a criminal. Janet and he wrapped their finds in two towels and crept downstairs with their chinking bundles, expecting someone to discover them any minute.

"I feel like a thief with the swag," Janet whispered. "Someone's going to shine a searchlight any second, and then the police will close in. *Are* there police here?"

"Yes," said Cat. "Do shut up."

But, as usual, there was no one about near the private door. They crept down the shiny passage and peeped outside. The space by the rhododendrons was empty. They crept out toward them. Trees that would hide Mr. Baslam would hide them and their loot.

They were three steps outside the door when a massed choir burst into song. Janet and Cat nearly jumped out of their skins. *"We belong to Chrestomanci Castle! We belong to Chrestomanci Castle!"* thundered forty voices. Some were deep, some were shrill, but all were very loud. They made a shattering noise. It took them a second or so to realize that the voices were coming from their bundles.

"Creeping antimacassars!" said Janet.

They turned around and ran for the door again, with the forty voices bawling in their ears.

Miss Bessemer opened the door. She stood tall and narrow and purple, waiting for them to come through it. There was nothing Janet and Cat could do but scuttle guiltily past her into the passage, where they put their suddenly silent bundles down on the floor and steeled themselves for trouble.

"What an *awful* noise, my loves!" said Miss Bessemer. "I haven't heard the like since a silly warlock tried to burgle us. What *were* you doing?"

Janet did not know who the stately purple lady was. She was too scared to speak. Cat had to say something. "We were wanting to play houses in the tree house," he said. "We needed some things for it." He was surprised how likely he made it sound.

"You should have told me, sillies!" said Miss Bessemer. "I could have given you some things that don't mind being taken outside. Run and put those back, and I'll look you out some nice furnishings for tomorrow."

They crept dismally back to Janet's room. "I just can't get used to the way everything's magic here," Janet moaned. "It's getting me down. Who was that long purple lady? I'm offering even money she's a sorceress."

"Miss Bessemer. The housekeeper," said Cat.

"Any hope that she'll give us splendid castoffs that will fetch twenty quid in the open market?" Janet asked. They both knew that was unlikely. They were no nearer thinking of another way to earn twenty pounds when the dressing gong went.

Cat had warned Janet what dinner was like. She had promised not to jump when footmen passed things over her, shoulder, and sworn not to try and talk about statues with Mr. Saunders. She assured Cat she would not mind hearing Bernard talk of stocks and shares. So Cat thought that for once he could be easy. He helped Janet dress and even had a shower himself, and when they went into the drawing room, he thought that they both did him credit.

But Mr. Saunders proved at last to have worn out his craze for statues. Instead, everyone began to talk about identical twins, and then about exact doubles who were no relation. Even Bernard forgot to talk about shares in his interest in this new subject.

"The really difficult point," he boomed, leaning forward with his eyebrows working up and down his forehead, "is how such people fit in with a series of other worlds."

And, to Cat's dismay, the talk turned to other worlds. He might have been interested at any other time. Now he dared not look at Janet, and could only wish that everyone would stop. But they talked eagerly, all of them, particularly Bernard and Mr. Saunders. Cat learned that a lot was known about other worlds. Numbers had been visited. Those which were best known had been divided into sets, called series, according to the events in History which were the same in them. It was very uncommon for people not to have at least one exact double in a world of the same series—usually people had a whole string of doubles, all along the set.

"But what about doubles outside a series?" Mr. Saunders said. "I have at least one double in Series Three, and I suspect the existence of another in—"

Janet sat up sharply, gasping. "Cat, help! It's like sitting on pins!"

Cat looked at Julia. He saw the little smile on her face, and the tail end of her handkerchief above the table. "Change places," he whispered, feeling rather tired. He stood up. Everyone stared.

"All of which makes me feel that a satisfactory classification has not yet been found," Mr. Saunders said, as he turned Cat's way.

"Do you think," said Cat, "that I could change places with J-Gwendolen, please? She can't quite hear what Mr. Saunders is saying from there."

"Yes, and it's rivetingly interesting," Janet gasped, shooting from her chair.

"If you find it essential," Chrestomanci said, a little annoyed.

Cat sat in Janet's chair. He could feel nothing wrong with it. Julia put her head down and gave him a long, unpleasant look, and her elbows worked as she crossly untied her handkerchief. Cat saw that she was going to hate him too, now. He sighed. It was one thing after another.

Nevertheless, when Cat fell asleep that night, he was not feeling hopeless. He could not believe things could get any worse—so they had to get better. Perhaps Miss Bessemer would give them something very valuable, and they could sell it. Or, better still, perhaps Gwendolen would be back when he woke up, and already solving all his problems.

But when he went to Gwendolen's room in the morning, it was still Janet, struggling to tie her garters and saying over her shoulder, "These things are probably very bad for people. Do you wear them too? Or are they a female torture? And one *useful* thing magic could do would be to hold one's stockings up. It makes you think that witches can't be very practical."

She did talk a lot, Cat thought. But it was better than having no one in Gwendolen's place.

At breakfast, neither Mary nor Euphemia were at all friendly and, as soon as they left the room, one of the curtains wrapped itself around Janet's neck and tried to strangle her. Cat took it away. It fought him like a live thing because Julia was holding both ends of her handkerchief and pulling hard on the knot.

"Oh, do stop it, Julia!" he begged her.

"Yes, do," Roger agreed. "It's silly and it's boring. I need to enjoy my food in peace."

"I'm quite willing to be friends," Janet offered.

"That makes one of us," said Julia. "No."

"Then be enemies!" Janet snapped, almost in Gwendolen's manner. "I thought at first that you might be nice, but I can see now that you're just a tedious, pigheaded, cold-hearted, horny-handed, cross-eyed *hag*!"

That, of course, was calculated to make Julia adore her.

Luckily, Mr. Saunders appeared earlier than usual. There had only been time for Janet's marmalade to turn to orange worms, and change back again when Cat gave her his instead, and for Janet's coffee to become rich brown gravy, and turn to coffee again when Cat drank it, before Mr. Saunders stuck his head around the door. At least, Cat thought it was lucky, until Mr. Saunders said, "Eric, Chrestomanci wants to see you now, in his study."

Cat stood up. His stomach, full of charmed marmalade as it was, made an unusually rapid descent to the Castle cellars. Chrestomanci's found out, he thought. He knows about the dragon's blood and about Janet, and he's going to look at me politely and— Oh, I do hope he *isn't* an enchanter!

"Where—where do I go?" he managed to say.

"Take him, Roger," said Mr. Saunders.

"And—and *why*?" Cat asked.

Mr. Saunders smiled. "You'll find out. Off you go."

CHAPTER 12

Chrestomanci's study was a large, sun-filled room with books in shelves all around it. There was a desk, but Chrestomanci was not sitting at it. He was sprawled on a sofa in the sun, reading a newspaper and wearing a green dressing gown with golden dragons on it. The gold embroidery of the dragons winked and glittered in the sun. Cat could not take his eyes off them. He stood just inside the door, not daring to go any farther, and he thought: He *has* found out about the dragon's blood.

Chrestomanci looked up and smiled. "Don't look so frightened," he said, laying down his newspaper. "Come and sit down."

He pointed to a large leather armchair. It was all in his friendliest way but, these days, Cat was sure this meant precisely nothing. He was sure that the friendlier Chrestomanci seemed, the angrier this meant he was. He stole over to the armchair and sat in it. It proved to be one of those deep, sloping kind of chairs. Cat slid backward down the slippery leather slope of its seat until he found he was having to look at Chrestomanci from between his knees. He felt quite defenseless. He thought he ought to say something, so he whispered, "Good morning."

"You don't look as if you thought so," observed Chrestomanci. "No doubt you have your reasons. But don't worry. This isn't exactly about the frog again. You see, I've been thinking about you—"

"Oh, you needn't!" Cat said from his half-lying position. He felt that if Chrestomanci were to fix his thoughts on something on the other side of the universe, it would hardly be too far away.

"It didn't hurt much," said Chrestomanci. "Thank you all the same. As I was saying, the frog affair set me thinking. And though I fear you probably have as little moral sense as your wretched sister, I wondered if I could trust you. Do you think I can trust you?"

Cat had no idea where this could be leading, except that from the way Chrestomanci put it, he did not seem to trust Cat very much. "Nobody's ever trusted me before," Cat said cautiously—except Janet, he thought, and only because she had no choice.

"But it might be worth trying, don't you think?" suggested Chrestomanci. "I ask because I'm going to start you on witchcraft lessons."

Cat had simply not expected this. He was horrified. His legs waved about in the chair with the shock. He managed to stop them, but he was still horrified. The moment Mr. Saunders started trying to teach him magic, it would be obvious that Cat had no witchcraft at all. Then Chrestomanci would start to think about the frog all over again. Cat cursed the chance that had made Janet draw in her breath and caused him to confess. "Oh, you mustn't do that!" he said. "It would be quite fatal. I mean, you can't trust me at all. I'm black-hearted. I'm evil. It was living with Mrs. Sharp that did it. If I learned witchcraft, there's no knowiing what I'd do. Look what I did to Euphemia."

"That," said Chrestomanci, "is just the kind of accident I'm anxious to prevent. If you learn how and what to do, you're far less likely to make that kind of mistake again."

"Yes, but I'd probably do it on purpose," Cat assured him. "You'll be putting the means in my hands."

"You have it there anyway," Chrestomanci said. "And witchcraft will out, you know. No one who has it can resist using it forever. What exactly makes you think you're so wicked?"

That question rather stumped Cat. "I steal apples," he said. "And," he suggested, "I was quite keen on some of the things Gwendolen did."

"Oh, me too," Chrestomanci agreed. "One wondered what she would think of next. How about her procession of nasties? Or those four apparitions?"

Cat shivered. He felt sick to think of them.

"Precisely," said Chrestomanci, and to Cat's dismay, he smiled warmly at him. "Right. We'll let Michael start you on Elementary Witchcraft on Monday."

"Oh, *please* don't!" Cat struggled out of the slippery chair in order to plead better. "I'll bring a plague of locusts. I'll be worse than Moses and Aaron."

Chrestomanci said musingly, "It might be quite useful if you parted the waters of the English Channel. Think of all the seasickness you'd save. Don't be so alarmed. We've no intention of teaching you to do things the way Gwendolen did."

Cat trailed forlornly back to the schoolroom to find them having Geography. Mr. Saunders was raging at Janet for not knowing where Atlantis was.

"How was I to know it's what I call America?" Janet asked Cat at lunchtime. "Though, mind you, that was a lucky guess when I said it was ruled by the Incas. What's the matter, Cat? You look ready to cry. He's not found out about Mr. Biswas, has he?"

"No, but it's quite as bad," said Cat, and he explained.

"This was all we needed!" said Janet. "Discovery threatens on all sides. But it may not be quite as bad as it seems, when I think. You might be able to work up a little magic if you practiced first. Let's see what we can do after school with Gwendolen's books that the dear, kind girl so obligingly left us."

Cat was quite glad when lessons started again. He was sick of changing plates with Janet, and Julia's handkerchief must have been worn to rags with the number of knots tied in it. After lessons, he and Janet collected the two magic books and took them up to Cat's room. Janet looked around it with admiration.

"I like this room much better than mine. It's cheerful. Mine makes me feel like the Sleeping Beauty and Cinderella, and they were both such sickeningly sweet girls. Now let's get down to work. What's a really simple spell?"

They knelt on the floor, leafing through a book each.

"I wish I could find how to turn buttons into sovereigns," said Cat. "We could pay Mr. Baslam then."

"Don't talk about it," said Janet. "I'm at our wits' end. How about this? *Simple flotation exercise. Take a small mirror and lay it so that your face is visible in it. Keeping face visible, move around widdershins three times, twice silently willing, the third time saying: 'Rise little mirror, rise in air, rise to my head and then stay there.' Mirror should then rise*— I think you ought to be able to manage that, Cat."

"I'll have a go," Cat said dubiously. "What's widdershins?"

"Anticlockwise," said Janet. "That I do know."

"I thought it meant crawling," Cat said humbly.

Janet looked at him consideringly. "I suppose you're quite small still," she said, "but you do worry me when you go all cowed. Has anyone done anything to you?"

"I don't think so," Cat said, rather surprised. "Why?"

"Well, I never had a brother," said Janet. "Fetch a mirror."

Cat got the hand mirror from his chest of drawers and laid it carefully in the middle of the floor. "Like that?"

Janet sighed. "That's what I mean. I knew you'd get it if I ordered you to. Do you mind not being so kind and obedient? It makes me nervous. Anyway—" She took up the book. "Can you see your face in it?"

"Almost nothing else," said Cat.

"Funny. I can see *my* face," said Janet. "Can I do it, too?"

"You're more likely to get it to work than I am," said Cat.

So they both circled the mirror, and they said the words in chorus. The door opened. Mary came in. Janet guiltily put the book behind her back.

"Yes, here he is," Mary said. She stood aside to let a strange young man come into the room. "This is Will Suggins," she said. "He's Euphemia's young man. He wants to talk to you, Eric."

Will Suggins was tall and burly and rather handsome. His clothes looked as if he had brushed them carefully after working in a bakery all day. He was not friendly. "It was you turned Euphemia into a frog, was it?" he said to Cat.

"Yes," said Cat. He dared say nothing else with Mary there.

"You're rather small," said Will Suggins. He seemed disappointed about it. "Anyway," he said, "whatever size you are, I'm not having Euphemia turned into things. I take exception to it. Understand?"

"I'm very sorry," said Cat. "I won't do it again."

"Too right you won't!" said Will Suggins. "You got off too light over this, by what Mary tells me. I'm going to teach you a lesson you won't forget in a hurry."

"No you're not!" said Janet. She marched up to Will Suggins and pushed *Magic for Beginners* threateningly toward him. "You're three times his size, and he's said he's sorry. If you touch Cat, I shall—" She took the book out of Will Suggins' chest in order to leaf hastily through it. "I shall induce complete immobility in the legs and trunk."

"And very pretty I shall look, I'm sure!" Will Suggins said, much amused. "How are you going to do that without your witchcraft, may I ask? And if you did, I daresay I could get out of it fast enough. I'm a fair warlock myself. Though," he said, turning to Mary, "you might have warned me he was this small."

"Not so small where witchcraft and mischief are concerned," said Mary. "Neither of them are. They're a pair of real bad lots."

"Well, I'll do it by witchcraft then. I'm easy," said Will Suggins. He searched in the pockets of his slightly floury jacket. "Ah!" he said, and fetched out what seemed to be a lump of dough. For a moment he shaped it vigorously in both powerful hands. Then he rolled it into a ball and threw it at Cat's feet. It landed on the carpet with a soft *plop.*

Cat looked at it in great apprehension, wondering what it was supposed to do.

"That'll lie there," said Will Suggins, "until three o'clock Sunday. Sunday's a bad time to be at witchcraft, but it's my free day. I shall be waiting for you then in Bedlam Field, in the form of a tiger. I make a good tiger. You can turn yourself into something as large as you like, or small and fast, if you prefer, and I'll teach you that lesson whatever you are. But if you don't come to Bedlam Field in the form of something, that lump of dough will start to work and you'll be a frog yourself—for as long as I feel like keeping you that way. Right, Mary. I'm through now."

Will Suggins turned and marched out of the room. Mary followed him, but she was unable to resist putting her head back around the door to say, "And see how you like that, Eric!" before she shut it.

Cat and Janet looked at one another and then at the lump of dough. "What am I going to *do*?" said Cat.

Janet threw her book onto Cat's bed and tried to pick up the lump of dough. But it had grown to the carpet. She could not shift it. "You'd only get this up by cutting a hole in the floor," she said. "Cat, this gets worse and worse. If you'll forgive my saying so, I've stopped loving your sugar-coated sister even one tiny bit!"

"It was my fault," said Cat. "I shouldn't have lied about Euphemia. That's what got me in this mess, not Gwendolen."

"Mess is not a strong enough word," said Janet. "On Sunday, you get mauled by a tiger. On Monday, it comes out that you can't do magic. And if the whole story doesn't come out then, it will on Wednesday, when Mr. Bedlam calls for his money. Do you think Fate has something up its sleeve for Tuesday too? I suppose if you go to meet him on Sunday in the form of yourself, he can't hurt you much, can he? It's better than waiting to be turned into a frog."

"I'd better do that," Cat agreed, looking at that ominous lump of dough. "I wish I really could turn into things, though. I'd go as a flea. He'd scratch himself to bits trying to find me."

Janet laughed. "Let's see if there's a spell for it." She turned around to fetch *Magic for Beginners* and hit her head on the mirror. It was hanging in the air, level with her forehead. "Cat! One of us *did* it! Look!"

Cat looked, without much interest. He had too much else on his mind. "I expect it was you. You're the same as Gwendolen, so you're bound to be able to work spells. But changing into things won't be in either of those books. That's Advanced Magic."

"Then I'll do the spell to get the mirror down," said Janet. "Not that I want to be a witch. The more I see of witchcraft, the more it seems just an easy way to be nasty."

She had opened the book, when there was a knock at the door. Janet seized the chair beside Cat's bed and stood on it, so as to hide the mirror. Cat hastily dropped to one knee on top of the lump of dough. Neither of them wanted any more trouble.

Janet doubled *Magic for Beginners* inside out so that it could have been any book, and waved it at Cat. "*Come into the garden, Maud,*" she proclaimed.

Taking this as an invitation, Miss Bessemer opened the door and came in. She was carrying an armful of things, with a chipped teapot hanging off one finger. "The furnishings I promised you, loves," she said.

"Oh," said Janet. "Oh, thanks very much. We were just having a poetry reading, you know."

"And I made sure you were talking to me!" Miss Bessemer said, laughing. "My name's Maud. Will these be all right on the bed?"

"Yes, thanks," said Cat.

Neither of them dared move. They twisted around to watch Miss Bessemer dump the armful on the bed and, still twisted, they thanked her profusely. As soon as Miss Bessemer had gone, they dived to see if, by any blessed chance, any of the pile was valuable. Nothing was. As Janet said, if they really had wanted to play houses, two stools and an old carpet would have been just the thing, but from a selling point of view, they were just a dead loss.

"It was kind of her to remember," Cat said as he packed the heap into his cupboard.

"Except that now we'll have to remember to play houses with them," Janet said morosely. "As if we hadn't enough to do. Now, I *will* get this mirror down. I will!"

But the mirror refused to come down. Janet tried all three spells in both books, and it still stayed hanging in the air level with her head.

"You try, Cat," said Janet. "We can't leave it there."

Cat roused himself from gloomily staring at the ball of dough. It was still round. There was no sign that he had knelt on it, and that alarmed him. He knew it must be a very strong charm. But when Janet appealed to him, he sighed and reached up to pull the mirror down. His experience with Julia had taught him that a simple spell could usually be broken quite simply.

The mirror refused to descend an inch. But it slid about in the air. Cat was interested. He hung on to it with both hands, pushed off with his feet, and went traveling across the room in a most agreeable way.

"That looks fun," said Janet.

"It is," said Cat. "You try."

They played with the mirror for some time after that. It could go as fast as they could push it, and it took the weight of both of them easily. Janet discovered that the best ride was to be had by standing on the chest of drawers and jumping. Then, provided you kept your feet up, you could swing across the room and land on Cat's bed. They were whirling together across the carpet, tangled up and laughing a good deal, when Roger knocked at the door and came in.

"I say, that's a good idea!" he said. "We've never thought of that. Can I have a go? And I met a peculiar cross-eyed man in the village, Gwendolen, and he gave me this letter for you."

Cat dropped off onto the carpet and took the letter. It was from Mr. Nostrum. Cat recognized the writing. He was so pleased that he said to Roger, "Have twenty goes if you want!" and rushed up to Janet with the letter. "Read it, quick! What does it say?"

Mr. Nostrum could get them out of their troubles. He might not be much of a necromancer, but he was surely able to turn Cat into a flea, if Janet asked him nicely. He would certainly have a charm that could make Cat look as if he could do magic. And though Mr. Nostrum was not rich, his brother William was. He could lend Cat twenty pounds, if he thought he was helping Gwendolen.

Cat sat on the bed beside Janet and they read the letter, while Roger trundled about the room dangling from the mirror and chuckling placidly at what fun it was. Mr. Nostrum wrote:

My dear and favorite pupil,

I am here, domiciled at the White Hart Inn. It is most important—I repeat, of the utmost importance—that you come to me here on Saturday afternoon, bringing your brother to be briefed by me.

Your affectionate and proud teacher,
Henry Nostrum

At this, Janet looked nervous and mystified and moaned gently.

"I hope it's not bad news," Roger said, sailing past with his feet hooked up behind him.

"No, it's the best news we could have had!" Cat said. He dug Janet in the ribs to make her smile. She smiled dutifully, but he could not make her see that it was good news, even when he had a chance to explain.

"If he taught Gwendolen, he'll know I'm not her," she said. "And if he doesn't know, he won't understand why you want to be turned into a flea. It is an odd thing to go and ask, even in this world. And he'd want to know why I couldn't do it to you. Couldn't we tell him the truth?"

"No, because it's Gwendolen he's fond of," Cat explained. Something told him that Mr. Nostrum would be almost as little pleased as Chrestomanci to find that Gwendolen had departed for another world. "And he's got some kind of plans for her."

"Yes, this briefing," Janet said irritably. "He obviously thinks I know all about it. If you ask me, Cat, it's just one more damned thing!"

Nothing could convince Janet that salvation was at hand. Cat was quite sure it was. He went to sleep rejoicing, and woke up happy. He still felt happy, even when he trod on the lump of dough and it was cold and froglike under his foot. He covered it up with *Magic for Beginners*. Then he had to turn his attention to the mirror. It would keep drifting out into the middle of the room. Cat had to tether it to the bookcase with his Sunday bootlace in the end.

He found Janet less happy than ever. Julia's latest idea was a mosquito. It met Janet as she came into breakfast, and it kept with her, whining in and biting, all through lessons, until Cat swatted it with his arithmetic book.

What with this and nasty looks from both Julia and Mary, and then having to meet Mr. Nostrum, Janet became both peevish and miserable.

"It's all right for you," she said morbidly, as they tramped down the avenue on their way to the village that afternoon. "You've been brought up with all this magic and you're used to it. But I'm not. And what scares me is that it's forever. And it scares me even more that it *isn't* forever. Suppose Gwendolen gets tired of her new world and decides to move on again? When that happens, off we shall be dragged, a whole string of us doubles, and I'll be having to cope in her world, and you'll have all your troubles over again with a new one."

"Oh, I'm sure that won't happen," Cat said, rather startled at the possibility. "She's bound to come back soon."

"Oh, *is* she?" said Janet. They came through the gates, and again mothers snatched children out of their sight, and the village green emptied as they reached it. "I *wish* I was back at home!" Janet wailed, almost in tears at the way everyone ran away.

CHAPTER 13

They were ushered into a private parlor in the White Hart. Mr. Henry Nostrum rolled pompously to meet them.

"My dear young friends!" He put his hands on Janet's shoulders and kissed her. Janet started backward, knocking her hat over one ear. Cat was a little shaken. He had forgotten Mr. Nostrum's seedy, shabby look, and the weird effect of his wandering left eye. "Sit down, sit down!" said Mr. Nostrum heartily. "Have some ginger beer."

They sat down. They sipped ginger beer, which neither of them liked. "What did you want me for, as well as Gwendolen?" Cat asked.

"Because," said Mr. Nostrum, "to come straight to the point and not to beat about the bush, we find, as we rather feared we would, that we are quite unable to make use of those three signatures which you were kind enough to donate to me for services rendered in the tuition line. The Person Who Inhabits That Castle Yonder, whose name I disdain to say, signs his name under unbreakable protections. You may call it prudent of him. But I fear it necessitates our using Plan Two. Which was why, my dear Cat, we were so glad to arrange for you to live at the Castle."

"What is Plan Two?" said Janet.

Mr. Nostrum's odd eye slipped sideways across Janet's face. He did not seem to realize she was not Gwendolen. Perhaps his wandering eye did not see very well. "Plan Two is just as I described it to you, my dear Gwendolen," he said. "We have not changed it one whit."

Janet had to try another way to find out what he was talking about. She was getting quite good at it. "I want you to describe it to Cat, though," she said. "He doesn't know about it, and he may need to because—because most unfortunately they've taken my witchcraft away."

Mr. Nostrum wagged a playful finger at her. "Yes, naughty girl. I've been hearing things about you in the village. A sad thing to lose, but let us hope it will only be temporary. Now—as to explaining to Young Chant—how shall I best go about it?" He thought, smoothing his frizzy wings of hair, as his habit was. Somehow, the way he did it showed Cat that whatever Mr. Nostrum was going to tell him, it would not be quite the truth. It was in the movement of Mr. Nostrum's hands, and in the very sit of his silver watch-chain across his shabby, rounded waistcoat.

"Well, Young Chant," said Mr. Nostrum, "this is the matter in a nutshell. There is a group, a clique, a collection of people, headed by the Master of the Castle, who are behaving very selfishly in connection with witchcraft. They are keeping all the best things to themselves, which of course makes them very dangerous—a threat to all witches, and a looming disaster to ordinary people. For instance, take dragon's blood. You know that it is banned. These people, with That Person at their head, had it banned, and yet—mark this well, Young Chant—they use it daily themselves. And—here is my point—they keep tight control of the ways to get to the worlds where dragon's blood comes from. An ordinary necromancer like myself can only get it at great risk and expense, and our exotic suppliers have to endanger themselves to get it for us. And the same goes for almost any product from another world.

"Now, I ask you, Young Chant, is this fair? No. And I'll tell you why not, young Eric. It is not fair that the ways of other worlds should be in the hands of a few. That is the crux of the matter: the ways to other worlds. We want them opened up, made free to everyone. And that is where you come in, Young Chant. The best and easiest way, the broadest Gateway to Elsewhere, if I may put it like that, is a certain enclosed garden in the grounds of this said Castle. I expect you have been forbidden to enter it—"

"Yes," said Cat. "We have been."

"And consider how unfair!" said Mr. Nostrum. "The Master of That Place uses it every day and travels where he pleases. So what I want you to do, Young Chant, and this is all Plan Two amounts to, is to go into that garden at two-thirty precisely on Sunday afternoon. Can you promise me to do that?"

"What good would that do?" asked Cat.

"It would break the seal of enchantment these dastardly persons have set on the Gateways to Elsewhere," Mr. Nostrum said.

"I've never quite understood," Janet said, with a very convincing wrinkle in her forehead, "how Cat could break the seals just by going into the garden."

Mr. Nostrum looked a little irritated. "By being an ordinary innocent lad, of course. My dear Gwendolen, I have stressed to you over and over again the importance of having an innocent lad at the center of Plan Two. You *must* understand."

"Oh, I do, I do," Janet said hastily. "And has it to be *this* Sunday at two-thirty?"

"As ever is," said Mr. Nostrum, smiling again. "It's a good strong time. Will you do that for us, Young Chant? Will you, by this simple act, set your sister and people like her free—free to do as they need in the practice of magic?"

"I'll get into trouble if I'm caught," said Cat.

"A bit of boyish cunning will see you through. Then, never fear, we'll take care of you afterward," Mr. Nostrum persuaded.

"I suppose I can try," said Cat. "But do you think you can help me a bit in return? Do you think your brother could very kindly lend us twenty pounds by next Wednesday?"

A vague, though affable, look affected Mr. Nostrum's left eye. It pointed benevolently to the farthest corner of the parlor. "Anything you please, dear boy. Just get into that garden, and the fruits of all the worlds will be yours for the picking."

"I need to be a flea half an hour later, and I want to look as if I can do magic on Monday," said Cat. "That's all I need, apart from the twenty pounds."

"Anything, anything! Just get into that garden for us," said Mr. Nostrum expansively.

With that, it seemed Cat and Janet had to be content. Cat made several efforts to fix Mr. Nostrum in a definite promise, but all he would say was, "Just get into that garden." Janet looked at Cat and they got up to go.

"Let us gossip," suggested Mr. Nostrum. "I have at least two items of interest to you."

"We haven't time," Janet lied firmly. "Come on, Cat."

Mr. Nostrum was used to Gwendolen being equally firm. He got up and led them to the Inn door like royalty and waved to them as they went out onto the green. "I'll see you on Sunday," he called after them.

"No you won't!" Janet whispered. Keeping her head down so that Gwendolen's broad hat hid her from Mr. Nostrum, she whispered to Cat, "Cat, if you do one thing that unbelievably dishonest man wants, you'll be a fool! I *know* he told you a pack of lies. I don't know what he's really after, but please don't do it."

"I know—" Cat was beginning, when Mr. Baslarn got up from a bench outside the White Hart and shambled after them.

"Wait!" he puffed, rolling beer fumes over them. "Young lady, young sir, I hope you're bearing in mind what I said to you. Wednesday. Don't forget Wednesday."

"No fear. It haunts my dreams," said Janet. "Please. We're busy, Mr. Bustle."

They walked quickly away across the green. The only other living soul in sight was Will Suggins, who came out of the backyard of the bread shop in order to stare meaningly after them.

"I think I've *got* to do what he wants," Cat said.

"Don't," said Janet. "Though I must say I can't see what else we can do."

"About the only thing left is running away," said Cat.

"Then let's do that—at once," said Janet.

They did not exactly run. They walked briskly out of the village on the road Cat thought pointed nearest to Wolvercote. When Janet objected that Wolvercote was the first place anyone at the Castle would think of looking, Cat explained about Mrs. Sharp's grand contacts in London. He knew Mrs. Sharp would smuggle them away somewhere, and no questions asked. He made himself very homesick by talking of Mrs. Sharp. He missed her dreadfully. He trudged along the country road, wishing it was Coven Street and wishing Janet was not walking beside him making objections.

"Well, you may be right," Janet said, "and I don't know where else we could go. How do we get to Wolvercote? Hitchhike?" When Cat did not understand, she explained that it meant getting lifts by waving your thumb.

"That would save a lot of walking," Cat agreed.

The road he had chosen shortly turned into a very country lane, rutted and grassy and lined with high hedges hung with red bryony berries. There was no traffic of any kind.

Janet managed not to point this out. "One thing," she said. "If we're going to make a proper go of this, do promise me you won't happen to mention You Know Who." When Cat did not understand this either, she explained, "The man Mr. Nostrum kept calling That Person and the Master of the Castle—you know!"

"Oh," said Cat. "You mean Chrest—"

"Quiet!" bawled Janet. "I do mean him, and you mustn't say it. He's an enchanter and he comes when you call him, stupid. Just think of the way that Mr. Nostrum was scared stiff to say his name."

Cat thought about this. Gloomy and homesick as he was, he was not anxious to agree with anything Janet said. She was not really his sister, after all. Besides, Mr. Nostrum had not been telling the truth. And Gwendolen had never said Chrestomanci was an enchanter. She would surely never have dared do all the magic she did if she thought he was. "I don't believe you," he said.

"All right. Don't," said Janet. "Just don't say his name."

"I don't mind," said Cat. "I hope I never see him again anyway."

The lane grew wilder as they walked. It was a crisp, warm afternoon. There were nuts in the hedges and great bushes of blackberries. Before they had gone another half mile, Cat found his feelings had changed entirely. He was free. His troubles had been left behind. He and Janet picked the nuts, which were just ripe enough to eat, and laughed a good deal over cracking them. Janet took her hat off—as she told Cat repeatedly, she hated hats—and they filled the crown of it with blackberries for later on. They laughed when the juice oozed through the hat and dripped down Janet's dress.

"I think running away is fun," said Cat.

"Wait till we're spending the night in a rat-infested barn," said Janet. "Flitterings and squeakings. Are there ghouls and goblins in this wor—? Oh, look! There's a car coming! Thumb—no, wave. They probably don't understand thumbing."

They waved furiously at the big black car that was whispering and bouncing along the ruts toward them. To their delight, it sighed to a stop beside them. The nearest window rolled down. They got a very rude shock when Julia put her head out of it.

Julia was pale and agitated. "Oh *please* come back!" she said. "I know you ran away because of me, and I'm *sorry*! I swear I won't do it anymore!"

Roger put his head out of the back window. "I kept telling her you would," he said. "And she didn't believe me. Do come back. Please."

The driver's door had opened by then. Milly came hurrying around the long bonnet of the car. She looked much more homely than usual, because her skirts were looped up for driving and she was wearing stout shoes and an old hat. She was as agitated as Julia. When she reached Janet and Cat, she flung an arm around each of them and hugged them so hard and thankfully that Cat nearly fell over.

"You poor darlings! Another time you get unhappy, you must come and tell me at *once!* And what a thing too! I was so afraid you'd got into real trouble, and then Julia told me it was *her*. I'm extremely vexed with her. A girl did that to me once and I know how miserable it made me. Now, please, please come back. I've got a surprise waiting for you at the Castle."

There was nothing Cat and Janet could do but climb into the back of the car and be driven back to the Castle. They were miserable. Cat's misery was increased by the fact that he began to feel sick from the moment Milly started to bump the car backward down the lane to a gate where she could turn it. The smell of blackberry coming from Janet's squashy hat made him feel worse.

Milly, Roger, and Julia were very relieved to have found them. They chattered joyfully the whole way. Through his sickness, Cat got the impression that, although none of them said so, what they were particularly glad about was to have found Janet and Cat before Chrestomanci came to hear they were gone. This did not make either Cat or Janet feel any better.

In five minutes, the car had whispered up the avenue and stopped at the main door of the Castle. The butler opened it for them just, Cat thought sadly, as Gwendolen would have wished. The butler, furthermore, ceremoniously took Janet's leaking hat away from her. "I'll see that these get to Cook," he said.

Milly told Janet that her dress would just pass muster and hurried them to what was called the Little Drawing Room. "Which means, of course, that it's a mere seventy feet square," she said. "Go in. Tea will be there for you."

They went in. In the middle of the big, square room, a wispy, skinny woman in beaded black clothes was sitting nervously on the edge of a gilded chair. She jumped around when the door opened.

Cat forgot he felt sick. "Mrs. Sharp!" he shouted, and ran to hug her.

Mrs. Sharp was overjoyed, in spite of her nervousness. "It's my Cat, then! Here, stand back, let me look at you, and you too, Gwendolen, love. My word, you do wear fine clothes to go playing about in! You're fatter, Cat. And Gwendolen, you've gone thin. I can understand that, dear, believe me! And would you just look at the tea they've brought for the three of us!"

It was a marvelous tea, even better than the tea on the lawn. Mrs. Sharp, in her old greedy way, settled down to eat as much as she could, and to gossip hard. "Yes, we came up on the train yesterday, Mr. Nostrum and me. After I got your postcard, Cat, I couldn't rest till I'd had a look at you both, and seeing as how my contacts and other things have been paying nicely, I felt I owed it to myself. They treated me like royalty when I turned up here at the door too. I can't fault them.

But I wish I cared for it in this Castle. Tell me, Gwendolen, love, does it get you like it gets me?"

"How does it get you?" Janet asked cautiously.

"I'm nerves all over," said Mrs. Sharp. "I feel weak and jumpy as a kitten—and that reminds me, Cat, but I'll tell you later. It's so *quiet* here. I kept trying to think what it was before you came—and you were a long time, my loves—and at last it came to me. It's an enchantment, that's what it is, a terrible strong one too, against us witches. I said, 'This Castle does not love witches, that's what it is!' and I felt for you, Gwendolen. Make him send you to school away somewhere. You'd be happier."

She chattered on. She was delighted to see them both, and she kept giving Cat particularly proud and affectionate looks. Cat thought she had convinced herself she had brought him up from a baby. After all, she had known him since he was born.

"Tell us about Coven Street," he said yearningly.

"I was coming to that," said Mrs. Sharp. "You remember Miss Larkins? Bad-tempered girl with red hair who used to tell fortunes? I never thought much of her myself. But someone did. She's been set up by a grateful client in a Salon in Bond Street. Coven Street's not good enough for her anymore. The luck some people have! But I've had a stroke of luck myself too. I told you in my letter—didn't I, Cat?—about being give five pounds for that old cat you turned our Cat's fiddle into, Gwendolen. Well, he was ever such a funny little man who bought him. While we were waiting to catch the old cat—you know how he never would come if you wanted him—this little man kept at me, telling me all about stocks and shares and capital investment and such like. Things I never could understand. He told me what I ought to be doing with that five pound he was giving me, and making my head go around with it. Well, I didn't think too much of it, but I thought I'd have a go. And I did what he said, as far as I could remember. And do you know, that five pounds has brought in one hundred! One hundred pounds, he got me!"

"He must have been a financial wizard," Janet said.

She meant it as a joke to cheer herself up. She needed cheering up for several reasons. But Mrs. Sharp took her literally. "He *was*, my dear! You're always so clever. I know he was, because I told Mr. Nostrum, and Mr. Nostrum did exactly what I did with five pounds of his own—or it may have been more—and he lost every penny of it. And another thing—"

Cat watched Mrs. Sharp as she chattered on. He was puzzled and sad. He was still just as fond of Mrs. Sharp. But he knew it would have been no use whatsoever running away to her. She was a weak, dishonest person. She would not have helped them. She would have sent them back to the Castle and tried to get money out of Chrestomanci for doing it. And the London contacts she was boasting of at that moment were just boasts. Cat wondered how much he had changed inside—and why he had—enough to know all this. But he did know, just as surely as if Mrs. Sharp had turned around in her gilded chair and assured him of it herself, and it upset him.

As Mrs. Sharp came to the end of the food, she seemed to become very nervous. Perhaps the Castle was getting her down. At length she got up and took a nervous trot to the distant window, absentmindedly taking her teacup with her.

"Come and explain this view," she called. "It's so grand I can't understand it." Cat and Janet obligingly went over to her. Whereupon Mrs. Sharp became astounded to find she had an empty teacup in her hand. "Oh, look at this," she said, shaking with nervousness. "I'll be carrying it away with me if I'm not careful."

"You'd better not," said Cat. "It's bound to be charmed. Everything you take outside shouts where it came from."

"Is that so?" All of a flutter, Mrs. Sharp passed Janet her cup and followed it up, very guiltily, with two silver spoons and the sugar tongs out of her handbag. "There, dear. Would you mind taking those back to the table?" Janet set off across the yards of carpet and, as soon as she was out of hearing, Mrs. Sharp bent and whispered, "Have you talked to Mr. Nostrum, Cat?"

Cat nodded.

Mrs. Sharp at once became nervous in a much more genuine way. "Don't do what he says, love," she whispered. "Not on *any* account. You hear me? It's a wicked, crying shame, and you're not to do it!" Then, as Janet came slowly back—slowly, because she could see Mrs. Sharp had something private to say to Cat—Mrs. Sharp burst out artificially, "Oh, those great immemorial oaks! They must be older than I am!"

"They're cedars," was all Cat could think of to say.

"Well, that was a nice tea, my loves, and lovely to see you," said Mrs. Sharp. "And I'm glad you warned me about those spoons. It's a mean, wicked trick, enchanting property, I always think. I must be going now. Mr. Nostrum's expecting me." And go Mrs. Sharp did, through the Castle hall and away down the avenue with such speed that it was clear she was glad to go.

"You can see the Castle really upsets her," Janet said, watching Mrs. Sharp's trotting black figure. "There is this quiet. I know what she means. But I think it's cheerful—or it would be if everything else wasn't so miserable. Cat, it would have been no good running away to her, I'm afraid."

"I know," said Cat.

"I thought you did," said Janet.

She was wanting to say more, but they were interrupted by Roger and Julia. Julia was so contrite and trying so hard to be friendly that neither Janet nor Cat had the heart to go off on their own. They played with hand mirrors instead. Roger fetched the mirror tethered to Cat's bookcase, and collected his own and Julia's and Gwendolen's too. Julia took a firm little reef in that handkerchief of hers and sent all four aloft in the playroom. Until supper, they had great fun whizzing around the playroom, not to speak of up and down the passage outside.

Supper was in the playroom that evening. There were guests to dinner again downstairs. Roger and Julia knew, but no one had mentioned it to Cat and Janet for fear the supposed Gwendolen might try to ruin it again.

"They always entertain a lot in the month before Halloween," Julia said as they finished the blackberry tart Cook had made specially out of Janet's hatful. "Shall we play soldiers now, or mirrors again?"

Janet was signaling so hard that she had something urgent to say that Cat had to refuse. "I'm awfully sorry. We've got to talk about something Mrs. Sharp told us. And don't say Gwendolen owns me. It's not that at all."

"We forgive you," Roger said. "We might forgive Gwendolen too, with luck."

"We'll come back when I've said it," said Janet.

They hurried along to her room, and Janet locked the door in case Euphemia tried to come in.

"Mrs. Sharp said I wasn't on any account to do what Mr. Nostrum says," Cat told her. "I think she came specially to tell me."

"Yes, she's fond of you," said Janet. "Oh—oh—oh *drat*!" She clasped her hands behind her back and marched up and down with her head bent. She looked so like Mr. Saunders teaching that Cat started to laugh. "Bother," said Janet. "Bother, bother, bother bother botherbotherbother!" She marched some more. "Mrs. Sharp is a highly dishonest person, almost as bad as Mr. Nostrum, and probably worse than Mr. Bistro, so if *she* thinks you oughtn't to do it, it must be bad. What are you laughing about?"

"You keep getting Mr. Baslam's name wrong," said Cat.

"He doesn't deserve to have it got right," Janet said, marching on.

"Oh, confusticate Mrs. Sharp! After I saw she wasn't any good for any kind of help, I was in such despair that I suddenly saw the ideal way out—and she's stopped it. You see, if that garden is a way to go to other worlds, you and I could go back to my world, and you could live there with me. Don't you think that was a good idea? You'd be safe from Chrestomanci and Mr. Baalamb, and I'm sure Will Suggins couldn't turn you into a frog there, either, could he?"

"No," Cat said dubiously. "But I don't think Mr. Nostrum was telling quite the truth. All sorts of things could be wrong."

"Don't I know it!" said Janet. "Especially after Mrs. Sharp. Mum and Dad would be another difficulty too—though I'm sure they'd like you when they understood. They must be fearfully puzzled by my Dear Replacement by now, as it is. And I did have a brother, who died when he was born, so perhaps they'd think you were *his* Dear Replacement."

"That's funny!" said Cat. "I nearly died being born too."

"Then you must be him," said Janet, swinging around at the end of her march. "They'd be delighted—I hope. And the best of it would have been that Gwendolen would have been dragged back here to face the music—and serve her right! This is all her fault."

"No, it isn't," said Cat.

"Yes, it *is*!" said Janet. "She did magic when she was forbidden to, and gave Mr. Blastoff dud earrings for something she wasn't supposed to have anyway, and dragged me here, and turned Euphemia into a frog, and got you into an even worse mess than I'm in. Will you stop being so loyal for a moment and *notice*!"

"It's no good getting angry," said Cat, and he sighed. He missed Gwendolen even more than he had missed Mrs. Sharp.

Janet sighed too, but with exasperation. She sat down at the dressing table with a thump and stared into her own cross face. She pushed its nose up and crossed her eyes. She had been doing this every spare minute. It relieved her feelings about Gwendolen a little.

Cat had been thinking. "I think it's a good idea," he said dolefully. "We'd better go to the garden. But I think you need some kind of magic to go to another world."

"Thus we find ourselves stumped," said Janet. "It's dangerous, and we can't anyway. But they'd taken Gwendolen's witchcraft away, and *she* did it. How? That's been puzzling me a lot."

"I expect she used dragon's blood," said Cat. "She still had that. Mr. Saunders has a whole jar of dragon's blood up in his workshop."

"Why didn't you *say* so?" Janet yelled, jumping around on her stool.

She really might have been Gwendolen. At the sight of her fierce face Cat missed Gwendolen more than ever. He resented Janet. She had been ordering him about all day. Then she tried to make out it was all Gwendolen's fault. He shrugged mulishly and went very unhelpful. "You didn't ask."

"But can you get some?"

"Maybe. But," Cat added, "I don't want to go to another world, really."

Janet drew a long, quiet breath and managed not to tell him to stay and be turned into a frog then. She made a very ingenious face at the mirror and counted up to ten. "Cat," she said carefully, "we really are in such a mess here that I can't see any other way out. Can you?"

"No," Cat admitted grudgingly. "I said I'd go."

"And thank you, dear Janet, for your kind invitation, I notice," Janet said. To her relief, Cat grinned. "But we'll have to be hideously careful about going," she said, "because I suspect that if Chrestomanci doesn't know what we're doing, Milly will."

"Milly?" said Cat.

"Milly," said Janet. "I think she's a witch." She ducked her head down and fiddled with the gold-backed hairbrush. "I know you think I go around seeing sorcery everywhere with my nasty, suspicious mind, like you did about Chrestomanci, but I really am sure, Cat. A sweet, kind honey of a witch, if you like. But she *is* one. How else did she know we were running away this afternoon?"

"Because Mrs. Sharp came and they wanted us," Cat said, puzzled.

"But we'd only been gone for an hour or so, and we could have been just going blackberrying. We hadn't even taken our nightclothes," Janet explained. "Now do you see?"

Though Cat was indeed sure that Janet had an obsession about witchcraft, and he was still feeling sulky and unhelpful, he could not help seeing that Janet had a point. "A very nice witch, then," he conceded. "I don't mind."

"But, Cat, you do see how difficult she's going to make it," Janet said. "Do you? You know, you should be called Mule, not Cat. If you don't want to know a thing, you don't. How did you get to be called Cat anyway?"

"That was just a joke Gwendolen made," said Cat. "She always said I'd got nine lives."

"Gwendolen made jokes?" Janet asked unbelievingly. She stopped, with an arrested look, and turned stiffly away from the mirror.

"Not usually," said Cat.

"Great heavens! I wonder!" said Janet. "In this place, where every other thing turns out to be enchanted, it almost must be! In which case, how horrible!" She pushed the mirror up until the glass faced the ceiling, jumped off the stool, and raced to the wardrobe. She dragged Gwendolen's box out of it and sorted fiercely through it. "Oh, I do hope I'm wrong! But I'm almost sure there were nine."

"Nine what?" asked Cat.

Janet had found the bundle of letters addressed to Miss Caroline Chant. The red book of matches was tucked in front of it. Janet took the little book carefully out and chucked the letters back in the box. "Nine matches," she said, as she opened the book. "And there are too! Oh, good Lord, Cat! Five of them are burned. Look."

She held the book out to Cat. He saw there were indeed nine matches in it. The heads of the first two were black. The third was charred right down to the base. The fourth had a black head again. But the fifth had burned so fiercely that the paper behind was singed and there was a hole in the sandpaper beneath it. It was a wonder the whole book had not caught fire—or at least the last four matches. They were as new, however. Their heads were bright red, with yellowish oily paper below, and bright white cardboard below that.

"It does look like a charm of some kind," Cat said.

"I know it is," said Janet. "These are your nine lives, Cat. How did you come to lose so many?"

Cat simply could not believe her. He was feeling surly and resistant anyway, and this was too much. "They can't be," he said. Even if he *had* nine lives, he knew he could only have lost three, and that was counting the time Gwendolen gave him cramps. The other two would be when he was born and on the paddleboat. But, as he thought this, Cat found he was remembering those four apparitions coming from the flaming bowl to join Gwendolen's gruesome procession. One had been a baby, one wet. The crippled one *had* seemed to have cramps. But why had there been four of them, when five matches were burned?

Cat began shivering, and this made him all the more determined to prove Janet wrong.

"You couldn't have died in the night once or twice without noticing?" Janet wondered.

"Of course I didn't." Cat reached down and took the book. "Look, I'll prove it to you." He tore the sixth match off and dragged it along the sandpaper.

Janet leapt up, shrieking to him to stop. The match burst into flame. So, almost at the same instant, did Cat himself.

CHAPTER 14

Cat screamed. Flames burst out of him all over. He screamed again, and beat at himself with flaming hands, and went on screaming. They were pale, shimmering, transparent flames. They burst out through his clothes, and his shoes, his hair, across his face, so that, in seconds, he was wrapped in pale flame from head to foot. He fell on the floor, still screaming, and rolled there, blazing.

Janet kept her presence of mind. She dragged up the nearest corner of the carpet and threw it over Cat. She had heard that this smothered flames. But it did not smother these. To Janet's horror, the pale, ghostly flames came straight through the carpet as if it was not there, and played on the black underside of it more fiercely than ever. They did not burn the carpet, nor did they burn Janet's hands as she frantically rolled Cat over in the carpet, and then over again. But no matter how much carpet she wrapped around Cat, the flames still came through, and Cat went on blazing and screaming. His head was half outside the flaming bundle she had made of him, and it was a sheaf of flames. She could see his screaming face inside the fire.

Janet did the only other thing she could think of. She jumped up and screamed herself. "Chrestomanci, Chrestomanci! Come *quickly*!"

The door burst open while she was still screaming.

Janet had forgotten it was locked, but the lock did not bother Chrestomanci. She could see it sticking out from the edge of the door as he flung it open. She had forgotten there were guests to dinner too. She remembered when she saw Chrestomanci's lace ruffles, and his black velvet suit which glimmered all over like an opal, blue, crimson, yellow, and green. But that did not seem to bother Chrestomanci either. He took one look at the flaming bundle on the floor and said "Good God!" Then he was down on his elegant knees unwrapping the carpet as frantically as Janet had wrapped it.

"I'm awfully sorry. I thought that would help," Janet stammered.

"It ought to have done," said Chrestomanci, rolling Cat over, with flames whirling through, over, and along his velvet arms. "How did he do it?"

"He struck one of the matches. I told him—"

"You stupid child!" Chrestomanci was so angry that Janet burst into tears. He lugged at the last of the carpet and Cat rolled free, flaming like a straw faggot. He was not really screaming anymore. He was making a long thin noise that had Janet covering her ears. Chrestomanci dived into the heart of the flames and found the book of matches. It was tightly clasped in Cat's right hand. "Thank God he didn't have it in the left one," he said. "Go and turn your shower on. Quick!"

"Of course. Of course," Janet sobbed, and raced to do it.

She fumbled with the taps and had just got a strong spray of cold water hissing into the sunken blue bath as Chrestomanci hurried in carrying Cat, in a ball of roaring flame. He dumped Cat down into the bath and held him there, turning him this way and that to get him wet all over.

Cat steamed and hissed. The water coming from the sprayhead shone like water against the sun, golden as the sun itself. It came down like a beam of light. And, as the bath began to fill up, Cat seemed to be turning and threshing in a pool of sunshine. He boiled it into golden bubbles. The room filled with steam. Coils of smoke drifted up from the bath, smelling thick and sweet. It was the same smell that Janet remembered from the morning she had first found herself there. As far as she could see through the smoke, Cat seemed to be turning black in the golden pool. But the water was wet. Chrestomanci was getting soaked.

"Don't you understand?" he said to Janet over his shoulder while he heaved at Cat to keep his head under the spray. "You shouldn't go telling him things like this until the Castle has had time to work on him. He wasn't ready to understand. You've given him the most appalling shock."

"I'm truly enormously sorry," Janet said, crying heavily.

"We'll just have to make the best of it," said Chrestomanci. "I'll try and explain to him. Run along to the speaking tube at the end of the corridor and tell them to send me some brandy and a pot of strong tea."

As Janet raced away, Cat found himself soaking wet, with water hissing down on him. He tried to roll away from it. Someone held him in it. A voice said insistently in his ear, "Cat. Cat, will you listen to me? Do you understand? Cat, you've only got three lives left now."

Cat knew that voice. "You told me I'd got five when you spoke to me through Miss Larkins," he grumbled.

"Yes, but you've only got three now. You'll have to be more careful," said Chrestomanci.

Cat opened his eyes and looked up at him. Chrestomanci was fearfully wet. The usually smooth black hair was hanging over his forehead in wriggles, with drips on the ends. "Oh. Was it you?" he said.

"Yes. You took a long time recognizing me, didn't you?" said Chrestomanci. "But then I didn't know you straight away when I saw you, either. I think you can come out of this water now."

Cat was too weak to get out of the bath alone. But Chrestomanci heaved him out, stripped off his wet clothes, dried him and wrapped him in another towel in no time at all. Cat's legs kept folding. "Up you come," said Chrestomanci, and carried him again, to the blue velvet bed, and tucked him in it. "Better now, Cat?"

Cat lay back, limp but luxurious, and nodded. "Thanks. You've never called me Cat before."

"Perhaps I should have done. You just might have understood." Chrestomanci sat beside the bed, looking very serious. "You do understand now?"

"The book of matches was my nine lives," Cat said. "And I've just burned one. I know it was stupid, but I didn't believe it. How *can* I have nine lives?"

"You have three," said Chrestomanci. "Get that into your head. You did have nine. In some manner and by someone, they were put into that book of matches, and that book I am now going to put in my secret safe, sealed with the strongest enchantments I know. But that will only stop people using them. It won't stop you losing them yourself."

Janet came hurrying in, still tearful, but very thankful to be of use. "It's coming," she said.

"Thank you," said Chrestomanci, and he gave her a long, thoughtful look. Janet was sure he was going to accuse her of not being Gwendolen, but what he said was, "You may as well hear this too, in order to prevent more accidents."

"Can I get you a towel first?" Janet said humbly. "You're so wet."

"I'm drying out, thank you," he said, smiling at her. "Now listen. People with nine lives are very important and very rare. They only happen when, for one reason or another, there are no counterparts of them living in any other world. Then the lives that would have been spread out over a whole set of worlds get concentrated in one person. And so do all the talents that those other eight people might have had."

Cat said, "But I haven't any talents," and Janet said at the same time, "How rare *are* these people?"

"Extremely rare," said Chrestomanci. "Apart from Cat, the only other person with nine lives that I know of on this world is myself."

"Really?" Cat was pleased and interested. "Nine?"

"I did have nine. I've only got two now. I was even more careless than Cat," Chrestomanci said. He sounded a little ashamed. "Now I have to take care to keep each life separately, in the safest place I can think of. I advise Cat to do the same."

Janet's ready brain promptly got to work on this. "Is one life here and the other downstairs having supper at this moment?"

Chrestomanci laughed. "It doesn't work like that. I—"

To Janet's disappointment, Euphemia hurried in with a tray and prevented Chrestomanci explaining how it did work. Mr. Saunders came in on Euphemia's heels, still unable to find evening clothes that covered his wrists and ankles.

"Is he all right?" Euphemia asked anxiously. "My Will was uttering threats, but if it was him I'll never speak to him again. And whatever happened to this carpet?"

Mr. Saunders was looking at the wrinkled and heaped up carpet too. "What did it?" he said. "There were surely enough charms in this carpet to stop any kind of accident."

"I know," said Chrestomanci. "But this was amazingly strong." The two of them looked at one another significantly.

Then everyone fussed over Cat. He had a most enjoyable time. Mr. Saunders sat him up on pillows, and Euphemia put him in a nightshirt and then stroked Cat's head, just as if he had never confessed to turning her into a frog. "It wasn't Will," Cat said to her. "It was me." Chrestomanci gave him a fierce swig of brandy and then made him drink a cup of sweet tea. Janet had a cup of tea too, and felt much better for it. Mr. Saunders helped Euphemia straighten the carpet, and then asked if he should strengthen the charms in it.

"Dragon's blood might do the trick," he suggested.

"Frankly, I don't think anything will," said Chrestomanci. "Leave it." He got up and turned the mirror straight. "Do you mind sleeping tonight in Cat's room?" he asked Janet. "I want to be able to keep an eye on Cat."

Janet looked from the mirror to Chrestomanci, and her face became very pink. "Er," she said. "I've been making faces—"

Chrestomanci laughed. Mr. Saunders was so amused that he had to sit on the blue velvet stool. "I suppose it serves me right," said Chrestomanci. "Some of the faces were highly original."

Janet laughed too, a little foolishly.

Cat lay, feeling comfortable and almost cheerful. For a while, everyone was there, settling him in. Then there seemed only to be Janet, talking as usual.

"I'm so glad you're all right," she said. "Why did I open my big mouth about those matches? I had the dreaded umjams when you suddenly flared up, and when the carpet didn't work, the only thing I could think of was to yell for Chrestomanci. I *was* right. He came before the words were out of my mouth, even though the door was locked. It was still locked when he opened it, but the lock isn't broken, because I tried it. So he *is* an enchanter. And he ruined a suit over you, Cat, and didn't seem to mind, so I think that when he isn't being like freezing fog over the Grampians, he's really very nice. This isn't for the benefit of the mirror. I mean it. I suppose that mirror is the magic equivalent of. . . ."

Cat thought he had been meaning to say something about freezing fog in the Grampians, but he drifted away to sleep while Janet talked, feeling snug and cared for.

He woke on Sunday morning, quite the opposite: cold and quivering. This afternoon he was due to be turned into a frog or face a tiger—and a rather heavy strong tiger Will Suggins would make too, he thought. Beyond the tiger—if there was a beyond—lay the horrors of Monday without magic. Julia and Roger might help there, except that it would be no use when Mr. Baslam came on Wednesday and demanded twenty pounds Cat knew he could not get. Mr. Nostrum was no help. Mrs. Sharp was even less. The only hope seemed to be to take Janet and some dragon's blood to the forbidden garden and try to get away.

Cat climbed out of bed to go and get some dragon's blood from Mr. Saunders' workshop. Euphemia came in with his breakfast on a tray, and he had to climb back into bed again. Euphemia was quite as kind as she had been last night. Cat felt bad. And when he had finished breakfast, Milly came. She scooped Cat off his pillows and hugged him.

"You poor silly darling! Thank goodness you're all right. I was aching to come and see you last night, but someone had to stay with our poor guests. Now, you're to stay in bed all today, and you must ask for anything you want. What would you like?"

"I couldn't have some dragon's blood, could I?" Cat asked hopefully.

Milly laughed. "Good heavens, Eric! You go and have that fearsome accident and then you ask for the most dangerous stuff in the world.

No, you may not have dragon's blood. It's one of the few things in the Castle that really are forbidden."

"Like Chrestomanci's garden?" Cat asked.

"*Not* quite like that," Milly answered. "The garden is old as the hills and stuffed with magic of every kind. That's dangerous in another way. Everything's stronger there. You'll be taken into the garden when you know enough magic to understand it. But dragon's blood is so harmful that I'm never happy even when Michael uses it. You're on no account to touch any."

Julia and Roger came in next, dressed ready for church, with armfuls of books and toys and a great many interested questions. They were so kind that Cat was quite unhappy by the time Janet arrived. He did not want to leave the Castle. He felt he was truly settling in to it.

"That lump of dough is still stuck to your carpet," Janet said gloomily, which made Cat feel rather less settled. "I've just been seeing Chrestomanci, and it *is* hard to be punished for other people's sins," Janet went on, "even though I've been rewarded with the sight of a sky-blue dressing gown with golden lions on it."

"I've not seen that one," said Cat.

"I think he has one for every day of the week," said Janet. "All he needed was a flaming sword. He forbade me to go to church. The vicar won't have me because of what Gwendolen did last Sunday. And I was so cross at being blamed for it that I'd got my mouth open to say I wasn't Gwendolen when I remembered that if I went to church I'd have to wear that stupid white hat with little holes in it—can he *hear* through that mirror, do you think?"

"No," said Cat. "Just see. Or he'd know all about you. I'm glad you're staying behind. We can go and get the dragon's blood while they're at church."

Janet kept watch at the window to see when the Family left. After about half an hour, she said, "Here they are at last, walking in a crowd down the avenue. All the men have got toppers, but Chrestomanci looks as if he's come out of a shop window. Who *are* they all, Cat? Who's the old lady in purple mittens, and the young one in green, and the little fellow who's always talking?"

"I've no idea," said Cat. He scrambled out of bed and scuttled up to his room to find some clothes. He felt perfectly well—marvelously well, in fact. He danced around his room while he put on his shirt. He sang putting on his trousers. Even the cold lump of dough on the carpet could not damp his spirits. He whistled tying his boots.

Janet came into the room as Cat was shooting out of it, pulling on his jacket and beaming with health. "I don't know," Janet said, as Cat shot past her and hammered away down the stairs. "Dying must agree with you, or something."

"Hurry up!" Cat called from the bottom of the stairs. "It's on the other side of the Castle from here. Milly says dragon's blood is very dangerous, so don't you touch it. I can spare a life on it and you can't."

Janet wanted to remark that Cat had not spared the last one very easily, but she never caught up with Cat sufficiently. Cat whirled through the green corridors and stormed up the winding stairs to Mr. Saunders' room, and Janet only reached him when he was actually inside it. Then there was too much else to take up her attention.

The room was heavy with the scent of stale magic. Though it was much the same as when Cat had seen it before, Mr. Saunders had tidied it a little for Sunday. The cresset was out. The torts and limbecks and other vessels were all clean. The books and scrolls had been piled in heaps on the second bench. The five-pointed star was still there, blazoned on the floor, but there was a new set of signs chalked on the third bench, and the mummified animal had been neatly laid at one end of it.

Janet was immensely interested. "It's like a laboratory," she said, "except that it isn't. What weird things! Oh, I see the dragon's blood. Does he need all that huge jar? He won't miss a bit out of that lot."

There was a rustling at the end of the third bench. Janet's head perked toward it. The mummified creature was twitching and spreading its filmy little wings.

"It did that before," said Cat. "I think it's all right."

He was not so sure, however, when the creature stretched and got to its doglike feet, yawning. The yawn showed them dozens of small, sharp teeth and also let out a cloud of bluish smoke. The creature ran pattering along the bench toward them. The little wings rattled on its back as it came, and two small puffs of smoke streamed behind it from its nostrils. It stopped at the edge of the bench to look up at them inquisitively from a melting glitter of golden eyes. They backed nervously away from it.

"It's alive!" said Janet. "I think it's a small dragon."

"Of course I am," said the dragon, which made both of them jump violently. Even more alarming, tiny flames played out of its mouth as it spoke, and they could feel the heat from them where they stood.

"I didn't know you could talk," said Cat.

"I speak English quite well," said the dragon, flickering flame. "Why do you want my blood?"

They looked guiltily at the great jar of powder on the shelf. "Is that all yours?" said Cat.

"If Mr. Saunders is making it give blood all the time, I think that's rather cruel," Janet said.

"Oh, that!" said the dragon. "That's powdered blood from older dragons. They sell it to people. You can't have any of that."

"Why not?" said Cat.

"Because I don't want you to," said the dragon, and a regular roll of fire came from its mouth, making them back away again. "How would you like to see me taking human blood and playing games with it?"

Though Cat felt the dragon had a point here, Janet did not. "It doesn't worry me," she said. "Where I come from we have blood transfusions and blood banks. Dad once showed me some of my blood under a microscope."

"It worries *me*," said the dragon, uttering another roll of fire. "My mother was killed by unlawful blood-stealers." It crept to the very end of the bench and stared up at Janet. The flickers in its golden eyes melted and changed and melted again. It was like being looked at by two small, golden kaleidoscopes. "I was too small to hold enough blood," it flickered softly to Janet, "so they left me. I'd have died if Chrestomanci hadn't found me. So you see why it worries me?"

"Yes," said Janet. "What do baby dragons feed on? Milk?"

"Michael tried me with milk, but I didn't like it," said the dragon. "I have minced steak now, and I'm growing beautifully. When I'm big enough, he's going to take me back, but meanwhile I'm helping him with his magic. I'm a great help."

"Are you?" said Janet. "What do you do?"

"I find old things he can't find himself." The dragon fell into a flickering croon. "I fetch him animals from the abyss—old golden creatures, things with wings, pearl-eyed monsters from the deep sea, and whispering plants from long ago." It stopped and looked at Janet with its head on one side. "That was easy," it remarked to Cat. "I've always wanted to do that, but no one let me before." It sighed a long blue fume of smoke. "I wish I was bigger. I could eat her now."

Cat took an alarmed look at Janet and found her staring like a sleepwalker, with a silly smile on her face. "Of all the mean tricks!" he said.

"I think I'll just have a nibble," said the dragon.

Cat realized it was being playful. "I'll wring your neck if you do," he said. "Haven't you got anything else to play with?"

"You sound just like Michael," said the dragon in a sulky roll of smoke. "I'm bored with mice."

"Tell him to take you for walks." Cat took Janet's arm and shook her. Janet came to herself with a little jump and seemed quite unaware that anything had happened to her. "And I can't help the way you feel," said Cat to the dragon. "I need some dragon's blood." He pulled Janet well out of range, just to be on the safe side, and picked up a little china crucible from the next bench.

The dragon hunched up irritably and scratched itself like a dog under the chin until its wings rattled. "Michael says dragon's blood always does harm somewhere," it said, "even when an adept uses it. If you're not careful, it costs a life."

Cat and Janet looked at one another through the smoke it had made with its speech. "Well, I can spare one," said Cat. He took the glass stopper off the big jar and scooped up some brown powder in the crucible. It had a strong, strange smell.

"I suppose Chrestomanci manages all right with two lives," Janet said nervously.

"But he's rather special," said the dragon. It was standing on the very edge of the bench, rattling with anxiety. Its golden eyes followed Cat's hands as he wrapped the crucible in his handkerchief and pushed the bundle cautiously into his pocket. It seemed so worried that Cat went over to it and, a little nervously, rubbed it under the chin where it had been scratching. The dragon stretched its neck and pressed against his fingers. The smoke came out of its nostrils in purring puffs.

"Don't worry," Cat said. "I've got three lives left, you see."

"That explains why I like you," said the dragon, and almost fell off the bench in its effort to follow Cat's fingers. "Don't go yet!"

"We've got to." Cat pushed the dragon back on the bench and patted its head. Once he was used to it, he found he did not mind touching its warm, horny hide a bit. "Good-bye."

"Good-bye," said the dragon.

They left it staring after them like a dog whose master has gone for a walk without it.

"I think it's bored," Cat said when he had shut the door.

"It's a shame! It's only a baby," said Janet. She stopped on the first turn of the stair. "Let's go back and take it for a walk. It was sweet!"

Cat was sure that if Janet did any such thing, she would come to herself to find the dragon browsing on her legs. "It wasn't that sweet," he said. "And we'll have to go to the garden straight away now. It's going to tell Mr. Saunders we took some dragon's blood as soon as it sees him."

"Yes, I suppose it does make a difference that it can talk," Janet agreed. "We'd better hurry then."

Cat walked very carefully through the Castle, down and out of doors, and kept a hand on his pocket in case of accidents. He was afraid he might arrive at the forbidden garden with one life less. He seemed to have lost three of his lives so easily. That kept puzzling him. From the look of those matches, losing life number five ought to have been as much of a disaster as losing the sixth one last night. But he had not noticed it go at all. He could not understand it. His lives did not seem to be properly attached to him, like ordinary people's. But at least he knew there were no other Cat Chants to be dragged into trouble in this world, when he left it.

CHAPTER 15

It was a glorious start-of-autumn day, with everything green and gold, hot and still. There was not a soul around, and very little sound except the lonely crunch of Cat's and Janet's feet as they hurried through the formal garden.

Halfway through the orchard, Janet said, "If the garden we want looks like a ruined castle, we're going away from it now."

Cat could have sworn they were heading straight for it but, sure enough, when he stopped and looked around, the high, sun-soaked old wall was right behind them. And now he came to think of it, he could not remember how he and Gwendolen had got to it before.

They turned back and walked toward the high wall. All they found was the long, low wall of the orchard. There was no gate in it, and the forbidden garden was beyond it. They went along the orchard wall to the nearest gate. Whereupon they were in the rose garden, and the ruined wall was behind them again, towering above the orchard.

"This couldn't be an enchantment to stop people getting into it, could it?" said Janet, as they plodded through the orchard again.

"I think it must be," said Cat. And they were in the formal garden again, with the high wall behind them.

"They'll be coming out of church before we've found it, at this rate," Janet said anxiously.

"Try keeping it in the corner of your eye and not going straight to it," said Cat.

They did that. They walked slantwise with the garden, not really looking at it. It seemed to keep pace with them. And suddenly they came out somehow beyond the orchard into a steep, walled path. Up at the top of it stood the high old wall, with its stairway masked by hollyhocks and bright with snapdragons, breathing warmth out of its crumbling stones into their worried faces. Neither of them dared look straight at the tall ruins, even while they were running up the path. But the wall was still there when they reached the end, and so was the overgrown stair.

The stair made a nerve-racking climb. They had to go up it twice as high as a house, with one side of themselves pressed against the hot stones of the wall, and a sheer drop on the other side. The stairs were frighteningly old and irregular. And they grew hotter and hotter. Toward the end, Cat had to keep his head tipped up to the trees hanging over the top of the ruins, because looking anywhere else began to make him dizzy. He had glimpses of the Castle in the distance from more angles than he would have thought possible. He suspected that the ruins he was on were moving about.

There was a notch in the wall at the top, not like a proper entrance at all. They swung themselves in through it, secret and guilty, and found the ground beyond worn smooth, as if other people had been coming that way for centuries. There were trees, thick and dark and close together. It was wonderfully cool. The smoothly worn path twined among them. Janet and Cat stole along it. As they went, the trees, as closely growing trees often seem to do when you walk among them, appeared to move this way and that and spread into different distances. But Cat was not altogether sure it was only an appearance.

One new distance opened into a dell. And then they were in the dell.

"What a lovely place!" Janet whispered. "But how peculiar!"

The little dip was full of spring flowers. Daffodils, scillas, snowdrops, hyacinths, and tiny tulips were all growing there in September in the most improbable profusion. There was a slight chill in the dip, which may have accounted for it. Janet and Cat picked their way among these flowers, shivering a little. There were the scents of spring, chilly and heady, clean and wild, but strong with magic. Before they had taken two steps, Cat and Janet were smiling gently. Another step and they were laughing.

"Oh, look!" said Janet. "There's a cat."

It was a large stripy tom. It stood arched suspiciously beside a clump of primroses, not sure whether to run away or not. It looked at Janet. It looked at Cat. And Cat knew it. Though it was firmly and definitely a cat, there was just a suggestion of a violin about the shape of its face.

He laughed. Everything made him happy in that place. "That's old Fiddle," he said. "He used to be my violin. What's he doing here?"

Janet knelt down and held out her hand. "Here, Fiddle. Here, puss." Fiddle's nature must have been softened by being in that dell. He let Janct rub his chin and stroke him. Then, in the most unheard-of-way, he let Janet pick him up and stand up hugging him. He even purred. Janet's face glowed. She could almost have been Gwendolen coming home from a witchcraft lesson, except that she looked kinder. She winked at Cat. "I love all kinds of Cat!"

Cat laughed. He put out his left hand and stroked Fiddle's head. It felt strange. He could feel the wood of the violin. He took his hand away quickly.

They went on through a white spread of narcissi, smelling like paradise, Janet still carrying Fiddle. There had been no white flowers until then. Cat began to be almost sure that the garden was moving around them of its own accord. When he stepped among bluebells, and then big red tulips, he was sure. He almost—but not quite—saw the trees softly and gently sliding about at the sides of what he could see. They slid him among buttercups and cow-parsley, into a sunny, sloping stretch. And here was a wild rose, tangled with a creeper covered in great blue flowers. Cat could definitely feel the sliding movement now. They were being moved around and down somehow. If he thought about the way the garden had also been moving about in the Castle grounds, he started to feel almost as sick as he did in the car. He found it was best just to keep walking and looking.

When they slid through the trees among flowers of high summer, Janet noticed too. "Aren't we getting a lightning tour of the year?" she said. "I feel as if I'm running down a moving staircase."

It was more than the ordinary year. Fig trees, olives, and date palms moved them around into a small desert, where there were cacti like tormented cucumbers and spiny green armchairs. Some had bright flowers on them. The sun burned down. But they had hardly time to get uncomfortable before the trees circled around them again and brought them into a richer, sadder light, and autumn flowers. They had barely got used to that when the trees put out berries, turned amber and lost their leaves. They moved toward a thick holly, full of red berries. It was colder. Fiddle did not like this part. He struggled out of Janet's arms and ran away to warmer climes.

"Which are the gates to other worlds?" Janet said, brought back to a sense of purpose.

"Soon, I think," said Cat. He felt them coming to the center of the garden. He had seldom felt anything magical so strongly.

The trees and bushes around them now were embalmed in frost. They could see bright berries in bright casings of ice. Yet Janet had scarcely time to rub her arms and shiver before a tree met them that was a wintry mass of pink blossom. Straight stalks of winter jasmine hung from the next, in lines of small yellow stars. And then came a mighty black thorn tree, twisted in all directions. It was just putting out a few white blossoms.

As it took them in under its dark hood, Janet looked up into its black twistings. "The one at Glastonbury looks like this," she said. "They say it blooms at Christmas."

Then Cat knew they were in the heart of the garden. They were in a small bowl of meadowland. All the trees were up around the edges, except one. And here it seemed the right season of the year, because the apples were just ripening on that one tree. It stood leaning over the center of the meadow, not quite overshadowing the queer ruin there. As Janet and Cat passed quietly toward this place, they found a little spring of water near the roots of the apple tree, which bubbled up from nowhere, and bubbled away again into the earth almost at once. Janet thought the clear water looked unusually golden. It reminded her of the water from the shower when it stopped Cat from burning.

The ruins were two sides of a broken archway. There was a slab of stone which must have fallen from the top of the arch lying nearby at the foot of the tree. There was no other sign of a gate.

"I think this is it," said Cat. He felt very sad to be leaving.

"I think it is too," Janet agreed in an awed, muffled voice. "I feel a bit miserable to be going, as a matter of fact. How *do* we go?"

"I'm going to try sprinkling a pinch of dragon's blood in the archway," said Cat.

He fumbled out the crucible wrapped in his handkerchief from his pocket. He smelled the strong smell of the dragon's blood and knew he was doing wrong. It was wrong to bring this harmful stuff into a place that was so strongly magic in such a different way.

But, since he did not know what else to do, Cat carefully took a pinch of the smelly brown powder between the finger and thumb of his right hand, wrapped the crucible away again with his left hand, and then, carefully and guiltily, sprinkled the powder between the pillars of broken stone.

The air between the pillars quivered like air that is hot. The piece of sunny meadow they could see beyond grew misty, then milky pale, then dark. The darkness cleared slowly, away into the corners of the space, and they found they could see into a huge room. There seemed acres of it. All of it was covered in a carpet of a rather ugly playing-card sort of design in red, blue, and yellow. The room was full of people. They reminded Cat of playing cards too, because they were dressed in stiff, bulky clothes in flat, bright colors. They were all trailing about, this way and that, looking important and agitated. The air between them and the garden was still quivering and, somehow, Cat knew they would not be able to get into the huge room.

"This is not right," said Janet. "Where is it?"

Cat was just about to say that he did not know either, when he saw Gwendolen. She was being carried by, quite near, on a sort of bed with handholds. The eight men carrying it all wore bulky golden uniforms. The bed was gold, with gold hangings and gold cushions. Gwendolen was dressed in even bulkier clothes than the rest, that were white and gold, and her hair was done up into a high golden headdress which may have been a crown. From the way she was behaving, she was certainly a queen. She nodded to some of the important people and they leapt eagerly to the side of her bed and listened with feverish intelligence to what she was saying. She waved to some others, and they ran to do things. She made a sign at another person and he fell on his knees, begging for mercy. He was still begging when other people dragged him away. Gwendolen smiled as if this amused her. By this time, the golden bed was right beside the archway, and the space was a turmoil of people racing to do what Gwendolen wanted.

And Gwendolen saw Cat and Janet. Cat knew she did, from the expression of surprise and faint annoyance on her face. Maybe she worked some magic of her own, or maybe the magic in the dragon's blood was simply used up. Whatever it was, the broken archway turned dark again, then milky, then to mist; and finally, there was nothing but meadow again between the pillars, and the air had stopped shimmering.

"That was Gwendolen," Cat said.

"I thought it was," Janet said unappreciatively. "She'll get fat if she has herself carried about like that all the time."

"She was enjoying herself," Cat said wistfully.

"I could see that," said Janet. "But how do we find my world?"

Cat was not at all sure. "Shall we try going around to the other side of the arch?"

"Seems reasonable," Janet agreed. She started to walk around the pillars, and stopped. "We'd better get it right this time, Cat. You can only afford one more try. Or didn't you lose a life on that one?"

"I didn't feel—" Cat began.

Then Mr. Nostrum was suddenly standing in the broken arch. He was holding the postcard Cat had sent to Mrs. Sharp, and he was cross and flustered.

"My dear boy," he said to Cat, "I told you two-thirty, not midday. It was the merest chance that I had my hand on your signature. Let us hope all is not lost." He turned and called over his shoulder, apparently into the empty meadow, "Come on, William. The wretched boy seems to have misunderstood me, but the spell is clearly working. Don't forget to bring the—ah—equipment with you."

He stepped out from between the pillars, and Cat backed away before him. Everything seemed to have gone very quiet. The leaves of the apple tree did not stir, and the small, small bubbling from the little spring changed to a soft, slow dripping. Cat had a strong suspicion that he and Janet had done something terrible. Janet was beyond the archway with her hands to her mouth, looking horrified. She was suddenly hidden by the large figure of Mr. William Nostrum, who popped into being from nowhere between the two pillars. He had a coil of rope around one arm, and there were shiny things sticking out of the pockets of his frock coat. His eyes were swiveling in an agitated way. He was a little out of breath.

"Premature but successful, Henry," he puffed. "The rest have been summoned."

William Nostrum stepped imposingly out beneath the apple tree beside his brother. The ground shook a little. The garden was quite silent. Cat backed away again and found that the little spring had stopped flowing. There was nothing but a muddy hole left. Cat was quite certain now that he and Janet had done something terrible.

Behind the Nostrums, other people came hurrying through the broken archway. The first one who came was one of the Accredited Witches from farther down Coven Street, puce in the face and very startled. She had been to church in her Sunday best: a monster of a hat with fruit and flowers in it, and a black and red satin dress. Most of the people who followed her were in Sunday best too: warlocks in blue serge and hard hats, witches in silk and bombazine and hats of all shapes and sizes, respectable-looking necromancers in frock coats like William Nostrum's, skinny sorcerers in black, and quite a sprinkling of impressive wizards, who had either been to church in long black cloaks, or playing golf in very freckled plus fours. They came crowding between the pillars, first by twos and threes and then by sixes and sevens, all a little hasty and startled. Among them Cat recognized most of the witches and fortune-tellers from Coven Street, though he did not see either Mrs. Sharp or Miss Larkins—but this may have been simply that, in no time at all, he was being jostled this way and that in the middle of a large and steadily growing crowd.

William Nostrum was shouting to each group who hurried through, "Spread out. Spread out up the meadow. Surround the gate there! Leave no avenue of escape."

Janet forced her way among them and seized Cat's arm. "Cat! What have we done? Don't tell me these aren't all witches and warlocks, because I won't believe you!"

"Ah, my dear Gwendolen!" said Mr. Henry Nostrum. "Plan Two is underway."

By this time, the sloping sides of the meadow were crowded with witches and warlocks. The ground quivered to their trampling and buzzed with their cheerful conversation. There were hundreds of them—a nodding of garish hats and shiny toppers, like the audience at the opening of a bazaar.

As soon as the last necromancer had hurried between the pillars, Henry Nostrum put a heavy possessive hand on Cat's shoulder. Cat wondered uneasily whether it was just an accident that it was the same hand which held his postcard to Mrs. Sharp. He saw that the Willing Warlock had stationed himself by one of the broken pillars, blue-chinned and cheerful as ever in his tight Sunday suit. Mr. William Nostrum had put as much of himself as would go behind the other pillar and, for some reason, he had taken off his heavy silver watch-chain and was swinging it in one hand.

"Now, my dear Gwendolen," said Henry Nostrum, "would you care for the honor of summoning Chrestomanci?"

"I—I'd rather not," said Janet.

"Then I'll take it upon myself," said Henry Nostrum, perfectly well pleased. He cleared his throat and shouted in a fluting tenor, "Chrestomanci! Chrestomanci! Come to me."

And Chrestomanci was standing between the pillars.

Chrestomanci must have been on his way up the avenue from church. He had his tall gray hat in one hand and, with the other, he was in the act of putting his prayer book into the pocket of his beautiful dove-gray coat. The assembled witches and necromancers greeted him with a sort of groaning sigh. Chrestomanci blinked around at them, in his mildest and most bewildered way. He became even vaguer and more bewildered when he happened to see Cat and Janet.

Cat opened his mouth to shout at Chrestomanci to go away. But the Willing Warlock leapt on Chrestomanci the moment he appeared. He was growling. His fingernails were growing into claws and his teeth into fangs.

Chrestomanci stuffed the prayer book into his pocket and turned his vague look on the Willing Warlock. The Willing Warlock stood still in midair and shrank. He shrank so fast, he made a whirring sound. Then he was a small brown caterpillar. He dropped to the grass and wriggled there. But, while he was still shrinking, William Nostrum pounced out from behind the other pillar and deftly wrapped his watch-chain around Chrestomanci's right hand.

"*Behind you!*" shrieked the Cat and Janet, too late.

After barely one wriggle, the caterpillar burst up out of the grass and became the Willing Warlock again, a little disheveled, but very pleased with himself. He threw himself on Chrestomanci again. As for Chrestomanci, it was plain that the watch-chain had somehow disabled him completely. There was a second or so of furious struggle in the archway, while the Willing Warlock tried to grab Chrestomanci in both brawny arms, and Chrestomanci tried to get the watch-chain off his wrist using his left hand, and William Nostrum hung on to it fiercely. None of them used any magic, and Chrestomanci seemed only able to shoulder the Willing Warlock weakly aside. After two attempts, the Willing Warlock wrapped his arms around Chrestomanci from behind and William Nostrum dragged a pair of silver handcuffs from his pocket and snapped them on both Chrestomanci's wrists.

There was a scream of triumph from under the nodding hats of the audience—the scream of true witchcraft, which made the sunlight tremble. Chrestomanci, even more disheveled than the Willing Warlock, was dragged out from between the pillars. His tall gray hat rolled near Cat's feet and Henry Nostrum stamped on it, with the greatest satisfaction. Cat tried to get out from under Henry Nostrum's hand while he did it. And he found he could not move. Mr. Nostrum had seen to that with Mrs. Sharp's postcard. Cat had to face the fact that he was as helpless as Chrestomanci seemed to be.

"So it is true!" Henry Nostrum said joyously, as the Willing Warlock bundled Chrestomanci toward the apple tree. "The touch of silver conquers Chrestomanci—the great Chrestomanci!"

"Yes. Isn't it a nuisance?" Chrestomanci remarked. He was dragged to the apple tree and pushed against it. William Nostrum hurried over to his brother and pulled the watch-chain off Henry's bulging waistcoat. Two silver watch-chains from two such ample brothers were more than enough to tie Chrestomanci to the tree. William Nostrum hastily twisted the ends into two charmed knots and stood back rubbing his hands. The audience screamed eldritch laughter and clapped. Chrestomanci sagged as if he were tired. His hair hung over his face, his tie was under his left ear, and there was green from the bark of the tree all over his dove-gray coat. Cat felt somehow ashamed to look at him in that state. But Chrestomanci seemed quite composed. "Now you've got me all tied up in silver, what do you propose doing?" he said.

William Nostrum's eyes swirled joyfully about. "Oh, the worst we can, my dear sir," he said. "Be assured of that. We're sick of you imposing restraints on us, you see. Why shouldn't we go out and conquer other worlds? Why shouldn't we use dragon's blood? Why shouldn't we be as wicked as we want? Answer me that, sir!"

"You might find the answer for yourself, if you thought," Chrestomanci suggested. But his voice was drowned in the yelling from the assembled witches and necromancers. While they shouted, Janet began edging quietly toward the tree. She supposed Cat dared not move with Henry Nostrum's hand on his shoulder, and she felt someone ought to do something.

"Oh, yes," said Henry Nostrum, cock-a-hoop with pleasure. "We are taking the arts of magic into our own hands today. This world will be ours by this evening. Come Halloween, dear sir, we shall be going out to conquer every other world we know. We are going to destroy you, my dear fellow, and your power. But before we do that, of course, we shall have to destroy this garden."

Chrestomanci looked thoughtfully down at his hands, hanging limply in the silver handcuffs. "I shouldn't advise that," he said. "This garden has things in it from the dawn of all the worlds. It's a good deal stronger than I am. You'd be striking at the roots of witchcraft—and you'd find it shockingly hard to destroy."

"Ah," said Henry Nostrum. "But we know we can't destroy you unless we destroy the garden, my wily sir. And don't think we don't know how to destroy the garden." He lifted his free hand and clapped Cat on the other shoulder with it. "The means are here."

Janet, at that moment, stumbled over the block of stone that lay in the grass near the apple tree. "Dratitude!" she said and fell heavily across it. The audience pointed and screamed with laughter, which annoyed her very much. She glared around the circle of Sunday bonnets and hats.

"Up you get, dear Gwendolen," Henry Nostrum said gleefully. "It's young Cat who has to go on there." He put an arm around the helpless Cat, plucked him off the ground, and carried him toward the block of stone. William Nostrum bustled up, beaming and uncoiling his rope. The Willing Warlock bounced up willingly to help too.

Cat was so terrified that he managed somehow to break the spell. He twisted out of Henry Nostrum's arms and ran for all he was worth toward the two pillars, trying to fetch out his dragon's blood as he ran. It was only a few steps to run. But naturally every witch, warlock, necromancer, and wizard there instantly cast a spell. The thick smell of magic coiled around the meadow. Cat's legs felt like two lead posts. His heart hammered. He felt himself running in slow motion, slower and slower, like a clockwork toy running down. He heard Janet scream at him to run, but he could not move any longer. He stuck just in front of the ruined archway, and he was stiff as a board. It was all he could do to breathe.

The Nostrum brothers and the Willing Warlock collected him from there, and wound the rope around his stiff body. Janet did her best to prevent them.

"Oh, please stop! What are you doing?"

"Now, now, Gwendolen," Henry Nostrum said, rather perplexed. "You know perfectly well. I explained to you most carefully that the garden has to be disenchanted by cutting the throat of an innocent child on that slab of stone there. You agreed it must be so."

"I didn't! It wasn't me!" said Janet.

"Be quiet!" Chrestomanci said from the tree. "Do you want to be put in Cat's place?"

Janet stared at him, and went on staring as all the implications struck her. While she stared, Cat, stiff as a mummy and wound in rope, was carried by the Willing Warlock and dumped rather painfully down on the block of stone. Cat stared resentfully at the Willing Warlock. He had always seemed so friendly. Apart from that, Cat was not as frightened as he might have been. Of course Gwendolen had known he had lives to spare. But he hoped his throat would heal after they cut it. He was bound to be very uncomfortable until it did. He turned his eyes up to Janet, meaning to give her a reassuring look.

To his astonishment, Janet was snatched away backward into nothingness. The only thing which remained of her was a yell of surprise. And the same yell rumbled around the meadow. Everyone there was quite as astonished as Cat.

"Oh, good!" Gwendolen said, from the other side of the stone. "I got here in time."

Everyone stared at her. Gwendolen came from between the pillars, dusting off the dragon's blood from her fingers with one of Cat's school essays. Cat could see his signature at the top: *Eric Emelius Chant, 26 Coven St., Wolvercote, England, Europe, The World, The Universe*—it was his, all right. Gwendolen still had her hair up in that strange headdress, but she had taken off the massive golden robes. She had on what must have amounted to underclothes in her new world. They were more magnificent than any of Chrestomanci's dressing gowns.

"Gwendolen!" exclaimed Henry Nostrum. He pointed to the space Janet had vanished from. "What—who—?"

"Just a replacement," Gwendolen explained, in her airiest way. "I saw her and Cat here just now, so I knew—" She noticed Chrestomanci limply tied to the apple tree. "Oh, good! You caught him! Just a moment." She marched over to Chrestomanci and held up her golden underclothes in order to kick him hard on both shins. "Take that! And that!" Chrestomanci did not try to pretend the kicks did not hurt. He doubled up. The toes of Gwendolen's shoes were as pointed as nails.

"Now, where was I?" Gwendolen said, turning back to the Nostrum brothers. "Oh, yes. I thought I'd better come back because I wanted to see the fun, and I remembered I'd forgotten to tell you Cat has nine lives. You'll have to kill him several times, I'm afraid."

"*Nine lives!*" shouted Henry Nostrum. "You foolish girl!"

After that, there was such a shouting and outcry from every witch and warlock in the meadow, that no one could have heard anything else. From where Cat lay, he could see William Nostrum leaning toward Gwendolen, red in the face, both eyes whirling, bawling furiously at her, and Gwendolen leaning forward to shout back. As the noise died down a little, he heard William Nostrum booming, "Nine lives! If he has nine lives, you stupid girl, *that means he's an enchanter in his own right!*"

"I'm not stupid!" Gwendolen yelled back. "I know that as well as you do! I've been using his magic ever since he was a baby. But I couldn't go on using it if you were going to kill him, could I? That's why I had to go away. I think it was nice of me to come back and tell you. So there!"

"How *can* you have used his magic?" demanded Henry Nostrum, even more put out than his brother.

"I just did," said Gwendolen. "He never minds."

"I *do* mind, rather," Cat said from his uncomfortable slab. "I *am* here, you know."

Gwendolen looked down at him as if she was rather surprised that he was. But before she could say anything to Cat, William Nostrum was loudly shushing for silence. He was very agitated. He took a long shiny thing out of his pocket and nervously bent it about.

"Silence!" he said. "We've gone too far to draw back now. We'll just have to discover the boy's weak point. We certainly can't kill him unless we find it. He must have one. All enchanters do." So saying, William Nostrum rounded on Cat and pointed the shiny thing at him. Cat was appalled to see that it was a long silver knife. The knife pointed at his face, even though William Nostrum's eyes did not. "What is your weak point, boy? Out with it."

Cat was not saying. It seemed the only chance he had of keeping any of his lives.

"I know," said Gwendolen. "I did it. I put all his lives into a book of matches. They were easier to use like that. It's in my room in the Castle. Shall I get it?"

Everyone Cat could see from his uncomfortable position looked relieved to hear this. "That's all right, then," said Henry Nostrum. "Can he be killed without burning a match?"

"Oh, yes," said Gwendolen. "He drowned once."

"So the question," said William Nostrum, very much relieved, "is simply how many lives he has left. How many have you, boy?" The knife pointed at Cat again.

Again Cat was not saying.

"He doesn't know," Gwendolen said impatiently. "I had to use quite a few. He lost one being born and another being drowned. And I used one to put him in the book of matches. It gave him cramps, for some reason. Then that toad tied up in silver there wouldn't give me magic lessons and took my witchcraft away, so I had to fetch another of Cat's lives in the night and make it send me to my nice new world. He was awfully disobliging about it, but he did it. And that was the end of that life. Oh, I nearly forgot! I put his fourth life into that violin he kept playing, to turn it into a cat—Fiddle—remember, Mr. Nostrum?"

Henry Nostrum clutched his two wings of hair. Consternation broke out around the meadow again. "You *are* a foolish girl! Someone took that cat away. We can't kill him at all!"

For a moment, Gwendolen looked very dashed. Then an idea struck her. "If I go away again, you can use my replacem—"

The watch-chains around Chrestomanci chinked. "Nostrum, you're upsetting yourself needlessly. It was I who had the cat-violin removed. The creature's around in the garden somewhere."

Henry Nostrum swung around to look at Chrestomanci suspiciously, still hanging on to his two wings of hair as if that kept his mind in place. "I doubt you, sir, very seriously. You are known to be a very wily person."

"You flatter me," said Chrestomanci. "Unfortunately I can't speak anything but the truth tied up in silver like this."

Henry Nostrum looked at his brother. "That is correct," William said, dubiously. "Silver constrains him to utter facts. Then I suppose the boy's missing life must be here somewhere."

This was enough for Gwendolen, the Willing Warlock, and for most of the witches and necromancers. Gwendolen said, "I'll go and find it, then," and minced up the meadow toward the trees as fast as she could in her pointed shoes, with the Willing Warlock bouncing ahead. As they pushed past a witch in a high green hat, the witch said, "That's right, dear. We must all hunt for the pussy." She turned to the crowd with a witch's piercing scream. "Hunt for pussy, everyone!"

And everyone raced off to do it, picking up skirts and holding on Sunday hats. The meadow emptied. The trees around it shook and waved and crashed. But the garden would not let anyone get very far. Brightly colored witches, cloaked wizards, and dark warlocks kept being spilled out of the trees into the meadow again. Cat heard Chrestomanci say, "Your friends seem very ignorant, Nostrum. The way out is widdershins. Perhaps you should tell them so. The cat will certainly be in summer or spring."

William Nostrum gave him a swirling glare and hurried off shouting, "Widdershins, brothers and sisters! Widdershins!"

"Let me tell you, sir," Henry Nostrum said to Chrestomanci, "you are beginning to annoy me considerably." He hovered for a second but, as quite a crowd of people, with Gwendolen and the Willing Warlock among them, were whirled out of the trees into the meadow again, and seemed very indignant about it, Henry Nostrum set off trotting toward them, calling, "No, my dear friends! My dear pupil! Widdershins. You have to go widdershins."

Cat and Chrestomanci were left alone for the time being by the broken arch and the apple tree.

CHAPTER 16

"Cat," said Chrestomanci, from almost behind Cat's head. "Cat!"

Cat did not want to talk. He was lying looking up at the blue sky through the leaves of the apple tree. Every so often it went blurred. Then Cat shut his eyes and tears ran out across both his ears. Now he knew how little Gwendolen cared about him, he was not sure he wanted any lives at all. He listened to the shouting and crashing among the trees and almost wished Fiddle would be caught soon. From time to time, he had an odd feeling that he was Fiddle himself—Fiddle furious and frightened, lashing out and scratching a huge fat witch in a flower hat.

"Cat," said Chrestomanci. He sounded almost as desperate as Fiddle. "Cat, I know how you're feeling. We hoped you wouldn't find out about Gwendolen for years yet. But you are an enchanter. I suspect that you're a stronger enchanter than I am when you set your mind to it. Could you use some of your magic now, before someone catches poor Fiddle? Please. As a great favor. Just to help me get out of this wretched silver, so that I can summon the rest of my power."

Cat was being Fiddle again while Chrestomanci talked. He climbed a tree, but the Willing Warlock and the Accredited Witch shook him out of it. He ran and he ran, and then jumped from between the Willing Warlock's grabbing hands, a huge jump, from somewhere immensely high. It was such a sickening jump that Cat opened his eyes. The apple leaves fluttered against the sky. The apple he could see was nearly ripe.

"What do you want me to do?" he said. "I don't know how to do anything."

"I know," said Chrestomanci. "I felt the same when they told me. Can you move your left hand at all?"

"Backward and forward," Cat said, trying. "I can't get it out of the rope though."

"No need," said Chrestomanci. "You've more ability in the little finger of that hand than most people—including Gwendolen—have in their entire lives. And the magic of the garden should help you. Just saw at the rope with your left hand and presume that the rope is made of silver."

Cat tipped his head back and looked at Chrestomanci unbelievingly. Chrestomanci was untidy and pale and very much in earnest. He must be telling the truth. Cat moved his left hand against the rope. It felt rough and ropish. He told himself it was not rough rope, it was silver. And the rope felt smooth. But sawing was rather a strain. Cat lifted his hand as far as he could get it and brought the edge of it down on the silver rope.

Clink. Jingle. The rope parted.

"Thank you," said Chrestomanci. "There go two watch-chains. But there seems to be a very firm spell on these handcuffs. Can you try again?"

The rope was a great deal looser. Cat fought his way out of it with a series of clatters and thumps—he was not sure quite what he had turned it into—and knelt up on the stone. Chrestomanci walked weakly toward him, with his hands still hanging limply in the handcuffs. At the same time, the Willing Warlock spilled out of the trees, arguing with the witch in the flower hat.

"I tell you the cat's dead. It fell a good fifty feet."

"But I tell you they always fall on their feet."

"Then why didn't it get up then?"

Cat realized there was no time to waste trying to imagine things. He put both hands to the handcuffs and wrenched.

"Ow!" said Chrestomanci.

But the handcuffs were off. Cat was suddenly very pleased with his newfound talent. He took the handcuffs in two and told them to be ferocious eagles. "Get after the Nostrums," he said. The left handcuff took off savagely as ordered, but the right half was still a silver handcuff and it fell on the grass. Cat had to pick it up in his left hand before it would do as it was told.

Cat looked around then to see what Chrestomanci was doing. He was standing under the apple tree, and the talkative little man called Bernard was stumbling down the hillside toward him. Bernard's Sunday cravat was comfortably undone. He was carrying a pencil and a newspaper folded open at the crossword. "Enchantment, five letters, ending in C," he was murmuring, before he looked up and saw Chrestomanci green with tree mold. He stared at the two watch-chains, Cat, the rope, and the numbers of people who were hurrying among the trees around the top of the meadow. "Bless my soul!" he said. "I'm sorry—I had no idea I was needed. You need the others too?"

"Rather quickly," said Chrestomanci.

The witch in the flower hat saw him standing away from the tree and raised her voice in a witch's scream. "They're getting away! Stop them!"

Witches, warlocks, necromancers, and wizards poured out into the meadow, with Gwendolen mincing among them, and hurriedly cast spells as they came. Muttering rolled around the garden. The smell of magic grew thick. Chrestomanci held up one hand as if he was asking for silence. The muttering grew instead, and sounded angry. But none of the people muttering came any nearer. The only ones who were still moving were William and Henry Nostrum, who kept spilling out from the trees, running hard and bawling faintly, each with a large flapping eagle after him.

Bernard chewed his pencil and his face looked ribby. "This is awful! There are so many of them!"

"Keep trying. I'm giving you all the help I can spare," Chrestomanci said, with an anxious look at the muttering crowd.

Bernard's bushy eyebrows bobbed up. "Ah!"

Miss Bessemer was standing above him on the slope. She had the works of a clock in one hand and a cloth in the other. Perhaps because of the slope, she seemed taller and more purple of dress than usual. She took in the situation at a glance. "You'll need a full muster to deal with this lot," she said to Chrestomanci.

A witch in the muttering crowd screamed, "He's getting help!" Cat thought it was Gwendolen. The smell of magic grew, and the muttering became like a long roll of thunder. The crowd seemed to be edging forward slowly, in a bobbing of fancy hats and a bristle of dark suits. The hand Chrestomanci was holding up to stop them began to shake.

"The garden's helping them too," said Bernard. "Put forth your best, Bessie-girl." He chewed his pencil and frowned intensely. Miss Bessemer wrapped her cloth neatly around her pieces of clock and grew noticeably taller.

And suddenly the rest of the Family began to appear around the apple tree, all in the middle of the peaceful Sunday things they had been doing when they were summoned. One of the younger ladies had a skein of wool between her hands, and one of the younger men was winding it. The next man was holding a billiard cue, and the other young lady had a lump of chalk. The old lady with mittens was crocheting a new pair of mittens. Mr. Saunders appeared with a thump. He had the dragon tucked playfully under one arm, and both of them looked startled to be fetched in the middle of a romp.

The dragon saw Cat. It wriggled out from under Mr. Saunders' arm, bounded across the grass, and jumped rattling and flaming into Cat's arms. Cat found himself staggering about under the apple tree with quite a heavy dragon squirming on his chest and enthusiastically licking his face with flame. It would have burned him badly if he had not remembered in time to tell the flames they were cool.

He looked up to see Roger and Julia appearing. They both had their arms stretched stiffly above their heads, because they had been playing mirrors again, and they were both very much astonished. "It's the garden!" said Roger. "And loads of people!"

"You never summoned us before, Daddy," said Julia.

"This is rather special," said Chrestomanci. He was holding his right hand up with his left one by now, and looking tired out. "I need you to fetch your mother. Quickly."

"We're holding them," Mr. Saunders said. He was trying to sound encouraging, but he was nervous. The muttering crowd was coming nearer.

"No, we aren't!" snapped the old lady in mittens. "We can't do anything more without Milly."

Cat had a feeling that everyone was trying to fetch Milly. He thought he ought to help, since they needed her so much, but he did not know what to do. Besides, the dragon's flames were so hot that he needed all his energy not to get burned.

Roger and Julia could not fetch Milly. "What's wrong?" said Julia. "We've always been able to before."

"All these people's spells are stopping us," said Roger.

"Try again," said Chrestomanci. "I can't. Something's stopping me too."

"Are you joining in the magic?" the dragon asked Cat. Cat was finding the heat of it really troublesome by now. His face was red and sore. But, as soon as the dragon spoke, he understood. He *was* joining in the magic. Only he was joining in on the wrong side, because Gwendolen was using him again. He was so used to her doing it that he barely noticed. But he could feel her doing it now. She was using so much of his power to stop Chrestomanci fetching Milly that Cat was getting burned.

For the first time in his life, Cat was angry about it. "She's no business to!" he told the dragon. And he took his magic back. It was like a cool draft in his face.

"Cat! Stop that!" Gwendolen screamed from the crowd.

"Oh, shut up!" Cat shouted back. "It's mine!"

At his feet, the little spring ran bubbling out of the grass again. Cat was looking down at it, wondering why it should, when he noticed a sort of gladness come over the anxious Family around him. Chrestomanci was looking upward, and a light seemed to have fallen across his face. Cat turned around and found Milly was there at last. He supposed it was some trick of the hillside that made her look tall as the apple tree. But it seemed no trick that she also looked kind as the end of a long day. She had Fiddle in her arms. Fiddle was draggled and miserable, but purring.

"I'm so sorry," Milly said. "I'd have come sooner if I'd known. This poor beast had fallen off the garden wall and I wasn't thinking of anything else."

Chrestomanci smiled, and let his hand go. He did not seem to need it to hold back the crowd anymore. They stood where they were, and their muttering had stopped. "It doesn't matter," he said. "But we must get to work now."

The Family got to work at once. Cat found it hard to describe or remember afterward just how they did. He remembered claps and peals of thunder, darkness, and mist. He thought Chrestomanci grew taller than Milly, tall as the sky—but that could have been because the dragon got extremely scared and Cat was kneeling in the grass to make it feel safer. From there he saw the Family from time to time, striding about like giants. Witches screamed and screamed. Warlocks and wizards roared and howled. Sometimes there was whirling white rain, or whirling white snow, or perhaps just whirling white smoke, whirling and whirling. Cat was sure the whole garden was spinning, faster and faster. Among the whirling and the whiteness came flying necromancers, or Bernard striding, or Mr. Saunders, billowing, with snow in his hair. Julia ran past, making knot after knot in her handkerchief. And Milly must have brought reinforcements with her. Cat glimpsed Euphemia, the butler, a footman, two gardeners and, to his alarm, Will Suggins once, breasting the whiteness in the howling, spinning, screaming garden.

The spinning got so fast that Cat was no longer giddy. It was spinning rock-steady, and humming. Chrestomanci stepped out of the whiteness and under the apple tree and held out one hand to Cat. He was wet and windswept, and Cat was still not sure how tall he was. "Can I have some of your dragon's blood?" Chrestomanci said.

"How did you know I'd got it?" Cat said guiltily, letting go of the dragon in order to get at his crucible.

"The smell," said Chrestomanci.

Cat passed his crucible over. "Here you are. Have I lost a life over it?"

"Not you," said Chrestomanci. "But it was lucky you didn't let Janet touch it." He stepped to the whirling, and emptied the whole crucible into it. Cat saw the powder snatched away and whirled. The mist turned brownish-red—and the humming to a terrible bell note that hurt Cat's ears. He could hear witches and warlocks howling with horror. "Let them roar," said Chrestomanci. He was leaning against the right-hand pillar of the archway. "Every single one of them has now lost his or her witchcraft. They'll complain to their MP's and there'll be questions asked in Parliament, but I daresay we shall survive it." He raised his hand and beckoned.

Frantic people in soaking-wet Sunday clothes came whirling out of the whiteness and were sucked through the broken arch like dead leaves in a whirlpool. More and more and more came. They sailed through in crowds. Out of the whirling many, Chrestomanci somehow collected the two Nostrums and put them down for a minute in front of Cat and the dragon. Cat was charmed to see one of his eagles sitting on Henry Nostrum's shoulders, pecking at his bald pate, and the other eagle fluttering around William, stabbing at the stouter parts of him.

"Call them off," said Chrestomanci.

Cat called them off, rather regretfully, and they fell on the grass as handcuffs. Then the handcuffs were swept away with the Nostrum brothers and whirled through the archway with them in the last of the crowd.

Last of all came Gwendolen. Chrestomanci stopped her too. As he did so, the whiteness cleared, the humming died away, and the rest of the Family began to collect on the sunny hillside, panting a little but not very wet. Cat thought the garden was probably still spinning. But perhaps it always did. Gwendolen stared around in horror.

"Let me go! I've got to go back and be queen."

"Don't be selfish," said Chrestomanci. "You've no right to keep snatching eight other people from world to world. Stay here and learn how to do it properly. And those courtiers of yours don't really do what you say, you know. They only pretend."

"I don't care!" Gwendolen screamed. She held up her golden clothes, kicked off her pointed shoes, and ran for the archway. Chrestomanci reached out to stop her. Gwendolen spun around and hurled her last handful of dragon's blood in his face and, while Chrestomanci was forced to duck and put one arm over his face, Gwendolen backed hastily through the archway. There was a mighty bang. The space between the pillars turned black. When everyone recovered, Gwendolen was gone. There was nothing but meadow between the pillars again. Even the pointed shoes had gone.

"What did the child do?" said the old lady with mittens, very shaken.

"Sealed herself in that world," said Chrestomanci. He was even more shaken. "Isn't that so, Cat?" he said.

Cat nodded mulishly. It had seemed worth it. He was not sure he wanted to see Gwendolen again.

"And look what that's done," said Mr. Saunders, nodding at the hillside.

Janet was stumbling down the slope, past Milly, and she was crying. Milly handed Fiddle carefully to Julia and put her arms around Janet. Janet sobbed heavily. The rest crowded around her. Bernard patted Janet's back and the old lady with mittens made soothing noises.

Cat stood on his own near the ruins, with the dragon looking inquiringly up at him from the grass. Janet had been happy in her own world. She had missed her mother and father. Now she was probably in this world for good, and Cat had done it. And Chrestomanci had called Gwendolen selfish!

"No, it's not that, quite, really," Janet said from the midst of the Family. She tried to sit down on the fallen block of stone, and got up quickly, remembering the way it was being used when she last saw it.

Cat had a very gallant idea. He sent for a blue velvet chair from Gwendolen's room and put it down on the grass beside Janet. Janet gave a tearful laugh. "That was kind." She started to sit in it.

"I belong to Chrestomanci Castle," said the chair. "I belong to Chresto—" Miss Bessemer looked at it sternly and it stopped.

Janet sat in the chair. It was a little wobbly because the grass was uneven. "Where's Cat?" she said anxiously.

"I'm here," said Cat. "I got the chair for you." He thought it was kind of Janet to look so relieved to see him.

"What do you say to a little lunch?" Milly asked Miss Bessemer. "It must be nearly two o'clock."

"Agreed," said Miss Bessemer, and made a stately half-turn toward the butler. He nodded. The footman and the gardeners staggered forward with great hampers like laundry baskets which, when the lids were thrown back, proved to be full of chickens, hams, meat pies, ice cream, fruit, and wine.

"Oh, beautiful!" said Roger.

Everyone sat around to eat the lunch. Most of them sat on the grass, and Cat made sure to sit as far away from Will Suggins as he could. Milly sat on the stone slab. Chrestomanci splashed some of the water from the bubbling spring over his face—which seemed to refresh him wonderfully—and sat leaning against the slab. The old lady with mittens produced a tuffet out of nowhere, which she said was more comfortable; and Bernard thoughtfully shook out the remains of the rope that Cat had left by the rock. It became a hammock. Bernard strung it between the pillars of the archway and lay in it, looking defiantly comfortable, even though he had the greatest difficulty keeping his balance and eating as well.

Fiddle was given a wing of chicken and took it into the apple tree to eat, out of the way of the dragon. The dragon was jealous of Fiddle. It divided its time between breathing resentful smoke up into the tree and leaning heavily against Cat, begging for chicken and meat pie.

"I warn you," said Mr. Saunders. "That is the most spoiled dragon in the world."

"I'm the *only* dragon in the world," the dragon said smugly.

Janet was still inclined to be tearful. "My dear, we do understand," said Milly, "and we're so very sorry."

"I can send you back," said Chrestomanci. "It's not quite so easy with Gwendolen's world missing from the series, but don't think it can't be done."

"No, no. That's all right," Janet gulped. "At least, it will be all right when I'm used to it. I was hoping to come back here—but it is rather a wrench. You see—" Her eyes filled and her mouth trembled. A handkerchief came out of the air and pushed itself into her hand. Cat did not know who had done it, but he wished he had thought of it. "Thanks," said Janet. "You see, Mum and Dad haven't noticed the difference." She blew her nose furiously. "I got back to my bedroom, and the other girl—she's called Romillia really—had been writing her diary. She got called away in midsentence and left it lying there, so I read it. And it was all about how scared she had been in case my parents noticed she wasn't me, and how glad she was when she was clever enough to make sure they didn't. She was utterly terrified of being sent back. She'd had a dreadful life as an orphan in her own world, and she was miserable there. She'd written things that made me feel really sorry for her. Mind you," Janet said severely, "she was just asking for trouble keeping a diary in the same house as my parents. I wrote a note in it telling her so, and I said if she *must* keep one, she'd better put it in one of my good hiding places. And then—and then I sat there and rather hoped I'd come back."

"That was kind of you," said Cat.

"It was, and you're truly welcome, my love," said Milly.

"You're sure?" Chrestomanci asked, looking searchingly at Janet over the chicken leg he was eating.

Janet nodded, quite firmly, though most of her face was still hidden in the handkerchief.

"You were the one I was most worried about," Chrestomanci said. "I'm afraid I didn't realize at once what had happened. Gwendolen had found out about the mirror, you see, and she worked the change in her bathroom. And anyway, none of us had the slightest idea Cat's powers were that strong. The truth only dawned on me during that unfortunate affair of the frog, and then of course I took a look at once to see what had happened to Gwendolen and the seven other girls. Gwendolen was in her element. And Jennifer, who came after Romillia, is as tough as Gwendolen and has always wished she was an orphan; whereas Queen Caroline, whom Gwendolen displaced, was as miserable as Romillia, and had run away three times already. And it was the same with the other five. They were all much better suited—except perhaps you."

Janet took her face out of the handkerchief and looked at him in large indignation. "Why couldn't you have *told* me you knew? I wouldn't have been nearly so scared of you! And you wouldn't believe the troubles Cat got into because of it—not to speak of me owing Mr. Bagwash twenty pounds and not knowing the Geography and History here! And you needn't laugh!" she said, as nearly everyone did.

"I apologize," said Chrestomanci. "Believe me, it was one of the most troubling decisions I've ever had to make. But who on earth is Mr. Bagwash?"

"Mr. Baslam," Cat explained reluctantly. "Gwendolen bought some dragon's blood from him and didn't really pay."

"He's asking outrageously much," said Milly. "And it is illegal, you know."

"I'll go and have a word with him tomorrow," Bernard said from his hammock. "Though he'll probably be gone by then. He knows I've got my eye on him."

"Why was it a troubling decision?" Janet asked Chrestomanci.

Chrestomanci tossed his chicken bone to the dragon and slowly wiped his fingers on a handkerchief with a gold-embroidered C in one corner. This gave him an excuse to turn Cat's way and stare, in his vaguest way, into the air above Cat's head. Since Cat was fairly clear by now that the vaguer Chrestomanci seemed about something, the more acutely he was attending to it, he was not altogether surprised when Chrestomanci said, "Because of Cat. We would have felt a good deal easier if Cat could have brought himself to tell someone what had happened. We gave him a number of opportunities to. But when he held his tongue, we thought perhaps he did know the extent of his powers after all."

"But I don't," said Cat.

And Janet, who was becoming thoroughly cheerful now she was being allowed to ask questions, said, "I think you were quite wrong. We both got so frightened that we came into this garden and nearly got you and Cat killed. You should have said."

"Perhaps," agreed Chrestomanci, and peeled a banana in a thoughtful way. He was still turned toward Cat. "Normally we're more than a match here for people like the Nostrums. I knew they were planning something through Gwendolen, and I thought Cat knew it too—my apologies, Cat. I wouldn't have had Gwendolen here for a minute, except that we had to have Cat. Chrestomanci *has* to be a nine-lived enchanter. No one else is strong enough for the post."

"Post?" said Janet. "Isn't it a hereditary title then?"

Mr. Saunders laughed, and threw his bone to the dragon too. "Heavens no! We're all Government employees here. The job Chrestomanci has is to make sure this world isn't run entirely by witches. Ordinary people have rights too. And he has to make sure witches don't get out into worlds where there isn't so much magic and play havoc there. It's a big job. And we're the staff that helps him."

"And he needs us like he needs two left legs," Bernard remarked, jerking about in the hammock as he tried to eat ice cream.

"Oh, come now!" said Chrestomanci. "I'd have been sunk without you today."

"I was thinking of the way you found the next Chrestomanci," Bernard said, spooning ice cream off his waistcoat. "You did it when we were just going around in circles."

"Nine-lived enchanters are not easy to find," Chrestomanci explained to Janet. "In the first place, they're very rare, and in the second, they have to use their magic before they can be found. And Cat didn't. We were actually thinking of bringing someone in from another world, when Cat happened to fall into the hands of a clairvoyant. Even then, we only knew where he was, not who. I'd no idea he was Eric Chant, or any relation of mine at all—though I suppose I might have remembered that his parents were cousins, which doubled the chance of their children being witches. And I must confess that Frank Chant wrote to me to say his daughter was a witch and seemed to be using her younger brother in some way. Forgive me, Cat. I ignored that letter because your father had been so very rude when I offered to make sure his children would be born without witchcraft."

"Just as well he was rude, you know," Bernard said.

"Was that what the letters were about?" said Cat.

"I don't understand," said Janet, "why you didn't say anything at all to Cat. Why couldn't you?"

Chrestomanci was still looking vaguely in Cat's direction. Cat could tell he was very wary indeed. "Like this," he said. "Remember we hadn't known one another very long. Cat appears to have no magic at all. Yet his sister works magic far beyond her own abilities, and goes on doing it even when her witchcraft is taken away. What am I to think? Does Cat know what he's doing? If he doesn't, why doesn't he? And if he does know, what is he up to? When Gwendolen removed herself, and nobody mentioned the fact, I hoped some of the answers might emerge. And Cat still does nothing—"

"What do you mean, nothing?" said Janet. "There were some fabulous horse chestnuts, and he kept stopping Julia."

"Yes, and I couldn't think what was happening," Julia said, rather ashamed.

Cat felt hurt and uncomfortable. "Leave me alone!" he said, and he stood up. Everyone, even Chrestomanci, went tense. The only person who did not was Janet, and Cat could hardly count her, because she was not used to magic. He found he was trying not to cry, which made him very much ashamed. "Stop treating me so carefully!" he said. "I'm not a fool, or a baby. You're all afraid of me, aren't you? You didn't tell me things and you didn't punish Gwendolen because you were afraid I'd do something dreadful. And I haven't. I don't know how to. I didn't know I could."

"My love, it was just that no one was sure," said Milly.

"Well, be sure now!" said Cat. "The only things I did were by mistake, like coming here in this garden—and turning Euphemia into a frog, I suppose, but I didn't know it was me."

"You're not to worry about that, Eric," said Euphemia from the hillside, where she was sitting with Will Suggins. "It was the shock upset me. I know enchanters are different from us witches. And I'll speak to Mary. I promise."

"Speak to Will Suggins too, while you're at it," said Janet. "Because he's going to turn Cat into a frog in revenge any minute now."

Euphemia bounced around on the hillside to look at Will. "What?" she said.

"What is this, Will?" Chrestomanci asked.

"I laid it on him—for three o'clock, sir," Will Suggins said apprehensively, "if he didn't meet me as a tiger."

Chrestomanci took out a large gold watch. "Hm. It's about due now. If you don't mind my saying so, that was a little foolish of you, Will.

Suppose you carry on. Turn Cat into a frog, or yourself into a tiger, or both. I shan't interfere."

Will Suggins climbed heavily to his feet and stood facing Cat, looking as if he would prefer to be several miles away. "Let the dough work, then," he said.

Cat was still feeling so upset and tearful that he wondered whether to oblige Will Suggins and become a frog. Or he could try being a flea instead. But it all seemed rather silly. "Why don't you be a tiger?" he said.

As Cat expected, Will Suggins made a beautiful tiger, long-backed and, sleek and sharply striped. He was heavy as he padded up and down the slope, but his legs slid so easily in the silky folds of his hide that he almost seemed light. But Will Suggins himself spoiled the effect by rubbing a distressed paw over his huge cat face and staring appealingly at Chrestomanci. Chrestomanci simply laughed. The dragon trotted up the hill to investigate this new beast. Will Suggins was so alarmed that he reared up on his great hind legs to get away from it. It looked so ungainly for a tiger to be doing that, that Cat turned him back to Will Suggins on the spot.

"It wasn't real?" asked the dragon.

"No!" said Will Suggins, mopping his face with his sleeve. "All right, lad, you win. How did you do it so quick?"

"I don't know," Cat said apologetically. "I've really no idea. Shall I learn when you teach me magic?" he asked Mr. Saunders.

Mr. Saunders looked a little blank. "Well—"

"No, Michael," said Chrestomanci, "is the right answer. It's quite clear Elementary Magic isn't going to mean much to Cat. I'll have to teach you myself, Cat, and we'll be starting on Advanced Theory, I think, by the look of it. You seem to start where most people leave off."

"But why didn't he know?" Janet demanded. "It always makes me angry not to know things, and I feel especially angry about this, because it seems so hard on Cat."

"It is, I agree," said Chrestomanci. "But it's something in the nature of enchanters' magic, I think. Something the same happened to me. I couldn't do magic either. I couldn't do anything. But they found I had nine lives—I lost them at such a rate that it soon became obvious—and they told me I had to be the next Chrestomanci when I grew up, which absolutely appalled me, because I couldn't work the simplest spell. So they sent me to a tutor, the most terrifying old person, who was supposed to find what the trouble was. And he took one look at me and snarled, 'Empty your pockets, Chant!' Which I did. I was too scared not to. I took out my silver watch, and one and sixpence, and a silver charm from my godmother, and a silver tiepin I had forgotten to wear, and a silver brace I was supposed to wear in my teeth. And as soon as they were gone, I did some truly startling things. As I remember, the roof of the tutor's house came off."

"Is it really true about silver, then?" Janet said.

"For me, yes," said Chrestomanci.

"Yes, poor darling," Milly said, smiling at him. "It's so awkward with money. He can only handle pound notes and coppers."

"He has to give us our pocket money in pennies, if Michael hasn't got it," said Roger. "Imagine sixty pennies in your pocket."

"The really difficult thing is mealtimes," said Milly. "He can't do a thing with a knife and fork in his hands—and Gwendolen would do awful things during dinner."

"How stupid!" said Janet. "Why on earth don't you use stainless steel cutlery?"

Milly and Chrestomanci looked at one another. "I never thought of it!" said Milly. "Janet, my love, it's a very good thing you're staying here!"

Janet looked at Cat and laughed. And Cat, though he was still a little lonely and tearful, managed to laugh too.

WITCH WEEK

EDITOR'S NOTE

Late one night in 1605, a soldier named Guy Fawkes was caught with some two tons of gunpowder that he had smuggled into a cellar beneath the Houses of Parliament in London. Fawkes was arrested, tried, and executed for his part in the Gunpowder Plot—a failed conspiracy to blow up King James I and most of his government the very next day, November 5. Centuries later, English people still set off fireworks, light bonfires, and burn "Guys" in effigy to celebrate November 5 as Guy Fawkes Day.

CHAPTER 1

The note said: *SOMEONE IN THIS CLASS IS A WITCH.* It was written in capital letters in ordinary blue ballpoint, and it had appeared between two of the geography books Mr. Crossley was marking. Anyone could have written it. Mr. Crossley rubbed his ginger moustache unhappily. He looked out over the bowed heads of Class 6B and wondered what to do about it.

He decided not to take the note to the headmistress. It was possibly just a joke, and Miss Cadwallader had no sense of humor to speak of. The person to take it to was the deputy head, Mr. Wentworth. But the difficulty there was that Mr. Wentworth's son was a member of 6B—the small boy near the back who looked younger than the rest was Brian Wentworth. No. Mr. Crossley decided to ask the writer of the note to own up. He would explain just what a serious accusation it was and leave the rest to the person's conscience.

Mr. Crossley cleared his throat to speak. Some of 6B looked up hopefully but Mr. Crossley had changed his mind then. It was journal time, and journal time was only to be interrupted for a serious emergency. Larwood House was very strict about that rule. Larwood House was very strict about a lot of things, because it was a boarding school run by the government for witch-orphans and children with other problems. The journals were to help the children with their problems. They were supposed to be strictly private. Every day, for half an hour, every pupil had to confide his or her private thoughts to their journals, and nothing else was done until everyone had. Mr. Crossley admired the idea heartily.

But the real reason that Mr. Crossley changed his mind was the awful thought that the note might be true. Someone in 6B could easily be a witch. Only Miss Cadwallader knew who exactly in 6B was a witch-orphan, but Mr. Crossley suspected that a lot of them were. Other classes had given Mr. Crossley feelings of pride and pleasure in being a schoolmaster; 6B never did. Only two of them gave him any pride at all: Theresa Mullett and Simon Silverson. They were both model pupils. The rest of the girls tailed dismally off until you came to empty chatterers like Estelle Green, or that dumpy girl, Nan Pilgrim, who was definitely the odd one out. The boys were divided into groups. Some had the sense to follow Simon Silverson's example, but quite as many clustered round that bad boy Dan Smith, and others again admired that tall Indian boy Nirupam Singh. Or they were loners like Brian Wentworth and that unpleasant boy Charles Morgan.

Here Mr. Crossley looked at Charles Morgan and Charles Morgan looked back, with one of the blank, nasty looks he was famous for. Charles wore glasses, which enlarged the nasty look and trained it on Mr. Crossley like a double laser beam. Mr. Crossley looked away hastily and went back to worrying about the note. Everyone in 6B gave up hoping for anything interesting to happen and went back to their journals.

28 October 1981, Theresa Mullett wrote in round, angelic writing. *Mr. Crossley has found a note in our geography books. I thought it might be from Miss Hodge at first, because we all know Teddy is dying for love of her, but he looks so worried that I think it must be from some silly girl like Estelle Green. Nan Pilgrim couldn't get over the vaulting horse again today. She jumped and stuck halfway. It made us all laugh.*

Simon Silverson wrote: *28. 10. 81. I would like to know who put that note in the geography books. It fell out when I was collecting them and I put it back in. If it was found lying about we could all be blamed. This is strictly off the record of course.*

I do not know, Nirupam Singh wrote musingly, *how anyone manages to write much in their journal, since everyone knows Miss Cadwallader reads them all during the holidays. I do not write my secret thoughts. I will now describe the Indian rope trick which I saw in India before my father came to live in England . . .*

Two desks away from Nirupam, Dan Smith chewed his pen a great deal and finally wrote, *Well I mean it's not much good if you've got to write your secret fealings, what I mean is it takes all the joy out of it and you don't know what to write. It means they aren't secret if you see what I mean.*

I do not think, Estelle Green wrote, *that I have any secret feelings today, but I would like to know what is in the note from Miss Hodge that Teddy has just found. I thought she scorned him utterly.*

At the back of the room, Brian Wentworth wrote, sighing, *Timetables just ran away with me, that is my problem. During geography I planned a bus journey from London to Baghdad via Paris. Next lesson I shall plan the same journey via Berlin.*

Nan Pilgrim meanwhile was scrawling, *This is a message to the person who reads our journals. Are you Miss Cadwallader, or does Miss Cadwallader make Mr. Wentworth do it?* She stared at what she had written, rather taken aback at her own daring. This kind of thing happened to her sometimes. Still, she thought, there were hundreds of journals and hundreds of daily entries. The chances of Miss Cadwallader reading this one had to be very small—particularly if she went on and made it really boring. *I shall now be boring,* she wrote. *Teddy Crossley's real name is Harold, but he got called Teddy out of the hymn that goes "Gladly my cross I'd bear." But of course everyone sings "Crossley my glad-eyed bear." Mr. Crossley is glad-eyed. He thinks everyone should be upright and honorable and interested in geography. I am sorry for him.*

But the one who was best at making his journal boring was Charles Morgan. His entry read, *I got up. I felt hot at breakfast. I do not like porridge. Second lesson was woodwork but not for long. I think we have games next.*

Looking at this, you might think Charles was either very stupid or very muddled, or both. Anyone in 6B would have told you that it had been a chilly morning and there had been cornflakes for breakfast. Second lesson had been PE, during which Nan Pilgrim had so much amused Theresa Mullett by failing to jump the horse, and the lesson to come was music, not games. But Charles was not writing about the day's work. He really was writing about his secret feelings, but he was doing it in his own private code so that no one could know.

He started every entry with *I got up*. It meant, I hate this school. When he wrote *I do not like porridge*, that was actually true, but porridge was his code-word for Simon Silverson. Simon was porridge at breakfast, potatoes at lunch, and bread at tea. All the other people he hated had code-words too. Dan Smith was cornflakes, cabbage, and butter. Theresa Mullett was milk.

But when Charles wrote *I felt hot,* he was not talking about school at all. He meant he was remembering the witch being burned. It was a thing that would keep coming into his head whenever he was not thinking of anything else, much as he tried to forget it. He had been so young that he had been in a stroller. His big sister Bernadine had been pushing him while his mother carried the shopping, and they had been crossing a road where there was a view down into the Market Square. There were crowds of people down there, and a sort of flickering. Bernadine had stopped the stroller in the middle of the street in order to stare. She and Charles had just time to glimpse the bonfire starting to burn, and they had seen that the witch was a large fat man. Then their mother came rushing back and scolded Bernadine on across the road. "You mustn't look at witches!" she said. "Only awful people do that!" So Charles had only seen the witch for an instant. He never spoke about it, but he never forgot it. It always astonished him that Bernadine seemed to forget about it completely. What Charles was really saying in his journal was that the witch came into his head during breakfast, until Simon Silverson made him forget again by eating all that toast.

When he wrote *woodwork second lesson*, he meant that he had gone on to think about the second witch—which was a thing he did not think about so often. *Woodwork* was anything Charles liked. They only had woodwork once a week, and Charles had chosen that for his code on the very reasonable grounds that he was not likely to enjoy anything at Larwood House any oftener than that. Charles had liked the second witch. She had been quite young and rather pretty, in spite of her torn skirt and untidy hair. She had come scrambling across the wall at the end of the garden and stumbled down the rockery to the lawn, carrying her smart shoes in one hand. Charles had been nine years old then, and he was minding his little brother on the lawn. Luckily for the witch, his parents were out.

Charles knew she was a witch. She was out of breath and obviously frightened. He could hear the yells and police whistles in the house behind. Besides, who else but a witch would run away from the police in the middle of the afternoon in a tight skirt? But he made quite sure. He said, "Why are you running away in our garden?"

The witch rather desperately hopped on one foot. She had a large blister on the other foot, and both her stockings were laddered. "I'm a witch," she panted. "Please help me, little boy!"

"Why can't you magic yourself safe?" Charles asked.

"Because I can't when I'm this frightened!" gasped the witch. "I tried, but it just went wrong! *Please*, little boy—sneak me out through your house and don't say a word, and I'll give you luck for the rest of your life. I promise."

Charles looked at her in that intent way of his which most people found blank and nasty. He saw she was speaking the truth. He saw, too, that she understood the look as very few people seemed to. "Come in through the kitchen," he said. And he led the witch, hobbling on her blister in her laddered stockings, through the kitchen and down the hall to the front door.

"Thanks," she said. "You're a love." She smiled at him while she put her hair right in the hall mirror, and after she had done something to her skirt that may have been witchcraft to make it seem untorn again, she bent down and kissed Charles. "If I get away, I'll bring you luck," she said. Then she put her smart shoes on again and went away down the front garden, trying hard not to limp. At the front gate, she waved and smiled at Charles.

That was the end of the part Charles liked. That was why he wrote *but not for long* next. He never saw the witch again, or heard what had happened to her. He ordered his little brother never to say a word about her—and Graham obeyed, because he always did everything Charles said and then he watched and waited for any sign of the witch or any sign of luck. None came. It was next to impossible for Charles to find out what might have happened to the witch, because there had been new laws since he glimpsed the first witch burning. There were no more public burnings. The bonfires were lit inside the walls of jails instead, and the radio would simply announce: "Two witches were burned this morning inside Holloway Jail." Every time Charles heard this kind of announcement he thought it was *his* witch. It gave him a blunt, hurtful feeling inside. He thought of the way she had kissed him, and he was fairly sure it made you wicked too, to be kissed by a witch. He gave up expecting to be lucky. In fact, to judge from the amount of bad luck he had had, he thought the witch must have been caught almost straightaway. For the blunt, hurtful feeling he had when the radio announced a burning made him refuse to do anything his parents told him to do. He just gave them his steady stare instead. And each time he stared, he knew they thought he was being nasty. They did not understand it the way the witch did. And, since Graham imitated everything Charles did, Charles's parents very soon decided Charles was a problem child and leading Graham astray. They arranged for him to be sent to Larwood House, because it was quite near.

When Charles wrote *games*, he meant bad luck. Like everyone else in 6B, he had seen Mr. Crossley had found a note. He did not know what was in the note, but when he looked up and caught Mr. Crossley's eye, he knew it meant bad luck coming.

Mr. Crossley still could not decide what to do about the note. If what it said was true, that meant inquisitors coming to the school. And that was a thoroughly frightening thought. Mr. Crossley sighed and put the note in his pocket. "Right, everyone," he said. "Put away your journals and get into line for music."

As soon as 6B had shuffled away to the school hall, Mr. Crossley sped to the staff room, hoping to find someone he could consult about the note.

He was lucky enough to find Miss Hodge there. As Theresa Mullett and Estelle Green had observed, Mr. Crossley was in love with Miss Hodge. But of course he never let it show. Probably the one person in the school who did not seem to know was Miss Hodge herself. Miss Hodge was a small neat person who wore neat gray skirts and blouses and her hair was even neater and smoother than Theresa Mullett's. She was busy making neat stacks of books on the staff room table, and she went on making them all the time Mr. Crossley was telling her excitedly about the note. She spared the note one glance.

"No, I can't tell who wrote it either," she said.

"But what shall I do about it?" Mr. Crossley pleaded. "Even if it's true, it's such a spiteful thing to write! And suppose it *is* true. Suppose one of them is—" He was in a pitiable state. He wanted so badly to attract Miss Hodge's attention, but he knew that words like *witch* were not the kind of words one used in front of a lady. "I don't like to say it in front of you."

"I was brought up to be sorry for witches," Miss Hodge remarked calmly.

"Oh, so was I! We all are," Mr. Crossley said hastily. "I just wondered how I should handle it—"

Miss Hodge lined up another stack of books. "I think it's just a silly joke," she said. "Ignore it. Aren't you supposed to be teaching 4C?"

"Yes, yes. I suppose I am," Mr. Crossley agreed miserably. And he was forced to hurry away without Miss Hodge's having looked at him once.

Miss Hodge thoughtfully squared off another stack of books, until she was sure Mr. Crossley had gone. Then she smoothed her smooth hair and hurried away upstairs to find Mr. Wentworth.

Mr. Wentworth, as deputy head, had a study where he wrestled with the schedules and various other problems Miss Cadwallader gave him. When Miss Hodge tapped on the door, he was wrestling with a particularly fierce one. There were seventy people in the school orchestra. Fifty of these were also in the school choir and twenty of those fifty were in the school play. Thirty boys in the orchestra were in various football teams, and twenty of the girls played hockey for the school. At least a third played basketball as well. The volleyball team were all in the school play. Problem: how do you arrange rehearsals and practices without asking most people to be in three places at once? Mr. Wentworth rubbed the thin patch at the back of his hair despairingly. "Come in," he said. He saw the bright, smiling, anxious face of Miss Hodge, but his mind was not on her at all.

"So spiteful of someone, and so awful if it's true!" he heard Miss Hodge saying. And then, merrily, "But I think I have a scheme to discover who wrote the note—it must be someone in 6B. Can we put our heads together and work it out, Mr. Wentworth?" She put her own head on one side, invitingly.

Mr. Wentworth had no idea what she was talking about. He scratched the place where his hair was going and stared at her. Whatever it was, it had all the marks of a scheme that ought to be squashed. "People only write anonymous notes to make themselves feel important," he said experimentally. "You mustn't take them seriously."

"But it's the perfect scheme!" Miss Hodge protested. "If I can explain—"

Not squashed yet, whatever it is, thought Mr. Wentworth. "No. Just tell me the exact words of this note," he said.

Miss Hodge instantly became crushed and shocked. "But it's awful!" Her voice fell to a dramatic whisper. "It says someone in 6B is a witch!"

Mr. Wentworth realized that his instinct had been right. "What did I tell you?" he said heartily. "That's the sort of stuff you can only ignore, Miss Hodge."

"But someone in 6B has a very sick mind!" Miss Hodge whispered.

Mr. Wentworth considered 6B, including his own son Brian. "They all have," he said. "Either they'll grow out of it, or we'll see them all riding round on broomsticks in the sixth grade." Miss Hodge started back. She was genuinely shocked at this coarse language. But she hastily made herself laugh. She could see it was a joke. "Take no notice," said Mr. Wentworth. "Ignore it, Miss Hodge." And he went back to his problem with some relief.

Miss Hodge went back to her stacks of books, not as crushed as Mr. Wentworth supposed she was. Mr. Wentworth had made a joke to her. He had never done that before. She must be getting somewhere. For—and this was a fact not known to Theresa Mullett or Estelle Green—Miss Hodge intended to marry Mr. Wentworth. He was a widower. When Miss Cadwallader retired, Miss Hodge was sure Mr. Wentworth would be head of Larwood House. This suited Miss Hodge, who had her old father to consider. For this, she was quite willing to put up with Mr. Wentworth's bald patch and his tense and harrowed look. The only drawback was that putting up with Mr. Wentworth also meant putting up with Brian. A little frown wrinkled Miss Hodge's smooth forehead at the thought of Brian Wentworth. Now there was a boy who quite deserved the way the rest of 6B were always on to him. Never mind. He could be sent away to another school.

Meanwhile, in music, Mr. Brubeck was asking Brian to sing on his own. 6B had trailed their way through "Here We Sit like Birds in the Wilderness." They had made it sound like a lament. "I'd prefer a wilderness to this place," Estelle Green whispered to her friend Karen Grigg. Then they sang "Cuckaburra Sits in the Old Gum Tree." That sounded like a funeral dirge. "What's a cuckaburra?" Karen whispered to Estelle.

"Another kind of bird," Estelle whispered back. "Australian."

"No, no, *no!*" shouted Mr. Brubeck. "Brian is the only one of you who doesn't sound like a cockerel with a sore throat!"

"Mr. Brubeck must have birds on the brain!" Estelle giggled. And Simon Silverson, who believed, strongly and sincerely, that nobody was worthy of praise except himself, gave Brian a scathingly jeering look.

But Mr. Brubeck was far too addicted to music to take any notice of what the rest of 6B thought. " 'The Cuckoo is a Pretty Bird,' " he announced. "I want Brian to sing this to you on his own."

Estelle giggled, because it was birds again. Theresa giggled too, because anyone who stood out for any reason struck her as exceedingly funny. Brian stood up with the song book in his hands. He was never embarrassed. But instead of singing, he read the words out in an incredulous voice.

" 'The cuckoo is a pretty bird, she singeth as she flies. She bringeth us good tidings, she telleth us no lies.' Sir, why are all these songs about birds?" he asked innocently. Charles thought that was a shrewd move of Brian's, after the way Simon Silverson had looked at him.

But it did Brian no good. He was too unpopular. Most of the girls said, "*Brian!*" in shocked voices. Simon said it jeeringly.

"Quiet!" shouted Mr. Brubeck. "Brian, get on and sing!" He struck notes on the piano.

Brian stood with the book in his hands, obviously wondering what to do. It was clear that he would be in trouble with Mr. Brubeck if he did not sing, and that he would be hit afterward if he did. And while Brian hesitated, the witch in 6B took a hand. One of the long windows of the hall flew open with a clap and let in a stream of birds. Most of them were ordinary birds: sparrows, starlings, pigeons, blackbirds, and thrushes, swooping round the hall in vast numbers and shedding feathers and droppings as they swooped. But among the beating wings were two curious furry creatures with large pouches, which kept uttering violent laughing sounds, and the red and yellow thing swooping among a cloud of sparrows and shouting "Cuckoo!" was clearly a parrot.

Luckily, Mr. Brubeck thought it was simply the wind which had let the birds in. The rest of the lesson had to be spent in chasing the birds out again. By that time, the laughing birds with pouches had vanished. Evidently the witch had decided they were a mistake. But everyone in 6B had clearly seen them. Simon said importantly, "If this happens again, we all ought to get together and—"

At this, Nirupam Singh turned round, towering among the beating wings. "Have you any proof that this is not perfectly natural?" he said.

Simon had not, so he said no more.

By the end of the lesson, all the birds had been sent out of the window again, except the parrot. The parrot escaped to a high curtain rail, where no one could reach it, and sat there shouting "Cuckoo!" Mr. Brubeck sent 6B away and called the caretaker to get rid of it. Charles trudged away with the rest, thinking that this must be the end of the games he had predicted in his journal. But he was quite wrong. It was only the beginning.

And when the caretaker came grumbling along with his small white dog trailing at his heels, to get rid of the parrot, the parrot had vanished.

CHAPTER 2

The next day was the day Miss Hodge tried to find out who had written the note. It was also the worst day either Nan Pilgrim or Charles Morgan had ever spent at Larwood House. It did not begin too badly for Charles, but Nan was late for breakfast.

She had broken her shoelace. She was told off by Mr. Towers for being late, and then by a monitor. By this time, the only table with a place was one where all the others were boys. Nan slid into the place, horribly embarrassed. They had eaten all the toast already, except one slice. Simon Silverson took that slice as Nan arrived. "Bad luck, fatso." From further down the table, Nan saw Charles Morgan looking at her. It was meant to be a look of sympathy, but, like all Charles's looks, it came out like a blank double-barreled glare. Nan pretended not to see it and did her best to eat wet, pale scrambled egg on its own.

At lessons, she discovered that Theresa and her friends had started a new craze. That was a bad sign. They were always more than usually pleased with themselves at the start of a craze—even though this one had probably started so that they need not think of witches or birds. The craze was white knitting, white and clean and fluffy, which you kept wrapped in a towel so that it would stay clean. The classroom filled with mutters of, "Two purl, one plain, twist two . . ."

But the day really got into its evil stride in the middle of the morning, during PE. Larwood House had that every day, like the journals. 6B joined with 6C and 6D, and the boys went running in the field, while the girls went together to the gym. The climbing ropes were let down there.

Theresa and Estelle and the rest gave glad cries and went shinnying up the ropes with easy swinging pulls. Nan tried to lurk out of sight against the wall bars. Her heart fell with a flop into her gym shoes. This was worse even than the vaulting horse. Nan simply could not climb ropes. She had been born without the proper muscles or something.

And, since it was that kind of day, Miss Phillips spotted Nan almost at once. "Nan, you haven't had a turn yet. Theresa, Delia, Estelle, come on down and let Nan have her turn on the ropes." Theresa and the rest came down readily. They knew they were about to see some fun.

Nan saw their faces and ground her teeth. This time, she vowed, she would do it. She would climb right up to the ceiling and wipe that grin off Theresa's face. Nevertheless, the distance to the ropes seemed several hundred shiny yards. Nan's legs, in the floppy divided skirts they wore for gym, had gone mauve and wide, and her arms felt like weak pink puddings. When she reached the rope, the knot on the end of it seemed to hang rather higher than her head. And she was supposed to stand on that knot somehow.

She gripped the rope in her fat, weak hands and jumped. All that happened was that the knot hit her heavily in the chest and her feet dropped sharply to the floor again. A murmur of amusement began among Theresa and her friends. Nan could hardly believe it. This was ridiculous—worse than usual! She could not even get off the floor now. She took a new grip on the rope and jumped again. And again. And again. And she leaped and leaped, bounding like a floppy kangaroo, and still the knot kept hitting her in the chest and her feet kept hitting the floor. The murmurs of the rest grew into giggles and then to outright laughter. Until at last, when Nan was almost ready to give up, her feet somehow found the knot, groped, gripped, and hung on. And there she clung, upside down like a sloth, breathless and sweating, from arms which did not seem to work anymore. This was terrible. And she still had to climb up the rope. She wondered whether to fall off on her back and die.

Miss Phillips was beside her. "Come on, Nan. Stand up on the knot."

Somehow, feeling it was superhuman of her, Nan managed to lever herself upright. She stood there, wobbling gently round in little circles, while Miss Phillips, her face level with Nan's trembling knees, kindly and patiently explained for the hundredth time exactly how to climb a rope.

Nan clenched her teeth. She *would* do it. Everyone else did. It must be possible. She shut her eyes to shut out the other girls' grinning faces and did as Miss Phillips told her. She took a strong and careful grip on the rope above her head. Carefully, she put the rope between the top of one foot and the bottom of the other. She kept her eyes shut. Firmly, she pulled with her arms. Crisply, she pulled her feet up behind. Gripped again. Reached up again, with fearful concentration. Yes, this was it! She was doing it at last! The secret must be to keep your eyes shut. She gripped and pulled. She could feel her body easily swinging upward toward the ceiling, just as the others did it.

But, around her, the giggles grew to laughter, and the laughter grew into screams, then shouts, and became a perfect storm of hilarity. Puzzled, Nan opened her eyes. All round her, at knee level, she saw laughing red faces, tears running out of eyes, and people doubled over yelling with mirth. Even Miss Phillips was biting her lip and snorting a little. And small wonder. Nan looked down to find her gym shoes still resting on the knot at the bottom of the rope. After all that climbing, she was still standing on the knot.

Nan tried to laugh too. She was sure it had been very funny. But it was hard to be amused. Her only consolation was that, after that, none of the other girls could climb the ropes either. They were too weak with laughing.

The boys, meanwhile, were running round and round the field. They were stripped to little pale blue running shorts and splashing through the dew in big spiked shoes. It was against the rules to run in anything but spikes. They were divided into little groups of laboring legs. The quick group of legs in front, with muscles, belonged to Simon Silverson and his friends, and to Brian Wentworth. Brian was a good runner in spite of his short legs. Brian was prudently trying to keep to the rear of Simon, but every so often the sheer joy of running overcame him and he went ahead. Then he would get bumped and jostled by Simon's friends, for everyone knew it was Simon's right to be in front.

The group of legs behind these were paler and moved without enthusiasm. These belonged to Dan Smith and his friends. All of them could have run at least as fast as Simon Silverson, but they were saving themselves for better things. They loped along easily, chatting among themselves. Today, they kept bursting into laughter.

Behind these again labored an assorted group of legs: mauve legs, fat legs, bright white legs, legs with no muscles at all, and the great brown legs of Nirupam Singh, which seemed too heavy for the rest of Nirupam's skinny body to lift. Everyone in the group was too breathless to talk. Their faces wore assorted expressions of woe.

The last pair of legs, far in the rear, belonged to Charles Morgan. There was nothing particularly wrong with Charles's legs, except that his feet were in ordinary school shoes and soaked through. He was always behind. He chose to be. This was one of the few times in the day when he could be alone to think. He had discovered that, as long as he was thinking of something else, he could keep up his slow trot for hours. And think. The only interruptions he had to fear were when the other groups came pounding past him and he was tangled up in their efforts for a few seconds. Or when Mr. Towers, encased in his nice warm tracksuit, came loping up alongside and called ill-advised encouragements to Charles.

So Charles trotted slowly on, thinking. He gave himself over to hating Larwood House. He hated the field under his feet, the shivering autumn trees that dripped on him, the white goalposts, and the neat line of pine trees in front of the spiked wall that kept everyone in. Then, when he swung round the corner and had a view of the school buildings, he hated them more. They were built of a purplish sort of brick. Charles thought it was the color a person's face would go if he was choking. He thought of the long corridors inside, painted caterpillar green, the thick radiators which were never warm, the brown classrooms, the frosty white dormitories, and the smell of school food, and he was almost in an ecstasy of hate. Then he looked at the groups of legs straggling round the field ahead, and he hated all the people in the school most horribly of all.

Upon that, he found he was remembering the witch being burned. It swept into his head unbidden, as it always did. Only today, it seemed worse than usual. Charles found he was remembering things he had not noticed at the time: the exact shape of the flames, just leaping from small to large, and the way the fat man who was a witch had bent sideways away from them. He could see the man's exact face, the rather blobby nose with a wart on it, the sweat on it, and the flames shining off the man's eyes and the sweat. Above all, he could see the man's expression. It was astounded. The fat man had not believed he was going to die until the moment Charles saw him. He must have thought his witchcraft could save him. Now he knew it could not. And he was horrified. Charles was horrified too. He trotted along in a sort of trance of horror.

But here was the smart red tracksuit of Mr. Towers loping along beside him. "Charles, what are you doing running in walking shoes?"

The fat witch vanished. Charles should have been glad, but he was not. His thinking had been interrupted, and he was not private anymore.

"I said why aren't you wearing your spikes?" Mr. Towers said.

Charles slowed down a little while he wondered what to reply. Mr. Towers trotted springily beside him, waiting for an answer. Because he was not thinking anymore, Charles found his legs aching and his chest sore. That annoyed him. He was even more annoyed about his spikes. He knew Dan Smith had hidden them. That was why that group were laughing. Charles could see their faces craning over their shoulders as they ran, to see what he was telling Mr. Towers. That annoyed him even more. Charles did not usually have this kind of trouble, the way Brian Wentworth did. His double-barreled nasty look had kept him safe up to now, if lonely. But he foresaw he was going to have to think of something more than just looking in future. He felt very bitter.

"I couldn't find my spikes, sir."

"How hard did you look?"

"Everywhere," Charles said bitterly. Why don't I say it was them? he wondered. And knew the answer. Life would not be worth living for the rest of the term.

"In my experience," said Mr. Towers, running and talking as easily as if he were sitting still, "when a lazy boy like you says everywhere, it means nowhere. Report to me in the locker room after school and find those spikes. You stay there until you find them. Right?"

"Yes," said Charles. Bitterly, he watched Mr. Towers surge away from him and run up beside the next group to pester Nirupam Singh.

He hunted for his spikes again during break. But it was hopeless. Dan had hidden them somewhere really cunning. At least, after break, Dan Smith had something else to laugh about besides Charles. Nan Pilgrim soon found out what. As Nan came into the classroom for lessons, she was greeted by Nirupam. "Hello," said Nirupam. "Will you do your rope trick for me too?"

Nan gave him a glare that was mostly astonishment and pushed past him without replying. How did he know about the ropes? she thought. The girls just never talked to the boys! How *did* he know?

But next moment, Simon Silverson came up to Nan, barely able to stop laughing. "My dear Dulcinea!" he said. "What a charming name you have! Were you called after the Archwitch?" After that, he doubled up with laughter, and so did most of the people nearby.

"Her name really is Dulcinea, you know," Nirupam said to Charles.

This was true. Nan's face felt to her like a balloon on fire. Nothing else, she was sure, could be so large and so hot. Dulcinea Wilkes had been the most famous witch of all time. No one was supposed to know Nan's name was Dulcinea. She could not think how it had leaked out. She tried to stalk loftily away to her desk, but she was caught by person after person, all laughingly calling out, "Hey, Dulcinea!" She did not manage to sit down until Mr. Wentworth was already in the room.

6B usually paid attention during Mr. Wentworth's lessons. He was known to be absolutely merciless. Besides, he had a knack of being interesting, which made his lessons seem shorter than other teachers'. But today, no one could keep their mind on Mr. Wentworth. Nan was trying not to cry. When, a year ago, Nan's aunts had brought her to Larwood House, even softer, plumper, and more timid than she was now, Miss Cadwallader had promised that no one should know her name was Dulcinea. Miss Cadwallader had *promised!* So how had someone found out? The rest of 6B kept breaking into laughter and excited whispers. Could Nan Pilgrim be a witch? Fancy anyone being called Dulcinea! It was as bad as being called Guy Fawkes! Halfway through the lesson, Theresa Mullett was so overcome by the thought of Nan's name that she was forced to bury her face in her knitting to laugh.

Mr. Wentworth promptly took the knitting away. He dumped the clean white bundle on the desk in front of him and inspected it dubiously. "What is it about this that seems so funny?" He unrolled the towel—at which Theresa gave a faint yell of dismay—and held up a very small fluffy thing with holes in it. "Just what is this?"

Everyone laughed.

"It's a bootee!" Theresa said angrily.

"Who for?" retorted Mr. Wentworth.

Everyone laughed again. But the laughter was short and guilty, because everyone knew Theresa was not to be laughed at.

Mr. Wentworth seemed unaware that he had performed a miracle and made everyone laugh at Theresa, instead of the other way round. He cut the laughter even shorter by telling Dan Smith to come out to the blackboard and show him two triangles that were alike. The lesson went on. Theresa kept muttering, "It's not funny! It's just not funny!" Every time she said it, her friends nodded sympathetically, while the rest of the class kept looking at Nan and bursting into muffled laughter.

At the end of the lesson, Mr. Wentworth uttered a few unpleasant remarks about mass punishments if people behaved like this again. Then, as he turned to leave, he said, "And by the way, if Charles Morgan, Nan Pilgrim, and Nirupam Singh haven't already looked at the main notice board, they should do so at once. They will find they are down for lunch on high table."

Both Nan and Charles knew then that this was not just a bad day—it was the worst day ever. Miss Cadwallader sat at high table with any important visitors to the school. It was her custom to choose three pupils from the school every day to sit there with her. This was so that everyone should learn proper table manners, and so that Miss Cadwallader should get to know her pupils. It was rightly considered a terrible ordeal. Neither Nan nor Charles had ever been chosen before. Scarcely able to believe it, they went to check with the notice board. Sure enough it read: *Charles Morgan 6B, Dulcinea Pilgrim 6B, Nirupam Singh 6B.*

Nan stared at it. So that was how everyone knew her name! Miss

Cadwallader had forgotten. She had forgotten who Nan was and everything she had promised, and when she came to stick a pin in the register—or whatever she did to choose people for high table—she had simply written down the names that came under her pin.

Nirupam was looking at the notice too. He had been chosen before, but he was no less gloomy than Charles or Nan. "You have to comb your hair and get your blazer clean," he said. "And it really is true you have to eat with the same kind of knife or fork that Miss Cadwallader does. You have to watch and see what she uses all the time."

Nan stood there, letting other people looking at the notices push her about. She was terrified. She suddenly knew she was going to behave very badly on high table. She was going to drop her dinner, or scream, or maybe take all her clothes off and dance among the plates. And she was terrified, because she knew she was not going to be able to stop herself.

She was still terrified when she arrived at high table with Charles and Nirupam. They had all combed their heads sore and tried to clean from the fronts of their blazers the dirt which always mysteriously arrives on the fronts of blazers, but they all felt grubby and small beside the stately company at high table. There were a number of teachers, and the bursar, and an important-looking man called Lord Something-or-other, and tall, stringy Miss Cadwallader herself. Miss Cadwallader smiled at them graciously and pointed to three empty chairs at her left side. All of them instantly dived for the chair furthest away from Miss Cadwallader. Nan, much to her surprise, won it, and Charles won the chair in the middle, leaving Nirupam to sit beside Miss Cadwallader.

"Now we know that won't do, don't we?" said Miss Cadwallader. "We always sit with a gentleman on either side of a lady, don't we? Dulcimer must sit in the middle, and I'll have the gentleman I haven't yet met nearest me. Clive Morgan, isn't it? That's right."

Suddenly, Charles, Nan, and Nirupam changed places. They stood there, while Miss Cadwallader was saying grace, looking out over the heads of the rest of the school, not very far below, but far enough to make a lot of difference. Perhaps I'm going to faint, Nan thought hopefully. She still knew she was going to behave badly, but she felt very odd as well—and fainting was a fairly respectable way of behaving badly.

She was still conscious at the end of grace. She sat down with the rest, between the glowering Charles and Nirupam. Nirupam had gone pale yellow with dread. To their relief, Miss Cadwallader at once turned to the important lord and began making gracious conversation with him.

The ladies from the kitchen brought round a tray of little bowls and handed everybody one.

What was this? It was certainly not a usual part of school dinner. They looked suspiciously at the bowls. They were full of yellow stuff, not quite covering little pink things.

"I believe it may be prawns," Nirupam said dubiously. "For a starter."

Here Miss Cadwallader reached forth a gracious hand. Their heads at once craned round to see what implement she was going to eat out of the bowl with. Her hand picked up a fork. They picked up forks too. Nan poked hers cautiously into her bowl. Instantly she began to behave badly. She could not stop herself. "I think it's custard," she said loudly. "Do prawns mix with custard?" She put one of the pink things into her mouth. It felt rubbery. "Chewing gum?" she asked. "No, I think they're jointed worms. Worms in custard."

"Shut up!" hissed Nirupam.

"But it's not custard," Nan continued. She could hear her voice saying it, but there seemed no way to stop it. "The tongue-test proves that the yellow stuff has a strong taste of sour armpits, combined with—yes—just a touch of old drains. It comes from the bottom of a dustbin."

Charles glared at her. He felt sick. If he had dared, he would have stopped eating at once. But Miss Cadwallader continued gracefully forking up prawns—unless they really were jointed worms—and Charles did not dare do differently. He wondered how he was going to put this in his journal. He had never hated Nan Pilgrim particularly before, so he had no code-word for her. Prawn? Could he call her prawn? He choked down another worm—prawn, that was—and he wished he could push the whole bowlful in Nan's face.

"A clean yellow dustbin," Nan announced. "The kind they keep the dead fish for biology in."

"Prawns are eaten curried in India," Nirupam said loudly.

Nan knew he was trying to shut her up. With a great effort, by cramming several forkfuls of worms—prawns, that was—into her mouth at once, she managed to stop herself from talking. She could hardly bring herself to swallow the mouthful, but at least it kept her quiet. Most fervently, she hoped that the next course would be something ordinary, which she would not have any urge to describe, and so did Nirupam and Charles.

But alas! What came before them in platefuls next was one of the school kitchen's more peculiar dishes. They produced it about once a month and its official name was hot-pot. With it came tinned peas and tinned tomatoes. Charles's head and Nirupam's craned toward Miss

Cadwallader again to see what they were supposed to eat this with. Miss Cadwallader picked up a fork. They picked up forks too, and then craned a second time, to make sure that Miss Cadwallader was not going to pick up a knife as well and so make it easier for everyone. She was not. Her fork dove gracefully under a pile of tinned peas. They sighed, and found both their heads turning toward Nan then in a sort of horrified expectation.

They were not disappointed. As Nan levered loose the first greasy ring of potato, the urge to describe came upon her again. It was as if she was possessed. "Now the aim of this dish," she said, "is to use up leftovers. You take old potatoes and soak them in washing-up water that has been used at least twice. The water must be thoroughly scummy." It's like the gift of tongues! she thought. Only in my case it's the gift of foul-mouth. "Then you take a dirty old tin and rub it round with socks that have been worn for a fortnight. You fill this tin with alternate layers of scummy potatoes and catfood, mixed with anything else you happen to have. Old doughnuts and dead flies have been used in this case—"

Could his code-word for Nan be hot-pot? Charles wondered. It suited her. No, because they only had hot-pot once a month—fortunately—and, at this rate, he would need to hate Nan practically every day. Why didn't someone stop her? Couldn't Miss Cadwallader hear?

"Now these things," Nan continued, stabbing her fork into a tinned tomato, "are small creatures that have been killed and cleverly skinned. Notice, when you taste them, the slight, sweet savor of their blood—"

Nirupam uttered a small moan and went yellower than ever.

The sound made Nan look up. Hitherto, she had been staring at the table where her plate was, in a daze of terror. Now she saw Mr. Wentworth sitting opposite her across the table. He could hear her perfectly. She could tell from the expression on his face. Why doesn't he stop me? she thought. Why do they let me go on? Why doesn't somebody do something, like a thunderbolt strike me, or eternal detention? Why don't I get under the table and crawl away? And, all the time, she could hear herself talking. "These did in fact start life as peas. But they have since undergone a long and deadly process. They lie for six months in a sewer, absorbing fluids and rich tastes, which is why they are called processed peas. Then—"

Here, Miss Cadwallader turned gracefully to them. Nan, to her utter relief, stopped in mid-sentence. "You have all been long enough in the school by now," Miss Cadwallader said, "to know the town quite well. Do you know that lovely old house in High Street?"

They all three stared at her. Charles gulped down a ring of potato. "Lovely old house?"

"It's called the Old Gate House," said Miss Cadwallader. "It used to be part of the gate in the old town wall. A very lovely old brick building."

"You mean the one with a tower on top and windows like a church?" Charles asked, though he could not think why Miss Cadwallader should talk of this and not processed peas.

"That's the one," said Miss Cadwallader. "And it's such a shame. It's going to be pulled down to make way for a supermarket. You know it has a king-pin roof, don't you?"

"Oh," said Charles. "Has it?"

"And a queen-pin," said Miss Cadwallader.

Charles seemed to have got saddled with the conversation. Nirupam was happy enough not to talk, and Nan dared do no more than nod intelligently, in case she started describing the food again. As Miss Cadwallader talked, and Charles was forced to answer while trying to eat tinned tomatoes—no, they were *not* skinned mice!—using just a fork, Charles began to feel he was undergoing a particularly refined form of torture. He realized he needed a hate-word for Miss Cadwallader too. Hot-pot would do for her. Surely nothing as awful as this could happen to him more than once a month? But that meant he had still not got a code-word for Nan.

They took the hot-pot away. Charles had not eaten much. Miss Cadwallader continued to talk to him about houses in the town, then about stately homes in the country, until the pudding arrived. It was set before Charles, white and bleak and swimming, with little white grains in it like the corpses of ants—Lord, he was getting as bad as Nan Pilgrim! Then he realized it was the ideal word for Nan.

"Rice pudding!" he exclaimed.

"It *is* agreeable," Miss Cadwallader said, smiling. "And so nourishing." Then, incredibly, she reached to the top of her plate and picked up a fork. Charles stared. He waited. Surely Miss Cadwallader was not going to eat runny rice pudding with just a fork? But she was. She dipped the fork in and brought it up, raining weak white milk.

Slowly, Charles picked up a fork too and turned to meet Nan's and Nirupam's incredulous faces. It was just not possible.

Nirupam looked wretchedly down at his brimming plate. "There is a story in the *Arabian Nights,*" he said, "about a woman who ate rice with a pin, grain by grain." Charles shot a terrified look at Miss Cadwallader, but she was talking to the lord again. "She turned out to be a ghoul," Nirupam said. "She ate her fill of corpses every night."

Charles's terrified look shot to Nan instead. "Shut up, you fool! You'll set her off again!"

But the possession seemed to have left Nan by then. She was able to whisper, with her head bent over her plate so that only the boys could hear, "Mr. Wentworth's using his spoon. Look."

"Do you think we dare?" said Nirupam.

"I'm going to," said Charles. "I'm hungry."

So they all used their spoons. When the meal was at last over, they were all dismayed to find Mr. Wentworth beckoning. But it was only Nan he was beckoning. When she came reluctantly over, he said, "See me at four in my study." Which was, Nan felt, all she needed. And the day was still only half over.

CHAPTER 3

That afternoon, Nan came into the classroom to find a broom laid across her desk. It was an old tatty broom, with only the bare minimum of twigs left in the brush end, which the groundsman sometimes used to sweep the paths. Someone had brought it in from the groundsman's shed. Someone had tied a label to the handle: *Dulcinea's Pony*. Nan recognized the round, angelic writing as Theresa's.

Amid sniggers and titters, she looked round the assembled faces. Theresa would not have thought of stealing a broom on her own. Estelle? No. Neither Estelle nor Karen Grigg was there. No, it was Dan Smith, by the look on his face. Then she looked at Simon Silverson and was not so sure. It could not have been both of them because they never, ever did anything together.

Simon said to her, in his suavest manner, grinning all over his face, "Why don't you hop on and have a ride, Dulcinea?"

"Yes, go on. Ride it, Dulcinea," said Dan.

Next moment, everyone else was laughing and yelling at her to ride the broom. And Brian Wentworth, who was only too ready to torment other people when he was not being a victim himself, was leaping up and down in the gangway between the desks, screaming, "Ride, Dulcinea! Ride!"

Slowly, Nan picked up the broom. She was a mild and peaceable person who seldom lost her temper—perhaps that was her trouble—but when she did lose it, there was no knowing what she would do. As she picked up the broom, she thought she just meant to stand it haughtily against the wall. But, as her hands closed round its knobby handle, her temper left her completely. She turned round on the jeering, hooting crowd, filled with roaring rage. She lifted the broom high above her head and bared her teeth. Everyone thought that was funnier than ever.

Nan meant to smash the broom through Simon Silverson's laughing face. She meant to bash in Dan Smith's head. But, since Brian Wentworth was dancing and shrieking and making faces just in front of her, it was Brian she went for. Luckily for him, he saw the broom coming down and leaped clear. After that, he was forced to back away up the gangway and then into the space by the door, with his arms over his head, screaming for mercy, while Nan followed him, bashing like a madwoman.

"Help! Stop her!" Brian screamed, and backed into the door just as Miss Hodge came through it carrying a large pile of English books. Brian backed into her and sat down at her feet in a shower of books. "Ow!" he yelled.

"What is going on?" asked Miss Hodge.

The uproar in the room was cut off as if with a switch. "Get up, Brian," Simon Silverson said righteously. "It was your own fault for teasing Nan Pilgrim."

"Really! Nan!" said Theresa. She was genuinely shocked. "Temper, temper!"

At that, Nan nearly went for Theresa with the broom. Theresa was only saved by the fortunate arrival of Estelle Green and Karen Grigg. They came scurrying in with their heads guiltily lowered and their arms wrapped round bulky bags of knitting wool. "Sorry we're late, Miss Hodge," Estelle panted. "We had permission to go shopping."

Nan's attention was distracted. The wool in the bags was fluffy and white, just like Theresa's. Why on earth, Nan wondered scornfully, did everyone have to imitate Theresa?

Miss Hodge took the broom out of Nan's unresisting hands and propped it neatly behind the door. "Sit down, all of you," she said. She was very put out. She had intended to come quietly into a nice quiet classroom and galvanize 6B by confronting them with her scheme. And here they were galvanized already, *and* with a witch's broom. There was clearly no chance of catching the writer of the note or the witch by surprise. Still, she did not like to let a good scheme go to waste.

"I thought we would have a change today," she said, when everyone was settled. "Our poetry book doesn't seem to be going down very well, does it?" She looked brightly round the class; 6B looked back cautiously. Some of them felt anything would be better than being asked to find poems beautiful. Some of them felt it depended on what Miss Hodge intended to do instead. Of the rest, Nan was trying not to cry, Brian was licking a scratch on his arm, and Charles was glowering.

Charles liked poetry because the lines were so short. You could think your own thoughts in the spaces round the print.

"Today," said Miss Hodge, "I want you all to do something yourselves."

Everyone recoiled. Estelle put her hand up. "Please, Miss Hodge. I don't know how to write poems."

"Oh, I don't want you to do that," said Miss Hodge. Everyone relaxed. "I want you to act out some little plays for me." Everyone recoiled again. Miss Hodge took no notice and explained that she was going to call them out to the front in pairs, a boy and a girl in each, and every pair was going to act out the same short scene. "That way," she said, "we shall have fifteen different pocket dramas." By this time, most of 6B were staring at her in wordless despair. Miss Hodge smiled round them and prepared to galvanize them. Really, she thought, her scheme might go quite well after all. "Now, we must choose a subject for our playlets. It has to be something strong and striking, with passionate possibilities. Suppose we act a pair of lovers saying good-bye?" Somebody groaned, as Miss Hodge had known somebody would. "Very well. Who has a suggestion?"

Theresa's hand was up, and Dan Smith's.

"A television star and her admirer," said Theresa.

"A murderer and a policeman making him confess," said Dan. "Are we allowed to torture?"

"No, we are not," said Miss Hodge, at which Dan lost interest. "Anyone else?"

Nirupam raised a long thin arm. "A salesman deceiving a lady over a car."

Well, Miss Hodge thought, she had not really expected anyone to make a suggestion that would give them away. She pretended to consider. "We-ell, so far the most dramatic suggestion is Dan's. But I had in mind something really tense, which we all know about quite well."

"We all know about murder," Dan protested.

"Yes," said Miss Hodge. She was watching everyone like a hawk now. "But we know even more about stealing, say, or lying, or witchcraft, or—" She let herself notice the broomstick again, with a start of surprise. It came in handy after all. "I know! Let us suppose that one of the people in our little play is suspected of being a witch, and the other is an inquisitor. How about that?"

Nothing. Not a soul in 6B reacted, except Dan. "That's the same as my idea," he grumbled. "And it's no fun without torture."

Miss Hodge made Dan into suspect number one at once. "Then you begin, Dan," she said, "with Theresa. Which are you, Theresa—witch or inquisitor?"

"Inquisitor, Miss Hodge," Theresa said promptly.

"It's not fair!" said Dan. "I don't know what witches do!"

Nor did he, it was clear. And it was equally clear that Theresa had no more idea what inquisitors did. They stood woodenly by the blackboard. Dan stared at the ceiling, while Theresa stated, "You are a witch." Whereupon Dan told the ceiling, "No I am not." And they went on doing this until Miss Hodge told them to stop. Regretfully, she demoted Dan from first suspect to last, and put Theresa down there with him, and called up the next pair.

Nobody behaved suspiciously. Most people's idea was to get the acting over as quickly as possible. Some argued a little, for the look of the thing. Others tried running about to make things seem dramatic. And first prize for brevity certainly went to Simon Silverson and Karen Grigg. Simon said, "I know you're a witch, so don't argue."

And Karen replied, "Yes, I am. I give in. Let's stop now."

By the time it came to Nirupam, Miss Hodge's list of suspects was all bottom and no top. Then Nirupam put on a terrifying performance as inquisitor. His eyes blazed. His voice alternately roared and fell to a sinister whisper. He pointed fiercely at Estelle's face. "Look at your evil eyes!" he bellowed. Then he whispered, "I see you, I feel you, I know you—you *are* a witch!" Estelle was so frightened that she gave a real performance of terrified innocence. But Brian Wentworth's performance as a witch outshone even Nirupam. Brian wept, he cringed, he made obviously false excuses, and he ended kneeling at Delia Martin's feet, sobbing for mercy, and crying real tears.

Everyone was astonished, including Miss Hodge. She would dearly have liked to put Brian at the top of her list of suspects, as either the witch or the one who wrote the note. But how bothersome for her plans if she had to go to Mr. Wentworth and say it was Brian. No, she decided. There was no genuine feeling in Brian's performance, and the same went for Nirupam. They were both just good actors.

Then it was the turn of Charles and Nan. Charles had seen it coming for some time now, that he would be paired with Nan. He was very annoyed. He seemed to be haunted by her today. But he did not intend to let that stop his performance from being a triumph of comic acting. He was depressed by the lack of invention everyone except Nirupam had shown. Nobody had thought of making the inquisitor funny. "I'll be inquisitor," he said quickly.

But Nan was still smarting from the broomstick. She thought Charles was getting at her and glared at him. Charles, on principle, never let anyone glare at him without giving his nastiest double-barreled stare in return. So they shuffled to the front of the class looking daggers at one another.

There Charles beat at his forehead. "Emergency!" he exclaimed. "There are no witches for the autumn bonfires. I shall have to find an ordinary person instead." He pointed at Nan. "You'll do," he said. "Starting from now, you're a witch."

Nan had not realized that the acting had begun. Besides, she was too hurt and angry to care. "Oh, no, I'm not!" she snapped. "Why shouldn't you be the witch?"

"Because I can prove you're a witch," Charles said, trying to stick to his part. "Being an inquisitor, I can prove anything."

"In that case," said Nan, angrily ignoring the fine acting, "we'll both be inquisitors, and I'll prove you're a witch too! Why not? You have four of the most evil eyes I ever saw. And your feet smell."

All eyes turned to Charles's feet. Since he had been forced to run round the field in the shoes he was wearing now, they were still rather wet. And, being warmed through, they were indeed exuding a small but definite smell.

"Cheese," murmured Simon Silverson.

Charles looked angrily down at his shoes. Nan had reminded him that he was in trouble over his missing running shoes. And she had spoiled his acting. He hated her. He was in an ecstasy of hate again. "Worms and custard and dead mice!" he said. Everyone stared at him, mystified. "Tinned peas soaked in sewage!" Charles said, beside himself with hatred. "Potatoes in scum. I'm not surprised your name's Dulcinea. It suits you. You're quite disgusting!"

"And so are you!" Nan shouted back at him. "I bet it was you who did those birds in music yesterday!" This caused shocked gasps from the rest of 6B.

Miss Hodge listened, fascinated. This was real feeling all right. And *what* had Charles said? It was clear to her now why the rest of 6B had clustered so depressingly at the bottom of her list of suspects. Nan and Charles were at the top of it. It was obvious. They were always the odd ones out in 6B. Nan must have written the note, and Charles must be the witch in question. And now let Mr. Wentworth pour scorn on her scheme!

"Please, Miss Hodge, the bell's rung," called a number of voices.

The door opened and Mr. Crossley came in. When he saw Miss Hodge, which he had come early in order to do, his face became a deep red, most interesting to Estelle and Theresa. "Am I interrupting a lesson, Miss Hodge?"

"Not at all," said Miss Hodge. "We had just finished. Nan and Charles, go back to your places." And she swept out of the room, without appearing to notice that Mr. Crossley had leaped to hold the door open for her.

Miss Hodge hurried straight upstairs to Mr. Wentworth's study. She knew this news was going to make an impression on him. But there, to her annoyance, was Mr. Wentworth dashing downstairs with a box of chalk, very late for a lesson with 3A.

"Oh, Mr. Wentworth," panted Miss Hodge. "Can you spare a moment?"

"Not a second. Write me a memo if it's urgent," said Mr. Wentworth, dashing on down.

Miss Hodge reached out and seized his arm. "But you must! You know 6B and my scheme about the anonymous note—"

Mr. Wentworth swung round on the end of her clutching hands and looked up at her irritably. "What about what anonymous note?"

"My scheme worked!" Miss Hodge said. "Nan Pilgrim wrote it, I'm sure. You must see her—"

"I'm seeing her at four o'clock," said Mr. Wentworth. "If you think I need to know, write me a memo, Miss Hodge."

"Eileen," said Miss Hodge.

"Eileen who?" said Mr. Wentworth, trying to pull his arm away. "You mean two girls wrote this note?"

"My name is Eileen," said Miss Hodge, hanging on.

"Miss Hodge," said Mr. Wentworth, "3A will be breaking windows by now!"

"But there's Charles Morgan too!" Miss Hodge cried out, feeling his arm pulling out of her hands. "Mr. Wentworth, I swear that boy recited a spell! Worms and custard and scummy potatoes, he said. All sorts of nasty things."

Mr. Wentworth succeeded in tearing his arm loose and set off downstairs again. His voice came back to Miss Hodge. "Slugs and snails and puppy-dogs' tails. Write it all down, Miss Hodge."

"Bother!" said Miss Hodge. "But I *will* write it down. He *is* going to notice!" She went at once to the staff room, where she spent the rest of the lesson composing an account of her experiment, in writing almost as round and angelic as Theresa's.

Meanwhile, in the 6B classroom, Mr. Crossley shut the door behind Miss Hodge with a sigh. "Journals out," he said. He had come to a decision about the note, and he did not intend to let his feelings about Miss Hodge interfere with his duty. So, before anyone could start writing in a journal and make it impossible for him to interrupt, he made

6B a long and serious speech. He told them how malicious and sneaky and unkind it was to write anonymous accusations. He asked them to consider how they would feel if someone had written a note about them. Then he told them that someone in 6B had written just such a note.

"I'm not going to tell you what was in it," he said. "I shall only say it accused someone of a very serious crime. I want you all to think about it while you write your journals, and after you've finished, I want the person who wrote the note to write me another note confessing who they are and why they wrote it. That's all. I shan't punish the person. I just want them to see what a serious thing they have done."

Having said this, Mr. Crossley sat back to do some marking, feeling he had settled the matter in a most understanding way. In front of him, 6B picked up their pens. Thanks to Miss Hodge, everyone thought they knew exactly what Mr. Crossley meant.

29 October, wrote Theresa. *There is a witch in our class. Mr. Crossley just said so. He wants the witch to confess. Mr. Wentworth confiscated my knitting this morning and made jokes about it. I did not get it back till lunchtime. Estelle Green has started knitting now. What a copycat that girl is. Nan Pilgrim couldn't climb the ropes this morning and her name is Dulcinea. That made us laugh a lot.*

29.10.81. Mr. Crossley has just talked to us very seriously, Simon Silverson wrote, *very seriously, about a guilty person in our class. I shall do my best to bring that person to justice. If we don't catch them we might all be accused. This is off the record of course.*

Nan Pilgrim is a witch, Dan Smith wrote. *This is not a private thought because Mr. Crossley just told us. I think she is a witch too. She is even called after the famous witch, but I can't spell it. I hope they burn her where we can see.*

Mr. Crossley has been talking about serious accusations, Estelle wrote. *And Miss Hodge has been making us all accuse one another. It was quite frightening. I hope none of it is true. Poor Teddy went awfully red when he saw Miss Hodge but she scorned him again.*

While everyone else was writing the same sort of things, there were four people in the class who were writing something quite different.

Nirupam wrote, *Today, no comment. I shall not even think about high table.*

Brian Wentworth, oblivious to everything, scribbled down how he would get from Timbuktu to Uttar Pradesh by bus, allowing time for roadworks on Sundays.

Nan sat for a considerable while wondering what to write. She wanted desperately to get some of today off her chest, but she could not at first think how to do it without saying something personal. At last she wrote, in burning indignation, *I do not know if 6B is average or not, but this is how they are. They are divided into girls and boys with an invisible line down the middle of the room and people only cross that line when teachers make them. Girls are divided into real girls (Theresa Mullett) and imitations (Estelle Green). And me. Boys are divided into real boys (Simon Silverson), brutes (Daniel Smith), and unreal boys (Nirupam Singh). And Charles Morgan. And Brian Wentworth. What makes you a real girl or boy is that no one laughs at you. If you are imitation or unreal, the rules give you a right to exist provided you do what the real ones or brutes say. What makes you into me or Charles Morgan is that the rules allow all the girls to be better than me and all the boys better than Charles Morgan. They are allowed to cross the invisible line to prove this. Everyone is allowed to cross the invisible line to be nasty to Brian Wentworth.*

Nan paused here. Up to then she had been writing almost as if she was possessed the way she had been at lunch. Now she had to think about Brian Wentworth. What was it about Brian that put him below even her? *Some of Brian's trouble,* she wrote, *is that Mr. Wentworth is his father, and he is small and perky and irritating with it. Another part is that Brian is really good at things and comes top in most things, and he ought to be the real boy, not Simon. But SS is so certain he is the real boy that he has managed to convince Brian too.* That, Nan thought, was still not quite it, but it was as near as she could get. The rest of her description of 6B struck her as masterly. She was so pleased with it that she almost forgot she was miserable.

Charles wrote, *I got up, I got up, I GOT UP.* That made it look as if he had sprung eagerly out of bed, which was certainly not the case, but he had so hated today that he had to work it off somehow. *My running shoes got buried in cornflakes. I felt very hot running round the field and on top of that I had lunch on high table. I do not like rice pudding. We have had games with Miss Hodge and rice pudding and there are still about a hundred years of today to go.* And that, he thought, about summed it up.

When the bell rang, Mr. Crossley hurried to pick up the books he had been marking in order to get to the staff room before Miss Hodge left it. And stared. There was another note under the pile of books. It was written in the same capitals and the same blue ballpoint as the first note. It said: *HA HA. THOUGHT I WAS GOING TO TELL YOU. DIDN'T YOU?*

Now what do I do? wondered Mr. Crossley.

CHAPTER 4

At the end of lessons, there was the usual stampede to be elsewhere. Theresa and her friends, Delia, Heather, Deborah, Julia, and the rest, raced to the lower school girls' playroom to grab the radiators there, so that they could sit on them and knit. Estelle and Karen hurried to get the chillier radiators in the corridor, and sat on them to cast on their stitches. Simon led his friends to the labs, where they added to Simon's collection of honor marks by helping tidy up. Dan Smith left his friends to play football without him, because he had business in the shrubbery, watching the senior boys meeting their senior girl friends there. Charles crawled reluctantly to the locker room to look for his running shoes again. Nan went, equally reluctantly, up to Mr. Wentworth's study.

There was someone else in with Mr. Wentworth when she got there. She could hear voices and see two misty shapes through the wobbly glass in the door. Nan did not mind. The longer the interview was put off the better. So she hung about in the passage for nearly twenty minutes, until a passing monitor asked her what she was doing there.

"Waiting to see Mr. Wentworth," Nan said. Then, of course, in order to prove it to the monitor, she was forced to knock at the door.

"Come in!" bawled Mr. Wentworth.

The monitor, placated, passed on down the passage. Nan put out her hand to open the door, but, before she could, it was pulled open by Mr. Wentworth himself and Mr. Crossley came out, rather red and laughing sheepishly.

"I still swear it wasn't there when I put the books down," he said.

"Ah, but you know you didn't look, Harold," Mr. Wentworth said. "Our practical joker relied on your not looking. Forget it, Harold. So there you are, Nan. Did you lose your way here? Come on in. Mr. Crossley's just going."

He went back to his desk and sat down. Mr. Crossley hovered for a moment, still rather red, and then hurried away downstairs, leaving Nan to shut the door. As she did so, she noticed that Mr. Wentworth was staring at three pieces of paper on his desk as if he thought they might bite him. She saw that one was in Miss Hodge's writing and that the other two were scraps of paper with blue capital letters on them, but she was much too worried on her own account to bother about pieces of writing.

"Explain your behavior at high table," Mr. Wentworth said to her.

Since there really was no explanation that Nan could see, she said, in a miserable whisper, "I can't, sir," and looked down at the parquet floor.

"Can't?" said Mr. Wentworth. "You put Lord Mulke off his lunch for no reason at all! Tell me another. Explain yourself."

Miserably, Nan fitted one of her feet exactly into one of the parquet oblongs in the floor. "I don't know, sir. I just said it."

"You don't know, you just said it," said Mr. Wentworth. "Do you mean by that that you found yourself speaking without knowing you were?"

This was meant to be sarcasm, Nan knew. But it seemed to be true as well. Carefully, she fitted her other shoe into the parquet block which slanted toward her first foot, and stood unsteadily, toe to toe, while she wondered how to explain. "I didn't know what I was going to say next, sir."

"Why not?" demanded Mr. Wentworth.

"I don't know," Nan said. "It was like—like being possessed."

"*Possessed!*" shouted Mr. Wentworth. It was the way he shouted just before he suddenly threw chalk at people. Nan went backward to avoid the chalk which came next. But she forgot that her feet were pointing inward and sat down heavily on the floor. From there, she could see Mr. Wentworth's surprised face, peering at her over the top of his desk. "What did that?" he said.

"Please don't throw chalk at me!" Nan said.

At that moment, there was a knock at the door and Brian Wentworth put his head round it into the room. "Are you free yet, Dad?"

"No," said Mr. Wentworth.

Both of them looked at Nan sitting on the floor. "What's she doing?" Brian asked.

"She says she's possessed. Go away and come back in ten minutes," Mr. Wentworth said. "Get up, Nan."

Brian obediently shut the door and went away. Nan struggled to her feet. It was almost as difficult as climbing a rope. She wondered a little how it felt to be Brian, with your father one of the teachers, but mostly she wondered what Mr. Wentworth was going to do to her. He had on his most harrowed, worried look, and he was staring again at the three papers on his desk.

"So you think you're possessed?" he said.

"Oh no," Nan said. "All I meant was it was *like* it. I knew I was going to do something awful before I started, but I didn't know what until I started describing the food. Then I tried to stop and I couldn't somehow."

"Do you often get taken that way?" Mr. Wentworth asked. Nan was about to answer indignantly No, when she realized that she had gone for Brian with the witch's broom in exactly the same way straight after lunch. And many and many a time, she had impulsively written things in her journal. She fitted her shoe into a parquet block again, and hastily took it away. "Sometimes," she said, in a low, guilty mutter. "I do sometimes—when I'm angry with people—I write what I think in my journal."

"And do you write notes to teachers too?" asked Mr. Wentworth.

"Of course not," said Nan. "What would be the point?"

"But someone in 6B has written Mr. Crossley a note," said Mr. Wentworth. "It accused someone in the class of being a witch."

The serious, worried way he said it made Nan understand at last. So that was why Mr. Crossley had talked like that and then been to see Mr. Wentworth. And they thought Nan had written the note. "The unfairness!" she burst out. "How *can* they think I wrote the note *and* call me a witch too! Just because my name's Dulcinea!"

"You could be diverting suspicion from yourself," Mr. Wentworth pointed out. "If I asked you straight out—"

"I am *not* a witch!" said Nan. "And I didn't write that note. I bet that was Theresa Mullett or Simon Silverson. They're both born accusers! Or Daniel Smith," she added.

"Now, I wouldn't have picked on Dan," Mr. Wentworth said. "I wasn't aware he could write."

The sarcastic way he said that showed Nan that she ought not to have mentioned Theresa or Simon. Like everyone else, Mr. Wentworth thought of them as the real girl and the real boy. "Someone accused *me*," she said bitterly.

"Well, I'll take your word for it that you didn't write the note," Mr. Wentworth said. "And next time you feel a possession coming on, take a deep breath and count up to ten, or you may be in serious trouble.

You have a very unfortunate name, you see. You'll have to be very careful in future. How did you come to be called Dulcinea? Were you called after the Archwitch?"

"Yes," Nan admitted. "I'm descended from her."

Mr. Wentworth whistled. "And you're a witch-orphan too, aren't you? I shouldn't let anyone else know that, if I were you. I happen to admire Dulcinea Wilkes for trying to stop witches being persecuted, but very few other people do. Keep your mouth shut, Nan—and don't ever describe food in front of Lord Mulke again either. Off you go now."

Nan fumbled her way out of the study and plunged down the stairs. Her eyes were so fuzzy with indignation that she could hardly see where she was going. "What does he take me for?" she muttered to herself as she went. "I'd rather admit to being descended from—from Attila the Hun or—or Guy Fawkes. Or anyone."

It was around that time that Mr. Towers, who had stood over Charles while Charles hunted unavailingly for his running shoes in the boys' locker room, finally smothered a long yawn and left Charles to go on looking by himself. "Bring them to me in the staff room when you've found them," he said.

Charles sat down on a bench, alone among gray lockers and green walls. He glowered at the slimy gray floor and the three odd football boots that always lay in one corner. He looked at nameless garments withering on pegs. He sniffed the smell of sweat and old socks. "I hate everything," he said. He had searched everywhere. Dan Smith had found a really cunning place for those shoes. The only way Charles was going to find them was by Dan telling him where they were.

Charles ground his teeth and stood up. "All right. Then I'll ask him," he said. Like everyone else, he knew Dan was in the shrubbery spying on seniors. Dan made no secret of it. He had got his uncle to send him a pair of binoculars so that he could get a really close view. And the shrubbery was only round the corner from the locker room. Charles thought he could risk going there, even if Mr. Towers suddenly came back. The real risk was from the seniors in the shrubbery. There was an invisible line round the shrubbery, just like the one Nan had described between the boys and the girls in 6B. Anyone younger than a senior who got found in the shrubbery could be most thoroughly beaten up by the senior who found them. Still, Charles thought, as he set off, Dan was not a senior either. That should help.

The shrubbery was a messy tangle of huge evergreen bushes, with wet grass in between. Charles's almost-dry shoes were soaked again before he found Dan. He found him quite quickly. Since it was a cold evening and the grass was so wet, there were only two pairs of seniors there, and they were all in the most trodden part, on either side of a mighty laurel bush. Ah! thought Charles. He crept to the laurel bush and pushed his face in among the wet and shiny leaves. Dan was there, among the dry branches inside.

"Dan!" whispered Charles.

Dan took his binoculars from his eyes with a jerk and whirled round. When he saw Charles's face leaning in among the leaves at him, beaming its nastiest double-barreled glare, he seemed almost relieved. "Pig off!" he whispered. "Magic out of here!"

"What have you done with my spikes?" said Charles.

"Whisper, can't you?" Dan whispered. He peered nervously through the leaves at the nearest pair of seniors. Charles could see them too. They were a tall, thin boy and a very fat girl—much fatter than Nan Pilgrim—and they did not seem to have heard anything. Charles could see the thin boy's fingers digging into the girl's fat where his arm was round her. He wondered how anyone could enjoy grabbing, or watching, such fatness.

"Where have you hidden my spikes?" he whispered.

But Dan did not care, as long as the seniors had not heard. "I've forgotten," he whispered. Beyond the bush, the thin boy leaned his head against the fat girl's head. Dan grinned. "See that? Mixing the breed." He put his binoculars to his eyes again.

Charles spoke a little louder. "Tell me where you've put my spikes, or I'll shout that you're here."

"Then they'll know you're here too, won't they?" Dan whispered. "I told you, magic off!"

"Not till you tell me," said Charles.

Charles saw that he had no option but to raise a yell and fetch the seniors into the bush. While he was wondering whether he dared, the second pair of seniors came hurrying round the laurel bush. "Hey!" said the boy. "There's some juniors in that bush. Sue heard them whispering."

"Right!" said the thin boy and the fat girl. And all four seniors dived at the bush.

Charles let out a squawk of terror and ran. Behind him, he heard cracking branches, leaves swishing, grunts, crunchings, and most unladylike threats from the senior girls. He hoped Dan had been caught. But even while he was hoping, he knew Dan had gotten away. Charles was in the open. The seniors had seen him and it was Charles they were after. He burst out of the shrubbery with all four of them after him. With a finger across his nose to hold his glasses on, he pelted for his life round the corner of the school.

There was nothing in front of him but a long wall and open space. The lower school door was a hundred yards away. The only possible place that was any nearer was the open door of the boys' locker room. Charles bolted through it without thinking. And skidded to a stop, realizing what a fool he had been. The seniors' feet were hammering round the corner, and the only way out of the locker room was the open door he had come in by. All Charles could think of was to dodge behind that door and stand there flat against the wall, hoping. There he stood, flattened and desperate, breathing in old sock and mildew and trying not to pant, while four pairs of feet slid to a stop outside the door.

"He's hiding in there," said the fat girl's voice.

"We can't go in. It's boys'," said the other girl. "You two go and bring him out."

There were breathless grunts from the two boys, and two pairs of heavy feet tramped in through the doorway. The thin boy, by the sound, tramped into the middle of the room. His voice rumbled round the concrete space.

"Where's he gotten to?"

"Must be behind the door," rumbled the other. The door was pulled aside. Charles stood petrified at the sight of the senior it revealed. This one was huge. He towered over Charles. He even had a sort of moustache. Charles shook with terror.

But the little angry eyes, high up above the moustache, stared down through Charles, seemingly at the floor and the wall. The bulky face twitched in annoyance. "Nope," said the senior. "Nothing here."

"He must have made it to the lower school door," said the thin boy.

"Magicking little witch!" said the other.

And, to Charles's utter amazement, the two of them tramped out of the locker room. There was some annoyed exclaiming from the two girls outside, and then all four of them seemed to be going away. Charles stood where he was, shaking, for quite a while after they seemed to have gone. He was sure it was a trick. But, five minutes later, they had still not come back. It was a miracle of some kind!

Charles tottered out into the middle of the room, wondering just what kind of miracle it was that could make a huge senior look straight through you. Now he knew it had happened, Charles was sure the senior had not been pretending. He really had not seen Charles standing there.

"So what did it?" Charles asked the nameless hanging clothes. "Magic?"

He meant it to be a scornful question, the kind of thing you say when you give the whole thing up. But, somehow, it was not. As he said it, a huge, terrible suspicion which had been gathering, almost unnoticed, at the back of Charles's head, like a headache coming on, now swung to the front of his mind, like a headache already there. Charles began shaking again.

"No," he said. "It wasn't that. It was something else!"

But the suspicion, now it was there, demanded to be sent away at once, now, completely. "All right," Charles said. "I'll prove it. I know how. I hate Dan Smith anyway."

He marched up to Dan's locker and opened it. He looked at the jumble of clothes and shoes inside. He had searched his locker twice now. He had searched all of them twice. He was sick of looking in lockers. He took up Dan's spiked running shoes, one in each hand, and backed away with them to the middle of the room.

"Now," he said to the shoes, "you vanish." He tapped them together, sole to spiked sole, to make it clear to them. "Vanish," he said. "Abracadabra." And, when nothing happened, he threw both shoes into the air, to give them every chance. "Hey presto," he said.

Both shoes were gone, in midair, before they reached the slimy floor.

Charles stared at the spot where he had last seen them. "I didn't mean it," he said hopelessly. "Come back."

Nothing happened. No shoes appeared.

"Oh well," said Charles. "Perhaps I did mean it."

Then, very gently, almost reverently, he went over and shut Dan's locker. The suspicion was gone. But the certainty which hung over Charles in its place was so heavy and so hideous that it made him want to crouch on the floor. He was a witch. He would be hunted like the witch he had helped and burned like the fat one. It would hurt. It would be horrible. He was very, very scared—so scared it was like being dead already, cold, heavy, and almost unable to breathe.

Trying to pull himself together, he took his glasses off to clean them. That made him notice that he was, actually, crouching on the floor beside Dan's locker. He dragged himself upright. What should he do? Might not the best thing be to get it over now, and go straight to Miss Cadwallader and confess?

That seemed an awful waste, but Charles could not seem to think of anything else to do. He shuffled to the door and out into the chilly evening. He had always known he was wicked, he thought. Now it was proved. The witch had kissed him because she had known he was evil too. Now he had grown so evil that he needed to be stamped out. He wouldn't give the inquisitors any trouble, not like some witches did. Witchcraft must show all over him anyway. Someone had already noticed and written that note about it. Nan Pilgrim had accused him of conjuring up all those birds in music yesterday. Charles thought he must have done that without knowing he had, just as he had made himself invisible to the seniors just now. He wondered how strong a witch he was. Were you more wicked, the stronger you were? Probably. But weak or powerful, you were burned just the same. And he was in nice time for the autumn bonfires. It was nearly Halloween now. By the time they had legally proved him a witch, it would be November 5, and that would be the end of it.

He did not know it was possible to feel so scared and hopeless.

Thinking and thinking, in a haze of horror, Charles shuffled his way to Miss Cadwallader's room. He stood outside the door and waited, without even the heart to knock. Minutes passed. The door opened. Seeing the misty oblong of bright light, Charles braced himself.

"So you didn't find them?" said Mr. Towers.

Charles jumped. Though he could not see what Mr. Towers was doing here, he said, "No, sir."

"I'm not surprised, if you took your glasses off to look," said Mr. Towers.

Tremulously, Charles hooked his glasses over his ears. They were ice cold. He must have had them in his hand ever since he took them off to clean. Now that he could see, he saw he was standing outside the staff room, not Miss Cadwallader's room at all. Why was that? Still he could just as easily confess to Mr. Towers. "Please, I deserve to be punished, sir. I—"

"Take a black mark for that," Mr. Towers said coldly. "I don't like boys who crawl. Now, either you can pay for a new pair of shoes, or you can write five hundred lines every night until the end of the term. Come to me tomorrow morning and tell me which you decide to do. Now get out of here."

He slammed the door of the staff room in Charles's face. Charles stood and looked at it. That was a fierce choice Mr. Towers had given him. And a black mark. But it had jolted his horror off sideways somehow. He felt his face going red. What a fool he was! Nobody knew he was a witch. Instinct had told him this, and taken his feet to the staff room instead of to Miss Cadwallader. But only luck had saved him confessing to Mr. Towers. He had better not be that stupid again. As long as he kept his mouth shut and worked no more magic, he would be perfectly safe. He almost smiled as he trudged off to supper.

But he could not stop thinking about it. Round and round and round, all through supper. How wicked was he? Could he do anything about it? Was it enough just not to do any magic? Could you go somewhere and be de-magicked, like clothes were dry-cleaned? If not, and he was found out, was it any use running away? Where did witches run to, after they had run through people's backyards? Was there any certain way of being safe?

"Oh magic!" someone exclaimed, just beside him. "I left my book in the playroom!" Charles jumped and hummed, like the school gong when it was hit, at the mere word.

"Don't swear," said the monitor in charge.

Then Theresa Mullett, from the end of the table, called out in a way that was not quite jeering, "Nan, won't you do something interesting and miraculous for us? We know you can." Charles jumped and hummed again.

"No, I can't," said Nan.

But Theresa, and Delia Martin too, kept on asking. "Nan, high table's got some lovely bananas. Won't you say a spell and fetch them over?"

"Nan, I feel like some ice cream. Conjure some up."

"Nan, do you really worship the devil?"

Each time they said any of these things, Charles jumped and hummed. Though he knew it was entirely to his advantage to have everyone think Nan Pilgrim was the witch, he wanted to scream at the girls to stop. He was very relieved, halfway through supper, when Nan jumped up and stormed out of the dining room.

Nan went straight to the deserted library. Very well, she thought. If everyone was so sure she was guilty, she could at least take advantage of it and do something she had always wanted to do and never dared to do before. She took down the encyclopedia and looked up Dulcinea Wilkes. Curiously enough, the fat book fell open at that page. It seemed as if a lot of people at Larwood House had taken an interest in the Archwitch. If so, they had all been as disappointed as Nan. The laws against witchcraft were so severe that most information about Nan's famous ancestress was banned. The entry was quite short.

WILKES, DULCINEA. 1760–1790. Notorious witch, known as the Archwitch. Born in Steeple Bumpstead, Essex, she moved to London in 1781, where she soon became well known for her nightly broomstick flights round St. Paul's and the Houses of Parliament. Brooms are still sometimes call "Dulcinea's Ponies." Dulcinea took a leading part in the Witches' Uprising of 1789. She was arrested and burned, along with the otber leaders. While she was burning, it is said that the lead on the roof of St. Paul's melted and ran off the dome. She continued to be burned in effigy every bonfire day until 1845, when the practice was discontinued owing to the high price of lead.

Nan sighed and put the encyclopedia back. When the bell rang, she went slowly to the classroom to do the work that had been set during the day. It was called devvy at Larwood House; no one knew why. Everyone else was there when Nan arrived. The room was full of the slap of exercise books around Brian Wentworth's head and Brian squealing. But the noise stopped as Nan came in, showing that Mr. Crossley had come in behind her.

"Charles Morgan," said Mr. Crossley. "Mr. Wentworth wants to see you."

Charles dragged his mind with a jolt from imaginary flames whirling round him. He got up and trudged off, like a boy in a dream, along corridors and through swinging doors to the part of the school where teachers who lived in the school had their private rooms. He had only been to Mr. Wentworth's room once before. He had to tear his mind away from thoughts of burning and look at the names on the doors. He supposed Mr. Wentworth wanted him because of his beastly shoes. Blast and magic Dan Smith! He knocked on the door.

"Come in!" said Mr. Wentworth.

He was sitting in an armchair smoking a pipe. The room was full of strong smoke. Charles was surprised to see how shabby Mr. Wentworth's room was. The armchair was worn out. There were holes in the soles of Mr. Wentworth's slippers, and holes in the hearthrug the slippers rested on. But the gas fire was churring away comfortably and the room was beautifully warm compared with the rest of school.

"Ah, Charles." Mr. Wentworth laid his pipe in an ashtray that looked like Brian's first attempt at pottery. "Charles, I was told this afternoon that you might be a witch."

CHAPTER 5

Charles had thought, in the locker room, that he had been as frightened as a person could possibly be. Now he discovered this was not so. Mr. Wentworth's words seemed to hit him heavy separate blows. Under the blows, Charles felt as if he were dissolving and falling away somewhere far, far below. He thought at first he was falling somewhere so sickeningly deep that the whole of his mind had become one long horrible scream. Then he felt he was rising up as he screamed. The shabby room was blurred and swaying, but Charles could have sworn he was now looking down on it from somewhere near the ceiling. He seemed to be hanging there, screaming, looking down on the top of his own head, and the slightly bald top of Mr. Wentworth's head, and the smoke writhing from the pipe in the ashtray. And that terrified him too. He must have divided into two parts. Mr. Wentworth was bound to notice.

To his surprise, the part of himself left standing on the worn carpet answered Mr. Wentworth quite normally. He heard his own voice, with just the right amount of amazement and innocence, saying, "Who, me? I'm not a witch, sir."

"I didn't say you were, Charles," Mr. Wentworth replied. "I just said someone said you were. From the account I was given, you had a public row with Nan Pilgrim, in the course of which you spoke of worms and dead mice, and a number of other unpleasant things."

The part of Charles left standing on the carpet answered indignantly, "Well I did. But I was only saying some of the things *she* said at lunch. You were there, sir. Didn't you hear her, sir?" Meanwhile, the part of Charles hovering near the ceiling was thanking whatever lucky stars looked after witches that Mr. Wentworth had chanced to sit opposite Nan Pilgrim at high table.

"I did," said Mr. Wentworth. "I recognized your reference at once. But my informant thought you were reciting a spell."

"But I wasn't, sir," protested the part of Charles on the carpet.

"But you sounded as if you were," Mr. Wentworth said. "You can't be too careful, Charles, in these troubled times. It sounds as if I'd better explain the position to you."

He picked up his pipe to help him in the explanation. In the way of pipes, it had gone out by then. Mr. Wentworth struck matches and puffed, and struck more matches and puffed. Smoke does not seem to mean fire where pipes are concerned. Mr. Wentworth used ten matches before the pipe was alight. As Charles watched, it dawned on him that Mr. Wentworth did not think he was a witch. Nor did Mr. Wentworth seem to have noticed the odd way he had split into two. Perhaps the part of him hovering near the ceiling was imaginary, and simply due to panic. As Charles thought this, he found the part of him near the ceiling slowly descending into the part of him standing normally on the carpet. By the time Mr. Wentworth risked putting his pipe out again by pressing the matchbox down on it, Charles found himself in one piece. He was still fizzing all over with terror, it is true, but he was feeling nothing like so peculiar.

"Now, Charles," said Mr. Wentworth. "You know witchcraft has always been illegal. But I think it's true to say that the laws against it have never been as strict as they are now. You've heard of the Witches' Uprising of course, in 1789, under the Archwitch Dulcinea Wilkes?"

Charles nodded. Everyone knew about Dulcinea. It was like being asked if you knew about Guy Fawkes.

"Now that," said Mr. Wentworth, "was a respectable sort of uprising in its way. The witches were protesting against being persecuted and burned. Dulcinea said, reasonably enough, that they couldn't help being born the way they were, and they didn't want to be killed for something they couldn't help. She kept promising that witches would use their powers only for good, if people would stop burning them. Dulcinea wasn't at all the awful creature everyone says, you know. She was young and pretty and clever—but she had a terribly hot temper. When people wouldn't agree not to burn witches, she lost her temper and worked a number of huge and violent spells. That was a mistake. It made people absolutely terrified of witchcraft, and when the uprising was put down, there were an awful lot of bonfires and some really strict laws. But you'll know all that."

Charles nodded again. Apart from the fact that he had been taught that Dulcinea was an evil old hag, and a stupid one, this was what everyone knew.

"But," said Mr. Wentworth, pointing his pipe at Charles, "what you may not know is that there was another, much more unpleasant uprising, just before you were born. Surprised? Yes, I thought you were. It was hushed up rather. The witches leading it were all unpleasant people, and their aim was to take over the country. The main conspirators were all civil servants and army generals, and the leader was a cabinet minister. You can imagine how scared and shocked everyone was at that."

"Yes, sir," said Charles. He had almost stopped being frightened by now. He found himself trying to imagine the prime minister as a witch. It was an interesting idea.

Mr. Wentworth put his pipe in his mouth and puffed out smoke expressively. "The minister was burned in Trafalgar Square," he said. "And Parliament passed the Witchcraft Emergency Act in an effort to stamp out witches for good. That act, Charles, is still in force today. It gives the inquisitors enormous powers. They can arrest someone on the mere suspicion of witchcraft—even if they're only your age, Charles."

"My age?" Charles said hoarsely.

"Yes. Witches keep on being born," said Mr. Wentworth. "And it was discovered that the minister's family had known he was a witch since he was eleven years old. A lot of research has been done since on witches. There are a hundred different kinds of witch-detectors. But most of the research has been toward discovering when witches first come into their powers, and it seems that most witches start at around your age, Charles. So, these days, the inquisitors keep a special eye on all schools. And a school like this one, where at least half the pupils are witch-orphans anyway, is going to attract their notice at once. Understand?"

"No, sir," said Charles. "Why are you telling me?"

"Someone thought you recited a spell," Mr. Wentworth said. "Think, boy! If I hadn't happened to know what you were really saying, you'd be under arrest by now. So now you'll have to be extra specially careful. Now do you see?"

"Yes, sir," said Charles. He was almost frightened again.

"Then off you go, back to devvy," said Mr. Wentworth. Charles turned round and trudged over the threadbare carpet to the door. "And Charles," called Mr. Wentworth. Charles turned round. "Take a black mark to remind you to be careful," said Mr. Wentworth.

Charles opened the door. Two black marks in one evening! If you got three black marks in a week, you went to Miss Cadwallader and were in real trouble. Two black marks! Both for things which were not his fault! Charles turned round while he was closing the door and directed the full force of his nastiest double-barreled glare at Mr. Wentworth. He was seething.

He trudged up the corridor to the swinging door, still seething. The swinging door swung as he reached it, and, to his surprise, Miss Hodge came through it. Miss Hodge did not live in school. As Estelle had speedily found out and told everyone, she lived with her old father in town. She was not usually here in the evenings at all.

"Charles!" said Miss Hodge. "How convenient! Have you been seeing Mr. Wentworth?"

It did not occur to Charles to wonder how Miss Hodge knew that. In his experience, teachers always knew far too much anyway. "Yes," he said.

"Then you can tell me which his room is," said Miss Hodge.

Charles pointed out the room and applied his shoulder to the swinging door. He had just forced his way out into the corridor beyond, when it swung again and again let Miss Hodge through.

"Charles, are you sure Mr. Wentworth was there? He didn't answer when I knocked."

"He was sitting by his fire," Charles said.

"Then perhaps I knocked at the wrong door," Miss Hodge said. "Can you come and show me? Would you mind very much?"

Yes, I would mind, Charles thought. He sighed and went back through the swinging door with Miss Hodge. Miss Hodge seemed pleased to have his company, which surprised him a little.

Miss Hodge was thinking how fortunate it was she had met Charles. Since the afternoon, she had been thinking carefully. And she saw that her next and most certain move toward marrying Mr. Wentworth was to go to him and impulsively take back her accusation against Charles. It was unpleasant to think of anyone being burned, even if Charles did have the most evil glare of any boy she knew. She would look so generous. And here she was, actually with Charles, to prove she bore him no malice.

Charles looked at Mr. Wentworth's name on the door and wondered how Miss Hodge could have gotten the wrong room.

"Oh," said Miss Hodge. "It was the right door. That's his name."

She knocked, and knocked again, with golden visions of her romance with Mr. Wentworth growing as, together, they tried to protect Charles from the clutches of the inquisitors. But there was no answer from the room. She turned to Charles in perplexity.

"Maybe he's gone to sleep," Charles said. "It was warm in there."

"Suppose we open the door and take a peep?" Miss Hodge said, fluttering a little.

"You do it," said Charles.

"No, you," said Miss Hodge. "I'll take all responsibility."

Charles sighed, and opened Mr. Wentworth's door for the second time that evening. A gust of cold, smoky air blew in their faces. The room was dark, except for a faint glow from the cooling gas fire. Even that vanished when Miss Hodge imperiously switched on the light and stood fanning the smoke away from her.

"Dear, dear," she said, looking round. "That man needs a woman's hand here. Are you sure he was here, Charles?"

"Just this minute," Charles said doggedly, but horror was beginning to descend on him. It was almost as if Mr. Wentworth had never been. He walked over to the bald patch of carpet in front of the fire and felt the fire. It was quite hot. Mr. Wentworth's pipe was lying in the pottery ashtray still, and that was warm too, but cooling in the icy air from the open window. Perhaps, Charles thought hopefully, Mr. Wentworth had just felt tired and gone to bed. There was a door in the opposite wall, beyond the blowing curtains of the window, which was probably the door to his bedroom.

But Miss Hodge boldly walked over and opened that door. It was a cupboard, stuffed with schoolbooks. "He didn't go this way," she said. "Has he a bedroom along the corridor, do you know?"

"He must have," said Charles. But he knew Mr. Wentworth had not gone down the corridor. He could not have come out of this room without Charles seeing him as he went to the swinging door, or Miss Hodge seeing him as she pushed past Charles the other way. There was only one other possibility. Charles had looked daggers at Mr. Wentworth. He had given him his very nastiest glare. And that glare had caused Mr. Wentworth to disappear, just as Dan's running shoes had disappeared. It was what they called the Evil Eye.

"I don't think there's any point in waiting," Miss Hodge said discontentedly. "Oh well. I can speak to him tomorrow."

Charles was only too glad to go. He was only too glad to accompany Miss Hodge down to the door where she had left her bicycle. He talked to her most politely all the way. It kept his mind off what he had done. And he thought that if he talked hard enough and made himself truly charming, Miss Hodge might not realize that Charles had been the last person to set eyes on Mr. Wentworth.

They talked of poems, football, bicycles, the caretaker's dog, and Mr. Hodge's garden. The result was that Miss Hodge mounted her bicycle and rode off, thinking that Charles Morgan was a very nice child once you got to know him. It made it all the better that she intended to withdraw her accusation against him. A teacher, she told herself, should always try to get to know her pupils.

Charles puffed out a big sigh of relief and trudged off again, weighted with new guilt. By the time he reached the classroom, nearly all the others had finished their work and were trooping off to choir practice. Charles had the room to himself, apart from Nan Pilgrim, who also seemed to be behindhand. They did not speak to one another, of course, but it was doubtful that either did much work. Nan was thinking miserably that if only she *was* a witch like Dulcinea Wilkes, she would not mind what anyone said. Charles was thinking about Mr. Wentworth.

First the birds in music, now Mr. Wentworth. Being invisible to the senior didn't count, because no one knew about that. What terrified Charles was that he would seem to keep using witchcraft by accident, where it showed. If only he could stop himself doing that, then he still might have a chance. Miss Hodge might give him an alibi over Mr. Wentworth, if he went on being nice to her. But how did you stop yourself working magic?

"This has been an awful day," Nan said, as she packed up to leave. "I'm so glad it's nearly over."

Charles stared at her, wondering how she knew. Then he packed up and left too. He was very much afraid that today was not over for him yet, by a long way. He had heard the inquisitors usually came for you in the night. So they would come for him, as soon as someone discovered Mr. Wentworth was missing. Charles thought about Mr. Wentworth all the time he was washing. He had rather liked Mr. Wentworth on the whole. He felt very bad about him. Perhaps the way to stop himself doing it again, to Mr. Crossley or someone, was to think hard about how it felt to be burned. It would hurt.

It hurts to be burned, he repeated to himself as he undressed. *It hurts to be burned.* He was shivering as he climbed into bed, and not only from the cold air in the long Spartan dormitory.

Brian Wentworth was being beaten up again a few beds along from him. Brian was crouching on his bed with his arms over his head, while Simon Silverson and his friends hit him with their pillows. They were laughing, but they meant it too. "Show off!" they were saying. "Bootlicker! Show off!"

Up till then, Charles had always been almost glad he was in this dormitory, and not in the one next door like Nirupam, where Dan Smith ruled with his friends from 6C and 6D. Now he wondered whether to sneak off and sleep in the lower school boys' playroom. Brian's yells—for Brian could never be hit quietly—kept cutting through Charles's miserable meditations and reminding him what he had done to Brian's father. It grew so bothersome that Charles nearly got out of bed and joined in hitting Brian too, just to relieve his feelings. But by this time he had gathered the reason for the pillows. Mr. Brubeck had asked Brian to sing a solo at the school concert, and Brian had unwisely agreed. Everyone else knew that it was Simon's right to sing solo.

This meant that hitting Brian would be sucking up to Simon. That Charles would not do. He went back to his desperate wonderings. There was no way of keeping Mr. Wentworth's disappearance secret that he could see. But there was quite a chance that no one would realize Charles had done it. So, if only he could think of some surefire way of stopping himself working magic by accident—that was it! Sure fire. It hurts to be burned.

Charles got out of bed. He unhooked his glasses from his bedrail, hooked them on his ears, and thumped across to the flurry of pillows.

"Can I borrow the emergency candle for five minutes?" he said loudly to Simon.

Simon of course was dormitory monitor. He paused in belaboring Brian and became official. "The candle's only for emergencies. What do you want it for?"

"You'll see if you give it to me," said Charles.

Simon hesitated, torn between curiosity and his usual desire never to give anyone anything. "You'll have to tell me what you want it for first. I can't let you have it for no reason."

"I'm not going to tell you," said Charles. "Just give it to me."

Simon considered. Long experience of Charles Morgan had shown him that when Charles said he was not going to tell, nothing would make him tell, not pillows or even wild horses. His curiosity, as Charles had hoped, was thoroughly aroused. "If I give it to you," he said righteously, "I shall be breaking the rules. You owe me compensation for risking getting into trouble, you know."

This was only to be expected. "What do you want?" said Charles.

Simon smiled graciously, wondering how great Charles's need was. "Your pocket money every week for the rest of term," he said. "How about that?"

"Too much," said Charles.

Simon turned away and picked up his pillow again. "Take it or leave it," he said. "That's my final offer."

"I'll take it," said Charles, hating Simon.

Simon turned back to him in astonishment. He had expected Charles either to protest or give up asking. His friends stared at Charles, equally astonished. In fact, by this time, nobody was hitting Brian anymore. Here was something really odd going on. Even Brian was staring at

Charles. How could anyone want a candle that much? "Very well," Simon said. "I'll accept your offer, Charles. But remember you promised in front of witnesses. You'd better pay up."

"I'll pay up," said Charles. "Every week when Mr. Crossley gives us our money. Now give me the candle."

Simon, with busy efficiency, fetched his key ring from his blazer and unlocked the cupboard on the wall where the first-aid kit and the candle were kept. If a miracle happened, Charles thought, and the inquisitors did not come for him after all, he had put himself in a true mess now. No pocket money until Christmas. That meant he could not pay for new running shoes. He would have to write five hundred lines every day for Mr. Towers. But he did not really believe he would be around to do that very long. Everyone said the inquisitors found witches whatever they did.

Simon put the candle in his hands. It was unlit, in a white enamel candle holder. Charles looked at it. He looked up to see Simon and all the other boys, even Brian, grinning.

"You forgot to ask for matches," Simon pointed out.

Charles looked at him. He glared. He did more than glare. It was the nastiest look he had ever given anyone. He hoped it would shrivel Simon on the spot.

All that happened was that Simon stepped backward from him. Even so, he looked as superior as ever. "But I'll give you the matches free," he said. "It's all part of the service." He tossed a box of matches toward Charles.

Charles put the candlestick down on the floor. With everyone staring at him, he struck a match and lit the candle. He knelt down beside it. *It hurts to be burned,* he thought. *It hurts to be burned.* He put out his finger and held it in the small yellow flame.

"Why on earth are you doing that?" asked Ronald West.

Charles did not answer. For a second, he thought the flame was not going to burn him. It just felt warm and wet. Then, quite suddenly, it was hot and it hurt very much indeed. It hurt, as Charles had expected, in quite a different way from cutting yourself or stubbing your toe. This was a much nastier pain, sharp and dull together, which brought Charles's back out in goose pimples and jangled the nerves all the way up his arm. Imagine this all over you, he thought. *It hurts to be burned.* He took hold of his wrist with his other hand and held it hard to stop himself snatching his finger out of the pain. *It hurts to be burned.* It did hurt too. It was making sweat prickle out just beneath his eyes.

"It must be for a dare or a bet," he heard Simon saying. "Which is it? Tell, or I'll put the candle away again."

"A bet," Charles answered at random. *It hurts to be burned. It hurts to be burned.* He thought this over and over, intent on branding it into his brain—or into whatever part of him it was that did magic. *It hurts to be*—Oh, it hurts!—*hurts to be burned.*

"Some people," Simon remarked, "make awfully stupid bets."

Charles ignored him and tried to keep his jerking finger steady. It was trying to jump out of the flame of its own accord. The finger was now red, with a white band across the red. He could hear a funny noise, a sort of tiny frizzling, as if his skin were frying. Then, suddenly, he could bear no more. He found himself snatching his finger away and blowing out the candle. The boys watching him all let out a sigh, as if they had been holding their breath.

"I suppose," Simon said discontentedly, as Charles handed him the candle back, "you make more money on this bet than you owe me now."

"No, I don't," Charles said quickly. He was afraid Simon would be after that money too. Simon was quite capable of telling Mr. Crossley about the candle if Charles did not pay. "I don't get anything. The bet was to burn my finger right off."

The monitor on duty appeared in the doorway, shouting, "Lights out! No more talking!"

Charles got into bed, sucking his burned finger, hoping and praying that he had now taught himself not to work magic by accident. His tongue could feel a big pulpy blister rising between the first and second joint of his finger. It hurt more than ever.

Simon said, out of the darkness, "I always knew Charles Morgan was mad. What a brainless thing to do!"

Ronald West said, "You don't expect brains in an animal."

"Animals have more sense," said Geoffrey Baines.

"Charles Morgan," said Simon, "is a lower life form."

These kinds of comments went on for some time. It was perfectly safe to talk because there was always such a noise from the next dormitory. Charles lay and waited for them to stop. He knew he was not going to sleep. Nor did he. Long after Simon and his friends had fallen silent, long after two monitors and the master in charge had come along and shut up the boys next door, Charles lay stiff as a log of wood, staring up into the shadows.

He was frightened—terrified. But the terror was now a dreary long-distance kind of terror, which he was sure he was going to feel all the time, for the rest of his life now. Suppose by some miracle, no inquisitors came for him; then he was going to be afraid that they would, every minute of every day, for years and years. He wondered if you learned to get used to it. He hoped so, because at this moment he felt like springing out of bed and confessing, just to get it over. What would Simon say if Charles jumped up shouting, "I'm a witch!" Probably he would think Charles was mad. It was funny that Simon had not disappeared too. Charles sucked his finger and puzzled over that. He certainly hated Simon enough. He had not hated Mr. Wentworth at all really—or only in the way you hate any master who gives you a black mark you do not deserve. Perhaps witchcraft had to be sort of clinical to work properly.

Then Charles thought of his other troubles. Two black marks in one day. No running shoes. No money. Five hundred lines a day. And none of it was his fault! It was not his fault he had been born a witch, either, for that matter. It was all so unfair! He wished he did not have to feel so guilty about Mr. Wentworth on top of it all. *It hurts to be burned.*

Charles's thoughts slowly grew less connected after this point. He realized afterward that he must have been asleep. But if it was sleep, it was only a light horrified doze, in which his thoughts kept on clanking about in his head, as if he were a piece of machinery with the switch jammed to ON. But he did not know he had been asleep. It seemed to him at the time that he sat up in bed after thinking things out in a perfectly orderly way. It was all quite obvious. He was a witch. He dared not be found out. Therefore he had to use some more witchcraft in order not to be found out. In other words, he had better go somewhere private like the toilets downstairs and conjure up first Mr. Wentworth and then his running shoes.

CHAPTER 6

Charles got up. He remembered to put on his glasses. He even thought of arranging his bedclothes in heaps to make it look as if he were still in bed. He could see to do that by the dim light shining in from the corridor. By that light, he could see to creep past the sleeping humps of all the other boys. He crept out into the corridor, which seemed light as day by comparison.

There was a lot of noise coming from the next dormitory. There was rustling, and some heavy thumps, followed by some giggles hurriedly choked off. Charles stopped. It sounded as if they were having one of their midnight feasts in there. The thumps would be the floorboards coming up so that they could get at their hidden food. It was a bad time to wander about. If the master in charge heard the noise, Charles would be caught too.

But the corridor remained empty. After a while, Charles dared to go on. He went along the corridor and down the dark pit of the concrete stairs at the end. It was cold. The heating, which was never warm anyway, was turned down for the night. The chill striking up through Charles's bare feet and in through his pajamas served to wake him up a little. He wondered if it was the pain in his finger which had awakened him in the first place. It was throbbing steadily. Charles held it against the cold wall to soothe it and, while his feet felt their way from stair to cold stair, he tried to plan what he would do. Mr. Wentworth was obviously the most important one to get back—if he could. But he did need those running shoes too.

"I'll practice on the shoes," Charles muttered. "If I get those, I'll try for Mr. Wentworth."

He stumbled off the end of the stairs and turned left toward the toilets. They were in a cross-passage down at the end. Charles was halfway to the corner, when the cross-passage became full of dull moving light. A half-lit figure loomed there, swinging a giant torch. The moving light caught the small white creature trundling at the figure's heels. The caretaker and his dog were on their way to inspect the toilets for vandals.

Charles turned and tiptoed the other way. The passage promptly filled with a shrill yap, like one very small clap of thunder. The dog had heard him. Charles ran. Behind him, he heard the caretaker shout, "Who's there?" and come clattering along the passage.

Charles ran. He ran past the end of the stairs, hoping the caretaker would think he had gone up them again, and went on, with his arms out in front of him, until he met the swinging door beyond. Gently, he pushed the door open a small way. Softly, he slid round it, holding the edge of the door so that it would not thump shut and give him away. Then he stood there hoping.

It was no good. The caretaker was not fooled. A muzz of light grew in the glass of the door. The shadow of the stair rails swung across it and fell away, and the light went on growing brighter as the caretaker advanced.

Charles let the door go and ran again, thumping along dark corridors until he had no idea where he was and could hardly breathe. He shook off the caretaker, but he lost himself. Then he ran round a corner and blinked in the orange light from a far-off streetlight shining through a window. Beyond the window was the unmistakable door of the lower school boys' playroom. Even in that dim light, Charles knew the kick marks at the bottom of the door, and the cracked glass in the upper panel where Nirupam Singh had tried to hit Dan Smith and missed. It seemed like home just then. There were worse places to practice magic in, Charles thought. He opened the door and crept in.

In the faint light, someone else jumped round to face him.

Charles jumped back against the door. He squeaked. The other person squeaked. "Who are you?" they both said at once. The Charles found the light switch. He moved it down and then back up in one swift waggle, dazzling both of them. What he saw made him lean against the door, confounded, blinking green darkness. The other person was Brian Wentworth. That was odd enough. But the oddest thing, in that dazzling moment of light, was that Charles had clearly seen that Brian was in tears. Charles was amazed. Brian, as was well known, never cried. He shrieked and yowled and yelled for mercy when he was hit, but he had never, ever been known to shed tears. Charles went very quickly from amazement to horror. For it clearly took something out of the ordinary to make Brian cry—and that thing must be that Brian had discovered his father was mysteriously missing.

"I came down to make it all right again," Charles said guiltily.

"What can *you* do?" said Brian's voice out of the dark, thick and throaty with crying. "The only reason you're better off than me is because you glare at people and they leave you alone. I wish I had a dirty look like yours. Then I could stop them getting at me and hitting me all the time!"

He began crying again, loud jerky sobs. Charles could hear the crying move off into the middle of the playroom, but he could not see Brian at first for the green dazzle. He really could not believe Brian minded being hit that much. It happened so often that Brian must be thoroughly used to it. By this time, he could see that Brian was crouching in the center of the concrete floor. Charles went over and crouched down facing him.

"Is that the only thing that's the matter?" he inquired cautiously.

"*Only!*" said Brian. "*Only thing!* What else do you want them to do? Tear me apart limb from limb or something! Sometimes I wish they would. I'd be dead then. I wouldn't have to put up with them getting at me then, hour after hour, day after day! I hate this school!"

"Yes," Charles said feelingly. "So do I." It gave him wonderful pleasure to say it, but it did not help bring the subject round to the disappearance of Mr. Wentworth. He took a deep breath to encourage himself. "Er—have you seen your father—?"

Brian broke in, almost with a scream. "Of *course* I've been to my magicking father! I go to him nearly every day and ask him to let me leave this place. I went to him this afternoon and asked him. I said why couldn't I go to Forest Road School, like Stephen Towers does, and you know what he said? He said Forest Road was a private school and he couldn't afford it. Couldn't afford it!" Brian said bitterly. "I ask you! *Why* can't he afford it, if Mr. Towers can? He must get paid twice as much as Mr. Towers! I bet he earns almost as much as Miss Cadwallader. And he says he can't afford it!"

Charles wondered. He remembered the threadbare hearthrug and the holes in Mr. Wentworth's slippers. That looked like poverty to him. But he supposed it could be meanness. And that brought him back to his guilt. With Mr. Wentworth gone, Brian would have to stay at Larwood House forever. "But have you seen your father since then?" he asked.

"No," said Brian. "He told me not to keep coming whining to him." And he began to cry again.

So Brian had not found out yet. Charles felt huge relief. There was still time to get Mr. Wentworth back. But that meant that it really was only being got at which was making Brian so unhappy. Despite the evidence, that surprised Charles. Brian always seemed so perky and unconcerned.

Brian was talking again, through his sobs. "Whatever I do," he said, "they get at me. I can't help my father being a teacher here! I can't help being good at things! I didn't *ask* Mr. Brubeck to give me a solo to sing. He just did. But of course magicking Simon Silverson thinks *he* ought to sing it. That's the thing I hate most," Brian said vehemently. "The way everyone does what Simon Silverson says!"

"I hate him too," said Charles. "Badly."

"Oh it doesn't matter how *we* feel," Brian said. "Simon's word is law. It's like that game—you know, *Simon Says*—where you have to do things if they say *Simon Says* first. And what is he anyway? A stuck up—"

"Prat," said Charles, "who sucks up to teachers—"

"With golden hair and a saintly expression. Don't forget the smug look," said Brian.

"Who could?" said Charles. "He kicks you in the pants, and then looks as if it's your fault his foot came up."

He was enjoying this. But he stopped enjoying it when Brian said, "Thanks for stopping them from hitting me this evening. What gave you the idea of burning your finger like that? And trust Simon Silverson to rip you off all your money just for a candle!" Brian hesitated a second and then added, "I suppose I'd better pay you half of it."

Charles managed to stop himself backing away. That would be really unkind. But what was he to do now? Brian clearly thought Charles had come downstairs in order to comfort him. Probably he would expect Charles to be his friend in the future. Well, Charles supposed, he had deserved it. This was what you got for putting the Evil Eye on people's fathers. But quite apart from Mr. Wentworth, quite apart from the fact that Brian was lowest of the low in 6B, even quite apart from the fact that Charles did not like Brian, Charles knew he could not be friends with anyone now. He was a witch. He could get anyone who was friends with him arrested too.

"You mustn't pay me anything," he said. "You don't owe me a thing."

Brian seemed distinctly relieved. "Then I'll tell you something instead," he said. "I've had enough of this place. If my father won't take me away, I'm going to *run* away."

"Where to?" said Charles. He had thought about running away himself, a while back, but he had had to give up the idea because there was nowhere to run away to.

"No idea," said Brian. "I shall just go."

"Don't be a fool," said Charles. This was one friendly thing he could say at least. "You have to plan it properly. If you just go, they'll call in tracker dogs and bring you straight back. Then you'll be punished."

"But I'll go mad if I stay here!" Brian said hysterically. Then he appeared to stop and consider, with his teeth chattering. "I think I see a way," he said.

By this time, both of them were shivering. It was cold in the playroom. Charles wondered how he could make Brian go back to bed without going himself. He could not think of a way. So they both went on crouching face to face in the middle of the concrete floor, until there was a sudden little pattering outside the cracked door. Both of them jumped.

"Caretaker's dog," whispered Charles.

Brian giggled. "Stupid creature. It looks just like Theresa Mullett's knitting."

Charles, before he could stop himself, gave a shriek of laughter. "It does! It does!"

"Shut up!" hissed Brian. "The caretaker's coming!"

Sure enough, the cracked glass of the door was showing misty torchlight. The dog began yapping furiously on the other side of it. It knew they were there.

Brian and Charles sprang up and fled, through the playroom and out its other door. As it thumped shut behind them, the cracked door thumped open and the hollow playroom echoed with the dog's little thunderclaps. Without a word, Charles ran one way and Brian ran another. Where Brian went, Charles never knew. He heard the second door thump open as he ran, and the patter of tiny feet behind him. Charles held his glasses on and ran desperately. It was just like the seniors in the shrubbery. What made everyone chase *him?* Did he smell of witch, or something?

He found an outside door, but it was locked. He pelted on. Behind him, in the distance, he could hear the caretaker bawling to his dog to come back. That made the dog hesitate. Charles, quite terrified by now, put on a spurt and hurled himself through the next door he came to.

There was a feeling of large cold space inside this door. Charles went forward a few cautious steps and hit his foot with a clang on a row of steel chairs. He stood frozen, waiting to be discovered. He could hardly hear for the blood banging in his ears at first. Then he found he could hear the dog yapping again, somewhere quite far off. It seemed to have lost him. At the same time, he found he could see the faint shapes of huge windows, high up, beyond the chairs. He was in the school hall.

It came to Charles that he was not going to get a better opportunity than this. Better summon up his shoes at once. No—forget the shoes. Mr. Wentworth was far more urgent. Get Mr. Wentworth, and when Mr. Wentworth appeared, perhaps Charles could put in a word about Brian.

It was at this point that Charles realized that he dared not fetch Mr. Wentworth back. If Mr. Wentworth did not know who had made him vanish, he *would* know as soon as he arrived back and found Charles.

"Flaming witches!" Charles moaned. "Why didn't I think?"

The dog, not too distant, gave another yap. Hunted and undecided, Charles shuffled forward and fell across more chairs. He was in a perfect maze of chairs. He stood where he was and tried to think.

He could still get the shoes, he thought. He could say he was sleepwalking with worry about them when the caretaker found him. Uncertainly, he held up both arms. That dog was definitely coming nearer again.

"Shoes," Charles said hurriedly, and his voice cracked with fear and cold and lack of breath. "Shoes. Come to me. Hey presto. Abracadabra. Shoes, I say!" The dog sounded almost outside the hall door now. Charles made dragging movements with his hands and then crossed them over his chest. "Shoes!"

A thing that, by the sound, could have been a shoe, fell on the chair next to him. Despite the yapping dog, Charles grinned with pleasure. The second shoe fell on the other side of him. Charles put out groping hands to find them. And two more fell on his head. Several more flopped down near his feet. Now he could hear shoes dropping down all round him. He seemed to be in the center of a rain of shoes. And the dog was scrabbling at the door now as it yapped. A Wellington boot, by the feel, hit Charles on the shoulder as he turned and groped along the chairs, stumbling over gym shoes, football boots, and lace-ups, with more and more dropping round him as he groped.

The caretaker was nearly at the door now. Charles could see the torchlight advancing through the glass. It helped him find his way. For he knew there was no question of any nonsense about sleepwalking now. He had to get out, and fast. He floundered among the pattering, flopping shoes, between the rows of chairs to the side of the hall, where he bolted for the door that the teachers came in by. Pitch dark descended on the other side of that door. Charles supposed he was in the staff room, but he never knew for sure. Stumbling, with his hands held out in front of him, dreamlike with panic, he fell over a stool. As he picked himself up, he remembered his second witch, the one who came through the garden. He should have thought about her earlier, he realized, as he knocked into a pile of books. She had said you couldn't work magic when you were frightened. She was right. Something had gone very wrong out there in the hall. Obviously, Charles thought, having a mad tangle with a coat of some kind, you needed to be cool and collected to be sure of getting it right. Oh thank Heaven! Here was a door.

Charles plunged out of the door and found himself not far from the main stairs. He fled up them. As he went, his thumb found the fat painful blister on his finger and he rubbed it as he ran upward. What a waste! What an utter waste of money! Burning his finger seemed to have taught him nothing at all. And here was the beautiful, welcoming green night light of the dormitory corridors. Not far now.

Charles did not remember getting into bed. His last clear thought was to wonder whether Brian had come back or whether he had run away on the spot. When the clanging bell dragged him awake in the morning, he had a sort of feeling that he had gone to sleep on the dormitory floor near the end of Brian's bed. But no. He was in his own bed. His glasses were hooked on the bedrail. He began to hope he had dreamed last night. But, long before he was awake enough to sit up and yawn, the room filled with indignant voices.

"I can't find my shoes!"

"I say, what's happened to all our shoes?"

"My slippers aren't here either!"

As Charles managed to sit up, Simon said, "Are you a shoe thief now, Brian?" and smacked Brian's head in a jolly, careless way, to show he did not think Brian was capable of being anything so enterprising. Brian was kneeling up in bed, looking as sleepy as Charles felt. He did not answer Simon or look at Charles.

In the next dormitory, they had no shoes either. And a senior could be heard coming down the corridor, shouting, "Hey! Have you lot pinched our shoes?"

Everyone was annoyed. Everyone thought there was a practical joke going on. Charles just hoped they would go on thinking that. Everyone was forced to go without shoes and slither around in socks. Charles's shoes were missing too—he was glad he seemed to have been that thorough and he was just dragging on a second pair of socks, when rumor spread along the corridor. In the way of rumors, it was quite mysterious. Nobody knew who started it.

"We're to go down to the hall. All the shoes are there."

Charles joined the slithering rush for the hall. That rush was joined in the downstairs passage by all the girls, also in socks, also making for the hall. The seniors naturally occupied the door of the hall. Everyone from the lower school streamed outside into the quadrangle to look through the hall windows. There, everyone's first reaction was simple awe.

A school with six hundred pupils owns an awful lot of shoes. There would be twelve hundred even if everyone simply had one pair. But at Larwood House, everyone had to have special shoes for almost everything they did. So you had to add to that number all the gym shoes, running shoes, tennis shoes, trainers, dancing shoes, spare shoes, best shoes, sandals, football boots, hockey boots, Wellington boots, and galoshes. The number of shoes is swiftly in thousands. Add to those all the shoes owned by the staff, too: Miss Cadwallader's characteristic footgear with heels like cotton-reels; the cook's extra-wide fitting; the groundsman's hobnails; Mr. Crossley's hand-made suede; Mr. Brubeck's brogues; the matron's sixteen pairs of stiletto heels; someone's purple fur boots; and even the odd pair of riding boots; not to speak of many more. And you have truly formidable numbers. The chairs in the hall were buried under a monstrous mountain of shoes.

Amid the general marveling, Theresa's voice was heard. "If this is someone's idea of a joke, I don't think it's funny. My bedsocks are all muddy!" She was wearing blue fluffy bedsocks over her school socks.

After this, there was something of a free-for-all. People scrambled in through doors and windows and slithered on the pile of shoes, digging for shoes they thought were theirs—or, failing that, simply a pair that would fit.

Until a voice began bellowing, "OUT! GET OUT ALL OF YOU! LEAVE ALL THE SHOES THERE!"

Charles was pushed backward by the rather slower rush to leave the hall, and had to crane to see who was shouting. It was Mr. Wentworth. Charles was so amazed that he stopped moving and was left by a sort of eddy inside the hall, just by the door. From there, he could clearly see Mr. Wentworth walking down the edge of the pile of shoes. He was wearing his usual shabby suit, but his feet were completely bare. Otherwise there was nothing wrong with him at all. After him came Mr. Crossley in bright yellow socks and Mr. Brubeck with a large hole in the heel of his left sock. After them came the caretaker. After him of course trundled the caretaker's dog, which was manifestly wishing to raise a leg against the pile of shoes.

"I don't know who done it!" the caretaker was protesting. "But I know there was people sneaking round my building half the night. The dog nearly caught one, right in this very hall."

"Did you come in here and investigate?" Mr. Wentworth said.

"Door was shut," said the caretaker. "Thought it was locked."

Mr. Wentworth turned from him in disgust. "Someone was pretty busy in here all last night," he said to Mr. Crossley, "and he didn't even look!"

"Thought it was locked," repeated the caretaker.

"Oh shut up!" snapped Mr. Wentworth. "And stop your dog peeing on that shoe. It's Miss Cadwallader's."

Charles slipped out into the corridor, trying to keep the grin on his face down to decent proportions. Mr. Wentworth was all right. He must have slipped off to bed after all last night, while Miss Hodge was asking Charles the way. And, better still, everyone thought the shoes had arrived in the hall quite naturally. Charles could have danced and sung.

But here was Dan Smith beside him. That sobered Charles somewhat. "Hey," said Dan. "Did those seniors catch you last night?"

"No, I ran away," Charles replied airily.

"You must have run pretty fast!" said Dan. It was grudging, but it was praise, coming from Dan. "Know anything about who did these shoes?" Dan asked, jerking his head toward the hall.

Charles would dearly have loved to say it was him and watch the respect grow on Dan's face. But he was not that much of a fool. "No," he said.

"I do," said Dan. "It was the witch in our class, I bet."

Mr. Wentworth appeared in the doorway of the hall. There were loud shushings up and down the packed corridor. "Breakfast is going to be late," Mr. Wentworth shouted. He looked very harrowed. "You can't expect the kitchen staff to work without shoes. You are all to go to your classrooms and wait there. Meanwhile, teachers and sixth graders are going to be working hard laying all the shoes out in the main quadrangle. When you are called—*when* you are called, understand?—you are to come by classes and pick out the shoes which are yours. Off you all go. Sixth grade stay behind."

Everyone milled off in a reluctant crowd. Charles was so pleased with himself that he risked grinning at Brian. But Brian was staring dreamily at the wall and did not notice. He did not move or even yell when Simon slapped him absentmindedly round the head. "Where's Nan Pilgrim?" Simon asked, laughing. "Turned herself invisible?"

Nan was keeping out of the way, lurking in the top corridor by the girls' bathrooms. From there, she had an excellent view of the quadrangle being covered with row upon row of shoes, and the kitchen ladies tiptoeing about the rows in stockings looking for their workshoes. It did not amuse her. Theresa's friend Delia Martin and Estelle's friend Karen Grigg had already made it quite plain that they thought it was Nan's doing. The fact that these two normally did not speak to one another, or to Nan either, only seemed to make it worse.

CHAPTER 7

Breakfast was ready before 6B had been called to find their shoes. Theresa was forced to walk through the corridors in her blue bedsocks. They were, by this time, quite black underneath, which upset her considerably. Breakfast was so late that assembly was cancelled. Instead, Miss Cadwallader stood up in front of high table, with her face all stringy with displeasure and one foot noticeably damp, and made a short speech.

"A singularly silly trick has been played on the school," she said. "The people who played it no doubt think it very funny, but they must be able to see by now what a stupid and dishonorable thing they have done. I want them to be honorable now. I want them to come to me and confess. And I want anyone else who knows or suspects who did it to be equally honorable and come and tell me what they know. I shall be in my study all morning. That is all."

"What is honorable," Nirupam said loudly, as everyone stood up, "about going and telling tales?"

By saying that, he did Nan a service, whether he meant to or not. No one in 6B wanted a name for telling tales. Nobody went to Miss Cadwallader. Instead, they all went out into the quadrangle, where a little freezing drizzle of rain was now falling, and walked up and down the rows of damp footgear, finding their shoes. Nan was forced to go too.

"Oh look! Here comes Archwitch Dulcinea," said Simon. "Why did you do it to your own shoes too, Dulcinea? Thought it would look more innocent, did you?"

And Theresa said, "Really, Nan! My bedsocks are ruined! It isn't funny!"

"Do something really funny now, Nan," Karen Grigg suggested.

"Hurry up!" Mr. Crossley shouted from the shelter of the porch. Everyone at once became very busy turning over shoes. The only one who did not was Brian. He simply wandered about, staring into space. In the end, Nirupam found his shoes for him and bundled them into Brian's lax arms.

"Are you all right?" Nirupam asked him.

"Who? Me? Oh yes," Brian said.

"Are you sure? One of your eyes is sort of set sideways," Nirupam said.

"Is it?" Brian asked vaguely, and wandered off.

Nirupam turned severely to Simon. "I think you hit him on the head once too often."

Simon laughed, a little uneasily. Nirupam was a head taller than he was. "Nonsense! There's nothing in his head to get hurt."

"Well, you watch it," said Nirupam, and might have said more, except that they were interrupted by an annoyed outcry from Dan Smith.

"I'll get someone for this!" Dan was shouting. He was very pale and cross after last night's midnight feast, and he looked quite savage. "I'll get them even if they're a magicking senior. Someone's gone off with my running shoes! I can't find them anywhere."

"Look again, carefully!" Mr. Crossley bawled from the porch.

This was a queer fact. Dan searched up and down the rows, and so did Charles, until their socks were soaked and their hair was trickling rain, but neither Dan's spikes nor Charles's were there. By this time, 7A, 7B, and 7C had been allowed out to collect their shoes too before they all got too wet, and almost the only footgear left was the three odd football boots, the riding boots, and a pair of luminous green trainers that nobody seemed to want. Dan uttered such threats that Charles was glad that it did not seem to occur to Dan that this had anything to do with Charles Morgan.

But it meant that Charles had to go to Mr. Towers next and confess that his running shoes had still not turned up. He was fed up as he stood and trickled rain outside the staff room. After all his trouble!

"I did look, sir," he assured Mr. Towers.

Mr. Towers glanced at Charles's soaking hair and rain-dewed glasses. "Anyone can stand in the rain," he said. "Are you paying for new ones or writing lines?"

"Doing lines," Charles said resentfully.

"In detention every evening until Christmas then," Mr. Towers said. The idea seemed to please him. "Wait." He dodged back into the staff room and came out again with a fat old book. "Here," he said, handing the book to Charles. "Copy five hundred lines of this out every evening. It will show you what a real schoolboy should be like. When you've copied it all, I'll give you the sequel."

Charles stood in front of the staff room and looked at the book. It was called *The Pluckiest Boy in School.* It smelled of mildew. Inside, the pages were furry and brownish, and the first line of the story went: "*What ripping fun!" exclaimed Watts Minor. "I'm down for scrum half this afternoon!"*

Charles looked from this to the fat, transparent, and useless blister on his finger and felt rather ill. "Magicking hell," he said.

"Good morning, Charles," said Miss Hodge, tripping toward the staff room, all fresh and unaware. "That looks like a nice old book. I'm glad to see you doing some serious reading at last."

She was most disconcerted to receive one of Charles's heaviest double-barreled glares. What a moody boy he was to be sure! she thought as she neatly stripped off her raincoat. She was equally surprised to find the staff room in some kind of uproar, with a pile of boots and shoes in the middle. Still, there was Mr. Wentworth at last, flying past on his way somewhere else. Miss Hodge stood in his way.

"Oh, Mr. Wentworth, I want to apologize for making that accusation against Charles Morgan." That was pretty generous of her, she thought, after the way Charles had just looked at her. She smiled generously at Mr. Wentworth.

To her annoyance, Mr. Wentworth simply said, "I'm glad to hear it," and brushed past her quite rudely. But he did have a lot on his mind, Miss Hodge realized, when Mr. Crossley told her excitedly all about the shoes. She did not hold it against Mr. Wentworth, She collected books—they had gotten spilled all over the floor somehow—and went off to give 6B another English lesson.

She arrived to find Simon Silverson holding aloft *The Pluckiest Boy in School.* "Listen to this!" he was saying. *"Swelling with pride, Watts Minor gazed into the eyes of his one true friend. Here was a boy above all, straight alike in body and mind—"*

Theresa and Delia were screaming with laughter, with their faces buried in their knitting. Charles was glaring blue murder.

"Really, Simon!" said Miss Hodge. "That was unworthy of you." Simon looked at her in astonishment. He knew he never did anything unworthy. "But, Charles," said Miss Hodge, "I do think you made rather an unfortunate choice of book." For the second time that day, Charles turned his glare on her. Miss Hodge flinched. Really, if she had not known now that Charles was a nice boy underneath, that glare of his would make her think seriously of the Evil Eye.

Nirupam held up his long arm. "Are we going to do acting again?" he asked hopefully.

"No, we are not," Miss Hodge said, with great firmness. "Get out your poetry books."

The lesson, and the rest of the morning, dragged past. Theresa finished her second bootee and cast on stitches for a sweater. Estelle knitted quite a lot of a baby's bonnet. Brian gave up staring at the wall and instead seemed to be attacked by violent industry. Whenever anyone looked at him, he was scribbling furiously in a different exercise book.

Charles sat and brooded, rather surprised at the things going on in his mind. He was not frightened at all now. He seemed to be accepting the fact he was a witch quite calmly after all. No one had noticed. They all thought the witch was Nan Pilgrim, because of her name, which suited Charles very well. But the really strange thing was the way he had stopped being worried by the witch he had seen being burned. He tried remembering him, cautiously at first, then boldly, when he found it did not bother him. Then he went on to the second witch, who came over the wall. Neither troubled him now. They were in the past: they were gone. It was like having a toothache that suddenly stops. In the peace that came with this, Charles saw that his mind must have been trying to tell him he was going to grow up a witch. And now that he knew, it stopped nagging him. Then, to see if this made him frightened, he thought of inquisitors. It hurts to be burned, he thought, and looked at his fat blister. It had taught him something after all. And that was: Don't get found out.

Good, thought Charles. And turned his mind to what he was going to do to Simon Silverson. Dan Smith next, but Simon definitely first. What could he do to Simon that would be worth nearly a whole term's pocket money? It was difficult. It had to be something bad enough, and yet with no connection with Charles. Charles was quite stumped at first. He wanted it to be artistic. He wanted Simon to suffer. He wanted everyone else to know about it, but not to know it was Charles who did it. What *could* he do?

The last lesson before lunch was the daily PE. Today, it was the boys' turn in the gym. They were to climb ropes too. Charles sat by the wallbars and pretended to tie his gym shoe. Unlike Nan, he could get up a rope if he wanted, but he did not want to. He wanted to sit and think what to do to Simon. Simon, of course, was one of the first to the ceiling. He saw Charles and shouted something down. The result was that someone from 6C came and dug Charles in the back.

"Simon says you're to stop lazing about."

"Simon says that, does he?" said Charles. He stood up. He was inspired. It was something Brian had said last night. That game, *Simon Says*. Suppose it was not just a game. Suppose everything Simon said really came true. At the very worst it ought to be pretty funny. At best, people might even think Simon was a witch.

Charles went up a rope. He dragged himself up it, nice and slow and gentle, so that he could go on thinking. He was obviously not going to be able to stand anywhere near Simon to put the spell on him. Someone would notice. But instinct told Charles that this was not the kind of magic you could work at a distance. It was too strong and personal. What he needed, in order to do it safely, was something which was not Simon himself, but something which belonged to Simon so personally that any witchcraft worked on it would work on Simon at the same time—a detachable piece of Simon, really. What removable parts had Simon? Teeth, toenails, fingernails, hair? He could hardly go up to Simon and pull any of those off him. Wait a minute! Hair. Simon combed his hair this morning. With any luck, there might be some hair stuck in Simon's comb.

Charles slid jubilantly down the rope—so fast that he was reminded again that it hurts to be burned. He had to blow on his hands to cool them. After lunch was the time. He could sneak up to the dormitory then.

After lunch proved to be important for Nan too. At lunch, she managed to escape Karen Grigg and Delia Martin by sitting at a table full of much older girls who did not seem to know Nan was there. They towered over her, talking of their own things. The food was almost as bad as yesterday, but Nan felt no urge to describe it. She rather wished she was dead. Then it occurred to her that if any of 6B went and told a teacher she was a witch, she would be dead, quite soon after that. She realized at once that she did not wish she was dead. That made her feel better. No one had gone to a teacher yet, after all. "It's only their usual silliness," she told herself. "They'll forget about it by Christmas. I'll just have to keep out of their way till they do."

Accordingly, after lunch, Nan sneaked upstairs to lurk in the passage outside the girls' bathrooms again. But Karen Grigg had been keeping tabs on her. She and Theresa appeared in the passage in front of Nan. When Nan turned round to make off, she found Delia and the other girls coming along the passage from the other end.

"Let's go in this bathroom," Theresa suggested. "We want to ask you something, Nan."

Nan could tell there was an ordeal coming. For a moment, she wondered whether to charge Theresa and Karen like a bull and burst past them. But they would only catch her tonight in the dormitory. Best get it over. "Okay," she said, and sauntered into the bathroom as if she did not care.

Almost at the same moment, Charles hastened furtively into the boys' dormitory. White and clean and cold, the beds stood like rows of deserted icebergs, each with its little white locker at its side. Charles hurried to Simon's. It was locked. Simon was an inveterate locker of things. Even his watch had a little key to lock it on his wrist. But Charles did not let that bother him. He held out his hand imperiously in front of the locked door. "Comb," he said. "Abracadabra."

Simon's comb came gliding out through the white wooden surface, like a fish swimming out of milk, and darted fishlike into Charles's hand. It was beautiful. Better still, there were three of Simon's curly golden hairs clinging to the teeth of the comb. Charles carefully pulled them off. He held the hairs in the finger and thumb of his left hand and carefully ran his right finger and thumb down the length of them. And down again. Over and over, he did it. "Simon Says," he whispered to them. "Simon Says, Simon Says. Whatever Simon says is true."

After about a minute, when he had done it often enough to give him the feeling that the spell was going to take, Charles carefully threaded the hairs back into the comb again. He did not intend to leave any evidence against himself. He had just finished, when Brian said, from behind him, "I want a bit of help from you, Charles."

Charles jumped as if Brian had shot him. He bent over, in white horror, to hide the comb in his hand and, with terrible guilty haste, gave it a push toward the locker. It went in, to his surprise, not quite like a fish this time—more like a comb being pushed through a door—but at least it went. "What do you want?" Charles said ungraciously to Brian.

"Take me down to the matron in the sick bay," Brian said.

It was a school rule that a person who felt ill had to find another person to take them to the matron. It had been made because, before that, the sick bay had been crowded with healthy people trying to get an afternoon off. The idea was that you could not deceive your friends. It did not work very well. Estelle Green, for instance, got Karen to take her to the matron at least twice a week. As far as Charles could see, Brian looked his usual pink and perky self, just like Estelle.

"You don't look ill to me," he said. He wanted to find Simon and see if the spell was working.

"How about this then?" said Brian. To Charles's surprise, he suddenly turned pale. He stared vaguely at the wall, with one eye pointing inward slightly. "This is it," Brian said. "Don't I look rather as if I'd been hypnotized?"

"You look as if you've been hit on the head," Charles said rudely. "Get Nirupam to take you."

"He looked after me this morning," said Brian. "I want as many witnesses as possible. I helped you last night. You help me now."

"You didn't help me last night," said Charles.

"Yes, I did," said Brian. "You came in and you went to sleep on the floor, just at the end of my bed. I got you in your bed. I even hooked your glasses on your bedrail for you." And he looked at Charles, very meaningfully.

Charles stared back. Brian was so thin and small that it was hard to believe he could lift anyone into bed. But, whether it was true or not, Charles realized that Brian had gotten him over a barrel. He knew Charles had been up last night. He had caught him with Simon's comb in his hands just now. Charles could not see why Brian wanted to go to the matron, but that was his own affair. "All right," he said. "I'll take you."

Inside the bathroom, on the other side of the quadrangle, the girls crowded in round Nan. "Where's Estelle?" asked Theresa.

"Outside, keeping watch," said Karen. "That's all she would do."

"What's this about?" Nan asked aggressively.

"We want you to do some proper witchcraft," said Theresa. "Here, where we can see you. We've none of us seen any before. And we know you can. Come on. We won't give you away."

The other girls joined in. "Come on, Nan. We won't tell."

The bathroom was a very public one. There were six baths in it, in a row. As the girls all crowded forward, Nan backed away, down the space between two of the baths. This was evidently just what they had wanted. Delia said, "That's it." Heather said, "Fetch it out." And Karen bent and pulled the groundsman's old broom out from under the left-hand bath. Julia and Deborah seized it and propped it across the two baths in front of Nan, penning her in. Nan looked from it to them.

"We want you to get on it and fly about," Theresa explained.

"Everyone knows that's what witches do," said Karen.

"We're asking you very nicely," said Theresa.

Typical Theresa double-think, Nan thought angrily. She was not asking her nicely. It was a smiling jeer. But if anyone asked Theresa afterward, she would say, with honest innocence, that she had been perfectly kind.

"We can prove you're a witch anyway, if you won't," Theresa said kindly.

"Yes, everyone knows that witches don't drown," said Delia. "You can put them right under water and they stay alive."

At this cue, Karen leaned over and put the plug in the nearest bath. Heather turned on the cold tap, just a little trickle, to show Nan they meant business.

"You know perfectly well," Nan said, "that I'm not a witch, and I can't fly on this broomstick. It's just an excuse to be nasty!"

"Nasty?" said Theresa. "Who's being nasty? We're asking you quite politely to ride the broomstick." Behind her, the tap trickled steadily into the bath.

"You can fetch all the shoes here again if you like," Delia said. "We don't mind which."

"But you've got to do *something,"* said Karen. "Or how would you like a nice deep cold bath with all your clothes on?"

Nan was annoyed enough by that to put one leg over the broomstick in order to climb out and get at Karen. Seeing it, Theresa gave a delighted jump and a giggle. "Oh, she's going to ride!"

The rest of them joined in. "She's going to ride it! Ride it, Nan!"

Very red in the face, Nan stood astride the broom and explained, "I am not going to ride. I do not know how to ride. You know I can't. I know I can't. Look. Look at me. I am sitting on the broomstick." Unwisely, she sat. It was extremely uncomfortable and she was forced to bounce upright again. This amused everyone highly. Angrier than ever, Nan shouted, "How *can* I ride a broomstick? I can't even climb a rope!"

They knew that. They were falling about laughing, when Estelle burst in, screaming with excitement. "Come and look, come and look! *Look* at what Simon Silverson's doing!"

This caused a stampede to the door, to look out of the windows in the corridor. Nan heard cries of "Good heavens! Just look at that!" This was followed by a further stampede as everyone raced off down to the quadrangle.

Nan was left astride an old broom propped on two baths.

"Thank goodness!" was the first thing she said. She had been precious near crying. "Stupid hussies!" she said next. "As if I could ride this thing. Look at it!" She jogged the broom. "Just an old broom!" Then she noticed the water still trickling into the bath behind her. She leaned sideways and back and turned off the tap.

That was the moment the old broom chose to rise sharply to the ceiling.

Nan shrieked. She was suddenly dangling head-down over a bath of cold water. The broom staggered a bit under her weight, but it went on climbing, swinging Nan right over the water. Nan bent her leg as hard as she could over its knobby stick, and managed to clench one hand in its sparse brushwood end. The broom reached the ceiling and leveled out. It did not leave room for Nan to climb on top of it, even if she had possessed the muscles. Blood thudded in her head from hanging upside down, but she did not dare let go.

"Stop it!" she squealed at the broom. "Please!"

It took no notice. It simply went on a solemn, lopsided, bumping flight all round the bathroom, with Nan dangling desperately underneath it and getting this-way-and-that glimpses of hard white baths frighteningly far below.

"I'm glad this didn't happen while the others were here," she gasped. "I must look a right idiot!" She began to laugh. She must look so silly. "Do go down," she said to the broom. "Suppose someone else comes in here."

The broom seemed struck by this. It gave a little start and slanted steeply down toward the floor. As soon as the floor was near enough, Nan clutched the handle in both hands and tried to unhook her leg. A mistake. The broom went steeply up again and hovered where it was just too high for Nan to dare to fall off. But her arms were getting tired and she had to do something. Wriggling and squirming, she managed to kick herself over, until she was more or less lying along the knobby handle, looking down at the row of baths. She hooked her feet on the brush and stayed there, panting.

Now what was she to do? This broom seemed determined to be ridden. There was a sad feeling about it. Once, long ago, it had been ridden, and it missed its witch.

"But that's all very well," Nan said to it. "I really daren't ride you now. Don't you understand? It's illegal. Suppose I promise to ride you tonight. Would you let me down then?"

There was a hesitating sort of hover to the broom.

"I swear to," said Nan. "Listen, I tell you what. You fly me down the passage to our dormitory. That will make a bit of a flight at least. Then you can hide yourself on top of the cupboard, right at the back. No one will see you there. And I'll promise to take you out tonight. What do you say?"

Though the broom could not speak, it evidently meant Yes! It turned and swept through the bathroom doorway in a glad swoop that made Nan seasick. It sped down the passage. She had to shut her eyes in order not to see the walls whirling by. It made a hair-raising turn into the dormitory. And it stopped there with such a jerk that Nan nearly fell round underneath it again.

"I see I shall have to train you," she gasped.

The broom gave an indignant buck and a bounce.

"I mean you'll have to train me," Nan said quickly. "Go down now. I have to get off you."

The broom hovered, questioning.

"I promised," Nan said.

At that, the broom came sweetly to the ground and Nan was able to get off, very wobbly in the legs. As soon as she was off, the broom fell to the floor, lifeless. "You poor thing!" Nan said. "I see. You need a rider to move at all. All right. Let's get you on top of the cupboard."

In this way, she missed the first manifestation of the *Simon Says* spell. Charles missed it too. Neither of them discovered how Simon first found out that everything he said came true. Charles left Brian with a thermometer in his mouth, staring cross-eyed at the wall, and trudged back to the quadrangle to find an excited group round Simon. At first, Charles thought that the brightness flaring at Simon's feet was simply the sun shining off a puddle. But it was not. It was a heap of gold coins. People were passing him pennies and stones and dead leaves.

To each thing as he took it, Simon said, "This is a gold coin. This is another gold coin." When that got boring he said, "This is a *rare* gold coin. These are pieces of eight. This is a doubloon . . ."

Charles shoved his way to the front of the crowd and watched, utterly disgusted. Trust Simon to turn things to his own advantage! Gold chinked down on the heap. Simon must have been a millionaire by this time.

With a great clatter of running feet, the girls arrived. Theresa, with her knitting bag hanging on her arm, pushed her way to the front, beside Charles. She was so astonished at the size of the pile of gold that she crossed the invisible line and spoke to Simon.

"How are you *doing* it, Simon?"

Simon laughed. He was like a drunk person by this time. "I've got the Golden Touch!" he said. Of course this immediately became the truth. "Just like that king in the story. Look." He reached for Theresa's knitting. Theresa indignantly snatched the knitting away and gave Simon a push at the same time. The result was that Simon touched her hand.

The knitting fell on the ground. Theresa screamed, and stood holding her hand out, and then screamed again because her hand was too heavy to hold up. It dropped down against her skirt, a bright golden metal hand, on the end of an ordinary human arm.

Out of the shocked silence which followed, Nirupam said, "Be very careful what you say, Simon."

"Why?" said Simon.

"Because everything you say becomes true," Nirupam said.

Evidently, Simon had not quite seen the extent of his powers. "You mean," he said, "I haven't got the Golden Touch." Instantly, he hadn't. "Let's test this," he said. He bent down and picked up Theresa's knitting. It was still knitting, in a slightly muddy bag.

"Put it down!" Theresa said faintly. "I shall go to Miss Cadwallader."

"No, you won't," said Simon, and that was true too. He looked at the knitting and considered. "This knitting," he announced, "is really two little caretaker's dogs."

The bag began to writhe about in his hands. Simon hurriedly dropped it with a sharp chink, onto the heap of gold. The bag heaved. Little shrill yappings came from inside it, and furious scrabbling. One little white bootee-dog burst out of it, shortly followed by a second. They ran on little minute legs, down the heap of gold and in among people's legs. Everyone got rather quickly out of their way. Everyone turned and watched as the two tiny white dogs went running and running into the distance across the quadrangle.

Theresa started to cry. "That was my knitting, you beast!"

"So?" Simon said, laughing.

Theresa lifted up her golden hand with her ordinary one and hit him with it. It was stupid of her, because she risked breaking her arm, but it was certainly effective. It nearly knocked Simon out. He sat down heavily on his heap of gold. "Ow!" said Theresa. "And I hope that hurt!"

"It didn't," said Simon, and got up smiling and, of course, unhurt.

Theresa went for him again, double-handed.

Simon skipped aside. "You haven't got one golden hand," he said.

There was suddenly space where Theresa's heavy golden hand had been. Her arm ended in a round pink wrist. Theresa stared at it. "How shall I knit?" she said.

"I mean," Simon said carefully, "that you have two ordinary hands."

Theresa looked at her two perfectly ordinary human hands and burst into strange, artificial-sounding laughter. "Somebody kill him for me!" she said.

"Quickly!"

Nobody offered to. Everybody was too shattered. Delia took Theresa's arm and led her tenderly away. The bell rang for afternoon lessons as they went.

"This is marvelous fun!" Simon said. "From now on, I'm all in favor of witchcraft."

Charles trudged off to lessons, wondering how he could cancel the spell.

CHAPTER 8

Simon arrived late for lessons. He had been making sure his heap of gold was safe. "I'm sorry, sir," he said to Mr. Crossley. And sorry he was. Tears came into his eyes, he was so sorry.

"That's all right, Simon," Mr. Crossley said kindly, and everyone else felt compelled to look at Simon with deep sympathy.

You can't win with people like Simon, Charles thought bitterly. Anyone else would have been in bad trouble by now. And it was exasperating the way nobody so much as dreamed of accusing Simon of witchcraft. They kept looking at Nan Pilgrim instead.

Nan felt much the same about Theresa. Theresa arrived ten minutes after Simon, very white and sniffing rather. She was led in tenderly by Delia, and received almost as much sympathy as Simon. "Just gave her an aspirin and sent her away!" Nan heard Delia whisper indignantly to Karen. "I do think she ought to have been allowed to lie down, after all she's been through!"

What about all *I've* been through? Nan thought. No, it was Theresa's right to be in the right, as much as it was Simon's.

Nan had been given the full story by Estelle. Estelle was always ready to talk in class, and she was particularly ready, now that Karen seemed to have joined Theresa's friends. She knitted away under her desk at her baby's bonnet, and whispered and whispered. Nor was she the only one. Mr. Crossley kept calling for quiet, but the whispers and rustling hardly abated at all. Notes kept arriving on Nan's desk. The first to arrive was from Dan Smith.

Make me the same as Simon and I'll be your friend forever, it said.

Most of the other notes said the same. All were very respectful. But one note was different. This one said, *Meet me round the back after lessons. I think you need help and I can advise you.* It was not signed. Nan wondered about it. She had seen the writing before, but she did not know whose it was.

She supposed she did need help. She really was a witch now. No one but a witch could fly a broomstick. She knew she was in danger and she knew she should be terrified. But she was not. She felt happy and strong, with a happiness and strength that seemed to be welling up from deep inside her. She kept remembering the way she had started to laugh when the broomstick went flying round the bathroom with herself dangling underneath it, and the way she seemed to understand by instinct what the broom wanted. Hair-raising as it had been, she had enjoyed it thoroughly. It was like coming into her birthright.

"Of course, Simon always said you were a witch," Estelle whispered.

That reduced Nan's joy a little. There was another witch in 6B, she did not doubt that. And that witch had, for some mad reason, made everything Simon said come true. He must be one of Simon's friends. And it was quite possible that Simon, while he was under the spell, had happened to say that Nan was a witch. So of course she would have become one.

Nan refused to believe it. She *was* a witch. She wanted to be one. She came from a long line of witches, stretching back beyond even Dulcinea Wilkes herself. She felt she had a *right* to be a witch.

All this while, Mr. Crossley was trying to give 6B a geography lesson. He had gotten to the point where he was precious near giving up and giving everyone detention instead. He had one last try. He could see that the unrest was centering on Simon, with a sub-center round Nan, so he tried to make use of it by asking Simon questions.

"Now the geography of Finland is very much affected by the last Ice Age. Simon, what happens in an Ice Age?"

Simon dragged his mind away from dreams of gold and glory. "Everything is very cold," he said. A blast of cold air swept through the room, making everyone's teeth chatter. "And goes on getting colder, I suppose," Simon added unwisely. The air in the room swiftly became icy. 6B's breath rolled out in steam. The windows misted over and froze, almost at once, into frosty patterns. Icicles began to grow under the radiators. Frost whitened the desks.

There was a chorus of shivers and groans, and Nirupam hissed, "*Watch* it!"

"I mean everything gets very hot," Simon said hastily.

Before Mr. Crossley had time to wonder why he was shivering, the cold was replaced by tropical heat. The frost slid away down the windows. The icicles tinkled off the radiators. For an instant, the room seemed fine and warm, until the frozen water evaporated. This produced a thick, steamy fog. In the murk, people were gasping. Some faces turned red, others white, and sweat ran on foreheads, adding to the fog.

Mr. Crossley put a hand to his forehead, thinking he might be getting the flu. The room seemed so dim suddenly. "Some theories do say that an Ice Age starts with extreme heat," he said uncertainly.

"But I say everything is normal for this time of year," Simon said, desperately trying to adjust the temperature.

Instantly it was. The classroom reverted to its usual way of being not quite warm enough, though still a little damp. Mr. Crossley found he felt better. "Stop talking nonsense, Simon!" he said angrily.

Simon, with incredulity, realized that he might get into trouble. He tried to pass the whole thing off in his usual lordly way. "Well, sir, nobody really knows a thing about Ice Ages, do they?"

"We'll see about that," Mr. Crossley said grimly. And of course nobody did. When he came to ask Estelle to describe an Ice Age, Mr. Crossley found himself wondering just why he was asking about something which did not exist. No wonder Estelle looked so blank. He rounded back on Simon. "Is this a joke of some kind? What are you thinking of?"

"Me? I'm not thinking of anything!" Simon said defensively. With disastrous results.

Ah! This is more like it! Charles thought, watching the look of complete vacancy growing on Simon's face.

Theresa saw Simon's eyes glaze and his jaw drop and jumped to her feet with a scream. "Stop him!" she screamed. "Kill him! Do something to him before he says another word!"

"Sit down, Theresa," said Mr. Crossley.

Theresa stayed standing up. "You wouldn't believe what he's done already!" she shouted. "And now look at him. If he says a word in that state—"

Mr. Crossley looked at Simon. The boy seemed to be pretending to be an idiot now. What was the matter with everyone? "Take that look off your face, Simon," he said. "You're not that much of a fool."

Simon was now in a state of perfect blankness. And in that state, people have a way of picking up and echoing anything that is said to them. "Not that much of a fool," he said slurrily. The vacancy of his face was joined by a look of deep cunning. Perhaps that was just as well, Charles thought. There was no doubt that Theresa had a point.

"Don't *speak* to him!" Theresa shouted. "Don't you understand?

It's every word he says! And—" She swung round and pointed at Nan. "It's all *her* fault!"

Before lunch, Nan would have quailed in front of Theresa's pointing finger and everyone's eyes turned on her. But she had ridden a broomstick now, and things were different. She was able to look scornfully at Theresa. "What nonsense!" she said.

Mr. Crossley was forced to agree that Nan was right. "Don't be ridiculous, Theresa," he said. "I told you to sit down." And he relieved his feelings by giving both Theresa and Simon an hour in detention.

"Detention!" Theresa exclaimed, and sat down with a bump. She was outraged.

Simon, however, uttered a cunning chuckle. "You think you've got me, don't you?" he said.

"Yes, I do," said Mr. Crossley. "Make it an hour and a half."

Simon opened his mouth to say something else. But here Nirupam intervened. He leaned over and whispered to Simon, "You're very clever. Clever people keep their mouths shut."

Simon nodded slowly, with immense, stupid wisdom. And, to Charles's disappointment, he seemed to take Nirupam's advice.

"Get your journals out," Mr. Crossley said wearily. There should be some peace now at least, he thought.

People opened their journals. They spread today's page in front of them. They picked up pens. And, at that point, even those who had not realized already, saw that there was almost nothing they dared write down. It was most frustrating. Here they were, with real, interesting events going on for once, and plenty of things to say, and almost none of it was fit for Miss Cadwallader's eyes. People chewed pens, shifted, scratched their heads, and stared at the ceiling. The most pitiable ones were those who were planning to ask Nan to endow them with the Golden Touch, or instant fame, or some other good thing. If they described any of the magic Nan was thought to have done, she would be arrested for witchcraft, and they would have killed the goose that laid the golden eggs.

Nan Pilgrim is not really a witch, Dan Smith wrote, after much hard thinking. He had rather a stomachache after last night's midnight feast and it made his mind go slow. *I never thought she was really, it was just Mr. Crossley having a joke. There was a pratical joke this morning, it must have been hard work pinching everyone's shoes like that and then someone pinched my spikes and got me really mad. The caretakers dog peed*—And there Dan stopped, remembering Miss Cadwallader would read this too. Got quite carried away there, he thought.

No comment again today, Nirupam wrote swiftly. *Someone is riding for a fall. Not that I blame them for this afternoon, but the shoes were silly.* He put down his pen and went to sleep. He had been up half the night eating buns from under the floorboards.

My bedsocks were ruined, Theresa complained in her angel-writing. *My knitting was destroyed. Today has been awful. I do not want to tell tales and I know Simon Silverson is not in his right mind but someone should* do *something. Teddy Crossley is useless and unfair and Estelle Green always thinks she knows best but she can't keep her knitting clean. The matron was unfair too. She sent me away with an aspirin and she let Brian Wentworth lie down and I was* really ill. *I shall never speak to Nan Pilgrim again.*

Most people, though they could not attain Theresa's eloquence, managed to write something in the end. But three people still sat staring at blank paper. These were Simon, Charles, and Nan.

Simon was very cunning. He was clever. He was thoroughly suspicious of the whole thing. They were trying to catch him out somehow. The safest and cleverest thing was not to commit anything to writing. He was sure of that. On the other hand, it would not do to let everyone know how clever he had gone. It would look peculiar. He ought to write just one thing. So, after more than half an hour of deep thought, he wrote: *Doggies*. It took him five minutes. Then he sat back, confident that he had fooled everyone.

Charles was stumped because he simply had no code for most of the things which had happened. He knew he had to write something, but the more he tried to think, the more difficult it seemed. At one point, he almost went to sleep like Nirupam. He pulled himself together. Think! Well, he could not write *I got up* for a start, because he had almost enjoyed today. Nor could he write *I didn't get up* because that made no sense. But he had better mention the shoes, because everyone else would. And he could talk about Simon under the code of potatoes. Mr. Towers could get a mention too.

It was nearly time for the bell before Charles sorted all this out. Hastily he scrawled: *Our shoes all went to play games. I thought about potatoes having hair hanging on a rope. I have games with a bad book.* As Mr. Crossley told them to put away their journals, Charles thought of something else and dashed it down. *I shall never be hot again.*

Nan wrote nothing at all. She sat smiling at her empty page, feeling no need to describe anything. When the bell went, as a gesture, she wrote down the date: October 30. Then she shut her journal.

The instant Mr. Crossley left the room, Nan was surrounded. "You got my note?" People clamored at her. "Can you make it that whenever I touch a penny it turns to gold? Just pennies."

"Can you make my hair go like Theresa's?"

"Can you give me three wishes every time I say Buttons?"

"I want big muscles like Dan Smith."

"Can you get us ice cream for supper?"

"I need good luck for the rest of my life."

Nan looked over at where Simon sat, hunched up with cunning and darting shrewd, stupid looks at Nirupam, who was sitting watchfully over him. If it was Simon who was responsible, there was no knowing when he would say something to cancel her witchcraft. Nan refused to believe it *was* Simon, but it was silly to make rash promises, whatever had made her a witch.

"There isn't time to work magic now," she told the clamoring crowd. And when that brought a volley of appeals and groans, she shouted, "It takes *hours*, don't you understand? You don't only have to mutter spells and brew potions. You have got to go out and pick strange herbs, and say stranger incantations, at dawn and full moon, before you can even begin. And when you've done all that, it doesn't necessarily work right away. Most of the time, you have to fly round and round the smoking herbs all night, chanting sounds of unutterable sweetness, before anything happens at all. Now do you see?" Utter silence greeted this piece of invention. Much encouraged, Nan added, "Besides, what have any of you done to deserve me going to all that trouble?"

"What indeed?" Mr. Wentworth asked, from behind her. "What exactly is going on here?"

Nan spun round. Mr. Wentworth was right in the middle of the room and had probably heard every word. Around her, everyone was slinking back to their seats. "That was my speech for the school concert, sir," she said. "Do you think it's any good?"

"It has possibilities," said Mr. Wentworth. "But it will need a little more working up to be quite good enough. Math books out, please."

Nan sank down into her seat, weak with relief. For one awful moment, she had thought Mr. Wentworth might have her arrested.

"I said math books out, Simon," Mr. Wentworth said. "Why are you giving me that awful cunning look? Is it such a peculiar thing to ask?"

Simon considered this. Nirupam, and a number of other people, doubled their legs under their chairs, ready to spring up and gag Simon if necessary. Theresa once more jumped to her feet.

"Mr. Wentworth, if he says another word, I'm not staying!"

Unfortunately, this attracted Simon's attention. "You," he said to Theresa, "stink."

"He seems to have spoken," said Mr. Wentworth. "Get out and

stand in the corridor, Theresa, with a black mark for bad behavior. Simon can have another, and the rest of us will have a lesson."

Theresa, redder in the face than anyone had ever seen her, raced for the door. She could not, however, beat the truly awful smell which rolled off her and filled the room as she ran.

"Pooh!" said Dan Smith.

Somebody kicked him, and everybody looked nervously at Mr. Wentworth to see if he could smell it too. But, as often happens to people who smoke a pipe, Mr. Wentworth had less than the average sense of smell. It was not for five minutes, during which he had written numerous things on the board and said many more, none of which 6B were in a fit state to attend to, that he said, "Estelle, put down that gray bag you're knitting and open a window, will you? There's rather a smell in here. Has someone let off a stink bomb?"

Nobody answered. Nirupam resourcefully passed Simon a note, saying, *Say there is no smell in here.*

Simon spelled it out. He considered it carefully, with his head on one side. He could see there was a trick in it somewhere. So he cunningly decided to say nothing.

Luckily, the open window, though it made the room almost as cold as Simon's Ice Age, did slowly disperse the smell. But nothing could disperse it from Theresa, who stood in the passage giving out scents of sludge, kippers, and old dustbins until the end of afternoon school.

When the bell had rung and Mr. Wentworth swept from the room, everyone relaxed with a groan. No one had known what Simon was going to say next. Even Charles had found it a strain. He had to admit that the results of his spell had taken him thoroughly by surprise.

Meanwhile, Delia and Karen, with most of Theresa's main friends, were determined to retrieve Theresa's honor. They surrounded Simon. "Take that smell off her at once," Delia said. "It's not funny. You've been on her all afternoon, Simon Silverson!"

Simon considered them. Nirupam leaped up so quickly that he knocked over his desk, and tried to put his hand over Simon's mouth. But he got there too late. "You girls," said Simon, "all stink."

The result was almost overpowering. So was the noise the girls made. The only girls who escaped were the lucky few, like Nan, who had already left the room. It was clear something had to be done. Most people were either smelling or choking. And Simon was slowly opening his mouth to say something else.

Nirupam left off trying to pick up his desk and seized hold of Simon by his shoulders. "You can break this spell," he said to him. "You could have stopped it straight away if you had any brain at all. But you would be greedy."

Simon looked at Nirupam in slow, dawning annoyance. He was being accused of being stupid. Him! He opened his mouth to speak.

"Don't *say* anything!" everyone near him shouted.

Simon gazed round at them, wondering what trick they were up to now. Nirupam shook him. "Say this after me," he said. And, when Simon's dull, cunning eyes turned to him, Nirupam said, slowly and loudly, "Nothing I said this afternoon came true. Go on. Say it."

"*Say* it!" everyone yelled.

Simon's slow mind was not proof against all this yelling. It gave in. "Nothing I said this afternoon came true," he said obediently.

The smell instantly stopped. Presumably everything else was also undone, because Simon at once became his usual self again. He had almost no memory of the afternoon. But he could see Nirupam was taking unheard-of liberties. He looked at Nirupam's hands, one on each of his shoulders, in surprise and annoyance. "Get off!" he said. "Take your face away."

The spell was still working. Nirupam was forced to let go and stand back from Simon. But, as soon as he had, he plunged back again and once more took hold of Simon's shoulders. He stared into Simon's face like a great dark hypnotist. "Now say," he said, " 'Nothing I say is going to come true in the future.' "

Simon protested at this. He had great plans for the future. "Now, look here!" he said. And of course Nirupam did. He looked at Simon with such intensity that Simon blinked as he went on with his protest. "But I'll fail every exam I ever ta-a-a-ake—!" His voice faded out into a sort of hoot, as he realized what he had said. For Simon loved passing exams. He collected A's and ninety percents as fervently as he collected honor marks. And what he had just said had stopped all that.

"Exactly," said Nirupam. "Now you've *got* to say it. Nothing I say—"

"Oh, all right. Nothing I say is going to come true in the future," Simon said peevishly.

Nirupam let go of him with a sigh of relief and went back to pick up his desk. Everyone sighed. Charles turned sadly away. Well, it had been good while it lasted.

"What's the matter?" Nirupam asked, catching sight of Charles's doleful face as he stood his desk on its legs again.

"Nothing," Charles said. "I—I've got detention." Then, with a good deal more pleasure, he turned to Simon. "So have you," he said.

Simon was scandalized. "What? I've never had detention all the time I've been at this school!"

It was explained to him that this was untrue. Quite a number of people were surprisingly ready to give Simon details of how he had rendered himself mindless and gained an hour and a half of detention from Mr. Crossley. Simon took it in very bad part and stormed off muttering.

Charles was about to trudge away after Simon, when Nirupam caught his arm. "Sit on the back bench," he said. "There's a store of comics in the middle, on the shelf underneath."

"Thanks," said Charles. He was so unused to people being friendly that he said it with enormous surprise and almost forgot to take Mr. Towers's awful book with him.

He trudged toward the old lab, where detention was held, and shortly found himself trudging behind Theresa Mullett. Theresa was proceeding toward detention, looking wronged and tragic, supported by a crowd of her friends, with Karen Grigg in addition.

"It's only for an hour," Charles heard Karen say consolingly.

"A whole *hour!*" Theresa exclaimed. "I shall never forgive Teddy Crossley for this! I hope Miss Hodge kicks him in the teeth!"

In order not to go behind Theresa's procession the whole way, Charles turned off halfway through the quadrangle and went by the way that was always called "round the back." It was a grassy space which had once been a second quadrangle. But the new labs and the lecture room and the library had been built in the space, sticking out into the grass at odd angles, so that the space had been pared down to a zigzag of grassy passage, where, for some reason, there was always a piercing wind blowing. It was a place where people only went to keep out of the way. So Charles was not particularly surprised to see Nan Pilgrim loitering about there. He prepared to glare at her as he trudged by. But Nan got in first with a very unfriendly look and moved off round the library corner.

I'm glad it wasn't Charles Morgan who wrote me that note, Nan thought, as Charles went on without speaking. I don't want any help from *him.*

She loitered out into the keen wind again, wondering if she needed help from anyone. She still felt a strong, confident inner witchiness. It was marvelous. It was like laughter bubbling up through everything she thought. She could not believe that it might be only Simon's doing. On the other hand, no one knew better than Nan how quickly inner confidence could drain away. Particularly if someone like Theresa laughed at you.

Another person was coming. Brian Wentworth this time. But he scurried by on the other side of the passage, to Nan's relief. She did not think Brian could help anyone. And—this place seemed unusually popular this evening—here was Nirupam Singh now, wandering up from the other direction, looking rather pleased with himself.

"I took the spell off Simon Silverson," he said to Nan. "I got him to say nothing he said was true."

"Good," said Nan. She wandered away round the library corner again. Did this mean she was no longer a witch then? She poked with one foot at the leaves and crisp packets the wind had blown into the corner. She could test it by turning them into something, she supposed.

But Nirupam had followed her round the corner. "No, wait," he said. "It was me that sent you that note."

Nan found this extremely embarrassing. She pretended to be very interested in the dead leaves. "I don't need help," she said gruffly.

Nirupam smiled and leaned against the library wall as if he were sunning himself. Nirupam had rather a strong personality, Nan realized. Though the sun was thin and yellow and the wind was whirling crisp packets about, Nirupam gave out such a strong impression of basking that Nan almost felt warm. "Everyone thinks you're a witch," he said.

"Well I *am*," Nan insisted, because she wanted to be sure of it herself.

"You shouldn't admit it," said Nirupam. "But it makes no difference. The point is, it's only a matter of time before someone goes to Miss Cadwallader and accuses you."

"Are you sure? They all want me to do things," said Nan.

"Theresa doesn't," said Nirupam. "Besides, you can't please everybody. Someone will get annoyed before long. I know this, because my brother tried to please all the servants. But one of them thought my brother was giving more to the other servants and told the police. And my brother was burned in the streets of Delhi."

"I'm sorry—I didn't know," said Nan. She looked across at Nirupam. His profile was like a chubby hawk, she thought. It looked desperately sad.

"My mother was burned too, for trying to save him," Nirupam said. "That was why my father came to this country, but things are just the same here. What I want to tell you is this—I have heard of a witches' underground rescue service in England. They help accused witches to escape, if you can get to one of their branches before the inquisitors come. I don't know where they send you, or whom to ask, but Estelle does. If you are accused, you must get Estelle to help."

"Estelle?" Nan said. She thought of Estelle's soft brown eyes and soft wriggly curls, and of Estelle's irritating chatter, and of Estelle's even more irritating way of imitating Theresa. She could not see Estelle helping anyone.

"Estelle is rather nice," said Nirupam. "I come round here and talk to her quite often."

"You mean Estelle talks to *you*," said Nan.

Nirupam grinned. "She does talk a lot," he agreed. "But she will help. She told me she likes you. She was sad you didn't like her."

Nan gaped. Estelle? It was not possible. No one liked Nan. But, now she remembered, Estelle had refused to come and threaten to drown her in the bathroom. "All right," she said. "I'll ask her. Thanks. But are you *sure* I'll be accused?"

Nirupam nodded. "There is this, you see. There are at least two other witches in 6B—"

"Two?" said Nan. "I mean, I know there's *one* more. It's obvious. But why *two?*"

"I told you," said Nirupam, "I've had experience of witches. Each one has their own style. It's like the way everyone's writing is different. And I tell you that it was not the same person who did the birds in music and the spell on Simon today. Those are two quite different outlooks on life. But both those people must know they have been very silly to do anything at all, and they will both be wanting to put the blame on you. It could well be one of them who accuses you. So you must be very careful. I will do my part and warn you if I hear of any trouble coming. Then you must ask Estelle to help you. Do you see now?"

"Yes, and I'm awfully grateful," said Nan. Regretfully, she saw she did not dare try turning the dead leaves into anything. And, in spite of her promise to the old broom, she had better not ride it again. She was quite frightened. Yet she still felt the laughing confidence bubbling up inside, even though there might not be anything now to be confident about. Watch it! she told herself. You must be mad!

CHAPTER 9

The old lab was not used for anything much except detention. But there was still a faint smell of old science clinging to it, from generations of experiments which had gone wrong. Charles slid onto the splintery back bench and propped Mr. Towers's awful book against the stump of an old gas pipe. The comics were there, stacked on the shelf underneath, just below a place where someone had spent industrious hours carving *Cadwallader is a bag* on the bench top. The rest of the people in the room were all at the front. They were mostly from 5B or 5C, and probably did not know about the comics.

Simon came in. Charles gave him a medium-strength glare to discourage him from the back bench. Simon went and sat haughtily in the very middle of the middle bench. Good. Then Mr. Wentworth came in. Not so good. Mr. Wentworth was carefully carrying a steaming mug of coffee, which everyone in the room looked at with mute envy. It would *have* to be Mr. Wentworth! Charles thought resentfully.

Mr. Wentworth set his cup of coffee carefully down on the teacher's bench and looked round to see who was doing time. He seemed surprised to see Simon and not at all surprised to see Charles. "Anyone need paper for lines?" he asked.

Charles did. He went up with most of 5B and was handed a lump of someone's old exam. The exam had used only one side of the paper, so, Charles supposed, it made sense to use the other side for lines. But it did, all the same, seem like a deliberate way of showing people how pointlessly they were wasting time here. Wasting wastepaper. And Charles could tell, as Mr. Wentworth gave the paper out, that he was in his nastiest and most harrowed mood.

Not good at all, Charles thought, as he slid back behind the back bench. For, though Charles had not particularly thought about it, it was obvious to him that he was going to use witchcraft to copy out Mr. Towers's awful book. What was the point of being a witch if you didn't make use of it? But he would have to go carefully with Mr. Wentworth in this mood.

The door opened. Theresa made an entry with her crowd of supporters.

Mr. Wentworth looked at them. "Come in," he said. "So glad you were able to make it, all of you. Sit down, Delia. Find a seat, Karen. Heather, Deborah, Julia, Theresa, and the rest can no doubt all squeeze in round Simon."

"*We* haven't got detention, sir," Delia said.

"We just came to bring Theresa," Deborah explained.

"Why? Didn't she know the way?" said Mr. Wentworth. "Well, you all have detention now—"

"But, sir! We only came—!"

"—unless you get out this second," said Mr. Wentworth.

Theresa's friends vanished. Theresa looked angrily at Simon, who was sitting in the place she would otherwise have chosen, and carefully selected a place at the end of the bench just behind him. "This is all your fault," she whispered to Simon.

"Drop dead!" said Simon.

It was, Charles thought, rather a pity that Nirupam had managed to break the *Simon Says* spell.

Silence descended, the woeful, restless silence of people who wish they were elsewhere. Mr. Wentworth opened a book and picked up his coffee. Charles waited until Mr. Wentworth seemed thoroughly into his book, and then brought out his ballpoint pen. He ran his finger and thumb down it, just as he had done with Simon's hair, down and down again. Write lines, he thought to it. Write five hundred lines out of this book. Write lines. Then, very grudgingly, he wrote out the first sentence for it—*"What ripping fun!" exclaimed Watts Minor. "I'm down for scrum half this afternoon!"*—to show it what to do. Then he cautiously let go of it. And the pen not only stood where he had left it but began to write industriously. Charles arranged Mr. Towers's book so that it would hide the scribbling pen. Then, with a sigh of satisfaction, he fetched out one of the comics and settled down as comfortably as Mr. Wentworth.

Five minutes later, he thought a thunderbolt hit him.

The pen fell down and rolled on the floor. The comic was snatched away. His right ear was in agony. Charles looked up—mistily, because his glasses were now hanging from his left ear—to find Mr. Wentworth towering over him. The pain in his ear was from the excruciatingly tight grip Mr. Wentworth had on it.

"Get up," Mr. Wentworth said, dragging at the ear.

Charles got up perforce. Mr. Wentworth led him, like that, by the ear, with his head painfully on one side, to the front of the room. Halfway there, Charles's glasses fell off his other ear. He almost didn't have the heart to catch them. In fact, he only saved them by reflex. He was fairly sure he would not be needing them much longer.

At the front, he could see just well enough to watch Mr. Wentworth cram the comic one-handed into the wastepaper basket. "Let that teach you to read comics in detention!" Mr. Wentworth said. "Now come with me." He led Charles, still by the ear, to the door. There, he turned round and spoke to the others in the room. "If anyone so much as stirs," he said, "while I'm gone, he or she will be here for double time, every night till Christmas." Upon this, he towed Charles outside.

He towed Charles some distance up the covered way outside. Then he let go of Charles's ear, took hold of his shoulders, and commenced shaking him. Charles had never been shaken like that. He bit his tongue. He thought his neck was breaking. He thought the whole of him was coming apart. He grabbed his left hand in his right one to try and hold himself together—and felt his glasses snap into two pieces. That was it, then. He could hardly breathe when Mr. Wentworth at last let go of him.

"I warned you!" Mr. Wentworth said, furiously angry. "I called you to my room and purposely warned you! Are you a complete fool, boy? How much more frightened do you have to be? Do you need to be in front of the inquisitors before you stop?"

"I—" gasped Charles. "I—" He had never known Mr. Wentworth could be this angry.

Mr. Wentworth went on, in a lifting undertone that was far more frightening than shouting, "Three times—three times today to *my* knowledge—you've used witchcraft. And the Lord knows how many times I *don't* know about. Are you *trying* to give yourself away? Have you the *least* idea what risk you run? What kind of a show-off are you? *All* the shoes in the school this morning—"

"That—that was a mistake, sir," Charles panted. "I—I was trying to find my spikes."

"A *stupid* thing to waste witchcraft on!" said Mr. Wentworth. "And not content with a public display like that, you *then* go and cast spells on Simon Silverson!"

"How did you know that was me?" said Charles.

"One look at your face, boy. And what's more, you were sitting there letting the unfortunate Nan Pilgrim take the blame. I call that thoroughly selfish and despicable! And now this! Writing lines where anyone could see you! You are lucky, let me tell you, boy, *very* lucky not to be down at the police station at this moment, waiting for the inquisitor. You *deserve* to be there. Don't you?" He shook Charles again. "Don't you?"

"Yes, sir," said Charles.

"And you will be," said Mr. Wentworth, "if you do one more thing. You're to forget about witchcraft, understand? Forget about magic. Try to be normal, if you know what that means. Because I promise you that if you do it again, you will be *really* in trouble. Is that clear?"

"Yes, sir," said Charles.

"Now get back in there and write properly!" Mr. Wentworth shoved Charles in front with one hand, and Charles could feel that hand shaking with anger. Frightening though that was, Charles was glad of it. He could barely see a thing without his glasses. When Mr. Wentworth burst back with him into the old lab, the room was just a large fuzzy blur. But he could tell everyone was looking at him. The air was thick with people thinking, I'm glad it wasn't me!

"Get back to your seat," Mr. Wentworth said, and let go of Charles with a sharp push.

Charles felt his way through swimming colored blurs, down to the other end of the old lab. Those crooked white squares must be the book and the old exam paper. But his pen, he remembered, had fallen on the floor. How was he to find it, in this state, let alone write with it?

"What are you standing there for?" Mr. Wentworth barked at him. "Put your glasses on and get back to work!"

Charles jumped with terror. He found himself diving for his seat, and hooking his glasses on as he dived. The world clicked into focus. He saw his pen lying almost under his feet and bent to pick it up. But surely, he thought, as he was half under the bench, his glasses had been in two pieces? He had heard a dreadfully final snapping noise. He thought he had felt them come apart. He put his hand up hurriedly and felt his glasses—there was no point taking them off and looking, because then he would not be able to see. They felt all right. Entire and whole. Either he had made a mistake, or the plastic had snapped and not the metal inside. Much relieved, Charles sat up with the pen in his hand.

And stared at what it had written by itself. *I am Watts down scrum Minor ripping this fun afternoon. I fun Minor am half this afternoon Watts* . . . and so on, for two whole pages. It was no good. Mr. Towers was bound to notice. Charles sighed and began writing. Perhaps he *should* stop doing witchcraft. Nothing seemed to go right.

Consequently, the rest of the evening was rather quiet. Charles sat in devvy running his thumb over the fat cushion of blister on his finger, not wanting to give up witchcraft and knowing he dared not go on. He felt such a mixture of regret and terror that it quite bewildered him. Simon was subdued too. Brian Wentworth was back, sitting scribbling industriously, with one eye still turned slightly inward, but Simon seemed to have lost his desire to hit Brian for the time being. And Simon's friends followed Simon's lead.

Nan kept quiet also, because of what Nirupam had said, but, however hard she reasoned with herself, she could not get rid of that bubbling inner confidence. It was still with her in the dormitory that night. It stayed, in spite of Delia, Deborah, Heather, and the rest, who began on her in their usual way.

"It was a bit much, that spell on Simon!"

"Really, Nan, I know we asked you, but you should *think* first."

"Look what he did to Theresa. And she lost her knitting over it."

And Nan, instead of submitting or apologizing, as she usually did, said, "What's put it into your pretty little heads that that spell was mine?"

"Because we know you're a witch," said Heather.

"Of course," said Nan. "But what gave you the idea I was the only one? You think, Heather, instead of just opening your little pink mouth and letting words trickle out. I told you, it takes *time* to make a spell. I told you about picking herbs and flying round and chanting, didn't I? And I left out the way you have to catch bats. That takes ages, even on a fast modern broomstick, because bats are so good at dodging. And you were with me in the bathroom, and with me all the time all this last week, and you *know* I haven't had time to catch bats or pick herbs, and you've *seen* I haven't been muttering and incantating. So you see? It wasn't me."

She could tell they were convinced, because they all looked so disappointed. Heather muttered, "And you said you couldn't fly that broomstick!" but she said nothing more. Nan was pleased. She seemed to have shut them up without losing her reputation as a witch.

All except Karen. Karen was newly admitted to the number of Theresa's friends. That made her very zealous. "Well, I think you should work a spell now," she said. "Theresa's lost a pair of bootees she spent hours knitting, and I think the least you can do is get them back for her."

"No trouble at all," Nan said airily. "But does Theresa want me to try?"

Theresa finished buttoning her pajamas and turned away to brush her hair. "She's not going to try, Karen," she said. "I should be *ashamed* to get my knitting back that way!"

"Lights out," said a monitor at the door. "Do these belong to anyone? The caretaker found them in his dog's basket." She held up two small gray fluffy things with holes in them.

The look everyone gave Nan, as Theresa went to claim her bootees, made Nan wonder if she had been wise to talk like that. And I don't even really know if I'm still a witch, she thought, as she got into bed. I'll keep my mouth shut in the future. And that broomstick stays on top of the cupboard. I don't care if I did promise it.

Right in the middle of the night, she was awakened by something prodding at her. Nan, in her sleep, rolled out of the way, and rolled again, until she woke up in the act of falling out of bed. There was a swift swishing noise. Something she only dimly saw in the near-dark dived over her and then dived under her. Nan woke up completely to find herself six feet off the floor and doubled over the broomstick, with her head hanging down one side and her feet the other. The knobby handle was a painful thing to be draped over. Nevertheless, Nan began to laugh. I *am* a witch after all! she thought joyfully.

"Put me down, you big fraud!" she whispered. "You were just playing for sympathy, pretending you needed a rider, weren't you? Put me down and go and fly yourself!"

The broomstick's answer was to rise up to the ceiling. Nan's bed looked like a small dim oblong from there. She knew she would miss it if she tried to jump off.

"You big bully!" she said. "I know I promised, but that was before—!"

The broom drifted suggestively toward the window. Nan became alarmed. The window was open because Theresa believed in fresh air. She had visions of herself being carted over the countryside, draped over the stick in nothing but pajamas. She gave in.

"All right. I'll fly you. But let me go down and get some blankets first. I'm not going to go like this!"

The broom whirled round and swooped back to Nan's bed. Nan's legs flew out and she landed on the mattress with a bounce. The broom did not trust her in the least. It hovered over her while she dragged the pink school blankets from her bed, and as soon as she had wrapped them round her, it made quite sure of her by darting underneath her and swooping up to the ceiling again. Nan was thrown backward. She nearly ended hanging underneath again.

"Go carefully!" she whispered. "Let me get settled."

The broom hovered impatiently while Nan tried to balance herself and get comfortable. She did not dare take too long over it. All the swooping and whispering were disturbing the other girls. Quite a few of them were turning over and murmuring crossly. Nan tried to sit on the broom and toppled over sideways. She got tangled in her blankets. In the end, she simply fell forward on her face and settled for lying along the handle again, in a bundle of blanket, with her feet hooked up on the brush.

Before she had even gotten comfortable like that, the broomstick swooped to the window, nudged it further open, and darted outside. There was pitch black night out there. It was cold, with a drizzle of rain falling. Nan wrinkled her face against it and tried to get used to being high up. The broom flew with a strange choppy movement, not altogether pleasant for a person lying on her face.

Nan talked, to take her mind off it. "How is this," she said, "for romantic dreams come true? I always thought of myself flying a broomstick on a warm summer night, outlined against an enormous moon, with a nightingale or so singing its head off. And look at us!" Underneath her, the broomstick jerked. It was obviously a shrug.

"Yes, I daresay it is the best we can do," Nan said. "But I don't feel very glamorous like this, and I'm getting wet. I bet Dulcinea Wilkes used to *sit* on her broom, gracefully, sidesaddle probably, with her long hair flowing out behind. And because it was London, she probably wore an elegant silk dress, with lots of lacy petticoats showing from underneath. Did you know I was descended from Dulcinea Wilkes?"

The rippling underneath her might have been the broom's way of nodding. But it could have been laughing at the contrast.

Nan found she could see in the dark now. She looked down and blenched. The broomstick felt very flimsy to be this high. It had soared and turned while she was talking, so that the square shapes of the school were a long way below and to one side. The pale spread of the playing field was directly underneath, and beyond that Nan could see the entire town, filling the valley ahead. The houses were all dark, with orange chains of streetlights in between. And in spite of the drifting drizzle, Nan could see as far as the blackness of Larwood Forest on the hill opposite.

"Let's fly over the forest," she said.

The broom swept off. Once you got used to it, it really would be a nice feeling, Nan told herself firmly, blinking against the drizzle. Secret, silent flight. It was in her blood. She held the end of the broom handle in both hands and tried to point it at the town. But the broom had other ideas. It wanted to go round the edge of the town. The result was that they flew sideways, jolting a little.

"Fly over the houses," said Nan.

The broom gave a shake that nearly sent her tumbling off. No.

"I suppose someone might look up and see us," Nan agreed. "All right. You win again. Bully." And it occurred to her that her dreams of flying against a huge full moon were really the most arrant romantic nonsense. No witch in her senses would do that, for fear the inquisitors might see her.

So they swooped over fields, and across the main road in a rush of rain. The rain at first came at Nan's face in separate drops out of the orange haze made by the streetlights. Then it was just wetness out of darkness, as they reached Larwood Forest, and the wetness brought a smell with it of autumn leaves and mushroom. But even a dark wood is not quite black at night. Nan could see paler trees, which still had yellow leaves, and she could clearly see mist caused by the rain smoking out above the trees. Some of it seemed to be real smoke. Nan smelled fire distinctly. A wet fire, burning smokily.

She suddenly felt rather quiet. "I say, that can't be a bonfire, can it? If it's after midnight, it is Halloween, isn't it?"

The idea seemed to upset the broom. It stopped with a jerk. For a second, its front end tipped downward as if it were thinking of landing. Nan had to grip hard in order not to slide off head first. Then it began actually flying backward, wagging its brush in agitated sweeps, so that Nan's feet were swirled from side to side.

"Stop it!" she said. "I shall be sick in a minute!"

They did, she knew, sometimes burn witch's brooms with the witch they belonged to. So she was not surprised when the broom swung round, away from the smell of smoke, and began flying back toward the school, in a stately sort of way, as if that was the way it had meant to go all along.

"You don't fool me," she said. "But you can go back if you want. I'm soaked."

The broom continued on its wet and stately way, high above the fields and the main road, until the pale flatness of the playing field appeared beneath them once more. Nan was just thinking that she would be in bed any minute now, when a new notion seemed to strike the broom. It dived a sickening fifty feet and put on speed. Nan found herself hurtling over the field, about twenty feet up, and oozing off backward with the speed. She hung on and shouted to it to stop. Nothing she said made any difference. The broom continued to hurtle.

"Oh really!" Nan gasped. "You are the most willful thing I've ever known! Stop!"

The rain beat in her face, but she could see something ahead now, all the same. It was something dark against the grass, and it was quite big, too big for a broom, although it was flying too, floating gently away across the field. The broom was racing toward it. As they plunged on, Nan saw that the thing was flat underneath, with the shape of a person on top of it. It got bigger and bigger. Nan decided it could only be a small carpet with a man sitting on it. She tugged and jerked at the broom handle, but there seemed nothing she could do to stop the broom.

The broom plunged gladly up alongside the dark shape. It *was* a man on a small carpet. The broom swooped round it, wagging its end so hard that Nan bit her tongue. It nuzzled and nudged and jogged at the carpet, jerking Nan this way and that as it went. And the carpet seemed equally delighted to meet the broom. It was jiggling and flapping, and rippling so that the man on top of it was rolled this way and that. Nan shrank down and clung to the broom, hoping that she just looked like a roll of blankets to whoever this witch on a carpet was.

But the man was becoming annoyed by the antics of the carpet and the broom. "Can't you control that thing yet?" he snapped.

Nan shrank down even further. Her bitten tongue made it hard to speak anyway, and she was almost glad of it. She knew that voice. It was Mr. Wentworth's.

"And I told you never to ride that thing in term time, Brian," Mr. Wentworth said. When Nan still did not say anything, he added, "I know, I know. But this wretched hearthrug insists on going out every night."

This is worse and worse! Nan thought. Mr. Wentworth thought she was Brian. So Brian must be—with a fierce effort, she managed to wrench the broom round, away from the hearthrug. With an even fiercer effort, she got it going again, toward the school. By kicking it hard with her bare toes, she kept it going. When she was some way away, she risked turning round and whispering, "Sorry." She hoped Mr. Wentworth would go on thinking she was Brian.

Mr. Wentworth called something after her as the broomstick lumbered away, but Nan did not even try to hear what it was. She did not want to know. She could still barely believe it. Besides, she needed all her attention to make the broom go. It was very reluctant. It flew across the field in a dismal, trudging way, which reminded Nan irresistibly of

Charles Morgan, but at least it went. Nan was pleased to discover that she could control it after all, when she had to.

It made particularly heavy weather of lifting Nan upward to her dormitory window. She almost believed it groaned. Some of the difficulty may have been real. All Nan's pink school blankets were soaked through by now and they must have weighed a great deal. But Nan remembered what an act the broom had put on in the afternoon and resolved to be pitiless. She drummed with her toes again. Up went the broom through the dark rainy night, up and up the wall, until at last they were outside the half-open dormitory window. Nan helped the broom shoulder the window open wider, and then swooped to the floor on her stomach. What a relief! she thought.

Someone whispered, "I put dry blankets on your bed."

Nan nearly fainted. After a pause to recover, she rolled herself off the broom and knelt up in her sopping blankets. A dim figure in regulation school pajamas was standing in front of her, bending down a little, so that Nan could see the hair was curly. Heather? No, don't be daft! Estelle. "Estelle?" she whispered.

"Hush!" whispered Estelle. "Come and help put these blankets in the airing cupboard. We can talk there."

"But the broom—?" Nan whispered.

"Send it away."

A good idea, Nan thought, if only the broom would obey. She picked it up, shedding soaking blankets as she went, and carried it to the window. "Go to the groundsman's shed," she told it in a severe whisper, and sent it off with a firm shove. Knowing the kind of broom it was, she would not have been surprised if it had simply clattered to the ground. But it obeyed her, rather to her astonishment—or at least, it flew off into the rainy night.

Estelle was already lugging the heap of blankets to the door. Nan tiptoed to help her. Together they dragged the heap down the passage and into the fateful bathroom. There, Estelle shut the door and daringly turned on the light.

"It'll be all right if we don't talk too loud," she said. "I'm awfully sorry—Theresa woke up while I was making your bed. I had to tell her you'd been sick. I said you were in the bathroom being sick again. Can you remember that if she asks tomorrow?"

"Thanks," said Nan. "That was kind of you. Did I wake you going out?"

"Yes, but it was training mostly," Estelle said. She opened the big airing cupboard. "If we fold these blankets and put them right at the back, no one's going to find them for weeks. They might even be dry by then, but with this school's heating there's no relying on that."

It was not a quick job. They had to take out the piles of pale pink dry blankets stacked in the cupboard, fold the heavy bright pink wet ones, put them in at the back, and then put all the dry ones back to hide them.

"Why did you say training woke you up?" Nan asked Estelle as they worked.

"Training with the witches' underground escape route," said Estelle. "My mum used to belong to it, and I used to help her. It took me right back, when I heard you going out—though it was usually people coming in that used to wake me up. And I knew you'd be wet when you came back, and need help. Mum brought me up to think of everything like that. We used to have witches coming in on brooms at all hours of the night, poor things. Most of them were as wet as you—and much more frightened, of course. Hold the blanket down with your chin. That's the best way to get it folded."

"Why did your mum send you away to this school?" Nan asked. "You must have been such a help."

Estelle's bright face saddened. "She didn't. The inquisitors sent me. They had a big campaign and broke up all our branch of the organization. My mum got caught. She's in prison now, for helping witches. But"—Estelle's soft brown eyes looked earnestly into Nan's face—"*please* don't say. I couldn't bear anyone else to know. You're the only one I've ever told."

CHAPTER 10

The next morning, Brian Wentworth did not get up. Simon threw a pillow at him as he lay there, but Brian did not stir.

"Wakey, wakey, Brian!" Simon said. "Get up, or I'll strip your bed off." When Brian still did not move, Simon advanced on his bed.

"Let him alone," Charles said. "He was ill yesterday."

"Anything you say, Charles," said Simon. "Your word is my command." And he pulled all the covers off Brian's bed.

Brian was not in it. Instead, there was a line of three pillows, artfully overlapped to give the shape of a body. Everyone gathered round and stared. Ronald West bent down and looked under the bed—as if he thought Brian might be there—and came up holding a piece of paper.

"Here," he said. "This must have come off with the bedclothes. Take a look!"

Simon snatched the paper from him. Everyone else craned and pushed to see it too. It was written in capital letters, in ordinary blue ballpoint, and it said: *HA HA. I HAVE GOT BRIAN WENTWORTH IN MY POWER. SIGNED, THE WITCH.*

The slightly tense look on Simon's face gave way to righteous concern. He had known at once that Brian's disappearance had nothing to do with him. "We're not going to panic," he said. "Someone get the master on duty."

There was instant emergency. Voices jabbered, rumors roared. Charles fetched Mr. Crossley, since everyone else seemed too astonished to think. After that, Mr. Crossley and monitors came and went, asking everyone when they had last seen Brian. People from the other dormitories crowded in the doorway, calling comments. Everyone was very eager to say something, but nothing very useful came out. A lot of people had noticed Brian was pale and cross-eyed the day before. Somebody said he had been ill and gone to the matron. A number of other people said he had come back later and seemed very busy writing. Everyone swore Brian had gone to bed as usual the night before.

Long before Mr. Crossley had sorted even this much out, Charles was tiptoeing hastily away downstairs. He felt sick. Up to last night, he had supposed Brian was trying to get himself invalided out of school. Now he knew better. Brian had run away, just as he had said he would. And he had taken the advice Charles had given him in the middle of the night before and confused his trail. But what had given Brian the idea of blaming the witch? Could it have been the shoes, and the sight of Charles muttering over some hairs from Simon's comb? Charles was fairly sure it was.

As Charles pushed through the boys in the corridor, he heard the words "witch" and "Nan Pilgrim" coming from all sides. Fine, as long as they went on blaming Nan. But would they? Charles took a look at his burned finger as he went down the stairs. The transparent juicy cushion of blister on it was fatter than ever. *It hurts to be burned.* Charles went the rest of the way down at a crazy gallop. He too remembered Brian scribbling and scribbling during devvy. Brian must have written pages. If there was one word about Charles Morgan in those pages, he was going to make sure no one else saw them. He pelted along the corridors. He flung himself into the classroom, squawking for breath.

Brian's desk was open. Nirupam was bending over it. He did not seem in the least surprised to see Charles. "Brian has been very eloquent," he said. "Come and see."

Behind the raised lid of the desk, Nirupam had lined up six exercise books, each of them open to a double page of hurried blue scrawl. *Help, help, help, help,* Charles read in the first. *The witch has the Evil Eye on me. HELP. I am being dragged away I know not where. HELP. My mind is in thrall. Nameless deeds are being forced upon me. HELP. The world is turning gray. The spell is working. Help . . .* And so on, for the whole two pages.

"There's yards of it!" said Charles.

"I know," said Nirupam, opening Brian's French book. "This is full of it too."

"Does it give names?" Charles asked tensely.

"Not so far," said Nirupam.

Charles was not going to take Nirupam's word for that. He picked up each book in turn and read the scrawl through. *Help. Wild chanting and horrible smells fill my ears. HELP. I can FEEL MYSELF GOING.*

The witch's will is strong. I must obey. Gray humming and horrible words. HELP. My spirit is being dragged from TIMBUKTU to UTTAR PRADESH. To utter destruction I mean. Help . . . It went on like this for all six books. Enough of it was in capitals for Charles to be quite sure that Brian had written the note under his bed himself.

After that, he read each of the rest of Brian's books as Nirupam finished with it. It was all the same kind of thing. To Charles's relief, Brian named no names. But there was still Brian's journal, at the bottom of the pile.

"If he's said anything definite, it will be in this," Nirupam said, picking up the journal. Charles reached out for it too. If necessary, he was going to force it out of Nirupam's hands by witchcraft. Or was it better just to make all the pages blank? But did he dare do either? His hand hesitated.

As Charles hesitated, they heard Mr. Crossley's voice out in the corridor. Charles and Nirupam frantically crammed the books back into Brian's desk and shut it. They raced to their own desks, sat down, got out books, and pretended to be busy finishing devvy from the night before.

"You boys should be going along to breakfast now," Mr. Crossley said, when he came in. "Go along."

Both of them had to go, without a chance of looking at Brian's journal. Charles wondered why Nirupam looked so frustrated. But he was too frightened on his own account to bother much about Nirupam's feelings.

In the corridor outside the dining hall, Mr. Wentworth rushed past them, looking even more harrowed than usual. Inside the dining hall, the rumor was going round that the police had just arrived.

"You wait," Simon said knowingly. "The inquisitor will be here before dinner time. You'll see."

Nirupam slid into a seat beside Nan. "Brian has written in all his school books about a witch putting a spell on him," he murmured to her.

Nan hardly needed this to show her the trouble she was in. Karen and Delia had already asked her several times what she had done to Brian. And Theresa had added, not looking at Nan, "Some people can't leave people alone, can they?"

"But he didn't name any names," Nirupam muttered, also not looking at Nan.

Brian didn't need to name names, Nan thought desperately. Everyone else would do that for him. And, if that was not enough, Estelle knew she had been out on the broomstick last night. She looked round for Estelle, but Estelle seemed to be avoiding her. She was at another table. At that, the last traces of witchy inner confidence left Nan completely. For once in her life, she had no appetite for breakfast. Charles was not much better. Whatever he tried to eat, the fat blister on his finger seemed to get in the way.

At the end of breakfast, another rumor went round: The police had sent for tracker dogs.

A short while after this, Miss Hodge arrived, to find the school in an uproar. It took her some time to find out what had happened, since Mr. Crossley was nowhere to be found. When Miss Phillips finally told her, Miss Hodge was delighted. Brian Wentworth had vanished! That is, Miss Hodge thought hastily, it was very sad and worrying of course, but it did give her a real excuse to attract Mr. Wentworth's attention again. Yesterday had been most frustrating. After Mr. Wentworth had brushed aside her generous apology over Charles Morgan, she had not been able to think of any other move toward getting him to marry her. But this was ideal. She could go to Mr. Wentworth and be terribly sympathetic. She could enter into his sorrow. The only difficulty was that Mr. Wentworth was not to be found, any more than Mr. Crossley. It seemed that they were both with the police in Miss Cadwallader's study.

As everyone went into the hall for assembly, they could see a police van in the quadrangle. Several healthy Alsatians were getting out of it, with their pink tongues draped over their large white fangs in a way that suggested they could hardly wait to get on and hunt something. A number of faces turned pale. There was a lot of nervous giggling.

"It doesn't matter if the dogs don't find anything," Simon could be heard explaining. "The inquisitor will simply run his witch-detector over everyone in the class, and they'll find the witch that way."

To Nan's relief, Estelle came pushing along the line and stood next to her. "Estelle—!" Nan began violently.

"Not now," Estelle whispered. "Wait for the singing."

Neither Mr. Wentworth nor Miss Cadwallader came into assembly. Mr. Brubeck and Mr. Towers, who sat in the main chairs instead, did not explain about that, and neither of them mentioned Brian. This seemed to make it all much more serious. Mr. Towers chose his favorite hymn. It was, to Nan's misery, "He Who Would Valiant Be." This hymn always caused Theresa to look at Nan and giggle, when it came to "To be a pilgrim." Nan had to wait for Theresa to do that before she dared to speak to Estelle, and, she thought, Theresa's giggle was rather nastier than usual.

"Estelle," Nan whispered, as soon as everyone had started the second verse. "Estelle, you don't think I went out—last night, the way I did—because of Brian, do you? I swear I didn't."

"I know you didn't," Estelle whispered back. "What would anyone want Brian *for*, anyway?"

"But everyone thinks I did! What shall I *do?*" Nan whispered back.

"It's PE second lesson. I'll show you then," said Estelle.

Charles was also whispering under cover of the singing, to Nirupam. "What are witch-detectors? Do they work?"

"Machines in black boxes," Nirupam said breathily at his hymn book. "And they always find a witch with them."

Mr. Wentworth had talked about witch-detectors too. So, Charles thought, if the rumor was right and the inquisitor got here before lunchtime, today was the end of Charles. Charles hated Brian. Selfish beast. Yes, all right, he had been selfish too, but Brian was even worse. There was only one thing to do now, and that was to run away as well. But those tracker dogs made that nearly impossible.

When they got to the classroom, Brian's desk had been taken away. Charles looked at the empty space in horror. Fingerprints! he thought. Nirupam had gone quite yellow.

"They took it to give the dogs the scent," said Dan Smith. He added thoughtfully, "They're trained to tear people to pieces, those police dogs. I wonder if they'll tear Brian up, or just the witch."

Charles looked at the blister on his finger and realized that burning was not the only thing that hurt. His first thought had been to run away during break. Now he decided to go in PE, next lesson. He wished there were not a whole lesson in between.

That lesson seemed to last about a year. And for most of that lesson, policemen were continually going past the windows with dogs on leads. Back and forth they went. Wherever Brian had gone, they seemed to be finding it hard to pick up his scent.

By this time, Nan's hands were shaking so that she could hardly hold her pen. Thanks to last night, she knew exactly why Brian had left no scent. It was that double-dealing broomstick. It must have flown Brian out before it came and woke her up. Nan was sure of it. She could have taken the police to the exact spot where Brian was. That was no bonfire she had smelled over Larwood Forest last night. It had been Brian's campfire. The broomstick had brought her right over the spot and then realized its mistake. That was why it had gotten so agitated and tried to fly away backward. She was so angry with Brian for getting her blamed that she wished she really could tell them where he was. But the moment she did that, she proved that she was a witch and incriminated Mr. Wentworth into the bargain. Oh, it was too bad of

Brian! Nan just hoped Estelle could think of some kind of rescue before someone accused her, and she started accusing Brian and Mr. Wentworth.

Just before the end of that lesson, the dogs must have found some kind of scent. When the girls walked round the outside of the school on their way to the girls' locker room, to change for PE, there was not a policeman or a dog in sight. As the line of girls went past the shrubbery, Estelle gently took hold of Nan's arm and pulled her toward the bushes. Nan let herself be pulled. She did not know if she was more relieved or more terrified. It was a little early in the day to find seniors in the shrubbery, but even so, surely somebody would notice.

"We have to go into town," Estelle whispered, as they pushed among the wet bushes. "To the Old Gate House."

"Why?" Nan asked, thrusting her way after Estelle.

"Because," Estelle whispered over her shoulder, "the lady there runs the Larwood branch of the witches' escape route."

They came out into the grass beside the huge laurel bush. Nan looked from Estelle's scared face to Estelle's trim blazer and school skirt. Then she looked down at her own plump shape. Different as they were, they were both obviously in Larwood House school uniforms. "But if someone sees us in town, they'll report us to Miss Cadwallader."

"I was hoping," Estelle whispered, "that you might be able to change us into ordinary clothes."

Nan realized that the only witchcraft she had ever done was to fly that broom. She had not the least idea how you changed clothes. But Estelle was relying on her and it really was urgent. Feeling an awful fool, Nan held out both shaking hands and said the first thing remotely like a spell that came into her head.

"Eeny, meeny, miney, mo,
Out of uniform we go!"

There was a swirling feeling around her. Estelle was suddenly in a small snowstorm that seemed to be made of little bits of rag. Navy blue rag, then dark rag. The rags settled like burnt paper, clinging to Estelle and hanging, and clinging to Nan too. And there they both were in seconds, dressed as witches, in long trailing black dresses, pointed black hats and all.

Estelle clapped both hands to her mouth to stop a giggle. Nan snorted with laughter. "This won't do! Try again," giggled Estelle.

"What do you want to wear?" Nan asked.

Estelle's eyes shone. "Riding clothes," she whispered ardently. "With a red jumper, please."

Nan stretched out her hands again. Now she knew she could do it, she felt quite confident.

"Agga, tagga, ragga, roast.
Wear the clothes you want the most."

The rag-storm began again. In Estelle's case, it started black and swirled very promisingly into pale brown and red. Around Nan, it seemed to be turning pink. When the storm stopped, there was Estelle, looking very trim and pretty in jodhpurs, red sweater, and hard hat, with her legs in shiny boots, pointing at Nan with a riding crop and making helpless bursting noises.

Nan looked down at herself. It seemed that the sort of clothes she wanted most was the dress she had imagined Dulcinea Wilkes wearing to ride her broomstick round London in. She was in a shiny pink silk balldress. The full skirt swept the wet grass. The tight pink bodice left her shoulders bare. It had blue bows up the front and lace in the sleeves. No wonder Estelle was laughing! Pink silk was definitely a mistake for someone as plump as Nan. Why pink? she wondered. Probably she had gotten that idea from the school blankets.

She had her hands stretched out to try again, when they heard Karen Grigg shouting outside the shrubbery. "Estelle! *Estelle!* Where are you? Miss Phillips wants to know where you've gotten to!"

Estelle and Nan turned and ran. Estelle's clothes were ideal for sprinting through bushes. Nan's were not. She lumbered and puffed behind Estelle, and wet leaves kept showering her bare shoulders with water. Her sleeves got in her way. Her skirt wrapped round her legs and kept catching on bushes. Just at the edge of the shrubbery, the dress got stuck on a twig and tore with such a loud ripping noise that Estelle whirled round in horror.

"Wait!" panted Nan. She wrenched the pink skirt loose and tore the whole bottom part of it off. She wrapped the torn bit like a scarf round her wet shoulders. "That's better."

After that, she could keep up with Estelle quite easily. They slipped through on to the school drive and pelted down it and out through the iron gates. Nan meant to stop and change the pink dress into something else in the road outside, but there was a man sweeping the pavement just beyond the gates. He stopped sweeping and stared at the two of them. A little further on, there were two ladies with shopping bags, who stared even harder. Nan put her head down in acute embarrassment as they walked past the ladies. She had strips of torn pink silk hanging down and clinging to the pale blue stockings she seemed to have changed her socks into. Below that, she seemed to have given herself pink ballet shoes.

"Will you call for me at my ballet class after you've had your riding lesson?" she said loudly and desperately to Estelle.

"I might. But I'm scared of your ballet teacher," Estelle said, playing up bravely.

They got past the ladies, but there were more people further down the road. The further they got into town, the more people there were. By the time they came to the shops, Nan knew she was not going to get a chance to change the pink balldress.

"You look awfully pretty. Really," Estelle said consolingly.

"No, I don't. It's like a bad dream," said Nan.

"In my bad dreams like that, I don't have any clothes on at all," said Estelle.

At last they reached the strange red brick castle which was the Old Gate House. Estelle, looking white and nervous, led Nan up the steps and under the pointed porch. Nan pulled the large bell pull hanging beside the pointed front door. Then they stood under the arch and waited, more nervous than ever.

For a long time, they thought nobody was going to answer the door. Then, after nearly five minutes, it opened, very slowly and creaking a great deal. A very old lady stood there, leaning on a stick, looking at them in some surprise.

Estelle was so nervous by then that she stuttered. "A—a w—way out in the n—name of D—Dulcinea," she said.

"Oh dear!" said the old lady. "My dears, I'm so sorry. The inquisitors broke up the organization here several years ago. If it wasn't for my age, I'd be in prison now. They come and check up on me every week. I daren't do a thing."

They stood and stared at her in utter dismay.

The old lady saw it. "If it's a real emergency," she said, "I can give you a spell. That's all I can think of. Would you like that?"

They nodded, dismally.

"Then wait a moment, while I write it down," said the old lady. She left the front door open and hobbled aside to a table at one side of the dark old hall. She opened a drawer in it and fumbled for some paper. She searched for a pen. Then she looked across at them. "You know, my dears, in order not to attract attention, you really should look as if you were collecting for charity. I can pretend to be writing you a check. Can either of you manage collecting boxes?"

"I can," said Nan. She had almost lost her voice with fright and dismay. She had to cough. She did not dare risk saying spells, standing there on the steps of the old house, up above the busy street. She simply waved a quivering hand and hoped.

Instant weight bore her hand down. A mighty collecting tin dangled from her arm, and another dangled from Estelle's. Each was as big as a tin of paint. Each had a huge red cross on one side and chinked loudly from their nervous trembling.

"That's better," said the old lady, and started, very slowly, to write.

The outsize tins did indeed make Nan and Estelle feel easier while they waited. People passing certainly looked up at them curiously, but most of them smiled when they saw the tins. And they were standing there for quite a long time, because, as well as writing very slowly, the old lady kept calling across to them.

"Do either of you know the Portway Oaks?" she called. They shook their heads. "Pity. You have to go there to say this," said the old lady. "It's a ring of trees just below the forest. I'd better draw you a map then." She drew, slowly. Then she called, "I don't know why they're called the Oaks. Every single tree there is a beech tree." Later still, she called, "Now I'm writing down the way you should pronounce it."

The girls still stood there. Nan was beginning to wonder if the old lady was really in league with the inquisitors and keeping them there on purpose, when the old lady at last folded up the paper and shuffled back to the front door.

"There you are, my dears. I wish I could do more for you."

Nan took the paper. Estelle produced a bright artificial smile. "Thanks awfully," she said. "What does it do?"

"I'm not sure," said the old lady. "It's been handed down in my family for use in emergencies, but no one has ever used it before. I'm told it's very powerful."

Like many old people, the old lady spoke rather too loudly. Nan and Estelle looked nervously over their shoulders at the street below, but nobody seemed to have heard. They thanked the old lady politely and, when the front door shut, they went drearily back down the steps, lugging their huge collecting tins.

"I suppose we'd better use it," said Estelle. "We daren't go back now."

CHAPTER 11

Charles jogged round the playing field toward the groundsman's hut. He hoped anyone who saw him would think he was out running for PE. For this reason, he had changed into his small sky-blue running shorts before he slipped away. When he had time, he supposed he could transform the shorts into jeans or something. But the important thing at the moment was to get hold of that mangy old broom people had been taunting Nan Pilgrim with the other day. If he got to that before anyone noticed he was missing, he could ride away on it and no dog on earth could pick up his trail.

He reached the hut, in its corner beside the kitchen gardens. He crept round it to its door. At the same moment, Nirupam crept round it from the opposite side, also in sky-blue shorts, and stretched out his long arm for the door too. The two of them stared at one another. All sorts of ideas for things to say streamed through Charles's mind, from explaining he was just dodging PE, to accusing Nirupam of kidnapping Brian. In the end, he said none of these things. Nirupam had hold of the doorlatch by then.

"Bags I the broomstick," Charles said.

"Only if there are two of them," said Nirupam. His face was yellow with fear. He pulled open the door and dodged into the hut. Charles dived in after him.

There was not even the one old broomstick. There were flowerpots, buckets, an old roller, a new roller, four rakes, two spades, a hoe, and an old wet mop propped in one of the buckets. And that was all.

"Who took it?" Charles said wildly.

"Nobody brought it back," said Nirupam.

"Oh, magic it all!" said Charles. "What shall we *do?*"

"Use something else," said Nirupam. "Or walk." He seized the nearest spade and stood astride it, bending and stretching his great long legs. "Fly," he told the spade. "Go on, fly, magic you!"

Nirupam had the right idea, Charles saw. A witch surely ought to be able to make anything fly. "I should think a rake would fly better," he said, and quickly grabbed hold of the wet mop for himself. The mop was so old that it had stuck to the bucket. Charles was forced to put one foot on the bucket and pull, before it came loose, and a lot of the head got left behind in the bucket. The result was a stick ending in a scraggly gray stump. Charles seized it and stood astride it. He jumped up and down. "Fly!" he told the mop. "Quick!"

Nirupam threw the spade down and snatched up the hoe. Together they jumped desperately round the hut. "Fly!" they panted. "Fly!"

In an old, soggy, dispirited way, the mop obeyed. It wallowed up about three feet into the air and wove toward the hut door. Nirupam was wailing in despair, when the hoe took off too, with a buck and a rush, as if it did not want to be left behind. Nirupam shot past Charles with his huge legs flailing. "It works!" he panted triumphantly, and went off in another kangaroo bound toward the kitchen gardens.

They were forbidden to go in the kitchen gardens, but it seemed the most secret way out of school. Charles followed Nirupam through the gate and down the gravel path, both of them trying to control their mounts. The mop wallowed and wove. It was like an old, old person, feebly hobbling through the air. The hoe either went by kangaroo surges, or it slanted and trailed its metal end along the path. Nirupam had to stick his feet out in front in order not to leave a scent on the ground. His eyes rolled in agony. He kept overtaking Charles and dropping behind. When they got to the wall at the end of the garden, both implements stopped. The mop wallowed about in the air. The hoe jittered its end on the gravel.

"They can't go high enough to get over," said Charles. "Now what?"

That might have been the end of their journey, had not the caretaker's dog been sniffing about in the kitchen gardens and suddenly caught their scent. It came racing down the long path toward them, yapping. The hoe and the mop took off like startled cats. They soared over the wall, with Charles and Nirupam hanging on anyhow, and went bucking off down the fields beyond. They raced toward the main road, the mop surging, the hoe plunging and trailing, clearing hedges by a whisker and missing trees by inches. They did not slow down until they had put three fields between them and the caretaker's dog.

"They must hate that dog as much as we do," Nirupam gasped. "Was it you that did the *Simon Says* spell?"

"Yes," said Charles. "Did you do the birds in music?"

"No," said Nirupam, much to Charles's surprise. "I did only one thing, and that was secret, but I daren't stay if the inquisitors are going to bring a witch-detector. They always get you with those."

"What did you do?" said Charles.

"You know that night all our shoes went into the hall," said Nirupam. "Well, we had a feast that night. Dan Smith made me get up the floorboards and get the food out. He says I have no right to be so large and so weak," Nirupam said resentfully, "and I was hating him for it, when I took the boards up and found a pair of running shoes, with spikes, hidden there with the food. I turned those shoes into a chocolate cake. I knew Dan was so greedy that he would eat it all himself. And he did eat it. He didn't let anyone else have any. You may have noticed that he wasn't quite himself the next day."

So much had happened to Charles that particular day, that he could not remember Dan seeming anything at all. He didn't have the heart to explain all the trouble Nirupam had caused him. "Those were my spikes," he said sadly. He wobbled along on the mop rather awed at the thought of iron spikes passing through Dan's stomach. "He must have a digestion like an ostrich!"

"The spikes were turned into cherries," said Nirupam. "The soles were the cream. The shoes as a whole became what is called a Black Forest gâteau."

Here they reached the main road and saw the tops of cars whipping past beyond the hedge. "We'll have to wait for a gap in that traffic," Charles said. "Stop!" he commanded the mop.

"Stop!" Nirupam cried to the hoe.

Neither implement took the slightest notice. Since Charles and Nirupam did not dare put their feet down for fear of leaving a scent for the dogs, they could find no way of stopping at all. They were carried helplessly over the hedge. Luckily, the road was down in a slight dip, and they had just enough height to clear the whizzing cars. Nirupam frantically bent his huge legs up. Charles tried not to let his legs dangle. Horns honked. He saw faces peering up at them, outraged and grinning. Charles suddenly saw how ridiculous they must look, both in their little blue shorts: himself with the disgraceful dirty old mop head wagging behind him; Nirupam lunging through the air in bunny hops, with a look of anguish on his face.

Horns were still sounding as they cleared the hedge on the other side of the road.

"Oh help!" gasped Nirupam. "Make for the woods, quick, before somebody gets the police!"

Larwood Forest was only a short hillside away and, luckily, their panic seemed to get through to the mop and the hoe. Both put on speed. The wagging and slewing of the mop nearly threw Charles off. The hoe helped itself along by digging its metal end fiercely into the ground, so that Nirupam went upward like someone on a pogo stick, yelping at each leap. Horns were still sounding from the road as first Nirupam, then Charles reached the trees and plunged in among them. By this time, Nirupam was so far ahead that Charles thought he had lost him. Probably just as well, Charles thought. They might be safer going separate ways. But the mop had other ideas. After dithering a bit, as if it had lost the scent, it set off again at top wallow. Charles was wagged round tree trunks and swayed through prickly undergrowth. Finally he was slewed through a bed of nettles. He yelled. Nirupam yelled too, just beyond the nettles. The hoe tipped him off into a blackberry bush and darted gladly toward an old threadbare broomstick which was leaning on the other side of the brambles. At the sight, the mop threw Charles into the nettles and went bouncing flirtatiously toward the broomstick too, looking just like a granny on an outing.

Charles and Nirupam picked themselves bad-temperedly up. They listened. The motorists on the road seemed to have got tired of sounding their horns. They looked. Beyond the jumping hoe and the nuzzling mop, there was a well-made campfire. Behind the fire, concealed by more brambles, was a small orange tent. Brian Wentworth was standing by the tent, glowering at them.

"I thought I'd got at least one of you arrested," Brian said. "Get lost, can't you! Or are you trying to get me caught?"

"No, we are not!" Charles said angrily. "We're— Hey, listen!"

Somewhere uphill, in the thick part of the wood, a dog gave one whirring, excited bark, and stopped suddenly. Birds were clapping up out of the trees. And Charles's straining ears could also hear a rhythmic swishing, as of heavy feet marching through undergrowth.

"That's the police," he said.

"You fools! You've brought them down on me!" Brian said in a screaming whisper. He grabbed the old broom from between the mop and the hoe and, in one practiced jump, he was on the broom and gliding away across the brambles.

"*He* did the birds in music," Nirupam said, and snatched the hoe. Charles seized the mop and both of them set off after Brian, wavering and hopping across the brambles and in among low trees. Charles kept his head down, because branches were raking at his hair, and thought that Nirupam must be right. Those birds had appeared promptly in time to save Brian's having to sing. And a parrot shouting "Cuckoo!" was exactly Brian's kind of thing.

They were catching up with the broom, not because they wanted to, but because the mop and the hoe were plainly determined to stay with the broom. They must have spent years together in the groundsman's hut and, Charles supposed irritably, they had got touchingly fond of one another. Nothing he or Nirupam could do would make either implement go a different way. Shortly, Brian was gliding among the trees only a few yards ahead of them.

He turned and glared at them. "Leave me alone! You've spoiled my escape and made me lose my tent. Go away!"

"It was the mop and the hoe," said Charles.

"The police are looking for you, not us," Nirupam panted. "What did you expect? You were missing."

"I didn't expect two great idiots crashing about the forest and bringing the police after me," Brian snarled. "Why couldn't you stay in school?"

"If you didn't want us, you shouldn't have written all that rubbish about a witch putting a spell on you," said Charles. "There's an inquisitor coming today because of you."

"Well, you advised me to do it," Brian said.

Charles opened his mouth and shut it again, quite unable to speak for indignation. They were coming to the edge of the woods now. He could see green fields through a mass of yellow hazel leaves, and he tried to turn the mop aside yet again. If they came out of the woods, they would be seen at once. But the mop obstinately followed the broom.

As they forced their way among whippy hazel boughs, Nirupam panted severely, "You ought to be glad to have some friends with you, Brian."

Brian laughed hysterically. "Friends! I wouldn't be friends with either of you if you paid me! Everyone in 6B laughs at you!"

As Brian said this, there was a sudden clamor of dog noises behind them in the wood. A voice shouted something about a tent. It was plain that the police had found Brian's camp. Brian and the broomstick put on speed and surged out into the field beyond. Charles and Nirupam found themselves being dragged anyhow through the hazel boughs as the mop and the hoe tried to keep up.

Scratched and breathless, they were whirled out into the field on the side of the woods that faced the town. Brian was some way ahead, flying low and fast downhill, toward a clump of trees in the middle of the field. The mop and the hoe surged after him.

"I know Brian is nasty, but I had always thought it was his situation before this," Nirupam remarked, in jerks, as the hoe kangaroo-hopped down the field.

Charles could not answer at once, because he was not sure that a person's character could be separate from his situation in quite this way. While he was wondering how you said this kind of thing aboard a speeding, wallowing mop, when you were hanging on with one hand and holding your glasses with the other, Brian reached the clump of trees and disappeared among them. They heard his voice again, shrill and annoyed, echoing out of the trees.

"Is Brian *trying* to bring the police after us?" Nirupam panted.

Both of them looked over their shoulders, expecting men and dogs to come charging out through the edge of the woods. There was nothing. Next moment, they were swishing through low branches covered with carroty beech leaves. The mop and the hoe jolted to a stop. Charles put his nettled legs down and stood up in a windy rustling space surrounded by pewter-colored tree trunks. He stared at Estelle Green, looking as if she had mislaid a horse. He stared at Nan Pilgrim in ragged pink silk, with the broomstick hopping and sidling affectionately round her.

Brian was standing angrily beside them. "Look at this!" he said to Charles and Nirupam. "The place is alive with you lot! Why can't you let a person run away in peace?"

"Will one of you please shut Brian up?" Estelle said, with great dignity. "We are just about to say a spell that will rescue us all."

"These trees are called the Portway Oaks," Nan explained, and bit the inside of her cheek in order not to laugh. Nirupam riding a hoe was one of the funniest things she had ever seen. And Charles Morgan's mop looked as if he had slain an old-age pensioner. But she knew she and Estelle looked equally silly, and the boys had not laughed at them.

Brian was still talking angrily. Nirupam let the hoe loose to jump delightedly around the broom and clapped one long brown hand firmly over Brian's mouth. "Go ahead," he said.

"And make it quick," said Charles.

Nan and Estelle bent over their fluttering piece of paper again. The old lady had written just one strange word three times at the top of the paper. Under that, as she had told them, she had written, in shaky capitals, how to say this word: KREST-OH-MAN-SEE. After that she had put, *Go to Portway Oaks and say word three times.* The rest of the paper was full of a very wobbly map.

Estelle and Nan pronounced the word together, three times. "Chrestomanci, Chrestomanci, Chrestomanci."

"Is that all?" asked Nirupam. He took his hand from Brian's face.

"Somebody swindled you!" Brian said. "That's no spell!"

It seemed as if a great gust of wind hit the clump of trees. The branches all round them lashed, and creaked with the strain, so that the air was full of the rushing of leaves. The dead orange leaves from the ground leaped in the air and swirled round them all, round and round, as if the inside of the clump were the center of a whirlwind. This was followed by a sudden stillness. Leaves stayed where they were, in the air, surrounding everyone. No one could see anything but leaves, and there was not a sound to be heard from anywhere. Then, very slowly, sound began again. There was a gentle rustling as the suspended leaves dropped back to the ground. Where they had been, there was a man standing.

He seemed utterly bewildered. His first act was to put his hands up and smooth his hair, which was a thing that hardly needed doing, since the wind had not disturbed even the merest wisp of it. It was smooth and black and shiny as new tar. Having smoothed his hair, this man rearranged his starched white shirt cuffs and straightened his already straight pale gray cravat. After that, he carefully pulled down his dove-mauve waistcoat and, equally carefully, brushed some imaginary dust off his beautiful dove-gray suit. All the while he was doing this, he was looking from one to the other of the five of them in increasing perplexity. His eyebrows rose higher with everything he saw.

They were all thoroughly embarrassed. Nirupam tried to hide behind Charles as the man looked at his little blue shorts. Charles tried to slither behind Brian. Brian tried to knock the mud off the knees of his jeans without looking as if he was. The man's eyes turned to Nan. They were bright black eyes, which did not seem quite as bewildered as the rest of the man's face, and they made Nan feel that she would rather have had no clothes on at all than a ragged pink balldress. The man looked on toward Estelle, as if Nan were too painful a sight. Nan looked at Estelle too. Estelle, as she set her hard hat straight, was gazing adoringly up into the man's handsome face.

That was all we needed! Nan thought. Evidently this was the kind of man that Estelle fell instantly in love with. So, not only had they somehow summoned up an over-elegant stranger, but they were no nearer being safe and, to crown it all, there would probably be no sense to be had from Estelle from now on.

"Bless my soul!" murmured the man. He was now staring at the mop, the hoe, and the broom, which were jigging about in a little group like an old folks' reunion. "I think you'd *definitely* better go," he said to them. All three implements vanished, with a faint whistling sound. The man turned to Nan. "What are we all doing here?" he said, a little plaintively. "And where are we?"

CHAPTER 12

A dog barked excitedly up the hill. Everyone except the stranger jumped.

"I think we must go now, sir," Nirupam said politely. "That was a police dog. They were looking for Brian, but I think they're looking for the rest of us now."

"What do you expect them to do if they find you?" the man asked.

"Burn us," said Charles, and his thumb ran back and forth over the fat blister on his finger.

"We're all witches, you see, except Estelle," Nan explained.

"So if you don't mind us leaving you—" said Nirupam.

"How very barbarous," said the man. "I think it would be much better if the police and their dogs simply didn't see this clump of trees where we all are, don't you?" He looked vaguely round to see what they thought of this idea. Everyone looked dubious, and Brian downright scornful. "I assure you," the man said to Brian, "that if you go into the field outside and look, you will not see these trees any more than the police will. If the word of an enchanter is not enough for you, go out and see for yourself."

"What enchanter?" Brian said rudely. But of course no one dared leave the trees. They all waited, with their backs prickling, while the voices of policemen came slowly nearer. Finally, they seemed to be just outside the trees.

"Nothing," they heard the policeman saying. "Everyone go back and concentrate on the woods. Hills and MacIver, you two go down and see what those motorists by the hedge are waving about. The rest of you get the dogs back to that tent and start again from there."

After that, the voices all went away. Everyone relaxed a little, and

Nan even began to hope that the stranger might be some help. But then he went all plaintive again. "Would one of you tell me where we are now?" he said.

"Just outside Larwood Forest," Nan said. "Hertfordshire."

"In England, the British Isles, the world, the solar system, the Milky Way, the Universe," Brian said scornfully.

"Ah yes," said the man. "But which one?" Brian stared. "I mean," the man said patiently, "do you happen to know *which* world, galaxy, universe, et cetera? There happen to be infinite numbers of them, and unless I know which this one is, I shall not find it very easy to help you."

This gave Charles a very strange feeling. He thought of outer space and bug-eyed monsters and his stomach turned over. His eyes ran over the man's elegant jacket, fascinated, trying to make out if there was room under it for an extra pair of arms. There was not. The man was obviously a human being. "You're not really from another world, are you?" he said.

"I am precisely that," said the man. "Another world full of people just like you, running side by side with this one. There are myriads of them. So which one *is* this one?"

As far as most of them knew, the world was just the world. Everyone looked blank, except Estelle. Estelle said shyly, "There is *one* other world. It's the one the witches' rescue people send witches into to be safe."

"Ah!" The man turned to Estelle, and Estelle blushed violently. "Tell me about this safe world."

Estelle shook her head. "I don't know any more," she whispered, overwhelmed.

"Then let's get at it another way," the man suggested. "You tell me all the events that led up to you summoning me here—"

"Is Chrestomanci your name then?" Estelle interrupted in an adoring whisper.

"I'm usually called that. Yes," said the man. "Was it you who summoned me then?"

Estelle nodded. "Some spell!" Brian said jeeringly.

Brian was plainly determined not to help in any way. He stayed scornfully silent while the rest of them explained the events which had led up to their being here. Nobody told Chrestomanci quite everything. Brian's contemptuous look made it all feel like a pack of lies anyway. Nan did not mention her meeting with Mr. Wentworth on his hearthrug. She felt rather noble not saying anything about that, considering the way Brian was behaving. She did not mention the way she had described the food, either, though Charles did. On the other hand, Charles did not feel the need to mention the *Simon Says* spell. Nirupam told Chrestomanci about that, but he somehow forgot to say that Dan Smith had eaten Charles's shoes. And when the rest of them had finished, Chrestomanci looked at Brian.

"Your narrative now, please," he said politely.

It was a very powerful politeness. Everyone had thought that Brian was not going to tell anything at all, but, grudgingly, he did. First he admitted to causing the birds in music. Then he claimed that Charles had advised him in the night to run away from school and confuse his trail by blaming the witch. And, while Charles was still stuttering with anger over that, Brian coolly explained that he had discovered Charles was a witch the next morning anyway and got Charles to take him to the matron so that the matron could see the effects of the Evil Eye at first hand. Finally, more grudgingly still, he confessed that he had written the anonymous note to Mr. Crossley and started everything. Then, as an afterthought, he turned on Nan.

"And you kept stealing my broomstick, didn't you?"

"It's not yours. It belongs to the school," said Nan.

At the same time, Charles was saying angrily to Chrestomanci, "It's not true I advised him to blame the witch!"

Chrestomanci was staring vaguely up into the beech trees and did not seem to hear. "The situation is quite impossible," he remarked. "Let us all go and see the old lady who used to run the witches' rescue service."

This struck them all as an excellent idea. It was clear the old lady could rescue them if she wanted. They agreed vigorously. Nirupam said, "But the police—"

"Invisibly, of course," said Chrestomanci. He was still obviously thinking of something else. He turned to walk away between the tree trunks, and, as he did so, everyone flicked out of sight. All that could be seen was the rustling circle of autumn beeches. "Come along," said Chrestomanci's voice.

There followed a minute or so of almost indescribable confusion. It started with Nan assuming she had no body and walking into a tree. She was just as solid as ever, and knocked herself quite silly for a second. "Oh, sorry!" she said to the tree. The rest of them somehow forced their way under the low branches and found themselves out in the field. There, the first thing everybody saw was two cars parked almost in the hedge below, and a number of people from the cars leaning over the hedge to talk to two policemen. From the way all the people kept pointing up at the woods, it was clear they were describing how they saw two witches ride across the road on a mop and a hoe. That panicked everyone. They all set off the other way, toward the town, in a hurry. But as soon as they did, they saw that there was no one ahead of them and waited for the rest to catch up. Then they heard someone speak some way ahead, and ran to catch up. But of course they could not tell where the people they were running after were. Shortly, nobody knew where anybody was or what to do about it.

"Perhaps," Chrestomanci's voice said out of the air, "you could all bring yourselves to hold hands? I have no idea where the Old Gate House is, you see."

Thankfully, everyone grabbed for everyone else. Nan found herself holding Brian's hand and Charles Morgan's. She had never thought the time would come when she would be glad to do that. Estelle had managed to be the one holding Chrestomanci's hand. That became clear when the line of them began to move briskly down to the path that led into town and Estelle's voice could be heard in front, piping up in answer to Chrestomanci's questions.

As soon as there was no chance of anyone else hearing them, Chrestomanci began asking a great many questions. He asked who was prime minister, and which were the most important countries, and what was the EEC, and how many world wars there had been. Then he asked about things from history. Before long, everyone was giving him answers, and feeling a little superior, because it was really remarkable the number of things Chrestomanci seemed not to know. He had heard of Hitler, though he asked Brian to refresh his memory about him, but he had only the haziest notion about Gandhi or Einstein, and he had never heard of Walt Disney or reggae. Nor had he heard of Dulcinea Wilkes. Nan explained about Dulcinea, and found herself saying, with great pride, that she was descended from Dulcinea.

Why am I saying that? she thought, in sudden alarm. I don't really know it's safe to tell him! And yet, as soon as she thought that, Nan began to see why she had said it. It was the way Chrestomanci was asking those questions. It reminded Nan of the time she had kept coming out in a rash, and her aunt had taken her to a very important specialist. The specialist had worn a very good suit, though it was nothing like as beautiful as Chrestomanci's, and he had asked questions in just the same way, trying to get at Nan's symptoms. Remembering this specialist made Nan feel a lot more hopeful. If you thought of Chrestomanci, in spite of his vagueness and his elegance, as a sort of specialist trying to solve their problems, then you could believe that he might just be able to help them. He was certainly a strong and expert witch. Perhaps he could make the old lady send them somewhere really safe.

When the path led them into the busy streets of the town, Chrestomanci stopped asking questions, but it was clear to Nan that he went on finding symptoms. He made everyone stop while he examined a truck parked by the supermarket. It was just an ordinary truck with Leyland on the front of it and Heinz Meanz Beanz on the side, but Chrestomanci murmured "Good Lord!" as if he was really astonished, before dragging them over to look through the windows of the supermarket. Then he towed them up and down in front of some cars. This part was really frightening. The car windows, the hubcaps, and the glass of the supermarket all showed faint, misty reflections of the six of them. They were quite sure some of the people who were shopping would notice any second.

At last, Chrestomanci let Estelle drag him up the street as far as the tatty draper's where nobody ever seemed to buy anything. "How long have you had decimal currency?" he asked. While they were telling him, the misty reflection in the draper's window showed his tall shape bending to look at some packets of tights and a dingy blue nylon nightdress. "What are these stockings made of?"

"Nylon, of course!" snapped Charles. He was wondering whether to let go of Nan's hand and run away.

Estelle, feeling much the same, heaved on Chrestomanci's hand and led them all in a rush to the doorway of the Old Gate House. She dragged them up the steps and hurriedly rang the bell before Chrestomanci could ask any more questions.

"There was no need to disturb her," Chrestomanci remarked. As he said it, the pointed porch dissolved away around them. Instead, they were in an old-fashioned drawing room, full of little tables with bobbly cloths on and ornaments on the cloth. The old lady was reaching for her stick and trying to lever herself out of her chair, muttering something about "An endless stream of callers today!"

Chrestomanci flicked into sight, tall and elegant and somehow very much in place in that old-fashioned room. Estelle, Nan, Charles, Nirupam, and Brian also flicked into sight, and they looked as much out of place as people could be. The old lady sank back in her chair and stared.

"Forgive the intrusion, madam," Chrestomanci said.

The old lady beamed up at him. "What a splendid surprise!" she said. "No one's appeared like this for years! Forgive me if I don't get up. My knees are very arthritic these days. Would you care for some tea?"

"We won't trouble you, madam," said Chrestomanci. "We came because I understand you are a keeper of some kind of way through."

"Yes, I am," said the old lady. She looked dubious. "If you all have to use it, I suppose you have to, but it will take us hours. It's down in the cellar, you see, hidden from the inquisitors under seven tons of coal."

"I assure you, we haven't come to ask you to heave coal, madam," said Chrestomanci. No, Charles thought, looking at Chrestomanci's white shirt cuffs. It will be us that does that. "What I really need to know," Chrestomanci went on, "is just which world it is on the other side of the way through."

"I haven't seen it," the old lady said regretfully. "But I've always understood that it's a world exactly like ours, only with no witchcraft."

"Thank you. I wonder—" said Chrestomanci. He seemed to have gone very vague again. "What do you know of Dulcinea Wilkes? Was there much witchcraft here before her day?"

"The Archwitch? Good gracious, yes!" said the old lady. "There were witches all over the place long before Dulcinea. I think it was Oliver Cromwell who made the first laws against witches, but it may be before that. Somebody did once tell me that Elizabeth I was probably a witch. Because of the storm which wrecked the Spanish Armada, you know."

Nan watched Chrestomanci nodding as he listened to this and realized that he was collecting symptoms again. She sighed, and wondered whether to offer to start shoveling the coal.

Chrestomanci sighed a little too. "Pity," he said. "I was hoping the Archwitch was the key to the problems here. Perhaps Oliver Cromwell—?"

"I'm afraid I'm not a historian," the old lady said firmly. "And you won't find many people who know much more. Witch history is banned. All those kinds of books were burned long ago."

Charles, who was as impatient as Nan, butted in here. "Mr. Wentworth knows a lot of witch history, but—"

"Yes!" Nan interrupted eagerly. "If you really want to know, you could summon Mr. Wentworth here. He's a witch too, so it wouldn't matter." Here she realized that Brian was giving her a glare almost up to Charles Morgan's standards, and that Charles himself was staring at her wildly. "Yes, he is," she said. "You know he is, Brian. I met him out flying on his hearthrug last night, and he thought I was you on your broomstick."

That explained everything, Charles thought. The night Mr. Wentworth had vanished, he had gone out flying. The window had been wide open and, now he understood, Charles could remember distinctly the bald place in front of the gas fire where the ragged hearthrug had been. And it explained that time in detention, too, when he had thought his glasses were broken. They *were* broken, and Mr. Wentworth had restored them by witchcraft.

"Can't you keep your big mouth shut?" Brian said furiously to Nan. He pointed to Chrestomanci. "How do we know he's safe? For all *we* know, he could be the Devil that you summoned up!"

"Oh, you flatter me, Brian," Chrestomanci said.

The old lady looked shocked. "What an unpleasant thing to say," she said to Brian. "Hasn't anyone ever told you that the Devil, however he appears, is *never* a perfect gentleman? Quite unlike this Mr.—er—Mr.—?" She looked at Chrestomanci with her eyebrows politely raised.

"Chrestomanci, madam," he said. "Which reminds me. I wish you would tell me how you came to give Estelle and Nan my name."

The old lady laughed. "Was that what the spell was? I had no idea. It has been handed down in my family from my great-grandmother's time, with strict instructions that it's only to be used in an emergency. And those two poor girls were in such trouble—but I refuse to believe you can be that old, my dear sir."

Chrestomanci smiled. "No. Brian will be sorry to hear that the spell must have been meant to call one of my predecessors. Now. Shall we go? We must go to your school and consult Mr. Wentworth, evidently."

They stared at him, even the old lady. Then, as it dawned on them that Chrestomanci was not going to let them go into the coal cellar to safety, everyone broke out into protest. Brian, Charles, and Nan said, "Oh no! Please!" The old lady said, "Aren't you taking rather a risk?" at the same moment as Nirupam said, "But I told you there's an inquisitor coming to school!" And Estelle added, "Couldn't we just all stay here quietly while *you* go and see Mr. Wentworth?"

Chrestomanci looked from Estelle to Nirupam, to Nan, and then at Brian and Charles. He seemed astounded, and not vague at all. The room seemed to go very quiet and sinister and unloving. "What's all this?" he said. It was so gentle that they all shivered. "I did understand you, didn't I? The five of you, between you, turn your school upside down. You cause what I am sure is a great deal of trouble to a great many teachers and policemen. You summon me a long way from some extremely important business, in a manner which makes it very difficult for me to get back. And now you all propose just to walk out and leave the mess you've made. Is that what you mean?"

"I didn't summon you," said Brian.

"It wasn't our fault," Charles said. "I didn't ask to be a witch."

Chrestomanci looked at him with faint, chilly surprise. "Didn't you?" The way he said it made Charles actually wonder, for a moment, if he had somehow chosen to be born a witch. "And so," said Chrestomanci, "you think your troubles give you a right to get this lady into much worse trouble with the inquisitors? Is that what you all say?"

Nobody said anything.

"I think we shall be going now," Chrestomanci said, "if you would all hold one another's hands again, please." Wordlessly, they all held out hands and took hold. Chrestomanci took hold of Brian's, but, before he took hold of Estelle's in the other hand, he took the old lady's veined and knobby hand and kissed it. The old lady was delighted. She winked excitedly at Nan over Chrestomanci's smooth head. Nan did not even feel up to smiling back. "Lead the way, Estelle," Chrestomanci said, straightening up and taking Estelle's hand. They found themselves invisible again. And, the same instant, they were outside in the street.

Estelle set off toward Larwood House. If it had been anybody else but Estelle in the lead, Charles thought, they might have thought of taking the line of them somewhere else—anywhere else—because Chrestomanci would not know. But Estelle led them straight to school, and everyone else shuffled after, too crushed and nervous to do anything else. Brian was the only one who protested. Whenever there were no people about, his voice could be heard saying that it wasn't *fair*. "What did you girls have to fetch him for?" he kept saying.

By the time they were through the school gates and shuffling up the drive, Brian gave up protesting. Estelle led them to the main door, the grand one, which was only used for parents or visitors like Lord Mulke. There were two police cars parked on the gravel beside it, but they were empty and there was no one about.

Here, in a sharp scuffling of gravel, Brian made a determined effort to run away. To judge by the sounds, and by the way Estelle came feeling her way along Nirupam and Nan, Chrestomanci was after Brian like a shot. Three thumps, and a scatter of small stones, and Chrestomanci suddenly reappeared, beside the nearest police car. He seemed to be on his own, but his right arm was stiffly bent and jerking a little, as the invisible Brian writhed on the end of it.

"I do advise you all to keep quite close to me," he said, as if nothing had happened. "You will only be invisible within ten yards of me."

"I can make myself invisible," Brian's voice said, from beside Chrestomanci's dove-gray elbow. "I'm a witch too."

"Quite probably," Chrestomanci agreed. "But I am not a witch, as it happens. I am an enchanter. And, among other differences, an enchanter is ten times as strong as a witch. Who is at the end of the line now? Charles. Charles, will you be good enough to walk up the steps to the door and ring the bell?"

Charles trudged forward, towing the others behind him, and rang the bell. There seemed nothing else to do.

The door was opened almost at once by the school secretary. Chrestomanci stood there, apparently alone, with his dove-gray suit quite unruffled and not a hair out of place, smiling pleasantly at the secretary. It was hard to believe that he had Brian gripped in one hand and Estelle clinging to the other, and three more people crowded uncomfortably around him. He bowed slightly.

"Name of Chant," he said. "I believe you were expecting me. I'm the inquisitor."

CHAPTER 13

The school secretary dissolved into dither. She gushed. It was just as well. Otherwise she might have heard five gasps out of the air round Chrestomanci.

"Oh, *do* come in, inquisitor," the secretary gushed. "Miss Cadwallader is expecting you. And I'm awfully sorry—we seem to have got your name wrong. We were told to expect a Mr. Littleton."

"Quite right," Chrestomanci said blandly. "Littleton is the regional inquisitor. But head office decided the matter was too grave to be merely regional. I'm the divisional inquisitor."

"Oh!" said the secretary, and seemed quite overawed. She ushered Chrestomanci in and through the tiled hall. Chrestomanci stepped after her, slow and stately, in a way that allowed plenty of time for everyone to squeeze round him into the hall and tiptoe beside him across the tiles. The secretary threw wide the door to Miss Cadwallader's study. "Mr. Chant, Miss Cadwallader. The divisional inquisitor." Chrestomanci went into the study even more slowly, lugging Brian and pulling Estelle. Nan and Nirupam squeezed after, and Charles just got in too by jamming himself against the doorpost as the secretary backed reverently out. He did not want to be left outside the circle of invisibility.

Miss Cadwallader sprang forward in a quite unusual flutter and shook hands with Chrestomanci. The rest of them heard Brian thump away sideways as Chrestomanci let go of him. "Oh, good morning, inquisitor!"

"Morning, morning," said Chrestomanci. He seemed to have gone vague again. He looked absently round the room while he was shaking hands. "Nice place you have here, Miss—er—Cudwollander."

This was true. Perhaps on the grounds that she had to persuade government officials and parents that Larwood House was a really good school, Miss Cadwallader had surrounded herself in luxury. Her carpet was like deep crimson grass. Her chairs were purple clouds of softness. She had marble statues on her mantelpiece and large gilt frames round her hundred or so pictures. She had a cocktail cabinet with a little refrigerator built into it and a coffeemaker on top. Her hi-fi and tape-deck took up most of one wall. Charles looked yearningly at her vast television with a crinoline doll on top. It seemed years since he had watched any television. Nan gazed at the wall of bright new books. Most of them seemed to be mystery stories. She would have loved to have a closer look at them, but she did not dare let go of Nirupam or Charles in case she never found them again.

"I'm so glad you approve, inquisitor," fluttered Miss Cadwallader. "My room is entirely at your disposal, if you wish to use it to interview children in. I take it that you will need to interview some of the children in 6B?"

"All the children in 6B," Chrestomanci said gravely, "and probably all their teachers too." Miss Cadwallader looked thoroughly dismayed by this. "I shall expect to interview everyone in the school before I'm through," Chrestomanci went on. "I shall stay here for as long as it takes—weeks, if necessary—to get to the bottom of this matter."

By this time, Miss Cadwallader was distinctly pale. She clasped her hands nervously. "Are you sure it's *that* serious, inquisitor? It *is* only a boy in 6B who disappeared in the night. His father happens to be one of our teachers here, which is really why we're so concerned. I know you were told that the boy left a large number of notes accusing a witch of abducting him, but the police have telephoned since to say they have found a camp in the forest with the boy's scent on it. Don't you think the whole thing could be cleared up quite easily and quickly?"

Chrestomanci gravely shook his head. "I have been kept abreast of the facts too, Miss—er—Kidwelly. The boy has still not turned up, has he? One can't be too careful in a case like this. I think someone in 6B knows more about this than you think."

Up to now, everyone listening had been feeling more and more relieved. If Miss Cadwallader had known there were four other people missing besides Brian, she would surely have said so. But their feelings changed at what Miss Cadwallader said next.

"You must interview a girl called Theresa Mullett straightaway, inquisitor, and I think you will find that the matter will be cleared up at once. Theresa is one of our *good* girls. She came to me during break and told me that the witch is almost certainly a child called Dulcinea Pilgrim. Dulcinea is *not* one of our good girls, inquisitor, I'm sorry to say. Some of her journal entries have been very free-spoken and disaffected. She questions everything and makes jokes about serious matters. If you like, I can send for Dulcinea's journal and you can see for yourself."

"I shall read all the journals in 6B," said Chrestomanci, "in good time. But is this all you have to go on, Miss—er—Collander? I can't find a girl a witch simply on hearsay and a few jokes. It's not professional. Have you no other suspects? Teachers, for instance—"

"Teachers here are all above suspicion, inquisitor." Miss Cadwallader said this very firmly, although her voice was a little shrill. "But 6B as a class are not. It is a sad fact, inquisitor, in a school like this, that a number of children come to us as witch-orphans, having had one or both parents burned. There are an unusual number of these in 6B. I would pick out, for your immediate attention, Nirupam Singh, who had a brother burned, Estelle Green, whose mother is in prison for helping witches escape, and a boy called Charles Morgan, who is almost as undesirable as the Pilgrim girl."

"Dear me! What a poisonous state of affairs!" said Chrestomanci. "I see I must get down to work at once."

"I shall leave you this room of mine to work in then, inquisitor," Miss Cadwallader said graciously. She seemed to have recovered from her flutter.

"Oh, I can't possibly trouble you," Chrestomanci said, quite as graciously. "Doesn't your deputy head have a study I could use?"

Intense relief shone through Miss Cadwallader's stately manner. "Yes, indeed he does, inquisitor. What an excellent idea! I shall take you to Mr. Wentworth myself, at once."

Miss Cadwallader swept out of her room, almost too relieved to be stately. Chrestomanci located Brian as easily as if he could see him, took his arm, and swept off after her. The other four were forced to tiptoe furiously to keep up. None of them wanted to see Mr. Wentworth. In fact, after what Miss Cadwallader had just said, the one thing they all longed to do was to sneak off and run away again. But the instant they got more than ten yards away from Chrestomanci, there they would be, in riding clothes, little blue shorts, and pink balldress, for Miss Cadwallader or anyone else they passed to see. That was enough to keep them all tiptoeing hard, along the corridors and up the stairs.

Miss Cadwallader rapped on the glass of Mr. Wentworth's study. "Come in!" said Mr. Wentworth's voice. Miss Cadwallader threw the door open and made ushering motions to Chrestomanci. Chrestomanci nodded vaguely and once more made a slow and imposing entry, with a slight dragging noise as he pulled the resisting Brian through the doorway. That gave the other four plenty of time to slip inside past Miss Cadwallader.

"I'll leave you with Mr. Wentworth for now, inquisitor," Miss Cadwallader said, in the doorway. Mr. Wentworth, at that, looked up from his schedules. When he saw Chrestomanci, his face went pale, and he stood up slowly, looking thoroughly harrowed. "Mr. Wentworth," said Miss Cadwallader, "this is Mr. Chant, who is the divisional inquisitor. Come to my study for sherry before lunch, both of you, please." Then obviously feeling she had done enough, Miss Cadwallader shut the door and went away.

"Good morning," Chrestomanci said politely.

"G—good morning," said Mr. Wentworth. His hands were trembling and rustling the schedules. He swallowed, loudly. "I—I didn't realize there were divisional inquisitors. New post, is it?"

"Oh, do you not have divisional ones?" Chrestomanci said. "What a shame. I thought it sounded so imposing."

He nodded. Everybody was suddenly visible again. Nan, Charles, and Nirupam all tried to hide behind one another. Brian was revealed tugging crossly to get his arm loose from Chrestomanci, and Estelle was hanging on to Chrestomanci's other hand again. She let go hurriedly and took her hard hat off. But it was quite certain that Mr. Wentworth did not notice any of these things. He backed against the window, staring from Chrestomanci to Brian, and he was more than harrowed now: he was terrified.

"What's going on?" he said. "Brian, what have you lent yourself to?"

"Nothing," Brian said irritably. "He isn't an inquisitor. He's an enchanter or something. It's not my fault he's here."

"What does he want?" Mr. Wentworth said wildly. "I haven't anything I can give him!"

"My dear sir," said Chrestomanci, "please try and be calm. I only want your help."

Mr. Wentworth pressed back against the window. "I don't know what you mean!"

"Yes, you do," Chrestomanci said pleasantly. "But let me explain. I am Chrestomanci. This is the title that goes with my post, and my job is controlling witchcraft. My world is somewhat more happily placed than yours, I believe, because witchcraft is not illegal there. In fact, this very morning I was chairing a meeting of the Walpurgis Committee, in the middle of making final arrangements for the Halloween celebrations, when I was rather suddenly summoned away by these pupils of yours—"

"Is that why you're wearing those beautiful clothes?" Estelle asked admiringly.

Everyone winced a little, except for Chrestomanci, who seemed to think it was a perfectly reasonable question. "Well, no, to be quite honest," he said. "I like to be well dressed, because I am always liable to be called elsewhere, the way you called me. But I have to confess that I have several times been fetched away in my dressing gown, in spite of all my care." He looked at Mr. Wentworth again, obviously expecting him to have calmed down by now. "There are real problems with this particular call," he said. "Your world is all wrong, in a number of ways. That's why I would appreciate your help, sir."

Unfortunately, Mr. Wentworth was by no means calm. "How dare you talk to me like this!" he said. "It's pure blackmail! You'll get no help from me!"

"Now that is unreasonable, sir," Chrestomanci said. "These children are in acute trouble. You are in the same trouble yourself. Your whole world is in even greater trouble. Please, try if you can, to forget that you have been scared for years, both for yourself and Brian, and listen to the questions I am going to ask you."

But Mr. Wentworth seemed unable to be reasonable. Nan looked at him sorrowfully. She had always thought he was such a firm person up till now. She felt quite disillusioned. So did Charles. He remembered Mr. Wentworth's hand on his shoulder, pushing him back into detention. He had thought that hand had been shaking with anger, but he realized now that it had been terror.

"It's a trick!" Mr. Wentworth said. "You're trying to get a confession out of me. You're using Brian. You *are* an inquisitor!"

Just as he said that, there was a little tap at the door, and Miss Hodge came brightly in. She had just given 6B an English lesson—the last one until next Tuesday, thank goodness! Naturally, she had noticed that four other people besides Brian were now missing. At first, she had assumed that they were all being questioned by the inquisitor. They were the obvious ones. But then someone in the staff room had remarked that the inquisitor still hadn't come. Miss Hodge saw at once that this was the excuse she needed to go to Mr. Wentworth and start sympathizing with him about Brian. She came in as soon as she had knocked, to make quite sure that Mr. Wentworth did not get away again.

The room for an instant seemed quite full of people, and poor Mr. Wentworth was looking so upset and shouting at what seemed to be the inquisitor after all. The inquisitor gave Miss Hodge a vague look and then waved his hand, just the smallest bit. After that, there did only seem to be the inquisitor and Mr. Wentworth in the room besides Miss

Hodge. But Miss Hodge knew what she had seen. She thought about it while she said what she had come to say.

"Oh, Mr. Wentworth, I'm afraid there are four more people missing from 6B now." And the four people had all been here in the room, Miss Hodge knew. Wearing such peculiar things too. And Brian had been there as well. That settled it. Mr. Wentworth might look upset, but he was not sorrowing about Brian. That meant that she either had to think of some other way to get his attention, or use the advantage she knew she had. The man who was supposed to be an inquisitor was politely putting forward a chair for her to sit in. A smooth villain. Miss Hodge ignored the chair. "I think I'm interrupting a witches' Sabbath," she said brightly.

The man with the chair raised his eyebrows as if he thought she was mad. A very smooth villain. Mr. Wentworth said, in a strangled sort of way, "This is the divisional inquisitor, Miss Hodge."

Miss Hodge laughed, triumphantly. "Mr. Wentworth! You and I both know that there's no such thing as a divisional inquisitor! Is this man annoying you? If so, I shall go straight to Miss Cadwallader. I think she has a right to know that your study is full of witches."

Chrestomanci sighed and wandered away to Mr. Wentworth's desk, where he idly picked up one of the schedules. Mr. Wentworth's eyes followed him as if Chrestomanci was annoying him very much, but he said, in a resigned way, "There's absolutely no point in going to Miss Cadwallader, Miss Hodge. Miss Cadwallader has known I'm a witch for years. She takes most of my salary in return for not telling anyone."

"I didn't know you—!" Miss Hodge began. She had not realized Mr. Wentworth was a witch too. That made quite a difference. She smiled more triumphantly than before. "In that case, let me offer you an alliance against Miss Cadwallader, Mr. Wentworth. You marry me, and we'll both fight her."

"Marry you?" Mr. Wentworth stared at Miss Hodge in obvious horror. "Oh no. You can't. I can't—"

Brian's voice said out of the air, "I'm not having *her* as a mother!"

Chrestomanci looked up from the schedules. He shrugged. Brian appeared on the other side of the room, looking as horrified as Mr. Wentworth. Miss Hodge smiled again. "So I was right!" she said.

"Miss Hodge," Mr. Wentworth said, shakily trying to sound calm and reasonable, "I'm sorry to disappoint you, but I can't marry anyone. My wife is still alive. She was arrested as a witch, but she managed to get away through someone's backyard and get to the witches' rescue service. So you see—"

"Well, you'd better pretend she was burned," Miss Hodge said. She was very angry. She felt cheated. She marched up to Mr. Wentworth's desk and took hold of the receiver of Mr. Wentworth's telephone. "You agree to marry me, or I ring the police about you. Now."

"No, please—!" said Mr. Wentworth.

"I mean it," said Miss Hodge. She tried to pick the receiver up off the telephone. It seemed to be stuck. Miss Hodge jiggled it angrily. It gave out a lot of tinkling, but it would not seem to move. Miss Hodge looked round to find Chrestomanci looking at her in an interested way. "You stop that!" she said to him.

"When you tell me one thing," Chrestomanci said. "You don't seem at all alarmed to find yourself in a roomful of witches. Why not?"

"Of course I'm not," Miss Hodge retorted. "I pity witches. Now will you please allow me to ring the police about Mr. Wentworth? He's been deceiving everyone for years!"

"But my dear young lady," said Chrestomanci, "so have you. The only sort of person who would behave as you do must be a witch herself."

Miss Hodge stared at him haughtily. "I have never used a spell in my life," she said.

"A slight exaggeration," Chrestomanci said. "You used one small spell, to make sure no one knew you were a witch."

Why didn't I think of that? Charles wondered, watching the look of fear and dismay grow in Miss Hodge's face. He was very shaken. He could not get used to the idea that his second witch had probably been Brian's mother.

Miss Hodge once more jiggled the telephone. It was still stuck. "Very well," she said. "I'm not afraid of you. You can disable all the phones in the school if you like, but you won't stop me going and telling everyone I meet about you and Mr. Wentworth and Brian, and the other four, unless Mr. Wentworth agrees to marry me this instant. I think I shall start with Harold Crossley." She made as if to turn away and leave the room. It was clear she meant it.

Chrestomanci sighed and put one finger down on the schedule he was holding, very carefully and precisely, in the middle of one of the rectangles marked *Miss Hodge 6B*. And Miss Hodge was not there anymore. The telephone gave out a small ting, and she was gone. At the same moment, Nan, Estelle, Nirupam, and Charles all found themselves visible again. It was clear to them that Miss Hodge was not just invisible in their place. The room felt empty of her, and a small gust of wind ruffling the papers on Mr. Wentworth's desk seemed to prove she was gone.

"Fancy her being a witch!" said Nirupam. "Where is she?"

Chrestomanci examined the schedule. "Er—next Tuesday, I believe. That should give us time to sort out this wretched situation. Unless we are very unlucky, of course." He looked at Mr. Wentworth. "Perhaps you would be ready to help us do that now, sir?"

But Mr. Wentworth sank into the chair behind his desk and covered his face with his hands.

"You never told me Mum got away," Brian said to him accusingly. "And you never said a word about Miss Cadwallader."

"You never told me you intended to go and camp in the forest," Mr. Wentworth said wearily. "Oh Lord! Where shall I get an extra teacher from? I've got to find someone to take Miss Hodge's lessons this afternoon somehow."

Chrestomanci sat in the chair he had put out for Miss Hodge. "It never ceases to amaze me," he said, "the way people always manage to worry about the wrong things. My dear sir, do you realize that you, your son, and four of your pupils are all likely to be burned unless we do something? And here you are worrying about schedules."

Mr. Wentworth lifted his harrowed face and stared past Chrestomanci. "How did she *do* it?" he said. "How does she keep it up? How *can* Miss Hodge be a teacher and not use witchcraft at all? I use it all the time. How else can I have eyes in the back of my head?"

"One of the great mysteries of our time," Chrestomanci agreed. "Now please listen to me. You are aware, I believe, that there is at least one other world besides this one. It seems to be your custom to send escaped witches there. I presume your wife is there. What you may not realize is that these are only two out of a multitude of worlds, all very different from one another. I come from one of the other ones myself."

To everyone's relief, Mr. Wentworth listened to this. "Alternative worlds, you mean?" he said. "There's been some speculation about that. If-worlds, counterfactuals, and so on. You mean they're real?"

"As real as you are," Chrestomanci said.

Nirupam was very interested in this. He doubled himself up on the floor beside Chrestomanci's beautifully creased trousers and said, "They are made from the great events in history, I believe, sir, where it is possible for things to go two ways. It is easiest to understand with battles. Both sides cannot win a battle, so each war makes two possible worlds, with a different side winning. Like the Battle of Waterloo. In our world, Napoleon lost it, but another world at once split off from ours, in which Napoleon won the battle."

"Exactly," said Chrestomanci. "I find that world a rather trying one. Everyone speaks French there and winces at my accent. The only place they speak English there, oddly enough, is in India, where they are very British and eat treacle pudding after their curry."

"I should like that," Nirupam said.

"Everyone to his taste," Chrestomanci said with a slight shudder. "But, as you will see, exactly who won the Battle of Waterloo made a great deal of difference between those two worlds. And that is the rule. A surprisingly small change always alters the new world almost out of recognition. Except in the case of this world of yours, where we all now are." He looked at Mr. Wentworth. "This is what I need your help about, sir. There is something badly wrong with this world. The fact that witches are extremely common, and illegal, should have made as much difference here as it does in my own world, where witches are equally common, but quite legal. But it does not. Estelle, perhaps you can tell us about the world where the witches' rescue service sends witches."

Estelle beamed up at him adoringly from where she was sitting cross-legged on the floor. "The old lady said it was just like this one, only with no witchcraft," she said.

"And that is just the trouble," said Chrestomanci. "I know that world rather well, because I have a young ward who used to belong in it. And since I have been here, I have discovered that events in history here, cars, advertisements, goods in shops, money—everything I can check—are all exactly the same as those in my ward's world. And this is quite wrong. No two worlds are ever this alike."

Mr. Wentworth was attending quite keenly now. He frowned. "What do you think has gone wrong?" And Nan thought, So he *was* finding out symptoms!

Chrestomanci looked round them all, vaguely and dubiously, before he said, "If you'll forgive me saying, your world should not exist." They all stared. "I mean it," Chrestomanci said, apologetically. "I have often wondered why there is so little witchcraft in my ward's world. I see now that it is all in this one. Something—I don't know what—has caused your world to separate from the other one, taking all the witchcraft with it. But instead of breaking off cleanly, it has somehow remained partly joined to the first world, so that it almost *is* that world. I think there has been some kind of accident. You shouldn't get a civilized world where witches are burned. As I said, it ought not to exist. So, as I have been trying to explain to you all along, Mr. Wentworth, I urgently need a short history of witchcraft, in order to discover what kind of accident happened here. Was Elizabeth I a witch?"

Mr. Wentworth shook his head. "Nobody knows for sure. But witchcraft didn't seem to be that much of a problem in her reign. Witches were mostly just old women in villages then. No—modern witchcraft really started soon after Elizabeth I died. There seems to have been a big increase in about 1606, when the first official bonfires started. The first Witchcraft Edict was passed in 1612. Oliver Cromwell passed more. There had been thirty-four Witchcraft Acts passed by 1760, the year Dulcinea Wilkes—"

But Chrestomanci held up one hand to stop him there. "Thank you. I know about the Archwitch. You've told me what I need to know. The present state of witchcraft began quite suddenly soon after 1600. That means that the accident we're looking for must have happened around then. Have you any idea what it might be?"

Mr. Wentworth shook his head again, rather glumly. "I haven't a notion. But—suppose you did know, what could you do about it?"

"One of two things," said Chrestomanci. "Either we could break this world away completely from the other one, which I don't consider a good idea, because then you would certainly all be burned—" Everybody shuddered, and Charles's thumb found itself running back and forth over the blister on his finger. "Or," said Chrestomanci, "and this is a much better idea, we could put your world back into the other one, where it really belongs."

"What would happen to us if you did?" asked Charles.

"Nothing much. You would simply melt quietly into the people you really are in that world," said Chrestomanci.

Everyone considered this in silence for a moment. "Can that really be done?" Mr. Wentworth asked hopefully.

"Well," said Chrestomanci, "it can, as long as we can find what caused the split in the first place. It will take strong magic. But it *is* Halloween and there ought to be a great deal of magic loose in this world particularly, and we can draw on that. Yes. I'm sure it can be done, though it may not be easy."

"Then let's do it," said Mr. Wentworth. The idea seemed to restore him to his usual self. He stood up, and his eyes roved grimly across the riding clothes, the sky-blue shorts and Brian's jeans, and rested incredulously upon the tattered pink balldress. "If you lot think you can appear in class like that," he said. He was back to being a schoolmaster again.

"Er, leave Brian, I think," Chrestomanci said quickly.

"You will have plenty of time to reconsider in detention," Mr. Wentworth finished. Nan, Estelle, Charles, and Nirupam all scrambled hurriedly to their feet. And as soon as they were standing up, they found they were wearing school uniforms. They looked round for Brian, but he did not seem to be there.

"I'm invisible again!" Brian said disgustedly, out of the air.

Chrestomanci was smiling. "Not bad, sir," he said to Mr. Wentworth. Mr. Wentworth looked pleased, and, as he shepherded the four of them to the door, he smiled back at Chrestomanci in quite a friendly way.

"Why is Brian allowed to stay invisible?" Estelle complained, as Mr. Wentworth marched them back toward the classroom.

"Because he gives Chrestomanci an excuse to go on staying here as an inquisitor," Nirupam whispered. "He is supposed to be finding what the witch has done with Brian."

"But don't tell Brian," Charles muttered, as they arrived outside the door of 6B. "He'd spoil it. He's like that." The truth was, he was not so sure he would not spoil things himself if he got the chance. Nothing had been changed. He was still in as much trouble as ever.

CHAPTER 14

Mr. Wentworth opened the door and ushered the four of them into the classroom, into a blast of stares and whispers. "I'm afraid I had to kidnap these four," Mr. Wentworth said to Mr. Crossley, who happened to be teaching the rest. "We've been arranging my study for the inquisitor to use."

Mr. Crossley seemed to believe this without question. 6B, to judge from their faces, felt it was an awful letdown. They had expected all four of them to have been arrested. But they made the best of it.

"Mr. Towers is looking for you two," Simon whispered righteously to Nirupam and Charles. And Theresa said to Estelle, "Miss Phillips wants you." Nan was lucky. Miss Phillips never remembered Nan if she could help it.

They had arrived back so late that there was only a short piece of lesson left before lunchtime. When the bell rang for lunch, Charles and Nirupam kept to the thickest crowds. Neither of them wanted Mr. Towers to see them. But Charles had his usual bad luck. Mr. Towers was on duty at the door of the dining hall. Charles was very relieved when he slipped past without Mr. Towers showing any interest in him at all.

Nirupam nudged Charles as they sat down after grace. Chrestomanci was sitting beside Miss Cadwallader at high table, looking bland and vague. Everyone craned to look at him. Word went round that this was the divisional inquisitor.

"I don't fancy getting on the wrong side of him," Dan Smith observed. "You can see that sleepy look's just there to fool you."

"He looks feeble," said Simon. "I'm not going to let him scare me."

Charles craned to look too. He knew what Simon meant, but he was quite sure by now that Chrestomanci's vague look was as deceptive as

Dan thought. Mr. Wentworth was up at high table too. Charles wondered where Brian was and how Brian would get any lunch.

Charles turned back to the table to hear Theresa saying, "He is so super looking, he makes me feel quite weak!"

To everyone's surprise, Estelle jumped to her feet and leaned across the table, glaring at Theresa. "Theresa Mullett!" she said. "You just dare be in love with the inquisitor and see what you get! He's mine. I met him first and *I* love him! So you just dare!"

Nobody said a word for a moment. Theresa was too astonished even to giggle. Everyone was so unused to seeing Estelle so fierce that even the monitor in charge could not think what to say.

During the silence, it became clear how Brian was going to get lunch. Charles and Nirupam felt themselves being pushed apart by an invisible body. Both of them were jabbed by invisible elbows as the body climbed on to the bench between them and sat. "You'll have to let me eat off your plates," whispered Brian's voice. "I hope it's not stew."

Luckily, Simon broke the silence just as Brian spoke. He said, in a jeering, not-quite-believing way, "And what took you all so long to arrange for Mr. Feeble Inquisitor?"

From the way everyone looked then, Nan knew nobody had believed Mr. Wentworth's excuse for an instant. She could see most of them suspected something like the truth. Help! thought Nan. "Well we had to put a lot of electric wiring into the study," she invented hastily. "He has to have a bright light arranged to shine into people's faces. It helps break them down."

"Not for electric shocks at all?" Dan asked hopefully.

"Some of it *may* have been," Nan admitted. "There were quite a lot of bare wires, and a sort of helmet thing with electrodes sticking out of it. Charles wired that. Charles is very good with electricity."

"And what else?" Dan asked breathlessly. He was far too fascinated by now to notice he was talking to a girl.

"The walls were all draped in black," invented Nan. "Estelle and I did that."

Lunch was served just then. It was potato pie. This was fortunate for Brian, who dared not use a knife and fork, but not so lucky for Charles and Nirupam. Both of them gave grunts of indignation as a large curved chunk vanished from their plates. Brian had taken a handful from each. They were more annoyed still, when lumps of potato began to flop down between them.

"Don't waste it!" snapped Nirupam.

"Can't you tell where your mouth is?" Charles whispered angrily.

"Yes. But I don't know where my hands are," Brian whispered back. "*You* try, if you think you're so clever!"

While they whispered, Nan was being eagerly questioned by Dan, and forced to invent more and more inquisitor's equipment for Mr. Wentworth's study. "Yes, there *were* these things with little chromium screws," she was saying. "I think you're right—those must have been thumbscrews. But some of them looked big enough to get an arm or a leg in. I don't think he stops at thumbs."

Nirupam dug Brian's invisible side with his elbow. "Listen to this!" he whispered. "It all has to be there if he calls Dan in."

"I'm not a fool," Brian's voice retorted with its mouth full.

"And of course there were a lot of other things we had to hang on the wall. All sizes of handcuffs," Nan went on. She was inspired now and her invention seemed boundless. She just could not seem to stop. Charles began to wonder if one small study could possibly hold all the things she was describing—or even only the half of it that Brian managed to remember.

Fortunately, Estelle, who was far too busy watching Chrestomanci to eat, caused a sudden diversion by shouting out, "Look, look! Miss Cadwallader's only using a fork, and *he's* using a knife and a fork! Oh, isn't he *brave!*"

At that, Nirupam seized the opportunity to try and shut Nan up. He gave her a sinister stare and said loudly, "You realize that the inquisitor will probably be questioning every one of us very searchingly indeed, after lunch is over."

Though Nirupam meant this simply as a warning to Nan, it caused a worried silence. A surprising number of people did not seem very keen on the treacle tart which followed the potato pie. Nirupam seized that opportunity too. He took third and fourth helpings and shared them with Brian.

Straight after lunch, Mr. Wentworth came and marshaled the whole of 6B into alphabetical order. The worried silence became a scared one. From the looks they saw on faces of the rest of the school, the scare was catching. Even seniors looked alarmed as 6B were marched away. They marched upstairs and were lined up half in the passage and half on the stairs, while Mr. Wentworth went into his study to tell Chrestomanci they were ready. Those at the front of the line were able to see that the wavy glass in the door was now black as night.

Then it turned out that Chrestomanci wanted to see them in reverse alphabetical order. They all had to march up and down and round again, so that Heather Young and Ronald West were at the front of the line instead of Geoffrey Barnes and Deborah Clifton. They did it with none of the usual grumbling and scuffling. Even Charles, who was quite certain that they were only marching to give Chrestomanci time to put all Nan's inventions in, found himself a little quiet and queasy, with his thumb rubbing at that blister. Heather and Ronald looked quite ill with terror. Dan Smith—who was third now that Brian was missing—asked Nirupam in an urgent whisper, "What's he going to do with us?"

Nirupam had no more idea than Dan. He had not even known that Chrestomanci really was going to question them. He tried to look sinister. "You'll see." Dan's face went cream-colored.

Chrestomanci did not see people for the same length of time. Heather disappeared into the study for what seemed an endless age, and she came out as frightened as she went in. Ronald was only in for a minute, and he came out from behind the darkened door looking relieved. He leaned across Dan and Nirupam to whisper to Simon, "No problem at all!"

"I knew there wouldn't be," Simon lied loftily.

"Quiet!" bellowed Mr. Wentworth. "Next—Daniel Smith."

Dan Smith was not gone long either, but he did not come out looking as if there were no problem. His face was more like cheese than cream.

Nirupam was gone for much longer than either Nan or Charles had expected. When he came out, he was frowning and uneasy. He was followed by Simon. There was another endless wait. During it, the bell rang for afternoon lessons, and was followed by the usual surge of hurrying feet. The silence of lessons which came after that had gone on for so long before Simon came out that there was not a soul in 6B who did not feel like an outcast. Simon came out at last. He was an odd color. He would not speak to any of the friends who were leaning out of the line wanting to know what had happened. He just walked to the wall like a sleepwalker and leaned against it, staring into space.

This did not make anyone feel better. Nan wondered what Chrestomanci was doing to people in there. By the time the three girls who came between her and Simon had all come out looking as bad as Heather Young, Nan was so scared that she could hardly make her legs work. But it was her turn. She had to go. She shuffled round the dark door somehow.

Inside, she stood and stared. Chrestomanci had indeed been very busy while 6B marched up and down outside. Mr. Wentworth's study was entirely lined with black curtains. A black carpet Nan had forgotten to invent covered the parquet floor. Hung on the walls and glimmering against the black background were manacles, a noose, festoons of chains, several kinds of scourge, and a cat-o'-nine-tails. There was a large can in one corner labeled *PETROL, DIV. INQ. OFFICE, FOR USE IN TORTURE ONLY.*

Chrestomanci himself was only dimly visible behind a huge glittering lamp, which reminded Nan uncomfortably of the light over an operating table. The light from it beamed onto Mr. Wentworth's desk, draped in more black cloth, where there was a sort of jeweler's display of shiny thumbscrews and other displeasing objects. The wired-up helmet was there. So was a bouquet of bare wires, spitting blue sparks. Behind those was a pile of fat black books.

"Can you see anything Brian forgot?" asked the dim shape of Chrestomanci.

Nan began to laugh. "I didn't say the carpet or the petrol!"

"Brian suggested a carpet. And I thought that corner looked a little bare," Chrestomanci admitted.

Nan pointed to the pile of black books. "What are those?"

"Disguised schedules," said Chrestomanci. "Oh—I see what you mean. Obviously they are Acts of Parliament and Witchcraft Edicts, torture manuals, and *The Observer's Guide to Witch-Spotting.* No inquisitor would be without them."

Nan could tell from his voice that he was laughing. "I accuse you of enjoying yourself," she said, "while everyone outside gibbers."

"I confess to that." Chrestomanci came round the desk under the light. He pushed the spitting bunch of wires casually aside—it did not appear to give him any kind of shock—and sat on the black-draped desk so that his face was level with Nan's. She suddenly found it almost impossible to look away. "I accuse you of enjoying yourself too," he said.

"Yes, I have!" Nan said defiantly. "For about the first time since I came to this beastly school!"

Chrestomanci looked at her almost anxiously. "You enjoy being a witch?" Nan nodded vigorously. "And you've enjoyed making things up and describing them—thumbscrews and so on?" Nan nodded again. "Which did you enjoy most?" Chrestomanci asked.

"Oh, being a witch," Nan declared. "It's made me feel—well—just so confident, I suppose."

"Describe the things you've invented so far to do as a witch," said Chrestomanci.

"I—" Nan looked at Chrestomanci, lit from one side by the strong light of the lamp and, from the other, by the flickering wires, and was rather puzzled to find how little she had done as a witch. All she had done, when you came down to it, was to ride a broomstick and to give herself and Estelle the wrong kind of clothes and some decidedly odd collecting tins. "I haven't had much time to do things yet," she said.

"But Charles Morgan has had about the same amount of time, and according to the things people have been telling me, he has been very inventive indeed," Chrestomanci said. "Wouldn't you say that, now that you've been a witch, and got your confidence, you might really prefer describing things even to witchcraft?"

Nan thought about it. "I suppose I would," she said, rather surprised. "If only we didn't have to do it in our journals!"

"Good," said Chrestomanci. "I think I can promise you one really good opportunity to describe things, nothing to do with journals. I told you it would take strong magic to put this world back into the one where it belongs. When I find the way to do it, I shall need everyone's help, in order to harness all the magic there is in the world to make the change. When the time comes, can I rely on you to explain all this?"

Nan nodded. She felt hugely flattered and responsible.

While she was feeling this way, Chrestomanci added, "Just as well you prefer describing things. I'm afraid you won't be a witch when the change comes." Nan stared at him. He was not joking. "I know you are descended from the Archwitch," Chrestomanci said, "but talents don't always descend in the same shape. Yours seem to have come to you in the form of making-up and describing. My advice is to stick with that, if you can. Now name me one character out of history."

Nan blinked at the change of subject. "Er—Christopher Columbus," she said miserably.

Chrestomanci took out a little gold notebook and unclipped a gold pencil. "Would you mind explaining who he was?" he said, a little helplessly.

It was astonishing the way Chrestomanci seemed not to know the most obvious things, Nan thought. She told him all about Christopher Columbus, as kindly as she could, and Chrestomanci wrote it down in his gold notebook. "Admirable," he murmured as he wrote. "Clear and vivid." The result was that Nan went out of the study one half delighted that Chrestomanci thought she was so good at describing things, and the other half desperately sad at not being a witch before long. Dan Smith's friend Lance Osgood, who was next one in, looked hard at Nan's face as she came out and did not know what to make of it.

Lance was not in the study long. Nor was Theresa Mullett, who came next. By this time, Estelle had just gotten up to the top of the stairs, near the end of the line. Estelle craned round the corner as Theresa came out, searching for signs of love in Theresa, but Theresa looked peevish and puzzled. Everyone saw that the inquisitor had not treated Theresa with proper respect. Delia was whispering across to Heather about it when Charles went in.

Charles was not in the least frightened by this time. He was sure by now that Chrestomanci was treating everybody exactly as he or she deserved. He grinned when he saw the study all draped in black, and pushed his glasses up his nose to look at the things hung on the walls.

Chrestomanci was a dim shape behind the lamp and the spitting wires. "You approve?" he said.

"It's not bad," said Charles. "Where's Brian?"

"Over here," said Brian's voice. Two pairs of handcuffs on the black-draped wall lifted and jingled. "How long is this going on? I'm magicking bored already, and you've only gotten to M."

"Why have you got him in here?" Charles asked Chrestomanci. He kept his finger on his glasses in order to give Brian his best double-barreled glare.

"I have my reasons," Chrestomanci said quietly. Quiet though it was, it made Charles feel as if something very cold and rather deadly was crawling down his back. "I want to talk to you," Chrestomanci continued, in the same quiet way, "about your *Simon Says* spell."

The cold spread from Charles's spine right through the rest of him, and settled particularly in his stomach. He knew that this interview was not going to be anything like the joke he had thought it would be. "What about it?" he muttered.

"I can't understand," Chrestomanci said, mild and puzzled and more deadly quiet than ever, "how you forgot to mention that spell. How did it come to slip your mind?"

It was like being embedded in ice. Charles tried to break out of the ice by blustering. "There was no point in telling you. It was only a spell—it wasn't important and Simon deserved it! And Nirupam took it off him anyway!"

"I beg your pardon. I wasn't aware that you had a defense," Chrestomanci said.

Sarcasm like this is hard enough to bear, and even worse if you know someone like Brian is listening in. Charles mustered another glare. But he found it hard to direct at Chrestomanci, hidden beyond the light, and swung it round at Brian again instead. Or rather, at the handcuffs where Brian might be. "It wasn't that important," he said.

Chrestomanci seemed more puzzled than ever. "Not important? My dear boy, what is so unimportant about a spell that could break the world up? You may know better, of course, but my impression is that Simon could easily have chanced to say something very silly, like—say—'Two and two are five.' If he had, everything to do with numbers would have fallen apart at once. And since everything can be counted, everything would have come apart—the earth, the sun in the sky, the cells in bodies, anything else you can think of. No doubt you have a mind above such things, but I can't help finding that quite important myself."

Charles glowered at the handcuffs to disguise how awful this made him feel. And Brian had heard every word! "I didn't realize—how could I? Simon had it coming to him, anyway. He deserved something." He was rather glad, as he said it, that no one knew he intended to do something to Dan Smith next.

"Simon deserved it?" wondered Chrestomanci. "Simon certainly has a large opinion of himself, but—Brian, you tell us. You have an ego at least as big as Simon's. Do you or Simon deserve to have such power put in your hands?"

"No," Brian's voice said sulkily. "Not to destroy the world."

Charles was cold all through with horror at what he had almost done. But he was not going to admit it. "Nirupam took it off him," he said, "before Simon did anything really."

"Brian seems to be learning," Chrestomanci remarked, "even if you are not, Charles. I grant you that, because magic is forbidden here, nobody has ever taught you what it can do or how to use it. But you could have worked it out. And you are still not thinking. Nirupam did *not* take that spell off Simon. He simply turned it back to front. *Nothing* the poor boy says comes true now. I have had to order him to keep his mouth shut."

"Poor boy!" Charles exclaimed. "You can't be sorry for him!"

"I am," said Brian's voice. "And if I hadn't been in the sick bay, I'd have tried to take it off him myself. I'd have managed better than Nirupam, too!"

"Now there, Charles," said Chrestomanci, "you have an excellent example quite apart from rights and wrongs, of why it is such a bad idea to do things to people. Everyone is now sorry for Simon. Which is not what you want at all, is it?"

"No." Charles looked down at the shadowy black carpet and decided regretfully to think again about Dan Smith. This time he would get it right.

"Make him take the spell off Simon," Brian suggested.

"I doubt if he could," said Chrestomanci. "It's a fearsomely strong thing. Charles must have powers way up in the enchanter class in order to have worked it at all." Charles kept his face turned to the carpet, hoping that would hide the huge smug grin he could feel spreading on his face. "It will take a number of special circumstances to get that spell off Simon," Chrestomanci continued. "For a start, Charles must want to take the spell off. And he doesn't. Do you, Charles?"

"No," said Charles. The idea of Simon having to hold his tongue for the rest of his life gave him such pleasure that he did not bother to listen to all the names Brian began calling him. He held his finger out, into the lamplight, and admired the way the strong light and the spitting wires made patterns in the yellow cushion of blister. Wickedness was branded into him, he thought.

Chrestomanci waited for Brian to run out of names to call Charles. Then he said, "I'm sorry you feel this way, Charles. We are all going to need your help when we try to put this world back where it belongs. Won't you reconsider?"

"Not after the way you went on at me in front of Brian," said Charles. And he went on admiring his blister.

Chrestomanci sighed. "You and Brian are both as bad as one another," he said. "People in Larwood House are always developing into witches, Mr. Wentworth tells me, but he tells me he has had no trouble in stopping any of them giving themselves away, until it came to you and Brian. Brian was so anxious to be noticed that he didn't care if he was burned—"

"Hey!" Brian said indignantly.

So Chrestomanci was trying to make it fair by getting at Brian now, Charles thought. It was a bit late for that. He was not going to help.

"So he is going to have to help, or stay invisible for the rest of his life," Chrestomanci went on. He ignored indignant, miserable noises from Brian and turned to Charles. "You, Charles, seem to have bottled yourself up, hating everything, until your witchcraft came along and blew the stopper off you. Now, either you are going to have to bottle yourself up again or be burned, *or* you are going to have to help us. Since your talent for witchcraft is so strong, it seems certain that in your right world, you will have an equally strong talent for something else, and you should find that easier. So which do you choose?"

Lose his witchcraft? Charles pressed one finger to his glasses and glared through the strong light at Chrestomanci. He did not think he even hated Simon or Dan as much as he hated Chrestomanci. "I'm going to go on being a witch! So there!"

The dim shape of Chrestomanci shrugged behind the light. "Warlock is the usual term for people who mess about the way you do. Very well. Now name me one historical personage, please."

"Jack the Ripper," snarled Charles.

The gold notebook flashed in the lamplight. "Thank you," said Chrestomanci. "Send the next person in as you go out."

As Charles turned and trudged to the door, Brian began calling him names again.

"Brian," Chrestomanci said quietly, "I told you I would take your voice away, and I shall if you speak to anyone else."

Typical! Charles thought angrily. He tore open the door, wondering what he dared do to Nan and Estelle for calling Chrestomanci here, and found himself staring into Delia Martin's face. He must have looked quite frightening. Delia went white. She actually spoke to him. "What's he like?"

"Magicking horrible!" Charles said loudly. He hoped Chrestomanci heard him.

CHAPTER 15

The rest of 6B shuffled slowly in and out of the study. Some came out white, some came out relieved. Estelle came out misty-eyed and beaming.

"Really!" said Theresa. "Some people!"

Estelle shot her a look of utter scorn and went up to Nan. She put both hands round one of Nan's ears and whispered wetly, "He says that where we're going, my mum won't be in prison!"

"Oh good!" said Nan, and she thought, in sudden excitement, *my* mum will still be alive, then!

Chrestomanci himself came out of the study with Geoffrey Barnes, who was last, and exchanged a deep look with Mr. Wentworth. Nan could tell that he had not found out how to change the world. She saw they were both worried.

"Right. In line and back to the classroom," shouted Mr. Wentworth. He was looking so harrowed, and hurried them down the stairs so fast, that Nan knew Chrestomanci's luck was running out. Perhaps the real inquisitor had arrived by now. The bell for the end of the first lesson rang as 6B marched through the corridors, which increased the urgent feeling. Other classes hurried past them, and gave them looks of pitying curiosity.

Simon's friends kept trying to talk to him as they went. Simon shook his head madly and pointed to his mouth. "He knows who the witch is, but his lips are sealed," Ronald West said wisely.

This caused Delia and Karen to skip out of line and walk beside Simon. "Tell us who the witch is, Simon," they whispered. "We won't say." The more Simon shook his head, the more they asked.

"Quiet!" barked Mr. Wentworth.

Everyone filed into the classroom. There stood Mr. Crossley, expecting to sit with 6B while they wrote their journals.

"You'd better treat this as a free period, Harold," Mr. Wentworth said to him. Mr. Crossley nodded, highly pleased, and went off to the staff room, hoping to catch Miss Hodge there.

"Poor Teddy," Estelle whispered to Nan. "He doesn't know she's in next Tuesday. Mind you, I don't think she'd ever have him anyway."

Chrestomanci came into the classroom, looking suave and vague. No one could have guessed from the look of him that time was running out and he was probably just as anxious as Mr. Wentworth. He coughed for attention. He got instant silence, complete and attentive. Mr. Wentworth looked a little envious.

"This is a miserable affair," Chrestomanci said. "We have a witch in our midst. And this witch has cast a spell on Simon Silverson—"

The room rustled with people turning to look at Simon. Charles glowered. Simon was looking almost happy again. He was in the limelight, where he belonged.

"Now, most unfortunately," Chrestomanci went on, "someone made a well-meant but misguided effort to break the spell and turned it back to front." Nirupam looked morbid. "You can't blame this person," said Chrestomanci, "but the result is most unhappy. It was a very strong spell. Everything Simon now says does not only *not* happen, but it never *has* happened. I have had to warn Simon not to open his mouth until we get to the bottom of the matter."

As he said this, Chrestomanci's eyes turned, vaguely and absently, toward Charles. Charles gave his blankest and nastiest look in reply. If Chrestomanci thought he could make him take the spell off this way, Chrestomanci could just think again. What Charles did not notice was that Chrestomanci's eyes moved toward Nan after that. Nobody else noticed at all, because three people had put their hands up: Delia, Karen, and Theresa. Delia spoke for all three.

"Mr. Inquisitor, sir, we told you who the witch is. It's Nan Pilgrim."

Estelle's desk went over with a crash. Books, journal, papers, and knitting skidded in all directions. Estelle stood in the middle of them, red with anger. "It is *not* Nan Pilgrim!" she shouted. "Nan never harmed anyone in her life! It's you lot that do the harm, spreading tales all the time, you and Theresa and Karen. And I'm ashamed I was ever friends with Karen!"

Nan put her hot face in her hands. Estelle was a bit too loyal for comfort.

"Pick that desk up, Estelle," said Mr. Wentworth.

Simon forgot himself and opened his mouth to make a jeering comment. Chrestomanci's eyes just happened to glance at him. Simon's mouth shut with a snap and his eyes popped.

And that was all the notice Chrestomanci took of the interruption. "If you will all attend," he said. Everyone did, immediately. "Thank you. Before we name the witch, I want you all to give the name of a second historical personage. You in the front, you begin—er—um—Theresa—er—Fish."

Everyone had already given one name. Everyone was convinced that the inquisitor would know the witch by the name they gave. It was obviously important not to name anybody wicked. So Theresa, although she was offended by the way the inquisitor got her name wrong, thought very carefully indeed. And, as usually happens, her mind was instantly filled with all the villains in history. She sat there dumbly, running through Burke and Hare, Crippen, Judas Iscariot, Nero, and Torquemada, and quite unable to think of anybody good.

"Come along—er—Tatiana," said Chrestomanci.

"Theresa," said Theresa. And then, with inspiration, "*Saint* Theresa, I mean."

Chrestomanci wrote that down in his gold notebook and pointed to Delia. "Saint George," said Delia.

"Didn't exist in any world," said Chrestomanci. "Try again."

Delia racked her brains and eventually came up with Lady Godiva. Chrestomanci's pointing finger moved on round the class, causing everyone the same trouble. Villains poured through their minds—Attila the Hun, Richard III, Lucrezia Borgia, Joseph Stalin—and when they did manage to think of anyone less villainous, it always seemed to be people like Anne Boleyn or Galileo, who had been put to death. Most people did not like to mention those either, though Nirupam, because he knew Chrestomanci was not really an inquisitor, took a risk and said Charles I. Chrestomanci turned to Mr. Wentworth after most names were mentioned, and Mr. Wentworth told him who they were. Most of 6B could not think why the inquisitor needed to do that, unless it was to prove that Mr. Wentworth was a mastermind, but Nan thought, He's collecting symptoms again. Why? Somebody in history must be very important, I think.

Charles watched Chrestomanci's finger point toward him. He thought, You don't get me like that! "Saint Francis," he said. Chrestomanci's finger simply moved on to Dan Smith.

Dan was stumped. "Please, sir, I've got a stomachache. I can't think."

The finger went on pointing.

"Oh," said Dan. "Er—Dick Turpin."

This evoked a gasp from 6B, and a near-groan of disappointment when Chrestomanci's finger moved on, across the gangway, and pointed to Estelle.

Estelle had picked up her desk and most of her books by now, but her knitting wool had rolled under several desks and come unwound as it went. Estelle was on her knees reeling it in, grayer than ever, and did not notice. Nan leaned down and poked her. Estelle jumped. "Is it me now? Sorry. Guy Fawkes—has anyone had Guy Fawkes yet?" She went back to her wool.

"One moment," said Chrestomanci. A curious hush seemed to grow in the room. "Can you tell me about Guy Fawkes?"

Estelle looked up again. Everyone was looking at her, wondering if she was the witch, but Estelle was only thinking about her wool. "Guy Fawkes?" she said. "They put him on a bonfire for blowing up the Houses of Parliament."

"Blowing them *up?*" said Chrestomanci. "But Guy Fawkes never managed to blow up Parliament in any world I ever heard of!"

Simon opened his mouth to say Estelle was quite right, and shut it again hastily. Estelle nodded. A number of people called out, "Yes, sir. He did, sir!"

Chrestomanci looked at Mr. Wentworth. Mr. Wentworth said, "In 1605, Guy Fawkes was smuggled into the Parliament cellars with some kegs of gunpowder, in order to blow up the government and the king. But he seems to have made a mistake. The gunpowder blew up in the night and destroyed both Houses, without killing anyone. Guy Fawkes got out unhurt, but they caught him almost at once."

It sounded like all the other times Mr. Wentworth had told Chrestomanci a piece of history, but somehow it was not. Chrestomanci's eyes had a special gleam, very bright and black, and he looked straight at Nan as he remarked, "A mistake, eh? That doesn't surprise me. That fellow Fawkes never could get anything right. So this is the world where he got things wronger even than usual." He pointed at Nan.

"Richard the Lionheart," said Nan. And she thought, He's got it! Guy Fawkes is the reason our world went different. But why? He'll want me to describe it and I don't know why. She thought and thought, while Chrestomanci was collecting names no one needed now from the rest of 6B. November 5, 1605. All Nan could remember was something her mother had once said, long ago, before the inquisitor took her away. Mum had said November 5 was the last day of Witch Week. Witch Week began on Halloween, and today was Halloween. Did that help? It must do, though Nan could not see how. But she knew she was right, and that Chrestomanci *had* found the answer, because he had such a smooth, pleased look as he stood beside Mr. Wentworth.

"Now," he said. "We shall reveal the witch."

He had gone vague again. He was slowly fetching a slim golden case from a dove-gray pocket and, if he was looking at anyone, it was at Charles now. Good, thought Nan. He's giving me time to think. And Charles thought, All right. Reveal me then. But I'm still not going to help.

Chrestomanci held the flat gold box out so that everyone could see it. "This," he said, "is the very latest modern witch-finder. Look at it carefully." Charles did. He was almost certain that the witch-finder was a gold cigarette case. "When I let go of this machine," Chrestomanci said, "it will travel by itself through the air, and it will point to everyone in turn, except Simon. When it points to a witch, it is programmed to make a noise. I want the witch it points to to come and stand beside me."

6B stared at the gold oblong, tense and excited. There were gasps. It had bobbled in Chrestomanci's hand. Chrestomanci let go of it and it stayed in the air, bobbing about by itself. Charles glowered. He understood. Brian. Brian was going to carry it invisibly round. That did it! If Chrestomanci thought he could get round Charles by giving Brian all the fun, he was going to be really disappointed.

The bobbing case upended itself. Charles saw it split open a fraction along the top edge, as Brian took a quick peep to see if it was indeed a cigarette case. It was. Charles glimpsed white cigarettes in it.

"Off you go," Chrestomanci said to it.

The gold box shut with a loud snap, making everybody jump, and then traveled swiftly to the first desk. It stopped level with Ronald West's head. It gave out a shrill beeping sound. Everybody jumped again, including Ronald and the gold box.

"Come out here," Chrestomanci said.

Ronald, looking quite dumbfounded, got out of his desk and stumbled toward Chrestomanci. "I never—!" he protested.

"Yes, you are, you know," Chrestomanci said. And he said to the gold box, "Carry on."

A little uncertainly, the box traveled to Geoffrey Barnes. It beeped again. Chrestomanci beckoned. Out came Geoffrey, white-faced but not protesting.

"How did it know?" he said drearily.

"Modern technology," said Chrestomanci.

This time the gold box went on without being told. It beeped, moved, and beeped again. Person after person got miserably up and trailed out to the front. Charles thought it was a dirty trick. Chrestomanci was just trying to break his nerve. The box was level with Lance Osgood now. Everyone waited for it to beep. And waited. The box stayed beside Lance, pointing until Lance's eyes were crossed with looking at it. But nothing happened.

"Go on," said Chrestomanci. "He's not a witch."

The box moved to Dan Smith. Here, it made the longest, loudest noise yet. Dan blenched. "I covered up my tracks!" he said.

"Out here," said Chrestomanci.

Dan got up slowly. "It's not fair! My stomach aches."

"No doubt you deserve it," said Chrestomanci. "By the noise, you've used witchcraft quite recently. What did you do?"

"Only hid a pair of running shoes," Dan mumbled. He did not look at Charles as he slouched up the gangway. Charles did not look at Dan either. He was beginning to see that Chrestomanci was not pretending that people were witches.

By now, the front of the class was quite crowded. The box went to Nirupam next. Nirupam was waiting for it. It beeped even louder for him than it had for Dan. The moment it did, Nirupam got up and fled with long strides to the front of the room, in order not to be asked what witchcraft he had done. Then the box came to Charles. The noise was deafening.

"All right, all right!" Charles muttered. He too trudged to the front of the class. So Chrestomanci was playing fair, but he was still obviously trying to teach Charles a lesson by devaluing witchcraft. Charles looked round the other people standing out in front. He knew his was the strongest magic of the lot. And he wanted to keep it. There were still a thousand things he could do with it. He did not want to blend with another world, even if they did not burn witches there. As to being burned—Charles looked down at his blister—he found he rather enjoyed being frightened, once he got used to it. It made life interesting.

Meanwhile, the gold box followed Charles down the gangway and pointed to Delia. There was silence. Delia did not try to hide her smirk. But the smirk came off her face when the box moved to Theresa. It gave one small clear beep.

Theresa stood up, scandalized. "Who? *Me!*"

"Only a very small, third-grade sort of witch," Chrestomanci told her comfortingly.

It did not comfort Theresa in the least. If she was to be a witch, she felt she should at least be a first-class one. It was a disgrace either way. She was really angry when the box moved to Karen and did not beep for Karen either. But she was equally annoyed when the box went on and beeped for Heather, Deborah, and all her other friends. She stood there with the most dreadful mixed feelings.

Then the box beeped for Estelle too. Theresa tossed her head angrily. But Estelle sprang up beaming. "Oh good! I'm a witch! I'm a witch!" She skipped out to the front, grinning all over her face.

"Some people!" Theresa said unconvincingly.

Estelle did not care. She laughed when the box beeped loudly for Nan and Nan came thoughtfully to join her. "I think most people in the world must be witches," Estelle whispered to her. Nan nodded. She was sure it was true. She was sure this fitted in with all the other things Chrestomanci had discovered, but she still could not think how to explain it.

This left four people scattered about the room. They were all, even Simon, looking peevish and left out.

"It's not fair!" said Karen.

"At least *we* won't be burned," said Delia.

Chrestomanci beckoned to the box. It wandered up the gangway and put itself in his hand. Chrestomanci put it back in his pocket while he looked round the crowd of witches. He ignored Charles. He had given him up. He looked at Nan and then across at Mr. Wentworth, who had been crowded against the door in the crush. "Well, Wentworth," he said. "This looks quite promising, doesn't it? We've got a fair amount of witchcraft to draw on here. I suggest we make our push now. If Nan is ready to explain to everyone—"

Nan was nothing like ready. She was about to say so, when the classroom door flew open. Mr. Wentworth was barged aside. And Miss Cadwallader stood in his place, stiff and upright and stringy with anger. "What are you all doing, 6B?" she said. "Back to your seats with the utmost rapidity."

Mr. Wentworth was behind the door, white and shaking. Everyone looked doubtfully at Chrestomanci. He had gone very vague. So everybody did the prudent thing and scuttled back to their desks. As they went, three more people came into the room behind Miss Cadwallader.

Miss Cadwallader faced Chrestomanci in angry triumph. "Mr. Chant," she said, "you are an imposter. Here is the real inquisitor. Inquisitor Littleton." She stood aside and shut the door, so that everyone could see the inquisitor.

Inquisitor Littleton was a small man in a blue pin-striped suit. He had a huge man on either side of him in the black uniform of the Inquisition. Each of these huge men had a gun holster, a truncheon, and a folded whip in his belt. At the sight of them, Charles's burnt finger doubled itself up and hid inside his fist like a guilty secret.

"You move, and I'll order you shot!" Inquisitor Littleton snapped at Chrestomanci. His voice was harsh. His little watery eyes glared at Chrestomanci from a little blunt face covered with bright red veins. His blue suit did not fit him very well, as if Inquisitor Littleton had shrunk and hardened some time after the suit was bought, into a new shape, dense with power.

"Good afternoon, inquisitor," Chrestomanci said politely. "I'd been half expecting you." He looked across his shoulder, to Simon. "Nod, if I'm right," he said. "Did you say an inquisitor would be here before lunch?"

Simon nodded, looking shattered.

Inquisitor Littleton narrowed his watery eyes. "So it was witchcraft that made my car break down?" he said. "I knew it!" He unslung a black box he was carrying on a strap over his shoulder. He pointed it at Chrestomanci and turned a knob. Everyone saw the violent twitching of the dials on top. "Thought so," grated Inquisitor Littleton. "It's a witch." He jerked his blunt chin at Mr. Wentworth. "Now get me that one."

One of the huge men reached out a huge hand and dragged Mr. Wentworth over from beside the door as easily as if Mr. Wentworth had been a guy stuffed with straw. Miss Cadwallader looked as if she would like to protest about this, but she gave it up as useless. Inquisitor Littleton trained his black box on Mr. Wentworth.

Before he could turn the knob, the black box was torn out of his hands. With its broken strap trailing, it hurried from the inquisitor to Chrestomanci.

"I think that was a mistake, Brian," said Chrestomanci.

Both huge men drew their guns. Inquisitor Littleton backed away and pointed at Chrestomanci. His face was purple, and full of a queer mixture of hate and horror and pleasure. "Look at that!" he shouted out. "It has a demon to wait on it! Oh, I've got you now!"

Chrestomanci looked almost irritated. "My good man," he said, "that really is a most ignorant assumption. Only a hedge wizard would stoop to using a demon."

"I'm not a demon!" shouted Brian's shrill voice. "I'm Brian Wentworth!"

Delia screamed. The huge man who was not holding Mr. Wentworth seemed to lose his nerve. Glaring with fear, he held his gun out in both hands, and aimed it at the black box.

"Throw it!" said Chrestomanci.

Brian obeyed. The black box sailed toward the window. The huge man was muddled into following it round with his gun. He fired. There was a tremendous crash. Quite a few people screamed this time. The black box exploded into a muddle of wire and metal plates and half of the window blew out. A gust of rain blew in.

"You fool!" said Inquisitor Littleton. "That was my very latest model witch-finder!" He glared at Chrestomanci. "Right. I've had enough of this foul thing. Get it for me."

The huge man put his gun back in its holster and marched toward Chrestomanci. Nirupam quickly stuck up a long arm. "Please. Just a moment. I think Miss Cadwallader may be a witch too."

Everyone at once looked at Miss Cadwallader. She said, "How dare you, child!" but she was as white as Mr. Wentworth.

And this, Nan realized, was where she came in. She was not sure how, but she surged to her feet all the same, in such haste that she nearly knocked her desk over like Estelle. Everyone stared at her. Nan felt terrible. For a long, long instant, she went on standing there without a thought in her head and without one scrap of confidence to help her. But she knew she could not just sit down again. She began to talk.

"Just a moment," she said. "Before you do another thing, I've got to tell you about Guy Fawkes. He's the reason almost everybody in the world is a witch, you know. The main thing about Guy Fawkes is that he was the kind of man who can never do anything right. He meant well, but he was a failure—"

"Make that girl shut up!" Inquisitor Littleton said, in his harsh, bossy voice. Nan looked at him nervously, and then at the two huge men. None of them moved. In fact, now that she looked, everyone seemed to be stuck and frozen exactly where they were when she first stood up. She looked at Chrestomanci. He was staring vaguely into the distance and did not seem to be doing anything either, but Nan was suddenly sure that Chrestomanci was somehow holding everything in one place to give her a chance to explain. That made her feel much better.

She had gone on talking all the time she was looking round, explaining about the Gunpowder Plot, and what a mistake the conspirators made choosing Guy Fawkes to do the blowing up. Now she seemed to be going on to explain about other worlds.

"There were an awful lot of Guy Fawkeses in an awful lot of worlds," she heard herself saying. "And he was a failure in every one. Some people are like that. There are millions of other worlds, you know. The big differences get made at the big events in history, where a battle gets either won or lost. Both things can't happen in one world, so a new one splits off and goes different after that. But there are all sorts of smaller things that can go two ways as well, which *don't* make a world split off. You've probably all had those kinds of dreams that are like your usual life, except that a lot of things are not the same, and you seem to know the future in them. Well, this is because these other worlds where two things can happen spread out from our own world like rainbows, and sort of flow into one another—"

Nan found herself rather admiring this description. She was inspired now. She could have talked for hours. But there was not much point unless she could persuade the rest of 6B to *do* something. Everyone was just staring at her.

"Now our world should really just be a rainbow-stripe in another proper world," she said. "But it isn't. And I'm going to tell you why, so that we can all do something about it. I told you Guy Fawkes was a failure. Well, the trouble was, he knew he was. And that made him very nervous, because he wanted to do at least this one thing right and blow up Parliament properly. He kept going over in his mind all the things that could go wrong: he could be betrayed, or the gunpowder could be damp, or his candle could go out, or his fuse might not light—he thought of all the possibilities, all the things that make the rainbow-stripes of not-quite different worlds. And in the middle of the night, he got so nervous that he went and lit the fuse, just to make sure it would light. He wasn't thinking that November 5, the day he was doing it, was the last day of Witch Week, when there is so much magic around in the world that all sorts of peculiar things happen—"

"Will somebody silence that girl!" said Inquisitor Littleton.

He made Charles jump. Charles had been sitting all this time trying to understand the way he was feeling. He seemed to have divided into two again, but inside himself, where it did not show. Half of him was plain terrified. It felt as if it had been buried alive, in screaming, shut-in despair. The other half was angry, angry with Chrestomanci, Miss Cadwallader, 6B, Inquisitor Littleton—everything. Now, when Inquisitor Littleton suddenly spoke in his loud grating voice, Charles looked at the inquisitor. He was a small man with a stupid face, in a blue suit which did not fit, who enjoyed arresting witches.

Charles found himself remembering his first witch again. The fat man who had been so astonished at being burned. And he suddenly understood the witch's amazement. It was because someone so ordinary, so plain stupid, as Inquisitor Littleton had the power to burn him. And that was all wrong.

"Oh come on, all of you!" said Nan. "Don't you see? When Guy Fawkes lit that fuse, that made a new spread of rainbow possibilities. In our proper world, the world we ought to belong to, the fuse should have gone straight out again, and the Houses of Parliament would have been perfectly safe. But once the fuse was alight, the night watchman could have smelled it, or Guy Fawkes could have put it out with water, or the thing could have happened which made us the way we are: Guy Fawkes could have stamped the fuse out, but left just one tiny spark alight, which went on burning and creeping toward the kegs of gunpowder—"

"I told you to shut that girl up!" said Inquisitor Littleton.

Charles was in one piece again now. He looked from the inquisitor to Chrestomanci. Chrestomanci did not look so elegant just then. His suit was crumpled as if he had fallen away inside it, and his face was pale and hollow. Charles could see sweat on his forehead. And he understood that Chrestomanci was putting out a huge effort and somehow holding the whole world still, to give Nan time to persuade 6B to use their combined witchcraft to change it. But 6B were still sitting there like dumb things. That was why Inquisitor Littleton had started talking again. He was obviously one of those people who were very hard to keep quiet, and Chrestomanci had had to let go of him in order to have strength to hold everything else.

"Will you be quiet, girl!" said Inquisitor Littleton.

"BOOM!" said Nan. "And up went Parliament, but with no people in it. It wasn't very important, because even Guy Fawkes wasn't killed. But remember it was Witch Week. That made it a much worse explosion than it should have been. In it, this whole stripe of the rainbow, where we are now, and all the magic anywhere near, got blown out of the rest of the world, like a sort of long colored splinter. But it wasn't blown quite free. It was still joined to the rest of the rainbow at both ends. And that's the way it still is. And we could put it back if only we could make it so that the explosion never happened. And because it's Halloween today, and there's even more magic about than usual—"

Charles saw that Chrestomanci was beginning to shake. He looked tired out. At this rate, Chrestomanci was not going to have any strength left to put their splinter of world back where it belonged. Charles jumped up. He wanted to apologize. It was obvious that someone with power like Chrestomanci's could easily have just gone away the moment Inquisitor Littleton arrived. Instead, he had chosen to stay and help them. But saying he was sorry would have to wait. Charles knew he had to do something. And thanks to Nan, he knew just what to do.

"Sit down, boy!" rasped Inquisitor Littleton.

Charles took no notice. He dived across the gangway and took hold of Simon Silverson by the front of his blazer. "Simon. Say what Guy Fawkes did. Quick!"

Simon gazed at Charles. He shook his head and pointed to his mouth.

"Go on! Say it, you fool!" said Charles, and he shook Simon.

Simon kept his mouth shut. He was afraid to say anything. It was like a bad dream. "Say what Guy Fawkes did!" Charles yelled at him. He gave up shaking Simon and poured witchcraft at him to make him say it. And Simon just shook his head.

Nirupam saw the point. "Say it, Simon!" he said. And that made all the rest of 6B understand what Charles was trying to do. Everyone stood up in their seats and shouted at Simon. "SAY IT, SIMON!" Mr. Wentworth shouted. Brian's voice joined in. Witchcraft was blasting at Simon from all sides, and even Karen and Delia were shouting at him. Nan joined in the shouting. She was bubbling with pride and delight. She had done this, just by describing what happened. It was as good as witchcraft any day. Everyone had understood that they could make this world part of the other one again—part of the world to which the witches' rescue service sent witches—by making Simon say what had *not* happened in that other world. "SAY IT, SIMON!" everyone screamed.

Simon opened his mouth. "I—oh, leave *off!*" He was terrified of what might happen, but once he had started to speak, all the witchcraft beating at him was too much for him. "He—he—Guy Fawkes blew up the Houses of Parliament."

Everything at once began to ripple.

It was as if the world had turned into a vast curtain, hanging in folds, with every fold in it rippling in and out. The ripples ran through desks, windows, walls, and people alike. Each person was rippled through. They were tugged, and rippled again, until everyone felt they were coming to pieces. By then, the ripples were so strong and steep that everyone could see right down into the folds. For just a moment, on the outside of each fold, was the classroom everyone knew, with the inquisitor and his huge men on the same fold as Miss Cadwallader, and Chrestomanci on another fold beside them. The inner parts of the folds were all different places.

Charles realized that if he were going to apologize to Chrestomanci, he had better do it at once. He turned round to say it. But the folds had already rippled flat and nothing was the same anymore.

CHAPTER 16

"I'm very sorry, sir," said one of the boys. He sounded as if he meant it, for a wonder.

Mr. Crossley jumped, and wondered if he had been asleep. He seemed to have had that kind of shiver that makes you say, "Someone walked over my grave." He looked up from the books he was marking.

The janitor was in the classroom. What was his name? He had a raucous voice and a lot of stupid opinions. Littleton, that was it. Littleton seemed to be clearing up broken glass. Mr. Crossley was puzzled, because he did not remember a window being broken. But when he looked over at the windows, he saw one of them was newly mended, with a lot of putty and many thumbprints.

"There you are, Mr. Crossley. All tidy now," Mr. Littleton rasped.

"Thank you, Littleton," Mr. Crossley said coldly. If you let Littleton get talking, he stayed and tried to teach the class. He watched the janitor collect his things and back himself through the door. Thank goodness!

"Thank you, Charles," said someone.

Mr. Crossley jerked round and discovered a total stranger in the room. This man was tall and tired-looking and seemed, from his clothes, to be on his way to a wedding. Mr. Crossley thought he must be a school governor and started to stand up politely.

"Oh, please don't get up," Chrestomanci said. "I'm just on my way out." He walked to the door. Before he went out of it, he looked round 6B and said, "If any of you want me again, a message to the Old Gate House should find me."

The door closed behind him. Mr. Crossley sat down to his marking again. He stared. There was a note on top of the topmost exercise book. He knew it had not been there before. It was written in ordinary blue ballpoint, in capital letters, and it gave Mr. Crossley the oddest feeling of having been in the same situation before. Why was that? He must have dozed off and had a dream. Yes. Now Mr. Crossley thought about it, he *had* had the strangest dream. He had dreamed he taught in a dreadful boarding school called Larwood House. He looked thankfully up at the bent, busy heads of 6B. This was, as he well knew, Portway Oaks Comprehensive, and everyone went home every evening. Thank goodness! Mr. Crossley hated the idea of teaching in a boarding school. You were always on the job.

He wondered who had written the note. And here, as his eyes went over the class, he had a momentary feeling of shock. A lot of faces were missing from his dream. He remembered a batch of tiresome girls: Theresa Mullett, Delia Martin, Heather Something, Karen Something Else. None of them was there. Nor was Daniel Smith.

Ah but—Mr. Crossley remembered now. Dan Smith should have been there. He was in the hospital. Two days ago, the stupid boy had eaten a handful of tintacks for a bet. No one had believed he had, at first. But when Mr. Wentworth, the headmaster, had put Dan in his car and driven him to be X-rayed, there he was, full of tintacks. Idiots some boys were!

And here was another mad thing about Mr. Crossley's dream: He had dreamed that Miss Cadwallader was head in place of Mr. Wentworth! Quite mad. Mr. Crossley knew perfectly well that Miss Cadwallader was the lady who ran The Gate House School for Girls, where Eileen Hodge was a teacher. Come to think of it, that must have been why he dreamed of Theresa Mullett and her friends. He had seen their faces staring out at him from the prim line of girls walking behind Eileen Hodge.

And now Mr. Crossley remembered something else that almost made him forget his dream and the mysterious note. Eileen Hodge had at last agreed to go out with him. He was to call for her on Tuesday, because she was going away for half-term. He was getting somewhere there at last!

But even through his pleasure about Eileen, the dream and the note kept nagging at Mr. Crossley. Why should it bother him who had written the note? He looked at Brian Wentworth, sitting next to his great friend Simon Silverson. The two of them were giggling about something. The note was quite probably one of Brian's jokes. But it could equally well be some deep scheme masterminded by Charles Morgan and Nirupam Singh. Mr. Crossley looked at those two.

Charles looked back at Mr. Crossley over his glasses and across the piece of paper he was supposed to be writing on. How much did Mr.

Crossley know? Charles's writing had gotten no further than the title: *Halloween Poem.* Neither had Nirupam's. On the floor between them was a pair of spiked running shoes and, filling them with wonder, was the name marked on the shoes: *Daniel Smith.* Both of them knew that Dan did not own any running shoes. Of course, Smith was not exactly an uncommon name, but—both of them were struggling with strange double memories.

Charles wondered particularly at the sense of relief and peace he had. He felt at ease inside. He also felt rather hungry. One part of his memory told him that this was because Brian Wentworth had invisibly eaten half his lunch. The other half suggested that it was because chess club had taken up most of the dinner hour. And here was an odd thing. Up till that moment, Charles had intended to be a chess grand master. Now those double memories caused him to change his mind. Someone—whose name he could not quite remember now—had suggested to him that he was going to have a very strong talent indeed for something, and it was not for chess, Charles was sure now. Perhaps he would be an inventor instead. Anyway, the chess club half of his memory, which seemed to be the important half, suggested that he hurry home early so he could eat the last of the cornflakes before his sister Bernadine hogged them.

"Guy Fawkes," Nirupam murmured.

Charles did not know if Nirupam was referring to witchcraft, or to Dan Smith's idea of half-term. They had been going to collect money for the guy, using Nirupam for a guy. Nirupam, in the Morgans' old stroller, made a beautiful long, thin, floppy guy. Now they were both wondering if they would have the nerve to do it on their own, without Dan to keep them up to it.

"Why did you have to bet Dan he couldn't eat tintacks?" Charles whispered to Nirupam.

"Because I didn't think he would!" Nirupam answered grumpily. He had been in a lot of trouble with Mr. Wentworth about that bet. "Could we get Estelle and Nan to help push me?"

"They're girls," Charles objected. But he considered the idea while he underlined *Halloween Poem* in red ink, with blood drops. Those two girls might just do it, at that. As he inked the last drop of blood, he noticed a blister on his finger. It had reached the flat, white, empty stage by now. Carefully, Charles inked it bright red. He was not sure he wanted to forget about things that soon.

Mr. Crossley was still considering the note. It could be another flight of fancy from Nan Pilgrim. Nan, as usual, since she had arrived at the school from Essex at the beginning of term, was sitting next to Estelle

Green. They were thick as thieves, those two. A good thing, because Estelle had been rather lonely before Nan arrived.

Nan glanced up at Mr. Crossley, and down again at her pen rushing across her paper. Fascinated, she read: *And in this part of the rainbow, Guy Fawkes stamped the fuse out, but a little, tiny smoldering spark remained. The spark crept and ate its way to the kegs of gunpowder. BOOM!!!*

"Estelle! Look at this!"

Estelle leaned over, looked, and goggled. "Do you know what I think?" she whispered. "When you grow up to be an author and write books, you'll think you're making the books up, but they'll all really be true, somewhere." She sighed. "My poem's going to be about a great enchanter."

Mr. Crossley suddenly wondered why he was worrying about the note. It was only a joke, after all. He cleared his throat. Everyone looked up hopefully. "Somebody," said Mr. Crossley, "seems to have sent me a Halloween message." And he read out the note. *"SOMEONE IN THIS CLASS IS A WITCH."*

6B thought this was splendid news. Hands shot up all over the room like a bed of beansprouts.

"It's me, Mr. Crossley!"

"Mr. Crossley, I'm the witch!"

"Can I be the witch, Mr. Crossley?"

"Me, Mr. Crossley, me, me, me!"

THE MAGICIANS OF CAPRONA

FOR JOHN

AUTHOR'S NOTE

The world of Chrestomanci is not the same as this one. It is a world parallel to ours, where magic is as normal as mathematics, and things are generally more old-fashioned. In Chrestomanci's world, Italy is still divided into numbers of small States, each with its Duke and capital city. In our world, Italy became one united country long ago.

Though the two worlds are not connected in any way, this story somehow got through. But it came with some gaps, and I had to get help filling them. Clare Davis, Gaynor Harvey, Elizabeth Carter and Graham Belsten discovered for me what happened in the magicians' single combat. And my husband, J. A. Burrow, with some advice from Basil Cottle, actually found the true words of the *Angel of Caprona.* I would like to thank them all very much indeed.

CHAPTER 1

Spells are the hardest thing in the world to get right. This was one of the first things the Montana children learnt. Anyone can hang up a charm, but when it comes to making that charm, whether it is written or spoken or sung, everything has to be just right, or the most impossible things happen.

An example of this is young Angelica Petrocchi, who turned her father bright green by singing a wrong note. It was the talk of all Caprona—indeed of all Italy—for weeks.

The best spells still come from Caprona, in spite of the recent troubles, from the Casa Montana or the Casa Petrocchi. If you are using words that really work, to improve reception on your radio or to grow tomatoes, then the chances are that someone in your family has been on a holiday to Caprona and brought the spell back. The Old Bridge in Caprona is lined with little stone booths, where long coloured envelopes, scrips and scrolls hang from strings like bunting. You can get spells there from every spell-house in Italy. Each spell is labelled as to its use and stamped with the sign of the house which made it. If you want to find out who made your spell, look among your family papers. If you find a long cherry-coloured scrip stamped with a black leopard, then it came from the Casa Petrocchi. If you find a leaf-green envelope bearing a winged horse, then the House of Montana made it. The spells of both houses are so good that ignorant people think that even the envelopes can work magic. This, of course, is nonsense. For, as Paolo and Tonino Montana were told over and over again, a spell is the right words delivered in the right way.

The great houses of Petrocchi and Montana go back to the first founding of the State of Caprona, seven hundred years or more ago.

And they are bitter rivals. They are not even on speaking terms. If a Petrocchi and a Montana meet in one of Caprona's narrow goldenstone streets, they turn their eyes aside and edge past as if they were both walking past a pig-sty. Their children are sent to different schools and warned never, ever to exchange a word with a child from the other house.

Sometimes, however, parties of young men and women of the Montanas and the Petrocchis happen to meet when they are strolling on the wide street called the Corso in the evenings. When that happens, other citizens take shelter at once. If they fight with fists and stones, that is bad enough, but if they fight with spells, it can be appalling.

An example of this is when the dashing Rinaldo Montana caused the sky to rain cowpats on the Corso for three days. It created great distress among the tourists.

"A Petrocchi insulted me," Rinaldo explained, with his most flashing smile. "And I happened to have a new spell in my pocket."

The Petrocchis unkindly claimed that Rinaldo had misquoted his spell in the heat of the battle. Everyone knew that all Rinaldo's spells were love-charms.

The grown-ups of both houses never explained to the children just what had made the Montanas and the Petrocchis hate one another so. That was a task traditionally left to the older brothers, sisters and cousins. Paolo and Tonino were told the story repeatedly, by their sisters Rosa, Corinna and Lucia, by their cousins Luigi, Carlo, Domenico and Anna, and again by their second-cousins Piero, Luca, Giovanni, Paula, Teresa, Bella, Angelo and Francesco. They told it themselves to six smaller cousins as they grew up. The Montanas were a large family.

Two hundred years ago, the story went, old Ricardo Petrocchi took it into his head that the Duke of Caprona was ordering more spells from the Montanas than from the Petrocchis, and he wrote old Francesco Montana a very insulting letter about it. Old Francesco was so angry that he promptly invited all the Petrocchis to a feast. He had, he said, a new dish he wanted them to try. Then he rolled Ricardo Petrocchi's letter up into long spills and cast one of his strongest spells over it. And it turned into spaghetti. The Petrocchis ate it greedily and were all taken ill, particularly old Ricardo—for nothing disagrees with a person so much as having to eat his own words. He never forgave Francesco Montana, and the two families had been enemies ever since.

"And that," said Lucia, who told the story oftenest, being only a year older than Paolo, "was the origin of spaghetti."

It was Lucia who whispered to them all the terrible heathen customs the Petrocchis had: how they never went to Mass or confessed; how they never had baths or changed their clothes; how none of them ever got married but just—in an even lower whisper—had babies like kittens; how they were apt to drown their unwanted babies, again like kittens, and had even been known to eat unwanted uncles and aunts; and how they were so dirty that you could smell the Casa Petrocchi and hear the flies buzzing right down the Via Sant' Angelo.

There were many other things besides, some of them far worse than these, for Lucia had a vivid imagination. Paolo and Tonino believed every one, and they hated the Petrocchis heartily, though it was years before either of them set eyes on a Petrocchi. When they were both quite small, they did sneak off one morning, down the Via Sant' Angelo almost as far as the New Bridge, to look at the Casa Petrocchi. But there was no smell and no flies buzzing to guide them, and their sister Rosa found them before they found it. Rosa, who was eight years older than Paolo and quite grown-up even then, laughed when they explained their difficulty, and good-naturedly took them to the Casa Petrocchi. It was in the Via Cantello, not the Via Sant' Angelo at all.

Paolo and Tonino were most disappointed in it. It was just like the Casa Montana. It was large, like the Casa Montana, and built of the same golden stone of Caprona, and probably just as old. The great front gate was old knotty wood, just like their own, and there was even the same golden figure of the Angel on the wall above the gate. Rosa told them that both Angels were in memory of the Angel who had come to the first Duke of Caprona bringing a scroll of music from Heaven—but the boys knew that. When Paolo pointed out that the Casa Petrocchi did not seem to smell much, Rosa bit her lip and said gravely that there were not many windows in the outside walls, and they were all shut.

"I expect everything happens round the yard inside, just like it does in our Casa," she said. "Probably all the smelling goes on in there."

They agreed that it probably did, and wanted to wait to see a Petrocchi come out. But Rosa said she thought that would be most unwise, and pulled them away. The boys looked over their shoulders as she dragged them off and saw that the Casa Petrocchi had four golden-stone towers, one at each corner, where the Casa Montana only had one, over the gate.

"It's because the Petrocchis are show-offs," Rosa said, dragging. "Come on."

Since the towers were each roofed with a little hat of red pan-tiles, just like their own roofs or the roofs of all the houses in Caprona, Paolo and Tonino did not think they were particularly grand, but they did not like to argue with Rosa. Feeling very let down, they let her drag them back to the Casa Montana and pull them through their own large knotty gate into the bustling yard beyond. There Rosa left them and ran up the steps to the gallery, shouting, "Lucia! Lucia, where are you? I want to *talk* to you!"

Doors and windows opened into the yard all round, and the gallery, with its wooden railings and pan-tiled roof, ran round three sides of the yard and led to the rooms on the top floor. Uncles, aunts, cousins large and small, and cats were busy everywhere, laughing, cooking, discussing spells, washing, sunning themselves or playing. Paolo gave a sigh of contentment and picked up the nearest cat.

"I don't think the Casa Petrocchi *can* be anything like this inside."

Before Tonino could agree, they were swooped on lovingly by Aunt Maria, who was fatter than Aunt Gina, but not as fat as Aunt Anna. "Where have you been, my loves? I've been ready for your lessons for half an hour or more!"

Everyone in the Casa Montana worked very hard. Paolo and Tonino were already being taught the first rules for making spells. When Aunt Maria was busy, they were taught by their father, Antonio. Antonio was the eldest son of Old Niccolo, and would be head of the Casa Montana when Old Niccolo died. Paolo thought this weighed on his father. Antonio was a thin, worried person who laughed less often than the other Montanas. He was different. One of the differences was that, instead of letting Old Niccolo carefully choose a wife for him from a spell-house in Italy, Antonio had gone on a visit to England and come back married to Elizabeth. Elizabeth taught the boys music.

"If I'd been teaching that Angelica Petrocchi," she was fond of saying, "she'd never have turned anything green."

Old Niccolo said Elizabeth was the best musician in Caprona. And that, Lucia told the boys, was why Antonio got away with marrying her. But Rosa told them to take no notice. Rosa was proud of being half English.

Paolo and Tonino were probably prouder to be Montanas. It was a grand thing to know you were born into a family that was known worldwide as the greatest spell-house in Europe—if you did not count the Petrocchis. There were times when Paolo could hardly wait to grow up and be like his cousin, dashing Rinaldo. Everything came easily to Rinaldo. Girls fell in love with him, spells dripped from his pen. He had composed seven new charms before he left school. And these days, as Old Niccolo said, making a new spell was not easy. There were so many already. Paolo admired Rinaldo desperately. He told Tonino that Rinaldo was a true Montana.

Tonino agreed, because he was more than a year younger than Paolo and valued Paolo's opinions, but it always seemed to him that it was

Paolo who was the true Montana. Paolo was as quick as Rinaldo. He could learn without trying spells which took Tonino days to acquire. Tonino was slow. He could only remember things if he went over them again and again. It seemed to him that Paolo had been born with an instinct for magic which he just did not have himself.

Tonino was sometimes quite depressed about his slowness. Nobody else minded in the least. All his sisters, even the studious Corinna, spent hours helping him. Elizabeth assured him he never sang out of tune. His father scolded him for working too hard, and Paolo assured him that he would be streets ahead of the other children when he went to school. Paolo had just started school. He was as quick at ordinary lessons as he was at spells.

But when Tonino started school, he was just as slow there as he was at home. School bewildered him. He did not understand what the teachers wanted him to do. By the first Saturday he was so miserable that he had to slip away from the Casa and wander round Caprona in tears. He was missing for hours.

"I can't help being quicker than he is!" Paolo said, almost in tears too.

Aunt Maria rushed at Paolo and hugged him. "Now, now, don't you start too! You're as clever as my Rinaldo, and we're all proud of you."

"Lucia, go and look for Tonino," said Elizabeth. "Paolo, you mustn't worry so. Tonino's soaking up spells without knowing he is. I did the same when I came here. Should I tell Tonino?" she asked Antonio. Antonio had hurried in from the gallery. In the Casa Montana, if anyone was in distress, it always fetched the rest of the family.

Antonio rubbed his forehead. "Perhaps. Let's go and ask Old Niccolo. Come on, Paolo."

Paolo followed his thin, brisk father through the patterns of sunlight in the gallery and into the blue coolness of the Scriptorium. Here his other two sisters, Rinaldo and five other cousins, and two of his uncles, were all standing at tall desks copying spells out of big leather-bound books. Each book had a brass lock on it so that the family secrets could not be stolen. Antonio and Paolo tiptoed through. Rinaldo smiled at them without pausing in his copying. Where other pens scratched and paused, Rinaldo's raced.

In the room beyond the Scriptorium, Uncle Lorenzo and Cousin Domenico were stamping winged horses on leaf-green envelopes. Uncle Lorenzo looked keenly at their faces as they passed and decided that the trouble was not too much for Old Niccolo alone. He winked at Paolo and threatened to stamp a winged horse on him.

Old Niccolo was in the warm mildewy library beyond, consulting over a book on a stand with Aunt Francesca. She was Old Niccolo's sister, and therefore really a great-aunt. She was a barrel of a lady, twice as fat as Aunt Anna and even more passionate than Aunt Gina. She was saying passionately, "But the spells of the Casa Montana always have a certain elegance. This is graceless! This is—"

Both round old faces turned towards Antonio and Paolo. Old Niccolo's face, and his eyes in it, were round and wondering as the latest baby's. Aunt Francesca's face was too small for her huge body, and her eyes were small and shrewd. "I was just coming," said Old Niccolo. "I thought it was Tonino in trouble, but you bring me Paolo."

"Paolo's not in trouble," said Aunt Francesca.

Old Niccolo's round eyes blinked at Paolo. "Paolo," he said, "what your brother feels is not your fault."

"No," said Paolo. "I think it's school really."

"We thought that perhaps Elizabeth could explain to Tonino that he can't avoid learning spells in this Casa," Antonio suggested.

"But Tonino has ambition!" cried Aunt Francesca.

"I don't think he does," said Paolo.

"No, but he is unhappy," said his grandfather. "And we must think how best to comfort him. I know." His baby face beamed. "Benvenuto."

Though Old Niccolo did not say this loudly, someone in the gallery immediately shouted, "Old Niccolo wants Benvenuto!" There was running and calling down in the yard. Somebody beat on a waterbutt with a stick. "Benvenuto! Where's that cat got to? Benvenuto!"

Naturally, Benvenuto took his time coming. He was boss cat at the Casa Montana. It was five minutes before Paolo heard his firm pads trotting along the tiles of the gallery roof. This was followed by a heavy thump as Benvenuto made the difficult leap down, across the gallery railing on to the floor of the gallery. Shortly, he appeared on the library window-sill.

"So there you are," said Old Niccolo. "I was just going to get impatient."

Benvenuto at once shot forward a shaggy black hind leg and settled down to wash it, as if that was what he had come there to do.

"Ah no, please," said Old Niccolo. "I need your help."

Benvenuto's wide yellow eyes turned to Old Niccolo. He was not a handsome cat. His head was unusually wide and blunt, with grey gnarled patches on it left over from many, many fights. Those fights had pulled his ears down over his eyes, so that Benvenuto always looked as if he were wearing a ragged brown cap. A hundred bites had left those ears notched like holly leaves. Just over his nose, giving his face a leering, lop-sided look, were three white patches. Those had nothing to do with Benvenuto's position as boss cat in a spell-house. They were the result of his partiality for steak. He had got under Aunt Gina's feet when she was cooking, and Aunt Gina had spilt hot fat on his head. For this reason, Benvenuto and Aunt Gina always pointedly ignored one another.

"Tonino is unhappy," said Old Niccolo.

Benvenuto seemed to feel this worthy of his attention. He withdrew his projecting leg, dropped to the library floor and arrived on top of the bookstand, all in one movement, without seeming to flex a muscle. There he stood, politely waving the one beautiful thing about him—his bushy black tail. The rest of his coat had worn to a ragged brown. Apart from the tail, the only thing which showed Benvenuto had once been a magnificent black Persian was the fluffy fur on his hind legs. And, as every other cat in Caprona knew to its cost, those fluffy breeches concealed muscles like a bulldog's.

Paolo stared at his grandfather talking face to face with Benvenuto. He had always treated Benvenuto with respect himself, of course. It was well known that Benvenuto would not sit on your knee, and scratched you if you tried to pick him up. He knew all cats helped spells on wonderfully. But he had not realised before that cats understood so much. And he was sure Benvenuto was answering Old Niccolo, from the listening sort of pauses his grandfather made. Paolo looked at his father to see if this was true. Antonio was very ill at ease. And Paolo understood from his father's worried face, that it was very important to be able to understand what cats said, and that Antonio never could. I shall have to start learning to understand Benvenuto, Paolo thought, very troubled.

"Which of you would you suggest?" asked Old Niccolo. Benvenuto raised his right front paw and gave it a casual lick. Old Niccolo's face curved into his beaming baby's smile. "Look at that!" he said. "He'll do it himself!" Benvenuto flicked the tip of his tail sideways. Then he was gone, leaping back to the window so fluidly and quickly that he might have been a paintbrush painting a dark line in the air. He left Aunt Francesca and Old Niccolo beaming, and Antonio still looking unhappy. "Tonino is taken care of," Old Niccolo announced. "We shall not worry again unless he worries us."

CHAPTER 2

Tonino was already feeling soothed by the bustle in the golden streets of Caprona. In the narrower streets, he walked down the crack of sunlight in the middle, with washing flapping overhead, playing that it was sudden death to tread on the shadows. In fact, he died a number of times before he got as far as the Corso. A crowd of tourists pushed him off the sun once. So did two carts and a carriage. And once, a long, gleaming car came slowly growling along, hooting hard to clear the way.

When he was near the Corso, Tonino heard a tourist say in English, "Oh look! Punch and Judy!" Very smug at being able to understand, Tonino dived and pushed and tunnelled until he was at the front of the crowd and able to watch Punch beat Judy to death at the top of his little painted sentry-box. He clapped and cheered, and when someone puffed and panted into the crowd too, and pushed him aside, Tonino was as indignant as the rest. He had quite forgotten he was miserable. "Don't shove!" he shouted.

"Have a heart!" protested the man. "I must see Mr Punch cheat the hangman."

"Then be quiet!" roared everyone, Tonino included.

"I only said—" began the man. He was a large damp-faced person, with an odd excitable manner.

"Shut up!" shouted everyone.

The man panted and grinned and watched with his mouth open Punch attack the policeman. He might have been the smallest boy there. Tonino looked irritably sideways at him and decided the man was probably an amiable lunatic. He let out such bellows of laughter at the smallest jokes, and he was so oddly dressed. He was wearing a shiny red silk suit with flashing gold buttons and glittering medals. Instead of the usual tie, he had white cloth folded at his neck, held in place by a brooch which winked like a tear-drop. There were glistening buckles on his shoes, and golden rosettes at his knees. What with his sweaty face and his white shiny teeth showing as he laughed, the man glistened all over.

Mr Punch noticed him too. "Oh what a clever fellow!" he crowed, bouncing about on his little wooden shelf. "I see gold buttons. Can it be the Pope?"

"Oh no it isn't!" bellowed Mr Glister, highly delighted.

"Can it be the Duke?" cawed Mr Punch.

"Oh no it isn't!" roared Mr Glister, and everyone else.

"Oh yes it is," crowed Mr Punch.

While everyone was howling *"Oh no it isn't!"* two worried-looking men pushed their way through the people to Mr Glister.

"Your Grace," said one, "the Bishop reached the Cathedral half an hour ago."

"Oh bother!" said Mr Glister. "Why are you lot always bullying me? Can't I just—until this ends? I love Punch and Judy."

The two men looked at him reproachfully.

"Oh—very well," said Mr Glister. "You two pay the showman. Give everyone here something." He turned and went bounding away into the Corso, puffing and panting.

For a moment, Tonino wondered if Mr Glister was actually the Duke of Caprona. But the two men made no attempt to pay the showman, or anyone else. They simply went trotting demurely after Mr Glister, as if they were afraid of losing him. From this, Tonino gathered that Mr Glister was indeed a lunatic—a rich one—and they were humouring him.

"Mean things!" crowed Mr Punch, and set about tricking the Hangman into being hanged instead of him. Tonino watched until Mr Punch bowed and retired in triumph into the little painted villa at the back of his stage. Then he turned away, remembering his unhappiness.

He did not feel like going back to the Casa Montana. He did not feel like doing anything particularly. He wandered on, the way he had been going, until he found himself in the Piazza Nuova, up on the hill at the western end of the city. Here he sat gloomily on the parapet, gazing across the River Voltava at the rich villas and the Ducal Palace, and at the long arches of the New Bridge, and wondering if he was going to spend the rest of his life in a fog of stupidity.

The Piazza Nuova had been made at the same time as the New Bridge, about seventy years ago, to give everyone the grand view of Caprona Tonino was looking at now. It was breath-taking. But the trouble was, everything Tonino looked at had something to do with the Casa Montana.

Take the Ducal Palace, whose golden-stone towers cut clear lines into the clean blue of the sky opposite. Each golden tower swept outwards at the top, so that the soldiers on the battlements, beneath the snapping red and gold flags, could not be reached by anyone climbing up from below. Tonino could see the shields built into the battlements, two a side, one cherry, one leaf-green, showing that the Montanas and the Petrocchis had added a spell to defend each tower. And the great white marble front below was inlaid with other marbles, all colours of the rainbow. And among those colours were cherry-red and leaf-green.

The long golden villas on the hillside below the Palace each had a leaf-green or cherry-red disc on their walls. Some were half hidden by the dark spires of the elegant little trees planted in front of them, but Tonino knew they were there. And the stone and metal arches of the New Bridge, sweeping away from him towards the villas and the Palace, each bore an enamel plaque, green and red alternately. The New Bridge had been sustained by the strongest spells the Casa Montana and the Casa Petrocchi could produce. At the moment, when the river was just a shingly trickle, they did not seem necessary. But in winter, when the rain fell in the Apennines, the Voltava became a furious torrent. The arches of the New Bridge barely cleared it. The Old Bridge—which Tonino could see by craning out and sideways—was often under water, and the funny little houses along it could not be used. Only Montana and Petrocchi spells deep in its foundations stopped the Old Bridge being swept away.

Tonino had heard Old Niccolo say that the New Bridge spells had taken the entire efforts of the entire Montana family. Old Niccolo had helped make them when he was the same age as Tonino. Tonino could not have done. Miserable, he looked down at the golden walls and red pan-tiles of Caprona below. He was quite certain that every single one hid at least a leaf-green scrip. And the most Tonino had ever done was help stamp the winged horse on the outside. He was fairly sure that was all he ever would do.

He had a feeling somebody was calling him. Tonino looked round at the Piazza Nuova. Nobody. Despite the view, the Piazza was too far for the tourists to come. All Tonino could see were the mighty iron griffins which reared up at intervals all round the parapet, reaching iron paws to the sky. More griffins tangled into a fighting heap in the centre of the square to make a fountain. And even here, Tonino could not get away from his family. A little metal plate was set into the stone beneath the huge iron claws of the nearest griffin. It was leaf-green. Tonino found he had burst into tears.

Among his tears, he thought for a moment that one of the more distant griffins had left its stone perch and come trotting round the parapet towards him. It had left its wings behind, or else had them tightly folded.

He was told, a little smugly, that cats do not need wings. Benvenuto sat down on the parapet beside him, staring accusingly.

Tonino had always been thoroughly in awe of Benvenuto. He stretched out a hand to him timidly. "Hallo, Benvenuto."

Benvenuto ignored the hand. It was covered with water from Tonino's eyes, he said, and it made a cat wonder why Tonino was being so silly.

"There are our spells everywhere," Tonino explained. "And I'll never be able— Do you think it's because I'm half English?"

Benvenuto was not sure quite what difference that made. All it meant, as far as he could see, was that Paolo had blue eyes like a Siamese and Rosa had white fur—

"Fair hair," said Tonino.

—and Tonino himself had tabby hair, like the pale stripes in a tabby, Benvenuto continued, unperturbed. And those were all cats, weren't they?

"But I'm so stupid—" Tonino began.

Benvenuto interrupted that he had heard Tonino chattering with those kittens yesterday, and he had thought Tonino was a good deal cleverer than they were. And before Tonino went and objected that those were only kittens, wasn't Tonino only a kitten himself?

At this, Tonino laughed and dried his hand on his trousers. When he held the hand out to Benvenuto again, Benvenuto rose up, very high on all four paws, and advanced to it, purring. Tonino ventured to stroke him. Benvenuto walked round and round, arched and purring, like the smallest and friendliest kitten in the Casa. Tonino found himself grinning with pride and pleasure. He could tell from the waving of Benvenuto's brush of a tail, in majestic, angry twitches, that Benvenuto did not altogether like being stroked—which made it all the more of an honour.

That was better, Benvenuto said. He minced up to Tonino's bare legs and installed himself across them, like a brown muscular mat. Tonino went on stroking him. Prickles came out of one end of the mat and treadled painfully at Tonino's thighs. Benvenuto continued to purr. Would Tonino look at it this way, he wondered, that they were both, boy and cat, a part of the most famous Casa in Caprona, which in turn was part of the most special of all the Italian States?

"I know that," said Tonino. "It's because I think it's wonderful too that I— Are we really so special?"

Of course, purred Benvenuto. And if Tonino were to lean out and look across at the Cathedral, he would see why.

Obediently, Tonino leaned and looked. The huge marble bubbles of the Cathedral domes leapt up from among the houses at the end of the Corso. He knew there never was such a building as that. It floated, high and white and gold and green. And on the top of the highest dome the sun flashed on the great golden figure of the Angel, poised there with spread wings, holding in one hand a golden scroll. It seemed to bless all Caprona.

That Angel, Benvenuto informed him, was there as a sign that Caprona would be safe as long as everyone sang the tune of the Angel of Caprona. The Angel had brought that song in a scroll straight from Heaven to the First Duke of Caprona, and its power had banished the White Devil and made Caprona great. The White Devil had been prowling round Caprona ever since, trying to get back into the city, but as long as the Angel's song was sung, it would never succeed.

"I know that," said Tonino. "We sing the *Angel* every day at school." That brought back the main part of his misery. "They keep making me learn the story—and all sorts of things—and I can't, because I know them already, so I can't learn properly."

Benvenuto stopped purring. He quivered, because Tonino's fingers had caught in one of the many lumps of matted fur in his coat. Still quivering, he demanded rather sourly why it hadn't occurred to Tonino to *tell* them at school that he knew these things.

"Sorry!" Tonino hurriedly moved his fingers. "But," he explained, "they keep saying you have to do them this way, or you'll never learn properly."

Well, it was up to Tonino of course, Benvenuto said, still irritable, but there seemed no point in learning things twice. A cat wouldn't stand for it. And it was about time they were getting back to the Casa.

Tonino sighed. "I suppose so. They'll be worried." He gathered Benvenuto into his arms and stood up.

Benvenuto liked that. He purred. And it had nothing to do with the Montanas being worried. The aunts would be cooking lunch, and Tonino would find it easier than Benvenuto to nick a nice piece of veal.

That made Tonino laugh. As he started down the steps to the New Bridge, he said, "You know, Benvenuto, you'd be a lot more comfortable if you let me get those lumps out of your coat and comb you a bit."

Benvenuto stated that anyone trying to comb him would get raked with every claw he possessed.

"A brush then?"

Benvenuto said he would consider that.

It was here that Lucia encountered them. She had looked for Tonino all over Caprona by then and she was prepared to be extremely angry. But the sight of Benvenuto's evil lop-sided countenance staring at her out of Tonino's arms left her with almost nothing to say. "We'll be late for lunch," she said.

"No we won't," said Tonino. "We'll be in time for you to stand guard while I steal Benvenuto some veal."

"Trust Benvenuto to have it all worked out," said Lucia. "What is this? The start of a profitable relationship?"

You could put it that way, Benvenuto told Tonino. "You could put it that way," Tonino said to Lucia.

At all events, Lucia was sufficiently impressed to engage Aunt Gina in conversation while Tonino got Benvenuto his veal. And everyone was too pleased to see Tonino safely back to mind too much. Corinna and Rosa minded, however, that afternoon, when Corinna lost her scissors and Rosa her hairbrush. Both of them stormed out on to the gallery. Paolo was there, watching Tonino gently and carefully snip the mats out of Benvenuto's coat. The hairbrush lay beside Tonino, full of brown fur.

"And you can really understand everything he says?" Paolo was saying.

"I can understand all the cats," said Tonino. "Don't move, Benvenuto. This one's right on your skin."

It says volumes for Benvenuto's status—and therefore for Tonino's—that neither Rosa nor Corinna dared say a word to him. They turned on Paolo instead. "What do you mean, Paolo, standing there letting him mess that brush up? Why couldn't you make him use the kitchen scissors?"

Paolo did not mind. He was too relieved that he was not going to have to learn to understand cats himself. He would not have known how to begin.

From that time forward, Benvenuto regarded himself as Tonino's special cat. It made a difference to both of them. Benvenuto, what with constant brushing—for Rosa bought Tonino a special hairbrush for him—and almost as constant supplies filched from under Aunt Gina's nose, soon began to look younger and sleeker. Tonino forgot he had ever been unhappy. He was now a proud and special person. When Old Niccolo needed Benvenuto, he had to ask Tonino first. Benvenuto flatly refused to do anything for anyone without Tonino's permission. Paolo was very amused at how angry Old Niccolo got.

"That cat has just taken advantage of me!" he stormed. "I ask him to do me a kindness and what do I get? Ingratitude!"

In the end, Tonino had to tell Benvenuto that he was to consider himself at Old Niccolo's service while Tonino was at school. Otherwise Benvenuto simply disappeared for the day. But he always, unfailingly, reappeared around half past three, and sat on the waterbutt nearest the gate, waiting for Tonino. And as soon as Tonino came through the gate, Benvenuto would jump into his arms.

This was true even at the times when Benvenuto was not available to anyone. That was mostly at full moon, when the lady cats wauled enticingly from the roofs of Caprona.

Tonino went to school on Monday, having considered Benvenuto's advice. And, when the time came when they gave him a picture of a cat and said the shapes under it went: Ker-a-ter, Tonino gathered up his courage and whispered, "Yes. It's a C and an A and a T. I know how to read."

His teacher, who was new to Caprona, did not know what to make of him, and called the Headmistress. "Oh," she was told. "It's another Montana. I should have warned you. They all know how to read. Most of them know Latin too—they use it a lot in their spells—and some of them know English as well. You'll find they're about average with sums, though."

So Tonino was given a proper book while the other children learnt their letters. It was too easy for him. He finished it in ten minutes and had to be given another. And that was how he discovered about books. To Tonino, reading a book soon became an enchantment above any spell. He could never get enough of it. He ransacked the Casa Montana and the Public Library, and he spent all his pocket money on books. It soon became well known that the best present you could give Tonino was a book—and the best book would be about the unimaginable situation where there were no spells. For Tonino preferred fantasy. In his favourite books, people had wild adventures with no magic to help or hinder them.

Benvenuto thoroughly approved. While Tonino read, he kept still, and a cat could be comfortable sitting on him. Paolo teased Tonino a little about being such a bookworm, but he did not really mind. He knew he could always persuade Tonino to leave his book if he really wanted him. Antonio was worried. He worried about everything. He was afraid Tonino was not getting enough exercise. But everyone else in the Casa said this was nonsense. They were proud of Tonino. He was as studious as Corinna, they said, and, no doubt, both of them would end up at Caprona University, like Great Uncle Umberto. The Montanas always had someone at the University. It meant they were not selfishly keeping the Theory of Magic to the family, and it was also very useful to have access to the spells in the University Library.

Despite these hopes for him, Tonino continued to be slow at learning spells and not particularly quick at school. Paolo was twice as quick at both. But as the years went by, both of them accepted it. It did not worry them. What worried them far more was their gradual discovery that things were not altogether well in the Casa Montana, nor in Caprona either.

CHAPTER 3

It was Benvenuto who first worried Tonino. Despite all the care Tonino gave him, he became steadily thinner and more ragged again. Now Benvenuto was roughly the same age as Tonino. Tonino knew that was old for a cat, and at first he assumed that Benvenuto was just feeling his years. Then he noticed that Old Niccolo had taken to looking almost as worried as Antonio, and that Uncle Umberto called on him from the University almost every day. Each time he did, Old Niccolo or Aunt Francesca would ask for Benvenuto and Benvenuto would come back tired out. So he asked Benvenuto what was wrong.

Benvenuto's reply was that they might let a cat have some peace, even if the Duke was a booby. And he was not going to be pestered by Tonino into the bargain.

Tonino consulted Paolo, and found Paolo worried too. Paolo had been noticing his mother. Her fair hair had lately become several shades paler with all the white in it, and she looked nervous all the time. When Paolo asked Elizabeth what was the matter, she said, "Oh nothing, Paolo—only all this makes it *so* difficult to find a husband for Rosa."

Rosa was now eighteen. The entire Casa was busy discussing a husband for her, and there did, now Paolo noticed, seem much more fuss and anxiety about the matter than there had been over Cousin Claudia, three years before. Montanas had to be careful who they married. It stood to reason. They had to marry someone who had some talent at least for spells or music; and it had to be someone the rest of the family liked; and, above all, it had to be someone with no kind of connection with the Petrocchis. But Cousin Claudia had found and married Arturo without all the discussion and worry that was going on over Rosa. Paolo could only suppose the reason was "all this," whatever Elizabeth had meant by that.

Whatever the reason, argument raged. Anxious Antonio talked of going to England and consulting someone called Chrestomanci about it. "We want a really strong spell-maker for her," he said. To which Elizabeth replied that Rosa was Italian and should marry an Italian. The rest of the family agreed, except that they said the Italian must be from Caprona. So the question was who.

Paolo, Lucia and Tonino had no doubt. They wanted Rosa to marry their cousin Rinaldo. It seemed to them entirely fitting. Rosa was lovely, Rinaldo handsome, and none of the usual objections could possibly be made. There were two snags, however. The first was that Rinaldo showed no interest in Rosa. He was at present desperately in love with a real English girl—her name was Jane Smith, and Rinaldo had some difficulty pronouncing it—and she had come to copy some of the pictures in the Art Gallery down on the Corso. She was a romantic girl. To please her, Rinaldo had taken to wearing black, with a red scarf at his neck, like a bandit. He was said to be considering growing a bandit moustache too. All of which left him with no time for a cousin he had known all his life.

The other snag was Rosa herself. She had never cared for Rinaldo. And she seemed to be the only person in the Casa who was entirely unconcerned about who she would marry. When the argument raged loudest, she would shake the blonde hair on her shoulders and smile. "To listen to you all," she said, "anyone would think I have no say in the matter at all. It's really funny."

All that autumn, the worry in the Casa Montana grew. Paolo and Tonino asked Aunt Maria what it was all about. Aunt Maria at first said that they were too young to understand. Then, since she had moments when she was as passionate as Aunt Gina or even Aunt Francesca, she told them suddenly and fervently that Caprona was going to the dogs. "Everything's going wrong for us," she said. "Money's short, tourists don't come here, and we get weaker every year. Here are Florence, Pisa and Siena all gathering round like vultures, and each year one of them gets a few more square miles of Caprona. If this goes on we shan't be a State any more. And on top of it all, the harvest failed this year. It's all the fault of those degenerate Petrocchis, I tell you! Their spells don't work any more. We Montanas can't hold Caprona up on our own! And the Petrocchis don't even try! They just keep turning things out in the same old way, and going from bad to worse. You can see they are, or that child wouldn't have been able to turn her father green!"

This was disturbing enough. And it seemed to be plain fact. All the years Paolo and Tonino had been at school, they had grown used to hearing that there had been this concession to Florence; that Pisa had demanded that agreement over fishing rights; or that Siena had raised taxes on imports to Caprona. They had grown too used to it to notice. But now it all seemed ominous. And worse shortly followed. News came that the Old Bridge had been seriously cracked by the winter floods.

This news caused the Casa Montana real dismay. For that bridge should have held. If it gave, it meant that the Montana charms in the foundations had given too. Aunt Francesca ran shrieking into the yard. "Those degenerate Petrocchis! They can't even sustain an old spell now! We've been betrayed!"

Though no one else put it quite that way, Aunt Francesca probably spoke for the whole family.

As if that was not enough, Rinaldo set off that evening to visit his English girl, and was led back to the Casa streaming with blood, supported by his cousins Carlo and Giovanni. Rinaldo, using curse words Paolo and Tonino had never heard before, was understood to say he had met some Petrocchis. He had called them degenerate. And it was Aunt Maria's turn to rush shrieking through the yard, shouting dire things about the Petrocchis. Rinaldo was the apple of Aunt Maria's eye.

Rinaldo had been bandaged and put to bed, when Antonio and Uncle Lorenzo came back from viewing the damage to the Old Bridge. Both looked very serious. Old Guido Petrocchi himself had been there, with the Duke's contractor, Mr Andretti. Some very deep charms had given. It was going to take the whole of both families, working in shifts, at least three weeks to mend them.

"We could have used Rinaldo's help," Antonio said.

Rinaldo swore that he was well enough to get out of bed and help the next day, but Aunt Maria would not hear of it. Nor would the doctor. So the rest of the family was divided into shifts, and work went on day and night. Paolo, Lucia and Corinna went to the bridge straight from school every day. Tonino did not. He was still too slow to be much use. But from what Paolo told him, he did not think he was missing much. Paolo simply could not keep up with the furious pace of the spells. He was put to running errands, like poor Cousin Domenico. Tonino felt very sympathetic towards Domenico. He was the opposite of his dashing brother Rinaldo in every way, and he could not keep up with the pace of things either.

Work had been going on, often in pouring rain, for nearly a week, when the Duke of Caprona summoned Old Niccolo to speak to him.

Old Niccolo stood in the yard and tore what was left of his hair.

Tonino laid down his book (it was called *Machines of Death* and quite fascinating) and went to see if he could help.

"Ah, Tonino," said Old Niccolo, looking at him with the face of a grieving baby, "I have gigantic problems. Everyone is needed on the Old Bridge, and that ass Rinaldo is lying in bed, and I have to go before the Duke with *some* of my family. The Petrocchis have been summoned too. We cannot appear less than they are, after all. Oh *why* did Rinaldo choose such a time to shout stupid insults?"

Tonino had no idea what to say, so he said, "Shall I get Benvenuto?"

"No, no," said Old Niccolo, more upset than ever. "The Duchess cannot abide cats. Benvenuto is no use here. I shall have to take those who are no use on the bridge. You shall go, Tonino, and Paolo and Domenico, and I shall take your Uncle Umberto to look wise and weighty. Perhaps that way we shan't look so very thin."

This was perhaps not the most flattering of invitations, but Tonino and Paolo were delighted nevertheless. They were delighted even though it rained hard the next day, the drilling white rain of winter. The dawn shift came in from the Old Bridge under shiny umbrellas, damp and disgruntled. Instead of resting, they had to turn to and get the party ready for the Palace.

The Montana family coach was dragged from the coach-house to a spot under the gallery, where it was carefully dusted. It was a great black thing with glass windows and monster black wheels. The Montana winged horse was emblazoned in a green shield on its heavy doors. The rain continued to pour down. Paolo, who hated rain as much as the cats did, was glad the coach was real. The horses were not. They were four white cardboard cut-outs of horses, which were kept leaning against the wall of the coach-house. They were an economical idea of Old Niccolo's father's. As he said, real horses ate and needed exercise and took up space the family could live in. The coachman was another cardboard cut-out—for much the same reasons—but he was kept inside the coach.

The boys were longing to watch the cardboard figures being brought to life, but they were snatched indoors by their mother. Elizabeth's hair was soaking from her shift on the bridge and she was yawning until her jaw creaked, but this did not prevent her doing a very thorough scrubbing, combing and dressing job on Paolo and Tonino. By the time they came down into the yard again, each with his hair scraped wet to his head and wearing uncomfortable broad white collars above their stiff Eton jackets, the spell was done. The spell-streamers had been carefully wound into the harness, and the coachman clothed in a paper coat covered with spells on the inside. Four glossy white horses were stamping as they were backed into their traces. The coachman was sitting on the box adjusting his leaf-green hat.

"Splendid!" said Old Niccolo, bustling out. He looked approvingly from the boys to the coach. "Get in, boys. Get in, Domenico. We have to pick up Umberto from the University."

Tonino said good-bye to Benvenuto and climbed into the coach. It smelt of mould, in spite of the dusting. He was glad his grandfather was so cheerful. In fact everyone seemed to be. The family cheered as the coach rumbled to the gateway, and Old Niccolo smiled and waved back. Perhaps, Tonino thought, something good was going to come from this visit to the Duke, and no one would be so worried after this.

The journey in the coach was splendid. Tonino had never felt so grand before. The coach rumbled and swayed. The hooves of the horses clattered over the cobbles just as if they were real, and people hurried respectfully out of their way. The coachman was as good as spells could make him. Though puddles dimpled along every street, the coach was hardly splashed when they drew up at the University, with loud shouts of "Woa there!"

Uncle Umberto climbed in, wearing his red and gold Master's gown, as cheerful as Old Niccolo. "Morning, Tonino," he said to Paolo. "How's your cat? Morning," he said to Domenico. "I hear the Petrocchis beat you up." Domenico, who would have died sooner than insult even a Petrocchi, went redder than Uncle Umberto's gown and swallowed noisily. But Uncle Umberto never could remember which younger Montana was which. He was too learned. He looked at Tonino as if he was wondering who he was, and turned to Old Niccolo. "The Petrocchis are sure to help," he said. "I had word from Chrestomanci."

"So did I," said Old Niccolo, but he sounded dubious.

The coach rumbled down the rainswept Corso and turned out across the New Bridge, where it rumbled even more loudly. Paolo and Tonino stared out of the rainy windows, too excited to speak. Beyond the swollen river, they clopped uphill, where cypresses bent and lashed in front of rich villas, and then among blurred old walls. Finally they rumbled under a great archway and made a crisp turn round the gigantic forecourt of the Palace. In front of their own coach, another coach, looking like a toy under the huge marble front of the Palace, was just drawing up by the enormous marble porch. This carriage was black too, with crimson shields on its doors, in which ramped black leopards. They were too late to see the people getting out of it, but they gazed with irritated envy at the coach itself and the horses. The horses were black, beautiful slender creatures with arched necks.

"I think they're *real* horses," Paolo whispered to Tonino.

Tonino had no time to answer, because two footmen and a soldier sprang to open the carriage door and usher them down, and Paolo jumped down first. But after him, Old Niccolo and Uncle Umberto were rather slow getting down. Tonino had time to look out of the further window at the Petrocchi carriage moving away. As it turned, he distinctly saw the small crimson flutter of a spell-streamer under the harness of the nearest black horse. So there! Tonino thought triumphantly. But he rather thought the Petrocchi coachman was real. He was a pale young man with reddish hair which did not match his cherry-coloured livery, and he had an intent, concentrating look, as if it was not easy driving those unreal horses. That look was too human for a cardboard man.

When Tonino finally climbed down on Domenico's nervous heels, he glanced up at their own coachman for comparison. He was efficient and jaunty. He touched a stiff hand to his green hat and stared straight ahead. No, the Petrocchi coachman was real all right, Tonino thought enviously.

Tonino forgot both coachmen as he and Paolo followed the others into the Palace. It was so grand, and so huge. They were taken through vast halls with shiny floors and gilded ceilings, which seemed to go on for miles. On either side of the long walls there were statues, or soldiers, or footmen, adding to the magnificence in rows. They felt so battered by all the grandeur that it was quite a relief when they were shown into a room only about the size of the Casa Montana yard. True, the floor was shiny and the ceiling painted to look like a sky full of wrestling angels, but the walls were hung with quite comfortable red cloth and there was a row of almost plain gilt chairs along each side.

Another party of people was shown into the room at the same time. Domenico took one look at them and turned his eyes instantly on the painted angels of the ceiling. Old Niccolo and Uncle Umberto behaved as if the people were not there at all. Paolo and Tonino tried to do the same, but they found it impossible.

So these were the Petrocchis, they thought, sneaking glances. There were only four of them, to their five. One up to the Montanas. And two of those were children. Clearly the Petrocchis had been as hard-pressed as the Montanas to come before the Duke with a decent party, and they had, in Paolo and Tonino's opinion, made a bad mistake in leaving one of their family outside with the coach. They were not impressive. Their University representative was a frail old man, far older than Uncle Umberto, who seemed almost lost in his red and gold gown. The most impressive one was the leader of the party, who must be Old Guido himself. But he was not particularly old, like Old Niccolo, and though he wore the same sort of black frock-coat as Old Niccolo and carried the same sort of shiny hat, it looked odd on Old Guido because he had a bright red beard. His hair was rather long, crinkly and black. And though he stared ahead in a bleak, important way, it was hard to forget that his daughter had once accidentally turned him green. Paolo and Tonino both sneaked fascinated glances, wondering what that red beard would look like as bright green.

The two children were both girls. Both had reddish hair. Both had prim, pointed faces. Both wore bright white stockings and severe black dresses and were clearly odious. The main difference between them was that the younger—who seemed about Tonino's age—had a large bulging forehead, which made her face even primmer than her sister's. It was possible that one of them was the famous Angelica, who had turned Old Guido green. The boys stared at them, trying to decide which it might be, until they encountered the prim, derisive stare of the elder girl. It was clear she thought they looked ridiculous. But Paolo and Tonino knew they still looked smart—they felt so uncomfortable—so they took no notice.

After they had waited a while, both parties began to talk quietly among themselves, as if the others were not there. Tonino murmured to Paolo, "Which one is Angelica?"

"I don't know," Paolo whispered.

"Didn't you see them at the Old Bridge then?"

"I didn't see any of them. They were all down the other—"

Part of the red hanging swung aside and a lady hurried in. "I'm so sorry," she said. "My husband has been delayed."

Everyone in the room bent their heads and murmured "Your Grace" because this was the Duchess. But Paolo and Tonino kept their eyes on her while they bent their heads, wanting to know what she was like. She had a stiff greyish dress on, which put them in mind of a statue of a saint, and her face might almost have been part of the same statue. It was a statue-pale face, almost waxy, as if the Duchess were carved out of slightly soapy marble. But Tonino was not sure the Duchess was really like a saint. Her eyebrows were set in a strong sarcastic arch, and her mouth was tight with what looked like impatience. For a second, Tonino thought he felt that impatience—and a number of other unsaintly feelings—pouring into the room from behind the Duchess's waxy mask like a strong rank smell.

The Duchess smiled at Old Niccolo. "Signor Niccolo Montana?" There was no scrap of impatience, only stateliness. Tonino thought to himself, I've been reading too many books. Rather ashamed, he watched

Old Niccolo bow and introduce them all. The Duchess nodded graciously and turned to the Petrocchis. "Signor Guido Petrocchi?"

The red-bearded man bowed in a rough, brusque way. He was nothing like as courtly as Old Niccolo. "Your Grace. With me are my great-uncle Dr Luigi Petrocchi, my elder daughter Renata, and my younger daughter Angelica."

Paolo and Tonino stared at the younger girl, from her bulge of forehead to her thin white legs. So *this* was Angelica. She did not look capable of doing anything wrong, or interesting.

The Duchess said, "I believe you understand why—"

The red curtains were once more swept aside. A bulky excited-looking man raced in with his head down, and took the Duchess by one arm. "Lucrezia, you must come! The scenery looks a treat!"

The Duchess turned as a statue might turn, all one piece. Her eyebrows were very high and her mouth pinched. "My lord Duke!" she said freezingly.

Tonino stared at the bulky man. He was now wearing slightly shabby green velvet with big brass buttons. Otherwise, he was exactly the same as the big damp Mr Glister who had interrupted the Punch and Judy show that time. So he had been the Duke of Caprona after all! And he was not in the least put off by the Duchess's, frigid look. "You must come and look!" he said, tugging at her arm, as excited as ever. He turned to the Montanas and the Petrocchis as if he expected them to help him pull the Duchess out of the room—and then seemed to realise that they were not courtiers. "Who are you?"

"These," said the Duchess—her eyebrows were still higher and her voice was strong with patience—"these are the Petrocchis and the Montanas awaiting your pleasure, my lord."

The Duke slapped a large, damp-looking hand to his shiny forehead. "Well I'm blessed! The people who make spells! I was thinking of sending for you. Have you come about this enchanter-fellow who's got his knife into Caprona?" he asked Old Niccolo.

"My lord!" said the Duchess, her face rigid.

But the Duke broke away from her, beaming and gleaming, and dived on the Petrocchis. He shook Old Guido's hand hugely, and then the girl Renata's. After that, he dived round and did the same to Old Niccolo and Paolo. Paolo had to rub his hand secretly on his trousers after he let go. He was wet. "And they say the young ones are as clever as the old ones," the Duke said happily. "Amazing families! Just the people I need for my play—my pantomime, you know. We're putting it on here for Christmas and I could do with some special effects."

The Duchess gave a sigh. Paolo looked at her rigid face and thought that it must be hard, dealing with someone like the Duke.

The Duke dived on Domenico. "Can you arrange for a flight of cupids blowing trumpets?" he asked him eagerly. Domenico swallowed and managed to whisper the word "illusion." "Oh good!" said the Duke, and dived at Angelica Petrocchi. "And you'll love my collection of Punch and Judys," he said. "I've got hundreds!"

"How nice," Angelica answered primly.

"My lord," said the Duchess, "these good people did not come here to discuss the theatre."

"Maybe, maybe," the Duke said, with an impatient, eager wave of his large hand. "But while they're here, I might as well ask them about that too. Mightn't I?" he said, diving at Old Niccolo.

Old Niccolo showed great presence of mind. He smiled. "Of course, Your Grace. No trouble at all. After we've discussed the State business we came for, we shall be happy to take orders for any stage-effects you want."

"So will we," said Guido Petrocchi, with a sour glance at the air over Old Niccolo.

The Duchess smiled graciously at Old Niccolo for backing her up, which made Old Guido look sourer than ever, and fixed the Duke with a meaning look.

It seemed to get through to the Duke at last. "Yes, yes," he said. "Better get down to business. It's like this, you see—"

The Duchess interrupted, with a gentle fixed smile. "Refreshments are laid out in the small Conference Room. If you and the adults like to hold your discussion there, I will arrange something for the children here."

Guido Petrocchi saw a chance to get even with Old Niccolo. "Your Grace," he barked stiffly, "my daughters are as loyal to Caprona as the rest of my house. I have no secrets from them."

The Duke flashed him a glistening smile. "Quite right! But they won't be half as bored if they stay here, will they?"

Quite suddenly, everyone except Paolo and Tonino and the two Petrocchi girls was crowding away through another door behind the red hangings. The Duke leaned back, beaming. "I tell you what," he said. "You must come to my pantomime, all of you. You'll love it! I'll send you tickets. Coming, Lucrezia."

The four children were left standing under the ceiling full of wrestling angels.

After a moment, the Petrocchi girls walked to the chairs against the wall and sat down. Paolo and Tonino looked at one another. They marched to the chairs on the opposite side of the room and sat down there. It seemed a safe distance. From there, the Petrocchi girls were dark blurs with thin white legs and foxy blobs for heads.

"I wish I'd brought my book," said Tonino.

They sat with their heels hooked into the rungs of their chairs, trying to feel patient. "I think the Duchess must be a saint," said Paolo, "to be so patient with the Duke."

Tonino was surprised Paolo should think that. He knew the Duke did not behave much like a duke should, while the Duchess was every inch a duchess. But he was not sure it was right, the way she let them know how patient she was being. "Mother dashes about like that," he said, "and Father doesn't mind. It stops him looking worried."

"Father's not a Duchess," said Paolo.

Tonino did not argue because, at that moment, two footmen appeared, pushing a most interesting trolley. Tonino's mouth fell open. He had never seen so many cakes together in his life before. Across the room, there were black gaps in the faces of the Petrocchi girls. Evidently they had never seen so many cakes either. Tonino shut his mouth quickly and tried to look as if he saw such sights every day.

The footmen served the Petrocchi girls first. They were very cool and seemed to take hours choosing. When the trolley was finally wheeled across to Paolo and Tonino, they found it hard to seem as composed. There were twenty different kinds of cake. They took ten each, with greedy speed, so that they had one of every kind between them and could swap if necessary. When the trolley was wheeled away, Tonino just managed to spare a glance from his plate to see how the Petrocchis were doing. Each girl had her white knees hooked up to carry a plate big enough to hold ten cakes.

They were rich cakes. By the time Paolo reached the tenth, he was going slowly, wondering if he really cared for meringue as much as he had thought, and Tonino was only on his sixth. By the time Paolo had put his plate neatly under his chair and cleaned himself with his handkerchief, Tonino, sticky with jam, smeared with chocolate and cream and infested with crumbs, was still doggedly ploughing through his eighth. And this was the moment the Duchess chose to sit smiling down beside Paolo.

"I won't interrupt your brother," she said, laughing. "Tell me about yourself, Paolo." Paolo did not know what to answer. All he could think of was the mess Tonino looked. "For instance," the Duchess asked helpfully, "does spell-making come easily to you? Do you find it hard to learn?"

"Oh no, Your Grace," Paolo said proudly. "I learn very easily."

Then he was afraid this might upset Tonino. He looked quickly at Tonino's pastry-plastered face and found Tonino staring gravely at the Duchess. Paolo felt ashamed and responsible. He wanted the Duchess to know that Tonino was not just a messy staring little boy. "Tonino learns slowly," he said, "but he reads all the time. He's read all the books in the Library. He's almost as learned as Uncle Umberto."

"How remarkable," smiled the Duchess.

There was just a trace of disbelief in the arch of her eyebrows. Tonino was so embarrassed that he took a big bite out of his ninth cake. It was a great pastry puff. The instant his mouth closed round it, Tonino knew that, if he opened his mouth again, even to breathe, pastry would blow out of it like a hailstorm, all over Paolo and the Duchess. He clamped his lips together and chewed valiantly. And, to Paolo's embarrassment, he went on staring at the Duchess. He was wishing Benvenuto was there to tell him about the Duchess. She muddled him. As she bent smiling over Paolo, she did not look like the haughty, rigid lady who had been so patient with the Duke. And yet, perhaps because she was not being patient, Tonino felt the rank strength of the unsaintly thoughts behind her waxy smile, stronger than ever.

Paolo willed Tonino to stop chewing and goggling. But Tonino went on, and the disbelief in the Duchess's eyebrows was so obvious, that he blurted out, "And Tonino's the only one who can talk to Benvenuto. He's our boss cat, Your—" He remembered the Duchess did not like cats. "Er—you don't like cats, Your Grace."

The Duchess laughed. "But I don't mind hearing about them. What about Benvenuto?"

To Paolo's relief, Tonino turned his goggle eyes from the Duchess to him. So Paolo talked on. "You see, Your Grace, spells work much better and stronger if a cat's around, and particularly if Benvenuto is. Besides Benvenuto knows all sorts of things—"

He was interrupted by a thick noise from Tonino. Tonino was trying to speak without opening his mouth. It was clear there was going to be a pastry-storm any second. Paolo snatched out his jammy, creamy handkerchief and held it ready.

The Duchess stood up, rather hastily. "I think I'd better see how my other guests are getting on," she said, and went swiftly gliding across to the Petrocchi girls.

The Petrocchi girls, Paolo noticed resentfully, were ready to receive her. Their handkerchiefs had been busy while the Duchess talked to Paolo, and now their plates were neatly pushed under their chairs too. Each had left at least three cakes. This much encouraged Tonino. He was feeling rather unwell. He put the rest of the ninth cake back beside the tenth and laid the plate carefully on the next chair. By this time, he had managed to swallow his mouthful.

"You shouldn't have told her about Benvenuto," he said, hauling out his handkerchief. "He's a family secret."

"Then you should have said something yourself instead of staring like a dummy," Paolo retorted. To his mortification both Petrocchi girls were talking merrily to the Duchess. The bulge-headed Angelica was laughing. It so annoyed Paolo that he said, "Look at the way those girls are sucking up to the Duchess!"

"I didn't do that," Tonino pointed out.

As Paolo wanted to say he wished Tonino had, he found himself unable to say anything at all. He sat sourly watching the Duchess talking to the girls across the room, until she got up and went gliding away. She remembered to smile and wave at Paolo and Tonino as she went. Paolo thought that was good of her, considering the asses they had made of themselves.

Very soon after that, the curtains swung aside and Old Niccolo came back, walking slowly beside Guido Petrocchi. After them came the two gowned great-uncles, and Domenico came after that. It was like a procession. Everyone looked straight ahead, and it was plain they had a lot on their minds. All four children stood up, brushed crumbs off, and followed the procession. Paolo found he was walking beside the elder girl, but he was careful not to look at her. In utter silence, they marched to the great Palace door, where the carriages were moving along to receive them.

The Petrocchi carriage came first, with its black horses patched and beaded with rain. Tonino took another look at its coachman, rather hoping he had made a mistake. It was still raining and the man's clothes were soaked. His red Petrocchi hair was brown with wet under his wet hat. He was shivering as he leant down, and there was a questioning look on his pale face, as if he was anxious to be told what the Duke had said. No, he was real all right. The Montana coachman behind stared into space, ignoring the rain and his passengers equally. Tonino felt that the Petrocchis had definitely come out best.

CHAPTER 4

When the coach was moving, Old Niccolo leaned back and said, "Well, the Duke is very good-natured, I'll say that. Perhaps he's not such a fool as he seems."

Uncle Umberto answered, with deepest gloom, "When my father was a boy, *his* father went to the Palace once a week. He was received as a friend."

Domenico said timidly, "At least we sold some stage-effects."

"That," said Uncle Umberto crushingly, "is just what I'm complaining of."

Tonino and Paolo looked from one to the other, wondering what had depressed them so.

Old Niccolo noticed them looking. "Guido Petrocchi wished those disgusting daughters of his to be present while we conferred with the Duke," he said. "I shall not—"

"Oh good Lord!" muttered Uncle Umberto, "One doesn't listen to a Petrocchi."

"No, but one trusts one's grandsons," said Old Niccolo. "Boys, old Caprona's in a bad way, it seems. The States of Florence, Pisa and Siena have now united against her. The Duke suspects they are paying an enchanter to—"

"Huh!" said Uncle Umberto. "Paying the Petrocchis."

Domenico, who had been rendered surprisingly bold by something, said, "Uncle, I could *see* the Petrocchis were no more traitors than we are!"

Both old men turned to look at him. He crumpled.

"The fact is," Old Niccolo continued, "Caprona is not the great State she once was. There are many reasons, no doubt. But we know, and the

Duke knows—even Domenico knows—that each year we set the usual charms for the defence of Caprona, and each year we set them stronger, and each year they have less effect. Something—or someone—is definitely sapping our strength. So the Duke asks what else we can do. And—"

Domenico interrupted with a squawk of laughter. "And we said we'd find the words to the *Angel of Caprona*!"

Paolo and Tonino expected Domenico to be crushed again, but the two old men simply looked gloomy. Their heads nodded mournfully. "But I don't understand," said Tonino. "The *Angel of Caprona's got* words. We sing them at school."

"Hasn't your mother taught you—?" Old Niccolo began angrily. "Ah, no, I forgot. Your mother is English."

"One more reason for careful marriages," Uncle Umberto said dismally.

By this time, what with the rain ceaselessly pattering down as well, both boys were thoroughly depressed and alarmed. Domenico seemed to find them funny. He gave another squawk of laughter.

"Be quiet," said Old Niccolo. "This is the last time I take you where brandy is served. No, boys, the *Angel* has not got the right words. The words you sing are a makeshift. Some people say that the glorious Angel took the words back to Heaven after the White Devil was vanquished, leaving only the tune. Or the words have been lost since. But everyone knows that Caprona cannot be truly great until the words are found."

"In other words," Uncle Umberto said irritably, "the *Angel of Caprona* is a spell like any other spell. And without the proper words, any spell is only at half force, even if it is of divine origin." He gathered up his gown as the coach jerked to a stop outside the University. "And we—like idiots—have pledged ourselves to complete what God left unfinished," he said. "The presumption of man!" He climbed out of the coach, calling to Old Niccolo, "I'll look in every manuscript I can think of. There must be a clue somewhere. Oh this confounded rain!"

The door slammed and the coach jerked on again.

Paolo asked, "Have the Petrocchis said they'll find the words too?"

Old Niccolo's mouth bunched angrily. "They have. And I should die of shame if they did it before we did. I—" He stopped as the coach lurched round the corner into the Corso. It lurched again, and jerked. Sprays of water flew past the windows.

Domenico leaned forward. "Not driving so well, is he?"

"Quiet!" said Old Niccolo, and Paolo bit his tongue in a whole succession of jerks. Something was wrong. The coach was not making the right noise.

"I can't hear the horses' hooves," Tonino said, puzzled.

"I thought that was it!" Old Niccolo snapped. "It's the rain." He let down the window with a bang, bringing in a gust of watery wind, and, regardless of faces staring up at him from under wet umbrellas, he leaned out and bellowed the words of a spell. "And drive quickly, coachman! There," he said, as he pulled the window up again, "that should get us home before the horses turn to pulp. What a blessing this didn't happen before Umberto got out!"

The noise of the horses' hooves sounded again, clopping over the cobbles of the Corso. It seemed that the new spell was working. But, as they turned into the Via Cardinale, the noise changed to a spongy *thump-thump,* and when they came to the Via Magica the hooves made hardly a sound. And the lurching and jerking began again, worse than ever. As they turned to enter the gate of the Casa Montana, there came the most brutal jerk of all. The coach tipped forward, and there was a crash as the pole hit the cobbles. Paolo got his window open in time to see the limp paper figure of the coachman flop off the box into a puddle. Beyond him, two wet cardboard horses were draped over their traces.

"That spell," said Old Niccolo, "lasted for days in my grandfather's time."

"Do you mean it's that enchanter?" Paolo asked. "Is he spoiling all our spells?"

Old Niccolo stared at him, full-eyed, like a baby about to burst into tears. "No, lad. I fancy not. The truth is, the Casa Montana is in as bad a way as Caprona. The old virtue is fading. It has faded generation by generation, and now it is almost gone. I am ashamed that you should learn it like this. Let's get out, boys, and start dragging."

It was a wretched humiliation. Since the rest of the family were all either asleep or at work on the Old Bridge, there was no one to help them pull the coach through the gate. And Domenico was no use. He confessed afterwards that he could not remember getting home. They left him asleep in the coach and dragged it in, just the three of them. Even Benvenuto dashing through the rain did not cheer Tonino much.

"One consolation," panted their grandfather. "The rain. There is no one about to see Old Niccolo dragging his own coach."

Paolo and Tonino did not find much consolation in that. Now they understood the growing unease in the Casa, and it was not pleasant. They understood why everyone was so anxious about the Old Bridge, and so delighted when, just before Christmas, it was mended at last. They understood, too, the worry about a husband for Rosa. As soon as the bridge was repaired, everyone went back to discussing that. And

Paolo and Tonino knew why everyone agreed that the young man Rosa must choose, must have, if he had nothing else, a strong talent for spells.

"To improve the breed, you mean?" said Rosa. She was very sarcastic and independent about it. "Very well, dear Uncle Lorenzo, I shall only fall in love with men who can make paper horses waterproof."

Uncle Lorenzo blushed angrily. The whole family felt humiliated by those horses. But Elizabeth was trying not to laugh. Elizabeth certainly encouraged Rosa in her independent attitude. Benvenuto informed Tonino it was the English way. Cats liked English people, he added.

"Have we really lost our virtue?" Tonino asked Benvenuto anxiously. He thought it was probably the explanation for his slowness.

Benvenuto said that he did not know what it was like in the old days, but he knew there was enough magic about now to make his coat spark. It seemed like a lot. But he sometimes wondered if it was being applied properly.

Around this time, twice as many newspapers found their way into the Casa. There were journals from Rome and magazines from Genoa and Milan, as well as the usual Caprona papers. Everyone read them eagerly and talked in mutters about the attitude of Florence, movements in Pisa and opinion hardening in Siena. Out of the worried murmurs, the word *War* began to sound, more and more frequently. And, instead of the usual Christmas songs, the only tune heard in the Casa Montana, night and day, was the *Angel of Caprona.*

The tune was sung, in bass, tenor and soprano. It was played slowly on flutes, picked out on guitars and lilted on violins. Every one of the Montanas lived in hope that he or she would be the person to find the true words. Rinaldo had a new idea. He procured a drum and sat on the edge of his bed beating out the rhythm, until Aunt Francesca implored him to stop. And even that did not help. Not one of the Montanas could begin to set the right words to the tune. Antonio looked so worried that Paolo could scarcely bear to look at him.

With so much worry about, it was hardly surprising that Paolo and Tonino looked forward daily to being invited to the Duke's pantomime. It was the one bright spot. But Antonio and Rinaldo went to the Palace—on foot—to deliver the special effects, and came back without a word of invitation. Christmas came. The entire Montana family went to church, in the beautiful marble-fronted Church of Sant' Angelo, and behaved with great devotion. Usually it was only Aunt Anna and Aunt Maria who were notably religious, but now everyone felt they had something to pray for. It was only when the time came to sing the *Angel of Caprona* that the Montana devotion slackened. An absent-minded look came over their faces, from Old Niccolo to the smallest cousin. They sang:

> *"Merrily his music ringing,*
> *See an Angel cometh singing,*
> *Words of peace and comfort bringing*
> *To Caprona's city fair.*
>
> *"Victory that faileth never,*
> *Friendship that no strife can sever,*
> *Lasting strength and peace for ever,*
> *For Caprona's city fair.*
>
> *"See the Devil flee astounded!*
> *In Caprona now is founded*
> *Virtue strong and peace unbounded—*
> *In Caprona's city fair."*

Every one of them was wondering what the real words were.

They came home for the family celebrations, and there was still no word from the Duke. Then Christmas was over. New Year drew on and passed too, and the boys were forced to realise that there would be no invitation after all. Each told himself he had *known* the Duke was like that. They did not speak of it to one another. But they were both bitterly disappointed.

They were roused from their gloom by Lucia racing along the gallery, screaming, "Come and look at Rosa's young man!"

"What?" said Antonio, raising his worried face from a book about the Angel of Caprona. "What? Nothing's decided yet."

Lucia leapt from foot to foot. She was pink with excitement. "Rosa's decided for herself! I knew she would. Come and see!"

Led by Lucia, Antonio, Paolo, Tonino and Benvenuto raced along the gallery and down the stone stairs at the end. People and cats were streaming through the courtyard from all directions, hurrying to the room called the Saloon, beyond the dining-room.

Rosa was standing near the windows, looking happy but defiant, with both hands clasped round the arm of an embarrassed-looking young man with ginger hair. A bright ring winked on Rosa's finger. Elizabeth was with them, looking as happy as Rosa and almost as defiant. When the young man saw the family streaming through the door and crowding towards him, his face became bright pink and his hand went up to loosen his smart tie. But, in spite of that, it was plain to everyone that, underneath, the young man was as happy as Rosa. And Rosa was so happy that she seemed to shine, like the Angel over the gate. This made everyone stare, marvelling. Which, of course, made the young man more embarrassed than ever.

Old Niccolo cleared his throat. "Now look here," he said. Then he stopped. This was Antonio's business. He looked at Antonio.

Paolo and Tonino noticed that their father looked at their mother first. Elizabeth's happy look seemed to reassure him a little. "Now, just who are you?" he said to the young man. "How did you meet my Rosa?"

"He was one of the contractors on the Old Bridge, Father," said Rosa.

"And he has enormous natural talent, Antonio," said Elizabeth, "and a beautiful singing voice."

"All right, all right," said Antonio. "Let the boy speak for himself, women."

The young man swallowed, and helped the swallow down with a shake of his tie. His face was now very pale. "My name is Marco Andretti," he said in a pleasant, if husky, voice. "I—I think you met my brother at the bridge, sir. I was on the other shift. That's how I came to meet Rosa." The way he smiled down at Rosa left everybody hoping that he would be fit to become a Montana.

"It'll break their hearts if Father says no," Lucia whispered to Paolo. Paolo nodded. He could see that.

Antonio was pulling his lip, which was a thing he did when his face could hold no more worry than it did already. "Yes," he said. "I've met Mario Andretti, of course. A very respectable family." He made that sound not altogether a good thing. "But I'm sure you're aware, Signor Andretti, that ours is a special family. We have to be careful who we marry. First, what do you think of the Petrocchis?"

Marco's pale face went fiery red. He answered with a violence which surprised the Montanas, "I hate their guts, Signor Montana!" He seemed so upset that Rosa pulled his arm down and patted it soothingly.

"Marco has personal family reasons, Father," she said.

"Which I'd prefer not to go into," Marco said.

"We—well, I'll not press you for them," Antonio said, and continued to pull his lip. "But, you see, our family must marry someone with at least some talent for magic. Have you any ability there, Signor Andretti?"

Marco Andretti seemed to relax at this. He smiled, and gently took Rosa's hands off his sleeve. Then he sang. Elizabeth had been right about his voice. It was a golden tenor. Uncle Lorenzo was heard to rumble that he could not think what a voice like that was doing outside the Milan Opera.

"A golden tree there grows, a tree
Whose golden branches bud with green. . ."

sang Marco. As he sang, the tree came into being, rooted in the carpet between Rosa and Antonio, first as a faint gold shadow, then as a rattling metal shape, dazzling gold in the shafts of sunlight from the windows. The Montanas nodded their appreciation. The trunk and each branch, even the smallest twig, was indeed pure gold. But Marco sang on, and as he sang, the gold twigs put out buds, pale and fist-shaped at first, then bright and pointed. Instants later, the tree was in leaf. It was moving and rattling constantly to Marco's singing. It put out pink and white flowers in clusters, which budded, expanded and dropped, as quickly as flames in a firework. The room was full of scent, then of petals fluttering like confetti. Marco still sang, and the tree still moved. Before the last petal had fallen, pointed green fruit was swelling where the flowers had been. The fruit grew brownish and swelled, and swelled and turned bulging and yellow, until the tree drooped under the weight of a heavy crop of big yellow pears.

". . . With golden fruit for everyone,"

Marco concluded. He put up a hand, picked one of the pears and held it, rather diffidently, out to Antonio.

There were murmurs of appreciation from the rest of the family. Antonio took the pear and sniffed it. And he smiled, to Marco's evident relief. "Good fruit," he said. "That was very elegantly done, Signor Andretti. But there is one more thing I must ask you. Would you agree to change your name to Montana? That is our custom, you see."

"Yes, Rosa told me," said Marco. "And—and this is a difficulty. My brother needs me in his firm, and he too wants to keep his family name. Would it be all right if I'm known as Montana when I'm here, and as—as Andretti when I'm at home with my brother?"

"You mean you and Rosa wouldn't live here?" Antonio asked, astonished.

"Not all the time. No," said Marco. From the way he said it, it was clear he was not going to change his mind.

This was serious. Antonio looked at Old Niccolo. And there were grave faces all round at the thought of the family being broken up.

"I don't see why they shouldn't," said Elizabeth.

"Well—my great-uncle did it," Old Niccolo said. "But it was not a success. His wife ran off to Sicily with a greasy little warlock."

"That doesn't mean *I'm* going to!" Rosa said.

The family wavered, with the tree gently rattling in their midst. Everyone loved Rosa. Marco was clearly nice. Nobody wanted to break their hearts. But this idea of living away from the Casa—!

Aunt Francesca heaved herself forward, saying, "I side with Elizabeth. Our Rosa has found herself a nice boy with more talent and a better voice than I've seen outside our family for years. Let them get married."

Antonio looked dreadfully worried at this, but he did not pull his lip. He seemed to be relaxing, ready to agree, when Rinaldo set the tree rattling furiously by pushing his way underneath it.

"Just a moment. Aren't we all being a bit trustful? Who *is* this fellow, after all? Why haven't we come across him and his talents before?"

Paolo hung his head and watched Rinaldo under his hair. This was Rinaldo in the mood he least admired. Rinaldo loud and aggressive, with an unpleasant twist to his mouth. Rinaldo was still a little pale from the cut on his head, but this went rather well with the black clothes and the red brigand's scarf. Rinaldo knew it did. He flung up his head with an air, and contemptuously brushed off a petal that had fallen on his black sleeve. And he looked at Marco, challenging him to answer.

The way Marco looked back showed that he was quite ready to stand up to Rinaldo. "I've been at college in Rome until recently," he said. "If that's what you mean."

Rinaldo swung round to face the family. "So he says," he said. "He's done a pretty trick for us, and said all the right things—but so would anyone in his place." He swung round on Marco. It was so dramatic that Tonino winced and even Paolo felt a little unhappy. "I don't trust you," said Rinaldo. "I've seen your face before somewhere."

"At the Old Bridge," said Marco.

"No, not there. It was somewhere else," said Rinaldo.

And this must be true, Tonino realised. Marco did have a familiar look. And Tonino could not have seen him at the Old Bridge, because Tonino had never been there.

"Do you want me to fetch my brother, or my priest, to vouch for me?" asked Marco.

"No," said Rinaldo rudely. "I want the truth."

Marco took a deep breath. "I don't want to be unfriendly," he said. The arm Rosa was not holding bent, and so did the fist on the end of it. Rinaldo gave it a look as if he welcomed it, and swaggered a step nearer.

"Please!" Rosa said uselessly.

Benvenuto moved in Tonino's arms. Into Tonino's head came a picture of a large stripy tomcat swaggering on the Casa roof—Benvenuto's roof. Tonino nearly laughed. Benvenuto's muscular back legs pushed him backwards into Paolo as Benvenuto took off. Benvenuto landed between Rinaldo and Marco. There was a gentle "Ah!" from the rest of the family. They knew Benvenuto would settle it.

Benvenuto deliberately ignored Rinaldo. Arching himself tall, with his tail straight up like a cypress tree, he minced to Marco's legs and rubbed himself round them. Marco undoubled his fist and bent to hold his hand out to Benvenuto. "Hallo," he said. "What's your name?" He paused, for Benvenuto to tell him. "I'm pleased to meet you, Benvenuto," he said.

The "Ah!" from the family was loud and long this time. It was followed by cries of, "Get out of it, Rinaldo! Don't make a fool of yourself! Leave Marco alone!"

Though Rinaldo was nothing like as easily crushed as Domenico, even he could not stand up to the whole family. When he looked at Old Niccolo and saw Old Niccolo waving him angrily aside, he gave up and shoved his way out of the room.

"Rosa and Marco," said Antonio, "I give my provisional consent to your marriage."

Upon that, everyone hugged everyone else, shook hands with Marco and kissed Rosa. Very flushed and happy, Marco plucked pear after pear from the golden tree and gave them to everyone, even the newest baby. They were delicious pears, ripe to perfection. They melted in mouths and dribbled down chins.

"I don't want to be a spoilsport," Aunt Maria said, slurping juice in Paolo's ear, "but a tree in the Saloon is going to be a nuisance."

But Marco had thought of that. As soon as the last pear was picked, the tree began to fade. Soon it was a clattering golden glitter, a vanishing shadow-tree, and then it was not there at all. Everyone applauded. Aunt Gina and Aunt Anna fetched bottles of wine and glasses, and the Casa drank to the health of Rosa and Marco.

"Thank goodness!" Tonino heard Elizabeth say. "I was so nervous for her!"

On the other side of Elizabeth, Old Niccolo was telling Uncle Lorenzo that Marco was a real acquisition, because he could understand cats. Tonino felt a little wistful at this. He went outside into the chilly yard. As he had expected, Benvenuto was now curled up in the sunny patch on the gallery steps. He undulated his tail in annoyance at Tonino. He had just settled down for a sleep.

But Marco could *not* understand cats, Benvenuto said irritably. He knew Benvenuto's name, because Rosa had told him, but he had no idea what Benvenuto had actually said to him. Benvenuto had told him that he and Rinaldo would get thoroughly scratched if they started a fight in the Casa—neither of them was boss cat here. Now, if Tonino would go away, a cat could get some sleep.

This was a great relief to Tonino. He now felt free to like Marco as much as Paolo did. Marco was fun. He was never in the Casa for very long, because he and his brother were building a villa out beyond the New Bridge, but he was one of the few people Tonino laid down his book to talk to. And that, Lucia told Rosa, was a compliment indeed.

Rosa and Marco were to be married in the spring. They laughed about it constantly as they swept in and out of the Casa together. Antonio and Uncle Lorenzo walked out to the villa where Mario Andretti lived, and arranged it all. Mario Andretti came to the Casa to settle the details. He was a large fat man—who drove a shrewd bargain, Aunt Francesca said—and quite different from Marco. The most notable thing about him was the long white motor car he came in.

Old Niccolo looked at that car reflectively. "It smells," he said. "But it looks more reliable than a cardboard horse." He sighed. He still felt deeply humiliated. All the same, after Mario Andretti had driven away, Tonino was very interested to be sent out to the post with two letters. One was addressed to Ferrari, the other to Rolls-Royce in England.

In the normal way, the talk in the Casa would have been all about that car and those two letters. But they passed unnoticed in the anxious murmurs about Florence, Siena and Pisa. The only topic able to drown out the talk of war was Rosa's wedding dress. Should it be long or short? With a train, or not? And what kind of veil? Rosa was quite as independent about that as she had been over Marco.

"I suppose I have no say in it at all," she said. "I shall have it knee-length one side and a train ten feet long on the other, I think. And no veil. Just a black mask."

This thoroughly offended Aunt Maria and Aunt Gina, who were the chief arguers. What with the noise they made, and the twanging the other side of the room, where Antonio had roped Marco in to help find the words to the *Angel,* Tonino was unable to concentrate on his book. He took it along the gallery to the library, hoping for peace there.

But Rinaldo was leaning on the gallery rail outside the library, looking remarkably sinister, and he stopped Tonino. "That Marco," he said. "I *wish* I could remember where I saw him. I've seen him in the Art

Gallery with Rosa, but it wasn't there. I know it was somewhere much more damaging than that."

Tonino had no doubt that Rinaldo knew all sorts of damaging places. He took his book into the library, hoping that Rinaldo would not remember the place, and settled down in the chilly mustiness to read.

The next moment, Benvenuto landed on his book with a thump.

"Oh get off!" said Tonino. "I start school tomorrow, and I want to finish this first."

No, said Benvenuto. Tonino was to go to Old Niccolo *at once.* A flurry of scrips, spells, yellow parchment rolls and then a row of huge red books passed behind Tonino's eyes. It was followed by a storm of enormous images. Giants were running, banging, smoking and burning, and they all wore red and gold. But not yet. They were preparing to fight, marching in great huge boots. Benvenuto was so urgent that it took all Tonino's skill to sort out what he meant.

"All right," said Tonino. "I'll tell him." He got up and pelted round the gallery, past Rinaldo, who said, "What's the hurry?" to Old Niccolo's quarters. Old Niccolo was just coming out.

"Please," said Tonino, "Benvenuto says to get out the war-spells. The Duke is calling up the Reserves."

Old Niccolo stood so very quiet and wide-eyed that Tonino thought he did not believe it. Old Niccolo was feeling for the door-frame. He seemed to think it was missing.

"You did hear me, did you?" Tonino asked.

"Yes," said Old Niccolo. "Yes, I heard. It's just so soon—so sudden. I wish the Duke had warned us. So war is coming. Pray God our strength is still enough."

CHAPTER 5

Benvenuto's news caused a stampede in the Casa Montana. The older cousins raced to the Scriptorium and began packing away all the usual spells, inks and pens. The aunts fetched out the special inks for use in war-spells. The uncles staggered under reams of fresh paper and parchment. Antonio, Old Niccolo and Rinaldo went to the library and fetched the giant red volumes, with *WAR* stamped on their spines, while Elizabeth raced to the music room with all the children to put away the ordinary music and set out the tunes and instruments of war.

Meanwhile, Rosa, Marco and Domenico raced out into the Via Magica and came back with newspapers. Everyone at once left what they were doing and crowded into the dining-room to see what the papers said.

They made a pile of people, all craning over the table. Rinaldo was standing on a chair, leaning over three aunts. Marco was underneath, craning anxiously sideways, head to head with Old Niccolo, as Rosa flipped over the pages. There were so many other people packed in and leaning over that Lucia, Paolo and Tonino were forced to squat with their chins on the table, in order to see at all.

"No, nothing," Rosa said, flipping over the second paper.

"Wait," said Marco. "Look at the Stop Press."

Everyone swayed towards it, pushing Marco further sideways. Then Tonino almost knew where he had seen Marco before.

"There it is," said Antonio.

All the bodies came upright, with their faces very serious.

"Reserve mobilised, right enough," said Rosa. "Oh, Marco!"

"What's the matter?" Rinaldo asked jeeringly from his chair. "Is Marco a Reservist?"

"No," said Marco. "My—my brother got me out of it."

Rinaldo laughed. "What a patriot!"

Marco looked up at him. "I'm a Final Reservist," he said, "and I hope you are too. If you aren't, it will be a pleasure to take you round to the Army Office in the Arsenal this moment."

The two glared at one another. Once again there were shouts to Rinaldo to stop making a fool of himself. Sulkily, Rinaldo climbed down and stalked out.

"Rinaldo *is* a Final Reservist," Paolo assured Marco.

"I thought he must be," Marco said. "Look, I must go. I—I must tell my brother. Rosa, I'll see you tomorrow if I can."

When Tonino fell asleep that night, the room next door to him was full of people talking of war and the *Angel of Caprona,* with occasional digressions about Rosa's wedding dress. Tonino's head was so full of these things that he was quite surprised, when he went to school, not to hear them talked of there. But no one seemed to have noticed there might be a war. True, some of the teachers looked grave, but that might have been just their natural feelings at the start of a new term.

Consequently, Tonino came home that afternoon thinking that maybe things were not so bad after all. As usual, Benvenuto leapt off the waterbutt and sprang into his arms. Tonino was rubbing his face against Benvenuto's nearest ragged ear, when he heard a carriage draw up behind him. Benvenuto promptly squirmed out of Tonino's arms. Tonino, very surprised, looked round to find him trotting, gently and politely, with his tail well up, towards a tall man who was just coming in through the Casa gate.

Benvenuto stood, his brush of tail waving slightly at the tip, his hind legs canted slightly apart under his fluffy drawers, staring gravely at the tall man. Tonino thought peevishly that, from behind, Benvenuto often looked pretty silly. The man looked almost as bad. He was wearing an exceedingly expensive coat with a fur collar and a tweed travelling cap with daft earflaps. And he bowed to Benvenuto.

"Good afternoon, Benvenuto," he said, as grave as Benvenuto himself. "I'm glad to see you so well. Yes, I'm very well thank you."

Benvenuto advanced to rub himself round the stranger's legs.

"No," said the man. "I beg you. Your hairs come off."

And Benvenuto stopped, without abating an ounce of his uncommon politeness.

By this time, Tonino was extremely resentful. This was the first time for years that Benvenuto had behaved as if anyone mattered more than Tonino. He raised his eyes accusingly to the stranger's. He met eyes even darker than his own, which seemed to spill brilliance over the rest of the man's smooth dark face. They gave Tonino a jolt, worse than the time the horses turned back to cardboard. He knew, beyond a shadow of doubt, that he was looking at a powerful enchanter.

"How do you do?" said the man. "No, despite your accusing glare, young man, I have never been able to understand cats—or not more than in the most general way. I wonder if you would be kind enough to translate for me what Benvenuto is saying."

Tonino listened to Benvenuto. "He says he's very pleased to see you again and welcome to the Casa Montana, sir." The *sir* was from Benvenuto, not Tonino. Tonino was not sure he cared for strange enchanters who walked into the Casa and took up Benvenuto's attention.

"Thank you, Benvenuto," said the enchanter. "I'm very pleased to be back. Though, frankly, I've seldom had such a difficult journey. Did you know your borders with Florence and Pisa were closed?" he asked Tonino. "I had to come in by sea from Genoa in the end."

"Did you?" Tonino said, wondering if the man thought it was his fault. "Where did you come from then?"

"Oh, England," said the man.

Tonino warmed to that. This then could not be the enchanter the Duke had talked about. Or could he? Tonino was not sure how far away enchanters could work from.

"Makes you feel better?" asked the man.

"Mother's English," Tonino admitted, feeling he was giving altogether too much away.

"Ah!" said the enchanter. "Now I know who you are. You're Antonio the Younger, aren't you? You were a baby when I saw you last, Tonino."

Since there is no reply to that kind of remark, Tonino was glad to see Old Niccolo hastening across the yard, followed by Aunt Francesca and Uncle Lorenzo, with Antonio and several more of the family hurrying behind them. They closed round the enchanter, leaving Tonino and Benvenuto beyond, by the gate.

"Yes, I've just come from the Casa Petrocchi," Tonino heard the stranger say. To his surprise, everyone accepted it, as if it were the most natural thing for the stranger to have done—as natural as the way he took off his ridiculous English hat to Aunt Francesca.

"But you'll stay the night with us," said Aunt Francesca.

"If it's not too much trouble," the stranger said.

In the distance, as if they already knew—as they unquestionably did in a place like the Casa Montana—Aunt Maria and Aunt Anna went clambering up the gallery steps to prepare the guest-room above. Aunt Gina emerged from the kitchen, held her hands up to Heaven, and dashed indoors again. Thoughtfully, Tonino gathered up Benvenuto and asked exactly who this stranger was.

Chrestomanci, of course, he was told. The most powerful enchanter in the world.

"Is he the one who's spoiling our spells?" Tonino asked suspiciously.

Chrestomanci, he was told—impatiently, because Benvenuto evidently thought Tonino was being very stupid—is always on our side.

Tonino looked at the stranger again—or rather, at his smooth dark head sticking out from among the shorter Montanas—and understood that Chrestomanci's coming meant there was a crisis indeed.

The stranger must have said something about him. Tonino found them all looking at him, his family smiling lovingly. He smiled back shyly.

"Oh, he's a good boy," said Aunt Francesca.

Then they all surged, talking, across the yard. "What makes it particularly difficult," Tonino heard Chrestomanci saying, "is that I am, first and foremost, an employee of the British Government. And Britain is keeping out of Italian affairs. But luckily I have a fairly wide brief."

Almost at once, Aunt Gina shot out of the kitchen again. She had cancelled the ordinary supper and started on a new one in honour of Chrestomanci. Six people were sent out at once for cakes and fruit, and two more for lettuce and cheese. Paolo, Corinna and Lucia were caught as they came in chatting from school and told to go at once to the butcher's. But, at this point, Rinaldo erupted furiously from the Scriptorium.

"What do you mean, sending all the kids off like this!" he bawled from the gallery. "We're up to our ears in war-spells here. I need copiers!"

Aunt Gina put her hands on her hips and bawled back at him. "And I need steak! Don't you stand up there cheeking me, Rinaldo Montana! English people always eat steak, so steak I must have!"

"Then cut pieces off the cats!" screamed Rinaldo. "I need Corinna and Lucia up here!"

"I tell you they are going to run after *me* for once!" yelled Aunt Gina.

"Dear me," said Chrestomanci, wandering into the yard. "What a very Italian scene! Can I help in any way?" He nodded and smiled from Aunt Gina to Rinaldo. Both of them smiled back, Rinaldo at his most charming.

"You would agree I need copiers, sir, wouldn't you?" he said.

"Bah!" said Aunt Gina. "Rinaldo turns on the charm and I get left to struggle alone! As usual! All right. Because it's war-spells, Paolo and Tonino can go for the steak. But wait while I write you a note, or you'll come back with something no one can chew."

"So glad to be of service," Chrestomanci murmured, and turned away to greet Elizabeth, who came racing down from the gallery waving a sheaf of music and fell into his arms. The heads of the five little cousins Elizabeth had been teaching stared wonderingly over the gallery rail. "Elizabeth!" said Chrestomanci. "Looking younger than ever!" Tonino stared as wonderingly as his cousins. His mother was laughing and crying at once. He could not follow the torrent of English speech. "Virtue," he heard, and "war" and, before long, the inevitable *"Angel of Caprona."* He was still staring when Aunt Gina stuck her note into his hand and told him to make haste.

As they hurried to the butcher's, Tonino said to Paolo, "I didn't know Mother knew anyone like Chrestomanci."

"Neither did I," Paolo confessed. He was only a year older than Tonino, after all, and it seemed that Chrestomanci had last been in Caprona a very long time ago. "Perhaps he's come to find the words to the *Angel,*" Paolo suggested. "I hope so. I don't want Rinaldo to have to go away and fight."

"Or Marco," Tonino agreed. "Or Carlo or Luigi or even Domenico."

Because of Aunt Gina's note, the butcher treated them with great respect. "Tell her this is the last good steak she'll see, if war is declared," he said, and he passed them each a heavy, squashy pink armload.

They arrived back with their armfuls just as a cab set down Uncle Umberto, puffing and panting, outside the Casa gate. "I am right, Chrestomanci *is* here? Eh, Paolo?" Uncle Umberto asked Tonino.

Both boys nodded. It seemed easier than explaining that Paolo was Tonino.

"Good, good!" exclaimed Uncle Umberto and surged into the Casa, where he found Chrestomanci just crossing the yard. "The *Angel of Caprona,*" Uncle Umberto said to him eagerly. "Could you—?"

"My dear Umberto," said Chrestomanci, shaking his hand warmly, "everyone here is asking me that. For that matter, so was everyone in the Casa Petrocchi too. And I'm afraid I know no more than you do. But I shall think about it, don't worry."

"If you could find just a line, to get us started," Uncle Umberto said pleadingly.

"I *will* do my best—" Chrestomanci was saying, when, with a great clattering of heels, Rosa shot past. From the look on her face, she had seen Marco arriving. "I promise you that," Chrestomanci said, as his head turned to see what Rosa was running for.

Marco came through the gate and stopped so dead, staring at Chrestomanci, that Rosa charged into him and nearly knocked him over. Marco staggered a bit, put his arms round Rosa, and went on staring at Chrestomanci. Tonino found himself holding his breath. Rinaldo was right. There *was* something about Marco. Chrestomanci knew it, and Marco knew he knew. From the look on Marco's face, he expected Chrestomanci to say what it was.

Chrestomanci indeed opened his mouth to say something, but he shut it again and pursed his lips in a sort of whistle instead. Marco looked at him uncertainly.

"Oh," said Uncle Umberto, "may I introduce—" He stopped and thought. Rosa he usually remembered, because of her fair hair, but he could not place Marco. "Corinna's fiancé," he suggested.

"I'm Rosa," said Rosa. "This is Marco Andretti."

"How do you do?" Chrestomanci said politely. Marco seemed to relax. Chrestomanci's eyes turned to Paolo and Tonino, standing staring. "Good heavens!" he said. "Everyone here seems to live such exciting lives. What have you boys killed?"

Paolo and Tonino looked down in consternation, to find that the steak was leaking on to their shoes. Two or three cats were approaching meaningly.

Aunt Gina appeared in the kitchen doorway. *"Where's my steak?"*

Paolo and Tonino sped towards her, leaving a pattering trail. "What was all that about?" Paolo panted to Tonino.

"I don't know," said Tonino, because he didn't, and because he liked Marco.

Aunt Gina shortly became very sharp and passionate about the steak. The leaking trail attracted every cat in the Casa. They were underfoot in the kitchen all evening, mewing pitifully. Benvenuto was also present, at a wary distance from Aunt Gina, and he made good use of his time. Aunt Gina erupted into the yard again, trumpeting.

"Tonino! *Ton-in-ooh!*"

Tonino laid down his book and hurried outside. "Yes, Aunt Gina?"

"That cat of yours has stolen a whole pound of steak!" Aunt Gina trumpeted, flinging a dramatic arm skyward.

Tonino looked, and there, sure enough, Benvenuto was, crouched on the pan-tiles of the roof, with one paw holding down quite a large lump of meat. "Oh dear," he said. "I don't think I can make him give it back, Aunt Gina."

"I don't want it back. Look where it's been!" screamed Aunt Gina.

"Tell him from me that I shall wring his evil neck if he comes near me again!"

"My goodness, you do seem to be at the centre of everything," Chrestomanci remarked, appearing beside Tonino in the yard. "Are you always in such demand?"

"I shall have hysterics," declared Aunt Gina. "And no one will get any supper." Elizabeth and Aunt Maria and Cousins Claudia and Teresa immediately came to her assistance and led her tenderly back indoors.

"Thank the Lord!" said Chrestomanci. "I'm not sure I could stand hysterics and starvation at once. How did you know I was an enchanter, Tonino? From Benvenuto?"

"No. I just knew when I looked at you," said Tonino.

"I see," said Chrestomanci. "This is interesting. Most people find it impossible to tell. It makes me wonder if Old Niccolo is right, when he talks of the virtue leaving your house. Would you be able to tell another enchanter when you looked at him, do you think?"

Tonino screwed up his face and wondered. "I might. It's the eyes. You mean, would I know the enchanter who's spoiling our spells?"

"I think I mean that," said Chrestomanci. "I'm beginning to believe there is someone. I'm sure, at least, that the spells on the Old Bridge were deliberately broken. Would it interfere with your plans too much, if I asked your grandfather to take you with him whenever he has to meet strangers?"

"I haven't got any plans," said Tonino. Then he thought, and he laughed. "I think you make jokes all the time."

"I aim to please," Chrestomanci said.

However, when Tonino next saw Chrestomanci, it was at supper—which was magnificent, despite Benvenuto and the hysterics—and Chrestomanci was very serious indeed. "My dear Niccolo," he said, "my mission *has* to concern the misuse of magic, not the balance of power in Italy. There would be no end of trouble if I was caught trying to stop a war."

Old Niccolo had his look of a baby about to cry. Aunt Francesca said, "We're not asking this personally—"

"But, my dear," said Chrestomanci, "don't you see that I can only do something like this as a personal matter? Please ask me personally. I shan't let the strict terms of my mission interfere with what I owe my friends." He smiled then, and his eyes swept round everyone gathered at the great table, very affectionately. He did not seem to exclude Marco. "So," he said, "I think my best plan for the moment is to go on to Rome. I know certain quarters there, where I can get impartial information, which should enable me to pin down this enchanter. At the moment, all we know is that he exists. If I'm lucky, I can prove whether Florence, or Siena, or Pisa is paying him—in which case, they and he can be indicted at the Court of Europe. And if, while I'm at it, I can get Rome, or Naples, to move on Caprona's behalf, be very sure I shall do it."

"Thank you," said Old Niccolo.

For the rest of supper, they discussed how Chrestomanci could best get to Rome. He would have to go by sea. It seemed that the last stretch of border, between Caprona and Siena, was now closed.

Much later that night, when Paolo and Tonino were on their way to bed, they saw lights in the Scriptorium. They tiptoed along to investigate. Chrestomanci was there with Antonio, Rinaldo and Aunt Francesca, going through spells in the big red books. Everyone was speaking in mutters, but they heard Chrestomanci say, "This is a sound combination, but it'll need new words." And on another page, "Get Elizabeth to put this in English, as a surprise-factor." And again, "Ignore the tune. The only tune which is going to be any use to you at the moment is the *Angel.* He can't block that."

"Why just those three?" Tonino whispered.

"They're best at making new spells," Paolo whispered back. "We need new war-spells. It sounds as if the other enchanter knows the old ones."

They crept to bed with an excited, urgent feeling, and neither of them found it easy to sleep.

Chrestomanci left the next morning before the children went to school. Benvenuto and Old Niccolo escorted him to the gate, one on either side, and the entire Casa gathered to wave him off. Things felt both flat and worrying once he was gone. That day, there was a great deal of talk of war at school. The teachers whispered together. Two had left, to join the Reserves. Rumours went round the classes. Someone told Tonino that war would be declared next Sunday, so that it would be a Holy War. Someone else told Paolo that all the Reserves had been issued with two left boots, so that they would not be able to fight. There was no truth in these things. It was just that everyone now knew that war was coming.

The boys hurried home, anxious for some real news. As usual, Benvenuto leapt off his waterbutt. While Tonino was enjoying Benvenuto's undivided attention again, Elizabeth called from the gallery, "Tonino! Someone's sent you a parcel."

Tonino and Benvenuto sprang for the gallery stairs, highly excited. Tonino had never had a parcel before. But before he got anywhere near it, he was seized on by Aunt Maria, Rosa and Uncle Lorenzo. They seized on all the children who could write and hurried them to the dining-room. This had been set up as another Scriptorium. By each chair was a special pen, a bottle of red war-ink and a pile of strips of paper. There the children were kept busy fully two hours, copying the same war-charm, again and again. Tonino had never been so frustrated in his life. He did not even know what shape his parcel was. He was not the only one to feel frustrated.

"Oh, why?" complained Lucia, Paolo and young Cousin Lena.

"I know," said Aunt Maria. "Like school again. Start writing."

"It's exploiting children, that's what we're doing," Rosa said cheerfully. "There are probably laws against it, so do complain."

"Don't worry, I will," said Lucia. "I am doing."

"As long as you write while you grumble," said Rosa.

"It's a new spell-scrip for the Army," Uncle Lorenzo explained. "It's very urgent."

"It's hard. It's all new words," Paolo grumbled.

"Your father made it last night," said Aunt Maria. "Get writing. We'll be watching for mistakes."

When finally, stiff-necked and with red splodges on their fingers, they were let out into the yard, Tonino discovered that he had barely time to unwrap the parcel before supper. Supper was early that night, so that the elder Montanas could put in another shift on the army-spells before bedtime.

"It's worse than working on the Old Bridge," said Lucia. "What's that, Tonino? Who sent it?"

The parcel was promisingly book-shaped. It bore the stamp and the arms of the University of Caprona. This was the only indication Tonino had that Uncle Umberto had sent it, for, when he wrenched off the thick brown paper, there was no letter, not even a card. There was only a new shiny book. Tonino's face beamed. At least Uncle Umberto knew this much about him. He turned the book lovingly over. It was called *The Boy Who Saved His Country,* and the cover was the same shiny, pimpled red leather as the great volumes of war-spells.

"Is Uncle Umberto trying to give you a hint, or something?" Paolo asked, amused. He and Lucia and Corinna leant over Tonino while he flipped through the pages. There were pictures, to Tonino's delight. Soldiers rode horses, soldiers rode machines; a boy hung from a rope and scrambled up the frowning wall of a fortress; and, most exciting of all, a boy stood on a rock with a flag, confronting a whole troop of ferocious-looking dragoons. Sighing with anticipation, Tonino turned to Chapter One: *How Giorgio uncovered an Enemy Plot.*

"*Supper!*" howled Aunt Gina from the yard. "Oh I shall go mad! Nobody attends to me!"

Tonino was forced to shut the lovely book again and hurry down to the dining-room. He watched Aunt Gina anxiously as she doled out minestrone. She looked so hectic that he was convinced Benvenuto must have been at work in the kitchen again.

"It's all right," Rosa said. "It's just she thought she'd got a line from the *Angel of Caprona.* Then the soup boiled over and she forgot it again."

Aunt Gina was distinctly tearful. "With so much to do, my memory is like a sieve," she kept saying. "Now I've let you all down."

"Of course you haven't, Gina my dear," said Old Niccolo. "This is nothing to worry about. It will come back to you."

"But I can't even remember what language it was in!" wailed Aunt Gina.

Everyone tried to console her. They sprinkled grated cheese on their soup and slurped it with special relish, to show Aunt Gina how much they appreciated her, but Aunt Gina continued to sniff and accuse herself. Then Rinaldo thought of pointing out that she had got further than anyone else in the Casa Montana. "None of the rest of us has any of the *Angel of Caprona* to forget," he said, giving Aunt Gina his best smile.

"Bah!" said Aunt Gina. "Turning on the charm, Rinaldo Montana!" But she seemed a good deal more cheerful after that.

Tonino was glad Benvenuto had nothing to do with it this time. He looked round for Benvenuto. Benvenuto usually took up a good position for stealing scraps, near the serving table. But tonight he was nowhere to be seen. Nor, for that matter, was Marco.

"Where's Marco?" Paolo asked Rosa.

Rosa smiled. She seemed quite cheerful about it. "He has to help his brother," she said, "with fortifications."

That brought home to Paolo and Tonino the fact that there was going to be a war. They looked at one another nervously. Neither of them was quite sure whether you behaved in the usual way in wartime, or not. Tonino's mind shot to his beautiful new book. *The Boy Who Saved His Country.* He slurped the title through his mind, just as he was slurping his soup. Had Uncle Umberto meant to say to him, find the words to the *Angel of Caprona,* and save your country, Tonino? It would indeed be the most marvellous thing if he, Tonino Montana, could find the words and save his country. He could hardly wait to see how the boy in the book had done it.

As soon as supper was over, he sprang up, ready to dash off and start reading. And once again he was prevented. This time it was because the children were told to wash up supper. Tonino groaned. And, again, he was not the only one.

"It isn't fair!" Corinna said passionately. "We slave all afternoon at spells, and we slave all evening at washing-up! I know there's going to be a war, but I still have to do my exams. How am I ever going to do my homework?" The way she flung out an impassioned arm made Paolo and Tonino think that Aunt Gina's manner must be catching.

Rather unexpectedly, Lucia sympathised with Corinna. "I think you're too old to be one of us children," she said. "Why don't you go away and do your homework and let me organize the kids?"

Corinna looked at her uncertainly. "What about your homework?"

"I've not got much. I'm not aiming for the University like you," Lucia said kindly. "Run along." And she pushed Corinna out of the dining-room. As soon as the door was shut, she turned briskly to the other children. "Come on. What are you lot standing gooping for? Everyone take a pile of plates to the kitchen. Quick march, Tonino. Move, Lena and Bernardo. Paolo, you take the big bowls."

With Lucia standing over them like a sergeant major, Tonino had no chance to slip away. He trudged to the kitchen with everyone else, where, to his surprise, Lucia ordered everyone to lay the plates and cutlery out in rows on the floor. Then she made them stand in a row themselves, facing the rows of greasy dishes.

Lucia was very pleased with herself. "Now," she said, "this is something I've always wanted to try. This is washing-up-made-easy, by Lucia Montana's patent method. I'll tell you the words. They go to the *Angel of Caprona.* And you're all to sing after me—"

"Are you sure we should?" asked Lena, who was a very law-abiding cousin.

Lucia gave her a look of scalding contempt. "If some people," she remarked to the whitewashed beams of the ceiling, "don't know true intelligence when they see it, they are quite at liberty to go and live with the Petrocchis."

"I only asked," Lena said, crushed.

"Well, don't," said Lucia. "This is the spell. . . ."

Shortly, they were all singing lustily:

"Angel, clean our knives and dishes,
Clean our spoons and salad-bowls,
Wash our saucepans, hear our wishes,
Angel, make our forks quite clean."

At first, nothing much seemed to happen. Then it became clear that the orange grease was certainly slowly clearing from the plates. Then the lengths of spaghetti stuck to the bottom of the largest saucepan started unwinding and wriggling like worms. Up over the edge of the saucepan they wriggled, and over the stone floor, to ooze themselves into the waste-cans. The orange grease and the salad-oil travelled after them, in rivulets. And the singing faltered a little, as people broke off to laugh.

"Sing, *sing*!" shouted Lucia. So they sang.

Unfortunately for Lucia, the noise penetrated to the Scriptorium. The plates were still pale pink and rather greasy, and the last of the spaghetti was still wriggling across the floor, when Elizabeth and Aunt Maria burst into the kitchen.

"Lucia!" said Elizabeth.

"You irreligious brats!" said Aunt Maria.

"I don't see what's so wrong," said Lucia.

"She doesn't see—Elizabeth, words fail!" said Aunt Maria. "How can I have taught her so little and so badly? Lucia, a spell is not *instead* of a thing. It is only to *help* that thing. And on top of that, you go and use the *Angel of Caprona,* as if it was any old tune, and not the most powerful song in all Italy! I—I could box your ears, Lucia!"

"So could I," said Elizabeth. "Don't you understand we need all our virtue—the whole combined strength of the Casa Montana—to put into the war-charms? And here you go frittering it away in the kitchen!"

"Put those plates in the sink, Paolo," ordered Aunt Maria. "Tonino, pick up those saucepans. The rest of you pick up the cutlery. And now you'll wash them properly."

Very chastened, everyone obeyed. Lucia was angry as well as chastened. When Lena whispered, "I *told* you so!" Lucia broke a plate and jumped on the pieces.

"Lucia!" snapped Aunt Maria, glaring at her. It was the first time any of the children had seen her look likely to slap someone.

"Well, how was I to know?" Lucia stormed. "Nobody ever explained—nobody *told* me spells were like that!"

"Yes, but you knew perfectly well you were doing something you shouldn't," Elizabeth told her, "even if you didn't know why. The rest of you, stop sniggering. Lena, you can learn from this too."

All through doing the washing-up properly—which took nearly an hour—Tonino was saying to himself, "And *then* I can read my book at last." When it was finally done, he sped out into the yard. And there was Old Niccolo hurrying down the steps to meet him in the dark.

"Tonino, may I have Benvenuto for a while, please?"

But Benvenuto was still not to be found. Tonino began to think he would die of book-frustration. All the children joined in hunting and calling, but there was still no Benvenuto. Soon, most of the grown-ups were looking for him too, and still Benvenuto did not appear. Antonio was so exasperated that he seized Tonino's arm and shook him.

"It's too bad, Tonino! You must have known we'd need Benvenuto. Why did you let him go?"

"I didn't! You *know* what Benvenuto's like!" Tonino protested, equally exasperated.

"Now, now, now," said Old Niccolo, taking each of them by a shoulder. "It is quite plain by now that Benvenuto is on the other side of town, making vile noises on a roof somewhere. All we can do is hope someone empties a jug of water on him soon. It's not Tonino's fault, Antonio."

Antonio let go Tonino's arm and rubbed both hands on his face. He looked very tired. "I'm sorry, Tonino," he said. "Forgive me. Let us know as soon as Benvenuto comes back, won't you?"

He and Old Niccolo hurried back to the Scriptorium. As they passed under the light, their faces were stiff with worry.

"I don't think I like war, Tonino," Paolo said. "Let's go and play table-tennis in the dining-room."

"I'm going to read my book," Tonino said firmly. He thought he would get like Aunt Gina if anything else happened to stop him.

CHAPTER 6

Tonino read half the night. With all the grown-ups hard at work in the Scriptorium, there was no one to tell him to go to bed. Corinna tried, when she had finished her homework, but Tonino was too deep in the book even to hear her. And Corinna went respectfully away, thinking that, as the book had come from Uncle Umberto, it was probably very learned.

It was not in the least learned. It was the most gripping story Tonino had ever read. It started with the boy, Giorgio, going along a mysterious alleyway near the docks on his way home from school. There was a peeling blue house at the end of the alley and, just as Giorgio passed it, a scrap of paper fluttered from one of its windows. It contained a mysterious message, which led Giorgio at once into a set of adventures with the enemies of his country. Each one was more exciting than the last.

Well after midnight, when Giorgio was holding a pass single-handed against the enemy, Tonino happened to hear his father and mother coming to bed. He was forced to leave Giorgio lying wounded and dive into bed himself. All night he dreamt of notes fluttering from the windows of peeling blue houses, of Giorgio—who was sometimes Tonino himself and sometimes Paolo—and of villainous enemies—most of whom seemed to have red beards and black hair, like Guido Petrocchi—and, as the sun rose, he was too excited to stay asleep. He woke up and went on reading.

When the rest of the Casa Montana began to stir, Tonino had finished the book. Giorgio had saved his country. Tonino was quivering with excitement and exhaustion. He wished the book was twice as long.

If it had not been time to get up, he would have gone straight back to the beginning and started reading the book again.

And the beauty of it, he thought, eating breakfast without noticing, was that Giorgio had saved his country, not only single-handed, but without a spell coming into it anywhere. If Tonino was going to save Caprona, that was the way he would like to do it.

Around Tonino, everyone else was complaining and Lucia was sulking. The washing-up spell was still about in the kitchen. Every cup and plate was covered with a thin layer of orange spaghetti grease, and the butter tasted of soap.

"What did she *use,* in Heaven's name?" groaned Uncle Lorenzo. "This coffee tastes of tomato."

"Her own words to the *Angel of Caprona,*" Aunt Maria said, and shuddered as she picked up her greasy cup.

"Lucia, you fool!" said Rinaldo. "That's the strongest tune there is."

"All right, all right. Stop going on at me. I'm sorry!" Lucia said angrily.

"So are the rest of us, unfortunately," sighed Uncle Lorenzo.

If only I could be like Giorgio, Tonino thought, as he got up from the table. I suppose what I should have to do is to find the words to the *Angel.* He went to school without seeing anything on the way, wondering how he could manage to do that, when the rest of his family had failed. He was realistic enough to know that he was simply not good enough at spells to make up the words in the ordinary way. It made him sigh heavily.

"Cheer up," said Paolo, as they went into school.

"I'm all right," Tonino said. He was surprised Paolo should think he was miserable. He was not miserable at all. He was wrapped in delightful dreams. Maybe I can do it by accident, he thought.

He sat in class composing strings of gibberish to the tune of the *Angel,* in hopes that some of it might be right. But that did not seem satisfactory, somehow. Then, in a lesson that was probably History—for he did not hear a word of it—it struck him, like a blinding light, what he had to do. He had to *find* the words, of course. The First Duke must have had them written down somewhere and lost the paper. Tonino was the boy whose mission it was to discover that lost paper. No nonsense about making up words, just straight detective work. And Tonino was positive that the book had been a clue. He must find a peeling blue house, and the paper with the words on would be somewhere near.

"Tonino," asked the teacher, for the fourth time, "where did Marco Polo journey to?"

Tonino did not hear the question, but he realised he was being asked something. *"The Angel of Caprona,"* he said.

Nobody at school got much sense out of Tonino that day. He was full of the wonder of his discovery. It did not occur to him that Uncle Umberto had looked in every piece of writing in the University Library, and not found the words to the *Angel*. Tonino knew.

After school, he avoided Paolo and his cousins. As soon as they were safely headed for the Casa Montana, Tonino set off in the opposite direction, towards the docks and quays by the New Bridge.

An hour later, Rosa said to Paolo, "What's the matter with Benvenuto? Look at him."

Paolo leant over the gallery rail beside her. Benvenuto, looking surprisingly small and piteous, was running backwards and forwards just inside the gate, mewing frantically. Every so often, as if he was too distracted to know what he was doing, he sat down, shot out a hind leg, and licked it madly. Then he leapt up and ran about again.

Paolo had never seen Benvenuto behave like this. He called out, "Benvenuto, what's the matter?"

Benvenuto swung round, crouching low on the ground, and stared urgently up at him. His eyes were like two yellow beacons of distress. He gave a string of mews, so penetrating and so demanding that Paolo felt his stomach turn uneasily.

"What *is* it, Benvenuto?" called Rosa.

Benvenuto's tail flapped in exasperation. He gave a great leap and vanished somewhere out of sight. Rosa and Paolo hung by their midriffs over the rail and craned after him. Benvenuto was now standing on the waterbutt, with his tail slashing. As soon as he knew they could see him, he stared fixedly at them again and uttered a truly appalling noise.

Wong wong wong wong-wong-wong!

Paolo and Rosa, without more ado, swung towards the stairs and clattered down them. Benvenuto's wails had already attracted all the other cats in the Casa. They were running across the yard and dropping from roofs before Paolo and Rosa were halfway down the stairs. They were forced to step carefully to the waterbutt among smooth furry bodies and staring, anxious green or yellow eyes.

"Mee-ow-ow!" Benvenuto said peremptorily, when they reached him.

He was thinner and browner than Paolo had ever seen him. There was a new rent in his left ear, and his coat was in ragged spikes. He looked truly wretched. "Mee-ow-ow!" he reiterated, from a wide pink mouth.

"Something's wrong," Paolo said uneasily. "He's trying to say something." Guiltily, he wished he had kept his resolution to learn to understand Benvenuto. But when Tonino could do it so easily, it had never been worth the bother. Now here was Benvenuto with an urgent message—perhaps word from Chrestomanci—and he could not understand it. "We'd better get Tonino," he said.

Benvenuto's tail slashed again. "Mee-ow-ow!" he said, with tremendous force and meaning. Around Paolo and Rosa, the pink mouths of all the other cats opened too. "MEE-OW-OW!" It was deafening. Paolo stared helplessly.

It was Rosa who tumbled to their meaning. "Tonino!" she exclaimed. "They're saying *Tonino*! Paolo, where's Tonino?"

With a jolt of worry, Paolo realised he had not seen Tonino since breakfast. And as soon as he realised that, Rosa knew it too. And, such was the nature of the Casa Montana, that the alarm was given then and there. Aunt Gina shot out of the kitchen, holding a pair of kitchen tongs in one hand and a ladle in the other. Domenico and Aunt Maria came out of the Saloon, and Elizabeth appeared in the gallery outside the Music Room with the five little cousins. The door of the Scriptorium opened, filled with anxious faces.

Benvenuto gave a whisk of his tail and leapt for the gallery steps. He bounded up them, followed by the other cats; and Paolo and Rosa hurried up too, in a sort of shoal of leaping black and white bodies. Everyone converged on Antonio's rooms. People poured out of the Scriptorium, Elizabeth raced round the gallery, and Aunt Maria and Aunt Gina clambered up the steps by the kitchen quicker than either had ever climbed in her life. The Casa filled with the sound of hollow running feet.

The whole family jammed themselves after Rosa and Paolo into the room where Tonino was usually to be found reading. There was no Tonino, only the red book lying on the window-sill. It was no longer shiny. The pages were thick at the edges and the red cover was curling upwards, as if the book was wet.

Benvenuto, with his jagged brown coat up in a ridge along his back and his tail fluffed like a fox's brush, landed on the sill beside the book and rashly put his nose forward to sniff at it. He leapt back again, shaking his head, crouching, and growling like a dog. Smoke poured up from the book. People coughed and cats sneezed. The book curled and writhed on the sill, amid clouds of smoke, exactly as if it were on fire. But instead of turning black, it turned pale grey-blue where it smoked, and looked slimy. The room filled with a smell of rotting.

"Ugh!" said everybody.

Old Niccolo barged members of his family right and left to get near it. He stood over it and sang, in a strong tenor voice almost as good as Marco's, three strange words. He sang them twice before he had to break off coughing. "Sing!" he croaked, with tears pouring down his face. "All of you."

All the Montanas obediently broke into song, three long notes in unison. And again. And again. After that, quite a number of them had to cough, though the smoke was distinctly less. Old Niccolo recovered and waved his arms, like the conductor of a choir. All who could, sang once more. It took ten repetitions to halt the decay of the book. By that time, it was a shrivelled triangle, about half the size it had been. Gingerly, Antonio leant over and opened the window beyond it, to let out the last of the smoke.

"What was it?" he asked Old Niccolo. "Someone trying to suffocate us all?"

"I thought it came from Umberto," Elizabeth faltered. "I never would have—"

Old Niccolo shook his head. "This thing never came from Umberto. And I don't think it was meant to kill. Let's see what kind of spell it is." He snapped his fingers and held out a hand, rather like a surgeon performing an operation. Without needing to be told, Aunt Gina put her kitchen tongs into his hand. Carefully, gently, Old Niccolo used the tongs to open the cover of the book.

"A good pair of tongs ruined," Aunt Gina said.

"Ssh!" said Old Niccolo. The shrivelled pages of the book had stuck into a gummy block. He snapped his fingers and held out his hand again. This time, Rinaldo put the pen he was carrying in it.

"And a good pen," he said, with a grimace at Aunt Gina.

With the pen as well as the tongs, Old Niccolo was able to pry the pages of the book apart without touching them and peel them over, one by one. Chins rested on both Paolo's shoulders as everyone craned to see, and there were chins on the shoulders of those with the chins. There was no sound but the sound of breathing.

On nearly every page, the printing had melted away, leaving a slimy, leathery surface quite unlike paper, with only a mark or so left in the middle. Old Niccolo looked closely at each mark and grunted. He grunted again at the first picture, which had faded like the print, but left a clearer mark. After that, though there was no print on any of the pages, the remaining mark was steadily clearer, up to the centre of the book, when it began to become more faded again, until the mark was barely visible on the back page.

Old Niccolo laid down the pen and the tongs in terrible silence.

"Right through," he said at length. People shifted and someone coughed, but nobody said anything. "I do not know," said Old Niccolo, "the substance this object is made of, but I know a calling-charm when I see one. Tonino must have been like one hypnotised, if he had read all this."

"He *was* a bit strange at breakfast," Paolo whispered.

"I am sure he was," said his grandfather. He looked reflectively at the shrivelled stump of the book and then round at the crowded faces of his family. "Now who," he asked softly, "would want to set a strong calling-charm on Tonino Montana? Who would be mean enough to pick on a child? Who would—?" He turned suddenly on Benvenuto, crouched beside the book, and Benvenuto cowered right down, quivering, with his ragged ears flat against his flat head. "Where were you last night, Benvenuto?" he asked, more softly still.

No one understood the reply Benvenuto gave as he cowered, but everyone knew the answer. It was in Antonio and Elizabeth's harrowed faces, in the set of Rinaldo's chin, in Aunt Francesca's narrowed eyes, narrowed almost out of existence, and in the way Aunt Maria looked at Uncle Lorenzo; but most of all, it was in the way Benvenuto threw himself down on his side, with his back to the room, the picture of a cat in despair.

Old Niccolo looked up. "Now isn't that odd?" he said gently. "Benvenuto spent last night chasing a white she-cat—over the roofs of the Casa Petrocchi." He paused to let that sink in. "So Benvenuto," he said, "who knows a bad spell when he sees one, was not around to warn Tonino."

"But *why*?" Elizabeth asked despairingly.

Old Niccolo went, if possible, quieter still. "I can only conclude, my dear, that the Petrocchis are being paid by Florence, Siena, or Pisa."

There was another silence, thick and meaningful. Antonio broke it. "Well," he said, in such a subdued, grim way that Paolo stared at him. "Well? Are we going?"

"Of course," said Old Niccolo. "Domenico, fetch me my small black spell-book."

Everyone left the room, so suddenly, quietly and purposefully that Paolo was left behind, not clear what was going on. He turned uncertainly to go to the door, and realised that Rosa had been left behind too. She was sitting on Tonino's bed, with one hand to her head, white as Tonino's sheets.

"Paolo," she said, "tell Claudia I'll have the baby, if she wants to go. I'll have all the little ones."

She looked up at Paolo as she said it, and she looked so strange that Paolo was suddenly frightened. He ran gladly out into the gallery. The family was gathering, still quiet and grim, in the yard. Paolo ran down there and gave his message. Protesting little ones were pushed up the steps to Rosa, but Paolo did not help. He found Elizabeth and Lucia and pushed close to them. Elizabeth put an arm round him and an arm round Lucia.

"Keep close to me, loves," she said. "I'll keep you safe." Paolo looked across her at Lucia and saw that Lucia was not frightened at all. She was excited. She winked at him. Paolo winked back and felt better.

A minute later, Old Niccolo took his place at the head of the family and they all hurried to the gate. Paolo had just forced his way through, jostling his mother on one side and Domenico on the other, when a carriage drew up in the road, and Uncle Umberto scrambled out of it. He came up to Old Niccolo in that grim, quiet way everyone seemed to be moving.

"Who is kidnapped? Bernardo? Domenico?"

"Tonino," replied Old Niccolo. "A book, with the University arms on the wrapping."

Uncle Umberto answered, "Luigi Petrocchi is also a member of the University."

"I bear that in mind," said Old Niccolo.

"I shall come with you to the Casa Petrocchi," said Uncle Umberto. He waved at the cab-driver to tell him to go. The man was only too ready to. He nearly pulled his horses over on their sides, trying to turn them too quickly. The sight of the entire Casa Montana grimly streaming into the street seemed altogether too much for him.

That pleased Paolo. He looked back and forth as they swung down the Via Magica, and pride grew in him. There were such a lot of them. And they were so single-minded. The same intent look was in every face. And though children pattered and young men strode, though the ladies clattered on the cobbles in elegant shoes, though Old Niccolo's steps were short and bustling, and Antonio, because he could not wait to come at the Petrocchis, walked with long lunging steps, the common purpose gave the whole family a common rhythm. Paolo could almost believe they were marching in step.

The concourse crowded down the Via Sant' Angelo and swept round the corner into the Corso, with the Cathedral at their backs. People out shopping hastily gave them room. But Old Niccolo was too angry to use the pavement like a mere pedestrian. He led the family into the middle of the road and they marched there like a vengeful army, forcing cars and carriages to draw into the kerbs, with Old Niccolo stepping proudly at their head. It was hard to believe that a fat old man with a baby's face could look so warlike.

The Corso bends slightly beyond the Archbishop's Palace. Then it runs straight again by the shops, past the columns of the Art Gallery on one side and the great gilded doors of the Arsenal on the other. They swung round that bend. There, approaching from the opposite direction, was another similar crowd, also walking in the road. The Petrocchis were on the march too.

"Extraordinary!" muttered Uncle Umberto.

"Perfect!" spat Old Niccolo.

The two families advanced on one another. There was utter silence now, except for the cloppering of feet. Every ordinary citizen, as soon as they saw the entire Casa Montana advancing on the entire Casa Petrocchi, made haste to get off the street. People knocked on the doors of perfect strangers and were let in without question. The manager of Grossi's, the biggest shop in Caprona, threw open his plate-glass doors and sent his assistants out to fetch in everyone nearby. After which he clapped the doors shut and locked a steel grille down in front of them. From between the bars, white faces stared out at the oncoming spell-makers. And a troop of Reservists, newly called up and sloppily marching in crumpled new uniforms, were horrified to find themselves caught between the two parties. They broke and ran, as one crumpled Reservist, and sought frantic shelter in the Arsenal. The great gilt doors clanged shut on them just as Old Niccolo halted, face to face with Guido Petrocchi.

"Well?" said Old Niccolo, his baby eyes glaring.

"Well?" retorted Guido, his red beard jutting.

"Was it," asked Old Niccolo, "Florence or Pisa that paid you to kidnap my grandson Tonino?"

Guido Petrocchi gave a bark of contemptuous laughter. "You mean," he said, "was it Pisa or Siena who paid *you* to kidnap my daughter Angelica?"

"Do you imagine," said Old Niccolo, "that saying that makes it any less obvious that you are a baby-snatcher?"

"Do you," asked Guido, "accuse me of lying?"

"Yes!" roared the Casa Montana. *"Liar!"*

"And the same to you!" howled the Casa Petrocchi, crowding up behind Guido, lean and ferocious, many of them red-haired. *"Filthy liars!"*

The fighting began while they were still shouting. There was no knowing who started it. The roars on either side were mixed with singing and muttering. Scrips fluttered in many hands. And the air was suddenly full of flying eggs. Paolo received one, a very greasy fried egg, right across the mouth, and it made him so angry that he began to shout egg-spells too, at the top of his voice. Eggs splattered down, fried eggs, poached eggs, scrambled eggs, new-laid eggs, and eggs so horribly bad that they were like bombs when they burst. Everyone slithered on the eggy cobbles. Egg streamed off the ends of people's hair and spattered everyone's clothes.

Then somebody varied it with a bad tomato or so. Immediately, all manner of unpleasant things were flying about the Corso: cold spaghetti and cowpats—though these may have been Rinaldo's idea in the first place, they were very quickly coming from both sides—and cabbages; squirts of oil and showers of ice; dead rats and chicken-livers. It was no wonder that the ordinary people kept out of the way. Egg and tomato ran down the grilles over Grossi's windows and splashed the white columns of the Art Gallery. There were loud clangs as rotten cabbages hit the brass doors of the Arsenal.

This was the first, disorganized phase of the battle, with everyone venting his fury separately. But, by the time everyone was filthy and sticky, their fury took shape a little. Both sides began on a more organized chant. It grew, and became two strong rhythmic choruses.

The result was that the objects flying about the Corso rose up into the air and began to rain down as much more harmful things. Paolo looked up to see a cloud of transparent, glittering, frozen-looking pieces tumbling out of the sky at him. He thought it was snow at first, until a piece hit his arm and cut it.

"Vicious beasts!" Lucia screamed beside him. "It's broken glass!"

Before the main body of the glass came down, Old Niccolo's penetrating tenor voice soared above the yells and the chanting. "Testudo!"

Antonio's full bass backed him up: "Testudo!" and so did Uncle Lorenzo's baritone. Feet tramped. Paolo knew this one. He bowed over, tramping regularly, and kept up the charm with them. The whole family did it. *Tramp, tramp, tramp.* "Testudo, testudo, testudo!" Over their bent heads, the glass splinters bounced and showered harmlessly off an invisible barrier. "Testudo." From the middle of the bowed backs, Elizabeth's voice rang up sweetly in yet another spell. She was joined by Aunt Anna, Aunt Maria and Corinna. It was like a soprano descant over a rhythmic tramping chorus.

Paolo knew without being told that he must keep up the shield-charm while Elizabeth worked her spell. So did everyone else. It was extraordinary, exciting, amazing, he thought. Each Montana picked up the slightest hint and acted on it as if it were orders. He risked glancing up and saw that the descant spell was working. Every glass splinter, as it hit the unseen shield Paolo was helping to make, turned into an angry hornet and buzzed back at the Petrocchis. But the Petrocchis simply turned them into glass splinters again and hurled them back. At the same time, Paolo could tell from the rhythm of their singing that some of them were working to destroy the shield charm. Paolo sang and tramped harder than ever.

Meanwhile, Rinaldo's voice and his father's were singing gently, deeply, at work on something yet again. More of the ladies joined in the hornet-song so that the Petrocchis would not guess. And all the while, the tramp, tramp of the shield charm was kept up by everyone else. It could have been the grandest chorus in the grandest opera ever, except that it all had a different purpose. The purpose came with a perfect roar of voices. The Petrocchis threw up their arms and staggered. The cobbles beneath them heaved and the solid Corso began to give way into a pit. Their instant reply was another huge sung chord, with discords innumerable. And the Montanas suddenly found themselves inside a wall of flame.

There was total confusion. Paolo staggered for safety, with his hair singed, over cobbles that quaked and heaved under his shoes. "Voltava!" he sang frantically. "Voltava!" Behind him, the flames hissed. Clouds of steam blotted out even the tall Art Gallery as the river answered the charm and came swirling up the Corso. Water was knee-deep round Paolo, up to his waist, and still rising. There was too much water. Someone had sung out of tune, and Paolo rather thought it was him. He saw his cousin Lena almost up to her chin in water and grabbed her. Towing Lena, he staggered through the current, over the heaving road, trying to make for the Arsenal steps.

Someone must have had the sense to work a cancel-spell. Everything suddenly cleared, steam, water and smoke together. Paolo found himself on the steps of the Art Gallery, not by the Arsenal at all. Behind him, the Corso was a mass of loose cobbles, shiny with mud and littered with cowpats, tomatoes and fried eggs. There could hardly have been more mess if Caprona had been invaded by the armies of Florence, Pisa and Siena.

Paolo felt he had had enough. Lena was crying. She was too young. She should have been left with Rosa. He could see his mother picking Lucia out of the mud, and Rinaldo helping Aunt Gina up.

"Let's go home, Paolo," whimpered Lena.

But the battle was not really finished. Montanas and Petrocchis were up and down the Corso in little angry, muddy groups, shouting abuse at one another.

"I'll give you broken glass!"

"You started it!"

"You lying Petrocchi swine! Kidnapper!"

"Swine yourself! Spell-bungler! Traitor!"

Aunt Gina and Rinaldo slithered over to what looked like a muddy boulder in the street and heaved at it. The vast bulk of Aunt Francesca arose, covered with mud and angrier than Paolo had ever seen her.

"You filthy Petrocchis! I demand single combat!" she screamed. Her voice scraped like a great saw-blade and filled the Corso.

CHAPTER 7

Aunt Francesca's challenge seemed to rally both sides. A female Petrocchi voice screamed, "We agree!" and all the muddy groups hastened towards the middle of the Corso again.

Paolo reached his family to hear Old Niccolo saying, "Don't be a fool, Francesca!" He looked more like a muddy goblin than the head of a famous family. He was almost too breathless to speak.

"They have insulted us and fought us!" said Aunt Francesca. "They deserve to be disgraced and drummed out of Caprona. And I shall do it! I'm more than a match for a Petrocchi!" She looked it, vast and muddy as she was, with her huge black dress in tatters and her grey hair half undone and streaming over one shoulder.

But the other Montanas knew Aunt Francesca was an old woman. There was a chorus of protest. Uncle Lorenzo and Rinaldo both offered to take on the Petrocchi champion in her place.

"No," said Old Niccolo. "Rinaldo, you were wounded—"

He was interrupted by catcalls from the Petrocchis. "Cowards! We want single combat!"

Old Niccolo's muddy face screwed up with anger. "Very well, they shall have their single combat," he said. "Antonio, I appoint you. Step forward."

Paolo felt a gush of pride. So his father was, as he had always thought, the best spell-maker in the Casa Montana. But the pride became mixed with alarm, when Paolo saw the way his mother clutched Antonio's arm, and the worried, reluctant look on his father's mud-streaked face.

"Go on!" Old Niccolo said crossly.

Slowly, Antonio advanced into the space between the two families, stumbling a little among the loose cobbles. "I'm ready," he called to the Petrocchis. "Who's your champion?"

It was clear that there was some indecision among the Petrocchis. A dismayed voice said, "It's *Antonio*!" This was followed by a babble of talk. From the turning of heads and the uncertain heaving about, Paolo thought they were looking for a Petrocchi who was unaccountably missing. But the fuss died away, and Guido Petrocchi himself stepped forward. Paolo could see several Petrocchis looking as alarmed as Elizabeth.

"I'm ready too," said Guido, baring his teeth angrily. Since his face was plastered with mud, it made him look quite savage. He was also large and sturdy. He made Antonio look small, gentle and fragile. "And I demand an unlimited contest!" snarled Guido. He seemed even angrier than Old Niccolo.

"Very well," Antonio said. There could have been the least shake in his voice. "You're aware that means a fight to the finish, are you?"

"Suits me perfectly," said Guido. He was like a giant saying "Fee-fi-fo-fum." Paolo was suddenly very frightened.

It was at this moment that the Ducal Police arrived. They had come in, quietly and cunningly, riding bicycles along the pavements. No one noticed them until the Chief of Police and his lieutenant were standing beside the two champions.

"Guido Petrocchi and Antonio Montana," said the lieutenant, "I arrest you—"

Both champions jumped, and turned to find blue braided uniforms on either side of them.

"Oh go away," said Old Niccolo, hastening forward. "What do you have to interfere for?"

"Yes, go away," said Guido. "We're busy."

The lieutenant flinched at Guido's face, but the Chief of Police was a bold and dashing man with a handsome moustache, and he had his reputation to keep up as a bold and dashing man. He bowed to Old Niccolo. "These two are under arrest," he said. "The rest of you I order to sink your differences and remember there is about to be a war."

"We're at war already," said Old Niccolo. "Go away."

"I regret," said the Chief of Police, "that that is impossible."

"Then don't say you weren't warned," said Guido.

There was a short burst of song from the adults of both families. Paolo wished he knew that spell. It sounded useful. As soon as it was over, Rinaldo and a swarthy young Petrocchi came over to the two policemen and towed them away backwards. They were as stiff as the tailor's dummies in the barred windows of Grossi's. Rinaldo and the other young man laid them against the steps of the Art Gallery and returned each to his family, without looking at one another. As for the rest of the Ducal Police, they seemed to have vanished, bicycles and all.

"Ready now?" said Guido.

"Ready," said Antonio.

And the single combat commenced.

Looking back on it afterwards, Paolo realised that it could not have lasted more than three minutes, though it seemed endless at the time. For, in that time, the strength, skill and speed of both champions was tried to the utmost. The first, and probably the longest, part was when the two were testing one another for an opening, and comparatively little seemed to happen. Both stood, leaning slightly forward, muttering, humming, occasionally flicking a hand. Paolo stared at his father's strained face and wondered just what was going on. Then, momentarily, Guido was a man-shaped red-and-white check duster. Someone gasped. But Antonio almost simultaneously became a cardboard man covered with green triangles. Then both flicked back to themselves again.

The speed of it astounded Paolo. A spell had not only been cast on both sides, but also a counter-spell, and a spell counter to that, all in the time it took someone to gasp. Both combatants were panting and looking warily at each other. It was clear they were very evenly matched.

Again there was a space when nothing seemed to happen, except a sort of flickering on both sides. Then suddenly Antonio struck, and struck so hard that it was plain he had all the time been building a strong spell, beneath the flicker of trivial spells designed to keep Guido occupied. Guido gave a shout and dissolved into dust, which swept away backwards in a spiral. But, somehow, as he dissolved, he threw *his* strong spell at Antonio. Antonio broke into a thousand little pieces, like a spilt jigsaw puzzle.

For an ageless time, the swirl of dust and the pile of broken Antonio hung in mid-air. Both were struggling to stay together and not to patter down on the uprooted cobbles of the Corso. In fact, they were still struggling to make spells too. When, at last, Antonio staggered forward in one piece, holding some kind of red fruit in his right hand, he had barely time to dodge. Guido was a leopard in mid-spring.

Elizabeth screamed.

Antonio threw himself to one side, heaved a breath and sang. *"Oliphans!"* His usually silky voice was rough and ragged, but he hit the right notes. A gigantic elephant, with tusks longer than Paolo was tall, cut off the low sun and shook the Corso as it advanced, ears spread, to trample the attacking leopard. It was hard to believe the great beast was indeed worried, thin Antonio Montana.

For a shadow of a second, the leopard was Guido Petrocchi, very white in the face and luridly red in the beard, gabbling a frantic song: "*Hickory-dickory-muggery mus!*" And he must have hit the right notes too. He seemed to vanish.

The Montanas were raising a cheer at Guido's cowardice, when the elephant panicked. Paolo had the merest glimpse of a little tiny mouse scampering aggressively at the great front feet of the elephant, before he was running for his life. The shrill trumpeting of Antonio seemed to tear his ears apart. Behind him, Paolo knew that the elephant was stark, staring mad, trampling this way and that among terrified Montanas. Lucia ran past him, carrying Lena clutched backwards against her front. Paolo grabbed little Bernardo by one arm and ran with him, wincing at the horrible brazen, braying squeal from his father.

Elephants are afraid of mice, horribly afraid. And there are very few people who can shift shape without taking the nature of the shape they shift to. It seemed that Guido Petrocchi had not only won, but got most of the Montanas trampled to death into the bargain.

But when Paolo next looked, Elizabeth was standing in the elephant's path, staring up at its wild little eyes. "Antonio!" she shouted. "*Antonio*, control yourself!" She looked so tiny and the elephant was coming so fast that Paolo shut his eyes.

He opened them in time to see the elephant in the act of swinging his mother up on to its back. Tears of relief so clouded Paolo's eyes that he almost failed to see Guido's next attack. He was simply aware of a shattering noise, a horrible smell, and a sort of moving tower. He saw the elephant swing round, and Elizabeth crouch down on its back. It was now being confronted by a vast iron machine, even larger than itself, throbbing with mechanical power and filling the Corso with nasty blue smoke. This thing ground slowly towards Antonio on huge moving tracks. As it came, a gun in its front swung down to aim between the elephant's eyes.

On the spur of the moment, Antonio became another machine. He was in such a hurry, and he knew so little about machines, that it was a very bizarre machine indeed. It was pale duck-egg blue, with enormous rubber wheels. In fact, it was probably made of rubber all through, because the bullet from Guido's machine bounced off it and crashed into the steps of the Arsenal. Most people threw themselves flat.

"Mother's *inside* that thing!" Lucia screamed to Paolo, above the noise.

Paolo realised she must be. Antonio had had no time to put Elizabeth down. And now he was barging recklessly at Guido, *bang*-bounce, *bang*-bounce. It must have been horrible for Elizabeth. Luckily, it only lasted a second. Elizabeth and Antonio suddenly appeared in their own shapes, almost under the mighty tracks of the Guido-machine. Elizabeth ran—Paolo had not known she could run so fast—like the wind towards the Arsenal. And it may have been Petrocchi viciousness, or perhaps simple confusion, but the great Guido-tank swung its gun down to point at Elizabeth.

Antonio called Guido a very bad name, and threw the tomato he still had in his hand. The red fruit hit, and splashed, and ran down the iron side. Paolo was just wondering what use that was, when the tank was not there any more. Nor was Guido. In his place was a giant tomato. It was about the size of a pumpkin. And it simply sat in the road and did not move.

That was the winning stroke. Paolo could tell it was from the look on Antonio's face as he walked up to the tomato. Disgusted and weary, Antonio bent down to pick up the tomato. There were scattered groans from the Petrocchis, and cheers, not quite certain and even more scattered, from the Montanas.

Then somebody cast yet another spell.

This time, it was a thick wet fog. No doubt, at the beginning, it would not have seemed so terrible, but, after all the rest, just when the fight was over, Paolo felt it was the last straw. All he could see, in front of his eyes, was thick whiteness. After he had taken a breath or so, he was coughing. He could hear coughing all round, and far off into the distance, which was the only thing which showed him he was not entirely alone. He turned his head from trying to see who else was coughing, and found he could not see Lucia. Nor could he find Bernardo, and he knew he had been holding Bernardo's arm a second before. As soon as he realised that, he found he had lost his sense of direction too. He was all alone, coughing and shivering, in cold white emptiness.

"I am *not* going to lose my head," Paolo told himself sternly. "My father didn't, and so I shan't. I shall find somewhere to shelter until this beastly spell is over. Then I shall go home. I don't care if Tonino *is* still missing—" He stopped then, because a thought came to him, like an astonishing discovery. "We're never going to find Tonino this way, anyway," he said. And he knew it was true.

With his hands stretched out in front of him and his eyes spread very wide in hopes of seeing something—which was unlikely, since they were streaming from the fog, and so was his nose—Paolo coughed and sniffed and shuffled his way forward until his toes came up against stone. Paolo looked down, but he could not see what it was. He tried lifting one foot, with his toes scraping against the obstruction. And, after a few inches, the obstruction stopped and his foot shot forward. It was a ledge, then. Probably the kerb. He had been near the edge of the road when he ran away from the elephant. He got both feet on the kerb and shuffled forward six inches—then he fell upstairs over what seemed to be a body.

It gave Paolo such a shock that he dared not move at first. But he soon realised that the body beneath him was shivering, as he was, and trying to cough and mutter at the same time. "Holy Mary—" Paolo heard, in a hoarse blurred voice. Very puzzled, Paolo put out a careful hand and felt the body. His fingers met cold metal buttons, uniform braid, and, a little above that, a warm face—which gave a croak as Paolo's cold hand met its mouth—and a large furry moustache beneath the nose.

Angel of Caprona! Paolo thought. It's the Chief of Police!

Paolo got himself to his knees on what must be the steps of the Art Gallery. There was no one around he could ask, but it did not seem fair to leave someone lying helpless in the fog. It was bad enough if you could move. So hoping he was doing the right thing, Paolo knelt and sang, very softly, the most general cancel-spell he could think of. It had no effect on the fog—that was evidently very strong magic—but he heard the Chief of Police roll over on his side and groan. Boots scraped as he tested his legs. "Mama mia!" Paolo heard him moan.

He sounded as if he wanted to be alone. Paolo left him and crawled his way up the Gallery steps. He had no idea he had reached the top, until he hit his elbow on a pillar and drove his head into Lucia's stomach at the same moment. Both of them said some extremely unpleasant things.

"When you've quite finished swearing," Lucia said at length, "you can get between these pillars with me and keep me warm." She coughed and shivered. "Isn't this awful? Who did it?" She coughed again. The fog had made her hoarse.

"It wasn't us," said Paolo. "We'd have known. Ow, my elbow!" He took hold of her for a guide and wedged himself down beside her. He felt better like that.

"The pigs," said Lucia. "I call this a mean trick. It's funny—you spend your life being told what pigs they are, and thinking they *can't* be, really. Then you meet them, and they're worse than you were told. Was it you singing just now?"

"I fell over the Chief of Police on the steps," said Paolo.

Lucia laughed. "I fell over the other one. I sang a cancel-spell too.

He was lying on all the corners of the stairs and it must have bruised him all over when I fell on him."

"It's bad enough when you can move," Paolo agreed. "Like being blind."

"Horrible," said Lucia. "That blind beggar in the Via Sant' Angelo—I shall give him some money tomorrow."

"The one with white eyes?" said Paolo. "Yes, so shall I. And I never want to see another spell."

"To tell you the truth," said Lucia, "I was wishing I dared burn the Library and the Scriptorium down. It came to me like a blinding flash just before I fell over that policeman—that no amount of spells are going to work on those beastly kidnappers."

"That's just what I thought!" exclaimed Paolo. "I know the only way to find Tonino—"

"Hang on," said Lucia. "I think the fog's getting thinner."

She was right. When Paolo leant forward, he could see two dark lumps below, where the Chief of Police and his lieutenant were sitting on the steps with their heads in their hands. He could see quite a stretch of the Corso beyond them—cobbles which were dark and wet-looking, but, to his surprise, neither muddy nor out of place.

"Someone's put it all back!" said Lucia.

The fog thinned further. They could see the glimmering doors of the Arsenal now, and the entire foggy width of the Corso, with every cobblestone back where it should be. Somewhere about the middle of it, Antonio and Guido Petrocchi were standing facing one another.

"Oh, they're not going to begin again, are they?" wailed Paolo.

But, almost at once, Antonio and Guido swung round and walked away from one another.

"Thank goodness!" said Lucia. She and Paolo turned to one another, smiling with relief.

Except that it was not Lucia. Paolo found himself staring into a white pointed face, and eyes darker, larger and shrewder than Lucia's. Surrounding the face were draggled dark red curls. The smile died from the face and horror replaced it as Paolo stared. He felt his own face behaving the same way. He had been huddling up against a Petrocchi! He knew which one, too. It was the elder of the two who had been at the Palace. Renata, that was her name. And she knew him too.

"You're that blue-eyed Montana boy!" she exclaimed. She made it sound quite disgusting.

Both of them got up. Renata backed into the pillars, as if she was trying to get inside the stone, and Paolo backed away along the steps.

"I thought you were my sister Lucia," he said.

"I thought you were my cousin Claudio," Renata retorted.

Somehow, they both made it sound as if it was the other one's fault.

"It wasn't my fault!" Paolo said angrily. "Blame the person who made the fog, not me. There's an enemy enchanter."

"I know. Chrestomanci said," said Renata.

Paolo felt he hated Chrestomanci. He had no business to go and say the same things to the Petrocchis as he said to the Montanas. But he hated the enemy enchanter even more. He had been responsible for the most embarrassing thing which had ever happened to Paolo. Muttering with shame, Paolo turned to run away.

"No, stop! *Wait*!" Renata said. She said it so commandingly that Paolo stopped without thinking, and gave Renata time to snatch hold of his arm. Instead of pulling away, Paolo stood quite still and attempted to behave with the dignity becoming to a Montana. He looked at his arm, and at Renata's hand holding it, as if both had become one composite slimy toad. But Renata hung on. "Look all you like," she said. "I don't care. I'm not letting go until you tell me what your family has done with Angelica."

"Nothing," Paolo said contemptuously. "We wouldn't touch one of you with a barge-pole. What have you lot done with Tonino?"

An odd little frown wrinkled Renata's white forehead. "Is that your brother? Is he really missing?"

"He was sent a book with a calling-spell in it," said Paolo.

"A book," said Renata slowly, "got Angelica too. We only realised when it shrivelled away."

She let go of Paolo's arm. They stared at one another in the blowing remains of the fog.

"It must be the enemy enchanter," said Paolo.

"Trying to take our minds off the war," said Renata. "Tell your family, won't you?"

"If you tell yours," said Paolo.

"Of course I will. What do you take me for?" said Renata.

In spite of everything, Paolo found himself laughing. "I think you're a Petrocchi!" he said.

But when Renata began to laugh too, Paolo realised it was too much. He turned to run away, and found himself facing the Chief of Police. The Chief of Police had evidently recovered his dignity. "Now then, you children. Move along," he said.

Renata fled, without more ado, red in the face with the shame of being caught talking to a Montana. Paolo hung on. It seemed to him that he ought to report that Tonino was missing.

"I said move along!" repeated the Chief of Police, and he pulled down his jacket with a most threatening jerk.

Paolo's nerve broke. After all, an ordinary policeman was not going to be much help against an enchanter. He ran.

He ran all the way to the Casa Montana. The fog and the wetness did not extend beyond the Corso. As soon as he turned into a side road, Paolo found himself in the bleak shadows and low red sun of a winter evening. It was like being shot back into another world—a world where things happened as they should, where one's father did not turn into a mad elephant, where, above all, one's sister did not turn out to be a Petrocchi. Paolo's face fired with shame as he ran. Of all the awful things to happen!

The Casa Montana came in sight, with the familiar Angel safely over the gate. Paolo shot in under it, and ran into his father. Antonio was standing under the archway, panting as if he too had run all the way home.

"Who—? Oh, Paolo," said Antonio. "Stay where you are."

"Why?" asked Paolo. He wanted to get in, where it was safe, and perhaps eat a large lump of bread and honey. He was surprised his father did not feel the same. Antonio looked tired out, and his clothes were torn and muddy rags. The arm he stretched out to keep Paolo in the gateway was half bare and covered with scratches. Paolo was going to protest, when he saw that something was indeed wrong. Most of the cats were in the gateway too, crouching around with their ears flattened. Benvenuto was patrolling the entrance to the yard, like a lean brown ferret. Paolo could hear him growling.

Antonio's scratched hand took Paolo by the shoulder and pulled him forward so that he could see into the yard. "Look."

Paolo found himself blinking at foot-high letters, which seemed to hang in the air in the middle of the yard. In the fading light, they were glowing an unpleasant, sick yellow.

STOP ALL SPELLS OR YOUR CHILD SUFFERS.
CASA PETROCCHI

The name was in sicker and brighter letters. They were meant to make no mistake about who had sent the message.

After what Renata had said, Paolo knew it was wrong. "It *wasn't* the Petrocchis," he said. "It's that enchanter Chrestomanci told us about."

"Yes, to be sure," said Antonio.

Paolo looked up at him and saw that his father did not believe him—

probably had not even attended to him. "But it's true!" he said. "He wants us to stop making war-spells."

Antonio sighed, and drew himself together to explain to Paolo. "Paolo," he said, "nobody but Chrestomanci believes in this enchanter. In magic, as in everything else, the simplest explanation is always best. In other words, why invent an unknown enchanter, when you have a known enemy with known reasons for hating you? Why shouldn't it be the Petrocchis?"

Paolo wanted to protest, but he was still too embarrassed about Renata to say that Angelica Petrocchi was missing too. He was struggling to find something that he *could* say, which might convince his father, when a square of light sprang up in the gallery as a door there opened.

"Rosa!" shouted Antonio. His voice cracked with anxiety.

The shape of Rosa appeared in the light, carrying Cousin Claudia's baby. The light itself was so orange and so right, beside the sick glow of the letters floating in the yard, that Paolo was flooded with relief. Behind Rosa, there was Marco, carrying another little one.

"Praised be!" said Antonio. He shouted, "Are you all right, Rosa? How did those words come here?"

"We don't know," Rosa called back. "They just appeared. We've been trying to get rid of them, but we can't."

Marco leant over the rails and called, "It's not true, Antonio. The Petrocchis wouldn't do a thing like this."

Antonio called back, "Don't go around saying that, Marco." He said it so forbiddingly that Paolo knew nothing he said was going to be believed. If he had had a chance of convincing Antonio, he had now lost it.

CHAPTER 8

When Tonino came to his senses—at, incidentally, the precise moment when the enchanted book began to shrivel away—he had, at first, a nightmare feeling that he was shut in a cardboard box. He rolled his head sideways on his arms. He seemed to be lying on his face on a hard but faintly furry floor. In the far distance, he could blurrily see someone else, leaning up against a wall like a doll, but he felt too queer to be very interested in that. He rolled his head round the other way and saw the panels of a wall quite near. That told him he was in a fairly long room. He rolled his head to stare down at the furry floor. It was patterned, in a pattern too big for his eyes to grasp, and he supposed it was a carpet of some kind. He shut his blurry eyes and tried to think what had happened.

He remembered going down near the New Bridge. He had been full of excitement. He had read a book which he thought was telling him how to save Caprona. He knew he had to find an alleyway with a peeling blue house at the end of it. It seemed a bit silly now. Tonino knew things never happened the way they did in books. Even then, he had been rather amazed to find that there *was* an alleyway with, really and truly, a peeling blue house at the end of it. And, to his huge excitement, there was a scrap of paper fluttering down at his feet. The book was coming true. Tonino had bent down and picked up the paper.

And, after that, he had known nothing till this moment.

That was really true. Tonino took himself through what had happened several times, but each time his memories stopped in exactly the same place—with himself picking up the scrap of paper. After that, it was all a vague sense of nightmare. By this time, he was fairly sure he had been the victim of a spell. He began to feel ashamed of himself. So he sat up.

He saw at once why he had seemed to dream he was shut up in a cardboard box. The room he was in was long and low, almost exactly the shape of a shoebox. The walls and ceiling were painted cream-colour—a sort of whitish cardboard-colour, in fact—but they seemed to be wood, because there were carvings picked out in gold paint on them. There was a crystal chandelier hanging from the ceiling, although the light came from four long windows in one of the longer walls; a rich carpet on the floor, and a very elegant dining-table and chairs by the wall opposite the windows. There were two silver candlesticks on the table. Altogether the place was extremely elegant—and wrong, somehow.

Tonino sat trying to puzzle out just what was wrong. The room was awfully bare. But that was not quite it. There was something strange about the daylight coming through the four long windows, as if the sun was somehow further away than it should be. But that was not quite it either. Tonino's eyes went to the four bands of too-faded sunlight falling through the windows on to the carpet, and then travelled along the carpet. At the end, he came to the person leaning up against the wall. It was Angelica Petrocchi, who had been at the Palace. Her eyes were closed beneath her bulge of forehead, and she looked ill. So she had been caught too.

Tonino looked back at the carpet. That was an odd thing. It was not really a carpet. It had been painted on the slightly furry substance of the floor. Tonino could see the brush-strokes in the sprawling pattern. And the reason he had thought the pattern was too big, was because it *was* too big. It was the wrong size for the rest of the room.

More puzzled than ever, Tonino struggled to his feet. He felt a little wobbly, so he put a hand on the gilded panels of the wall to steady himself. That felt furry too, except where it was gold. The gold was flat, but not quite hard, like—Tonino thought, but no other likeness came to him—like paint. He ran his hand over the apparently carved panel. It was a total cheat. It was not even wood, and the carving was painted on, in lines of brown, blue and gold. Whoever had caught him was trying to seem richer than they were, but doing it very badly.

There were movements at the other end of the room. Angelica Petrocchi was wavering to her feet, and she too was running her hand over the painted carving. Very anxiously and cautiously, she turned and looked at Tonino.

"Will you let me go now, please?" she said.

There was a little wobble in her voice that showed Tonino she was very frightened. So was he, now he came to think of it. "I can't let you go," he said. "I didn't catch you. Neither of us can go. There isn't a door."

That was the wrong thing he had been trying not to notice. And as soon as he said it, he wished he had kept his mouth shut. Angelica screamed. And the sound sent Tonino into a panic too. There was no door! He was shut into a cardboard box with a Petrocchi child!

Tonino may have screamed as well—he was not sure. When he caught up with himself, he had one of the elegant chairs in his hands and was battering at the nearest window with it. That was more frightening than ever. The glass did not break. It was made of some slightly rubbery stuff, and the chair bounced off. Beyond him, the Petrocchi girl was banging away at another window with one of the silver candlesticks, screaming all the time. Outside the window, Tonino could clearly see the smug spire-shape of a little cypress tree, lit by afternoon sun. So they were in one of those rich villas near the Palace, were they? Just let him get *out*! He lifted the chair and smashed it against the window with all his strength.

He made no impression on the window, but the chair came to pieces. Two ill-glued legs fell off it, and the rest crumpled to splintery matchwood. Tonino thought it was disgustingly badly made. He threw it to the painted carpet and fetched another chair. This time, for variety, he attacked the wall beside the window. Pieces of that chair came away and flew about, and Tonino was left with its painted seat—painted to look like embroidery, just as the floor was painted to look like carpet. He drove it into the wall, again and again. It made large brown dents. Better still, the wall shook and leapt about, sounding muffled and hollow, as if it were made of something very cheap. Tonino beat at it and yelled. Angelica beat at the wall and the window impartially with her candle-stick, and went on screaming.

They were stopped by a terrible hammering. Someone seemed to be dealing hundreds of thunderous blows on the ceiling. The room was like the inside of a drum. It was too loud to bear. The Petrocchi girl dropped her candlestick and rolled on the floor. Tonino found himself crouching down, with his hands to his ears, looking up at the chandelier jiggling overhead. He thought his head would burst.

The pounding stopped. There was no sound except a whimper, which Tonino rather thought came from him.

A great huge voice spoke through the ceiling. "That's better. Now be quiet, or you won't get any food. And if you try any more tricks, you'll be punished. Understand?"

Tonino and Angelica both sat up. *"Let us out!"* they screamed.

There was no answer, only a distant shuffling. The owner of the huge voice seemed to be going away.

"A mean trick with an amplifying spell," Angelica said. She picked up the candlestick and looked at it with disgust. The branched part was bent at right-angles to the base. "What *is* this place?" she said. "Everything's so shoddy."

They got up and went to the windows again, in hopes of a clue. Several little spire-shaped trees were clearly to be seen, just outside, and a sort of terrace beyond that. But, peer as they might, all they could make out further off was queer blue distance, with one or two square-shaped mountains catching the sun on a glossy corner or so. There seemed to be no sky.

"It's a spell," said Angelica. Her voice suggested she might be going to panic again. "A spell to stop us knowing where we are."

Tonino supposed it must be. There was no other way of accounting for the strange absence of view. "But I'm sure I know," he said, "by those trees. We're in one of those rich villas by the Palace."

"You're right," agreed Angelica. The panic had left her voice. "I shall never envy those people again. Their lives are all show."

They turned from the windows and discovered that the vast banging had dislodged one of the wall panels behind the dining-table. It hung open like a door. They shoved one another out of the way to reach it first. But there was only a cupboard-sized bathroom, without a window.

"Good," said Angelica. "I was wondering what we'd do. And at least we'll have water." She reached out to one of the taps over the small washbasin. It came away in her hand. Under it was a blob of glue on white china. It was clear the tap had never been meant to be used. Angelica stared at it with such a ridiculous look of bewilderment that Tonino laughed. She drew herself up at that. "Don't you laugh at me, you beastly Montana!" She stalked out into the main room and threw the useless tap on to the table with a clump. Then she sat in one of the two remaining chairs and rested her elbows gloomily on the table.

After a while, Tonino did the same. The chair creaked under him. So did the table. Though its surface was painted to look like smooth mahogany, close to, it was all blobs of varnish and huge splinters. "There's nothing that's not shoddy," he said.

"Including you, Whatyoumecall Montana!" Angelica said. She was still angry.

"My name's Tonino," Tonino said.

"It's the last twist of the knife, being shut up with a Montana!" Angelica said. "Whatever your name is. I shall have to put up with all your filthy habits."

"Well, I've got to put up with yours," Tonino said irritably. It suddenly struck him that he was all alone, far from the friendly bustle of the Casa Montana. Even when he was hidden in a corner of the Casa with a book, he knew the rest of the family was all round him. And Benvenuto would be purring and pricking him, to remind him he was not alone. Dear old Benvenuto. Tonino was afraid he was going to cry—in front of a Petrocchi too. "How did they catch you?" he said, to take his mind off it.

"With a book." A slight, woeful smile appeared on Angelica's tight white face. "It was called *The Girl Who Saved Her Country,* and I thought it was from Great-Uncle Luigi. I still think it was a good story." She looked defiantly at Tonino.

Tonino was annoyed. It was not pleasant to think he had been caught by the same spell as a Petrocchi. "Me too," he said gruffly.

"And *I* haven't got any filthy habits!" snapped Angelica.

"Yes you have. All the Petrocchis have," said Tonino. "But I expect you don't realise because they're normal to you."

"I like that!" Angelica picked up the broken tap, as if she had half a mind to throw it.

"I don't care about your habits," said Tonino. Nor did he. All he wanted to do was find some way out of this nightmare room and go home. "How shall we get out of here?"

"Through the ceiling," Angelica said sarcastically.

Tonino looked upwards. There was that chandelier. If they could give it a pull, it might well rip a hole in the shoddy ceiling.

"Don't be stupid," said Angelica. "If there's a spell out in front, there's bound to be one up there to stop us getting out."

Tonino feared she was right, but it was worth a try. He climbed from his chair on to the table. He thought he could reach the chandelier from there if he stood up. There was a violent creaking. Before Tonino could begin to stand up, the table swayed away sideways, as if all four of its legs were loose.

"Get down!" said Angelica.

Tonino got down. It was clear the table would fall to pieces if he stayed on it. Gloomily he pushed the crooked legs straight again. "So that's no good," he said.

"Unless," said Angelica, suddenly bright and pert, "we steady it with a spell."

Tonino transferred his miserable look from the table-legs to her sharp little face. He sighed. The subject had been bound to come up. "You'll have to do the spell," he said. Angelica stared at him. He could feel his face heating up. "I hardly know any spells," he said. "I—I'm slow."

He had expected Angelica to laugh, and she did. But he thought she need not have laughed in such a mean, exultant way, nor keep saying, "Oh that's good!" like that.

"What's so funny?" he said. "You can laugh! I know all about you turning your father green. You're no better than me!"

"Want to bet?" said Angelica, still laughing.

"No," said Tonino. "Just make the spell."

"I can't," said Angelica. It was Tonino's turn to stare, and Angelica's turn to blush. A thin bright pink spread right up the bulge of her forehead, and she put her chin up defiantly. "I'm hopeless at spells," she said. "I've never got a spell right in my life." Seeing Tonino still staring, she said, "It's a pity you didn't bet. I'm *much* worse than you are."

Tonino could not credit it. "How?" he said. "Why? Can't you learn spells either, then?"

"Oh, I can *learn* them all right." Angelica took up the broken tap again and scribbled angrily with it, great yellow scratches in the varnished top of the table. "I know hundreds of spells," she said, "but I always get them wrong. For a start, I'm tone-deaf. I can't sing a tune right to save my life. Like now." Carefully, as if she was a craftsman doing a fine carving, she peeled up a long yellow curl of varnish from the table, using the tap as a gouge. "But it's not only that," she said angrily, following her work intently. "I get words wrong too—everything wrong. And my spells always work, that's the worst of it. I've turned all my family all colours of the rainbow. I've turned the baby's bath into wine, and the wine into gravy. I turned my own head back to front once. I'm much worse than you. I *daren't* do spells. About all I'm good for is understanding cats. And I even turned my cat purple too."

Tonino watched her working away with the tap, with rather mixed feelings. If you looked at it practically, this was the worst possible news. Neither of them had a hope against the powerful spell-maker who had caught them. On the other hand, he had never met anyone who was worse at spells than he was. He thought, a little smugly, that at least he had never made a mistake in a spell, and that made him feel good. He wondered how the Casa Montana would feel if he kept turning them all colours of the rainbow. He imagined the stern Petrocchis must hate it. "Doesn't your family mind?" he asked.

"Not much," Angelica said, surprisingly. "They don't mind it half as much as I do. Everyone has a good laugh every time I make a new mistake—but they don't let anyone talk about it outside the Casa. Papa says I'm notorious enough for turning him green, and he doesn't like me to be even *seen* anywhere until I've grown out of it.

"But you went to the Palace," said Tonino. He thought Angelica must be exaggerating.

"Only because Cousin Monica was having her baby and everyone was so busy on the Old Bridge," said Angelica. "He had to take Renata off her shift and get my brother out of bed to drive the coach, in order to have enough of us."

"There were five of us," Tonino said, smugly.

"Our horses collapsed in the rain." Angelica turned from her gouging and looked at Tonino keenly. "So my brother said yours were bound to have collapsed too, because *you* only had a cardboard coachman."

Uncomfortably, Tonino knew Angelica had scored a point. "Our coachman collapsed too," he admitted.

"I thought so," said Angelica, "from the look on your face." She went back to scraping the table, conscious of victory.

"It wasn't our fault!" Tonino protested. "Chrestomanci says there's an enemy enchanter."

Angelica took such a slice out of the varnish that the table swooped sideways and Tonino had to push it straight. "And he's got us now," she said. "And he's taken care to get the two who are no good at spells. So how do we get out of here and spite him, Tonino Montana? Any ideas?"

Tonino sat with his chin in his hands and thought. He had read enough books, for goodness sake. People were always being kidnapped in books. And in his favourite books—this was like a bad joke—they escaped without using magic of any kind. But there was no door. That was what made it seem impossible. Wait a moment! The vast voice had promised them food. "If they think we're behaving," he said, "they'll bring us supper probably. And they've got to bring the food in somehow. If we watch where it comes in, we ought to be able to get out the same way."

"There's bound to be a spell on the entrance," Angelica said gloomily.

"Do stop bleating away about spells!" said Tonino. "Don't you Petrocchis ever talk about anything else?"

Angelica did not reply, but simply scraped away with her tap. Tonino sat wanly in his creaking chair thinking over the few spells he really knew. The most useful seemed to be a simple cancel-spell.

"A cancel-spell," Angelica said irritatingly, scratching carefully with the tap. The floor round her feet was heaped with yellow curls of varnish. "That might hold the entrance open. Or isn't a cancel-spell one of the ones you know?"

"I know a cancel-spell," said Tonino.

"So does my baby brother," said Angelica. "He'd probably be more use."

Their supper arrived. It appeared, without warning, on a tray, floating towards them from the windows. It took Tonino completely by surprise.

"Spell!" Angelica squawked at him. "Don't just stare!"

Tonino sang the spell. Hurried and surprised though he was, he was *sure* he got it right. But it was the tray the spell worked on. The tray, and the food on it, began to grow. Within seconds, it was bigger than the table-top. And it still floated towards the table, growing as it came. Tonino found himself backing away from two steaming bath-sized bowls of soup and two great orange thickets of spaghetti, all of which were getting steadily vaster the nearer they came. By now, there was not much room round the edges of the tray. Tonino backed against the end wall, wondering if Angelica's trouble with spells was catching. Angelica herself was squashed against the bathroom door. Both of them were in danger of being cut in two.

"Get down on the floor!" Tonino shouted.

They slithered hurriedly down the wall, underneath the tray, which hung over them like a too-low ceiling. The huge odour of spaghetti was quite oppressive.

"What have you done?" Angelica said, coming towards Tonino on hands and knees. "You didn't get it right."

"Yes, but if it gets much bigger, it might break the room open," said Tonino.

Angela sank back on her knees and looked at him with what was nearly respect. "That's almost a good idea."

But it was only almost. The tray certainly met all four walls. They heard it thump against them. There was a deal of swaying, creaking and squeezing, from the tray and from the walls, but the walls did not give. After a moment it was clear that the tray was not being allowed to get any bigger.

"There *is* a spell on this room," Angelica said. It was not meant to be I-told-you-so. She was miserable.

Tonino gave up and sang the cancel-spell, carefully and correctly. The tray shrank at once. They were left kneeling on the floor looking at a reasonable-sized supper laid neatly in the centre of the table. "We might as well eat it," he said.

Angelica annoyed him thoroughly again by saying, as she picked up her spoon, "Well, I'm glad to know I'm not the only person who gets my spells wrong."

"I know I got it right," Tonino muttered into his spoon, but Angelica chose not to hear.

After a while, he was even more annoyed to find, every time he looked up, that Angelica was staring at him curiously. "What's the matter now?" he said at last, quite exasperated.

"I was waiting to see your filthy eating habits," she said. "But I think you must be on your best behaviour."

"I always eat like this!" Tonino saw that he had wound far too much spaghetti on his fork. He hurriedly unwound it.

The bulge of Angelica's forehead was wavy with frown-lines. "No you don't. Montanas always eat disgustingly because of the way Old Ricardo Petrocchi made them eat their words."

"Don't talk nonsense," said Tonino. "Anyway, it was Old Francesco Montana who made the Petrocchis eat *their* words."

"It was not!" Angelica said heatedly. "It was the first story I ever learnt. The Petrocchis made the Montanas eat their spells disguised as spaghetti."

"No they didn't. It was the other way round!" said Tonino. "It was the first story I ever learnt too."

Somehow, neither of them felt like finishing their spaghetti. They laid their forks down and went on arguing.

"And because of eating those spells," said Angelica, "the Montanas went quite disgusting and started eating their uncles and aunts when they died."

"We do not!" said Tonino. "You eat babies."

"How dare you!" said Angelica. "You eat cowpats for pizzas, and you can smell the Casa Montana right on the Corso."

"The Casa Petrocchi smells all down the Via Sant' Angelo," said Tonino, "and you can hear the flies buzzing from the New Bridge. You have babies like kittens and—"

"That's a lie!" shrieked Angelica. "You just put that about because you don't want people to know that the Montanas never get married properly!"

"Yes we do!" bawled Tonino. "It's you who don't!"

"I like that!" yelled Angelica. "I'll have you know, my brother got married, in church, just after Christmas. So there!"

"I don't believe you," said Tonino. "And my sister's going to get married in Spring, so—"

"I was a *bridesmaid!*" screamed Angelica.

While they argued, the tray quietly floated off the table and vanished somewhere near the windows. Tonino and Angelica looked irritably round for it, extremely annoyed that they had once again missed noticing how it got in and out.

"Now look what you've done!" said Angelica.

"It's your fault for telling lies about my family," said Tonino.

CHAPTER 9

"If you're not careful," said Angelica, glowering under the bulge of her forehead, "I shall sing the first spell that comes into my head. And I hope it turns you into a slug."

That was a threat indeed. Tonino quailed a little. But the honour of the Montanas was at stake. "Take back what you said about my family," he said.

"Only if you take back what you said about mine," said Angelica. "Swear by the Angel of Caprona that none of those dreadful lies are true. Look. I've got the Angel here. Come and swear." Her pink finger jabbed down at the table-top. She reminded Tonino of his school teacher on a bad day.

He left his creaking chair and leant over to see what she was pointing at. Angelica fussily dusted away a shower of yellow varnish to show him that she indeed had the Angel, scratched with the useless tap into the top of the table. It was quite a good drawing, considering that the tap was not a good gouge and had shown a tendency to slip about. But Tonino was not prepared to admire it. "You've forgotten the scroll," he said.

Angelica jumped up, and her flimsy chair crashed over backwards. "That does it! You've asked for it!" She marched over to the empty space by the windows and took up a position of power. From there, with her hands raised, she looked at Tonino to see if he was going to relent. Tonino would have liked to relent. He did not want to be a slug. He sought about in his mind for some way of giving in which did not look like simple cowardice. But, as with everything, he was too slow. Angelica flounced round, so that her arms were no longer at quite the right angle.

"Right," she said. "I shall make it a cancel-spell, to cancel you out." And she began to sing.

Angelica's voice was horrible, sharp and flat by turns, and wandering from key to key. Tonino would have liked to interrupt her, or at least distract her by making noises, but he did not quite dare. That might only make things worse. He waited while Angelica squawked out a couple of verses of a spell which seemed to centre round the words *turn the spell round, break the spell off.* Since he was a boy and not a spell, Tonino rather hoped it would not do anything to him.

Angelica raised her arms higher for the third verse and changed key for the sixth time. "Turn the spell off, break the spell round—"

"That's wrong," said Tonino.

"Don't you dare put me off!" snapped Angelica, and turned round to say it, which sent the angle of her arms more thoroughly wrong than ever. One hand was now pointing at a window. "I command the unbinding of that which was bound," she sang, cross and shrill.

Tonino looked quickly down at himself, but he seemed to be still there, and the usual colour. He told himself that he had known all along that such a bungled spell could not possibly work.

There came a great creaking from the ceiling, just above the windows. The whole room swayed. Then, to Tonino's amazement, the entire front wall of the room, windows and all, split away from the side walls and the ceiling, and fell outwards with a soft clatter—a curiously soft sound for the whole side of a house. A draught of musty-smelling air blew in through the open space.

Angelica was quite as astonished as Tonino. But that did not prevent her turning to him with a smug and triumphant smile. "See? My spells always work."

"Let's get out," said Tonino. "Quick. Before somebody comes."

They ran out across the painted panels between the windows, across the marks Tonino had made with the chair. They stepped down off the surprisingly clean, straight edge, where the wall had joined the ceiling, on to the terrace in front of the house. It appeared to be made of wood, not of stone as Tonino had expected. And beyond that—

They stopped, just in time, at the edge of a huge cliff. Both of them swayed forward, and caught at one another. The cliff went down sheer, into murky darkness. They could not see the bottom. Nor could they see much more when they looked straight ahead. There was a blaze of red-gold sunlight there, dazzling them.

"There's still a spell on the view," said Tonino.

"In that case," said Angelica, "let's just keep walking. There must be a road or a garden that we can't see."

There certainly should have been something of the kind, but it neither felt nor looked like that. Tonino was sure he could sense vast hollow spaces below the cliff. There were no city sounds, and only a strangely musty smell.

"Coward!" said Angelica.

"You go," said Tonino.

"Only if you go too," she said.

They hovered, glaring at one another. And, as they hovered, the blaze of sunlight was cut off by an immense black shape. *"Naughty!"* said a vast voice. "Bad children shall be punished."

A force almost too strong to feel swept them away on to the fallen wall. The fallen wall rose briskly back into its place, sweeping Angelica and Tonino with it, helplessly sliding and rolling, until they thumped on to the painted carpet. By that time, Tonino was so breathless and dizzy that he hardly heard the wall snap back into place with a click.

After that, the dizziness grew worse. Tonino knew he was in the grip of another spell. He struggled against it furiously, but whoever was casting it was immensely strong. He felt surging and bumping. The light from the windows changed, and changed again. Almost he could have sworn, the room was being *carried.* It stopped with a jolt. He heard Angelica's voice gabbling a prayer to Our Lady, and he did not blame her. Then there was a mystifying gap in what Tonino knew.

He came to himself because whoever was casting the spell wanted him to. Tonino was quite sure of that. The punishment would not be so much fun, unless Tonino knew about it.

He was in a confusion of light and noise—there was a huge blur of it to one side—and he was racing up and down a narrow wooden platform, dragging (of all things!) a string of sausages. He was wearing a bright red nightgown and there was a heaviness on the front of his face. Each time he reached one end of the wooden platform, he found a white cardboard dog there, with a frill round its neck. The dog's cardboard mouth opened and shut. It was making feeble cardboard attempts to get the sausages.

The noise was terrific. Tonino seemed to be making some of it himself. "What a clever fellow! What a clever fellow!" he heard himself squawking, in a voice quite unlike his own. It was like the noise you make singing into paper over a comb. The rest of the noise was coming from the lighted space to one side. Vast voices were roaring and laughing, mixed with tinny music.

"This is a dream!" Tonino told himself. But he knew it was not. He had a fair idea what was happening, though his head still felt muzzy and his eyes were blurred. As he raced back down the little platform, he turned his bleary eyes inwards, towards the heaviness on his face. Sure enough, blurred and doubled, he could see a great red and pink nose there. He was Mr Punch.

Naturally, then, he tried to dig in his heels and stop racing up and down, and to lift his hand and wrench off the huge pink nose. He could not do either. More than that, whoever was making him be Mr Punch promptly took mean pleasure in making him run faster and whirl the sausages about harder.

"Oh, very good!" yelled someone from the lighted space.

Tonino thought he knew that voice. He sped towards the cardboard Dog Toby again, whirled the sausages away from its cardboard jaws and waited for his head and eyes to stop feeling so fuzzy. He was sure they would. The mean person wanted him conscious. "What a clever fellow!" he squawked. As he raced down the stage the other way, he snatched a look across his huge nose towards the lighted space, but it was a blur. So he snatched a look towards the other side.

He saw the wall of a golden villa there, with four long windows. Beside each window stood a little dark cypress tree. Now he knew why the strange room had seemed so shoddy. It was only meant as scenery. The door on the outside wall was painted on. Between the villa and the stage was a hole. The person who was working the puppets ought to have been down there, but Tonino could only see empty blackness. It was all being done by magic.

Just then he was distracted by a cardboard person diving upwards from the hole, squawking that Mr Punch had stolen his sausages. Tonino was forced to stand still and squawk back. He was glad of a rest by then. Meanwhile, the cardboard dog seized the sausages and dived out of sight with them. The audience clapped and shouted, "Look at Dog Toby!" The cardboard person sped past Tonino squawking that he would fetch the police.

Once again, Tonino tried to look out at the audience. This time, he could dimly see a brightly lit room and black bulky shapes sitting in chairs, but it was like trying to see something against the sun. His eyes watered. A tear ran down the pink beak on his face. And Tonino could feel that the mean person was delighted to see that. He thought Tonino was crying. Tonino was annoyed, but also rather pleased; it looked as if the person could be fooled by his own mean thoughts. He stared out, in spite of the dazzle, trying to see the mean person, but all he could clearly see was a carving up near the roof of the lighted room. It was the Angel of Caprona, one hand held out in blessing, the other holding the scroll.

Then he was jumped round to face Judy. On the other side of him, the wall had gone from the front of the villa. The scene was the room he knew only too well, with the chandelier artistically alight.

Judy was coming along the stage holding the white rolled-up shape of the baby. Judy wore a blue nightdress and a blue cap. Her face was mauve, with a nose in the middle of it nearly as large and red as Tonino's. But the eyes on either side of it were Angelica's, alternately blinking and wide with terror. She blinked beseechingly at Tonino as she squawked, "I have to go out, Mr Punch. Mind you mind the baby!"

"Don't want to mind the baby!" he squawked.

All through the long silly conversation, he could see Angelica's eyes blinking at him, imploring him to think of a spell to stop this. But of course Tonino could not. He did not think Rinaldo, or even Antonio, could stop anything as powerful as this. Angel of Caprona! he thought. Help us! That made him feel better, although nothing stopped the spell. Angelica planted the baby in his arms and dived out of sight.

The baby started to cry. Tonino first squawked abuse at it, then took it by the end of its long white dress and beat its brains out on the platform. The baby was much more realistic than Dog Toby. It may have been only cardboard, but it wriggled and waved its arms and cried most horribly. Tonino could almost have believed it was Cousin Claudia's baby. It so horrified him that he found he was repeating the words of the *Angel of Caprona* as he swung the baby up and down. And those might not have been the right words, but he could feel they were doing something. When he finally flung the white bundle over the front of the stage, he could see the shiny floor the baby fell on, away below. And when he looked up at the clapping spectators, he could see them too, equally clearly.

The first person he saw was the Duke of Caprona. He was sitting on a gilded chair, in a glitter of buttons, laughing gigantically. Tonino wondered how he could laugh like that at something so horrible, until he remembered that he had stood himself, a score of times, and laughed himself sick, at just the same thing. But those had been only puppets. Then it dawned on Tonino that the Duke thought they *were* puppets. He was laughing at the skill of the showman.

"What a clever fellow!" squawked Tonino, and was made to dance about gleefully, without wanting to in the least. But as he danced, he looked sharply at the rest of the audience, to see who it was who knew he was not a puppet.

To his terror, a good half of them knew. Tonino met a knowing look on the faces of the three grave men surrounding the Duke, and the same on the elegantly made-up faces of the two ladies with the Duchess. And the Duchess—as soon as Tonino saw the amused arch of the Duchess's eyebrows and the little, secret smile on her mouth, he knew she was the one doing it. He looked her in the eyes. Yes, she was an enchantress. That was what had so troubled him about her when he saw her before. And the Duchess saw him look, and smiled less secretly, because Tonino could do nothing about it.

That really frightened Tonino. But Angelica came swooping upwards again, with a large stick clutched in her arms, and he had no time to think.

"What have you done with the baby?" squawked Angelica. And she belaboured Tonino with the stick. It really hurt. It knocked him to his knees and went on bashing at him. Tonino could see Angelica's lips moving. Though her silly squeaky voice kept saying, "I'll teach you to kill the baby!" her mouth was forming the words of the *Angel of Caprona.* That was because she knew what came next.

Tonino said the words of the *Angel* too and tried to stay crouched on the floor. But it was no good. He was made to spring up, wrest the stick from Judy and beat Angelica with it. He could see the Duke laughing, and the courtiers smiling. The Duchess's smile was very broad now, because, of course, Tonino was going to have to beat Angelica to death.

Tonino tried to hold the stick so that it would only hit Angelica lightly. She might be a Petrocchi and a thoroughly irritating girl, but she had not deserved this. But the stick leapt up and down of its own accord, and Tonino's arms went with it. Angelica fell on her knees and then on her face. Her squawks redoubled, as Tonino smote away at her back, and then her voice stopped. She lay with her head hanging down from the front of the platform, looking just like a puppet. Tonino found himself having to kick her down the empty space between the false villa and the stage. He heard the distant *flop* as she fell. And then he was forced to skip and cackle with glee, while the Duchess threw back her head and laughed as heartily as the Duke.

Tonino hated her. He was so angry and so miserable that he did not mind at all when a cardboard policeman appeared and he chased him with the stick too. He laid into the policeman as if he was the Duchess and not a cardboard doll at all.

"Are you all right, Lucrezia?" he heard the Duke say.

Tonino looked sideways as he dealt another mighty swipe at the policeman's cardboard helmet. He saw the Duchess wince as the stick landed. He was not surprised when the policeman was immediately whisked away and he himself forced into a violent capering and even louder squawking. He let himself do it. He felt truly gleeful as he squawked, "What a clever fellow!" for what felt like the thousandth time. For he understood what had happened. The Duchess *was* the policeman, in a sort of way. She was putting some of herself into all the puppets to make them work. But he must not let her know he knew. Tonino capered and chortled, doing his best to seem terrified, and kept his eyes on that carving of the Angel, high up over the door of the room.

And now the hooded Hangman-puppet appeared, dragging a little wooden gibbet with a string noose dangling from it. Tonino capered cautiously. This was where the Duchess did for him unless he was very careful. On the other hand, if this Punch and Judy show went as it should, he might just do for the Duchess.

The silly scene began. Tonino had never worked so hard at anything in his life. He kept repeating the words of the *Angel* in his head, both as a kind of prayer and as a smoke-screen, so that the Duchess would not understand what he was trying to do. At the same time, he thought, fiercely and vengefully, that the Hangman was not just a puppet—it was the Duchess herself. And, also at the same time, he attended to Mr Punch's conversation with all his might. This had to go right.

"Come along, Mr Punch," croaked the Hangman. "Just put your head in this noose."

"How do I do that?" asked Mr Punch and Tonino, both pretending hard to be stupid.

"You put your head in here," croaked the Hangman, putting one hand through the noose.

Mr Punch and Tonino, both of them quivering with cunning, put his head first one side of the noose, then the other. "Is this right? Is this?" Then, pretending even harder to be stupid, "I can't see how to do it. You'll have to show me."

Either the Duchess was wanting to play with Tonino's feelings, or she was trying the same cunning. They went through this several times. Each time, the Hangman put his hand through the noose to show Mr Punch what to do. Tonino did not dare look at the Duchess. He looked at the Hangman and kept thinking, That's the Duchess, and reciting the *Angel* for all he was worth. At last, to his relief, the Duke became restive.

"Come on, Mr Punch!" he shouted.

"You'll have to put your head in and show me," Mr Punch and Tonino said, as persuasively as he knew how.

"Oh well," croaked the Hangman. "Since you're so stupid." And he put his cardboard head through the noose.

Mr Punch and Tonino promptly pulled the rope and hanged him. But Tonino thought, This is the *Duchess*! and went as limp and heavy as he could. For just a second, his full puppet's weight swung on the end of the rope.

It only lasted that second. Tonino had a glimpse of the Duchess on her feet with her hands to her throat. He felt real triumph. Then he was thrown, flat on his face, across the stage, unable to move at all. There he was forced to lie. His head hung down from the front of the stage, so that he could see very little. But he gathered that the Duchess was being led tenderly away, with the Duke fussing round her.

I think I feel as pleased as Punch, he thought.

CHAPTER 10

Paolo never wanted to remember that night afterwards. He was still staring at the sick yellow message in the yard, when the rest of the family arrived. He was crowded aside to let Old Niccolo and Aunt Francesca through, but Benvenuto spat at them like hot fat hitting fire and would not let them pass.

"Let be, old boy," Old Niccolo said. "You've done your best." He turned to Aunt Francesca. "I shall never forgive the Petrocchis," he said. "Never." Paolo was once again struck by how wretched and goblin-like his grandfather looked. He had thought Old Niccolo was helping vast, panting, muddy Aunt Francesca along, but he now wondered if it was not the other way round. "Well. Let's get rid of this horrible message," Old Niccolo said irritably to the rest of them.

He raised his arms to start the family on the spell and collapsed. His hands went to his chest. He slid to his knees, and his face was a strange colour. Paolo thought he was dead until he saw him breathing, in uneven jerks. Elizabeth, Uncle Lorenzo and Aunt Maria rushed to him.

"Heart attack," Uncle Lorenzo said, nodding over at Antonio. "Get that spell going. We've got to get him indoors."

"Paolo, run for the doctor," said Elizabeth.

As Paolo ran, he heard the burst of singing behind him. When he came back with the doctor, the message had vanished and Old Niccolo had been carried up to bed. Aunt Francesca, still muddy, with her hair hanging down one side, was roving up and down the yard like a moving mountain, crying and wringing her hands.

"Spells are forbidden," she called out to Paolo. "I've stopped everything."

"And a good thing too!" the doctor said sourly. "A man of Niccolo Montana's age has no business to be brawling in the streets. And make your great-aunt lie down," he said to Paolo. "She'll be in bed next."

Aunt Francesca would only go to the Saloon, where she refused even to sit down. She raged up and down, wailing about Old Niccolo, weeping about Tonino, declaring that the virtue had gone from the Casa Montana for good, and uttering terrible threats against the Petrocchis. Nobody else was much better. The children cried with tiredness. Elizabeth and the aunts worried about Old Niccolo, and then about Aunt Francesca. In the Scriptorium, among all the abandoned spells, Antonio and the uncles sat rigid with worry, and the rest of the Casa was full of older cousins wandering about and cursing the Petrocchis.

Paolo found Rinaldo leaning moodily on the gallery rail, in spite of it being dark now and really quite cold. "Curse those Petrocchis," he said gloomily to Paolo. "We can't even earn a living now, let alone help if there's a war."

Paolo, in spite of his misery, was very flattered that Rinaldo seemed to think him old enough to talk family business to. He said, "Yes, it's awful," and tried to lean on the rail in the same elegant attitude as Rinaldo. It was not easy, since Paolo was not nearly tall enough, but he leant and prepared the arguments he would use to persuade Rinaldo that Tonino was in the hands of an enemy enchanter. That was not easy either. Paolo knew that Rinaldo would not listen to him if he dropped the least small hint that he had talked to a Petrocchi—and besides, he would have died rather than told his cousin. But he knew that, if he persuaded Rinaldo, Rinaldo would rescue Tonino in five dashing minutes. Rinaldo was a true Montana.

While he thought, Rinaldo said angrily, "What possessed that stupid brat Tonino to read that blessed book? I shall give him something to think about when we get him back!"

Paolo shivered in the cold. "Tonino always reads books." Then he shifted a bit—the elegant attitude was not at all comfortable—and asked timidly, "How shall we get him back?" This was not at all what he had planned to say. He was annoyed with himself.

"What's the use?" Rinaldo said. "We know where he is—in the Casa Petrocchi. And if he's uncomfortable there, it's his own fault!"

"But he's not!" Paolo protested. As far as he could see in the light from the yard lamp, Rinaldo turned and looked at him jeeringly. The discussion seemed to be getting further from the way he had planned it every second. "An enemy enchanter's got him," he said. "The one Chrestomanci talked about."

Rinaldo laughed. "Load of old crab-apples, Paolo. Our friend had been talking to the Petrocchis. He invented his convenient enchanter because he wanted us all working for Caprona. Most of us saw through it at once."

"Then who made that mist on the Corso?" Paolo said. "It wasn't us, and it wasn't them."

But Rinaldo only said, "Who said it wasn't them?"

As Paolo could not say it was Renata Petrocchi, he could not answer. Instead, he said rather desperately, "Come with me to the Casa Petrocchi. If you used a finding-spell, you could *prove* Tonino isn't there."

"What?" Rinaldo seemed astounded. "What kind of fool do you take me for, Paolo? I'm not going to take on a whole family of spell-makers single-handed. And if I go there and use a spell, and they do something to Tonino, everyone's going to blame me, aren't they? For something we know anyway. It's not worth it, Paolo. But I tell you what—"

He was interrupted by Aunt Gina trumpeting below in the yard. "Notti's is the only chemist open by now. Tell him it's for Niccolo Montana!"

With some relief, Paolo dropped the elegant attitude entirely and leant over the rail to watch Lucia and Corinna hurry through the yard with the doctor's prescription. The sight gave his stomach a wrench of worry. "Do you think Old Niccolo's going to die, Rinaldo?"

Rinaldo shrugged. "Could be. He's pretty old. It's about time the old idiot gave up anyway. I shall be one step closer to being head of the Casa Montana then."

A peculiar thing happened inside Paolo's head then. He had never given much thought to who might follow Antonio—for it was clear his father would follow Old Niccolo—as head of the Casa Montana. But he had never, for some reason, thought it might be Rinaldo. Now he tried to imagine Rinaldo doing the things Old Niccolo did. And as soon as he did, he saw Rinaldo was quite unsuitable. Rinaldo was vain, and selfish—and cowardly, provided he could be a coward and still keep up a good appearance. It was as if Rinaldo had said a powerful spell to clear Paolo's eyes.

It never occurred to Rinaldo, expert spell-maker though he was, that a few ordinary words could make such a difference. He bent towards Paolo and dropped his voice to a melodious murmur. "I was going to tell you, Paolo. I'm going round enlisting all the young ones. We're going to swear to work a secret revenge on the Petrocchis. We'll do something worse than make them eat their words. Are you with me? Will you swear to join the plan?"

Maybe he was in earnest. It would suit Rinaldo to work in secret, with lots of willing helpers. But Paolo was sure that this plan was a step in Rinaldo's plans to be head of the Casa. Paolo sidled away along the rail.

"Are you game?" Rinaldo whispered, laughing a little.

Paolo sidled beyond grabbing-distance. "Tell you later." He turned and scudded away. Rinaldo laughed and did not try to catch him. He thought Paolo was scared.

Paolo went down into the yard, feeling more lonely than he had felt in his life. Tonino was not there. Tonino was not vain, or selfish, or cowardly. And nobody would help him find Tonino. Paolo had not noticed until now how much he depended on Tonino. They did everything important together. Even if Paolo was busy on his own, he knew Tonino was there somewhere, sitting reading, ready to put his book down if Paolo needed him. Now there seemed to be nothing for Paolo to do. And the whole Casa reeked of worry.

He went to the kitchen, where there seemed, at last, to be something happening. All his small cousins were there. Rosa and Marco were trying to make soup for them.

"Come in and help, Paolo," Rosa said. "We're going to put them to bed after soup, but we're having a bit of trouble."

Both she and Marco were looking tired and flustered. Most of the little ones were grizzling, including the baby. The trouble was Lucia's spell. Paolo understood this because Marco dumped the baby in his arms. Its wrapper was covered with orange grease. "Yuk!" said Paolo.

"I know," said Rosa. "Well, Marco, better try again. Clean saucepan. Clean water. The very last packet of soup-powder—don't make that face, Paolo. We've got through all the vegetables. They just sail away to the waste-bins, and they're mouldy before they get there."

Paolo looked nervously at the door, wondering if the enemy enchanter was powerful enough to overhear him. "Try a cancel-spell," he whispered.

"Aunt Gina went through them all this afternoon," said Rosa. "No good. Little Lucia used the *Angel of Caprona,* you see. We're trying Marco's way now. Ready, Marco?"

Rosa opened the packet of soup and held it over the saucepan. As the dry pink powder poured into the water, Marco leant over the saucepan and sang furiously. Paolo watched them nervously. This was just what the message told them not to do, he was sure. When all the powder was in the water, Rosa and Marco peered anxiously into the saucepan. "Have we done it?" asked Marco.

"I think—" Rosa began, and ended in a yell of exasperation. "Oh *no*!" The little pasta shells in the powder had turned into real sea-shells, little grey ones. "With *creatures* in!" Rosa said despairingly, dipping a spoonful out. "Where *is* Lucia?" she said. "Bring her here. Tell her I— No, don't. Just fetch her, Paolo."

"She's gone to the chemist," said Paolo.

There was shouting in the yard. Paolo passed the greasy baby to the nearest cousin and shot outside, dreading another sick yellow message about Tonino. Or there was just a chance the noise was Lucia.

It was neither. It was Rinaldo. The uncles must have left the Scriptorium, for Rinaldo was making a bonfire of spells in the middle of the yard. Domenico, Carlo and Luigi were busily carrying armfuls of scrips, envelopes and scrolls down from the gallery. Paolo recognised, already curling among the flames, the army-charms he and the other children had spent such a time copying. It was a shocking waste of work.

"This is what the Petrocchis have forced us to!" shouted Rinaldo, striking an attitude beside the flames. It was evidently part of his plan to enlist the young ones.

Paolo was glad to see Antonio and Uncle Lorenzo hurry out of the Saloon.

"Rinaldo!" shouted Antonio. "Rinaldo, we're worried about Umberto. We want you to go to the University and enquire."

"Send Domenico," said Rinaldo, and turned back to the flames.

"No," said Antonio. "You go." There was something about the way he said it that caused Rinaldo to back away from him.

"I'll go," said Rinaldo. He held up one hand, laughing. "I was only joking, Uncle Antonio."

He left at once. "Take those spells back," Uncle Lorenzo said to the other three cousins. "I hate to see good work wasted." Domenico, Carlo and Luigi obeyed without a word. Antonio and Uncle Lorenzo went to the bonfire and tried to stamp out the flames, but they were burning too strongly. Paolo saw them look at one another, rather guiltily, and then lean forward and whisper a spell over the fire. It flicked out as if it had been turned off with a switch. Paolo sighed worriedly. It was plain that no one in the Casa Montana could drop the habit of using spells. He wondered how long it would be before the enemy enchanter noticed.

"Fetch a light!" Antonio shouted to Domenico. "And sort out the ones that aren't burnt."

Paolo went back to the kitchen before they asked him to help. The bonfire had given him an idea.

"There is quite a bit of mince," Rosa was saying. "Dare we try with that?"

"Why don't you," said Paolo, "take the food to the dining-room? I'll light a fire there, and you can cook it on that."

"The boy's a genius!" said Marco.

They did that. Rosa cooked by relays and Marco made cocoa. The children were fed first, Paolo included. Paolo sat on one of the long benches, thinking it was almost enjoyable—except if he thought of Tonino, or Old Niccolo in bed upstairs. He was very pleased and surprised when a sudden bundle of claw and warm-iron muscle landed on his knee. Benvenuto was missing Tonino too. He rubbed against Paolo with a kind of desperation, but he would not purr.

Rosa and Marco were getting up to put the young ones to bed, when there was a sudden great clanging, outside in the night.

"Good Heavens!" said Rosa, and opened the yard door.

The noise flooded in, an uneven metal sound, hasty and huge. The nearest—*clang-clang-clang*—was so near that it could only be the bell of Sant' Angelo's. Behind it, the bell of the Cathedral tolled. And beyond that, now near, now faint and tinny, every bell in every church in Caprona beat and boomed and clashed and chimed. Corinna and Lucia came racing in, their faces bright with cold and excitement.

"We're at war! The Duke's declared war!"

Marco said he thought he had better go. "Oh no, don't!" Rosa cried out. "Not yet. By the way, Lucia—"

Lucia took a quick look at the cooking in the hearth. "I'll go and take Aunt Gina the prescription," she said, and prudently ran away.

Marco and Rosa looked at one another. "Three States against us and no spells to fight with," said Marco. "We're not likely to have a long and happy marriage, are we?"

"Mr Notti says the Final Reserve is being called up tomorrow," Corinna said encouragingly. She caught Rosa's eye. "Come on, you kids," she said to four cousins at random. "Bed time."

While the young ones were being put to bed, Paolo sat nursing Benvenuto, feeling more dismal than ever. He wondered if there would be soldiers from Florence and Pisa and Siena in Caprona by tomorrow. Would guns fire in the streets? He thought of big marble chips shot off the Cathedral, the New Bridge broken, despite all the spells in it, and swarthy enemy soldiers dragging Rosa off screaming. And he saw that all this could really have happened by the end of the week.

Here, he became quite certain that Benvenuto was trying to tell him something. He could tell from the accusing stare of Benvenuto's yellow eyes. But he simply could not understand.

"I'll try," he said to Benvenuto. "I really will try."

He had, fleetingly, the feeling that Benvenuto was glad. Encouraged by this, Paolo bent his head and stared at Benvenuto's urgent face. But it did no good. All that Paolo could get out of it was a picture in his mind—a picture of somewhere with a coloured marble front, very large and beautiful.

"The Church of Sant' Angelo?" he said doubtfully.

While Benvenuto's tail was still lashing with annoyance, Rosa and Marco came back. "Oh dear!" Rosa said to Marco. "There's Paolo taking all the troubles of the Casa on his shoulders again!"

Paolo looked up in surprise.

Marco said, "You look just like Antonio sometimes."

"I can't understand Benvenuto," Paolo said despairingly.

Marco sat on the table beside him. "Then he'll have to find some other way of telling us what he wants," he said. "He's a clever cat—the cleverest I've ever known. He'll do it." He put out a hand and Benvenuto let him stroke his head. "Your ears," said Marco, "Sir Cat, are like sea-holly without the prickles."

Rosa perched on the table too, on the other side of Paolo. "What is it, Paolo? Tonino?"

Paolo nodded. "Nobody will believe me that the enemy enchanter's got him."

"We do," said Marco.

Rosa said, "Paolo, it's just as well he's got Tonino and not you. Tonino'll take it much more calmly."

Paolo was a little bewildered. "Why do you two believe in the enchanter and no one else does?"

"What makes you think he exists?" Marco countered.

Even to Rosa and Marco, Paolo could not bring himself to tell of his embarrassing encounter with a Petrocchi. "There was a horrible fog at the end of the fight," he said.

Rosa and Marco jumped round delightedly. Their hands met with a smack over Paolo's head. "It worked! It worked!" And Marco added, "We were hoping someone would mention a certain fog! Did there seem to have been a large-scale cancel-spell with it, by any chance?"

"Yes," said Paolo.

"*We* made that fog," Rosa said. "Marco and me. We were hoping to stop the fighting, but it took us ages to make it, because all the magic in Caprona was going into the fight."

Paolo digested this. That took care of the one piece of proof that did not depend on the word of a Petrocchi. Perhaps the enchanter did not exist after all. Perhaps Tonino really was at the Casa Petrocchi. He remembered that Renata had not said Angelica was missing until the fog cleared and she knew who he was. "Look," he said. "Will you two come to the Casa Petrocchi with me and see if Tonino's there?"

He was aware that Rosa and Marco were exchanging some kind of look above his head. "Why?" said Rosa.

"Because," said Paolo. "Because." The need to persuade them cleared his wits at last. "Because Guido Petrocchi said Angelica Petrocchi was missing too."

"I'm afraid we can't," Marco said, with what sounded like real regret. "You'd understand, if you knew how pressing our reasons are, believe me!"

Paolo did not understand. He knew that, with these two, it was not cowardice, or pride, or anything like that. That only made it more maddening. "Oh, nobody will help!" he cried out.

Rosa put her arm around him. "Paolo! You're just like Father. You think you have to do everything yourself. There is one thing we can do."

"Call Chrestomanci?" said Marco.

Paolo felt Rosa nod. "But he's in Rome," he objected.

"It doesn't matter," said Marco. "He's that kind of enchanter. If he's near enough and you need him enough, he comes when you call."

"I must cook!" said Rosa, jumping off the table.

Just before the second supper was ready, Rinaldo came back, in great good spirits. Uncle Umberto and old Luigi Petrocchi had had another fight, in the dining-hall of the University. That was why Uncle Umberto had not turned up to see how Old Niccolo was. He and Luigi were both in bed, prostrated with exhaustion. Rinaldo had been drinking wine with some students who told him all about the fight. The students' supper had been ruined. Cutlets and pasta had flown about, followed by chairs, tables and benches. Umberto had tried to drown Luigi in a soup tureen, and Luigi had replied by hurling the whole of the Doctors' supper at Umberto. The students were going on strike. They did not mind the fight, but Luigi had shown them that the Doctors' food was better than theirs.

Paolo listened without truly attending. He was thinking about Tonino and wondering if he dared depend on the word of a Petrocchi.

CHAPTER 11

After a while, someone came and picked Tonino up. That was unpleasant. His legs and arms dragged and dangled in all directions, and he could not do anything about it. He was plunged somewhere much darker. Then he was left to lie amid a great deal of bumping and scraping, as if he were in a box which was being pushed across a floor. When it stopped, he found he could move. He sat up, trembling all over.

He was in the same room as before, but it seemed to be much smaller. He could tell that, if he stood up, his head would brush the little lighted chandelier in the ceiling. So he was larger now; where he had been three inches tall before, he must now be more like nine. The puppets must be too big for their scenery, and the false villa meant to look as if it was some distance away. And, with the Duchess suddenly taken ill, none of her helpers had bothered what size Tonino was. They had simply made sure he was shut up again.

"Tonino," whispered Angelica.

Tonino whirled round. Half the room was full of a pile of lax puppet bodies. He scanned the cardboard head of the policeman, then his enemy the Hangman, and the white sausage of the baby, and came upon Angelica's face halfway up the pile. It was her own face, though swollen and tearstained. Tonino clapped his hand to his nose. To his relief, the red beak was gone, though he still seemed to be wearing Mr Punch's scarlet nightgown.

"I'm sorry," he said. His teeth seemed to be chattering. "I tried not to hurt you. Are your bones broken?"

"No—o," said Angelica. She did not sound too sure. "Tonino, what happened?"

"I hanged the Duchess," Tonino said, and he felt some vicious triumph as he said it. "I didn't kill her though," he added regretfully.

Angelica laughed. She laughed until the heap of puppets was shaking and sliding about. But Tonino could not find it funny. He burst into tears, even though he was crying in front of a Petrocchi.

"Oh dear," said Angelica. "Tonino, stop it! Tonino—please!" She struggled out from among the puppets and hobbled looming through the room. Her head banged the chandelier and sent it tinkling and casting mad shadows over them as she knelt down beside Tonino. "Tonino, please stop. She'll be furious as soon as she feels better." Angelica was wearing Judy's blue cap and Judy's blue dress still. She took off the blue cap and held it out to Tonino. "Here. Blow on that. I used the baby's dress. It made me feel better." She tried to smile at him, but the smile went hopelessly crooked in her swollen face. Angelica's large forehead must have hit the floor first. It was now enlarged by a huge red bump. Under it, the grin looked grotesque.

Tonino understood it was meant for a smile and smiled back, as well as he could for his chattering teeth.

"Here." Angelica loomed back through the room to the pile of puppets and heaved at the Hangman. She returned with his black felt cape. "Put this on."

Tonino wrapped himself in the cape and blew his nose on the blue cap and felt better.

Angelica heaved more puppets about. "I'm going to wear the policeman's jacket," she said. "Tonino—have you thought?"

"Not really," said Tonino. "I sort of know."

He had known from the moment he looked at the Duchess. She was the enchanter who was sapping the strength of Caprona and spoiling the spells of the Casa Montana. Tonino was not sure about the Duke—probably he was too stupid to count. But in spite of the Duchess's enchantments, the spells of the Casa Montana—and the Casa Petrocchi—must still be strong enough to be a nuisance to her. So he and Angelica had been kidnapped to blackmail both houses into stopping making spells. And if they stopped, Caprona would be defeated. The frightening part was that Tonino and Angelica were the only two people who knew, and the Duchess did not care that they knew. It was not only that even someone as clever as Paolo would never think of looking in the Palace, inside a Punch and Judy show: it must mean that the two of them would be dead before anyone found them.

"We absolutely have to get away," said Angelica. "Before she's better from being hanged."

"She'll have thought of that," said Tonino.

"I'm not sure," said Angelica. "I could tell everyone was startled to death. They let me see you being put through thc floor, and I think we could get out that way. It will be easier now we're bigger."

Tonino fastened the cape round him and struggled to his feet, though he felt almost too tired and bruised to bother. His head hit the chandelier too. Huge flickering shadows fled round the room, and made the heap of puppets look as if they were squirming about. "Where did they put me through?" he said.

"Just where you're standing," said Angelica.

Tonino backed against the windows and looked at the place. He would not have known there was any opening. But, now Angelica had told him, he could see, disguised by the painted swirls of the carpet and confused by the swinging light, the faintest black line. The outline made an oblong about the size of the shoddy dining-table. The tray of supper must have come through that way too.

"Sing an opening spell," Angelica commanded him.

"I don't know one," Tonino was forced to confess.

He could tell by the stiff way Angelica stood that she was trying not to say a number of nasty things. "Well I don't dare," she said. "You saw what happened last time. If I do anything, they'll catch us again and punish us by making us be puppets. And I couldn't bear another time."

Tonino was not sure he could bear it either, even though, now he thought about it, he was not sure it had been a punishment. The Duchess had probably intended to make them perform anyway. She was quite mean enough. On the other hand, he was not sure he could stand another of Angelica's botched spells, either. "Well, it's only a trap-door," he said. "It must be held up by one of those little hooks. Let's try bashing at it with the candlesticks."

"And if there's a spell on it?" said Angelica. "Oh, come on. Let's try."

They seized a candlestick each and knelt beside the windows, knocking diligently at the scarcely-seen black line. The cardboard was tough and pulpy. The candlesticks shortly looked like metal weeping-willow trees. But they succeeded in making a crumbly hollow in the middle of one edge of the hidden door. Tonino thought he could see a glimmer of metal showing. He raised his bent candlestick high to deliver a mighty blow.

"Stop!" hissed Angelica.

There were large shuffling footsteps somewhere. Tonino lowered the candlestick by gentle fractions and scarcely dared breathe. A distant voice grumbled. . . . "Mice then" . . . "Nothing here. . . ." It was suddenly very much darker. Someone had switched off a light, leaving them only with the bluish glimmer of the little chandelier. The footsteps shuffled. A door bumped, and there was silence.

Angelica laid her candlestick down and began trying to tear at the cardboard with her fingers. Tonino got up and wandered away. It was no good. Someone was going to hear them, whatever they did. The Palace was full of footmen and soldiers. Tonino would have given up then and waited for the Duchess to do her worst. Only now he was standing up, the cardboard room seemed so small. Half of it was filled with the puppets. There was hardly room to move. Tonino wanted to hurl himself at the walls and scream. He did make a movement, and knocked the table. Because he was so much bigger and heavier now, the table swayed and creaked.

"I know!" he said. "Finish drawing the Angel."

The bump on Angelica's forehead turned up to him. "I'm not in the mood for doodling."

"Not a doodle, a spell," Tonino explained. "And then pull the table over us while we make a hole in the trap-door."

Angelica did not need telling that the Angel was the most potent spell in Caprona. She threw the candlestick aside and scrambled up. "That might just work," she said. "You know, for a Montana, you have very good ideas." Her head hit the chandelier again. In the confusion of swinging shadows, they could not find the tap Angelica had been drawing with. Tonino had to jam his head and arm into the tiny bathroom and pull off the other useless tap.

Even when the shadows stopped swinging, the Angel scratched on the table was hard to see. It now looked faint and small.

"He needs his scroll," said Angelica. "And I'd better put in a halo to make sure he's holy."

Angelica was now so much bigger and stronger that she kept dropping the tap. The halo, when she had scratched it in, was too big, and the scroll would not go right. The table swayed this way and that, the tap ploughed and skidded, and there was a danger the Angel would end up a complete mess.

"It's so fiddly!" said Angelica. "Will that do?"

"No," said Tonino. "It needs the scroll more unrolled. Some of the words show on our Angel."

Because he was quite right, Angelica lost her temper. "All right! Do it yourself, if you're so clever, you horrible Montana!"

She held the tap out to Tonino and he snatched it from her, quite as angry. "Here," he said, ploughing up a long curl of varnish. "Here's the hanging bit. And the words go sideways. You can see *Carmen pa, Venit ang, Cap* and a lot more, but there won't be room for it."

"Our Angel," said Angelica, "says *cis saeculare, elus cantare* and *virtus data* near the end." Tonino scratched away and took no notice. It was hard enough shaping tiny letters with a thing like a tap, without listening to Angelica arguing. "Well it does!" said Angelica. "I've often wondered why it's not the words we sing—"

The same idea came to both of them. They stared at one another, nose to nose across the scratched varnish.

"*Finding* the words means *looking* for them," said Tonino.

"And they were over our gates all the time! Oh how *stupid*!" exclaimed Angelica. "Come on. We *must* get out now!"

Tonino left the scroll with *Carmen* scraped on it. There was really no room for any more. They dragged the creaking, swaying table across the hole they had made in the floor and set to work underneath it, hacking lumps out of the painted floor. Shortly, they could see a bar of silvery metal stretching from the trap door to the floor underneath them. Tonino forced the end of his candlestick down between the battered cardboard edges and heaved sideways at the metal.

"There's a spell on it," he said.

"Angel of Caprona," Angelica said at the same moment.

And the bar slipped sideways. A big oblong piece of the floor dropped away from in front of their knees and swung, leaving a very deep dark hole.

"Let's get the Hangman's rope," said Angelica.

They edged along to the pile of puppets and disentangled the string from the little gibbet. Tonino tied it to the table leg.

"It's a long way down," he said dubiously.

"It's only a few feet *really,*" Angelica said. "And we're not heavy enough to hurt. I went all floppy when you kicked me off the stage and—well—I didn't break anything anyway."

Tonino let Angelica go first, swinging down into the dark space like an energetic blue monkey. *Crunch* went the shoddy table. *Creeeak.* And it swayed towards the leg where the rope was tied.

"Angel of Caprona!" Tonino whispered.

The table plunged, one corner first, down into the space. The cardboard room rattled. And, with a rending and creaking of wood, the table stuck, mostly in the hole, but with one corner out and wedged against the sides. There was a thump from below. Tonino was fairly sure he was stuck in the room for good now.

"I'm down," Angelica whispered up. "You can pull the rope up. It nearly reaches the floor."

Tonino leaned over and fumbled the string up from the table leg. He was sure there had been a miracle. That leg ought to have broken off, or the table ought to have gone down the hole. He whispered "Angel of Caprona!" again as he slid down under the table into the dark.

The table creaked hideously, but it held together. The string burnt Tonino's hands as he slid, and then it was suddenly not there. His feet hit the floor almost at once. "Oof!" he went. His feet felt as if they had been knocked up through his legs.

Down there, they were standing on the shiny floor of a Palace room. The towering walls of the Punch and Judy show were on three sides of them. Instead of a back wall, there was a curtain, intended to hide the puppet-master, and very dim light was coming in round its edges. They pulled one end of the curtain aside. It felt coarse and heavy, like a sack. Behind it was the wall of the room. The puppet show had evidently been simply pushed away to one side. There was just space for Angelica and Tonino to squeeze past the ends of the show, into a large room lit by moonlight falling in strong silver blocks across its shiny floor.

It was the same room where the court had watched the Punch and Judy show. The puppet show had not been put away. Tonino thought of the time he and Angelica had tottered on the edge of the stage, looking into nothingness. They could have been killed. That seemed another miracle. Then, they must have been in some kind of storeroom. But, when the Duchess was so mysteriously taken ill, no one had bothered to put them back there.

The moonlight glittered on the polished face of the Angel, high up on the other side of the room, leaning out over some big double doors. There were other doors, but Tonino and Angelica set out, without hesitation, towards the Angel. Both of them took it for a guide.

"Oh bother!" said Angelica, before they reached the first block of moonlight. "We're still small. I thought we'd be the right size as soon as we got out, didn't you?"

Tonino's one idea was to get out, whatever his size. "It'll be easier to hide like this," he said. "Someone in your Casa can easily turn you back." He pulled the Hangman's cloak round him and shivered. It was colder out in the big room. He could see the moon through the big windows, riding high and cold in a wintry dark blue sky. It was not going to be fun running through the streets in a red nightgown.

"But I *hate* being this small!" Angelica complained. "We'll never be able to get down stairs."

She was right to complain, as Tonino soon discovered. It seemed a mile across the polished floor. When they reached the double doors, they were tired out. High above them, the carved Angel dangled a scroll they could not possibly read, and no longer looked so friendly. But the doors were open a crack. They managed to push the crack wider by leaning their backs against the edge of both doors. It was maddening to think they could have opened them with one hand if only they had been the proper size.

Beyond was an even bigger room. This one was full of chairs and small tables. The only advantage of being doll-sized was that they could walk under every piece of furniture in a straight line to the far-too-distant door. It was like trudging through a golden moonlit forest, where every tree had an elegant swan-bend to its trunk. The floor seemed to be marble.

Before they reached the door, they were quarrelling again from sheer tiredness.

"It's going to take all *night* to get out of here!" Angelica grumbled.

"Oh shut up!" said Tonino. "You make more fuss about things than my Aunt Gina!"

"Is your Aunt Gina bruised all over because you hit her?" Angelica demanded.

When they came to the half-open door at last, there was only another room, slightly smaller. This one had a carpet. Gilded sofas stood about like Dutch barns, and large frilly armchairs. Angelica gave a wail of despair.

Tonino stood on tiptoe. There seemed to be cushions on some of the seats. "Suppose we hid under a cushion for the night?" he suggested, trying to make peace.

Angelica turned on him furiously. "Stupid! No wonder you're slow at spells! We may be small, but they'll find us *because* of that. We must *stink* of magic. Even my baby brother could find us, and he may be a baby but he's cleverer than you!"

Tonino was too angry to answer. He simply marched away into the carpet. At first it was a relief to his sore feet, but it soon became another trial. It was like walking through long, tufty grass—and anyone who has done that for a mile or so will know how tiring that can be. On top of that, they had to keep going round puffy armchairs that seemed as big as houses, frilly footstools and screens as big as hoardings. Some of these things would have made good hiding-places, but they were both too angry and frightened to suggest it.

Then, when they reached the door at last, it was shut. They threw themselves against the hard wood. It did not even shake.

"Now what?" said Tonino, leaning his back against it. The moon was going down by now. The carpet was in darkness. The bars of moonlight from the far-off windows only touched the tops of armchairs, or picked out the gold on the sofa backs, or the glitter from a shelf of coloured glass vases. It would be quite dark soon.

"There's an Angel over there," Angelica said wearily.

She was right. Tonino could just see it, as coloured flickers on wood, lit by moonlight reflected off the shelf of glass vases. There was another door under the Angel, or rather a dark space, because that door was wide open. Too tired even to speak, Tonino set off again, across another mile of tufty carpet, past beetling cliffs of furniture, to the other side of the room.

By the time they reached that open door, they were so tired that nothing seemed real any more. There were four steps down beyond the door. Very well. They went down them somehow. At the bottom was an even more brutally tufted carpet. And the window here was the other side from the moon. It was quite dark.

Angelica sniffed the darkness. "Cigars."

It could have been scillas for all Tonino cared. All he wanted was the next door. He set off, feeling round the walls for it, with Angelica stumbling after. They bumped into one huge piece of furniture, felt their way round it, and banged into another, which stuck even further into the room. And so they went, stumbling and banging, climbing across two rounded metal bars, wading in carpet, until they arrived at the four steps again. It was quite a small room—for the Palace—and it had only one door. Tonino felt for the first step, as high as his head, and did not think he had the strength to get up them again. The Angel had not been a guide after all.

"That part that stuck out," said Angelica. "I don't know what it was, but it was hollow, like a box. Shall we risk hiding in it?"

"Let's find it," said Tonino.

They found it, or something like it, by walking into it. It was a steep-sided box which came up to their armpits. There was a large piece of metal, like a very wide door-knocker, hung on the front of it. When they felt inside, they felt sheets of stiff leather, and crisper stuff that was possibly paper.

"I think it's an open drawer," said Tonino.

Angelica did not answer. She simply climbed in. Tonino heard her flapping and crackling among the paper—if it was paper. Well! he thought. And it was Angelica who said they smelt of magic. But he was so tired that he climbed in too, and fell into a warm crumply nest where Angelica was already asleep. Tonino was almost too tired by now to care if they were found or not. But he had the sense to drag a piece of parchment over them both before he went to sleep too.

CHAPTER 12

Tonino woke up feeling chilly and puzzled. The light was pale and yellow because his sheet seemed to be over his face. Tonino gazed up at it, thinking it was a surprisingly flat, stiff sheet. It had large black letters on it too. His eyes travelled along the letters. *DECLARATION OF WAR (Duplicate Copy),* he read.

Then he knew, with a jump, that he was nine inches high and lying in a drawer in the Palace. And it was light! Someone would find them. In fact, someone nearly had. That was what had woken him. He could hear someone moving about the room, making obscure thumps and shuffles, and occasionally whistling a snatch of the *Angel of Caprona.* Whoever it was had reached the drawer now. Tonino could hear the floor creak under him and a dress rustling, loud and near. He moved his head, gently and stiffly, and found Angelica's frightened face resting on crumpled paper an inch or so away. The rustling dress proved the person was a woman. It must be the Duchess looking for them.

"That Duke!" said the person, in a voice no Duchess would use. "There never was such an untidy man!" Her breathing came suddenly nearer. Before either Tonino or Angelica could think what to do, the drawer moved. Helplessly, they were shunted inwards, feet first, into darkness, and the drawer shut with a bang behind their heads.

"Help!" whispered Angelica.

"Ssh!"

The maid was still in the room. They could hear her move something, and then a tinkle of notes as she dusted a piano. Then a bump. And finally nothing. When they were quite sure she was gone, Angelica whispered, "What do we do now?"

There was room to sit up in the drawer, but not much else. Above their heads was a slit of light where the drawer met the desk, or whatever it was, and no way of opening it. But they could see quite well. Light was coming in at the back, beyond their feet. They tried bracing their hands against the wood overhead and heaving, but the drawer was made of solid, spicy-smelling wood and they could not budge it.

"We keep being shut in places without doors!" Angelica cried out. And she went floundering through the papers to the back of the drawer, where the light came in. Tonino crawled after her.

As soon as they got there, they realised this was the way out. The end of the drawer was lower than the front, and it did not reach the back of the wooden desk it was part of. There was quite a big gap there. When they put their heads into the space, they could see the ends of the other drawers above theirs going up like a ladder, and a slit of daylight at the top.

They squeezed through into the gap and climbed, side by side. It was as easy as climbing a ladder. They were one drawer away from the slit of daylight—which was going to be a tight squeeze—when they heard someone else in the room.

"They came down here, madam," said a lady's voice.

"Then we've caught them," replied the Duchess. "Look very carefully."

Tonino and Angelica hung from the back of the drawers by their fingers and toes, not daring to move. Silk dresses rustled as the Duchess and her lady moved round the room.

"There's nothing this end at all, madam,"

"And I swear this window hasn't been opened," said the Duchess. "Open all the drawers in the desk."

There was a sharp rumble above Tonino's head. Dusty white light flooded down from the open top drawer. Papers were loudly tossed over. "Nothing," said the lady. The top drawer slammed in again. Tonino and Angelica had been hanging on to the second drawer. They climbed down to the next as fast and quietly as they could. The second drawer rumbled open, and slammed shut, nearly deafening them. The drawer they were on jerked. Luckily, it was stiff. The lady tugged and rattled at it, and that gave Tonino and Angelica just time to climb frantically up to the second drawer again and cling there. And there they hung, in the dark narrow space, while the lady opened the third drawer, slammed it shut, and pulled out the bottom drawer. They craned over their arms and watched the white light flood in from below.

"Look at this!" cried the lady. "They've been here! It's like a mouse-nest!"

Silks rustled as the Duchess hurried over. "Curse it!" she said. "Not long ago too! I can smell them even through the cigars. Quick! They can't be far away. They must have got out before the room was cleaned."

The drawer rumbled in, bringing dusty darkness with it. There was a flurry of silks as the two women hurried away up the steps to the room with the armchairs, and the quiet, firm *clap* of the door closing.

"Do you think it's a trap?" Angelica whispered.

"No," said Tonino. He was sure the Duchess had not guessed where they were. But they were shut in this room now, by the sound, and he had no idea how they would get the door open.

All the same, even a shut room was great open spaces compared with the narrow slit at the back of the drawers. Angelica and Tonino pushed and squeezed and forced themselves through the narrow daylight slit, and finally crawled out on the top of a writing-desk. Before their eyes had got used to the light, Tonino stubbed his toe on a vast pen like a telegraph pole and then tripped over a paper-knife like an ivory plank. Angelica bumped into a china ornament standing at the back of the desk. It swayed. She swayed. She flung her arms round it. When her eyes stopped watering, she found she was hugging a china Mr Punch, nose, red nightgown and all, about the same height as she was. There was a china Judy standing at the other end of the desk.

"We can't get away from these things!" she said.

The desk was covered in smooth red leather, very easy on the feet, and held a huge white blotter, which was even more comfortable to walk on. A chair with a matching red seat stood in front of the desk. Tonino saw they could easily jump down on to it. Even more easily, they could climb down the handles of the drawers. On the other hand, the piano the maid had dusted stood right beside the desk, and the window was round the corner from the piano. To reach the window was only a long stride from the piano. Though the window was shut, it had quite an easy-looking catch, if only they could reach it.

"Look!" said Angelica, pointing disgustedly.

A whole row of Punch and Judys stood along the top of the piano. Two were puppets on stands, very old and valuable by the look of them; two more were actually made of gold; and two others were rather arty clay models, which made Punch look like a leering ordinary man and Judy uncomfortably like the Duchess. And the music which was open on the piano was headed *Arnolfini—Punch and Judy Suite.*

"I think this is the Duke's study," said Angelica. And both of them got the giggles.

Still giggling, Tonino stepped on to the piano and started to walk to the window. *Do—ti—so—fa,* went the piano.

"Come back!" Angelica laughed.

Tonino came back—*fa—so—ti—do*—nearly in hysterics.

The door of the room opened and someone hurried down the steps. Angelica and Tonino could think of nothing better to do than stand stiffly where they were, hoping to be taken for more Punch and Judys. And, luckily, the man who came in was busy and worried. He slapped a pile of papers on the desk, without so much as glancing at the two new puppets, and hurried out again, gently closing the door behind him.

"Phew!" said Angelica.

They walked round to the front of the papers and looked at them curiously. The top one said:

Report of Campaign at 08.00 hours. Summary:
Troops advancing on all fronts to repel invasion.
Heavy Artillery and Reservists moving up in support.
Pisan front reports heavy losses. Fleet sighted—
Pisan?—steaming for mouth of Voltava.

"We're at war!" said Tonino. "Why?"

"Because the Duchess has got us, of course," said Angelica. "And our families daren't make war-spells. Tonino, we must get *out.* We must tell them where the words to the *Angel* are!"

"But why does the Duchess want Caprona beaten?" Tonino said.

"I don't know," said Angelica. "There's something wrong about her, I know that. Aunt Bella said there was an awful fuss when the Duke decided to marry her. Nobody likes her."

"Let's see if we can open the window," said Tonino. He set off along the piano again. DO-ti-so-*fa-me-re*—

"Quiet!" said Angelica.

Tonino discovered that, if he put each foot down very slowly, the notes did not sound. He was halfway along the keyboard, and Angelica had one foot stretched out to follow, when they heard someone opening the door again. There was no time to be careful. Angelica fled back to the desk. Tonino, with a terrible discord, scrambled across the black notes and squeezed behind the music on the stand.

He was only just in time. When he looked—he was standing with his feet and head sideways, like an Ancient Egyptian—the Duke of Caprona himself was standing in front of the desk. Tonino thought the Duke seemed both puzzled and sad. He was tapping the *Report of Campaign* against his teeth and did not seem to notice Angelica standing between the Punch and the Judy on his desk, although Angelica's eyes were blinking against the glitter from the Duke's buttons.

"But I didn't declare war!" the Duke said to himself. "I was watching that puppet-show. How could I—?" He sighed and bit the *Report* worriedly between two rows of big shiny teeth. "Is my mind going?" he asked. He seemed to be talking to Angelica. She had the sense not to answer. "I must go and ask Lucrezia," the Duke said. He flung the *Report* down at Angelica's feet and hurried out of the study.

Tonino slid cautiously down the piano-lid on to the keys again—*ker-pling.* Angelica was now standing at the end of the piano, pointing at the window. She was speechless with horror.

Tonino looked—and for a moment he was as frightened as Angelica. There was a brown monster glaring at him through the glass, wide-faced, wide-eyed and shaggy. The thing had eyes like yellow lamps.

Faintly, through the glass, came a slightly irritable request to pull himself together and open the window.

"Benvenuto!" shouted Tonino.

"Oh—it's only a cat," Angelica quavered. "How terrible it must feel to be a mouse!"

"Just a cat!" Tonino said scornfully. "That's Benvenuto." He tried to explain to Benvenuto that it was not easy to open windows when you were nine inches high.

Benvenuto's impatient answer was to shove Tonino's latest magic exercise book in front of Tonino's mind's eye, open at almost the first page.

"Oh, thanks," Tonino said, rather ashamed. There were three opening-spells on that page, and none of them had stuck in his head. He chose the easiest, shut his eyes so that he could read the imaginary page more clearly, and sang the spell.

Gently and easily, the window swung open, letting in a gust of cold wind. And Benvenuto came in with the wind, almost as lightly. As Benvenuto trod gently up the scale towards him, Tonino had another moment when he knew how mice felt. Then he forgot it in the gladness of seeing Benvenuto. He stretched his arms wide to rub behind Benvenuto's horny ears. Benvenuto put his sticky black nose to Tonino's face, and they both stood, delighted, holding down a long humming discord on the piano.

Benvenuto said that Paolo was not quick enough; he could not make him understand where Tonino was. Tonino must send Paolo a message. Could Tonino write this size?

"There's a pen on the desk here," Angelica called.

And Tonino remembered her saying she could understand cats.

Rather anxiously, Benvenuto wanted to know if Tonino minded him talking to a Petrocchi.

The question astonished Tonino for a moment. He had clean forgotten that he and Angelica were supposed to hate one another. It seemed a waste of time, when they were both in such trouble. "Not at all," he said.

"Do get off that piano, both of you," said Angelica. "The humming's horrible."

Benvenuto obliged, with one great flowing leap. Tonino struggled after him with his elbows hooked over the piano-lid, pushing himself along against the black notes. By the time he reached the desk, Benvenuto and Angelica had exchanged formal introductions, and Benvenuto was advising them not to try getting out of the window. The room was three floors up. The stonework was crumbling, and even a cat had some trouble keeping his feet. If they would wait, Benvenuto would fetch help.

"But the Duchess—" said Tonino.

"And the Duke," said Angelica. "This is the Duke's study."

Benvenuto considered the Duke harmless on his own. He thought they were in the safest place in the Palace. They were to stay hidden and write him a note small enough to carry in his mouth.

"Wouldn't it be better if we tied it round your neck?" Angelica asked.

Benvenuto had never submitted to anything round his neck, and he was not going to start now. Anyway, someone in the Palace might see the message.

So Tonino put one foot on the *Report of Campaign* and succeeded, by heaving with both hands, in tearing off a corner of it. Angelica passed him the huge pen, which he had to hold in both hands, with the end resting on his shoulder. Then she stood on the paper to keep it steady while Tonino wielded the pen. It was such hard work, that he kept the message as short as possible. *In Duke's Palace. Duchess enchantress. T.M. & A.P.*

"Tell them about the words to the *Angel*," said Angelica. "Just in case."

Tonino turned the paper over and wrote *Words to Angel on Angel over gate. T & A.* Then, exhausted with heaving the pen up and down, he folded the piece of paper with that message inside and the first one outside, and trod it flat. Benvenuto opened his mouth. Angelica winced at that pink cavern with its arched wrinkly roof and its row of white fangs, and let Tonino place the message across Benvenuto's prickly tongue. Benvenuto gave Tonino a loving glare and sprang away. He struck one ringing chord from the piano, around middle C, made the slightest thump on the window-sill, and vanished.

Tonino and Angelica were staring after him and did not notice, until it was too late, that the Duke had come back.

"Funny," said the Duke. "There's a new Punch now, as well as a new Judy."

Tonino and Angelica stood stiff as posts, one on each end of the blotter, in agonizingly uncomfortable attitudes.

Fortunately, the Duke noticed the open window. "Blessed maids and their fresh air!" he grumbled, and went over to shut it. Tonino seized the opportunity to stand on both feet, Angelica to uncrick her neck. Then they both jumped. An unmistakable gunshot cracked out, from somewhere below. And another. The Duke bent out of the window and seemed to be watching something. "Poor pussy," he said. He sounded sad and resigned. "Why couldn't you keep away, puss? She hates cats. And they make such a din, too, shooting them." Another shot cracked out, and then several more. The Duke stood up, shaking his head sadly. "Ah well," he said, as he shut the window. "I suppose they do eat birds."

He came back across the study. Tonino and Angelica could not have moved if they tried. They were both too stricken.

The Duke's face folded into shiny wrinkles. He had noticed the corner torn from the *Report*. "I've been eating paper now!" he said. His sad, puzzled face turned towards Tonino and Angelica. "I think I do forget things," he said. "I talk to myself. That's a bad sign. But I really don't remember you two at all. At least, I remember the new Judy, but," he said to Tonino, "I don't remember you at all. How did you get here?"

Tonino was far too upset about Benvenuto to think. After all, the Duke really was speaking to him. "Please, sir," he said, "I'll explain—"

"Shut *up*!" snapped Angelica. "I'll say a spell!"

"—only please tell me if they shot my cat," said Tonino.

"I think so," said the Duke. "It looked as if they got it." Here he took a deep breath and turned his eyes carefully to the ceiling, before he looked at Tonino and Angelica again. Neither of them moved. Angelica was glaring at Tonino, promising him spells unimaginable if he said another word. And Tonino knew he had been an utter idiot anyway. Benvenuto was dead and there was no point in moving—no point in anything.

The Duke, meanwhile, slowly pulled a large handkerchief out of his pocket. A slightly crumpled cigar came out with it and flopped on the desk. The Duke picked it up and put it absent-mindedly between his glistening teeth. And then he had to take it out again to wipe his shiny face. "Both of you spoke," he said, putting the handkerchief away and fetching out a gold lighter. "You know that?" he said, putting the cigar back into his mouth. He gave a furtive look round, clicked the lighter, and lit the cigar. "You are looking," he said, "at a poor dotty Duke." Smoke rolled out with his words, as much smoke as if the Duke had been a dragon.

Angelica sneezed. Tonino thought he was going to sneeze. He drew a deep breath to stop himself and burst out coughing.

"Ahah!" cried the Duke. "Got you!" His large wet hands pounced, and seized each of them round the legs. Holding them like that, firmly pinned to the blotter, he sat down in the chair and bent his triumphant shiny face until it was level with theirs. The cigar, cocked out of one side of his mouth, continued to roll smoke over them. They flailed their arms for balance and coughed and coughed. "Now what are you?" said the Duke. "Another of her fiendish devices for making me think I'm potty? Eh?"

"No we're not!" coughed Tonino, and Angelica coughed, "Oh, please stop that smoke!"

The Duke laughed. "The old Chinese cigar-torture," he said gleefully, "guaranteed to bring statues to life." But his right hand moved Tonino, stumbling and swaying, across the blotter to Angelica, where his left hand gathered him in. His right hand took the cigar out of his mouth and laid it on the edge of the desk. "Now," he said. "Let's have a look at you."

They scrubbed their streaming eyes and looked fearfully up at his great grinning face. It was impossible to look at all of it at once. Angelica settled for his left eye, Tonino for his right eye. Both eyes bulged at them, round and innocent, like Old Niccolo's.

"Bless me!" said the Duke. "You're the spell-makers' children who were supposed to come to my pantomime! Why didn't you come?"

"We never got an invitation, Your Grace," Angelica said. "Did you?" she asked Tonino.

"No," Tonino said mournfully.

The Duke's face sagged. "So that's why it was. I wrote them myself too. That's my life in a nutshell. None of the orders I give ever get carried out, and an awful lot of things get done that I never ordered at all." He opened his hand slowly. The big warm fingers peeled damply off their legs. "You feel funny wriggling about in my hand," he said. "There, if I let you go, will you tell me how you got here?"

They told him, with one or two forced pauses when he took a puff at his cigar and set them coughing again. He listened wonderingly. It was not like explaining things to a huge grown-up Duke. Tonino felt as if he was telling a made-up story to his small cousins. From the way the Duke's eyes popped, and the way he kept saying "Go on!" Tonino was sure the Duke was believing it no more than the little Montanas believed the story of Giovanni the Giant Killer.

Yet, when they had finished, the Duke said, "That Punch and Judy show started at eight-thirty and went on till nine-fifteen. I know, because there was a clock just over you. They say I declared war at nine o'clock last night. Did either of you notice me declaring war?"

"No," they said. "Though," Angelica added sourly, "I was being beaten to death at the time and I might not have noticed."

"My apologies," said the Duke. "But did either of you hear gunfire? No. But firing started around eleven and went on all night. It's still going on. You can see it, but not hear it, from the tower over this study. Which means another damn spell, I suppose. And I think I'm supposed to sit here and not notice Caprona being blown to pieces around me." He put his chin in his hands and stared at them miserably. "I know I'm a fool," he said, "but just because I love plays and puppet-theatres, I'm not an idiot. The question is, how do we get you two out of here without Lucrezia knowing?"

Tonino and Angelica were almost too surprised and grateful to speak. And while they were still trying to say thank you, the Duke jumped upright, staring pop-eyed.

"She's coming! I've got an instinct. Quick! Get in my pockets!"

He turned round sideways to the desk and held one pocket of his coat stretched against it, between two fingers. Angelica hastily lifted the pocket-flap and slid down between the two layers of cloth. The Duke stubbed out his cigar on the edge of the desk and popped it in after her. Then he turned round and held the other pocket open for Tonino. As Tonino crouched down in fuzzy darkness, he heard the door open and the voice of the Duchess.

"My lord, you've been smoking cigars in here again."

CHAPTER 13

Paolo woke up that morning knowing that he was going to have to look for Tonino himself. If his father, and Rinaldo, and then Rosa and Marco, all refused to try, then there was no use asking anyone else.

He sat up and realised that the Casa was full of unusual noises. Below in the yard, the gate was open. He could hear the voices of Elizabeth, Aunt Anna, Aunt Maria and Cousin Claudia, who were bringing the day's bread.

"Just look at the Angel!" he heard his mother say. "Now what did that?"

"It's because we've stopped our spells," said Cousin Claudia.

Following that came a single note of song from Aunt Anna, cut off short with a squeak. Aunt Maria said angrily, "No spells, Anna! Think of Tonino!"

This was intriguing, but what really interested Paolo were the noises behind the voices: marching feet, orders being shouted, a drum beating, horses' hooves, heavy rumbling and some cursing. Paolo shot out of bed. It must be the army.

"Hundreds of them," he heard Aunt Anna say.

"Most of them younger than my Domenico," said Aunt Maria. "Claudia, take this basket while I shut the gate. All going to face three armies without a war-scrip between them. I could cry!"

Paolo shot along the gallery, pulling on his jacket, and hurried down the steps into the cold yellow sunlight. He was too late. The gate was barred and the war-noises shut out. The ladies were crossing the yard with their baskets.

"Where do you think you're going?" Elizabeth called to him. "No one's going out today. There's going to be fighting. The schools are all closed."

They put down their baskets to open the kitchen door. Paolo saw them recoil, with cries of dismay.

"Good Lord!" said Elizabeth.

"Don't anyone tell Gina!" said Aunt Maria.

At the same moment, someone knocked heavily at the Casa gate.

"See who that is, Paolo," called Aunt Anna.

Paolo went under the archway and undid the flap of the peephole. He was pleased to have this chance to see the army, and pleased that the schools were shut. He had not intended to go to school today anyway.

There was a man in uniform outside, who shouted, "Open and receive this, in the name of the Duke!" Behind him, Paolo caught glimpses of shiny marching boots and more uniforms. He unbarred the gate.

Meanwhile, it became plain that Aunt Gina was not to be kept away from the kitchen. Her feet clattered on the stairs. There was a stunned pause. Then the whole Casa filled with her voice.

"Oh my God! Mother of God! *Insects!*" It even drowned the noise of the military band that was marching past as Paolo opened the gate.

The man outside thrust a sheet of paper at Paolo and darted off to hammer on the next door. Paolo looked at it. He had a mad idea that he had just been handed the words to the *Angel.* After that, he went on staring, oblivious alike of Aunt Gina—who was now screaming what she was going to do to Lucia—and of the great gun that went rumbling past, pulled by four straining horses.

State of Caprona, Paolo read, *Form FR_3 Call Up of Final Reservists. The following to report to the Arsenal for immediate duty at 03.00 hrs, January 14th, 1979: Antonio Montana, Lorenzo Montana, Piero Montana, Ricardo Montana, Arturo Montana (ne Notti), Carlo Montana, Luigi Montana, Angelo Montana, Luca Montana, Giovanni Montana, Piero Iacopo Montana, Rinaldo Montana, Domenico Montana, Francesco Montana.*

That was everyone! Paolo had not realised that even his father was a Final Reservist.

"Shut the gate, Paolo!" shrieked Aunt Maria.

Paolo was about to obey, when he remembered that he had not yet looked at the Angel. He dodged outside and stared up, while half a regiment of infantry marched past behind him. It looked as if, in the night, every pigeon in Caprona had chosen to sit on that one golden carving. It was plastered with bird-droppings. They were particularly thick, not unnaturally, on the outstretched arm holding the scroll, and the scroll was a crusty white mass. Paolo shuddered. It seemed like an omen. He did not notice one of the marching soldiers detach himself from the column and come up behind him.

"I should close the gate, if I were you," said Chrestomanci.

Paolo looked up at him and wondered why people looked so different in uniform. He pulled himself together and dragged the two halves of the gate shut. Chrestomanci helped him slot the big iron bars in to lock it. As he did, he said, "I was at the Casa Petrocchi around dawn, so there's no great need for explanations. But I would like to know what's the matter in the kitchen this time."

Paolo looked. Eight baskets piled high with round tan-coloured loaves stood outside the kitchen. There were agitated noises from inside it, and a curious long droning-sound. "I think it's Lucia's spell again," he said.

He and Chrestomanci set off across the yard. Before they had gone three steps, the aunts burst out of the kitchen and rushed towards him. Antonio and the uncles hurried down from the gallery, and cousins arrived from everywhere else. Aunt Francesca surged out of the Saloon. She had spent the night there, and looked as if she had. Chrestomanci was soon in the middle of a crowd and holding several conversations at once.

"You were quite right to call me," he said to Rosa, and to Aunt Francesca, "Old Niccolo is good for years yet, but you should rest." To Elizabeth and Antonio, he said, "I know about Tonino," and to Rinaldo, "This is my fourth uniform today. There's heavy fighting in the hills and I had to get through somehow. What possessed the Duke," he asked the uncles, "to declare war so soon? I could have got help from Rome if he'd waited." None of them knew, and they all told him so at once. "I know," said Chrestomanci. "I know. No war-spells. I think our enemy enchanter has made a mistake over Tonino and Angelica. If it does nothing else, it allows me a free hand." Then, as the clamour showed no sign of abating, he said, "By the way, the Final Reserve has been called up," and nodded to Paolo to give the paper to Antonio.

In the sober hush that this produced, Chrestomanci pushed his way to the kitchen and put his head inside. "My goodness me!" Paolo heard him murmur.

Paolo ducked under all the people crowding round Antonio and looked into the kitchen under Chrestomanci's elbow. He looked into a wall of insects. The place was black with them, and glittering, and crawling, and dense with different humming. Flies of all kinds, mosquitoes, wasps and midges filled the air-space. Beetles, ants, moths and a hundred other crawling things occupied the floor and shelves and sink.

Peering through the buzzing clouds, Paolo was almost sure he saw a swarm of locusts on the cooking-stove. It was even worse than he had imagined the Petrocchi kitchen when he was little.

Chrestomanci drew a deep breath. Paolo suspected he was trying not to laugh. They both looked round for Lucia, who was standing on one leg among the breadbaskets, wondering whether to run away. "I am sure," Chrestomanci said to her—he *was* trying not to laugh; he had to start again. "I am sure people have talked to you about misusing spells. But—just out of interest—what did you use?"

"She used her own words to the *Angel of Caprona*!" Aunt Maria said, bursting angrily out of the crowd. "Gina's nearly out of her mind!"

"All the children did it," Lucia said defiantly. "It wasn't only me."

Chrestomanci looked at Paolo, and Paolo nodded. "A considerable tribute to the powers of the younger Montanas," said Chrestomanci. He turned and snapped his fingers into the buzzing, crawling kitchen. Not much happened. The air cleared enough for Paolo to see that it was indeed locusts on the cooker, but that was all. Chrestomanci's eyebrows went up a little. He tried again. This time nothing happened at all. He retreated from the buzzing, looking thoughtful.

"With all due respect," he said to Paolo and Lucia, "to the *Angel of Caprona*, it should not be this powerful on its own. I'm afraid this spell will just have to wear itself out." And he said to Aunt Maria, "No wonder the enemy enchanter is so much afraid of the Casa Montana. Does this mean there won't be any breakfast?"

"No, no. We'll make it in the dining-room," Aunt Maria said, looking very flustered.

"Good," said Chrestomanci. "There's something I have to say to everyone, when they're all there."

And when everyone was gathered round the tables to eat plain rolls and drink black coffee made over the dining-room fire, Chrestomanci stood in front of the fire, holding a coffee-cup, and said, "I know few of you believe Tonino is not in the Casa Petrocchi, but I swear to you he is not, and that Angelica Petrocchi is also missing. I think you are quite right to stop making spells until they are found, but I want to say this: even if I found Tonino and Angelica this minute, all the spells of the Casa Montana and the Casa Petrocchi are not going to save Caprona now. There are three armies, and the fleet of Pisa, closing in on her. The *only thing* which is going to help you is the true words to the *Angel of Caprona*. Have you all understood?"

They all had. Everyone was silent. Nobody spoke for some time. Then Uncle Lorenzo began grumbling. Moths had got into his Reservist uniform. "Someone took the spell out," he complained. "I shan't be fit to be seen."

"Does it matter?" asked Rinaldo. His face was very white and he was not having anything but coffee. "You'll only be seen dead anyway."

"But that's just it!" said Uncle Lorenzo. "I don't want to be seen dead in it!"

"Oh be quiet!" Domenico snapped at him. Uncle Lorenzo was so surprised that he stopped talking. Breakfast finished in gloomy murmurs.

Paolo got up and slid behind the bench where Chrestomanci was sitting. "Excuse me, sir. Do you know where Tonino is?"

"I wish I did," said Chrestomanci. "This enchanter is good. So far, I have only two clues. Last night, when I was coming up through Siena, somebody worked two very strange spells somewhere ahead of me."

"Tonino?" Paolo said eagerly.

Chrestomanci shook his head. "The first one was definitely Angelica. She has what you might call an individual style. But the other one baffled me. Do you think your brother is capable of working anything strong enough to get through an enchanter's spells? Angelica did it through sheer weirdness. Could Tonino, do you think?"

"I shouldn't think so," said Paolo. "He doesn't know many spells, but he always gets them right and they work—"

"Then it remains a mystery," said Chrestomanci. He sighed. Paolo thought he looked tired.

"Thanks," he said, and slipped off, carefully thinking careless thoughts about what would he do now school was closed. He did not want anyone to notice what he meant to do.

He slipped through the coach-house, past the crumpled horses and coachman, past the coach, and opened the little door in the wall at the back. He was half through it, when Rosa said doubtfully, at the front of the coach-house, "Paolo? Are you in there?"

No, I'm not, Paolo thought, and shut the little door after him as gently as he knew how. Then he ran.

By this time, there were hardly any soldiers in the streets, and hardly anyone else either. Paolo ran past yellow houses, heavily shuttered, in a quiet broken by the uneasy ringing of bells. From time to time, he thought he could hear a dull, distant noise—a sort of booming, with a clatter in its midst. Wherever the houses opened out and Paolo could see the hills, he saw soldiers—not as soldiers, but as crawling, twinkling lines, winding upwards—and some puffs of smoke. He knew Chrestomanci was right. The fighting was very near.

He was the only person about in the Via Cantello. The Casa Petrocchi was as shuttered and barred as the Casa Montana. And their

Angel was covered with bird-lime too. Like the Montanas, they had stopped making spells. Which showed, thought Paolo, that Chrestomanci was right about Angelica too. He was much encouraged by that as he hammered on the rough old gate.

There was no sound from inside, but, after a second or so, a white cat jumped to the top of the gate, and crouched in the gap under the archway, looking down with eyes even bluer than Paolo's.

Those eyes reminded Paolo that his own eyes were likely to give him away. He did not think he dared disguise them with a spell, in case the Petrocchis noticed. So he swallowed, told himself that he had to find the one person who was likely to help him look for Tonino, and said to the cat, "Renata. Could I speak to Renata?"

The white cat stared. Maybe it made some remark. Then it jumped down inside the Casa, leaving Paolo with an uncomfortable feeling that it knew who he was. But he waited. Before he had quite decided to go away again, the peephole was unlatched. To his relief, it was Renata's pointed face that looked through the bars at him.

"Whoops!" she said. "I see why Vittoria fetched *me*. What a relief you came!"

"Come and help find Tonino and Angelica," said Paolo. "Nobody will listen."

"Ung." Renata pulled a strip of her red hair into her mouth and bit it. "We're forbidden to go out. Think of an excuse."

"Your teacher's ill and scared of the war and wants us to sit with her," said Paolo.

"That might do," said Renata. "Come in while I ask." Paolo heard the gate being unbarred. "Her name's Mrs Grimaldi," Renata whispered, holding the gate open for him. "She lives in the Via Sant' Angelo and she's ever so ugly, in case they ask. Come in."

Considerably to his amazement, Paolo entered the Casa Petrocchi, and was even more amazed not to be particularly frightened. He felt as if he was about to do an exam, keyed up, and knowing he was in for it, but that was all.

He saw a yard and a gallery so like his own that he could almost have believed he had been magically whisked back home. There were differences, of course. The gallery railings were fancy wrought-iron, with iron leopards in them at intervals. The cats that sat sunning themselves on the waterbutts were mostly ginger or tabby—whereas in the Casa Montana, Benvenuto had left his mark, and the cats were either black or black and white. And there was a gush of smell from the kitchen—frying onions—the like of which Paolo had not smelt since Lucia cast her unlucky spell.

"Mother!" shouted Renata.

But the first person who appeared was Marco. Marco was galloping down the steps from the gallery with a pair of long shiny boots in one hand, and a crumpled red uniform over his arm. "Mother!" Marco bellowed, in the free and easy way people always bellow for their mothers. "Mother! There's moth in my uniform! Who took the spell out of it?"

"Stupid!" Renata said to him. "We put every single spell away last night." And she said to Paolo, "That's my brother Marco."

Marco turned indignantly to Renata. "But moths take months—!" And he saw Paolo. It was hard to tell which of them was more dismayed.

At that moment, a red-haired, worried-looking lady came across the yard, carrying a little boy. The baby had black hair and the same bulging forehead as Angelica. "I don't know, Marco," she said. "Get Rosa to mend it. What is it, Renata?"

Marco interrupted. "Rosa," he said, looking fixedly at Paolo, "is with her *sister*. Who's your friend, Renata?"

Paolo could not resist. "I'm Paolo Andretti," he said wickedly. Marco rewarded him with a look which dared him to say another word.

Renata was relieved, because she now knew what to call Paolo. "Paolo wants me to come and help look after Mrs Grimaldi. She's ill in bed, Mother."

Paolo could see by the way Marco's eyes went first wide and then almost to slits, that Marco was extremely alarmed by this and determined to stop Renata. But Paolo could not see how Marco could do anything. He could not give away that he knew who Paolo was without giving away himself and Rosa too. It made him want to laugh.

"Oh poor Mrs Grimaldi!" said Mrs Petrocchi. "But, Renata, I don't think—"

"Doesn't Mrs Grimaldi realise there's a war on?" Marco said. "Did Paolo tell you she was ill?"

"Yes," Paolo said glibly. "My mother's great friends with Mrs Grimaldi. She's sorry for her because she's so ugly."

"And of course she knows about the war," Renata said. "I kept telling you, Marco, how she dives under her desk if she hears a bang. She's scared stiff of guns."

"And it's all been too much for her, Mother says," Paolo added artistically.

Marco tried another tack. "But why does Mrs Grimaldi want *you*, Renata? Since when have you been teacher's pet?"

Renata, who was obviously as quick as Paolo, said, "Oh, I'm not. She just wants me to amuse her with some spells—"

At this, Mrs Petrocchi and Marco both said, "You're not to use spells! Angelica—"

"—but of course I won't," Renata continued smoothly. "I'll just sing songs. She likes me to sing. And Paolo's going to read to her out of the Bible. Do say we can go, Mother. She's lying in bed all on her own."

"Well—" said Mrs Petrocchi.

"The streets aren't safe," said Marco.

"There was no one about at all," Paolo said, giving Marco a look to make him watch it. Two could play at that.

"Mother," said Renata, "you *are* going to mend Marco's uniform, aren't you?"

"Yes, yes, of course," said Mrs Petrocchi.

Renata at once took this as permission to go with Paolo. "Come on, Paolo," she said, and raced under Marco's nose to what was obviously the coach-house. Paolo whizzed after her.

Marco, however, was not defeated. Before Renata's hand was on the latch of the big door, an obvious uncle was leaning over the gallery. "Renata! Be a good girl and find me my tobacco." An obvious aunt shot out of the kitchen. She looked like Aunt Gina with red hair, and she hooted in the same way. "Renata! Have you taken my good knife?" Two young cousins shot out of another door. "Renata, you said you'd play dressing-up!" and Mrs Petrocchi, looking anxious and undecided, was holding the baby boy out, saying, "Renata, you'll have to mind Roberto while I'm sewing."

"I can't stop now!" Renata shouted back. "Poor Mrs Grimaldi!" She wrenched open the big door and pushed Paolo inside. "What's going on?" she whispered.

It was obvious to Paolo what was going on. It was so like the Casa Montana. Marco had broadcast—not an alarm, because he dared not—a sort of general uneasiness about Renata. "Marco's trying to stop us," he said.

"I know *that*," Renata said, hurrying him past the sleek Petrocchi coach and—to Paolo's interest—past four black cardboard horses as crumpled and muddy as the Casa Montana ones. "*Why* is he? How does he know?"

Behind them was a perfect clamour of Petrocchi voices, all wanting Renata. "He just does," Paolo said. "Be quick!"

The small door to the street had a big stiff key. Renata took it in both hands and struggled to turn it. "Does he know *you*?" she said sharply.

Like an answer, Marco's voice sounded from behind the coach.

"Renata!" Then, much more softly, "Paolo—Paolo Montana, come here!"

The door came open. "Run, if you're coming!" Paolo said. They shot out into the street, both running hard. Marco came to the door and shouted something, but he did not seem to be following. Nevertheless, Paolo kept on running, which forced Renata to run too. He did not want to talk. He wanted to absorb the shock of Marco. Marco Andretti was really Marco Petrocchi—he must be Guido's eldest son! Rosa Montana and Marco Petrocchi. How did they do it? How ever did they *manage* it? he kept wondering. And also—more soberly—How ever will they get away with it?

"All right. That will do," Renata panted. By this time they had crossed the Corso and were down beside the river, trotting along empty quaysides towards the New Bridge. Renata slowed down, and Paolo did too, quite breathless. "Now," she said, "tell me how Marco knew you, or I won't come a step further."

Paolo looked at her warily. He had already discovered that Renata was, as Aunt Gina would say, sharp enough to cut herself, and he did not like the way she was looking at him. "He saw me at the Palace of course," Paolo said.

"No he didn't," said Renata. "He drove the coach. He knows your name *and* he knows why you came, doesn't he? How?"

"I think he must have been standing behind us on the Art Gallery steps, and we didn't see him in the fog," said Paolo.

Renata's shrewd eyes continued the look Paolo did not like. "Good try," she said. Paolo tried to break off the look by turning and sauntering on along the quays. Renata followed him, saying, "And I was meant to get all embarrassed and not ask any more. You're sharp enough to cut yourself, Mr Montana. But what a pity. Marco wasn't in the fight. They wanted him for the single combat, that's how I know, and he wasn't there, so Papa had to do it. And I can tell that you don't want me to know how Marco knows you. And I can tell Marco doesn't, or he'd have stopped me going by saying who you were. So—"

"You're the one who's going to cut yourself," Paolo said over his shoulder, "by being too clever. I don't know how Marco knew me, but he was being kind not say—" He stopped. He sniffed. He was level with an alleyway, where a peeling blue house bulged out on to the jetty. Paolo felt the air round that alley with a sense he hardly knew he had, inborn over generations of spellmaking. A spell had been set here—a strong spell, not long ago.

Renata came up behind. "You're not going to wriggle out—" She stopped too. "Someone made a spell here!"

"Was it Angelica? Can you tell?" Paolo asked.

"Why?" said Renata.

Paolo told her what Chrestomanci had said. Her face went red, and she prodded with her toe at a mooring-chain in the path. "Individual style!" she said. "Him and his jokes! It's not Angelica's fault. She was born that way. And it's not everyone who can get a spell to work by doing everything wrong. I think she's a sort of back-to-front genius, and I told the Duchess of Caprona so when she laughed, too!"

"But is the spell hers?" asked Paolo. He could hear gunfire, from somewhere down the river, mixed with the dull booming from the hills. It was a blunt, bonking *clomp, clomp*, like a giant chopping wood. His head went up to listen as he said, "I know it's not Tonino. His feel careful."

"No," said Renata, and her head was up too. "It's a bit stale, isn't it? And it doesn't feel very nice. The war sounds awfully close. I think we ought to get off the quays."

She was probably right. Paolo hesitated. He was sure they were hot on the trail. The stale spell had a slight sick feeling to it, which reminded him of the message in the yard last night.

And while he hesitated, the war seemed suddenly right on top of them. It was deafening, brazen, horrible. Paolo thought of someone holding one end of an acre of sheet-metal and flapping it, or of gigantic alarm-clocks. But that did not do justice to the noise. Nor did it account for some huge metallic screeches. He and Renata ducked and put their hands to their ears, and enormous things whirled above them. They went on, whatever they were, out above the river. Paolo and Renata crouched on the quay, staring at them.

They flapped across in a group—there were at least eight of them—gonging and screeching. Paolo thought first of flying machines and then of the Montana winged horse. There seemed to be legs dangling beneath the great black bodies, and their metal wings were whirling furiously. Some of them were not flying so well. One lost height, despite madly clanging with its wings, and dropped into the river with a splash that threw water all over the New Bridge and spattered Renata and Paolo. Another one lost height and whirled its iron tail for balance. Paolo recognised it as one of the iron griffins from the Piazza Nuova, as it, too, fell into a spout of water.

Renata began to laugh. "Now that *is* Angelica!" she said. "I'd know her spells anywhere."

They leapt up and raced for the long flight of stairs up to the Piazza Nuova. The din from the griffins was still drowning all but the nearest gunfire. Renata and Paolo ran up the steps, turning round at every landing to see what was happening to the rest of the griffins. Two more came down in the river. A further two plunged into the gardens of rich villas. But the last two were going well. When Paolo next looked, they seemed to be struggling to gain altitude in order to get over the hills beyond the Palace. The distant clanging was fast and furious, and the metal wings a blur.

Paolo and Renata turned and climbed again. "What is it? A call for help?" panted Paolo.

"Must be," gasped Renata. "Angelica's spells—always—mad kind of reasonableness."

An echoing clang brought them whirling round. Another griffin was down, but they did not see where. Fascinated, they watched the efforts of the last one. It had now reached the marble front of the Duke's Palace, and it was not high enough to clear it. The griffin seemed to know. It put out its claws and seemed to be clutching at the zig-zag marble battlements. But that did no good. They saw it, a distant black blot, go sliding down the coloured marble facade—they could even hear the grinding—down and down, until it crashed on to the roof of the marble gateway, where it drooped and lay still. Above it, even from here, they could see two long lines of scratches, all down the front of the Palace.

"Wow!" said Paolo.

He and Renata climbed up into the strangely bare Piazza Nuova. It was now nothing but a big paved platform surrounded by a low wall. At intervals round the wall were the snapped-off stumps of the griffins' pedestals, each with a broken green or crimson plaque lying beside it. In the middle, what had been a tangled griffin-fountain was now a jet of water from a broken pipe.

"Just look at all these spells she's broken!" exclaimed Renata. "I didn't think she could do anything this strong!"

Paolo looked across at the scratched Palace, rather enviously. There were spells in the marble to stop that kind of thing. Angelica must have broken them all. The odd thing was that he could not feel the spell. The Piazza Nuova ought to have reeked of magic, but it just felt empty. He stared round, puzzled. And there, trotting slowly and wearily along the low wall, was a familiar brown shape with a trailing bush of a tail.

"Benvenuto!" he said.

For a moment, it looked as if Benvenuto was going to walk straight past Paolo, as he so often did. But that must have been because he was tired. He stopped. He glared urgently at Paolo. Then he carefully opened his mouth and spat out a small folded scrap of paper. After that, he lay down and lost interest in the world. Paolo could see his brown sides heaving when he picked up the paper.

Renata looked over Paolo's shoulder as Paolo—rather disgustedly, because it was wet—unfolded the paper. The writing was definitely Tonino's, though it was far too small. And, though Paolo did not know it, not much of Tonino's message had survived. He and Renata read:

ords to Angel on Angel over

It was small wonder that Paolo and Renata misunderstood. From the Piazza Nuova, now the griffins were gone, an Angel was clearly visible. It stood, golden and serene, guarding a Caprona which was already surrounded in the smoke from gunfire, on top of the great dome of the Cathedral.

"Do you think we can get up there?" said Paolo.

Renata's face was white. "We'd better try. But I warn you, I'm no good at heights."

They hurried down among the red roofs and golden walls, leaving Benvenuto asleep on the wall. After a while, Benvenuto picked himself up and trotted away, restored. It took more than a few ill-aimed rifles to finish Benvenuto.

When Paolo and Renata reached the cobbled square in front of the Cathedral, the great bell in the bell-tower beside it was tolling. People were gathering into the church to pray for Caprona, and the Archbishop of Caprona himself was standing by the door blessing everyone who entered. Renata and Paolo joined the line. It seemed the easiest way to get in. They had nearly reached the door, when Marco dashed into the square towing Rosa. Rosa saw Renata's hair and pointed. She was too blown to speak. Marco grinned. "Your spell wins," he said.

CHAPTER 14

The warm pocket holding Tonino swayed and swooped as the Duke stood up. "Of course I smoked a cigar," he said to the Duchess, injured. "Anyone would smoke a cigar, if they found they'd declared war without knowing they had, and knew they were bound to be beaten." His voice came rumbling to Tonino's ears through his body, more than from outside.

"I've told you it's bad for your health," said the Duchess. "Where are you going?"

"Me? Oh," said the Duke. The pockets swooped, then swooped again, as he climbed the steps to the door. "Off to the kitchens. I feel peckish."

"You could send for food," said the Duchess, but she did not sound displeased. Tonino knew she had guessed they had been in the study all along and wanted the Duke out of it while she found them.

He heard the door shut. The pocket swung rhythmically as the Duke walked. It was not too bad once Tonino was used to it. It was a large pocket. There was almost room in it for Tonino, and the Duke's lighter, and his handkerchief, and another cigar, and some string, and some money, and a rosary, and some dice. Tonino made himself comfortable with the handkerchief as a cushion and wished the Duke would not keep patting at him to see if he was there.

"Are you all right in there?" the Duke rumbled at last. "Nobody about. You can stick your heads out. I thought of the kitchens because you didn't seem to have had any breakfast."

"You are kind," Angelica's voice came faintly. Tonino worked himself to his feet and put his head out under the flap of the pocket. He still could not see Angelica—the Duke's generous middle was in the way—but he heard her say, "You keep rather a lot of things in your pockets, don't you? Do you happen to know what I've got stuck to my foot?"

"Er—toffee, I suspect," said the Duke. "Please oblige me by eating it."

"Thanks," Angelica said doubtfully.

"I say," said Tonino. "Why didn't the Duchess know we were in your pockets? She could smell us before."

The Duke's loud laugh rumbled through him. The gilded wall Tonino could see began to jolt upward, and upward, and upward. The Duke was walking downstairs. "Cigars, lad!" the Duke said. "Why do you think I smoke them? She can't smell anything through them, and she hates that. She tried setting a spell on me to make me stop once, but I got so bad-tempered she had to take it off."

"Excuse me, sir," came Angelica's voice from the other side of the Duke. "Won't someone notice if you walk downstairs talking to yourself?"

The Duke laughed again. "Not a soul! I talk to myself all the time—and laugh, too, if something amuses me. They all think I'm potty anyway. Now, have you two thought of a way to get you out of here? The safest way would be to fetch your families here. Then I could hand you over in secret, and she'd be none the wiser."

"Can't you just send for them?" Tonino suggested. "Say you need them to help in the war."

"She'd smell a rat," said the Duke. "She says your war-charms are all washed-up anyway. Think of something that's nothing to do with the war."

"Special effects for another pantomime," Tonino suggested, rather hopelessly. But he could see that even the Duke was not likely to produce a play while Caprona was being invaded.

"I know," said Angelica. "I shall cast a spell."

"No!" said Tonino. "Anything might happen!"

"That doesn't matter," said Angelica. "My family would know it's me, and they'd come here like a shot."

"But you might turn the Duke green!" said Tonino.

"I really wouldn't mind," the Duke put in mildly.

He came to the bottom of the stairs and went with long, charging strides through rooms and corridors of the Palace. Angelica and Tonino each held on to an edge of their pockets and shouted arguments round him.

"But you could help me," said Angelica, "and your part would go right. Suppose we made it a calling-charm to fetch all the rats and mice in Caprona to the Palace. If you did the calling, we'd fetch something."

"Yes, but what would it be?" said Tonino.

"We could make it in honour of Benvenuto," shouted Angelica, hoping to please him.

But Tonino thought of Benvenuto lying somewhere on a Palace roof and became more obstinate than ever. He shouted that he was not going to do anything so disrespectful.

"Are you telling me you can't do a calling-spell?" shrieked Angelica. "Even my baby brother—"

They were shouting so loudly that the Duke had to tell them to shush twice. The military man hurrying up to the Duke stared slightly. "No need to stare, Major," the Duke said to him. "I said Shush and I meant Shush. Your boots squeak. What is it?"

"I'm afraid the forces of Caprona are in retreat in the south, Your Grace," said the soldier. "And our coastal batteries have fallen to the Pisan fleet."

Both pockets drooped as the Duke's shoulders slumped. "Thank you," he said. "Report to me personally next time you have news." The Major saluted and went, glancing at the Duke once or twice over his shoulder. The Duke sighed. "There goes another one who thinks I'm mad. Didn't you two say you were the only ones who knew where to find the words to the *Angel*?"

Tonino and Angelica put their heads out of his pockets again. "Yes," they said.

"Then," said the Duke, "will you please agree on a spell. You really must get out and get those words while there's still some of Caprona left."

"All right," said Tonino. "Let's call mice." He had not seen it was so urgent.

So the Duke stood in a wide window-bay and lit the cigar-stub from under Angelica with the lighter from under Tonino, to cover up the spell. Tonino leant out of his pocket and sang, slowly and carefully, the only calling-spell he knew. Angelica stood in the other pocket with her arms upraised and spoke, quickly, confidently and—quite certainly—wrong. Afterwards, she swore it was because she nearly laughed.

Another man approached. Tonino thought it was one of the courtiers who had watched the puppet show, but he was never sure, because the Duke flipped his pocketflaps down over their heads and began singing himself.

"Merrily his music ringing,
See an Angel cometh singing . . ."

roared the Duke. Even Angelica did not sing so much out of tune. Tonino had the greatest difficulty in keeping up his own song. And it was certainly around then that the spell seemed to go wrong. Tonino had the sudden feeling that his words were pulling a great weight.

The Duke broke off his abominable singing to say, "Ah, Pollio, there's nothing like a good song while Caprona burns! Nero did it, and now me."

"Yes, Your Grace," the man said feebly. They heard him scuttle away.

"And he's *sure* I'm mad," said the Duke. "Finished?"

Just then, Tonino's words came loose, with a sort of jerk, and he knew the spell had worked in some way or another. "Yes," he said.

But nothing seemed to happen. The Duke said philosophically that it would take a mouse quite a while to run from the Corso to the Palace, and strode on to the kitchens. They thought he was mad there, too, Tonino could tell. The Duke asked for two bread rolls and two pats of butter and solemnly put one into each pocket. No doubt they thought he was madder still when he remarked to no one: "There's a cigar-cutter in my right pocket that spreads butter quite well."

"Indeed, Your Grace?" they heard someone say dubiously.

Just then, someone rushed in screaming about the griffins from the Piazza Nuova. They were flying across the river, straight for the Palace. There was a general panic. Everyone screamed and yammered and said it was an omen of defeat. Then someone else rushed in yelling that one griffin had actually reached the Palace and was sliding down the marble front. There was more outcry. The next thing, everyone said, the great gold Angel from the Cathedral would fly away too.

Tonino was taking advantage of the confusion to bash a piece off his roll with the Duke's lighter, when the Duke bellowed, *"Nonsense!"* There was sudden quiet. Tonino dared not move, because everyone was certainly looking at the Duke.

"Don't you see?" said the Duke. "It's just an enemy trick. But we in Caprona don't frighten that easily, do we? Here—you—go and fetch the Montanas. And you go and get the Petrocchis. Tell them it's urgent. Tell as many of them to come as possible. I shall be in the North gallery." And he went striding off there, while Angelica and Tonino jigged against bread and tried not to tread in the butter.

When he got to the gallery, the Duke sat down on a window-seat. Angelica and Tonino stood half out of his pockets and managed to eat their bread and butter. The Duke amiably handed the cigar-cutter from one to the other and, in between whiles, seemed lost in thought, staring at the white puffs of shells bursting on the hills behind Caprona.

Angelica was inclined to be smug. "I told you," she said to Tonino, "my spells always work."

"Iron griffins," said Tonino, "aren't mice."

"No, but I've never done anything as big as that before," said Angelica. "I'm glad it didn't knock the Palace down."

The Duke said gloomily, "The guns of Pisa are going to do that soon. I can see gunboats on the river, and I'm sure they aren't ours. I wish your families would be quick."

But it was half an hour before a polite footman came up to the Duke, causing him to flip his pocket-flaps down and scatter buttery crumbs in all directions. "Your Grace, members of the Montana and Petrocchi families are awaiting you in the Large Reception Saloon."

"Good!" said the Duke. He leapt up and ran so fast that Tonino and Angelica had to brace their feet on the seams of his pockets and hang on hard to the edges. They lost their footing several times, even though the Duke tried to help them by holding his pockets as he ran. They felt him clatter to a stop. "Blast!" he said. "This is always happening!"

"What?" asked Tonino breathlessly. He felt jerked out of shape.

"They've told me the wrong room!" said the Duke and set off again on another swaying, jolting run. They felt him dive forward through a doorway. His pockets swung. Then they swung the other way as he slid and stopped. "Lucrezia, this is too bad! Is this why you always tell me the wrong room?"

"My lord," came the coldest voice of the Duchess from some way off, "I can't answer for the slackness of the footmen. What is the matter?"

"This," said the Duke. "These—" They felt him shaking. "Those were the Montanas and the Petrocchis, weren't they? Don't fob me off, Lucrezia. I sent for them. I know."

"And what if they were?" said the Duchess, rather nearer. "Do you wish to join them, my lord?"

They felt the Duke backing away. "No. No indeed! My dear, your will is always my pleasure. I—I just want to know why. They only came about some griffins."

The Duchess's voice moved away again as she answered. "Because, if you must know, Antonio Montana recognised me."

"But—but—" said the Duke, laughing uneasily, "everyone knows you, my dear. You're the Duchess of Caprona."

"I mean, he recognised me for what I am," said the Duchess from the distance. The sound of a door shutting followed.

"Look!" said the Duke in a shaky whisper. "Just look!" While he was still saying it, Angelica and Tonino were bracing their feet on the seams of his pockets and pushing their heads out from under the flaps.

They saw the same polished room where they had once waited and eaten cakes, the same gilded chairs and angelic ceiling. But this time the polished floor was littered with puppets. Puppets lay all over it, limp grotesque things, scattered this way and that as people might lie if they had suddenly fallen. They were in two groups. Otherwise there was no way of telling which puppet was who. There were Punches, Judys, Hangmen, Sausage-men, Policemen, and an odd Devil or so, over and over again. From the numbers, it looked as if both families had realised that Tonino and Angelica were behind the mysterious griffins and had sent nearly every grown-up in the Casas.

Tonino could not speak. Angelica said, "That hateful woman! Her mind seems to run on puppets."

"She sees people that way," the Duke said miserably. "I'm sorry, both of you. She's been too many for us. Terrible female! I can't think why I married her—but I suppose that was a spell too."

"Do you think she suspects you've got us?" Tonino asked. "She must be wondering where we are."

"Maybe, maybe," said the Duke. He marched up and down the room, while they leant out of his pockets and looked down at the crowd of strewn floppy puppets. "She doesn't care now, of course," he said. "She's done for both families anyway. Oh, I am a fool!"

"It's not your fault," said Angelica.

"Oh, but it *is*," said the Duke. "I never show the slightest resolution. I always take the easiest way— What is it?" Darkness descended as he flipped his pocket-flaps down.

"Your Grace," said the Major whose boots squeaked, "the Pisan fleet is landing men down beyond the New Quays. And our troops to the south are being rolled back into the suburbs."

They felt the Duke droop. "Almost done, in fact," he said. "Thanks— No, wait, Major! Could you be a good fellow and go to the stables and order out my coach? The lackeys have all run away, you know. Ask for it at the door in five minutes."

"But, Your Grace—" said the Major.

"I intend to go down into the city and speak with the people," said the Duke. "Give them what's-it-called. Moral support."

"A very fine aim, sir," said the Major, with a great deal more warmth. "In five minutes, sir." His boots went squeaking swiftly off.

"Did you hear that?" said the Duke. "He called me 'sir'! Poor fellow. I told him a set of whoppers and he couldn't take his eyes off all those puppets, but he called me 'sir,' and he'll get that coach and he won't tell *her*. Cardboard box!"

The hangings whipped by as the Duke charged through a doorway into another room. This one had a long table down the middle. "Ah!" said the Duke, and charged towards a stack of boxes by the wall. The boxes proved to have wine-glasses in them, which the Duke proceeded feverishly to unload on to the table.

"I don't understand," Tonino said.

"Box," said the Duke. "We can't leave your families behind, for her to revenge herself on. I'm going to be resolute for once. I'm going to get in the coach and go, and dare her to stop me." So saying, he stormed back to the reception room with the empty box and knelt down to collect the puppets. Angelica was bounced on the floor as his coat swung. "Sorry," said the Duke.

"Pick them up gently," said Tonino. "It hurts if you don't."

Tenderly and hastily, using both hands for each puppet, the Duke packed the puppets in layers in the cardboard box. In the process, Montanas got very thoroughly mixed with Petrocchis, but there was no way of preventing that. All three of them were expecting the Duchess to come in any moment. The Duke kept looking nervously round and then muttering to himself, "Resolute!" He was still muttering it when he set off, awkwardly carrying the cardboard box in his arms. "Funny to think," he remarked, "that I'm carrying almost every spell-maker in Caprona at the moment."

Boots squeaked towards them. "Your coach is waiting, sir," said the voice of the Major.

"Resolute," said the Duke. "I mean, thank you. I shall think of you in heaven, Major, since I'm sure that's where most of us are going soon. Meanwhile, can you do two more things for me?"

"Sir?" said the Major alertly.

"First, when you think of the Angel of Caprona, what do you think of?"

"The song or the figure, sir?" the Major asked, more wary now than alert.

"The figure."

"Why—" The Major was becoming sure that the Duke was mad again. "I—I think of the golden Angel on the Cathedral, Your Grace."

"Good man!" the Duke cried out. "So do I! The other thing is, can you take this box and stow it in my coach for me?" Neither Tonino nor Angelica could resist peeping out to see how the Major took this request. Unfortunately, his face was hidden behind the box as the Duke thrust it at him. They felt they had missed a rare sight. "If anyone asks," the Duke said, "it's gifts for the war weary people."

"Yes, Your Grace." The Major sounded amused and indulgent, humouring the Duke in his madness, but they heard his boots squeaking briskly off.

"Thank the lord!" said the Duke. "I'm not going to be caught with them. I can feel her coming."

Thanks to the Duke's charging run, it was some minutes before the Duchess caught up with them. Tonino, squinting out under the flap, could see the great marble entrance hall when the Duke skidded to a stop. He dropped the flap hastily when he heard the cold voice of the Duchess. She sounded out of breath but triumphant.

"The enemy is by the New Bridge, my lord. You'll be killed if you go out now."

"And I'll be killed if I stay here too," said the Duke. He waited for the Duchess to deny this, but she said nothing. They heard the Duke swallow. But his resolution held. "I'm going," he said, a mite squeakily, "to drive down among my people and comfort their remaining hours."

"Sentimental fool," said the Duchess. She was not angry. It was what she thought the Duke was.

This made the Duke bluster. "I may not be a good ruler," he said, "but this is what a good ruler should do. I shall—I shall pat the heads of children and join in the singing of the choir."

The Duchess laughed. "And much good may it do you, particularly if you sing," she said. "Very well. You can get killed down there instead of up here. Run along and pat heads."

"Thank you, my dear," the Duke said humbly. He surged forward again, *thump, thump, thump,* down marble steps. They heard the sound of hooves on gravel and felt the Duke shaking. "Let's go, Carlo," he said. "What is it? What are you pointing—? Oh yes. So it is a griffin. How remarkable. Drive on, can't you." He surged upwards. Coach-springs creaked and a door clapped shut. The Duke surged down. They heard him say "Oh good!" as he sat, and the rather-too-familiar sound of cardboard being hit, as he patted the box on the seat beside him. Then the coach started, with a shrilling of wheels on gravel and a battering of hooves. They felt the Duke sigh with relief. It made them bounce. "You can come out now," said the Duke.

They climbed cautiously out on to his wide knees. The Duke kindly moved over to the window so that they could see out. And the first thing that met their eyes was an iron griffin, very crumpled and bent, lying in quite a large crater in the Palace yard.

"You know," said the Duke, "if my Palace wasn't going to be broken up anyway by Pisans, or Sienese, or Florentines, I'd get damages off you two. The other griffin has scraped two great ditches all down my facade." He laughed and patted at his glossy face with his handkerchief. He was still very nervous.

As the coach rolled out of the yard on to the road, they heard gunfire. Some of it sounded near, a rattle of shots from below by the river. Most of it was far and huge, a long grumble from the hills. The bangs were so close together that the sound was nearly continuous, but every so often, out of the grumble, came a very much nearer *clap-clap-clap*. It made all three of them jump each time.

"We *are* taking a pounding," the Duke said unhappily.

The coach slowed down. They could hear the prim voice of the coachman among the other noise. "I fear the New Bridge is under fire, Your Grace. Where exactly are we bound?"

The Duke pushed down the window. The noise doubled. "The Cathedral. Go upriver and see if we can cross by the Old Bridge." He pushed the window shut. "Phew! I don't envy Carlo up there on the box!"

"Why are we going to the Cathedral?" Angelica asked anxiously. "We want to look at the Angels on our Casas."

"No," said the Duke. "She'll have thought of those. That's why I asked the Major. It seems to me that the one place where those words are always safe and always invisible *must* be on the Cathedral Angel. You think of it at once, but it's up there and far away, so you forget it."

"But it's *miles* up!" said Angelica.

"It's got a scroll, though," said Tonino. "And the scroll looks to be more unrolled than the ones on our Angels."

"I'm afraid it's bound to be about the only place she might have forgotten," said the Duke.

They rattled along briskly, except for one place, where there was a shell crater in the road. Somehow, Carlo got them round it.

"Good man, Carlo," said the Duke. "About the one good man she hasn't got rid of."

The noise diminished a little as the coach went down to the river and the Piazza Martia—at least, Angelica and Tonino guessed that was where it was; they found they were too small to see any great distance. They could tell they were on the Old Bridge, by the rumble under the wheels and the little shuttered houses on either side. The Duke several times craned round, whistled and shook his head, but they could not see why. They recognised the Cathedral, when the coach wheeled towards it across the cobbles, because it was so huge and snowy white. Its great bell was still tolling. A large crowd, mostly of women and children, was slowly moving towards its door. As the coach drew up, it was near enough for Tonino and Angelica to see the Archbishop of Caprona in his spreading robes, standing at the door, sprinkling each person with holy water and murmuring a blessing.

"Now there's a brave man," said the Duke. "I wish I could do as well. Look, I'll pop you two out of this door and then get out of the other one and keep everyone busy while you get up on the dome. Will that do?" He had the door nearest the Cathedral open as he spoke.

Tonino and Angelica felt lost and helpless. "But what shall we do?"

"Climb up there and read out those words," said the Duke. He leant down, encircled them with his warm wet hands, and planted them out on the cold cobbles. They stood shivering under the vast hoop of the coach-wheel. "Be sensible," he whispered down to them. "If I ask the Archbishop to put up ladders, she'll guess." That of course was quite true. They heard him surge to the other door and that door crash open.

"He always does everything so *hugely*," Angelica said.

"People of Caprona!" shouted the Duke. "I've come here to be with you in your hour of sorrow. Believe me, I didn't choose what has happened today—"

There was a mutter from the crowd, even a scatter of cheering. "He's doing it quite well," said Angelica.

"We'd better do our bit," said Tonino. "There's only us left now."

CHAPTER 15

Tonino and Angelica pattered over to the vast marble cliff of the Cathedral and doubtfully approached a long, sloping buttress. That was the only thing they could see which gave them some chance of climbing up. Once they were close to it, they saw it was not difficult at all. The marble looked smooth, but, to people as small as they were, it was rough enough to give a grip to their hands and feet.

They went up like monkeys, with the cold air reviving them. The truth was that, though they had had an eventful morning, it had also been a restful and stuffy one. They were full of energy and they weighed no more than a few ounces. They were scarcely panting as they scampered up the long cold slope of the lowest dome. But there the rest of the Cathedral rose before them, a complicated glacier of white and rose and green marble. They could not see the Angel at all.

Neither of them knew which way to climb next. They hung on to a golden cross and stared up. And there, brown-black hair and white fur hurtled up to them. Gold eyes glared and blue eyes gazed. A black nose and a pink nose dabbed at them.

"Benvenuto!" shouted Tonino. "Did you—?"

"Vittoria!" cried Angelica, and threw her arms round the neck of the white cat.

But the cats were hasty and very worried. Things tumbled into their heads, muddled, troubled things about Paolo and Renata, Marco and Rosa. Would Tonino and Angelica please come on, and *hurry*!

They began an upward scamper which they would never have believed possible. With the cats to guide them, they raced up long lead groins, and over rainbow buttresses, like dizzy bridges, to higher domes. Always the cats implored them to hurry, and always they were there if the footing was difficult. With his hand on Benvenuto's wiry back, Tonino went gaily up marble glacis and through tiny drain-holes hanging over huge drops, and raced up high curving surfaces, where the green marble ribs of a dome seemed as tall as a wall beside him. Even when they began the long toil up the slope of the great dome itself, neither of them was troubled. Once, Angelica stumbled and saved herself by catching hold of Vittoria's silky tail; and once Benvenuto took Tonino's red nightgown in his teeth and heaved him aside from a deep drain. But up here it was rounded and remote. Tonino felt as if he was on the surface of the moon, in spite of the pale winter sky overhead and the wind singing. The rumble of guns was almost beyond the scope of his small ears.

At last, they scrambled between fat marble pillars on to the platform at the very top of the dome. And there was the golden Angel above them. The Angel's tremendous feet rested on a golden pedestal rather higher than Tonino's normal height. There was a design round the pedestal, which Tonino absently took in, of golden leopards entwined with winged horses. But he was looking up beyond, to the Angel's flowing robes, the enormous wings outspread to a width of twenty feet or more, the huge hand high above his head, raised in blessing, and the other hand flung out against the sky, further away still, holding the great unrolled scroll. Far above that again, shone the Angel's vast and tranquil face, unheedingly beaming its blessing over Caprona.

"He's enormous!" Angelica said. "We'll never get up to that scroll, if we tried all day!"

The cats, however, were nudging and hustling at them, to come to a place further round the platform. Wondering, they trotted round, almost under the Angel's scroll. And there was Paolo's head above the balustrade, with his hair blown back in a tuft and his face exceedingly pale. He had one arm clutched over the marble railing. The other stretched away downward. Tonino peered between the marble pillars to see why. And there was the miserable humped huddle of Renata hanging on to Paolo.

"But she's terrified of heights!" said Angelica. "How *did* she get this high?"

Vittoria told Angelica she was to get Renata up at once.

Angelica stuck her upper half out between the pillars. Being small certainly had its advantages. Distances which were mercilessly huge to Renata and Paolo were too far away to worry Angelica. The dome was like a whole small world to her.

Paolo said, carefully patient, "I can't hold on much longer. Do you think you can have another try?" The answer from Renata was a sobbing shudder.

"Renata!" shouted Angelica.

Renata's scared face turned slowly up. "Something's happened to my eyes now! You look tiny."

"I *am* tiny!" yelled Angelica.

"Both of them are!" Paolo said, staring at Tonino's head.

"Pull me up quick," said Renata. The size of Angelica and Tonino so worried Renata and Paolo that both of them forgot they were hundreds of feet in the air. Paolo heaved on Renata and Renata shoved at Paolo, and they scrambled over the marble rail in a second. But there, Renata looked up at the immense golden Angel and had an instant relapse. "Oh—oh!" she wailed and sank down in a heap against the golden pedestal.

Tonino and Angelica huddled behind her. The warmth of climbing had worn off. They were feeling the wind keenly through their scanty nightshirts.

Benvenuto leapt across Renata to them. Something else had to be done, and done quickly.

Tonino went again and looked through the marble pillars, where the dome curved away and down like an icefield with ribs of green and gold. There, coming into view over the curve, was a bright red uniform, making Marco's carroty hair look faded and sallow against it. The uniform went with Marco's hair even less well than the crimson he had worn as a coachman. Tonino knew who Marco was in that instant. But that bothered him less than seeing Marco flattened to the surface and looking backwards, which Tonino was sure was a mistake. Beyond Marco's boots, fair hair was wildly blowing. Rosa's flushed face came into sight.

"I'm all *right.* Look after yourself," Rosa said.

Benvenuto was beside Tonino. They were to come up quicker than that. It was important.

"Get Rosa and Marco up here quickly!" Tonino shrieked to Paolo. He did not know if he had caught the feeling from the cats or not, but he was sure Rosa and Marco were in danger.

Paolo went unwillingly to the railing and flinched at the height. "They've been following us and shouting the whole way," he said. "Get up here quickly!" he shouted.

"Thank you very much!" Marco shouted back. "Whose fault is it we're up here anyway?"

"Is Renata all right?" Rosa yelled.

Angelica and Tonino pushed themselves between the pillars. "Hurry up!" they screamed.

The sight of them worked on Rosa and Marco as it had done on Renata and Paolo. They stared at the two tiny figures, and got to their feet as they stared. Then, stooping over, with their hands hanging, they came racing up the last of the curve for a closer look. Marco tumbled over the rail and said, as he was pulling Rosa over, "I couldn't believe my eyes at first! We'd better do a growing-spell before—"

"Get down!" said Paolo. Benvenuto's message was so urgent that he had caught it too. Both cats were crouching, stiff and low, and even Benvenuto's flat ears were flattened. Rosa stooped down. Marco grudgingly went on one knee.

"Look here, Paolo—" he began.

A savage gale hit the dome. Freezing wind shrieked across the platform, howled in the spaces between the marble pillars, and scoured across the curve of the dome below. The Angel's wings thrummed with it. It brought stabs of rain and needles of ice, hurling so hard that Tonino was thrown flat on his face. He could hear ice rattling on the Angel and spitting on the dome. Paolo snatched him into shelter behind himself. Renata feebly scrabbled about until she found Angelica and dragged her into shelter by one arm. Marco and Rosa bowed over. It was quite clear that anyone climbing the dome would have been blown off.

The wind passed, wailing like a wolf. They raised their heads into the sun.

The Duchess was standing on the platform in front of them. She had melting ice winking and trickling from her hair and from every fold of her marble-grey dress. The smile on her waxy face was not pleasant.

"Oh no," she said. "The Angel is not going to help anyone this time. Did you think I'd forgotten?"

Marco and Rosa looked up at the Angel's golden arm holding the great scroll above them. If they had not understood before, they knew now. From their suddenly thoughtful faces, Tonino knew they were finding spells to use on the Duchess.

"Don't!" squeaked Angelica. "She's an enchantress!"

The Duchess's lips pursed in another unpleasant little smile. "More than that," she said. She pointed up at the Angel. "Let the words be removed from the scroll," she said.

There was a click from the huge golden statue, followed by a grating sound, as if a spring had been released. The arm holding the scroll began to move, gently and steadily downwards, making the slightest grinding noise as it moved. They could hear it easily, in spite of a sudden clatter of gunfire from the houses beyond the river. Downwards and inwards, travelled the Angel's arm, until it stopped with a small *clunk.* The scroll now hung, flashing in the sun, between them and the Duchess. There were large raised letters on it. *Angelus,* they saw. *Capronensi populo.* It was as if the Angel were holding it out for them to read.

"Exactly," said the Duchess, though Tonino thought, from the surprised arch of her eyebrows, that this was not at all what she expected. She pointed again at the scroll, with a long white finger like a white wax pencil. "Erase," she said. "Word by word."

Their heads all tipped anxiously as they looked at the lines of writing. The first word read *Carmen.* And, sure enough, the golden capital C was sinking slowly away into the metal background. Paolo moved. He had to do something. The Duchess glanced at him, a contemptuous flick of the eyebrows. Paolo found he was twisted to the spot, with jabbing cramp in both legs.

But he could still speak, and he remembered what Marco and Rosa had said last night. Without daring to draw breath, he screamed as loud as he could. *"Chrestomanci!"*

There was more wind. This was one keen blaring gust. And Chrestomanci was there, beyond Renata and the cats. There was so little room on the platform that Chrestomanci rocked, and quickly took hold of the marble balustrade. He was still in uniform, but it was muddy and he looked extremely tired.

The Duchess whirled round and pointed her long finger at him. "You! I misled you!"

"Oh you did," Chrestomanci said. If the Duchess had hoped to catch him off balance, she was too late. Chrestomanci was steady now. "You led me a proper wild-goose-chase," he said, and put out one hand, palm forwards, towards her pointing finger. The long finger bent and began dripping white, as if it were wax indeed. The Duchess stared at it, and then looked up at Chrestomanci almost imploringly. "No," Chrestomanci said, sounding very tired. "I think you've done enough harm. Take your true form, please." He beckoned at her, like someone sick of waiting.

Instantly, the Duchess's body was seething out of shape. Her arms gathered inwards. Her face lengthened, and yet still remained the same waxy, sardonic face. Whiskers sprang from her upper lip, and her eyes lit red, like bulging lamps. Her marble skirts turned white, billowed and gathered soapily to her ankles, revealing her feet as long pink claws. And all the time, she was shrinking. Two teeth appeared at the end of her lengthened white face. A naked pink tail, marked in rings like an earthworm, snaked from behind the soapy bundle of her skirts and lashed the marble floor angrily. She shrank again.

Finally, a huge white rat with eyes like red marbles, leapt to the marble railing and crouched, chittering and glaring with its humped back twitching.

"The White Devil," said Chrestomanci, "which the Angel was sent to expel from Caprona. Right, Benvenuto and Vittoria. She's all yours. Make sure she never comes back."

Benvenuto and Vittoria were already creeping forward. Their tails swept about and their eyes stared. They sprang. The rat sprang too, off the parapet with a squeal, and went racing away down the dome. Benvenuto raced with it, long and low, keeping just beside the pink whip of its tail. Vittoria raced the other side, a snowy sliver making the great rat look yellow, running at the rat's shoulder. They saw the rat turn and try to bite her. And then, suddenly, the three were joined by a dozen smaller rats, all running and squealing. They only saw them for an instant, before the whole group ran over the slope of the dome and disappeared.

"Her helpers from the Palace," said Chrestomanci.

"Will Vittoria be safe?" said Angelica.

"She's the best ratter in Caprona, isn't she?" said Chrestomanci. "Apart from Benvenuto, that is. And by the time the Devil and her friends get to the ground, they'll have every cat in Caprona after them. Now—"

Tonino found he was the right size again. He clung to Rosa's hand. Beyond Rosa, he could see Angelica, also the right size, shivering and pulling her flimsy blue dress down over her knees, before she grabbed for Marco's hand. The wind was far worse on a larger body. But what made Tonino grab at Rosa was not that. The dome was not world-sized any more. It was a white hummock wheeling in a grey-brown landscape. The hills round Caprona were pitilessly clear. He could see flashes of flame and running figures which seemed to be almost beside him, or just above him, as if the tiny white dome had reeled over on its side. Yet the houses of Caprona were immeasurably deep below, and the river seemed to stand up out of them. The New Bridge appeared almost overhead, suffused in clouds of smoke. Smoke rolled in the hills and swirled giddily out of the downside-upside houses beyond the Old Bridge, and, worst of all, the boom and clap, the rattle and yammer of guns was now nearly deafening. Tonino no longer wondered what had scared Renata and Paolo so. He felt as if he was spinning to his death.

He clung to Rosa's hand and looked desperately up at the Angel. That at least was still huge. The scroll, which it still held patiently towards them, was almost as big as the side of a house.

"—Now," said Chrestomanci, "the best thing you can do, all of you, is to sing those words, quickly."

"What? Me too?" said Angelica.

"Yes, all of you," said Chrestomanci.

They gathered, the six of them, against the marble parapet, facing the golden scroll, with the New Bridge behind them, and began, somewhat uncertainly, to fit those words to the tune of the *Angel of Caprona.* They matched like a glove. As soon as they realised this, everyone sang lustily. Angelica and Renata stopped shivering. Tonino let go of Rosa's hand, and Rosa put her arm over his shoulders instead. And they sang as if they had always known those words. It was only a version of the usual words in Latin, but it was what the tune had always asked for.

"Carmen pacis saeculare
Venit Angelus cantare,
Et deorsum pacem dare
Capronensi populo.

"Dabit pacem eternalem,
Sine morbo immortalem,
Sine pugna triumphalem,
Capronensi populo.

"En diabola albata
De Caprona expulsata,
Missa pax et virtus data
Capronensi populo."

When they had finished, there was silence. There was not a sound from the hills, or the New Bridge, or the streets below. Every noise had stopped. So they were all the more startled at the tinny slithering with which the Angel slowly rolled up the scroll. The shining outstretched wings bent and settled against the Angel's golden shoulders, where the Angel gave them a shake to order the feathers. And that noise was not the sound of metal, but the softer rattling of real pinions. It brought with it a scent of such sweetness that there was a moment when they were not aware of anything else.

In that moment, the Angel was in flight. As the huge golden wings passed over them, the scent came again and, with it, the sound of singing. It seemed like hundreds of voices, singing tune, harmony and descant to the *Angel of Caprona.* They had no idea if it was the Angel alone, or something else. They looked up and watched the golden figure wheel and soar and wheel, until it was only a golden glint in the sky. And there was still utter silence, except for the singing.

Rosa sighed. "I suppose we'd better climb down." Renata began to shiver again at the thought.

Chrestomanci sighed too. "Don't worry about that."

They were suddenly down again, on solid cobbles, in the Cathedral forecourt. The Cathedral was once more a great white building, the houses were high, the hills were away beyond, and the people surrounding them were anything but quiet. Everyone was running to where they could see the Angel, flashing in the sun as he soared. The Archbishop was in tears, and so was the Duke. They were wringing one another's hands beside the Duke's coach.

And Chrestomanci had brought them to earth in time to see another miracle. The coach began to work and bounce on its springs. Both doors burst open. Aunt Francesca squeezed out of one, and Guido Petrocchi fell out after her. From the other door tumbled Rinaldo and the red-haired Petrocchi aunt. After them came mingled Montanas and Petrocchis, more and more and more, until anyone could see that the coach could not possibly have held that number. People stopped crowding to see the Angel and crowded to look at the Duke's coach instead.

Rosa and Marco looked at one another and began to back away among the spectators. But Chrestomanci took them each by a shoulder. "It'll be all right," he said. "And if it isn't, I'll set you up in a spell-house in Venice."

Antonio disentangled himself from a Petrocchi uncle and hurried with Guido towards Tonino and Angelica. "Are you all right?" both of them said. "Was it you who fetched the griffins—?" They broke off to stare coldly at one another.

"Yes," said Tonino. "I'm sorry you were turned into puppets."

"She was too clever for us," said Angelica. "But be thankful you got your proper clothes back afterwards. Look at us. We—"

They were pulled apart then by aunts and cousins, fearing they were contaminating one another, and hurriedly given coats and sweaters by uncles. Paolo was swept away from Renata too, by Aunt Maria. "Don't go near her, my love!"

"Oh well," said Renata, as she was pulled away too. "Thanks for helping me up the dome, anyway."

"Just a moment!" Chrestomanci said loudly. Everyone turned to him, respectful but irritable. "If each spell-house," he said, "insists on regarding the other as monsters, I can promise you that Caprona will shortly fall again." They stared at him, Montanas and Petrocchis, equally indignant. The Archbishop looked at the Duke, and both of them began to edge towards the shelter of the Cathedral porch.

"What are you talking about?" Rinaldo said aggressively. His dignity was damaged by being a puppet anyway. The look in his eye seemed to promise cowpats for everyone—with the largest share for Chrestomanci.

"I'm talking about the Angel of Caprona," said Chrestomanci. "When the Angel alighted on the Cathedral, in the time of the First Duke of Caprona, bearing the safety of Caprona with him, history clearly states that the Duke appointed two men—Antonio Petrocchi and Piero Montana—to be keepers of the words of the Angel and therefore keepers of the safety of Caprona. In memory of this, each Casa has an Angel over its gate, and the great Angel stands on a pedestal showing the Petrocchi leopard entwined with the Montana winged horse." Chrestomanci pointed upwards. "If you don't believe me, ask for ladders and go and see. Antonio Petrocchi and Piero Montana were fast friends, and so were their families after them. There were frequent marriages between the two Casas. And Caprona became a great city and a strong State. Its decline dates from that ridiculous quarrel between Ricardo and Francesco."

There were murmurs from Montanas and Petrocchis alike, here, that the quarrel was *not* ridiculous.

"Of course it was," said Chrestomanci. "You've all been deceived from your cradles up. You've let Ricardo and Francesco fool you for two centuries. What they really quarrelled about we shall never know, but I know they both told their families the same lies. And you have all gone on believing their lies and getting deeper and deeper divided, until the White Devil was actually able to enter Caprona again."

Again there were murmurs. Antonio said, "The Duchess *was* the White Devil, but—"

"Yes," said Chrestomanci. "And she has gone for the moment, because the words were found and the Angel awakened by members of both families. I suspect it could only have been done by Montanas and Petrocchis united. The rest of you could have sung the right words separately, until you were all blue in the face, and nothing would have happened. The Angel respects only friendship. The young ones of both families are luckily less bigoted than the rest of you. Marco and Rosa have even had the courage to fall in love and get married—"

Up till then, both families had listened—restively, it was true, because it was not pleasant to be lectured in front of a crowd of fellow-citizens, not to speak of the Duke and the Archbishop—but they had listened. But at this, pandemonium broke out.

"*Married!*" screamed the Montanas. "She's a *Montana*!" screamed the Petrocchis. Insults were yelled at Rosa and at Marco. Anyone who wished to count would have found no less than ten aunts in tears at once, and all cursing as they wept. Rosa and Marco were both white. It needed only Rinaldo to step up to Marco, glowering, and he did. "This scum," he said to Rosa, "knocked me down and cut my head open. And you marry it!"

Chrestomanci made haste to get between Marco and Rinaldo. "I'd hoped someone would see reason," he said to Rosa. He seemed very tired. "It had better be Venice."

"Get out of my way!" said Rinaldo. "You double-dealing sorcerer!"

"Please move, sir," said Marco. "I don't need to be shielded from an idiot like him."

"Marco," said Chrestomanci, "have you thought what two families of powerful magicians could do to you and Rosa?"

"Of course we have!" Marco said angrily, trying to push Chrestomanci aside.

But a strange silence fell again, the silence of the Angel. The Archbishop knelt down. Awed people crowded to one side or another of the Cathedral yard. The Angel was returning. He came from far off down the Corso, on foot now, with his wing-tips brushing the cobbles and the chorus of voices swelling as he approached. As he passed through the Cathedral court, it was seen that in every place where a feather had touched the stones there grew a cluster of small golden flowers. Scent gushed over everyone as the Angel drew near and halted by the Cathedral porch, towering and golden.

There he turned his remote smiling face to everyone present. His voice was like one voice singing above many. "Caprona is at peace. Keep our covenant." At that he spread his wings, making them all dizzy with the scent. And he was next seen moving upwards, over lesser domes and greater, to take his place once more on the great dome, guarding Caprona in the years to come.

This is really the end of the story, except for one or two explanations.

Marco and Rosa had to tell their story many times, at least as often as Tonino and Angelica told theirs. Among the first people they told it to was Old Niccolo, who was lying restlessly in bed and only kept there because Elizabeth sat beside him all the time. "But I'm quite well!" he kept saying.

So, in order to keep him there, Elizabeth had first Tonino and then Rosa and Marco come and tell him their stories.

Rosa and Marco had met when they were both working on the Old

Bridge. Falling in love and deciding to marry had been the easiest part, over in minutes. The difficulty was that they had to provide themselves with a family each which had nothing to do with either Casa. Rosa contrived a family first. She pretended to be English. She became very friendly with the English girl at the Art Gallery—the same Jane Smith that Rinaldo fancied so much. Jane Smith thought it was a great joke to pretend to be Rosa's sister. She wrote long letters in English to Guido Petrocchi, supposed to be from Rosa's English father, and visited the Casa Petrocchi herself the day Rosa was introduced there.

Rosa and Marco planned the introductions carefully. They used the pear-tree spell—which they worked together—in both Casas, to Jane's amusement. But the Petrocchis, though they liked the pear-tree, were not kind to Rosa at first. In fact, some of Marco's aunts were so unpleasant that Marco was quite disgusted with them. That was why Marco was able to tell Antonio so vehemently that he hated the Petrocchis. But the aunts became used to Rosa in time. Renata and Angelica became very fond of her. And the wedding was held just after Christmas.

All this time, Marco had been unable to find anyone to act as a family for him. He was in despair. Then, only a few days before the wedding, his father sent him with a message to the house of Mario Andretti, the builder. And Marco discovered that the Andrettis had a blind daughter. When Marco asked, Mario Andretti said he would do anything for anyone who cured his daughter.

"Even then, we hardly dared hope," said Marco. "We didn't know if we could cure her."

"And apart from that," said Rosa, "the only time we dared both go there was the night after the wedding."

So the wedding was held in the Casa Petrocchi. Jane Smith helped Rosa make her dress and was a bridesmaid for her, together with Renata, Angelica and one of Marco's cousins. Jane thoroughly enjoyed the wedding and seemed, Rosa said dryly, to find Marco's cousin Alberto at least as attractive as Rinaldo, whereas Rosa and Marco could think of almost nothing but little Maria Andretti. They hurried to the Andrettis' house as soon as the celebrations were over.

"And I've never known anything so difficult," said Rosa. "We were at it all night—"

Elizabeth was unable to contain herself here. "And I never even knew you were out!" she said.

"We took good care you didn't," said Rosa. "Anyway, we hadn't done anything like that before, so we had to look up spells in the University. We tried seventeen and none of them worked. In the end we had to make up one of our own. And all the time, I was thinking:

suppose this doesn't work on the poor child either, and we've played with the Andrettis' hopes."

"Not to speak of our own," said Marco. "Then our spell worked. Maria yelled out that the room was all colours and there were things like trees in it—she thought people looked like trees—and we all jumped about in the dawn, hugging one another. And Andretti was as good as his word, and did his brother-act so well here that I told him he ought to be on the stage."

"He took *me* in," Old Niccolo said, wonderingly.

"But someone was bound to find out in the end," said Elizabeth. "What did you mean to do then?"

"Just hoped," said Marco. "We thought perhaps people might get used to it—"

"In other words, you behaved like a couple of young idiots," said Old Niccolo. "What is that terrible stench?" And he leapt up and raced out on to the gallery to investigate, with Elizabeth, Rosa and Marco racing after him to stop him.

The smell, of course, was the kitchen-spell again. The insects had vanished and a smell of drains had taken their place. All day long, the kitchen belched out stinks, which grew stronger towards evening. It was particularly unfortunate, because the whole of Caprona was preparing to feast and celebrate. Caprona was truly at peace. The troops from Florence, and Pisa and Siena, had all returned home—somewhat bewildered and wondering how they had been beaten—and the people of Caprona were dancing in the streets.

"And we can't even cook, let alone celebrate!" wailed Aunt Gina.

Then an invitation arrived from the Casa Petrocchi. Would the Casa Montana be pleased to join in the celebrations at the Casa Petrocchi? It was a trifle stiff, but the Casa Montana did please. What could be more fortunate? Tonino and Paolo suspected that it was Chrestomanci's doing. The only difficulty was to stop Old Niccolo getting out of bed and going with the rest of them. Everyone said Elizabeth had done enough. Everyone, even Aunt Francesca, wanted to go. Then, more fortunately still, Uncle Umberto turned up, and old Luigi Petrocchi with him. They said they would sit with Old Niccolo—and on him if necessary. They were too old for dancing.

So everyone else went to the Casa Petrocchi, and it proved a celebration to remember. The Duke was there, because Angelica had insisted on it. The Duke was so grateful to be invited that he had brought with him as much wine and as many cakes as his coach would hold, and six footmen in a second coach to serve it.

"The Palace is awful," he said. "No one in it but Punch and Judys. Somehow I don't fancy them like I used to."

What with the wine, the cakes, and the good food baked in the Casa Petrocchi kitchen, the evening became very merry. Somebody found a barrel-organ and everyone danced to it in the yard. And, if the six footmen forgot to serve cakes and danced with the rest, who was to blame them? After all, the Duke was dancing with Aunt Francesca—a truly formidable sight.

Tonino sat with Paolo and Renata beside a charcoal brazier, watching the dancing. And while they sat, Benvenuto suddenly emerged from the shadows and sat down by the brazier, where he proceeded to give himself a fierce and thorough wash.

They had done a fine, enjoyable job on that white rat, he informed Tonino, as he stuck one leg high above his gnarled head and subjected it to punishing tongue-work. She'd not be back again.

"But is Vittoria all right?" Renata wanted to know.

Fine, was Benvenuto's answer. She was resting. She was going to have kittens. They would be particularly good kittens because Benvenuto was the father. Tonino was to make sure to get one for the Casa Montana.

Tonino asked Renata for a kitten then and there, and Renata promised to ask Angelica. Whereupon, Benvenuto, having worked over both hind legs, wafted himself on to Tonino's knees, where he made himself into a tight brown mat and slept for an hour.

"I wish I could understand him," said Paolo. "He tried to tell me where you were, but all I did was see a picture of the front of the Palace."

"But that's how he always tells things!" said Tonino. He was surprised Paolo had not known. "You just have to read his pictures."

"What's he saying now?" Renata asked Paolo.

"Nothing," said Paolo. "Snore, snore." And they all laughed.

Sometime later, when Benvenuto had woken up and drifted off to try his luck in the kitchen, Tonino wandered into a room nearby, without quite knowing why he did. As soon as he got inside, though, he knew it was no accident. Chrestomanci was there, with Angelica and Guido Petrocchi, and so was Antonio. Antonio was looking so worried that Tonino braced himself for trouble.

"We were discussing you, Tonino," said Chrestomanci. "You helped Angelica fetch the griffins, didn't you?"

"Yes," said Tonino. He remembered the damage they had done and felt alarmed.

"And you helped in the kitchen spell?" asked Chrestomanci.

Tonino said "Yes" again. Now he was sure there was trouble.

"And when you hanged the Duchess," Chrestomanci said, to Tonino's confusion, "how did you do that?"

Tonino wondered how he could be in trouble over that too, but he answered, "By doing what the puppet show made me do. I couldn't get out of it, so I had to go along with it, you see."

"I do," said Chrestomanci, and he turned to Antonio rather triumphantly. "You see? And that was the White Devil! What interests me is that it was someone else's spell each time." Then before Tonino could be too puzzled, he turned back to him. "Tonino," he said, "it seems to me that you have a new and rather useful talent. You may not be able to work many spells on your own, but you seem to be able to turn other people's magic to your own use. I think if they had let you help on the Old Bridge, for instance, it would have been mended in half a day. I've been asking your father if he'd let you come back to England with me, so that we could find out just what you can do."

Tonino looked at his father's worried face. He hardly knew what to think. "Not for good?" he said.

Antonio smiled. "Only for a few weeks," he said. "If Chrestomanci's right, we'll need you here badly."

Tonino smiled too. "Then I don't mind," he said.

"But," said Angelica, "it was me who fetched the griffins really."

"What were you really fetching?" asked Guido.

Angelica hung her head. "Mice." She looked resigned when her father roared with laughter.

"I wanted to talk about you too," said Chrestomanci. He said to Guido, "Her spells always work, don't they? It occurs to me you might learn from Angelica."

Guido scratched his beard. "How to turn things green and get griffins, you mean?"

Chrestomanci picked up his glass of wine. "There are risks, of course, to Angelica's methods. But I meant she can show you that a thing need not be done in the same old way in order to work. I think, in time, she will make you a whole new set of spells. Both houses can learn from her." He raised his wine glass. "Your health, Angelica. Tonino. The Duchess thought she was getting the weakest members of both Casas, and it turned out quite the opposite."

Antonio and Guido raised their glasses too. "I'll say this," said Guido. "But for you two, we wouldn't be celebrating tonight."

Angelica and Tonino looked at each other and made faces. They felt very shy and very, very pleased.

THE LIVES OF CHRISTOPHER CHANT

FOR LEO,
WHO GOT HIT ON THE HEAD
WITH A CRICKET BAT

NOTE

Everything in this book happens
at least twenty-five years
before the story told in *Charmed Life*.

CHAPTER 1

It was years before Christopher told anyone about his dreams. This was because he mostly lived in the nurseries at the top of the big London house, and the nursery maids who looked after him changed every few months.

He scarcely saw his parents. When Christopher was small, he was terrified that he would meet Papa out walking in the Park one day and not recognize him. He used to kneel down and look through the banisters on the rare days when Papa came home from the City before bedtime, hoping to fix Papa's face in his mind. All he got was a foreshortened view of a figure in a frock coat with a great deal of well-combed black whisker, handing a tall black hat to the footman, and then a view of a very neat white parting in black hair, as Papa marched rapidly under the stairway and out of sight. Beyond knowing that Papa was taller than most footmen, Christopher knew little else.

Some evenings, Mama was on the stairs to meet Papa, blocking Christopher's view with wide silk skirts and a multitude of frills and draperies. "Remind your master," she would say icily to the footman, "that there is a Reception in this house tonight and that he is required for once in his life to act as host."

Papa, hidden behind Mama's wide clothing, would reply in a deep gloomy voice, "Tell Madam I have a great deal of work brought home from the office tonight. Tell her she should have warned me in advance."

"Inform your master," Mama would reply to the footman, "that if I'd warned him, he would have found an excuse not to be here. Point out to him that it is my money that finances his business and that I shall remove it if he does not do this small thing for me."

Then Papa would sigh. "Tell Madam I am going up to dress," he would say. "Under protest. Ask her to stand aside from the stairs."

Mama never did stand aside, to Christopher's disappointment. She always gathered up her skirts and sailed upstairs ahead of Papa, to make sure Papa did as she wanted. Mama had huge lustrous eyes, a perfect figure and piles of glossy black curls. The nursery maids told Christopher Mama was a Beauty. At this stage in his life, Christopher thought everyone's parents were like this; but he did wish Mama would give him a view of Papa just once.

He thought everyone had the kind of dreams he had, too. He did not think they were worth mentioning. The dreams always began the same way. Christopher got out of bed and walked round the corner of the night nursery wall—the part with the fireplace, which jutted out—on to a rocky path high on the side of a valley. The valley was green and steep, with a stream rushing from waterfall to waterfall down the middle, but Christopher never felt there was much point in following the stream down the valley. Instead he went up the path, round a large rock, into the part he always thought of as The Place Between. Christopher thought it was probably a leftover piece of the world, from before somebody came along and made the world properly. Formless slopes of rock towered and slanted in all directions. Some of it was hard and steep, some of it piled and rubbly, and none of it had much shape. Nor did it have much color—most of it was the ugly brown you get from mixing every color in a paintbox. There was always a formless wet mist hanging round this place, adding to the vagueness of everything. You could never see the sky. In fact, Christopher sometimes thought there might not *be* a sky: he had an idea that the formless rock went on and on in a great arch overhead—but when he thought about it, that did not seem possible.

Christopher always knew in his dream that you could get to Almost Anywhere from The Place Between. He called it Almost Anywhere because there was one place that did not want you to go to it. It was quite near, but he always found himself avoiding it. He set off sliding, scrambling, edging across bulging wet rock, and climbing up or down, until he found another valley and another path. There were hundreds of them. He called them the Anywheres.

The Anywheres were mostly quite different from London. They were hotter or colder, with strange trees and stranger houses. Sometimes the people in them looked ordinary, sometimes their skin was bluish or reddish and their eyes were peculiar, but they were always very kind to Christopher. He had a new adventure every time he went on a dream. In the active adventures people helped him escape through cellars of odd buildings, or he helped them in wars, or in rounding up dangerous animals. In the calm adventures, he got new things to eat and people gave him toys. He lost most of the toys as he was scrambling back home over the rocks, but he did manage to bring back the shiny shell necklace the silly ladies gave him, because he could hang it round his neck.

He went to the Anywhere with the silly ladies several times. It had blue sea and white sand, perfect for digging and building in. There were ordinary people in it, but Christopher only saw them in the distance. The silly ladies came and sat on rocks out of the sea and giggled at him while he made sand castles.

"Oh clistoffer!" they would coo, in lisping voices. "Tell uth what make you a clistoffer." And they would all burst into screams of high laughter.

They were the only ladies he had seen without clothes on. Their skins were greenish and so was their hair. He was fascinated by the way the ends of them were big silvery tails that could curl and flip almost like a fish could, and send powerful sprays of water over him from their big finned feet. He never could persuade them that he was not a strange animal called a clistoffer.

Every time he went to that Anywhere, the latest nursery maid complained about all the sand in his bed. He had learned very early on that they complained even louder when they found his pajamas muddy, wet and torn from climbing through The Place Between. He took a set of clothes out on to the rocky path and left them there to change into. He had to put new clothes there every year or so, when he grew out of the latest torn and muddy suit, but the nursery maids changed so often that none of them noticed. Nor did they notice the strange toys he brought back over the years. There was a clockwork dragon, a horse that was really a flute, and the necklace from the silly ladies which, when you looked closely, was a string of tiny pearl skulls.

Christopher thought about the silly ladies. He looked at his latest nursemaid's feet, and he thought that her shoes were about big enough to hide the flippers at the end of her tail. But you could never see any more of any lady because of her skirts. He kept wondering how Mama and the nursery maid walked about on a big limber tail and flippers, instead of legs and feet.

His chance to find out came one afternoon when the nursery maid put him into an unpleasant sailor-suit and led him downstairs to the drawing room. Mama and some other ladies were there with someone called Lady Badgett, who was a kind of cousin of Papa's. She had asked to see Christopher. Christopher stared at her long nose and her wrinkles. "Is she a witch, Mama?" he asked loudly.

Everyone except Lady Badgett—who went more wrinkled than ever—said, "Hush dear!" After that, Christopher was glad to find they seemed to have forgotten him. He quietly lay down, on his back on the carpet, and rolled from lady to lady. When they caught him, he was under the sofa gazing up Lady Badgett's petticoats. He was dragged out of the room in disgrace, very disappointed to discover that all the ladies had big thick legs, except Lady Badgett: her legs were thin and yellow like a chicken's.

Mama sent for him in her dressing room later that day. "Oh Christopher, how *could* you!" she said. "I'd just got Lady Badgett to the point of calling on me, and she'll never come again. You've undone the work of years!"

It was very hard work, Christopher realized, being a Beauty. Mama was very busy in front of her mirror with all sorts of little cut glass bottles and jars. Behind her, a maid was even busier, far busier than the nursery maids ever were, working on Mama's glossy curls. Christopher was so ashamed to have wasted all this work that he picked up a glass jar to hide his confusion.

Mama told him sharply to put it down. "Money isn't everything, you see, Christopher," she explained. "A good place in Society is worth far more. Lady Badgett could have helped us both. Why do you think I married your Papa?"

Since Christopher had simply no idea what could have brought Mama and Papa together, he put out his hand to pick up the jar again. But he remembered in time that he was not supposed to touch it, and picked up a big pad of false hair instead. He turned it round in his hands while Mama talked.

"You are going to grow up with Papa's good family and my money," she said. "I want you to promise me now that you will take your place in Society alongside the very best people. Mama intends you to be a great man—Christopher, are you listening?"

Christopher had given up trying to understand Mama. He held the false hair out instead. "What's this for?"

"Bulking out my hair," Mama said. "Please attend, Christopher. It's very important you begin *now* preparing yourself for the future. Put that hair *down*."

Christopher put the pad of hair back. "I thought it might be a dead rat," he said. And somehow Mama must have made a mistake because, to Christopher's great interest, the thing really *was* a dead rat. Mama and her maid both screamed. Christopher was hustled away while a footman came running with a shovel.

After that, Mama called Christopher to her dressing room and talked to him quite often. He stood trying to remember not to fiddle with the jars, staring at his reflection in her mirror, wondering why his curls were black and Mama's rich brown, and why his eyes were so much more like coal than Mama's. Something seemed to stop there ever being another dead rat, but sometimes a spider could be encouraged to let itself down in front of the mirror, whenever Mama's talk became too alarming. He understood that Mama cared very urgently about his future. He knew he was going to have to enter Society with the best people. But the only Society he had heard of was the Aid the Heathen Society that he had to give a penny to every Sunday in church, and he thought Mama meant that.

Christopher made careful inquiries from the nursery maid with the big feet. She told him Heathens were savages who ate people. Missionaries were the best people, and they were the ones Heathens ate. Christopher saw that he was going to be a missionary when he grew up. He found Mama's talk increasingly alarming. He wished she had chosen another career for him.

He also asked the nursery maid about the kind of ladies who had tails like fish. "Oh you mean mermaids!" the girl said, laughing. "Those aren't real."

Christopher knew mermaids were not real, because he only met them in dreams. Now he was convinced that he would meet Heathens too, if he went to the wrong Almost Anywhere. For a time, he was so frightened of meeting Heathens that when he came to a new valley from The Place Between, he lay down and looked carefully at the Anywhere it led to, to see what the people were like there before he went on. But after a while, when nobody tried to eat him, he decided that the Heathens probably lived in the Anywhere which stopped you going to it, and gave up worrying until he was older.

When he was a little older, people in the Anywheres sometimes gave him money. Christopher learned to refuse coins. As soon as he touched them, everything just stopped. He landed in bed with a jolt and woke up sweating. Once this happened when a pretty lady who reminded him of Mama tried laughingly to hang an earring in his ear. Christopher would have asked the nursery maid with big feet about it, but she had left long ago. Most of the ones who came after simply said, "Don't bother me now—I'm busy!" when he asked them things. Until he learned to read, Christopher thought this was what all nursery maids did: they stayed a month, too busy to talk, and then set their mouths in a nasty line and flounced out. He was amazed to read of Old Retainers, who stayed with families for a whole lifetime arid could be persuaded to tell long (and sometimes very boring) stories about the family in the past. In his house, none of the servants stayed more than six months.

The reason seemed to be that Mama and Papa had given up speaking to one another even through the footman. They handed the servants notes to give to one another instead. Since it never occurred to either Mama or Papa to seal the notes, sooner or later someone would bring the note up to the nursery floor and read it aloud to the nursery maid. Christopher learned that Mama was always short and to the point.

"Mr. Chant is requested to smoke cigars only in his own room." Or, "Will Mr. Chant please take note that the new laundry maid has complained of holes burned in his shirts." Or, "Mr. Chant caused me much embarrassment by leaving in the middle of my Breakfast Party."

Papa usually let the notes build up and then answered the lot in a kind of rambling rage. "My dear Miranda, I shall smoke where I please and it is the job of that lazy laundry maid to deal with the results. But then your extravagance in employing foolish layabouts and rude louts is only for your own selfish comfort and never for mine. If you wish me to remain at your parties, try to employ a cook who knows bacon from old shoes and refrain from giving that idiotic tinkling laugh all the time."

Papa's replies usually caused the servants to leave overnight.

Christopher rather enjoyed the insight these notes gave him. Papa seemed more like a person, somehow, even if he was so critical. It was quite a blow to Christopher when he was cut off from them by the arrival of his first Governess.

Mama sent for him. She was in tears. "Your Papa has overreached himself this time," she said. "It's a mother's place to see to the education of her child. I want you to go to a good school, Christopher. It's most important. But I don't want to *force* you into learning. I want your ambition to flower as well. But your Papa comes crashing in with his *grim* notions and goes behind my back by appointing this Governess who, knowing your Papa, is bound to be *terrible*! Oh my poor child!"

Christopher realized that the Governess was his first step towards becoming a missionary. He felt solemn and alarmed. But when the Governess came, she was simply a drab lady with pink eyes, who was far too discreet to talk to servants. She only stayed a month, to Mama's jubilation.

"Now we can really start your education," Mama said. "I shall choose the next Governess myself."

Mama said that quite often over the next two years, for Governesses came and went just like nursery maids before them. They were all drab, discreet ladies, and Christopher got their names muddled up. He decided that the chief difference between a Governess and a nursery maid was that a Governess usually burst into tears before she left—and that was the only time a Governess ever said anything interesting about Mama and Papa.

"I'm sorry to do this to you," the third—or maybe the fourth—Governess wept, "because you're a nice little boy, even if you *are* a bit remote, but the *atmosphere* in this house! Every night *he's* home—which thank God is rarely!—I have to sit at the dining table with them in utter silence. And *she* passes me a note to give to *him*, or *he* passes me one for *her*. Then they open the notes and look daggers at one another and then at me. I can't stand any more!"

The ninth—or maybe the tenth—Governess was even more indiscreet. "I know they hate one another," she sobbed, "but *she's* no call to hate me too! She's one of those who can't abide other women. And she's a sorceress, I think—I can't be sure, because she only does little things—and *he's* at least as strong as *she* is. He may even be an enchanter. Between them they make such an atmosphere—it's no wonder they can't keep any servants! Oh Christopher, forgive me for talking like this about your parents!"

All the Governesses asked Christopher to forgive them and he forgave them very readily, for this was the only time now that he had news of Mama and Papa. It gave him a wistful sort of feeling that perhaps other people had parents who were not like this. He was also sure that there was some sort of crisis brewing. The hushed thunder of it reached as far as the schoolroom, even though the Governesses would not let him gossip with the servants any more. He remembered the night the crisis broke, because that was the night when he went to an Anywhere where a man under a yellow umbrella gave him a sort of candlestick of little bells. It was so beautiful that Christopher was determined to bring it home. He held it in his teeth as he scrambled across the rocks of The Place Between. To his joy, it was in his bed when he woke up. But there was quite a different feeling to the house. The twelfth Governess packed and left straight after breakfast.

CHAPTER 2

Christopher was called to Mama's dressing room that afternoon. There was a new Governess sitting on the only hard chair, wearing the usual sort of ugly grayish clothes and a hat that was uglier than usual. Her drab cotton gloves were folded on her dull bag and her head hung down as if she were timid or put-upon, or both. Christopher found her of no interest. All the interest in the room was centered on the man standing behind Mama's chair with his hand on Mama's shoulder.

"Christopher, this is my brother," Mama said happily. "Your Uncle Ralph."

Mama pronounced it Rafe. It was more than a year before Christopher discovered it was the name he read as Ralph. Uncle Ralph took his fancy completely. To begin with, he was smoking a cigar. The scents of the dressing room were changed and mixed with the rich, incense-like smoke, and Mama was not protesting by even so much as sniffing. That alone was enough to show that Uncle Ralph was in a class by himself. Then he was wearing tweeds, strong and tangy and almost fox-colored, which were a little baggy here and there, but blended beautifully with the darker foxiness of Uncle Ralph's hair and the redder foxiness of his mustache. Christopher had seldom seen a man in tweeds or without whiskers. This did even more to assure him that Uncle Ralph was someone special. As a final touch, Uncle Ralph smiled at him like sunlight on an autumn forest. It was such an engaging smile that Christopher's face broke into a return smile almost of its own accord.

"Hallo old chap," said Uncle Ralph, rolling out blue smoke above Mama's glossy hair. "I know this is not the best way for an uncle to recommend himself to a nephew, but I've been sorting the family affairs out, and I'm afraid I've had to do one or two quite shocking things, like bringing you a new Governess and arranging for you to start school in the autumn. Governess over there. Miss Bell. I hope you like one another. Enough to forgive me anyway."

He smiled at Christopher in a sunny, humorous way which had Christopher rapidly approaching adoration. All the same, Christopher glanced dubiously at Miss Bell. She looked back, and there was an instant when a sort of hidden prettiness in her almost came out into the open. Then she blinked pale eyelashes and murmured, "Pleased to meet you," in a voice as uninteresting as her clothes.

"She'll be your last Governess, I hope," said Mama. Because of that, Christopher ever after thought of Miss Bell as the Last Governess. "She's going to prepare you for school. I wasn't meaning to send you away yet, but your uncle says—Anyway, a good education is important for your career and, to be blunt with you, Christopher, your Papa has made a most *vexatious* hash of the money—which is mine, not his, as you know—and lost practically all of it. Luckily I had your uncle to turn to and—"

"And once turned to, I don't let people down," Uncle Ralph said, with a quick flick of a glance at the Governess. Maybe he meant she should not be hearing this. "Fortunately, there's plenty left to send you to school, and then your Mama is going to recoup a bit by living abroad. She'll like that—eh, Miranda? And Miss Bell is going to be found another post with glowing references. Everyone's going to be fine."

His smile went to all of them one by one, full of warmth and confidence. Mama laughed and dabbed scent behind her ears. The Last Governess almost smiled, so that the hidden prettiness half emerged again. Christopher tried to grin a strong manly grin at Uncle Ralph, because that seemed to be the only way to express the huge, almost hopeless adoration that was growing in him. Uncle Ralph laughed, a golden brown laugh, and completed the conquest of Christopher by fishing in a tweed pocket and tipping his nephew a bright new sixpence.

Christopher would have died rather than spend that sixpence. Whenever he changed clothes, he transferred the sixpence to the new pockets. It was another way of expressing his adoration of Uncle Ralph. It was clear that Uncle Ralph had stepped in to save Mama from ruin, and this made him the first good man that Christopher had met. And on top of that, he was the only person outside the Anywheres who had bothered to speak to Christopher in that friendly man-to-man way.

Christopher tried to treasure the Last Governess too, for Uncle Ralph's sake, but that was not so easy. She was so very boring. She had a drab, calm way of speaking, and she never raised her voice or showed impatience, even when he was stupid about Mental Arithmetic or Levitation, both of which all the other Governesses had somehow missed out on.

"If a herring and a half cost three-ha'pence, Christopher," she explained drearily, "that's a penny and a half for a fish and a half. How much for a whole fish?"

"I don't know," he said, trying not to yawn.

"Very well," the Last Governess said calmly. "We'll think again tomorrow. Now look in this little mirror and see if you can't make it rise in the air just an inch."

But Christopher could not move the mirror any more than he could understand what a herring cost. The Last Governess put the mirror aside and quietly went on to puzzle him about French. After a few days of this, Christopher tried to make her angry, hoping she would turn more interesting when she shouted. But she just said calmly, "Christopher, you're getting silly. You may play with your toys now. But remember you only take one out at a time, and you put that back before you get out another. That is our rule."

Christopher had become rapidly and dismally accustomed to this rule. It reduced the fun a lot. He had also become used to the Last Governess sitting beside him while he played. The other Governesses had seized the chance to rest, but this one sat in a hard chair efficiently mending his clothes, which reduced the fun even more. Nevertheless, he got the candlestick of chiming bells out of the cupboard, because that was fascinating in its way. It was so arranged that it played different tunes, depending on which bell you touched first. When he had finished with it, the Last Governess paused in her darning to say, "That goes in the middle of the top shelf. Put it back before you take that clockwork dragon." She waited to listen to the chiming that showed Christopher had done what she said. Then, as she drove the needle into the sock again, she asked in her dullest way, "Who gave you the bells, Christopher?"

No one had ever asked Christopher about anything he had brought back from the Anywheres before. He was rather at a loss. "A man under a yellow umbrella," he answered. "He said they bring luck on my house."

"What man where?" the Last Governess wanted to know—except that she did not sound as if she cared if she knew or not.

"An Almost Anywhere," Christopher said. "The hot one with the smells and the snake charmers. The man didn't say his name."

"That's not an answer, Christopher," the Last Governess said calmly, but she did not say anything more until the next time, two days later, when Christopher got out the chiming bells again. "Remember where they go when you've finished with them," she said. "Have you thought yet where the man with yellow umbrella was?"

"Outside a painted place where some gods live," Christopher said, setting the small silvery bellcups ringing. "He was nice. He said it didn't matter about money."

"Very generous," remarked the Last Governess. "Where was this painted house for gods, Christopher?"

"I told you. It was an Almost Anywhere," Christopher said.

"And I told you that that is not an answer," the Last Governess said. She folded up her darning. "Christopher, I insist that you tell me where those bells came from."

"Why do you want to know?" Christopher asked, wishing she would leave him in peace.

"Because," the Last Governess said with truly ominous calm, "you are not being frank and open like a nice boy should be. I suspect you stole those bells."

At this monstrous injustice, Christopher's face reddened and tears stood in his eyes. "I *haven't*!" he cried out. "He *gave* them to me! People always give me things in the Anywheres, only I drop most of them. Look." And regardless of her one-toy-at-a-time rule, he rushed to the cupboard, fetched the horse flute, the mermaids' necklace and the clockwork dragon, and banged them down in her darning basket. "Look! These are from other Anywheres."

The Last Governess gazed at them with terrible impassiveness. "Am I to believe you have stolen these, too?" she said. She put the basket and the toys on the floor and stood up. "Come with me. This must be reported to your Mama at once."

She seized Christopher's arm and in spite of his yells of "I *didn't*, I *didn't*!" she marched him inexorably downstairs.

Christopher leaned backwards and dragged his feet and implored her not to. He knew he would never be able to explain to Mama. All the notice the Last Governess took was to say, "Stop that disgraceful noise. You're a big boy now."

This was something all the Governesses agreed on. But Christopher no longer cared about being big. Tears poured disgracefully down his cheeks and he screamed the name of the one person he knew who saved people. "Uncle Ralph! I'll explain to Uncle Ralph!"

The Last Governess glanced down at him at that. Just for a moment, the hidden prettiness flickered in her face. But to Christopher's despair, she dragged him to Mama's dressing room and knocked on the door.

Mama turned from her mirror in surprise. She looked at Christopher, red faced and gulping and wet with tears. She looked at the Last Governess. "Whatever is going on? Is he ill?"

"No, madam," the Last Governess said in her dullest way. "Something has happened which I think your brother should be informed of at once."

"Ralph?" said Mama. "You mean I'm to write to Ralph? Or is it more urgent than that?"

"Urgent, madam, I think," the Last Governess said drearily. "Christopher says that he is willing to confess to his uncle. I suggest, if I may make so bold, that you summon him now."

Mama yawned. This Governess bored her terribly. "I'll do my best," she said, "but I don't answer for my brother's temper. He lives a very busy life, you know." Carelessly, she pulled one of her dark glossy hairs out of the silver backed brush she had been using. Then, much more carefully, she began teasing hairs out of her silver and crystal hair-tidy. Most of the hairs were Mama's own dark ones, but Christopher, watching Mama's beautiful pearly nails delicately pinching and pulling at the hairs, while he sobbed and swallowed and sobbed again, saw that one of the hairs was a much redder color. This was the one Mama pulled out. She laid it across her own hair from the brush. Then, picking up what seemed to be a hatpin with a glittery knob, she laid that across both hairs and tapped it with one sharp, impatient nail. "Ralph," she said. "Ralph Weatherby Argent. Miranda wants you."

One of the mirrors of the dressing table turned out to be a window, with Uncle Ralph looking through it, rather irritably, while he knotted his tie. "What is it?" he said. "I'm busy today."

"When *aren't* you?" asked Mama. "Listen, that Governess is here looking like a wet week as usual. She's brought Christopher. Something about a confession. *Could* you come and sort it out? It's beyond me."

"*Is* she?" said Uncle Ralph. He leaned sideways to look through the mirror—or window, or whatever—and when he saw Christopher, he winked and broke into his sunniest smile. "Dear, dear. This does look upsetting. I'll be along at once."

Christopher saw him leave the window and walk away to one side. Mama had only time to turn to the Last Governess and say, "There, I've done my best!" before the door of her dressing room opened and Uncle Ralph strode in.

Christopher quite forgot his sobs in the interest of all this. He tried to think what was on the other side of the wall of Mama's dressing room. The stairs, as far as he knew. He supposed Uncle Ralph *could* have a secret room in the wall about one foot wide, but he was much more inclined to think he had been seeing real magic. As he decided this, Uncle Ralph secretly passed him a large white handkerchief and walked cheerfully into the middle of the room to allow Christopher time to wipe his face.

"Now what's all this about?" he said.

"I have no idea," said Mama. "She'll explain, no doubt."

Uncle Ralph cocked a ginger eyebrow at the Last Governess. "I found Christopher playing with an artifact," the Governess said tediously, "of a kind I have never seen before, made of a metal that is totally unknown to me. He then revealed he had three more artifacts, each one different from the other, but he was unable to explain how he had come by them."

Uncle Ralph looked at Christopher, who hid the handkerchief behind his back and looked nervously back. "Enough to get anyone into hot water, old chap," Uncle Ralph said. "Suppose you take me to look at these things and explain where they do come from?"

Christopher heaved a great happy sigh. He had known he could count on Uncle Ralph to save him. "Yes please," he said.

They went back upstairs with the Last Governess processing ahead and Christopher hanging gratefully on to Uncle Ralph's large warm hand. When they got there, the Governess sat quietly down to her sewing again as if she felt she had done her bit. Uncle Ralph picked up the bells and jingled them. "By Jove!" he said "These sound like nothing else in the universe!" He took them to the window and carefully examined each bell. "Bull's-eye!" he said. "You clever woman! They *are* like nothing else in the universe. Some kind of strange alloy, I think, different for each bell. Handmade by the look of them." He pointed genially to the tuffet by the fire. "Sit there, old chap, and oblige me by explaining what you did to get these bells here."

Christopher sat down, full of willing eagerness. "I had to hold them in my mouth while I climbed through The Place Between," he explained.

"No, no," said Uncle Ralph. "That sounds like near the end. Start with what you did in the beginning before you got the bells."

"I went down the valley to the snake-charming town," Christopher said.

"No, before that, old chap," said Uncle Ralph. "When you set off from here. What time of day was it, for instance? After breakfast? Before lunch?"

"No, in the night," Christopher explained. "It was one of the dreams."

In this way, by going carefully back every time Christopher missed out a step, Uncle Ralph got Christopher to tell him in detail about the dreams, and The Place Between, and the Almost Anywheres he came to down the valleys. Since Uncle Ralph, far from being angry, seemed steadily more delighted, Christopher told him everything he could think of.

"What did I tell you!" he said, possibly to the Governess. "I can always trust my hunches. Something *had* to come out of a heredity like this! By Jove, Christopher old chap, you must be the only person in the world who can bring back solid objects from a spirit trip! I doubt if even old de Witt can do that!"

Christopher glowed to find Uncle Ralph so pleased with him, but he could not help feeling resentful about the Last Governess., "*She* said I stole them."

"Take no notice of her. Women are always jumping to the wrong conclusions," Uncle Ralph said, lighting a cigar. At this, the Last Governess shrugged her shoulders up and smiled a little. The hidden prettiness came out stronger than Christopher had ever seen it, almost as if she was human and sharing a joke. Uncle Ralph blew a roll of blue smoke over them both, beaming like the sun coming through clouds. "Now the next thing, old chap," he said, "is to do a few experiments to test this gift of yours. Can you control these dreams of yours? Can you say *when* you're about to go off to your Almost Anywheres—or can't you?"

Christopher thought about it. "I go when I want to," he said.

"Then have you any objection to doing me a test run, say tomorrow night?" Uncle Ralph asked.

"I could go tonight," Christopher offered.

"No, tomorrow," said Uncle Ralph. "It'll take me a day to get things set up. And when you go, this is what I want you to do." He leaned forward and pointed his cigar at Christopher, to let him know he was serious. "You set out as usual when you're ready and try to do two experiments for me. First, I'm going to arrange to have a man waiting for you in your Place Between. I want you to see if you can find him. You may have to shout to find him—I don't know: I'm not a spirit traveler myself—but anyway, you climb about and see if you can make contact with him. *If* you do, then you do the second experiment. The man will tell you what that is. And if they both work, then we can experiment some more. Do you think you can do that? You'd like to help, wouldn't you, old chap?"

"Yes!" said Christopher.

Uncle Ralph stood up and patted his shoulder. "Good lad. Don't let anyone deceive you, old chap. You have a very exciting and important gift here. It's so important that I advise you not to talk about it to anyone but me and Miss Bell over there. Don't tell anyone, not even your Mama. Right?"

"Right," said Christopher. It was wonderful that Uncle Ralph thought him important. He was so glad and delighted that he would have done far more for Uncle Ralph than just not tell anyone. That was easy. There was no one to tell.

"So it's our secret," said Uncle Ralph, going to the door. "Just the three of us—and the man I'm going to send, of course. Don't forget you may have to look quite hard to find him, will you?"

"I won't forget," Christopher promised eagerly.

"Good lad," said Uncle Ralph, and went out of the door in a waft of cigar smoke.

CHAPTER 3

Christopher thought he would never live through the time until tomorrow night. He burned to show Uncle Ralph what he could do. If it had not been for the Last Governess, he would have made himself ill with excitement, but she managed to be so boring that she somehow made everything else boring too. By the time Christopher went to bed that next night, he was almost wondering if it was worth dreaming.

But he did dream, because Uncle Ralph had asked him to, and got out of bed as usual and walked round the fireplace to the valley, where his clothes were lying on the rocky path as usual. By now this lot of clothes were torn, covered with mud and assorted filth from a hundred Almost Anywheres, and at least two sizes too small. Christopher put them on quickly, without bothering to do up buttons that would not meet. He never wore shoes because they got in the way as he climbed the rocks. He pattered round the crag in his bare feet into The Place Between.

It was formless and unfinished as ever, all slides and jumbles of rock rearing in every direction and high overhead. The mist billowed as formlessly as the rocks. It was one of the times when rain slanted in it, driven this way and that by the hither-thither winds that blew in The Place Between. Christopher hoped he would not have to spend too long here hunting for Uncle Ralph's man. It made him feel so small, besides being cold and wet. He dutifully braced himself on a slide of rubbly sand and shouted.

"Hallo!"

The Place Between made his voice sound no louder than a bird cheeping. The windy fog seemed to snatch the sound away and bury it in a flurry of rain. Christopher listened for a reply, but for minutes on end the only noise was the hissing hum of the wind. He was wondering whether to shout again, when he heard a little cheaping thread of sound, wailing its thin way back to him across the rocks. "Hallo-o-o!" It was his own shout. Christopher was sure of it. Right from the start of his dreams, he had known that The Place Between liked to have everything that did not belong sent back to the place it came from. That was why he always climbed back to bed faster than he did when he climbed out to a new valley. The Place pushed him back.

Christopher thought about this. It probably did no good to shout. If Uncle Ralph's man was out there in the mist, he would not be able to stand and wait for very long, without getting pushed back to the valley he came from. So the man would have to wait in the mouth of a valley and hope that Christopher found him. Christopher sighed. There were such thousands and thousands of valleys, high up, low down, turning off at every angle you could think of, and some valleys turned off other valleys—and that was only if you crawled round the side of the Place that was nearest. If you went the other way, towards the Anywhere that did not want people, there were probably many thousands more. On the other hand, Uncle Ralph would not want to make it too difficult. The man must be quite near.

Determined to make Uncle Ralph's experiment a success if he could, Christopher set off, climbing, sliding, inching across wet rock with his face close to the cold hard smell of it. The first valley he came to was empty. "Hallo?" he called down it. But the river rushed down green empty space and he could see no one was there. He backed out and climbed up and sideways to the next. And there, before he reached the opening, he could see someone through the mist, dark and shiny with rain, crouching on a rock and scrabbling for a handhold overhead.

"Hallo?" Christopher asked.

"Well I'll be—Is that Christopher?" the person asked. It was a strong young man's voice. "Come on out where we can see one another."

With a certain amount of heaving and slipping, both of them scrambled round a bulge of rock and dropped down into another valley, where the air was calm and warm. The grass here was lit pink by a sunset in the distance.

"Well, well," said Uncle Ralph's man. "You're about half the size I expected. Pleased to meet you, Christopher. I'm Tacroy." He grinned down at Christopher. Tacroy was as strong and young as his voice, rather squarely and sturdily built, with a roundish brown face and merry-looking hazel eyes. Christopher liked him at once—partly because Tacroy was the first grown man he had met who had curly hair like his own. It was not quite like. Where Christopher's hair made loose black rounds, Tacroy's hair coiled tight, like a mass of little pale brown springs. Christopher thought Tacroy's hair must hurt when a Governess or someone made him comb it. This made him notice that Tacroy's curls were quite dry. Nor was there any trace of the shiny wetness that had been on his clothes a moment before. Tacroy was wearing a greenish worsted suit, rather shabby, but it was not even damp.

"How did you get dry so quickly?" Christopher asked him.

Tacroy laughed. "I'm not here quite as bodily as you seem to be. And you're soaked through. How was that?"

"The rain in The Place Between," Christopher said. "You were wet there, too."

"Was I?" said Tacroy. "I don't visualize at all on the Passage—it's more like night with a few stars to guide by. I find it quite hard to visualize even here on the World Edge—though I can see you quite well of course, since we're both willing it." He saw that Christopher was staring at him, not understanding more than a word of this, and screwed his eyes up thoughtfully. This made little laughing wrinkles all round Tacroy's eyes. Christopher liked him better than ever. "Tell me," Tacroy said, waving a brown hand towards the rest of the valley, "what do you see here?"

"A valley," Christopher said, wondering what Tacroy saw, "with green grass. The sun's setting and it's making the stream down the middle look pink."

"Is it now?" said Tacroy. "Then I expect it would surprise you very much to know that all I can see is a slightly pink fog."

"Why?" said Christopher.

"Because I'm only here in spirit, while you seem to be actually here in the flesh," Tacroy said. "Back in London, my valuable body is lying on a sofa in a deep trance, tucked up in blankets and warmed by stone hot-water bottles, while a beautiful and agreeable young lady plays tunes to me on her harp. I insisted on the young lady as part of my pay. Do you think you're tucked up in bed somewhere too?"

When Tacroy saw that this question made Christopher both puzzled and impatient, his eyes screwed up again. "Let's get going," he said. "The next part of the experiment is to see if you can bring a prepared package back. I've made my mark. Make yours, and we'll get down into this world."

"Mark?" said Christopher.

"Mark," said Tacroy. "If you don't make a mark, how do you think you will find your way in and out of this world, or know which one it is when you come to it?"

"Valleys are quite easy to find," Christopher protested. "And I can tell that I've been to this Anywhere before. It's got the smallest stream of all of them."

Tacroy shrugged with his eyes screwed right up. "My boy, you're giving me the creeps. Be kind and please me and scratch the number nine on a rock or something. I don't want to be the one who loses you."

Christopher obligingly picked up a pointed flint and dug away at the mud of the path until he had made a large wobbly 9 there. He looked up to find Tacroy staring as if he was a ghost. "What's the matter?"

Tacroy gave a short wild-sounding laugh. "Oh nothing much. I can *see* it, that's all. That's only unheard of, that's all. Can *you* see *my* mark?"

Christopher looked everywhere he could think of, including up at the sunset sky, and had to confess that he could see nothing like a mark.

"Thank Heaven!" said Tacroy. "At least *that's* normal! But I'm still seriously wondering what you are. I begin to understand why your uncle got so excited."

They sauntered together down the valley. Tacroy had his hands in his pockets and he seemed quite casual, but Christopher got the feeling, all the same, that Tacroy usually went into an Anywhere in some way that was quicker and quite different. He caught Tacroy glancing at him several times, as if Tacroy was not sure of the way to go and was waiting to see what Christopher did. He seemed very relieved when they came to the end of the valley and found themselves on the rutty road among the huge jungle trees. The sun was almost down. There were lights at the windows of the tumbledown old inn in front of them.

This was one of the first Anywheres Christopher had been to. He remembered it hotter and wetter. The big trees had been bright green and dripping. Now they seemed brown and a bit wilted, as far as he could tell in the pink light. When he followed Tacroy on to the crazily built wooden veranda of the inn, he saw that the blobs of colored fungus that had fascinated him last time had all turned dry and white. He wondered if the Landlord would remember him.

"Landlord!" Tacroy shouted. When nothing happened, he said to Christopher, "Can you bang on the table? I can't."

Christopher noticed that the bent boards of the veranda creaked under his own feet, but not under Tacroy's. It did seem as if Tacroy was not really here in some way. He picked up a wooden bowl and rapped hard on the twisted table with it. It was another thing that made Tacroy's eyes screw up.

When the Landlord shuffled out, he was wrapped in at least three knitted shawls and too unhappy to notice Christopher, let alone remember him.

"Ralph's messenger," Tacroy said. "I believe you have a package for me."

"Ah yes," shivered the Landlord. "Won't you come inside out of this exceptionally bitter weather, sir? This is the hardest winter anyone has known for years."

Tacroy's eyebrows went up and he looked at Christopher. "I'm quite warm," Christopher said.

"Then we'll stay outside," Tacroy said. "The package?"

"Directly, sir," shivered the Landlord. "But won't you take something hot to warm you up? On the house, sir."

"Yes please," Christopher said quickly. Last time he was here he had been given something chocolatish which was not cocoa but much nicer. The Landlord nodded and smiled and shuffled shivering back indoors. Christopher sat at the table. Even though it was almost dark now, he felt deliciously warm. His clothes were drying nicely. Crowds of fleshy moth-things were flopping at the lighted windows, but enough light came between them for him to see Tacroy sit down in the air and then slide himself sideways on to the chair on the other side of the table.

"You'll have to drink whatever-it-is for me," Tacroy said.

"That won't worry me," Christopher said. "Why did you tell me to write the number nine?"

"Because this set of worlds is known as Series Nine," Tacroy explained. "Your uncle seems to have a lot of dealings here. That was why it was easy to set the experiment up. If it works, I think he's planning a whole set of trips, all along the Related Worlds. You'd find that a bit boring, wouldn't you?"

"Oh no. I'd like it," Christopher said. "How many are there after nine?"

"Ours is Twelve," said Tacroy. "Then they go down to One, along the other way. Don't ask me why they go back to front. It's traditional."

Christopher frowned over this. There were a great many more valleys than that in The Place Between, all arranged higgledy-piggledy too, not in any neat way that made you need to count up to twelve. But he supposed there must be some way in which Tacroy knew best—or Uncle Ralph did.

The Landlord shuffled hastily out again. He was carrying two cups that steamed out a dark chocolate smell, although this lovely aroma was rather spoiled by a much less pleasant smell coming from a round leather container on a long strap, which he dumped on the table beside the cups. "Here we are," he said. "That's the package and here's to take the chill off you and drink to further dealings, sir. I don't know how you two can stand it out here!"

"We come from a cold and misty climate," Tacroy said. "Thanks," he added to the Landlord's back, as the Landlord scampered indoors again. "I suppose it must be tropical here usually," he remarked as the door slammed. "I wouldn't know. I can't feel heat or cold in the spirit. Is that stuff nice?"

Christopher nodded happily. He had already drained one tiny cup. It was dark, hot, and delicious. He pulled Tacroy's cup over and drank that in sips, to make the taste last as long as possible. The round leather bottle smelled so offensive that it got in the way of the taste. Christopher put it on the floor out of the way.

"You can lift it, I see, *and* drink," Tacroy said, watching him. "Your uncle told me to make quite sure, but I haven't any doubt myself. He said you lose things on the Passage."

"That's because it's hard carrying things across the rocks," Christopher explained. "I need both hands for climbing."

Tacroy thought. "Hm. That explains the strap on the bottle. But there could be all sorts of other reasons. I'd love to find out. For instance, have you ever tried to bring back something alive?"

"Like a mouse?" Christopher suggested. "I could put it in my pocket."

A sudden gleeful look came into Tacroy's face. He looked, Christopher thought, like a person about to be thoroughly naughty. "Let's try it," he said. "Let's see if you can bring back a small animal next. I'll persuade your uncle that we need to know that. I think I'll die of curiosity if we don't try it, even if it's the last thing you do for us!"

After that Tacroy seemed to get more and more impatient. At last he stood up in such a hurry that he stood right through the chair as if it wasn't there. "Haven't you finished yet? Let's get going."

Christopher regretfully stood the tiny cup on his face to get at the last drops. He picked up the round bottle and hung it round his neck by the strap. Then he jumped off the veranda and set off down the rutty road, full of eagerness to show Tacroy the town. Fungus grew like corals on all the porches. Tacroy would like that.

Tacroy called after him. "Hey! Where are you off to?" Christopher stopped and explained. "No way," said Tacroy. "It doesn't matter if the fungus is sky-blue-pink. I can't hold this trance much longer, and I want to make sure you get back too."

This was disappointing. But when Christopher came close and peered at him, Tacroy did seem to be developing a faint, fluttery look, as if he might dissolve into the dark, or turn into one of the moth-things beating at the windows of the inn. Rather alarmed by this, Christopher put a hand on Tacroy's sleeve to hold him in place. For a moment, the arm hardly felt as if it was there—like the feathery balls of dust that grew under Christopher's bed—but after that first moment it firmed up nicely. Tacroy's outline grew hard and black against the dark trees. And Tacroy himself stood very still.

"I do believe," he said, as if he did not believe it at all, "that you've done something to fix me. What did you do?"

"Hardened you up," Christopher said. "You needed it so that we could go and look at the town. Come on."

But Tacroy laughed and took a firm grip on Christopher's arm—so firm that Christopher was sorry he had hardened him. "No, we'll see the fungus another time. Now I know you can do this too, it's going to be much easier. But I only contracted for an hour this trip. Come on."

As they went back up the valley, Tacroy kept peering round. "If it wasn't so dark," he said, "I'm sure I'd be seeing this as a valley, too. I can hear the stream. This is amazing!" But it was clear that he could not see The Place Between. When they got to it, Tacroy went on walking as if he thought it was still the valley. When the wind blew the mist aside, he was not there any more.

Christopher wondered whether to go back into Nine, or on into another valley. But it did not seem such fun without company, so he let The Place Between push him back home.

CHAPTER 4

By the next morning, Christopher was heartily sick of the smell—it was more of a reek really—from the leather bottle. He put it under his head, but it was still so bad that he had to get up and cover it with a pillow before he could get to sleep.

When the Last Governess came in to tell him to get up, she found it at once by the smell. "Dear Heavens above!" she said, dragging it out by its strap. "Would you credit this! I didn't believe even your uncle could ask for a whole bottleful of this stuff! Didn't he think of the danger?"

Christopher blinked up at her. He had never seen her so emotional. All her hidden prettiness had come out and she was staring at the bottle as if she did not know whether to be angry or scared or pleased. "What's in it?" he said.

"Dragons' blood," said the Last Governess. "And it's not even dried! I'm going to get this straight off to your uncle while you get dressed, or your Mama will throw fits." She hurried away with the bottle at arm's length, swinging on its strap. "I think your uncle's going to be very pleased," she called over her shoulder.

There was no doubt about that. A day later a big parcel arrived for Christopher. The Last Governess brought it up to the schoolroom with some scissors and let him cut the string for himself, which added much to the excitement. Inside was a huge box of chocolates, with a vast red bow and a picture of a boy blowing bubbles on the top. Chocolates were so rare in Christopher's life that he almost failed to notice the envelope tucked into the bow. It had a gold sovereign in it and a note from Uncle Ralph.

"Well done!!!!" it said. "Next experiment in a week. Miss Bell will tell you when. Congratulations from your loving uncle."

This so delighted Christopher that he let the Last Governess have first pick from the chocolates. "I think," she said dryly, as she picked the nutty kind that Christopher never liked, "that your Mama would like to be offered one before too many are gone." Then she plucked the note out of Christopher's fingers and put it in the fire as a hint that he was not to explain to Mama what he had done to earn the chocolates.

Christopher prudently ate the first layer before he offered the box to Mama. "Oh dear, these are so bad for your teeth!" Mama said, while her fingers hovered over the strawberry and then the truffle. "You do seem to have taken your uncle's fancy—and that's just as well, since I've had to put all my money in his hands. It'll be your money one day," she said as her fingers closed on the fudge. "Don't let my brother spoil him too much," she said to the Last Governess. "And I think you'd better take him to a dentist."

"Yes, madam," said the Last Governess, all meek and drab.

It was clear that Mama did not have the least suspicion what the chocolates were really about. Christopher was pleased to have been so faithful to Uncle Ralph's wishes, though he did wish Mama had not chosen the fudge. The rest of the chocolates did not last quite the whole week, but they did take Christopher's mind off the excitement of the next experiment. In fact, when the Last Governess said calmly, the next Friday before bedtime, "Your uncle wants you to go on another dream tonight," Christopher felt more businesslike than excited. "You are to try to get to Series Ten," said the Last Governess, "and meet the same man as before. Do you think you can do that?"

"Easy!" Christopher said loftily. "I could do it standing on my head."

"Which is getting a little swelled," remarked the Last Governess. "Don't forget to brush your hair and clean your teeth and don't get too confident. This is not really a game."

Christopher did honestly try not to feel too confident, but it *was* easy. He went out on to the path, where he put on his muddy clothes, and then climbed through The Place Between looking for Tacroy. The only difficulty was that the valleys were not arranged in the right order. Number Ten was not next one on from Nine, but quite a way lower down and further on. Christopher almost thought he was not going to find it. But at length he slid down a long slope of yellowish scree and saw Tacroy shining wetly through the mist as he crouched uncomfortably on the valley's lip. He held out a dripping arm to Christopher.

"Lord!" he said. "I thought you were never coming. Firm me up, will you? I'm fading back already. The latest girl is nothing like so effective."

Christopher took hold of Tacroy's cold woolly-feeling hand. Tacroy began firming up at once. Soon he was hard and wet and as solid as Christopher, and very pleased about it too. "This was the part your uncle found hardest to believe," he said while they climbed into the valley. "But I swore to him that I'd be able to see—Oh—Um. What do you see, Christopher?"

"It's the Anywhere where I got my bells," Christopher said, smiling round the steep green slopes. He remembered it perfectly. This Anywhere had a particular twist to the stream halfway down. But there was something new here—a sort of mistiness just beside the path. "What's that?" he asked, forgetting that Tacroy could not see the valley.

But Tacroy evidently could see the valley now he was firmed up. He stared at the mistiness with his eyes ruefully wrinkled. "Part of your uncle's experiment that doesn't seem to have worked," he said. "It's supposed to be a horseless carriage. He was trying to send it through to meet us. Do you think you can firm that up too?"

Christopher went to the mistiness and tried to put his hand on it. But the thing did not seem to be there enough for him to touch. His hand just went through.

"Never mind," said Tacroy. "Your uncle will just have to think again. And the carriage was only one of three experiments tonight." He insisted that Christopher write a big 10 in the dirt of the path, and then they set off down the valley. "If the carriage had worked," Tacroy explained, "we'd have tried for something bulky. As it is, I get my way and we try for an animal. Lordy! I'm glad you came when you did. I was almost as bad as that carriage. It's all that girl's fault."

"The lovely young lady with the harp?" asked Christopher.

"Alas, no," Tacroy said regretfully. "She took a fit when you firmed me up last time. It seems my body there in London went down to a thread of mist and she thought I was a goner. Screamed and broke her harp strings. Left as soon as I came back. She said she wasn't paid to harbor ghosts, pointed out that her contract was only for one trance, and refused to come back for twice the money. Pity. I hoped she was made of sterner stuff. She reminded me very much of another young lady with a harp who was once the light of my life." For a short while, he looked as sad as someone with such a merry face could. Then he smiled. "But I couldn't ask either of them to share my garret," he said. "So it's probably just as well."

"Did you need to get another one?" Christopher asked.

"I can't do without, unfortunately, unlike you," Tacroy said. "A professional spirit traveler has to have another medium to keep him anchored—music's the best way—and to call him back in case of trouble, and keep him warm, and make sure he's not interrupted by tradesmen with bills and so forth. So your uncle found this new girl in a bit of a hurry. She's stern stuff all right. Voice like a hatchet. Plays the flute like someone using wet chalk on a blackboard." Tacroy shuddered slightly. "I can hear it faintly all the time if I listen."

Christopher could hear a squealing noise too, but he thought it was probably the pipes of the snake charmers who sat in rows against the city wall in this Anywhere. They could see the city now. It was very hot here, far hotter than Nine. The high muddy-looking walls and the strange-shaped domes above them quivered in the heat, like things under water. Sandy dust blew up in clouds, almost hiding the dirty-white row of old men squatting in front of baskets blowing into pipes. Christopher looked nervously at the fat snakes, each one swaying upright in its basket.

Tacroy laughed. "Don't worry. Your uncle doesn't want a snake any more than you do!"

The city had a towering but narrow gate. By the time they reached it both were covered in sandy dust and Christopher was sweating through it, in trickles. Tacroy seemed enviably cool. Inside the walls it was even hotter. This was the one drawback to a thoroughly nice Anywhere. The shady edges of the streets were crowded with people and goats and makeshift stalls under colored umbrellas, so that Christopher was forced to walk with Tacroy down the blinding stripe of sun in the middle. Everyone shouted and chattered cheerfully. The air was thick with strange smells, the bleating of goats, the squawks of chickens, and strange clinking music. All the colors were bright, and brightest of all were the small gilded dollhouse things at the corners of streets. These were always heaped with flowers and dishes of food. Christopher thought they must belong to very small gods.

A lady under an electric blue umbrella gave him some of the sweetmeat she was selling. It was like a crisp bird's nest soaked in honey. Christopher gave some to Tacroy, but Tacroy said he could only taste it the way you tasted food in dreams, even when Christopher firmed him up again.

"Does Uncle Ralph want me to fetch a goat?" Christopher asked, licking honey from his fingers.

"We'd have tried if the carriage had worked," Tacroy said. "But what your uncle's really hoping for is a cat from one of the temples. We have to find the Temple of Asheth."

Christopher led the way to the big square where all the large houses for gods were. The man with the yellow umbrella was still there, on the steps of the largest temple. "Ah yes. That's it," Tacroy said. But when Christopher set off hopefully to talk to the man with the yellow umbrella again, Tacroy said, "No, I think our best bet is to get in round the side somewhere."

They found their way down narrow side alleys that ran all round the temple. There were no other doors to the temple at all, nor did it have any windows. The walls were high and muddy-looking and totally blank except for wicked spikes on the top. Tacroy stopped quite cheerfully in a baking alley where someone had thrown away a cartload of old cabbages and looked up at the spikes. The ends of flowering creepers were twined among the spikes from the other side of the wall.

"This looks promising," he said, and leaned against the wall. His cheerful look vanished. For a moment he looked frustrated and rather annoyed. "Here's a turnup," he said. "You've made me too solid to get through, darn it!" He thought about it, and shrugged. "This was supposed to be experiment three anyway. Your uncle thought that if you could broach a way between the worlds, you could probably pass through a wall too. Are you game to try? Do you think you can get in and pick up a cat without me?"

Tacroy seemed very nervous and worried about it. Christopher looked at the frowning wall and thought that it was probably impossible. "I can try," he said, and largely to console Tacroy, he stepped up against the hot stones of the wall and tried to push himself through them. At first it *was* impossible. But after a moment, he found that if he turned himself sort of sideways in a peculiar way, he began to sink into the stones. He turned and smiled encouragingly at Tacroy's worried face. "I'll be back in a minute."

"I don't like letting you go on your own," Tacroy was saying, when there came a noise like SHLUCK! and Christopher found himself on the other side of the wall all mixed up in creepers. For a second he was blinded in the sun there. He could see and hear and feel that things were moving all over the yard in front of him, rushing away from him in a stealthy, blurred way that had him almost paralyzed with terror. Snakes! he thought, and blinked and squinted and blinked again, trying to see them properly.

They were only cats, running away from the noise he had made coming through the wall. Most of them were well out of reach by the time he could see. Some had climbed high up the creepers and the rest had bolted for the various dark archways round the yard. But one white cat was slower than the others and was left trotting uncertainly and heavily across the harsh shadow in one corner. That was the one to get. Christopher set off after it.

By the time he had torn himself free of the creepers, the white cat had taken fright. It ran. Christopher ran after it, through an archway hung with more creepers, across another, shadier yard, and then through a doorway with a curtain instead of a door. The cat slipped round the curtain. Christopher flung the curtain aside and dived after it, only to find it was so dark beyond that he was once more blinded.

"Who are *you*?" said a voice from the darkness. It sounded surprised and haughty. "You're not supposed to be here."

"Who are *you*?" Christopher said cautiously, wishing he could see something beside blue and green dazzle.

"I'm the Goddess of course," said the voice. "The Living Asheth. What are you doing here? I'm not supposed to see *anyone* but priestesses until the Day of Festival."

"I only came to get a cat," said Christopher. "I'll go away when I have."

"You're not allowed to," said the Goddess. "Cats are sacred to Asheth. Besides, if it's Bethi you're after, she's mine, and she's going to have kittens again."

Christopher's eyes were adjusting. If he peered hard at the corner where the voice came from, he could see someone about the same size as he was, sitting on what seemed to be a pile of cushions, and pick out the white hump of the cat clutched in the person's arms. He took a step forward to see better.

"Stay where you are," said the Goddess, "or I'll call down fire to blast you!"

Christopher, much to his surprise, found he could not move from the spot. He shuffled his feet to make sure. It was as if his bare soles were fastened to the tiles with strong rubbery glue. While he shuffled, his eyes started working properly. The Goddess was a girl with a round, ordinary face and long mouse-colored hair. She was wearing a sleeveless rust brown robe and rather a lot of turquoise jewelry, including at least twenty bracelets and a little turquoise-studded coronet. She looked a bit younger than he was—much too young to be able to fasten someone's feet to the floor. Christopher was impressed. "How did you do it?" he said.

The Goddess shrugged. "The power of the Living Asheth," she said. "I was chosen from among all the other applicants because I'm the best vessel for her power. Asheth picked me out by giving me the mark of a cat on my foot. Look." She tipped herself sideways on her cushions and stretched one bare foot with an anklet round it towards Christopher.

It had a big purple birthmark on the sole. Christopher did not think it looked much like a cat, even when he screwed his eyes up so much that he felt like Tacroy. "You don't believe me," the Goddess said, rather accusingly.

"I don't know," said Christopher. "I've never met a Goddess before. What do you do?"

"I stay in the Temple unseen, except for one day every year, when I ride through the city and bless it," said the Goddess. Christopher thought that this did not sound very interesting, but before he could say so, the Goddess added, "It's not much fun, actually, but that's the way things are when you're honored like I am. The Living Asheth always has to be a young girl, you see."

"Do you stop being Asheth when you grow up then?" Christopher asked.

The Goddess frowned. Clearly she was not sure. "Well, the Living Asheth never *is* grown up, so I suppose so—they haven't said." Her round solemn face brightened up. "That's something to look forward to, eh Bethi?" she said, stroking the white cat.

"If I can't have that cat, will you let me have another one?" Christopher asked.

"It depends," said the Goddess. "I don't think I'm allowed to give them away. What do you want it for?"

"My uncle wants one," Christopher explained. "We're doing an experiment to see if I can fetch a live animal from your Anywhere to ours. Yours is Ten and ours is Twelve. And it's quite difficult climbing across The Place Between, so if you do let me have a cat, could you lend me a basket too, please?"

The Goddess considered. "How many Anywheres are there?" she asked in a testing kind of way.

"Hundreds," said Christopher, "but Tacroy thinks there's only twelve."

"The priestesses say there are twelve known Otherwheres," the Goddess said, nodding. "But Mother Proudfoot is fairly sure there are many more than that. Yes, and how did you get into the Temple?"

"Through the wall," said Christopher. "Nobody saw me."

"Then you could get in and out again if you wanted to?" said the Goddess.

"Easy!" said Christopher.

"Good," said the Goddess. She dumped the white cat in the cushions and sprang to her feet, with a smart jangle and clack from all her jewelry. "I'll swop you a cat," she said. "But first you must swear by the Goddess to come back and bring me what I want in exchange, or I'll keep your feet stuck to the floor and shout for the Arm of Asheth to come and kill you."

"What do you want in exchange?" asked Christopher.

"Swear first," said the Goddess.

"I swear," said Christopher. But that was not enough. The Goddess hooked her thumbs into her jeweled sash and stared stonily. She was actually a little shorter than Christopher, but that did not make the stare any less impressive. "I swear by the Goddess that I'll come back with what you want in exchange for the cat—will that do?" said Christopher. "Now what do you want?"

"Books to read," said the Goddess. "I'm bored," she explained. She did not say it in a whine, but in a brisk way that made Christopher see it was true.

"Aren't there any books here?" he said.

"Hundreds," the Goddess said gloomily. "But they're all educational or holy. And the Living Goddess isn't allowed to touch *anything* in this world outside the Temple. Anything in this *world*. Do you understand?"

Christopher nodded. He understood perfectly. "Which cat can I have?"

"Throgmorten," said the Goddess. Upon that word, Christopher's feet came loose from the tiles. He was able to walk beside the Goddess as she lifted the curtain from the doorway and went out into the shady yard. "I don't mind you taking Throgmorten," she said. "He smells and he scratches and he bullies all the other cats. I hate him. But we'll have to be quick about catching him. The priestesses will be waking up from siesta quite soon. Just a moment!" She dashed aside into an archway in a clash of anklets that made Christopher jump. She whirled back almost at once, a whirl of rusty robe, flying girdle, and swirling mouse-colored hair. She was carrying a basket with a lid. "This should do," she said. "The lid has a good strong fastening." She led the way through the creeper-hung archway into the courtyard with the blinding sunlight. "He's usually lording it over the other cats somewhere here," she said. "Yes, there he is—that's him in the corner."

Throgmorten was ginger. He was at that moment glaring at a black and white female cat, who had lowered herself into a miserable crouch while she tried to back humbly away. Throgmorten swaggered towards her, lashing a stripy snakelike tail, until the black and white cat's nerve broke and she bolted. Then he turned to see what Christopher and the Goddess wanted.

"Isn't he horrible?" said the Goddess. She thrust the basket at Christopher. "Hold it open and shut the lid down quick after I've got him into it."

Throgmorten was, Christopher had to admit, a truly unpleasant cat. His yellow eyes stared at them with a blank and insolent leer, and there was something about the set of his ears—one higher than the other—which told Christopher that Throgmorten would attack viciously anything that got in his way. This being so, he was puzzled that Throgmorten should remind him remarkably much of Uncle Ralph. He supposed it must be the gingerness.

At this moment, Throgmorten sensed they were after him. His back arched incredulously. Then he fairly levitated up into the creepers on the wall, racing and scrambling higher and higher, until he was far above their heads.

"No you *don't*!" said the Goddess.

And Throgmorten's arched ginger body came flying out of the creepers like a furry orange boomerang and landed slap in the basket. Christopher was deeply impressed—so impressed that he was a bit slow getting the lid down. Throgmorten came pouring out over the edge of the basket again in an instant ginger stream. The Goddess seized him and crammed him back, whereupon a large number of flailing ginger legs—at least seven, to Christopher's bemused eyes—clawed hold of her bracelets and her robe and her legs under the robe, and tore pieces off them. Christopher waited and aimed for an instant when one of Throgmorten's heads—he seemed to have at least three, each with more fangs than seemed possible—came into range. Then he banged the basket lid on it, hard. Throgmorten, for the blink of an eye, became an ordinary dazed cat instead of a fighting devil. The Goddess shook him off into the basket. Christopher slapped the lid on. A huge ginger paw loaded with long pink razors at once oozed itself out of the latch hole and tore several strips off Christopher while he fastened the basket.

"Thanks," he said, sucking his wounds.

"I'm glad to see the back of him," said the Goddess, licking a slash on her arm and mopping blood off her leg with her torn robe.

A melodious voice called from the creeper-hung archway. "Goddess dear! Where are you?"

"I have to go," whispered the Goddess. "Don't forget the books. You swore to a swop. *Coming!*" she called, and went running back to the archway, clash-tink, clash-tink.

Christopher turned quickly to the wall and tried to go through it. And he could not. No matter how he tried turning that peculiar sideways way, it would not work. He knew it was Throgmorten. Holding a live cat snarling in a basket made him part of this Anywhere and he had to obey its usual rules. What was he to do? More melodious voices were calling to the Goddess in the distance, and he could see people moving inside at least two more of the archways round the yard. He never really considered putting the basket down. Uncle Ralph wanted this cat. Christopher ran for it instead, sprinting for the nearest archway that seemed to be empty.

Unfortunately the jigging of the basket assured Throgmorten that he was certainly being kidnapped. He protested about it at the top of his voice—and Christopher would never have believed that a mere cat could make such a powerful noise. Throgmorten's voice filled the dark passages beyond the archway, wailing, throbbing, rising to a shriek like a dying vampire's, and then falling to a strong curdled contralto howl. Then it went up to a shriek again. Before Christopher had run twenty yards, there were shouts behind him, and the slap of sandals and the thumping of bare feet. He ran faster than ever, twisting into a new passage whenever he came to one, and sprinting down that, but all the time Throgmorten kept up his yells of protest from the basket, showing the pursuers exactly where to follow. Worse, he fetched more. There were twice the number of shouts and thumping feet behind by the time Christopher saw daylight ahead. He burst out into it, followed by a jostling mob.

And it was not really daylight, but a huge confusing temple, full of worshippers and statues and fat painted pillars. The daylight was coming from great open doors a hundred yards away. Christopher could see the man with the yellow umbrella outlined beyond the doors and knew exactly where he was. He dashed for the doors, dodging pillars and sprinting round people praying. "Wong-*wong*—WONG-*WONG*!" howled Throgmorten from the basket in his hand.

"Stop thief!" screamed the people chasing him. "Arm of Asheth!"

Christopher saw a man in a silver mask, or maybe a woman—a silver-masked person anyway—standing on a flight of steps carefully aiming a spear at him. He tried to dodge, but there was no time, or the spear followed him somehow. It crashed into his chest with a jolting thud.

Things seemed to go very slowly then. Christopher stood still, clutching the howling basket, and stared disbelievingly at the shaft of the spear sticking out of his chest through his dirty shirt. He saw it in tremendous detail. It was made of beautifully polished brown wood, with words and pictures carved along it. About halfway up was a shiny silver handgrip which had designs that were almost rubbed out with wear. A few drops of blood were coming out where the wood met his shirt. The spearhead must be buried deep inside him. He looked up to see the masked person advancing triumphantly towards him. Beyond, in the doorway, Tacroy must have been fetched by the noise. He was standing frozen there, staring in horror.

Falteringly, Christopher put out his free hand and took hold of the spear by the handgrip to pull it out. And everything stopped with a bump.

CHAPTER 5

It was early morning. Christopher realized that what had woken him was angry cat noises from the basket lying on its side in the middle of the floor. Throgmorten wanted out. Instantly. Christopher sat up beaming with triumph because he had proved he could bring a live animal from an Anywhere. Then he remembered he had a spear sticking out of his chest. He looked down. There was no sign of a spear. There was no blood. Nothing hurt. He felt his chest. Then he undid his pajamas and looked. Incredibly he saw only smooth pale skin without a sign of a wound.

He was all right. The Anywheres were really only a kind of dream after all. He laughed.

"Wong!" Throgmorten said angrily, making the basket roll about.

Christopher supposed he had better let the beast out. Remembering those spiked tearing claws, he stood up on his bed and unhitched the heavy bar that held the curtains. It was hard to maneuver with the curtains hanging from it and sliding about, but Christopher rather thought he might need the curtains to shield him from Throgmorten's rage, so he kept them in a bunch in front of him. After a bit of swaying and prodding, he managed to get the brass point at the end of the curtain bar under the latch of the lid and open the basket.

The cat sounds stopped. Throgmorten seemed to have decided that this was a trick. Christopher waited, gently bouncing on his bed and clutching the bar and the bundle of curtain, for Throgmorten to attack. But nothing happened. Christopher leaned forward cautiously until he could see into the basket. It contained a round ginger bundle gently moving up and down. Throgmorten, disdaining freedom now he had it, had curled up and gone to sleep.

"All right then," said Christopher. "*Be* like that!" With a bit of a struggle, he hitched the curtain pole back on its supports again and went to sleep himself.

Next time he woke, Throgmorten was exploring the room. Christopher lay on his back and warily watched Throgmorten jump from one piece of furniture to another all round the room. As far as he could tell, Throgmorten was not angry any more. He seemed simply full of curiosity. Or maybe, Christopher thought, as Throgmorten gathered himself and jumped from the top of the wardrobe to the curtain pole, Throgmorten had a bet on with himself that he could get all round the night nursery without touching the floor. As Throgmorten began scrambling along the pole, hanging on to it and the curtains with those remarkable claws of his, Christopher was sure of it.

What happened then was definitely not Throgmorten's fault. Christopher knew it was his own fault for not putting the curtain pole back properly. The end furthest from Throgmorten and nearest Christopher came loose and plunged down like a harpoon, with the curtains rattling along it and Throgmorten hanging on frantically. For an instant, Christopher had Throgmorten's terror-stricken eyes glaring into his own as Throgmorten rode the pole down. Then the brass end hit the middle of Christopher's chest. It went in like the spear. It was not sharp and it was not heavy, but it went right into him all the same. Throgmorten landed on his stomach an instant later, all claws and panic. Christopher thought he screamed. Anyway either he or Throgmorten made enough noise to fetch the Last Governess running. The last thing Christopher saw for the time being was the Last Governess in her white night dress, gray with horror, moving her hands in quick peculiar gestures and gabbling very odd words . . .

. . . He woke up a long time later, in the afternoon by the light, very sore in front and not too sure of very much, to hear Uncle Ralph's voice.

"This is a damned nuisance, Effie, just when things were looking so promising! Is he going to be all right?"

"I think so," the Last Governess replied. The two of them were standing by Christopher's bed. "I got there in time to say a staunching spell and it seems to be healing." While Christopher was thinking, Funny, I didn't know she was a witch! she went on, "I haven't dared breathe a word to your sister."

"Don't," said Uncle Ralph. "She has her plans for him cut and dried, and she'll put a stop to mine if she finds out. Drat that cat! I've got things set up all over the Related Worlds on the strength of that first run and I don't want to cancel them. You think he'll recover?"

"In time," said the Last Governess. "There's a strong spell in the dressing."

"Then I shall have to postpone everything," Uncle Ralph said, not sounding at all pleased. "At least we've got the cat. Where's the thing got to?"

"Under the bed. I tried to fetch it out but I just got scratched for my pains," said the Last Governess.

"Women!" said Uncle Ralph. "I'll get it." Christopher heard his knees thump on the floor. His voice came up from underneath. "Here. Nice pussy. Come here, pussy."

There was a very serious outbreak of cat noises.

Uncle Ralph's knees went thumping away backwards and his voice said quite a string of bad words. "The creature's a perfect devil!" he added. "It's torn lumps off me!" Then his voice came from higher up and further away. "Don't let it get away. Put a holding spell on this room until I get back."

"Where are you going?" the Last Governess asked.

"To fetch some thick leather gloves and a vet," Uncle Ralph said from by the door. "That's an Asheth Temple cat. It's almost priceless. Wizards will pay five hundred pounds just for an inch of its guts or one of its claws. Its eyes will fetch several thousand pounds each—so make sure you set a good tight spell. It may take me an hour or so to find a vet."

There was silence after that. Christopher dozed. He woke up feeling so much better that he sat up and took a look at his wound. The Last Governess had efficiently covered it with smooth white bandage. Christopher peered down inside it with great interest. The wound was a round red hole, much smaller than he expected. It hardly hurt at all.

While he wondered how to find out how deep it was, there was a piercing wail from the windowsill behind him. He looked round. The window was open—the Last Governess had a passion for fresh air—and Throgmorten was crouched on the sill beside it, glaring appealingly. When he saw Christopher was looking, Throgmorten put out one of his razor-loaded paws and scraped it down the space between the window and the frame. The empty air made a sound like someone scratching a blackboard.

"Wong," Throgmorten commanded.

Christopher wondered why Throgmorten should think he was on his side. One way and another, Throgmorten had half-killed him.

"Wong?" Throgmorten asked piteously.

On the other hand, Christopher thought, none of the half-killing had been Throgmorten's fault. And though Throgmorten was probably the ugliest and most vicious cat in any Anywhere, it did not seem fair to kidnap him and drag him to a strange world and then let him be sold to wizards, parcel by parcel.

"All right," he said and climbed out of bed. Throgmorten stood up eagerly, with his thin ginger snake of a tail straight up behind. "Yes, but I'm not sure how to break spells," Christopher said, approaching very cautiously. Throgmorten backed away and made no attempt to scratch. Christopher put his hand out to the open part of the window. The empty space felt rubbery and gave when he pressed it, but he could not put his hand through even if he shoved it hard. So he did the only thing he could think of and opened the window wider. He felt the spell tear like a rather tough cobweb.

"Wong!" Throgmorten uttered appreciatively. Then he was off. Christopher watched him gallop down a slanting drain and levitate to a windowsill when the drain stopped. From there it was an easy jump to the top of a bay window and then to the ground. Throgmorten's ginger shape went trotting away into the bushes and squeezed under the next-door fence, already with the air of looking for birds to kill and other cats to bully. Christopher put the window carefully back the way it had been and got back to bed.

When he woke up next Mama was outside the door saying anxiously, "How is he? I hope it's not infectious."

"Not in the least, madam," said the Last Governess.

So Mama came in, filling the room with her scents—which was just as well, since Throgmorten had left his own penetrating odor under the bed—and looked at Christopher. "He seems a bit pale," she said. "Do we need a doctor?"

"I saw to all that, madam," said the Last Governess.

"Thank you," said Mama. "Make sure it doesn't interrupt his education."

When Mama had gone, the Last Governess fetched her umbrella and poked it under the bed and behind the furniture, looking for Throgmorten. "Where has it *got* to?" she said, climbing up to jab at the space on top of the wardrobe.

"I don't know," Christopher said truthfully, since he knew Throgmorten would be many streets away by now. "He was here before I went to sleep."

"It's vanished!" said the Last Governess. "A cat can't just vanish!"

Christopher said experimentally, "He was an Asheth Temple cat."

"True," said the Last Governess. "They *are* wildly magic by all accounts. But your uncle's not going to be at all pleased to find it gone."

This made Christopher feel decidedly guilty. He could not go back to sleep, and when, about an hour later, he heard brisk heavy feet approaching the door, he sat up at once, wondering what he was going to say to Uncle Ralph. But the man who came in was not Uncle Ralph. He was a total stranger—No, it was Papa! Christopher recognized the black whiskers. Papa's face was fairly familiar too, because it was quite like his own, except for the whiskers and a solemn, anxious look. Christopher was astonished because he had somehow thought—without anyone ever having exactly said so—that Papa had left the house in disgrace after whatever went wrong with the money.

"Are you all right, son?" Papa said, and the hurried, worried way he spoke, and the way he looked round nervously at the door, told Christopher that Papa had indeed left the house and did not want to be found here. This made it plain that Papa had come specially to see Christopher, which astonished Christopher even more.

"I'm quite well, thank you," Christopher said politely. He had not the least idea how to talk to Papa, face to face. Politeness seemed safest.

"Are you sure?" Papa asked, staring attentively at him. "The lifespell I have for you showed—In fact it stopped, as if you were—um—Frankly I thought you might be dead."

Christopher was more astonished still. "Oh no, I'm feeling much better now," he said.

"Thank God for that!" said Papa. "I must have made an error setting the spell—it seems a habit with me just now. But I have drawn up your horoscope, too, and checked it several times, and I must warn you that the next year and a half will be a time of acute danger for you, my son. You must be very careful."

"Yes," said Christopher. "I will." He meant it. He could still see the curtain rod coming down if he shut his eyes. And he had to keep trying not to think at all of the way the spear had stuck out of him.

Papa leaned a little closer and looked furtively at the door again. "That brother of your Mama's—Ralph Argent—I hear he's managing your Mama's affairs," he said. "Try to have as little to do with him as you can, my son. He is not a nice person to know." And having said that, Papa patted Christopher's shoulder and hurried away. Christopher was quite relieved. One way and another, Papa had made him very uncomfortable. Now he was even more worried about what he would say to Uncle Ralph.

But to his great relief, the Last Governess told him that Uncle Ralph was not coming. He said that he was too annoyed about losing Throgmorten to make a good sick-visitor. Christopher sighed thankfully and settled down to enjoy being an invalid. He drew pictures, he ate grapes, he read books, and he spun out his illness as long as he could. This was not easy. The next morning his wound was only a round itchy scab, and on the third day it was hardly there at all. On the fourth day, the Last Governess made him get up and have lessons as usual; but it had been lovely while it lasted.

On the day after that, the Last Governess said, "Your uncle wants to try another experiment tomorrow. He wants you to meet the man at Series Eight this time. Do you think you feel well enough?"

Christopher felt perfectly well, and provided nobody wanted him to go near Series Ten again, he was quite willing to go on another dream.

Series Eight turned out to be the bleak and stony Anywhere up above Nine. Christopher had not cared for it much when he had explored it on his own, but Tacroy was so glad to see him that it would have made up for a far worse place.

"Am I glad to see you!" Tacroy said, while Christopher was firming him up. "I'd resigned myself to being the cause of your death. I could *kick* myself for persuading your uncle to get you to fetch an animal! Everyone knows living creatures cause all sorts of problems, and I've told him we're never going to try that again. Are you really all right?"

"Fine," said Christopher. "My chest was smooth when I woke up." In fact the funny thing about both accidents was that Throgmorten's scratches had taken twice as long to heal as either wound. But Tacroy seemed to find this so hard to believe and to be so full of self blame that Christopher got embarrassed and changed the subject. "Have you still got the young lady who's stern stuff?"

"Sterner than ever," Tacroy said, becoming much more cheerful at once. "The wretched girl's setting my teeth on edge with that flute at this moment. Take a look down the valley. Your uncle's been busy since you—since your accident."

Uncle Ralph had perfected the horseless carriage. It was sitting on the sparse stony grass beside the stream as firm as anything, though it looked more like a rough wooden sled than any kind of carriage. Something had been done so that Tacroy was able to take hold of the rope fastened to the front. When he pulled, the carriage came gliding down the valley after him without really touching the ground.

"It's supposed to return to London with me when I go back to my garret," he explained. "I know that doesn't seem likely, but your uncle swears he's got it right this time. The question is, will it go back with a load on it, or will the load stay behind? That's what tonight's experiment is to find out."

Christopher had to help Tacroy haul the sled up the long stony trail beyond the valley. Tacroy was never quite firm enough to give a good pull. At length they came to a bleak stone farm crouched halfway up the hill, where a group of thick-armed silent women were waiting in the yard beside a heap of packages carefully wrapped in oiled silk. The packages smelled odd, but that smell was drowned by the thick garlic breath from the women. As soon as the sled came to a stop, garlic rolled out in waves as the women picked up the packages and tried to load them on the sled. The parcels dropped straight through it and fell on the ground.

"No good," said Tacroy. "I thought you were warned. Let Christopher do it."

It was hard work. The women watched untrustingly while Christopher loaded the parcels and tied them in place with rope. Tacroy tried to help, but he was not firm enough and his hands went through the parcels. Christopher got tired and cold in the strong wind. When one of the women gave a stern, friendly smile and asked him if he would like to come indoors for a drink, he said yes gladly.

"Not today, thank you," Tacroy said. "This thing's still experimental and we're not sure how long the spells will hold. We'd better get back." He could see Christopher was disappointed. As they towed the sled away downhill, he said, "I don't blame you. Call this just a business trip. Your uncle aims to get this carriage corrected by the way it performs tonight. My devout hope is that he can make it firm enough to be loaded by the people who bring the load, and then we can count you out of it altogether."

"But I like helping," Christopher protested. "Besides, how would you pull it if I'm not there to firm you up?"

"There is that," Tacroy said. He thought about it while they got to the bottom of the hill and he started plodding up the valley with the rope straining over his shoulder. "There's something I must say to you," he panted. "Are you learning magic at all?"

"I don't think so," Christopher said.

"Well you should be," Tacroy panted. "You must have the strongest talent I've ever encountered. Ask your mother to let you have lessons."

"I think Mama wants me to be a missionary," Christopher said.

Tacroy screwed his eyes up over that. "Are you sure? Might you have misheard her? Wouldn't the word be *magician*?"

"No," said Christopher. "She says I'm to go into Society."

"Ah Society!" Tacroy panted wistfully. "I have dreams of myself in Society, looking handsome in a velvet suit and surrounded by young ladies playing harps."

"Do missionaries wear velvet suits?" asked Christopher. "Or do you mean Heaven?"

Tacroy looked up at the stormy gray sky. "I don't think this conversation is getting anywhere," he remarked to it. "Try again. Your uncle tells me you're going away to school soon. If it's any kind of a decent school, they should teach magic as an extra. Promise me that you'll ask to be allowed to take it."

"All right," said Christopher. The mention of school gave him a jab of nerves somewhere deep in his stomach. "What are schools like?"

"Full of children," said Tacroy. "I won't prejudice you." By this time he had labored his way to the top of the valley, where the mists of The Place Between were swirling in front of them. "Now comes the tricky part," he said. "Your uncle thought this thing might have more chance of arriving with its load if you gave it a push as I leave. But before I go—next time you find yourself in a Heathen Temple and they start chasing you, drop everything and get out through the nearest wall. Understand? By the looks of things, I'll be seeing you in a week or so."

Christopher put his shoulder against the back of the carriage and shoved as Tacroy stepped off into the mist holding the rope. The carriage tilted and slid downwards after him. As soon as it was in the mists it looked all light and papery like a kite, and like a kite it plunged and wallowed down out of sight.

Christopher climbed back home thoughtfully. It shook him to find he had been in the Anywhere where the Heathens lived without knowing it. He had been right to be nervous of Heathens. Nothing, he thought, would possess him to go back to Series Ten now. And he did wish that Mama had not decided that he should be a missionary.

CHAPTER 6

From then on, Uncle Ralph arranged a new experiment every week. He had, Tacroy said, been very pleased because the carriage and the packages had arrived in Tacroy's garret with no hitch at all. Two wizards and a sorcerer had refined the spell on it until it could stay in another Anywhere for up to a day. The experiments became much more fun. Tacroy and Christopher would tow the carriage to the place where the load was waiting, always carefully wrapped in packages the right size for Christopher to handle. After Christopher had loaded them, he and Tacroy would go exploring.

Tacroy insisted on the exploring. "It's his perks," he explained to the people with the packages. "We'll be back in an hour or so." In Series One they went and looked at the amazing ring-trains, where the rings were on pylons high above the ground and miles apart, and the trains went hurtling through them with a noise like the sky tearing without even touching the rings. In Series Two they wandered a maze of bridges over a tangle of rivers and looked down at giant eels resting their chins on sandbars, while even stranger creatures grunted and stirred in the mud under the bridges. Christopher suspected that Tacroy enjoyed exploring as much as he did. He was always cheerful during this part.

"It makes a change from sloping ceilings and peeling walls. I don't get out of London very much," Tacroy confessed while he was advising Christopher how to build a better sand castle on the seashore in Series Five. Series Five turned out to be the Anywhere where Christopher had met the silly ladies. It was all islands. "This is better than a Bank Holiday at Brighton any day!" Tacroy said, looking out across the bright blue crashing waves. "Almost as good as an afternoon's cricket. I wish I could afford to get away more."

"Have you lost all your money then?" Christopher asked sympathetically.

"I never had any money to lose," Tacroy said. "I was a foundling child."

Christopher did not ask any more just then, because he was busy hoping that the mermaids would appear the way they used to. But though he looked and waited, not a single mermaid came.

He went back to the subject the following week in Series Seven. As they followed a gypsy-looking man who was guiding them to see the Great Glacier, he asked Tacroy what it meant to be a foundling child.

"It means someone found me," Tacroy said cheerfully. "The someone in my case was a very agreeable and very devout Sea Captain, who picked me up as a baby on an island somewhere. He said the Lord had sent me. I don't know who my parents were."

Christopher was impressed. "Is that why you're always so cheerful?"

Tacroy laughed. "I'm mostly cheerful," he said. "But today I feel particularly good because I've got rid of the flute-playing girl at last. Your uncle's found me a nice grandmotherly person who plays the violin quite well. And maybe it's that, or maybe it's your influence, but I feel firmer with every step."

Christopher looked at him, walking ahead along the mountain path. Tacroy looked as hard as the rocks towering on one side and as real as the gypsy-looking man striding ahead of them both. "I think you're getting better at it," he said.

"Could be," said Tacroy. "I think you've raised my standards. And yet, do you know, young Christopher, until you came along, I was considered the best spirit traveler in the country?"

Here the gypsy man shouted and waved to them to come and look at the glacier. It sat above them in the rocks in a huge dirty-white *V*. Christopher did not think much of it. He could see it was mostly just dirty old snow—though it was certainly very big. Its giant icy lip hung over them, almost transparent gray, and water dribbled and poured off it. Series Seven was a strange world, all mountains and snow, but surprisingly hot too. Where the water poured off the glacier, the heat had caused a great growth of strident green ferns and flowing tropical trees. Violent green moss grew scarlet cups as big as hats, all dewed with water. It was like looking at the North Pole and the Equator at once. The three of them seemed tiny beneath it.

"Impressive," said Tacroy. "I know two people who are like this thing. One of them is your uncle."

Christopher thought that was a silly thing to say. Uncle Ralph was nothing like the Giant Glacier. He was annoyed with Tacroy all the following week. But he relented when the Last Governess suddenly presented him with a heap of new clothes, all sturdy and practical things. "You're to wear these when you go on the next experiment," she said. "Your uncle's man has been making a fuss. He says you always wear rags and your teeth were chattering in the snow last time. We don't want you ill, do we?"

Christopher never noticed being cold, but he was grateful to Tacroy. His old clothes had got so much too small that they got in the way when he climbed through The Place Between. He decided he liked Tacroy after all.

"I say," he said, as he loaded packages in a huge metal shed in Series Four, "can I come and visit you in your garret? We live in London, too."

"You live in quite a different part," Tacroy said hastily. "You wouldn't like the area my garret's in at all."

Christopher protested that this didn't matter. He wanted to see Tacroy in the flesh and he was very curious to see the garret. But Tacroy kept making excuses. Christopher kept on asking, at least twice every experiment, until they went to bleak and stony Series Eight again, where Christopher was exceedingly glad of his warm clothes. There, while Christopher stood over the farmhouse fire warming his fingers round a mug of bitter malty tea, gratitude to Tacroy made him say yet again, "Oh *please* can't I visit you in your garret?"

"Oh do stow it, Christopher," Tacroy said, sounding rather tired of it all. "I'd invite you like a shot, but your uncle made a condition that you only see me like this while we're on an experiment. If I told you where I live, I'd lose this job. It's as simple as that."

"I could go round all the garrets," Christopher suggested cunningly, "and shout Tacroy and ask people until I found you."

"You could *not*," said Tacroy. "You'd draw a complete blank if you tried. Tacroy is my spirit name. I have quite a different name in the flesh."

Christopher had to give in and accept it, though he did not understand in the least.

Meanwhile, the time when he was to go to school was suddenly almost there. Christopher tried carefully not to think of it, but it was hard to forget when he had to spend such a lot of time trying on new clothes. The Last Governess sewed name tapes—C. CHANT—on the clothes and packed them in a shiny black tin trunk—also labeled C. CHANT in bold white letters. This trunk was shortly taken away by a carrier whose thick arms reminded Christopher of the women in Series Eight, and the same carrier took away all Mama's trunks, too, only hers were addressed to Baden-Baden while Christopher's said "Penge School, Surrey."

The day after that, Mama left for Baden-Baden. She came to say good-bye to Christopher, dabbing her eyes with a blue lace handkerchief that matched her traveling suit. "Remember to be good and learn a lot," she said. "And don't forget your Mama wants to be very proud of you when you grow up." She put her scented cheek down for Christopher to kiss and said to the Last Governess, "Mind you take him to the dentist now."

"I won't forget, madam," the Last Governess said in her dreariest way. Somehow her prettiness never seemed to come out in front of Mama.

Christopher did not enjoy the dentist. After banging and scraping round Christopher's teeth as if he was trying to make them all fall out, the dentist made a long speech about how crooked and out of place they were, until Christopher began to think of himself with fangs like Throgmorten's. He made Christopher wear a big shiny tooth-brace, which he was supposed never to take out, even at night. Christopher hated the brace. He hated it so much that it almost took his mind off his fears about school.

The servants covered the furniture with dust sheets and left one by one, until Christopher and the Last Governess were the only people in the house. The Governess took him to the station in a cab that afternoon and put him on the train to school.

On the platform, now the time had come, Christopher was suddenly scared stiff. This really was the first step on the road to becoming a missionary and being eaten by Heathens. Terror seemed to drain the life out of him, down from his face, which went stiff, and out through his legs, which went wobbly. It seemed to make his terror worse that he had not the slightest idea what school was like.

He hardly heard the Last Governess say, "Good-bye, Christopher. Your uncle says he'll give you a month at school to settle down. He'll expect you to meet his man as usual on October the eighth in Series Six. October the eighth. Have you got that?"

"Yes," Christopher said, not attending to a word, and got into the carriage like someone going to be executed.

There were two other new boys in the carriage. The small thin one called Fenning was so nervous that he had to keep leaning out of the window to be sick. The other one was called Oneir, and he was restfully ordinary. By the time the train drew into the school station, Christopher was firm friends with them both. They decided to call themselves the Terrible Three, but in fact everyone in the school called them the Three Bears. "Someone's been sitting in *my* chair!" they shouted whenever the three came into a room together. This was because Christopher was tall, though he had not known he was before, and Fenning was small, while Oneir was comfortably in the middle.

Before the end of the first week, Christopher was wondering what he had been so frightened of. School had its drawbacks, of course, like its food, and some of the masters, and quite a few of the older boys, but those were nothing beside the sheer fun of being with a lot of boys your own age and having two real friends of your own. Christopher discovered that you dealt with obnoxious masters and most older boys the way you dealt with Governesses: you quite politely told them the truth in the way they wanted to hear it, so that they thought they had won and left you in peace. Lessons were easy. In fact most of the new things Christopher learned were from the other boys. After less than three days, he had learned enough—without quite knowing how—to realize that Mama had never intended him to be a missionary at all. This made him feel a bit of a fool, but he did not let it bother him. When he thought of Mama, he thought much more kindly of her, and threw himself into school with complete enjoyment.

The one lesson he did not enjoy was magic. Christopher found, rather to his surprise, that someone had put him down for magic as an extra. He had a dim notion that Tacroy might have arranged it. If so, Christopher showed no sign of the strong gift for magic Tacroy thought he had. The elementary spells he had to learn bored him nearly to tears.

"Please control your enthusiasm, Chant," the magic master said acidly. "I'm heartily sick of looking at your tonsils." Two weeks into the term, he suggested Christopher give up magic.

Christopher was tempted to agree. But he had discovered by then that he was good at other lessons, and he hated the thought of being a failure even in one thing. Besides, the Goddess had stuck his feet to the spot by magic, and he wanted very much to learn to do that, too. "But my mother's paying for these lessons, sir," he said virtuously. "I will try in future." He went away and made an arrangement with Oneir, whereby Christopher did Oneir's algebra and Oneir made the boring spells work for Christopher. After that, he cultivated a vague look to disguise his boredom and stared out of the window.

"Wool gathering again, Chant?" the magic teacher took to asking. "Can't you muster an honest yawn these days?"

Apart from this one weekly lesson, school was so entirely to Christopher's taste that he did not think of Uncle Ralph or anything to do with the past for well over a month. Looking back on it later, he often thought that if he had known what a short time he was going to be at that school, he would have taken care to enjoy it even more.

At the start of November, he got a letter from Uncle Ralph:

Old chap,

What exactly are you playing at? I thought we had an arrangement. The experiments have been waiting for you since October and a lot of people's plans have been thrown out. If something's wrong and you can't do it, write and tell me. Otherwise get off your hambones, there's a good chap, and contact my man as usual next Thursday.

Your affectionate but puzzled uncle,
Ralph

This caused Christopher quite a rush of guilt. Oddly enough, though he did think of Tacroy going uselessly into trances in his garret, most of his guilt was about the Goddess. School had taught him that you did not take swears and swops lightly. He had sworn to swop Throgmorten for books, and he had let the Goddess down, even though she was only a girl. School considered that far worse than not doing what your uncle wanted. In his guilt, Christopher realized that he was going to have to spend Uncle Ralph's sovereign at last, if he was to give the Goddess anything near as valuable as Throgmorten. A pity, because he now knew that a gold sovereign was big money. But at least he would still have Uncle Ralph's sixpence.

The trouble was, school had also taught him that girls were a Complete Mystery and quite different from boys. He had no idea what books girls liked. He was forced to consult Oneir, who had an older sister.

"All sorts of slush," Oneir said, shrugging. "I can't remember what."

"Then could you come down to the bookshop with me and see if you can see some of them?" Christopher asked.

"I might," Oneir agreed. "What's in it for me?"

"I'll do your geometry tonight as well as your algebra," Christopher said.

On this understanding, Oneir went down to the bookshop with Christopher in the space between lessons and tea. There he almost immediately picked out *The Arabian Nights* (Unexpurgated). "This one's good," he said. He followed it with something called *Little Tanya and the Fairies,* which Christopher took one look at and put hastily back on the shelf. "I know my sister's read that one," Oneir said, rather injured. "Who's the girl you want it for?"

"She's about the same age as us," Christopher said and, since Oneir was looking at him for a further explanation and he was fairly sure Oneir was not going to believe in someone called the Goddess, he added, "I've got this cousin called Caroline." This was quite true. Mama had once shown him a studio photo of his cousin, all lace and curls. Oneir was not to know that this had nothing whatsoever to do with the sentence that had gone before.

"Wait a sec then," Oneir said, "and I'll see if I can spot some of the real slush." He wandered on along the shelf, leaving Christopher to flip through *The Arabian Nights.* It did look good, Christopher thought. Unfortunately he could see from the pictures that it was all about somewhere very like the Goddess's own Anywhere. He suspected the Goddess would call it educational. "Ah, here we are! This is sure-fire slush!" Oneir called, pointing to a whole row of books. "These *Millie* books. Our house is full of the things."

Millie Goes to School, Christopher read, *Millie of Lowood House, Millie Plays the Game.* He picked up one called *Millie's Finest Hour.* It had some very brightly colored schoolgirls on the front and in small print: "Another moral and uplifting story about your favorite schoolgirl. You will weep with Millie, rejoice with Millie, and meet all your friends from Lowood House School again . . . "

"Does your sister really like these?" he asked incredulously.

"Wallows in them," said Oneir. "She reads them over and over again and cries every time."

Though this seemed a funny way to enjoy a book, Christopher was sure Oneir knew best. The books were two and sixpence each. Christopher chose out the first five, up to *Millie in the Upper Fourth,* and bought *The Arabian Nights* for himself with the rest of the money. After all, it *was* his gold sovereign. "Could you wrap the *Millie* books in something waterproof?" he asked the assistant. "They have to go to a foreign country." The assistant obligingly produced some sheets of waxed paper and, without being asked, made a handle for the parcel out of string.

That night Christopher hid the parcel in his bed. Oneir pinched a candle from the kitchens and read aloud from *The Arabian Nights,* which turned out to have been a remarkably good buy. "Unexpurgated" seemed to mean that all sorts of interestingly dirty bits had been put in. Christopher was so absorbed that he almost forgot to work out how he might get to The Place Between from the dormitory. It was probably important to go round a corner. He decided the best corner was the one beyond the washstands, just beside Fenning's bed, and then settled down to listen to Oneir until the candle burned out. After that, he would be on his way.

To his exasperation, nothing happened at all. Christopher lay and listened to the snores, the mutters, and the heavy breathing of the other boys for hours. At length he got up with the parcel and tiptoed across the cold floor to the corner beyond Fenning's bed. But he knew this was not right, even before he bumped into the washstands. He went back to bed, where he lay for further hours, and nothing happened even when he went to sleep.

The next day was Thursday, the day he was supposed to meet Tacroy. Knowing he would be too busy to deliver the books that night, Christopher left them in his bedside locker and read aloud from *The Arabian Nights* himself, so that he could control the time when everyone went to sleep. And so he did. All the other boys duly began to snore and mutter and puff as they always did, and Christopher was left lying awake alone, unable to get to The Place Between or to fall asleep either.

By this time he was seriously worried. Perhaps the only way to get to the Anywheres was from the night nursery of the house in London. Or perhaps it was an ability he had simply grown out of. He thought of Tacroy in a useless trance and the Goddess vowing the vengeance of Asheth on him, and he heard the birds beginning to sing before he got to sleep that night.

CHAPTER 7

The next morning Matron noticed Christopher stumbling about, aching-eyed and scarcely awake. She pounced on him. "Can't sleep, can you?" she said. "I always watch the ones with tooth-braces. I don't think these dentists realize how uncomfortable they are. I'm going to come and take that away from you before lights-out tonight and you can come and fetch it in the morning. I make Mainwright Major do that too—it works wonders, you'll see."

Christopher had absolutely no faith in this idea. Everyone knew this was one of the bees in Matron's bonnet. But, to his surprise, it worked. He found himself dropping asleep as soon as Fenning began reading *The Arabian Nights.* He had just presence of mind to fumble the parcel of books from his locker, before he was dead to the world. And here an even more surprising thing happened. He got out of bed, carrying the parcel, and walked across the dormitory without anyone appearing to notice him at all. He walked right beside Fenning, and Fenning just went on reading with the stolen candle balanced on his pillow. Nobody seemed to realize when Christopher walked round the corner, out of the dormitory and on to the valley path.

His clothes were lying in the path and he put them on, hanging the parcel from his belt so that he would have both hands free for The Place Between. And there was The Place Between.

So much had happened since Christopher had last been here that he saw it as if this was the first time. His eyes tried to make sense of the shapeless way the rocks slanted, and couldn't. The formlessness stirred a formless kind of fear in him, which the wind and the mist and the rain beating in the mist made worse. The utter emptiness was more frightening still. As Christopher set off climbing and sliding down to

Series Ten, with the wind wailing round him and the fog drops making the rocks wet and slippery, he thought he had been right to think, when he was small, that this was the part left over when all the worlds were made. The Place Between was exactly that. There was no one here to help him if he slipped and broke a leg. When the parcel of books unbalanced him, and he did slip, and skidded twenty feet before he could stop, his heart was in his mouth. If he had not known that he had climbed across here a hundred times, he would have known he was mad to try.

It was quite a relief to clamber into the hot valley and walk down to muddy-walled city. The old men were still charming snakes outside it. Inside was the same hot clamor of smells and goats and people under umbrellas. And Christopher found he was still afraid, except that now he was afraid of someone pointing at him and shouting, "There's the thief that stole the Temple cat!" He kept feeling that spear thudding into his chest. He began to get annoyed with himself. It was as if school had taught him how to be frightened.

When he got to the alley beside the Temple wall—where turnips had been thrown away this time—he was almost too scared to go on. He had to make himself push into the spiked wall by counting to a hundred and then telling himself he had to go. And when he was most of the way through, he stopped again, staring through the creepers at the cats in the blazing sun, and did not seem to be able to go on. But the cats took no notice of him. No one was about. Christopher told himself that it was *silly* to come all this way just to stand in a wall. He pulled himself out of the creepers and tiptoed to the overgrown archway, with the parcel of books butting him heavily with every step.

The Goddess was sitting on the ground in the middle of the shady yard, playing with a large family of kittens. Two of them were ginger, with a strong look of Throgmorten. When she saw Christopher, the Goddess jumped to her feet with an energetic clash of jewelry, scattering kittens in all directions.

"You've brought the books!" she said. "I never thought you would."

"I always keep my word," Christopher said, showing off a little.

The Goddess watched him unhitch the parcel from his belt as if she could still scarcely believe it. Her hands trembled a little as she took the waxy parcel, and trembled even more as she knelt on the tiles and tore and ripped and pulled until the paper and string came off. The kittens seized on the string and the wrappings and did all sorts of acrobatics with them, but the Goddess had eyes only for the books. She knelt and gazed. "Ooh! Five of them!"

"Just like Christmas," Christopher remarked.

"What's Christmas?" the Goddess asked absently. She was absorbed in stroking the covers of the books. When she had done that, she opened each one, peeped inside, and then shut it hastily as if the sight was too much. "Oh, I remember," she said. "Christmas is a Heathen festival, isn't it?"

"The other way around," said Christopher. "You're the Heathens."

"No we're not. Asheth's true," said the Goddess, not really attending. "Five," she said. "That should last me a week if I read slowly on purpose. Which is the best one to start with?"

"I brought you the first five," Christopher said. "Start with *Millie Goes to School.*"

"You mean there are *more*!" the Goddess exclaimed. "How many?"

"I didn't count—about five," Christopher said.

"*Five!* You don't want another cat, do you?" said the Goddess.

"No," Christopher said firmly. "One Throgmorten is quite enough, thanks."

"But I've nothing else to swop!" said the Goddess. "I *must* have those other five books!" She jumped up with an impetuous clash of jewelry and began wrestling to unwind a snakelike bracelet from the top of her arm. "Perhaps Mother Proudfoot won't notice if this is missing. There's a whole chest of bracelets in there."

Christopher wondered what she thought he would do with the bracelet. Wear it? He knew what school would think of that. "Hadn't you better read these books first? You might not like them," he pointed out.

"I know they're perfect," said the Goddess, still wrestling.

"I'll bring you the other books as a present," Christopher said hastily.

"But that means I'll have to do something for you. Asheth always pays her debts," the Goddess said. The bracelet came off with a twang. "Here. I'll *buy* the books from you with this. Take it." She pushed the bracelet into Christopher's hand.

The moment it touched him, Christopher found himself falling through everything that was there. The yard, the creepers, the kittens, all turned to mist—as did the Goddess's round face, frozen in the middle of changing from eagerness to astonishment—and Christopher fell out of it, down and down, and landed violently on his bed in the dark dormitory. CRASH!

"What was that?" said Fenning, quavering a little, and Oneir remarked, apparently in his sleep, "Help, someone's fallen off the ceiling."

"Shall I fetch Matron?" asked someone else.

"Don't be an ass. I just had a dream," Christopher said, rather irritably, because it had given him quite a shock. It was a further shock to find he was in pajamas and not in the clothes he *knew* he had put on in the valley. When the other boys had settled down, he felt all over his bed for the parcel of books, and when they did not seem to be there, felt for the bracelet instead. He could not find that either. He searched again in the morning, but there was no sign of it. He supposed that was not so surprising, when he thought how much Uncle Ralph had said Throgmorten was worth. Twelve-and-sixpenceworth of books was a pretty poor swop for several thousand poundsworth of cat. Something must have noticed that he was cheating the Goddess.

He knew he was going to have to find the money for those other five books somehow and take them to the Goddess. Meanwhile, he had missed Tacroy, and he supposed he had better try to meet him next Thursday instead. He was not looking forward to it. Tacroy was bound to be pretty annoyed by now.

When Thursday came, Christopher nearly forgot Tacroy. It was only by accident that he happened to fall asleep during a particularly tedious story in *The Arabian Nights. The Arabian Nights* had become the dormitory's favorite reading. They took it in turns to steal a candle and read aloud to the others. It was Oneir's turn that night, and Oneir read all on one note like the school Chaplain reading the Bible. And that night he was deep into a confusing set of people who were called Calendars—Fenning made everyone groan by suggesting they got their name from living in the part of the world where dates grew—and Christopher dropped off to sleep. Next thing he knew, he was walking out into the valley.

Tacroy was sitting in the path beside the heap of Christopher's clothes. Christopher eyed those clothes and wondered how they got there. Tacroy was sitting with his arms wrapped round his knees as if he were resigned to a long wait, and he seemed quite surprised to see Christopher.

"I didn't expect to see you!" he said, and he grinned, though he looked tired.

Christopher felt ashamed and awkward. "I suppose you must be pretty angry—" he began.

"Stow it," said Tacroy. "I get paid for going into trances and you don't. It's just a job for me—though I must say I miss you being around to firm me up." He stretched his legs out across the path, and Christopher could see stones and grass through the green worsted trousers. Then he stretched his arms above his head and yawned. "You don't really want to go on with these experiments, do you?" he asked. "You've been busy with school, and that's much more fun than climbing into valleys of a night, isn't it?"

Because Tacroy was being so nice about it, Christopher felt more ashamed than ever. He had forgotten how nice Tacroy was. Now he thought about it, he had missed him quite badly. "Of course I want to go on," he said. "Where are we going tonight?"

"Nowhere," said Tacroy. "I'm nearly out of this trance as it is. This was just an effort to contact you. But if you really want to go on, your uncle is sending the carriage to Series Six next Thursday—you know, the place that's living in an Ice Age. You *do* want to go on—really?" Tacroy looked up at Christopher with his eyes screwed into anxious lines. "You don't have to, you know."

"Yes, but I will," Christopher said. "See you next Thursday." And he dashed back to bed, where, to his delight, something seemed to be happening to the Calendars at last.

The rest of that term passed very swiftly, from lesson to lesson, from tale to tale in *The Arabian Nights,* from Thursday to Thursday. The longest parts were the weekly magic lessons. Climbing across The Place Between to meet Tacroy the first Thursday, Christopher still felt quite frightened, but it made a difference knowing that Tacroy was waiting for him outside the fifth valley along. Soon he was used to it again, and the experiments went on as before.

Someone had arranged for Christopher to stay for the Christmas holidays with Uncle Charles and Aunt Alice, the parents of his cousin Caroline. They lived in a big house in the country quite near, in Surrey too, and Cousin Caroline, in spite of being three years younger and a girl, turned out to be good fun. Christopher enjoyed learning all the things people did in the country, including snowballing with the stable lads and Caroline, and trying to sit on Caroline's fat pony, but he was puzzled that no one mentioned Papa. Uncle Charles was Papa's brother. He realized that Papa must be in disgrace with his whole family. In spite of this, Aunt Alice made sure he had a good Christmas, which was kind of her. Christopher's most welcome Christmas present was another gold sovereign inside a card from Uncle Ralph. That meant he could afford more books for the Goddess.

As soon as school started again, he went down to the bookshop and bought the other five *Millie* books, and had them wrapped in waxed paper like the others. That was another twelve-and-sixpence towards the cost of Throgmorten. At this rate, he thought, he would be carrying parcels of books across The Place Between for the rest of his life.

In the Temple, the Goddess was in her dimly lit room bent over *Millie's Finest Hour.* When Christopher came in, she jumped and stuffed the book guiltily under her cushions. "Oh it's only you!" she said. "Don't ever come in quietly like that again, or I shall be a Dead

Asheth on the spot! Whatever happened last time? You turned into a ghost and went down through the floor."

"I've no idea," said Christopher, "except that I fell on my bed with a crash. I've brought you the other five books."

"*Wonderfu—*!" the Goddess began eagerly. Then she stopped and said soberly, "It's very kind of you, but I'm not sure Asheth wants me to have them, after what happened when I tried to give you the bracelet."

"No," said Christopher. "I think Asheth must know that Throgmorten's worth thousands of pounds. I could bring you the whole school library and it still wouldn't pay for him."

"Oh," said the Goddess. "In that case—How *is* Throgmorten, by the way?"

Since Christopher had no idea, he said airily, "Trotting around bullying other cats and scratching people," and changed the subject before the Goddess realized he was only guessing. "Were the first five books all right?"

The Goddess's round face became all smile, so much smile that her face could hardly hold it and she spread her arms out as well. "They're the most marvelous books in this world! It's like really *being* at Lowood House School. I cry every time I read them."

Oneir had got it right, Christopher thought, watching the Goddess unwrap the new parcel with little cries of pleasure and much chinking of bracelets. "Oh Millie *does* get to be Head Girl!" she cried out, picking up *Head Girl Millie.* "I've been wondering and wondering whether she would. She must have got the better of that awful prig Delphinia after all." She stroked the book lovingly, and then took Christopher by surprise by asking, "What happened when you took Throgmorten? Mother Proudfoot told me that the Arm of Asheth killed the thief."

"They tried," Christopher said awkwardly, trying to sound casual.

"In that case," said the Goddess, "you were very brave to honor the swop and you deserve to be rewarded. Would you like a reward—not a swop or a payment, a reward?"

"If you can think of one," Christopher said cautiously.

"Then come with me," said the Goddess. She got up briskly, clash-tink. She collected the new books and the old one from among the cushions, and gathered up the paper and the string. Then she threw the whole bundle at the wall. All of it, all six books and the wrappings, turned over on itself and shut itself out of sight, as if a lid had come down on an invisible box. There was nothing to tell that any of it had been there. Once again Christopher was impressed. "That's so Mother Proudfoot won't know," the Goddess explained as she led the way into the shady yard. "I like her a lot, but she's very stern and she's into everything."

"How do you get the books back?" asked Christopher.

"I beckon the one I want," said the Goddess, pushing through the creeper in the archway. "It's a by-product of being the Living Asheth."

She led him across the blazing yard, among the cats, to an archway he remembered rather too well for comfort. It was the one he had fled into with Throgmorten yowling in the basket. Christopher began to be nervously and gloomily certain that the Goddess's idea of a reward was nothing like his own. "Won't there be a lot of people?" he asked, hanging back rather.

"Not for a while. They snore for hours in the hot season," the Goddess said confidently.

Christopher followed her reluctantly along a set of dark passages, not quite the way he had run before, he thought, though it was hard to be sure. At length they came to a wide archway hung with nearly transparent yellow curtains. There was a rich gleam of daylight beyond. The Goddess parted the curtains and waved Christopher through, tink-clash. There seemed to be an old, dark tree in front of them, so old that it was thoroughly worm-eaten and had lost most of its branches. And something was making a suffocating smell, a little like church incense, but much thicker and stronger. The Goddess marched round the tree, down some shallow steps, and into the space full of rich daylight, which was blocked off by more yellow curtains a few yards away, like a tall golden room. Here she turned round to face the tree.

"This is the Shrine of Asheth," she said. "Only initiates are allowed here. This is your reward. Look. Here I am."

Christopher turned round and felt decidedly cheated. From this side, the tree turned out to be a monstrous statue of a woman with four arms. From the front it looked solid gold. Clearly the Temple had not bothered to coat the back of the wooden statue with gold, but they had made up for it on the front. Every visible inch of the woman shone buttery yellow gold, and she was hung with golden chains, bracelets, anklets and earrings. Her skirt was cloth-of-gold and she had a big ruby embedded in each of her four golden palms. More precious stones blazed from her high crown. The Shrine was made so that daylight slanted dramatically down from the roof, touching each precious stone with splendor, but veiled by the thick smoke climbing from golden burners beside the woman's huge golden feet. The effect was decidedly Heathen.

After waiting a moment for Christopher to say something, the Goddess said, "This is Asheth. She's me and I'm her, and this is her Divine Aspect. I thought you'd like to meet me as I really am."

Christopher turned to the Goddess, meaning to say, No you're not: you haven't got four arms. But the Goddess was standing in the smoky yellow space with her arms stretched out to the side in the same position as the statue's top pair of arms, and she did indeed have four arms. The lower pair were misty and he could see the yellow curtain through them, but they had the same sort of bracelets and they were arranged just like the statue's lower pair of arms. They were obviously as real as Tacroy before he was firmed up. So he looked up at the statue's smooth golden face. He thought it looked hard and cruel behind its blank golden stare.

"She doesn't look as clever as you," he said. It was the only thing he could think of that was not rude.

"She's got her very stupid expression on," the Goddess said. "Don't be fooled by that. She doesn't want people to know how clever she really is. It's a very useful expression. I use it a lot in lessons when Mother Proudfoot or Mother Dowson go boring on."

It *was* a useful expression, Christopher thought, a good deal better than his vague look which he used in magic lessons. "How do you make it?" he asked with great interest.

Before the Goddess could reply, footsteps padded behind the statue. A strong voice, musical but sharp, called out, "Goddess? What are you doing in the Shrine at this hour?"

Christopher and the Goddess went into two separate states of panic. Christopher turned to plunge out through the other set of yellow curtains, heard sandals slapping about out there too, and turned back in despair. The Goddess whispered, "Oh *blast* Mother Proudfoot! She seems to know where I am by *instinct* somehow!" and she spun round in circles trying to wrestle a bracelet off her upper arm.

A long bare foot and most of a leg in a rust-colored robe appeared round the golden statue. Christopher gave himself up for lost. But the Goddess, seeing she was never going to get the bracelet off in time, snatched his hand and held it against the whole heap of jingling jewelry on her arm.

Just as before, everything turned misty and Christopher fell through it, into his bed in the dormitory. Crash!

"I wish you wouldn't *do* that!" Fenning said, waking up with a jump. "Can't you control those dreams of yours?"

"Yes," Christopher said, sweating at his narrow escape. "I'm never going to have a dream like that again." It was a silly setup anyway—a live girl pretending to be a goddess, who was nothing but a worm-eaten wooden statue. He had nothing against the Goddess herself. He admired her quick thinking, and he would have liked to learn both the very stupid expression and how you did that vanishing trick with the books. But it was not worth the danger.

CHAPTER 8

For the rest of the Spring term, Christopher went regularly to the Anywheres with Tacroy, but he did not try to go to one on his own. By now Uncle Ralph seemed to have a whole round of experiments set up. Christopher met Tacroy in Series One, Three, Five, Seven and Nine, and then in Eight, Six, Four and Two, always in that order, but not always in the same place or outside the same valley. In each Anywhere people would be waiting with a pile of packages which, by the weight and feel, had different things inside each time. The parcels in Series One were always knobby and heavy, and in Four they were smooth boxes. In Series Two and Five, they were squashy and smelled of fish, which made sense since both those Anywheres had so much water in them. In Series Eight, the women always breathed garlic and those parcels had the same strong odor every time. Beyond that, there seemed no rule. Christopher got to know most of the people who supplied the packages, and he laughed and joked with them as he loaded the horseless carriage. And as the experiments went on, Uncle Ralph's wizards gradually perfected the carriage. By the end of the term, it moved under its own power and Tacroy and Christopher no longer had to drag it up the valleys to The Place Between.

In fact, the experiments had become so routine that they were not much of a change from school. Christopher thought of other things while he worked, just as he did in magic lessons and English and Chapel at school.

"Why don't we ever go to Series Eleven?" he asked Tacroy as they walked up one of the valleys from Series One with another heavy knobby load gliding behind on the carriage.

"Nobody goes to Eleven," Tacroy said shortly. Christopher could see he wanted to change the subject. He asked why. "Because," said Tacroy, "because they're peculiar, unfriendly people there, I suppose—if you can call them people. Nobody knows much about them because they make damn sure nobody sees them. And that's all I know, except that Eleven's not a Series. There's only one world." Tacroy refused to say more than that, which was annoying, because Christopher had a strong feeling that Tacroy did know more. But Tacroy was in a bad mood that week. His grandmotherly lady had gone down with flu and Tacroy was making do with the stern flute-playing young lady. "Somewhere in our world," he said, sighing, "there is a young lady who plays the harp and doesn't mind if I turn transparent, but there are too many difficulties in the way between us."

Probably because Tacroy kept saying things like this, Christopher now had a very romantic image of him starving in his garret and crossed in love. "*Why* won't Uncle Ralph let me come and see you in London?" he asked.

"I told you to stow it, Christopher," Tacroy said, and he stopped further talk by stepping out into the mists of The Place Between with the carriage billowing behind him.

Tacroy's romantic background nagged at Christopher all that term, particularly when a casual word he dropped in the dormitory made it clear that none of the other boys had ever met a foundling child. "I wish I was one," Oneir said. "I wouldn't have to go into my father's business then." After that, Christopher felt he would not even mind meeting the flute-playing young lady.

But this was driven out of his mind when there proved to be a muddle over the arrangements for the Easter holidays. Mama wrote and said he was to come to her in Genoa, but at the last moment she turned out to be going to Weimar instead, where there was no room for Christopher. He had to spend nearly a week at school on his own after everyone had gone home, while the school wrote to Uncle Charles, and Uncle Charles arranged for Papa's other brother, Uncle Conrad, to have him in four days' time. Meanwhile, since the school was closing, Christopher was sent to stay with Uncle Ralph in London.

Uncle Ralph was away, to Christopher's disappointment. Most of his house was shut up, with locked doors everywhere, and the only person there was the housekeeper. Christopher spent the few days wandering round London by himself.

It was almost as good as exploring an Anywhere. There were parks and monuments and street musicians, and every road, however narrow, was choked with high-wheeled carts and carriages. On the second day Christopher found himself at Covent Garden market, among piles of fruit and vegetables, and he stayed there till the evening, fascinated by the porters. Each of them could carry at least six loaded baskets in a tall pile on his head, without even wobbling. At last, he turned to come away and saw a familiar sturdy figure in a green worsted suit walking down the narrow street ahead of him.

"Tacroy!" Christopher screamed and went racing after him.

Tacroy did not appear to hear. He went walking on, with his curly head bent in a rather dejected way, and turned the corner into the next narrow street before Christopher had caught up. When Christopher skidded round the corner, there was no sign of him. But he knew it had been, unmistakably, Tacroy. The garret must be somewhere quite near. He spent the rest of his stay in London hanging round Covent Garden, hoping for another glimpse of Tacroy, but it did no good. Tacroy did not appear again.

After that, Christopher went to stay at Uncle Conrad's house in Wiltshire, where the main drawback proved to be his cousin Francis. Cousin Francis was the same age as Christopher, and he was the kind of boy Fenning called "a stuck-up pratterel." Christopher despised Francis on this account, and Francis despised Christopher for having been brought up in town and never having ridden to hounds. In fact, there was another reason too, which emerged when Christopher fell heavily off the quietest pony in the stables for the seventh time.

"Can't do magic, can you?" Francis said, looking smugly down at Christopher from the great height of his trim bay gelding. "I'm not surprised. It's your father's fault for marrying that awful Argent woman. No one in my family has anything to do with your father now."

Since Christopher was fairly sure that Francis had used magic to bring him off the pony, there was not much he could do but clench his teeth and feel that Papa was well shot of this particular branch of the Chants. It was a relief to go back to school again.

It was more than a relief. It was the cricket season. Christopher became obsessed with cricket almost overnight. So did Oneir. "It's the King of Games," Oneir said devoutly, and went and bought every book on the subject that he could afford. He and Christopher decided they were going to be professional cricketers when they grew up. "And my father's business can just go hang!" Oneir said.

Christopher quite agreed, only in his case it was Mama's plans for Society. I've made up my mind for myself! he thought. It was like being released from a vow. He was quite surprised to find how determined and ambitious he was. He and Oneir practiced all day, and Fenning, who was no good really, was persuaded to run after the balls. In between they talked cricket, and at night Christopher had normal ordinary dreams, all about cricket.

It seemed quite an interruption on the first Thursday, when he had to give up dreams of cricket and meet Tacroy in Series Five.

"I saw you in London," Christopher said to him. "Your garret's near Covent Garden, isn't it?"

"Covent Garden?" Tacroy said blankly. "It's nowhere near there. You must have seen someone else." And he stuck to that, even when Christopher described in great detail which street it was and what Tacroy had looked like. "No," he said. "You must have been running after a complete stranger."

Christopher *knew* it had been Tacroy. He was puzzled. But there seemed no point in going on arguing. He began loading the carriage with fishy-smelling bundles and went back to thinking about cricket. Naturally, not thinking what he was doing, he let go of a bundle in the wrong place. It fell half through Tacroy and slapped to the ground, where it lay leaking an even fishier smell than before. "Pooh!" said Christopher. "What is this stuff?"

"No idea," said Tacroy. "I'm only your uncle's errand boy. What's the matter? Is your mind somewhere else tonight?"

"Sorry," Christopher said, collecting the bundle. "I was thinking of cricket."

Tacroy's face lit up. "Are you bowler or batsman?"

"Batsman," said Christopher. "I want to be a professional."

"I'm a bowler myself," said Tacroy. "Slow leg-spin, and though I say it myself, I'm not half bad. I play quite a lot for—well, it's a village team really, but we usually win. I usually end up taking seven wickets—and I can bat a bit too. What are you, an opener?"

"No, I fancy myself as a stroke player," Christopher said.

They talked cricket all the time Christopher was loading the carriage. After that they walked on the beach with the blue surf crashing beside them and went on talking cricket. Tacroy several times tried to demonstrate his skill by picking up a pebble, but he could not get firm enough to hold it. So Christopher found a piece of driftwood to act as a bat and Tacroy gave him advice on how to hit.

After that, Tacroy gave Christopher a coaching session in whatever Anywhere they happened to be, and both of them talked cricket nonstop. Tacroy was a good coach. Christopher learned far more from him than he did from the Sports master at school. He had more and more splendid ambitions of playing professionally for Surrey or somewhere, cracking the ball firmly to the boundary all round the ground. In fact, Tacroy taught him so well, that he began to have quite real, everyday ambitions of getting into the school team.

They were reading Oneir's cricket books aloud in the dormitory now. Matron had discovered *The Arabian Nights* and taken it away, but nobody minded. Every boy in the dormitory, even Fenning, was cricket mad. And Christopher was most obsessed of all.

Then disaster struck. It began with Tacroy saying, "By the way, there's a change of plan. Can you meet me in Series Ten next Thursday? Someone seems to be trying to spoil your uncle's experiments, so we have to change the routine."

Christopher was distracted from cricket by slight guilt at that. He knew he ought to make a further payment for Throgmorten, and he was afraid that the Goddess might have supernatural means of knowing he had been to Series Ten without bringing her any more books. He went rather warily to the valley.

Tacroy was not there. It took Christopher a good hour of climbing and scrambling to locate him at the mouth of quite a different valley. By this time Tacroy had become distinctly misty and unfirm.

"Dunderhead," Tacroy said while Christopher hastily firmed him up. "I was going to lose this trance any second. You *know* there's more than one place in a series. What got into you?"

"I was probably thinking of cricket," Christopher said.

The place beyond the new valley was nothing like as primitive and Heathen-seeming as the place where the Goddess lived. It was a vast dockside with tremendous cranes towering overhead. Some of the biggest ships Christopher had ever seen, enormous rusty iron ships, very strangely shaped, were tied up to cables so big that he had to step over them as if they were logs. But he knew it was still Series Ten when the man waiting with an iron cart full of little kegs said, "Praise Asheth! I thought you were never coming!"

"Yes, make haste," Tacroy said. "This place is safer than that Heathen city, but there may be enemies around all the same. Besides, the sooner you finish, the sooner we can get to work on your forward defensive play."

Christopher hurried to roll the little kegs from the iron cart to the carriage. When all the kegs were in, he hurried to fasten the straps that held the loads on it. And, of course, because he was hurrying, one of the straps slithered out of his hand and fell back on the other side of the carriage. He had to lean right over the load to get it. He could hear iron clanking in the distance and a few shouts, but he thought nothing of it, until Tacroy suddenly sprang into sight beside him.

"Off there! Get off!" Tacroy shouted, tugging uselessly at Christopher with misty hands.

Christopher, still lying across the kegs, looked up to see a giant hook on the end of a chain traveling towards him faster than he could run.

That was really all he knew about it. The next thing he knew—rather dimly—was that he was lying in the path in his own valley beside his pajamas. He realized that the iron hook must have knocked him out and it was lucky that he had been more or less lying across the carriage or Tacroy would never have got him home. A little shakily, he got back into his pajamas. His head ached, so he shambled straight back to bed in the dormitory.

In the morning he did not even have a headache. He forgot about it and went straight out after breakfast to play cricket with Oneir and six other boys.

"Bags I bat first!" he shouted.

Everyone shouted it at the same time. But Oneir had been carrying the bat and he was not going to let go. Everyone, including Christopher, grabbed at him. There was a silly laughing tussle, which ended when Oneir swung the bat round in a playful, threatening circle.

The bat met Christopher's head with a heavy THUK. It hurt. He remembered hearing several other distinct cracks, just over his left ear, as if the bones of his skull were breaking up like an ice puddle. Then, in a way that was remarkably like the night before, he knew nothing at all for quite a long time.

When he came round, he knew it was much later in the day. Though the sheet had somehow got over his face, he could see late evening light coming in through a window high up in one corner. He was very cold, particularly his feet. Someone had obviously taken his shoes and socks off to put him to bed. But where had they put him? The window was in the wrong place for the dormitory—or for any other room he had slept in for that matter. He pushed the sheet off and sat up.

He was on a marble slab in a cold, dim room. It was no wonder he felt cold. He was only wearing underclothes. All round him were other marble slabs, most of them empty. But some slabs had people lying on them, very still and covered all over with white sheets.

Christopher began to suspect where he might be. Wrapping the sheet round him for what little warmth it gave, he slid down from the marble slab and went over to the nearest white slab with a person on it. Carefully he pulled back the sheet. This person had been an old tramp and he was dead as a doornail—Christopher poked his cold, bristly face to make sure. Then he told himself to keep quite calm, which was a sensible thing to tell himself, but much too late. He was already in the biggest panic of his life.

There was a big metal door down at the other end of the cold room. Christopher seized its handle and tugged. When the door turned out to be locked, he kicked it and beat at it with both hands and rattled the handle. He was still telling himself to be sensible, but he was shaking all over, and the panic was rapidly getting out of control.

After a minute or so, the door was wrenched open by a fat, jolly-looking man in a white overall, who stared into the room irritably. He did not see Christopher at first. He was looking over Christopher's head, expecting someone taller.

Christopher wrapped the sheet round himself accusingly. "What do you mean by locking this door?" he demanded. "Everybody's dead in here. They're not going to run away."

The man's eyes turned down to Christopher. He gave a slight moan. His eyes rolled up to the ceiling. His plump body slid down the door and landed at Christopher's feet in a dead faint.

Christopher thought *he* was dead too. It put the last touch to his panic. He jumped over the man's body and rushed down the corridor beyond, where he found himself in a hospital. There a nurse tried to stop him, but Christopher was beyond reason by then. "Where's school?" he shrieked at her. "I'm missing cricket practice!" For half an hour after that the hospital was in total confusion, while everyone tried to catch a five-foot corpse clothed mostly in a flying sheet, which raced up and down the corridors shrieking that it was missing cricket practice.

They caught him at last outside the Maternity Ward, where a doctor hastily gave him something to make him sleep. "Calm down, son," he said. "It's a shock to us too, you know. When I last saw you, your head was like a run-over pumpkin."

"I'm missing cricket practice, I tell you!" Christopher said.

He woke up next day in a hospital bed. Mama and Papa were both there, facing one another across it, dark clothes and whiskers on one side, scents and pretty colors on the other. As if to make it clear to Christopher that this was a bad crisis, the two of them were actually speaking to one another.

"Nonsense, Cosimo," Mama was saying. "The doctors just made a mistake. It was only a bad concussion after all and we've both had a fright for nothing."

"The school Matron said he was dead too," Papa said somberly.

"And she's a flighty sort of type," Mama said. "I don't believe a word of it."

"Well I do," said Papa. "He has more than one life, Miranda. It explains things about his horoscope that have always puzzled—"

"Oh *fudge* to your wretched horoscopes!" Mama cried. "Be quiet!"

"I shall not be quiet where I know the truth!" Papa more or less shouted. "I have done what needs to be done and sent a telegram to de Witt about him."

This obviously horrified Mama. "What a wicked thing to do!" she raged. "And without consulting me! I tell you I shall *not* lose Christopher to your gloomy connivings, Cosimo!"

At this point both Mama and Papa became so angry that Christopher closed his eyes. Since the stuff the doctor had given him was still making him feel sleepy, he dropped off almost at once, but he could still hear the quarrel, even asleep. In the end he climbed out of bed, slipping past Mama and Papa without either of them noticing, and went to The Place Between. He found a new valley there, leading to somewhere where there was some kind of circus going on. Nobody in that world spoke English, but Christopher got by quite well, as he had often done before, by pretending to be deaf and dumb.

When he came slipping back, the room was full of soberly dressed people who were obviously just leaving. Christopher slipped past a stout, solemn young man in a tight collar, and a lady in a gray dress who was carrying a black leather instrument case. Neither of them knew he was there. By the look of things, the part of him left lying in the bed had just been examined by a specialist. As Christopher slipped round Mama and got back into bed, he realized that the specialist was just outside the door, with Papa and another man in a beard.

"I agree that you were right in the circumstance to call me in," Christopher heard an old, dry voice saying, "but there is only one life present, Mr. Chant. I admit freakish things can happen, of course, but we have the report of the school magic teacher to back up our findings in this case. I am afraid I am not convinced at all . . ." The old dry voice went away up the corridor, still talking, and the other people followed, all except Mama.

"What a relief!" Mama said. "Christopher, are you awake? I thought for a moment that that dreadful old man was going to get hold of you, and I would never have forgiven your Papa! Never! I don't want you to grow up into a boring law-abiding *policeman* sort of person, Christopher. Mama wants to be proud of you."

CHAPTER 9

Christopher went back to school the next day. He was rather afraid that Mama was going to be disappointed in him when he turned out to be a professional cricketer, but that did not alter his ambition in the least.

Everyone at school treated him as if he were a miracle. Oneir apologized, almost in tears. That was the only thing which made Christopher uncomfortable. Otherwise he basked in the attention he got. He insisted on playing cricket just as before, and he could hardly wait for next Thursday to come so that he could tell Tacroy all his adventures.

On Wednesday morning the Headmaster sent for Christopher. To his surprise, Papa was there with the Head, both of them standing uneasily beside the Head's mahogany desk.

"Well, Chant," the Head said, "we shall be sorry to lose our nine-days' wonder so quickly. Your father has come to fetch you away. It seems you are to go to a private tutor instead."

"What? Leave school, sir?" Christopher said. "But it's cricket practice this afternoon, sir!"

"I have suggested to your father that you might remain at least until the end of term," the Head said, "but it seems that the great Dr. Pawson will not agree to it."

Papa cleared his throat. "These Cambridge Dons," he said. "We both know what they are, Headmaster." He and the Head smiled at one another, rather falsely.

"Matron is packing you a bag now," said the Head. "In due course, your box and your school report will be sent after you. Now we must say good-bye, as I gather your train leaves in half an hour." He shook hands with Christopher, a brisk, hard, Headmasterly shake, and Christopher was whisked away, there and then, in a cab with Papa, without even a chance to say good-bye to Oneir and Fenning. He sat in the train seething about it, staring resentfully at Papa's whiskered profile.

"I was hoping to get into the school cricket team," he said pointedly, when Papa did not seem to be going to explain.

"Shame about that," Papa said, "but there will be other cricket teams no doubt. Your future is more important than cricket, my son."

"My future *is* cricket," Christopher said boldly. It was the first time he had come right out with his ambition to an adult. He went hot and cold at his daring in speaking like this to Papa. But he was glad, too, because this was an important step on the road to his career.

Papa gave a melancholy smile. "There was a time when I myself wanted to be an engine driver," he said. "These whims pass. It was more important to get you to Dr. Pawson before the end of term. Your Mama was planning to take you abroad with her then."

Christopher's teeth clenched so tightly with anger that his tooth-brace cut his lip. Cricket a whim indeed! "Why is it so important?"

"Dr. Pawson is the most eminent Diviner in the country," said Papa. "I had to pull a few strings to get him to take you on at such short notice, but when I put the case to him, he himself said that it was urgent not to give de Witt time to forget about you. De Witt will revise his opinion of you when he finds you have a gift for magic after all."

"But I can't *do* magic," Christopher pointed out.

"And there must be some reason why not," said Papa. "On the face of it, your gifts should be enormous, since I am an enchanter, and so are both my brothers, while your Mama—this I will grant her—is a highly gifted sorceress. And *her* brother, that wretched Argent fellow, is an enchanter, too."

Christopher watched houses rushing past behind Papa's profile as the train steamed into the outskirts of London, while he tried to digest this. No one had told him about his heredity before. Still, he supposed there were duds born into the most wizardly families. He thought he must be a dud. So Papa was truly an enchanter? Christopher resentfully searched Papa for the signs of power and riches that went with an enchanter, and the signs did not seem to be there. Papa struck him as threadbare and mournful. The cuffs of his frock coat were worn and his hat looked dull and unprosperous. Even the black whiskers were thinner than Christopher remembered, with streaks of gray in them.

But the fact was, enchanter or not, Papa had snatched him out of school in the height of the cricket season, and from the way the Head had talked, he was not expected to go back. Why not? Why had Papa taken it into his head to do this to him?

Christopher brooded about this while the train drew into the Great Southern terminus and Papa towed him through the bustle to a cab. Galloping and rattling towards St. Pancras Cross, he realized that it was going to be difficult even to see Tacroy and get some cricket coaching that way. Papa had told him to have nothing to do with Uncle Ralph, and Papa was an enchanter.

In the small sooty carriage of the train to Cambridge, Christopher asked resentfully, "Papa, what made you decide to take me to Dr. Pawson?"

"I thought I had explained," Papa said. That, for a while seemed all he was going to say. Then he turned towards Christopher, sighing rather, and Christopher saw that he had just been gathering himself for a serious talk. "Last Friday," he said, "you were certified dead, my son, by two doctors and a number of other people. Yet when I arrived to identify your body on Saturday, you were alive and recovering and showing no signs of injury. This made me certain that you had more than one life—the more so as I suspect that this has happened once before. Tell me, Christopher, that time last year when they told me a curtain pole had fallen on you—you were mortally injured then, weren't you? You may confess to me. I shan't be angry."

"Yes," Christopher said reluctantly. "I suppose I was."

"I thought so!" Papa said with dismal satisfaction. "Now, my son, those people who are lucky enough to have several lives are always, invariably, highly gifted enchanters. It was clear to me last Saturday that you are one. This was why I sent for Gabriel de Witt. Now Monsignor de Witt—" Here Papa lowered his voice and looked nervously round the sooty carriage as if he thought Monsignor de Witt could hear—"is the strongest enchanter in the world. He has nine lives. Nine, Christopher. This makes him strong enough to control the practice of magic throughout this world and several others. The Government has given him that task. For this reason you will hear some people call him the Chrestomanci. The post bears that title."

"But," said Christopher, "what has all this and the kress toe mancy got to do with pulling me out of school?"

"Because I wish de Witt to take an interest in your case," said Papa. "I am a poor man now. I can do nothing for you. I have made considerable sacrifices to afford Dr. Pawson's fee, because I think de Witt was wrong when he said you were a normal boy with only one life. My hope is that Dr. Pawson can prove he was wrong and that de Witt can then be persuaded to take you on to his staff. If he does, your future is assured."

Take me on to his staff, Christopher thought. Like Oneir in his father's business having to start as an office boy. "I don't think," he said, "that I want my future assured like that."

His father looked at him sorrowfully. "There speaks your Mama in you," he said. "Proper tuition should cure that sort of levity."

This did nothing to reconcile Christopher to Papa's plans. But I said that for *myself*! he thought angrily. It had nothing to *do* with Mama! He was still in a state of seething resentment when the train steamed into Cambridge, and he walked with Papa through streets full of young men in gowns like the coats people wore in Series Seven, past tall turreted buildings that reminded him of the Temple of Asheth, except that the Cambridge buildings had more windows. Papa had rented rooms in a lodging house, a dark, mingy place that smelled of old dinners.

"We shall be staying here together while Dr. Pawson sorts you out," he told Christopher. "I have brought ample work with me, so that I can keep a personal eye on your well-being."

This about put the lid on Christopher's angry misery. He wondered if he dared go to The Place Between to meet Tacroy on Thursday with a full-grown enchanter keeping a careful eye on him. To crown it all, the lodging house bed was even worse than the beds at school and twanged every time he moved. He went to sleep thinking he was about as miserable as he could be. But that was before he saw Dr. Pawson and realized his miseries had only just begun.

Papa delivered him to Dr. Pawson's house in the Trumpington Road at ten the next morning. "Dr. Pawson's learning gives him a disconcerting manner at times," Papa said, "but I know I can trust my son to bear himself with proper politeness notwithstanding."

This sounded ominous. Christopher's knees wobbled while the housemaid showed him into Dr. Pawson's room. It was a bright, bright room stuffed full of clutter. A harsh voice shouted out of the clutter.

"Stop!"

Christopher stood where he was, bewildered.

"Not a step further. And keep your *knees* still, boy! Lord, how the young do fidget!" the harsh voice bellowed. "How am I to assess you if you won't stay still? Now, what do you say?"

The largest thing among the clutter was a fat armchair. Dr. Pawson was sitting in it, not moving a muscle except for a quiver from his vast purple jowls. He was probably too fat to move. He was vastly, hugely, grossly fat. His belly was like a small mountain with a checked waistcoat stretched over it. His hands reminded Christopher of some purple bananas he had seen in Series Five. His face was stretched, and purple too, and out of it glared two merciless, watery eyes.

"How do you do, sir?" Christopher said, since Papa trusted him to be polite.

"No, *no*!" shouted Dr. Pawson. "This is an examination, not a social call. What's your problem—Chant your name is, isn't it? State your problem, Chant."

"I can't do magic, sir," Christopher said.

"So can't a lot of people. Some are born that way," Dr. Pawson bawled. "Do better than that, Chant. Show me. Don't do some magic and let me see."

Christopher hesitated, out of bewilderment mostly.

"Go on, boy!" howled Dr. Pawson. "Don't do it!"

"I can't not do something I can't do," Christopher said, thoroughly harassed.

"Of course you can!" yelled Dr. Pawson. "That's the essence of magic. Get on with it. Mirror on the table beside you. Levitate it and be quick about it!"

If Dr. Pawson hoped to startle Christopher into succeeding, he failed. Christopher stumbled to the table, looked into the elegant silver-framed mirror that was lying there, and went through the words and gestures he had learned at school. Nothing at all happened.

"Hm," said Dr. Pawson. "Don't do it again."

Christopher realized he was supposed to try once more. He tried, with shaking hands and voice, and exasperated misery growing inside him. This was hopeless! He hated Papa for dragging him off to be terrorized by this appalling fat man. He wanted to cry, and he had to remind himself, just as if he were his own Governess, that he was far too big for that. And, as before, the mirror simply lay where it was.

"Um," said Dr. Pawson. "Turn round, Chant. No, *right* round, boy, slowly, so that I can see all of you. Stop!"

Christopher stopped and stood, and waited. Dr. Pawson shut his watery eyes and lowered his purple chins. Christopher suspected he had gone to sleep. There was utter silence in the room except for clocks ticking among the clutter. Two clocks were the kind with all the works showing, one was a grandfather, and one was a mighty marble timepiece that looked as if it had come off someone's grave. Christopher nearly jumped out of his skin when Dr. Pawson suddenly barked at him like the clap of doom.

"EMPTY YOUR POCKETS, CHANT!"

Eh? thought Christopher. But he did not dare disobey. He began hurriedly unloading the pockets of his Norfolk jacket: Uncle Ralph's sixpence which he always kept, a shilling of his own, a grayish handkerchief, a note from Oneir about algebra, and then he was down to shaming things like string and rubber bands and furry toffees. He hesitated.

"All of it!" yelled Dr. Pawson. "Out of every single pocket. Put it all down on the table."

Christopher went on unloading: a chewed rubber, a bit of pencil, peas for Fenning's pea-shooter, a silver threepenny bit he had not known about, a cough drop, fluff, more fluff, string, a marble, an old pen nib, more rubber bands, more fluff, more string. And that was it.

Dr. Pawson's eyes glared over him. "No, that's *not* all! What else have you got on you? Tiepin. Get rid of that too."

Reluctantly Christopher unpinned the nice silver tiepin Aunt Alice had given him for Christmas. And Dr. Pawson's eyes continued to glare at him.

"Ah!" Dr. Pawson said. "And that stupid thing you have on your teeth. That's got to go too. Get it out of your mouth and put it on the table. What the devil's it *for* anyway?"

"To stop my teeth growing crooked," Christopher said rather huffily. Much as he hated the tooth-brace, he hated even more being criticized about it.

"What's wrong with crooked teeth?" howled Dr. Pawson, and he bared his own teeth. Christopher rather started back from the sight. Dr. Pawson's teeth were brown, and they lay higgledy-piggledy in all directions, like a fence trampled by cows. While Christopher was blinking at them, Dr. Pawson bellowed, "Now do that levitation spell again!"

Christopher ground his teeth—which felt quite straight by contrast and very smooth without the brace—and turned to the mirror again. Once more he looked into it, once more said the words, and once more raised his arms aloft. And as his arms went up, he felt something come loose with them—come loose with a vengeance.

Everything in the room went upwards except Christopher, the mirror, the tiepin, the tooth-brace and the money. These slid to the floor as the table surged upwards, but were collected by the carpet which came billowing up after it. Christopher hastily stepped off the carpet and stood watching everything soar around him—all the clocks, several tables, chairs, rugs, pictures, vases, ornaments, and Dr. Pawson too. He and his armchair both went up, majestically, like a balloon, and bumped against the ceiling. The ceiling bellied upwards and the chandelier plastered itself sideways against it. From above came crashings, shrieks, and an immense airy grinding. Christopher could feel that the roof of the house had come off and was on its way to the sky, pursued by the attics. It was an incredible feeling.

"STOP THAT!" Dr. Pawson roared. Christopher guiltily took his arms down.

Instantly everything began raining back to the ground again. The tables plunged, the carpets sank, vases, pictures and clocks crashed to the floor all round. Dr. Pawson's armchair plummeted with the rest, followed by pieces of the chandelier, but Dr. Pawson himself floated down smoothly, having clearly done some prudent magic of his own. Up above, the roof came down thunderously. Christopher could hear tiles falling and chimneys crashing, as well as smashings and howls from upstairs. The upper floors seemed now to be trying to get through to the ground. The walls of the room buckled and oozed plaster, while the windows bent and fell to pieces. It was about five minutes before the slidings and smashings died away, and the dust settled even more slowly. Dr. Pawson sat among the wreckage and the blowing dust and stared at Christopher. Christopher stared back, very much wanting to laugh.

A little old lady suddenly materialized in the armchair opposite Dr. Pawson's. She was wearing a white nightgown and a lacy cap over her white hair. She smiled at Christopher in a steely way. "So it was you, child," she said to Christopher. "Mary-Ellen is in hysterics. Don't *ever* do that again, or I'll put a Visitation on you. I'm still famed for my Visitations, you know." Having said this, she was gone as suddenly as she had come.

"My old mother," said Dr. Pawson. "She's normally bedridden, but as you can see, she's very strongly moved. As is almost everything else." He sat and stared at Christopher a while longer, and Christopher went on struggling not to laugh. "Silver," Dr. Pawson said at last.

"Silver?" asked Christopher.

"Silver," said Dr. Pawson. "Silver's the thing that's stopping you, Chant. Don't ask me why at the moment. Maybe we'll never get to the bottom of it, but there's no question about the facts. If you want to work magic, you'll have to give up money except for coppers and sovereigns, throw away that tiepin, and get rid of that stupid brace."

Christopher thought about Papa, about school, about cricket, in a flood of anger and frustration which gave him courage to say, "But I don't think I do want to work magic, sir."

"Yes you do, Chant," said Dr. Pawson. "For at least the next month." And while Christopher was wondering how to contradict him without being too rude, Dr. Pawson gave out another vast bellow. "YOU HAVE TO PUT EVERYTHING BACK, CHANT!"

And this is just what Christopher had to do. For the rest of the morning he went round the house, up to every floor and then outside into the garden, while Dr. Pawson trundled beside him in his armchair and showed him how to cast holding-spells to stop the house falling down. Dr. Pawson never seemed to leave that armchair. In all the time Christopher spent with him, he never saw Dr. Pawson walk. Around midday, Dr. Pawson sent his chair gliding into the kitchen, where a cook-maid was sitting dolefully in the midst of smashed butter crocks, spilled milk, bits of basin and dented saucepans, and dabbing at her eyes with her apron.

"Not hurt in here are you?" Dr. Pawson barked. "I put a holder on first thing to make sure the range didn't burst and set the house on fire—that sort of thing. That held, didn't it? Water pipes secure?"

"Yes, sir," gulped the cook-maid. "But lunch is ruined, sir."

"We'll have to have a scratch lunch for once," said Dr. Pawson. His chair swung round to face Christopher. "By this evening," he said, "this kitchen is going to be mended. Not holding-spells. Everything as new. I'll show you how. Can't have the kitchen out of action. It's the most important place in the house."

"I'm sure it is, sir," Christopher said, eyeing Dr. Pawson's mountain of a stomach.

Dr. Pawson glared at him. "I can dine in college," he said, "but my mother needs her nourishment."

For the rest of that day Christopher mended the kitchen, putting crockery back together, recapturing spilled milk and cooking sherry, taking dents out of pans, and sealing a dangerous split at the back of the range. While he did, Dr. Pawson sat in his armchair warming himself by the range fire and barking things like, "Now put the eggs together, Chant. You'll need the spell to raise them first, then the dirt-dispeller you used on the milk. *Then* you can start the mending-spell." While Christopher labored, the cook-maid, who was obviously even more frightened of Dr. Pawson than Christopher was, edged round him trying to bake a cake and prepare the roast for supper.

One way and another, Christopher probably learned more practical magic that day than he had in two and a half terms at school. By the evening he was exhausted. Dr. Pawson barked, "You can go back to your father for now. Be here at nine tomorrow prompt. There's still the rest of the house to see to."

"Oh Lord!" Christopher groaned, too weary to be polite. "Can't someone help me at all? I've learned my lesson."

"What gave you the idea there was only one lesson to learn?" bawled Dr. Pawson.

Christopher tottered back to the lodging house carrying the tooth-brace, the money, and the tiepin wrapped in the gray handkerchief. Papa looked up from a table spread with horoscope sheets. "Well?" he asked with gloomy eagerness.

Christopher fell into a lumpy chair. "Silver," he said. "Silver stops me working magic. And I hope I *have* got more than one life because Dr. Pawson's going to kill me at this rate."

"Silver?" said Papa. "Oh dear! Oh dear, dear!" He was very sad and silent all through the cabbage soup and sausages the lodging house provided for supper. After supper, he said, "My son, I have a confession to make. It is my fault that silver stops you working magic. Not only did I cast your horoscope when you were born, but I also cast every other spell I knew to divine your future. And you can imagine my horror when each kind of forecast foretold that silver would mean danger or death to you." Papa paused, drumming his fingers on the horoscope sheets and staring absently at the wall. "Argent," he said musingly. "Argent means silver. Could I have got it wrong?" He pulled himself sadly back together. "Well it is too late to do anything about that, except to warn you again to have nothing to do with your Uncle Ralph."

"But why is it your fault?" Christopher asked, very uncomfortable at the way Papa's thoughts were going.

"There is no getting round Fate," Papa said, "as I should have known. I cast my strongest spells and put forth all my power to make silver neutral to you. Silver—any contact with silver—seems to transform you at once into an ordinary person without a magic gift at all—and I see now that this could have its dangers. I take it you *can* work magic when you are not touching silver?"

Christopher gave a weary laugh. "Oh yes. Like anything."

Papa brightened a little. "That's a relief. Then my sacrifice here was not in vain. As you know, Christopher, I very foolishly lost your Mama's money and my own by investing it where I thought my horoscopes told me to." He shook his head sadly. "Horoscopes are tricky, particularly with money. Be that as it may, I am finished. I regard myself as a failure. You are all I have left to live for, my son. Any success I am to know, I shall know through you."

If Christopher had not been so tired, he would have found this decidedly embarrassing. Even through his weariness, he found he was annoyed that he was expected to live for Papa and not on his own account. Would it be fair, he wondered, to use magic to make yourself a famous cricketer? You could make the ball go anywhere you wanted. Would Papa regard this as success? He knew perfectly well that Papa would not. By this time, his eyes were closing themselves and his head was nodding. When Papa sent him off to bed, Christopher fell on to the twanging mattress and slept like a log. He had meant, honestly meant, to go to The Place Between and tell Tacroy all that had happened, but either he was just too tired or too scared that Papa would guess. Whatever the reason was, he did not have any dreams of any kind that night.

CHAPTER 10

For the next three weeks, Dr. Pawson kept Christopher so hard at work mending the house that he fell into bed each night too weary to dream. Each morning when Christopher arrived, Dr. Pawson was sitting in his armchair in the hall, waiting for him.

"To work, Chant!" he would bark.

Christopher took to replying, "Really, sir? I thought we were going to have a lazy day like yesterday." The strange thing about Dr. Pawson was that he did not mind this kind of remark in the least. Once Christopher got used to him, he discovered that Dr. Pawson rather liked people to stand up to him, and once he had discovered that, Christopher found that he did not really hate Dr. Pawson—or only in the way you hate a violent thunderstorm you happen to be caught in. He found he quite liked rebuilding the house, though perhaps the thing which he really liked was working magic that actually did something. Every spell he did had a real use. That made it far more interesting than the silly things he had tried to learn at school. And the hard work was much easier to bear when he was able to say things to Dr. Pawson that would have caused masters at school to twist his ears and threaten to cane him for insolence.

"Chant!" Dr. Pawson howled from his armchair in the middle of the lawn. "Chant! The chimney pots on the right are crooked."

Christopher was balanced on the tiles of the roof, shivering in the wind. It was raining that day, so he was having to maintain a shelter-spell for the roof and for the lawn while he worked. And he had put the chimneys straight four times already. "Yes, sir, of course, sir!" he screamed back. "Would you like them turned to gold too, sir?"

"None of that or I'll make you *do* it!" Dr. Pawson yelled.

When Christopher came to mend Dr. Pawson's mother's room, he made the mistake of trying to treat old Mrs. Pawson the same way. She was sitting up in a bed heaped with plaster from the ceiling, looking quite comfortable and composed, knitting something striped and long. "I saved the looking-glass, child," she remarked with a pleasant smile, "but that is as far as my powers stretch. Be good enough to mend the chamber pot first, and count yourself fortunate, child, that it had not been used. You will find it under the bed."

Christopher fished it out in three broken white pieces and got to work.

"Mend it quite straight," old Mrs. Pawson said, her knitting needles clattering away. "Make sure the handle is not crooked and the gold rim round the top is quite regular. Please do not leave any uncomfortable lumps or unsightly bulges, child."

Her voice was gentle and pleasant and it kept interrupting the spell. At length Christopher asked in exasperation, "Would you like it studded with diamonds too? Or shall I just give it a posy of roses in the bottom?"

"Thank you, child," said Mrs. Pawson. "The posy of roses, please. I think that's a charming idea."

Dr. Pawson, sitting by in his armchair, was full of glee at Christopher's discomfiture. "Sarcasm never pays, Chant," he bawled. "Roses require a creation-spell. Listen carefully."

After that, Christopher had to tackle the maids' rooms. Then he had to mend all the plumbing. Dr. Pawson gave him a day off on Sundays so that Papa could take him to church. Christopher, now he knew what he could do, toyed with the idea of making the church spire melt like a candle, but he never quite dared to do it, with Papa pacing soberly beside him. Instead, he experimented in other ways. Every morning, while he was walking up the Trumpington Road, he tried to coax the trees that lined it into a different pattern. He got so good at it that before long he could shunt them up the road in a long line and crowd them into a wood at the end. In the evenings, tired though he was, he could not resist trying to make the lodging house supper taste better. But food magic was not easy. "What *do* they put in sausages these days?" Papa remarked. "These taste of strawberry."

Then came a morning when Dr. Pawson shouted from his chair in the hall, "Right, Chant, from now on you finish the mending in the afternoons. In the mornings we teach you some control."

"Control?" Christopher said blankly. By this time the house was nearly finished and he was hoping that Dr. Pawson would soon have finished with him too.

"That's right," Dr. Pawson bawled. "You didn't think I'd let you loose on the world without teaching you to control your power, did you? As you are now, you're a menace to everyone. And don't tell me you haven't been trying to see what you can do, because I won't believe you."

Christopher looked at his feet and thought of what he had just been doing with the trees in the Trumpington Road. "I've hardly done anything, sir."

"Hardly anything! What do boys know of restraint?" said Dr. Pawson. "Into the garden. We're going to raise a wind, and you're going to learn to do it without moving so much as a blade of grass."

They went into the garden, where Christopher raised a whirlwind. He thought it rather expressed his feelings. Luckily it was quite small and only destroyed one rose bed. Dr. Pawson canceled it with one flap of his purple banana hand. "Do it again, Chant."

Learning control was boring, but it was a good deal more restful. Dr. Pawson obviously knew this. He began setting Christopher homework to do in the evenings. All the same, even after disentangling the interlacing spells in the problems he had been set, Christopher began to feel for the first time that he had some brain left over to think with. He thought about silver first. Keeping Uncle Ralph's silver sixpence in his pocket had stopped him doing such a lot. And that beastly tooth-brace had stopped him doing even more. What a waste! No wonder he had not been able to take the books to the Goddess until Matron made him take the brace out.

He must have been using magic to get to the Anywheres all these years without knowing it—except that he *had* known it, in an underneath sort of way. Tacroy had known, and he had been impressed. And the Goddess must have realized, too, when her silver bracelet turned Christopher into a ghost. Here Christopher tried to go on thinking about the Goddess, but he found he kept thinking of Tacroy instead. Tacroy would now have gone into a trance uselessly for three weeks running. Tacroy made light of it, but Christopher suspected that going into a trance took a lot out of a person. He really would have to let Uncle Ralph know what had happened.

Glancing over at Papa, who was hard at work with a special pen marking special symbols on horoscopes under the big oil lamp, Christopher started writing a letter to Uncle Ralph, pretending it was part of his homework. The oil lamp cast shadows on Papa's face, removing the threadbare look and making him look unusually kind and stern. Christopher told himself uneasily that Papa and Uncle Ralph just did not like one another. Besides, Papa had not actually forbidden him to write to Uncle Ralph.

All the same, it took several nights to write the letter. Christopher did not want to seem disloyal to Papa. In the end, he simply wrote that Papa had taken him away from school to be taught by Dr. Pawson. It was a lot of effort for such a short letter. He posted it next day on his way up the Trumpington Road with a sense of relief and virtue.

Three days later, Papa had a letter from Mama. Christopher could tell at once from Papa's face that Uncle Ralph had told Mama where they were. Papa threw the letter on the fire and fetched his hat. "Christopher," he said, "I shall be coming with you to Dr. Pawson's today."

This made Christopher certain that Mama was in Cambridge too. As he walked up the Trumpington Road beside Papa, he tried to work out what his feelings were about that. But he did not have much time to think. A strong wind, scented with roses, swept round the pair of them, hurling Christopher sideways and snatching Papa's hat from his head. Papa made a movement to chase his hat—which was just rolling under a brewer's dray—and then dived round and seized Christopher's arm instead.

"Hats are expendable," he said. "Keep walking, son."

They kept walking, with the wind hurling and buffeting round them. Christopher could actually feel it trying to curl around him in order to pull him away. But for Papa's grip on his arm, he would have been carried across the road. He was impressed. He had not known Mama's magic was this strong.

"I can control it if you want," he called to Papa above the noise. "Dr. Pawson taught me wind control."

"No, Christopher," Papa panted sternly, looking strange and most undignified, with his coat flapping and his hair blowing in all directions. "A gentleman *never* works magic against a woman, particularly his own Mama."

Gentlemen, it seemed to Christopher, made things unreasonably difficult for themselves in that case. The wind grew stronger and stronger, the nearer they got to the gate of Dr. Pawson's house. Christopher thought they would never cover the last yard or so. Papa was forced to seize the gatepost to hold them both in place while he tried to undo the latch. Whereupon the wind made a last, savage snatch. Christopher felt his feet leave the ground, and knew he was about to soar away. He made himself very heavy just in time. He did it because it was a contest, really, because he did not like being on the losing side. He would not at all have minded seeing Mama. But he very much hoped Papa would not notice the rather large dents his feet had made in the ground just outside the gate.

Inside the gate there was no more wind. Papa smoothed his hair and rang the doorbell.

"Aha!" shouted Dr. Pawson from his armchair while Mary-Ellen was opening the door. "The expected trouble has come to pass, I see. Chant, oblige me by going upstairs and reading aloud to my mother while I talk to your father."

Christopher went up the stairs as slowly as he dared, hoping to hear what was being said. All he caught was Dr. Pawson's voice, hardly shouting at all. "I've been in touch almost daily for a week, but they still can't—" After that the door shut. Christopher went on up the stairs and knocked at the door of old Mrs. Pawson's room.

She was sitting up in bed, still knitting. "Come and sit on that chair so that I can hear you," she said in her gentle voice, and gave him a gentle but piercing smile. "The Bible is here on the bedside table. You may start from the beginning of Genesis, child, and see how far you can get. I expect the negotiations will take time. Such things always do."

Christopher sat down and began to read. He was stumbling among the people who begat other people when Mary-Ellen came in with coffee and biscuits and gave him a welcome break. Ten minutes later, old Mrs. Pawson took up her knitting and said, "Continue, child." Christopher had got well into Sodom and Gomorrah and was beginning to run out of voice, when old Mrs. Pawson cocked her white head on one side and said, "Stop now, child. They want you downstairs in the study."

Much relieved and very curious, Christopher put the Bible down and shot to the ground floor. Papa and Dr. Pawson were sitting facing one another in Dr. Pawson's crowded room. It had become more cluttered than ever over the last weeks, since it was stacked with pieces of clocks and ornaments from all over the house, waiting for Christopher to mend. Now it looked more disorganized still. Tables and carpets had been pushed to the walls to leave a large stretch of bare floorboards, and a design had been chalked on the boards. Christopher looked at it with interest, wondering what it had to do with Mama. It was a five-pointed star inside a circle. He looked at Papa, who was obviously delighted about something, and then at Dr. Pawson, who was just as usual.

"News for you, Chant," said Dr. Pawson. "I've run a lot of tests on you these last weeks—don't stare, boy, you didn't know I was doing it—and every one of those tests gives you nine lives. Nine lives and some of the strongest magic I've met. Naturally I got in touch with Gabriel de Witt. I happen to know he's been looking for a successor for years. Naturally all I got was a lot of guff about the way they'd already tested you and drawn a blank. That's Civil Servants for you. They need a bomb under them before they'll change their minds. So today, after the bother with your Mama had given me the excuse we needed, I had a good old shout at them. They caved in, Chant. They're sending a man to fetch you to Chrestomanci Castle now."

Here Papa broke in as if he could not stop himself. "It's just what I've been hoping for, my son! Gabriel de Witt is to become your legal guardian, and in due course you will be the next Chrestomanci."

"Next Chrestomanci?" Christopher echoed. He stared at Papa, knowing there was no chance of deciding on a career for himself now. It was all settled. His visions of himself as a famous cricketer faded and fell and turned to ashes. "But I don't want—"

Papa thought Christopher did not understand. "You will become a very important man," he said. "You will watch over all the magic in this world and prevent any harm being done with it."

"But—" Christopher began angrily.

It was too late. The misty shape of a person was forming inside the five-pointed star. It solidified into a pale plump young man with a long face, very soberly dressed in a gray suit and a wide starched collar that looked much too tight for him. He was carrying a thing like a telescope. Christopher remembered him. The young man was one of the people who had been in the hospital room after everyone had thought Christopher was dead.

"Good morning," the young man said, stepping out of the star. "My name is Flavian Temple. Monsignor de Witt has sent me to examine your candidate."

"EXAMINE HIM!" shouted Dr. Pawson. "I've already DONE that! What do you people take me for?" He rolled his angry eyes at Papa. "Civil Servants!"

Flavian Temple obviously found Dr. Pawson quite as alarming as Christopher did. He flinched a bit. "Yes, doctor, we know you have. But my instructions are to verify your findings before proceeding. If this lad could just step into the pentagram."

"Go on, son," said Papa. "Stand inside the star."

With a furious, helpless feeling, Christopher stepped into the chalked pattern and stood there while Flavian Temple sighted down the telescope-thing at him. There must be a way of making yourself look as if you only had one life, he thought. There *had* to be! But he had no idea what it was you did.

Flavian Temple frowned. "I can only make it seven lives."

"He's already lost TWO, you fat young fool!" Dr. Pawson bellowed. "Didn't they tell you anything? Tell him, Chant."

"I've lost two lives already," Christopher found himself saying. There was some kind of spell on the pattern. Otherwise he would have denied everything.

"SEE?" howled Dr. Pawson.

Flavian Temple managed to turn a wince into a polite bow. "I do see, doctor. That being the case, I will of course take the boy to be interviewed by Monsignor de Witt. Any final decision has to be Monsignor de Witt's."

Christopher perked up at this. Perhaps it was not settled after all. But Papa seemed to think it was. He came and laid an arm round Christopher's shoulders. "Good-bye, my son. This makes me a very proud and happy man. Say good-bye to Dr. Pawson."

Dr. Pawson behaved as if it were settled too. His chair trundled forward and he held out a big purple banana finger to Christopher. "Bye, Chant. Take no notice of the official way they go on. This Flavian's a fool Civil Servant like the rest of them."

As Christopher shook the purple finger, old Mrs. Pawson materialized, sitting on the arm of Dr. Pawson's chair in her crisp white nightdress, holding her knitting wrapped into a stripey bundle. "Good-bye, child," she said. "You read very nicely. Here is the present I've knitted for you. It's full of protection spells." She leaned forward and draped the knitting round Christopher's neck. It was a scarf about ten feet long, striped in the colors of the rainbow.

"Thank you," Christopher said politely.

"Just move up—er, Christopher—but don't leave the pentagram," said Flavian. He stepped back inside the chalk marks, taking up more than half the space, and took hold of Christopher's arm to keep him inside it. Old Mrs. Pawson waved a withered hand. And without anything more being said, Christopher found himself somewhere quite different. It was even more disconcerting than being carried off from school by Papa.

He and Flavian were standing in a much bigger pentagram that was made of white bricks, or tiles, built into the floor of a lofty space with a glass dome high overhead. Under the glass dome, a majestic pink marble staircase curled up to the next floor. Stately paneled doors with statues over them opened off the space all round—the most stately had a clock above it as well as a statue—and an enormous crystal chandelier hung from the glass dome on a long chain. Behind Christopher, when he twisted round to look, was a very grand front door. He could see he was in the front hall of a very big mansion, but nobody thought to tell him where he was.

There were people standing round the tiled pentagram, waiting for them. And a stately, dismal lot they looked too! Christopher thought. All of them, men and women alike, were dressed in black or gray. The men wore shiny white collars and cuffs and the women all wore neat black lace mittens. Christopher felt their eyes on him, sizing up, disapproving, coldly staring. He shrank into a very small grubby boy under those eyes and realized that he had been wearing the same set of clothes ever since he had left school.

Before he had a chance to do more than look around, a man with a little pointed gray beard stepped up to him and took the striped scarf away. "He won't be needing this," he said, rather shocked about it.

Christopher thought the man was Gabriel de Witt and was all prepared to hate him, until Flavian said, "No, of course, Dr. Simonson," apologizing for Christopher. "The old lady gave it to him, you know. Shall I—?"

Christopher decided to hate the bearded man anyway.

One of the ladies, a small plump one, stepped forward then. "Thank you, Flavian," she said in a final, bossy sort of way. "I'll take Christopher to Gabriel now. Follow me, young man." She turned and went swishing off towards the pink marble stairs. Flavian gave Christopher a nudge, and Christopher stepped out of the tiled pattern and followed her, feeling about a foot high and dirty all over. He knew his collar was sticking up at one side, and that his shoes were dusty, and he could feel the hole in his left sock sliding out of its shoe and showing itself to everyone in the hall as he went upstairs after the lady.

At the top of the stairs was a very tall solid-looking door, the only one in a row of doors that was painted black. The lady swished up to the black door and knocked. She opened it and pushed Christopher firmly inside. "Here he is, Gabriel," she said. Then she shut the door behind him and went away, leaving Christopher alone in an oval-shaped room where it seemed to be twilight or sunset.

The room was paneled in dark brown wood, with a dark brown carpet on the floor. The only furniture seemed to be a huge dark desk. As Christopher came in, a long thin figure reared up from behind the desk—about six-foot-six of skinny old man, Christopher realized, when his heart stopped thumping. The old man had a lot of white hair and the whitest face and hands Christopher had ever seen. His eyebrows jutted and his cheeks stood out in wide peaks, making the eyes between them look sunken and staring. Below that was a hooked beak of nose. The rest of the old man's face went into a small, sharp point, containing a long grim mouth. The mouth opened to say, "I am Gabriel de Witt. So we meet again, Master Chant."

Christopher knew he would have remembered if he had ever seen this old man before. Gabriel de Witt was even more memorable than Dr. Pawson. "I've never seen you in my life before," he said.

"I have met you. You were unconscious at the time," Gabriel de Witt said. "I suppose this accounts for our being so strangely mistaken in you. I can see now at a glance that you do indeed have seven lives and should have nine."

There were quite a lot of windows in the twilight room, Christopher saw, at least six of them, in a high curving row near the ceiling. The ceiling was a sort of orange, which seemed to keep all the light from the windows to itself. All the same, it was a mystery to Christopher how a room with quite so many windows could end up being so very dark.

"In spite of this," Gabriel de Witt said, "I am very dubious about taking you on. Your heredity frankly appalls me. The Chants give themselves out as a race of respectable enchanters, but they produce a black sheep every generation, while the Argents, though admittedly gifted, are the kind of people I would not nod to in the street. These traits have come out in both your parents. I gather your father is bankrupt and your mother a contemptible social climber."

Even Cousin Francis had not said anything quite as bald as this. Anger flared through Christopher. "Oh thank you, sir," he said. "There's nothing I like more than a polite warm welcome like that."

The old man's eagle eyes stared. He seemed puzzled. "I felt it only fair to be frank with you," he said. "I wished you to understand that I have agreed to become your legal guardian because we do not consider either of your parents a fit person to have charge of the future Chrestomanci."

"Yes, sir," said Christopher, angrier than ever. "But you needn't bother. I don't want to be the next Chrestomanci. I'd rather lose all my lives first."

Gabriel de Witt simply looked impatient. "Yes, yes, this is often the way, until we realize the job needs doing," he said. "I refused the post myself when it was first offered to me, but I was in my twenties and you are a mere child, even less capable of deciding than I was. Besides, we have no choice in the matter. You and I are the only nine-lifed enchanters in all the Related Worlds." He made a gesture with one white hand. A small bell chimed somewhere and the plump young lady swished into the room. "Miss Rosalie here is my chief assistant," Gabriel de Witt said. "She will show you to your room and get you settled in. I have allotted Flavian Temple to you as a tutor, though I can ill spare him, and I will of course be teaching you myself twice a week as well."

Christopher followed Miss Rosalie's swishing skirt past the line of doors and down a long corridor. Nobody seemed to care what he felt. He wondered whether to show them by raising another whirlwind. But there was a spell on this place, a strong, thick spell. After Dr. Pawson's teaching, Christopher was sensitive to all spells, and though he was not sure what this one did, he was fairly sure it would make things like whirlwinds pretty useless. "Is this Chrestomanci Castle?" he asked angrily.

"That's right," Miss Rosalie said. "The Government took it over two hundred years ago after the last really wicked enchanter was beheaded." She turned to smile at him over her shoulder. "Gabriel de Witt's a dear, isn't he? I know he seems a bit dry at first, but he's adorable when you get to know him."

Christopher stared. *Dear* and *adorable* seemed to him the last words he would ever use to describe Gabriel de Witt.

Miss Rosalie did not see him stare. She was throwing open a door at the end of the corridor. "There," she said, rather proudly. "I hope you like it. We're not used to having children here, so we've all been racking our brains over how to make you feel at home."

There was not much sign of it, Christopher thought, staring round a large brown room with one high white bed looking rather lonely in one corner. "Thanks," he said glumly. When Miss Rosalie left him, he found there was a brown spartan washroom at the other end of the room and a shelf by the window. There was a teddy bear on the shelf, a game of Snakes and Ladders and a copy of *The Arabian Nights* with all the dirty bits taken out. He put them in a heap on the floor and jumped on them. He knew he was going to hate Chrestomanci Castle.

CHAPTER 11

For the first week, Christopher could think of nothing else but how much he hated Chrestomanci Castle and the people in it. It seemed to combine the worst things about school and home, with a few special awfulnesses of its own. It was very grand and very big, and except when he was doing lessons, Christopher was forced to wander about entirely on his own, missing Oneir and Fenning and the other boys and cricket acutely, while the Castle people got on with their grown-up affairs as if Christopher was not there at all. He had nearly all his meals alone in the schoolroom, just like home, except that the schoolroom looked out on to the empty, shaven Castle lawns.

"We thought you'd be happier not having to listen to our grown-up talk," Miss Rosalie told him as they walked up the long drive from church on Sunday. "But of course you'll have Sunday lunch with us."

So Christopher sat at the long table with everyone else in their sober Sunday clothes and thought it would have made no difference if he hadn't been there. Voices hummed among the chinking cutlery, and not one of them spoke to him.

"And you have to add copper to sublimate, whatever the manuals say," the bearded Dr. Simonson was telling Flavian Temple, "but after that you can, I find, put it straight to the pentacle with a modicum of fire."

"The Wraith's illegal dragons' blood is simply flooding the market now," said a young lady across the table. "Even the honest suppliers are not reporting it. They know they can evade taxes."

"But the correct words present problems," Dr. Simonson told Flavian.

"I know statistics are misleading," said a younger man beside Christopher, "but my latest sample had twice the legal limit of poison balm. You only have to extrapolate to see how much the gang is bringing in."

"The flaming tincture *must* then be passed through gold," Dr. Simonson proclaimed, and another voice cut across his saying, "That magic mushroom essence certainly came from Ten, but I think the trap we set there stopped that outlet." While Dr. Simonson added, "If you wish to proceed without copper, you'll find it far more complicated."

Miss Rosalie's voice rang through his explanation from the other end of the table. "But Gabriel, they had actually butchered a whole tribe of mermaids! I know it's partly our wizards' fault for being willing to pay the earth for mermaid parts, but the Wraith really has to be stopped!"

Gabriel's dry voice answered in the distance, "That part of the operation has been closed down. It's the weapons coming in from One that present the biggest problem."

"My advice is that you then start with pentacle and fire," Dr. Simonson droned on, "using the simpler form of words to start the process, but . . ."

Christopher sat silent, thinking that if he did get to be the next Chrestomanci he would forbid people to talk about their work at mealtimes. Ever. He was glad when he was allowed to get up from the table and go. But when he did, the only thing to do was to wander about, feeling all the spells on the place itching at him like gnat bites. There were spells in the formal gardens to keep weeds down and encourage worms, spells to keep the giant cedars on the lawns healthy, and spells all round the grounds to keep intruders out. Christopher thought he could have broken that set quite easily and simply run away, except that the sensitivity he had learned from Dr. Pawson showed him that breaking that boundary spell would set alarms ringing in the lodge at the gate and probably all over the Castle too.

The Castle itself had an old crusty part with turrets and a newer part which were fused together into a rambling whole. But there was an extra piece of castle that stood out in the gardens and looked even older, so old that there were trees growing on top of its broken walls. Christopher naturally wanted to explore this part, but there was a strong misdirection spell on it, which caused it to appear behind him, or to one side, whenever he tried to get to it. So he gave up and wandered indoors, where the spells, instead of itching, pressed down on him like a weight. He hated the Castle spells most of all. They would not allow him to be as angry as he felt. They made everything blunt and muffled. In order to express his hatred, Christopher fell back more and more on silent scorn. When people did speak to him, and he had to answer, he was as sarcastic as he knew how to be.

This did not help him get on with Flavian Temple. Flavian was a kind and earnest tutor. In the ordinary way, Christopher would have quite liked him, even though Flavian wore his collars too tight and tried far too hard to be hushed and dignified like the rest of Gabriel de Witt's people. But he hated Flavian for being one of those people—and he very soon discovered that Flavian had no sense of humor at all.

"You wouldn't see a joke if it jumped up and bit you, would you?" Christopher said, the second afternoon. Afternoons were always devoted to magic theory or magic practical.

"Oh, I don't know," Flavian said. "Something in *Punch* made me smile last week. Now, to get back to what we were saying—how many worlds do you think make up the Related Worlds?"

"Twelve," said Christopher, because he remembered that Tacroy sometimes called the Anywheres the Related Worlds.

"Very good!" said Flavian. "Though, actually, there are more than that, because each world is really a set of worlds, which we call a Series. The only one which is just a single world is Eleven, but we needn't bother with that. All the worlds were probably one world to begin with—and then something happened back in prehistory which could have ended in two contradictory ways. Let's say a continent blew up. Or it didn't blow up. The two things couldn't both be true at once in the same world, so that world became two worlds, side by side but quite separate, one with that continent and one without. And so on, until there were twelve."

Christopher listened to this with some interest, because he had always wondered how the Anywheres had come about. "And did the Series happen the same way?" he asked.

"Yes indeed," said Flavian, obviously thinking Christopher was a very good pupil. "Take Series Seven, which is a mountain Series. In prehistory, the earth's crust must have buckled many more times than it did here. Or Series Five, where all the land became islands, none of them larger than France. Now these are the same right across the Series, but the course of history in each world is different. It's history that makes the differences. The easiest example is our own Series, Twelve, where our world, which we call World A, is orientated on magic—which is normal for most worlds. But the next world, World B, split off in the Fourteenth Century and turned to science and machinery. The world beyond that, World C, split off in Roman times and became divided into large empires. And it went on like that up to nine. There are usually nine to a Series."

"Why are they numbered back to front?" Christopher asked.

"Because we *think* One was the original world of the twelve," Flavian said. "Anyway it was the Great Mages of One who first discovered the other worlds, and they did the numbering."

This was a much better explanation than the one Tacroy had given. Christopher felt obliged to Flavian for it. So that when Flavian asked, "Now what do you think makes us call these twelve the Related Worlds?" Christopher felt he owed him an answer.

"They all speak the same languages," he said.

"*Very* good!" said Flavian. His pale face went pink with surprise and pleasure. "You *are* a good pupil!"

"Oh, I'm absolutely brilliant," Christopher said bitterly.

Unfortunately, when Flavian turned to practical magic on alternate afternoons, Christopher was anything but brilliant. With Dr. Pawson he had become used to spells that really did something. But with Flavian he went back to small elementary magics of the kind he had been doing at school. They bored Christopher stiff. He yawned and he spilled things and usually, keeping a special vague look on his face so that Flavian would not notice what he was doing, he made the spells work without going through more than half the steps.

"Oh no," Flavian said anxiously, when he did notice. "That's enchanter's magic. We'll be starting on that in a couple of weeks. But you have to know basic witchcraft first. It's most important for you to know whether a witch or wizard is misusing the craft when you come to be the next Chrestomanci."

That was the trouble with Flavian. He was always saying, "When you come to be the next Chrestomanci." Christopher felt bitterly angry. "Is Gabriel de Witt going to die soon?" he said.

"I don't imagine so. He still has eight lives left," said Flavian. "Why do you ask?"

"It was a whim," Christopher said, thinking angrily of Papa.

"Oh dear," Flavian said, worrying because he was failing to keep his pupil interested. "I know—we'll go out into the gardens and study the properties of herbs. You may like that part of witchcraft better."

Down into the gardens they went, into a raw gray day. It was one of those summers that was more like winter than many winters are. Flavian stopped under a huge cedar and invited Christopher to consider the ancient lore about cedarwood. Christopher was in fact quite interested to hear that cedar was part of the funeral pyre from which the Phoenix was reborn, but he was not going to let Flavian see he was. As Flavian talked, his eye fell on the separate ruined piece of castle, and he knew that if he asked about that Flavian would only tell him that they would be doing misdirection spells next month—which put another thing he wanted to know into his mind.

"When am I going to learn how to fasten a person's feet to the spot?" he asked.

Flavian gave him a sideways look. "We won't be doing magic that affects other people until next year," he said. "Come over to the laurel bushes now and let's consider those."

Christopher sighed as he followed Flavian over to the big laurels by the drive. He might have known Flavian was not going to teach him anything useful! As they approached the nearest bush, a ginger cat emerged from among the shiny leaves, stretching and glaring irritably. When it saw Flavian and Christopher, it advanced on them at a trot, purpose all over its savage, lop-eared face.

"Look out!" Flavian said urgently.

Christopher did not need telling. He knew what this particular cat could do. But he was so astonished at seeing Throgmorten here at Chrestomanci Castle that he forgot to move. "Who—whose cat is that?" he said.

Throgmorten recognized Christopher too. His tail went up, thinner and more snaky than ever, and he stopped and stared. "Wong?" he said incredulously. And he advanced again, but in a much more stately way, like a Prime Minister greeting a foreign President. "Wong," he said.

"Careful!" said Flavian, prudently backing behind Christopher. "It's an Asheth Temple cat. It's safest not to go near it."

Christopher of course knew that, but Throgmorten was so evidently meaning to be polite that he risked squatting down and cautiously holding out his hand. "Yes, wong to you too," he said. Throgmorten put forward his moth-eaten-looking orange nose and dabbed at Christopher's hand with it.

"Great heavens! The thing actually likes you!" said Flavian. "Nobody else dares get within yards of it. Gabriel's had to give all the outdoor staff special shielding spells or they said they'd leave. It tears strips off people through ordinary spells."

"How did it get here?" Christopher said, letting Throgmorten politely investigate his hand.

"Nobody knows—at least not how it wandered in here from Series Ten," Flavian said. "Mordecai found it in London, brave man, and brought it here in a basket. He recognized it by its aura, and he said if *he* could, then most wizards would, too, and they'd kill it for its magical properties. Most of us think that wouldn't be much loss, but Gabriel agreed with Mordecai."

Christopher had still not learned the names of all the sober-suited men round the Sunday lunch-table. "Which one is Mr. Mordecai?" he said.

"Mordecai Roberts—he's a particular friend of mine, but you won't have met him yet," said Flavian. "He works for us in London these days. Perhaps we could get on with herb lore now."

At that moment, a strange noise broke from Throgmorten's throat, a sound like wooden cogwheels not connecting very well. Throgmorten was purring. Christopher was unexpectedly touched. "Does he have a name?" he asked.

"Most people just call him That Thing," said Flavian.

"I shall call him Throgmorten," said Christopher, at which Throgmorten's cogwheels went round more noisily than ever.

"It suits him," said Flavian. "Now, please—consider this laurel."

With Throgmorten sauntering amiably beside him, Christopher heard all about laurels and found it all much easier to take. It amused him the way Flavian took care to keep well out of reach of Throgmorten.

From then on, in a standoffish way, Throgmorten became Christopher's only friend in the Castle. They both seemed to have the same opinion of the people in it. Christopher once saw Throgmorten encounter Gabriel de Witt coming down the pink marble stairs. Throgmorten spat and flew at Gabriel's long thin legs, and Christopher was charmed and delighted at the speed with which those long thin legs raced up the stairs again to get away.

Christopher hated Gabriel more every time he had a lesson with him. He decided that the reason Gabriel's room always seemed so dark in spite of all its windows was because it reflected Gabriel's personality. Gabriel never laughed. He had no patience with slowness, or mistakes, and he seemed to think Christopher ought to know everything he taught him at once, by instinct. The trouble was that, the first week, when Flavian and Gabriel were teaching him about the Related Worlds, Christopher *had* known all about them, from the Anywheres, and this seemed to have given Gabriel the idea that Christopher was a good learner. But after that, they went on to the different kinds of magics, and Christopher just could not seem to get it through his head why witchcraft and enchanters' magic were not the same, or how wizardry differed from sorcery and both from magicians' magic.

It was always a great relief to Christopher when his lesson with Gabriel was over. Afterwards, Christopher usually sneaked Throgmorten indoors and the two of them explored the Castle together. Throgmorten was not allowed inside the Castle, which was why Christopher liked to have him there. Once or twice, with luck and cunning from both of them, Throgmorten spent the night on the end of Christopher's bed, purring like a football rattle. But Miss Rosalie had a way of knowing where Throgmorten was. She nearly always arrived wearing gardening gloves and chased Throgmorten out with a broom. Luckily Miss Rosalie was often busy straight after lessons, so Throgmorten galloped beside Christopher down the long corridors and through the rambling attics, thrusting his face into odd corners and remarking "Wong!" from time to time.

The Castle was huge. The weighty, baffling spells hung heavily over most of it, but there were parts that nobody used where the spells seemed to have worn thin. Christopher and Throgmorten were both happiest in those parts. The third week, they discovered a big round room in a tower, which looked to have been a wizard's workshop at one time. It had shelves round the walls, three long workbenches, and a pentagram painted on the stone floor. But it was deserted and dusty and stuffy with the smell of old, old magic.

"Wong," Throgmorten said happily.

"Yes," Christopher agreed. It seemed a waste of a good room. When I'm the next Chrestomanci, he thought, I shall make sure this room is used. Then he was angry with himself, because he was not going to *be* the next Chrestomanci. He had caught the habit from Flavian. But I could make this a secret workshop of my own, he thought. I could sneak stuff up here bit by bit.

The next day, he and Throgmorten went exploring for a new attic where there might be things Christopher could use to furnish the tower room. And they discovered a second tower up a second, smaller winding stair. The spells were worn away almost entirely here, because this tower was ruinous. It was smaller than the other tower room and half its roof was missing. Half the floor was wet with that afternoon's rain. Beyond that there was what had once been a mullioned window. It was now a slope of wet rubbly wall with one stone pillar standing out of it.

"Wong wong!" Throgmorten uttered approvingly. He went trotting over the wet floor and jumped up on to the broken wall.

Christopher followed him eagerly. They both climbed out on to the slope of rubble beyond what was left of the window and looked down at the smooth lawn and the tops of the cedar trees. Christopher caught a glimpse of the separate piece of castle with the misdirection spell on it. It was almost out of sight beyond the knobby stonework of the tower, but he thought he should be high enough to see into it over the trees growing on top of it. Holding on to the pillar that had been part of the window, he stepped further out on the broken slope and leaned right out to see.

The pillar snapped in half.

Christopher's feet shot forward on the slippery stones. He felt himself plunge through the air and saw the cedars rushing past upside down. Bother! he thought. Another life! He remembered that the ground stopped him with a terrible jolt. And he had a vague notion that Throgmorten somehow followed him down and then proceeded to make an appalling noise.

CHAPTER 12

They said he had broken his neck this time. Miss Rosalie told him that the spells on the Castle should have stopped him falling, or at least alerted people when he did fall. But as the spells were worn out there, it had been Throgmorten's howls that had fetched a horrified gardener. Because of this, Throgmorten was respectfully allowed to spend that night on the end of Christopher's bed, until the maids complained of the smell in the morning. Then Miss Rosalie appeared with her gardening gloves and her broom and chased Throgmorten out.

Christopher thought resentfully that there was very little difference between the way the Castle people treated Throgmorten and the way they treated him. The bearded Dr. Simonson, when he was not instructing everyone how to put tinctures to fire, turned out to be a medical magician. He came the following morning and, in an off-handed disapproving way, examined Christopher's neck.

"As I thought," he said. "Now the new life has taken over there is no sign of the break. Better stay in bed today because of the shock. Gabriel is going to want to talk to you about this escapade."

Then he went away and nobody else came near Christopher apart from maids with trays, except Flavian, who came and stood in the doorway sniffing cautiously at the strong odor Throgmorten had left in the room.

"It's all right," Christopher said. "Miss Rosalie's just chased him out."

"Good," said Flavian and he came over to Christopher's bed carrying a big armful of books.

"Oh wonderful!" Christopher said, eyeing the armful. "Lots of lovely work. I've been lying here itching to get on with some algebra!"

Flavian looked a little injured. "Well, no," he said. "These are things from the Castle library that I thought you might like." And he went away.

Christopher looked through the books and found they were all stories from different parts of the world. Some were from different worlds. All of them looked pretty good. Christopher had not realized there was anything worth reading in the Castle library before, and as he settled down to read, he decided he would go and have a look for himself tomorrow.

But the smell of Throgmorten interrupted him. The combination of the smell and the books kept reminding him of the Goddess, and he kept remembering that he still had not paid for a hundredth part of Throgmorten. It took him quite an effort to forget about Series Ten and concentrate on his book, and as soon as he did, Miss Rosalie came in, flushed and breathless from a long pursuit of Throgmorten, and interrupted him again.

"Gabriel wants to see you about that fall," she said. "You're to go to his office at nine o'clock tomorrow." As she turned to go, she said, "I see you've got some books. Is there anything else I can get you? Games? You've got Snakes and Ladders, haven't you?"

"It takes two to play that," Christopher told her pointedly.

"Oh dear," Miss Rosalie said. "I'm afraid I don't know much about games." Then she went away again.

Christopher laid his book down and stared round his brown empty room, hating the Castle and all the people in it quite passionately. The room now had his school trunk in one corner, which made it seem emptier than ever by reminding him of all the company he was missing at school. There was an ideal corner for getting to the Anywheres between the trunk and the bare fireplace. He wished he could run away to somewhere even magic could not find him, and never come back.

Then he realized that he *could* get away, after a fashion, by going to an Anywhere. He wondered why he had not tried all the time he had been at the Castle. He put it down to the Castle spells. They muffled your mind so. But now, either the shock of breaking his neck, or the new life he could feel sturdily and healthily inside him, or both, had started him thinking again. Perhaps he could go to an Anywhere and stay there for good.

The trouble was, when he went to the Anywheres, he seemed to have to leave a piece of himself behind in bed. But it *must* be possible to take the whole of yourself. From the things Flavian and Gabriel had said when they talked about the Related Worlds, Christopher was sure that some people did go to worlds in the other Series. He would just have to wait and learn how it was done. Meanwhile, there was nothing to stop him looking round for a suitable Anywhere to escape to.

Christopher read his books innocently until the maid came and turned out his gaslight for the night. Then he lay staring into the dark, trying to detach the part of himself that could go to the Anywheres. For quite a while, he could not do it. The Castle spell lay heavy on him, squashing all the parts of him into a whole. Then, as he got sleepier, he realized the way, and slipped out sideways from himself and went padding round the corner between the trunk and the fireplace.

There, it was like walking into a sheet of thick rubber that bounced him back into the room. The Castle spells again. Christopher set his teeth, turned his shoulder into the rubberiness, and pushed. And pushed, and pushed, and walked forward a little with each push, but quietly and gently, not to alert anyone in the Castle—until, after about half an hour, he had the spell stretched as thin as it would go. Then he took a pinch of it in each hand and tore it gently apart.

It was wonderful to walk out through the split he had made, into the valley and find his clothes still lying there, a little damp and too small again, but *there*. He put them on. Then, instead of going into The Place Between, he set off the other way, down the valley. It stood to reason that the valley led to one of the other worlds in Series Twelve. Christopher hoped it would be World B. One of his cunning ideas had been to hide quite near in the non-magical world, where he was sure no one, even Gabriel de Witt, would think of looking.

Probably it was World B, but he only stayed there half a minute. When he got to the end of the valley it was raining, pouring—souping down steadily sideways. Christopher found himself in a city full of rushing machines, speeding all round him on wheels that hissed on the wet black road. A loud noise made him look round just in time to see a huge red machine charging down on him out of the white curtain of rain. He saw a number on it and the words TUFNELL PARK, and sheets of water flew over him as he got frantically out of its way.

Christopher escaped up the valley again, soaking wet. World B was the worst Anywhere he had ever been in. But he still had his other cunning idea, and that was to go to Series Eleven, the world nobody ever went to. He went up the valley and round the jutting rock into The Place Between.

The Place was so desolate, so shapeless and so empty, that if he had not just been somewhere even more terrible he might have turned back. As it was, Christopher felt the same lonely horror he had felt the first time he had gone to The Place Between from school. But he ignored it and set off resolutely in the direction of the Anywhere that did not want you to get to it. He was sure now that this must be Eleven.

The way was across the mouth of his own valley, down, and then up a cliff of sheer slippery rock. Christopher had to cling with fingers and toes that were already cold and wet from World B. The Anywhere above kept pushing him away and the wind sweeping across reminded him of Mama's attack in Cambridge. Up, cling. Feel for a foothold. Then a handhold. Cling. Up.

Halfway up his foot slipped. A new gust of wind made his cold fingers too weak to hang on, and he fell.

He pitched down further than he had climbed up, upside down on to the back of his head. When he got to his knees, things in his neck grated and his head wobbled about. It felt very queer.

Somehow he made it back to the jutting crag, helped by the way The Place Between always pushed him back where he came from. Somehow he put his pajamas on again and got through the slit in the Castle spells, back into bed. He fell asleep with a strong suspicion that he had broken his neck again. Good, he thought. Now I won't have to go and see Gabriel de Witt in the morning.

But there was nothing at all wrong with him when he woke up. Christopher would have been very puzzled had he not been dreading seeing Gabricl. Hc crawled along to breakfast and found there was a pretty, scented letter from Mama on his tray. Christopher picked it up eagerly, hoping it would take his mind off Gabriel. And it did not, or not straight away. He could tell it had been opened and then stuck down again. He could feel the spell still hanging about it. Hating the people in the Castle more than ever, he unfolded the letter.

Dear Christopher,

The laws are so unjust. Only your Papa's signature was required to sell you into slavery with that dreadful old man, and I have still not forgiven your Papa. Your Uncle sends his sympathies and hopes to hear from you by next Thursday. Be polite to him, dear.

Your affectionate
Mama

Christopher was very pleased to think that Gabriel had read himself being called "that dreadful old man" and he was impressed at the cunning way Uncle Ralph had sent his message through Mama. As he ate his breakfast, he rejoiced at the thought of seeing Tacroy again next

Thursday. What a lucky thing he had made that split in the Castle spells! And "slavery" was the right word for it, he thought, as he got up to go to Gabriel's office.

But on the way, he found himself thinking of the Goddess again, very guiltily this time. He really would have to take her some more books. Throgmorten was a cat worth paying for.

In his twilight room, Gabriel stood up behind his great black desk. That was a bad sign, but Christopher now had so many other things to think of that he was not as scared as he might have been. "Really, Christopher," Gabriel said in his driest voice, "a boy your age should know better than to climb about in a ruined tower. The result is that you have foolishly and carelessly wasted a life and now have only six left. You will need those lives when you are the next Chrestomanci. What have you to say for yourself?"

Christopher's anger rose. He felt it being pushed down again by the Castle spells, and that made him angrier than ever. "Why don't you make Throgmorten the next Chrestomanci?" he said. "He's got nine lives too."

Gabriel stared at him a second. "This is not a matter for jokes," he said. "Do you not realize the trouble you have caused? Some of my staff will have to go to the towers, and to the attics and cellars, in case you take it into your head to climb about there, too, and it will take them days to make it all safe." At this, Christopher thought ruefully that they would certainly find and mend the split he had made and he would have to make another. "Please attend," said Gabriel. "I can ill spare any of my staff at this time. You are too young to be aware of this, but I wish to explain that we are all working full stretch just now in an effort to catch a gang of interworld villains." He looked at Christopher fiercely. "You have probably never heard of the Wraith."

After three boring Sunday lunches, Christopher felt he knew all about the Wraith. It was what everyone talked of all the time. But he sensed that Gabriel was quite likely to get sidetracked from telling him off if he went on explaining about the gang, so he said, "No, I haven't, sir."

"The Wraith is a gang of smugglers," Gabriel said. "We know they operate through London, but that is about all we know, for they are slippery as eels. In some way, despite all our traps and watchfulness, they smuggle in illicit magical produce by the hundredweight from all over the Related Worlds. They have brought in cartloads of dragons' blood, narcotic dew, magic mushrooms, eel livers from Series Two, poison balm from Six, dream juice from Nine and eternal fire from Ten. We set a trap in Ten, which took out at least one of their operatives, but that did not stop them. The only success we have had is in Series Five, where the Wraith was butchering mermaids and selling the parts in London. There we were helped by the local police and were able to put a stop to it. But—" By this time, Gabriel had his eyes fixed on the sunset light of his ceiling and seemed lost in his worries. "But this year," he said, "we have had reports of the most appalling weapons that the Wraith is bringing in from Series One, each one capable of destroying the strongest enchanter, and we still cannot lay hands on the gang." Here, to Christopher's dismay, Gabriel turned his eyes down to him. "You see what mischief your careless climbing could do? While we rush round the Castle on your account, we could miss our one chance of catching this gang. You should learn to think of others, Christopher."

"I do," Christopher said bitterly, "but none of you think of me. When most people die, they don't get told off for it."

"Go down to the library," said Gabriel, "and write one hundred times 'I must look before I leap.' And kindly shut the door when you leave."

Christopher went to the door and opened it, but he did not shut it. He left it swinging so that Gabriel would hear what he said as he went towards the pink marble staircase. "I must be the only person in the *world*," he called out, "EVER to be punished for breaking my neck!"

"Wong," agreed Throgmorten, who was waiting for him on the landing.

Christopher did not see Throgmorten in time. He tripped over him and went crashing and sliding the whole way down the staircase. As he went, he could hear Throgmorten wailing again. Oh *no*! he thought.

When his next life took over, he was lying on his back near the pentacle in the hall, looking up into the glass dome. Almost the first thing he saw was the clock over the library, which said half past nine. It seemed as if every time he lost a life, the new one took over more quickly and easily than the last. The next thing he saw was everyone in the Castle, standing round him staring solemnly. Just like a funeral! he thought.

"Did I break my neck again?" he asked.

"You did," said Gabriel de Witt, stepping up to lean over him. "Really, after what I had just said to you, it is too bad! Can you get up?"

Christopher turned over and got to his knees. He felt slightly bruised but otherwise all right. Dr. Simonson strode over and felt his neck. "The fracture has vanished already," he said. Christopher could tell from his manner that he was not going to be allowed to stay in bed this time.

"Very well," said Gabriel. "Go to the library now, Christopher, and write the lines I gave you. In addition write one hundred times 'I have only five lives remaining.' That might teach you prudence."

Christopher limped to the library and wrote the lines at one of the red leather tables on paper headed *Government Property.* As he wrote, his mind was elsewhere, thinking how odd it was that Throgmorten always seemed to be there when he lost a life. And there was that time in Series Ten. Just before the hook hit him, a man had mentioned Asheth. Christopher began to be afraid he might be under a curse from Asheth. It made another very good reason for taking the Goddess some more books.

When the lines were done, Christopher got up and inspected the bookshelves. The library was large and lofty and seemed to contain thousands of books. But Christopher discovered that there were really ten times as many as the ones you saw. There was a spell-plate at the end of each shelf. When Christopher put his hand on one, the books at the right of the shelf moved up and vanished and new books appeared on the left. Christopher found the storybook section and stood with his hand on the plate, keeping the line of books slowly moving until he found the kind he wanted.

It was a long row of fat books by someone called Angela Brazil. Most of them had *School* in the title. Christopher knew at a glance they were just right for the Goddess. He took three and spread the others out. Each of them was labelled *Rare Book: Imported from World XIIB,* which made Christopher hope that they might just be valuable enough to pay for Throgmorten at last.

He carried the books up to his room in a pile of others he thought he might like to read himself, and it seemed just his luck that he had to meet Flavian in the corridor. "Lessons as usual this afternoon," Flavian said cheerfully. "Dr. Simonson doesn't seem to think they'll harm you."

"Slavery as usual!" Christopher muttered as he went into his room.

But in fact that afternoon was not so bad. In the middle of practical magic, Flavian said suddenly, "Are you interested in cricket at all?"

What a question! Christopher felt his face light up even while he was answering coolly, "No, I'm only passionate about it. Why?"

"Good," said Flavian. "The Castle plays the village on Saturday, down on the village green. We thought you might like to work the scoreboard for us."

"Only if someone takes me out through the gate," Christopher said acidly. "The spell stops me going through on my own. Otherwise, yes—like a shot."

"Oh Lord! I should have got you a pass!" Flavian said. "I didn't realize you liked to go out. I go on long hikes all the time. I'll take you with me next time I go—there are all sorts of outdoor practicals we can do—only I think you'd better master witch sight first."

Christopher saw that Flavian was trying to bribe him. They were on enchanter's magic now. Christopher had had no trouble learning how to conjure things from one place to another—it was a little like the levitation he had worked so spectacularly for Dr. Pawson, and not unlike raising a wind, too—and he had learned with only a little more difficulty how to make things invisible. He thought he would not have too much trouble conjuring fire, either, as soon as Flavian allowed him to try. But he could not get the hang of witch sight. It was quite simple, Flavian kept telling him. It was only making yourself see through a magical disguise to what was really there. But when Flavian put an illusion spell on his right hand and held that hand out as a lion's paw, a lion's paw was all Christopher could see.

Flavian did it over and over again. Christopher yawned and looked vague and kept seeing a lion's paw. The only good thing was that while his mind wandered he hit on the perfect way to keep those books for the Goddess dry in The Place Between.

CHAPTER 13

That night Christopher went round the corner between his trunk and the fireplace all prepared to tear a new split in the Castle spells. To his surprise, the split was still there. It looked as though the Castle people had no idea he had made it. Very gently, not to disturb it, he tore two long strips off it, one wide and one narrow. Then, with a vague shimmering piece of spell in each hand, he went back to the books and wrapped them in the wide piece. The narrow piece he used like string to tie the parcel up, leaving a loose length to tie to his belt. When he spat on the parcel, the spit rolled off it in little round balls. Good.

Then it was like old times, climbing across the rocks the well-known way, in clothes that had got even shorter and tighter since yesterday night. It did not worry Christopher at all that he had fallen last time. He knew this way too well. And again like old times, the old men were still charming snakes in front of the city walls. They must do it for religion or something, Christopher supposed, because they did not seem to want money for it. Inside the gates, the city was still the same loud smelly place, full of goats and umbrellas, and the small shrines at the street corners were still surrounded with offerings. The only difference was that it did not seem quite so hot here as last time, though it was still plenty hot enough for someone who had just come from an English summer.

Yet, oddly enough, Christopher was not comfortable here. He was not frightened of people throwing spears. It was because, after the hushed dignity and dark clothes at the Castle, this city made every nerve he had jangle. He had a headache long before he got to the Temple of Asheth. It made him need to rest a bit among the latest pile of old cabbages in the alley, before he could muster the inclination to push his way through the wall and the creepers. The cats were still sunning themselves in the yard. No one was about.

The Goddess was in a room further along from her usual one. She was on a big white cushion that was probably a bed, with more white cushions to prop her up and a shawl over her in spite of the heat. She had grown too, though not as much as Christopher. But he thought she might be ill. She was lying there, staring into nothing, and her face was not as round as he remembered, and a good deal paler.

"Oh thanks," she said, as if she was thinking of something else, when Christopher dumped the parcel of books on her shawl. "I've nothing to swop."

"I'm still paying for Throgmorten," Christopher said.

"Was he that valuable?" the Goddess said listlessly. In a slow, lackluster way she began stripping the spell off the books. Christopher was interested to see that she had no more trouble tearing it than he had. Being the Living Asheth obviously meant you were given strong magic. "These look like good books," the Goddess said politely. "I'll read them—when I can concentrate."

"You're ill, aren't you?" said Christopher. "What have you got?"

"Not germs," the Goddess said weakly. "It's the Festival. It was three days ago. You know it's the one day in the year when I go out, don't you? After months and months all quiet and dark here in the Temple, there I am suddenly out in the sun, riding in a cart, dressed in huge heavy clothes and hung with jewels, with my face covered with paint. Everyone shouts. And they all jump up on the cart and try to touch me—for luck, you know, and not as if I was a person." Tears began slowly rolling down her face. "I don't think they notice I'm alive. And it goes on all day, the shouting and the sun and hands banging at me until I'm bruised all over." The tears rolled faster. "It used to be exciting when I was small," she said. "But now it's too much."

The Goddess's white cat came galloping into the room and jumped possessively onto her lap. The Goddess stroked it weakly. Like Throgmorten sitting on my bed, Christopher thought. Temple cats know when their people are upset. He thought he could understand a little, after his own feelings in the city just now, the way the Festival had felt to the Goddess.

"I think it's being inside all year and then suddenly going out," the Goddess explained as she stroked Bethi.

Christopher had meant to ask if it was the curse of Asheth that kept killing him all the time, but he could see this was not the moment. The Goddess needed her mind taken off Asheth. He sat down on the tiles beside her cushions. "It was clever of you to see that silver stopped me doing magic," he said. "I didn't know myself—not until Papa took me to Dr. Pawson." Then he told her about the levitation spell.

The Goddess smiled. When he told her about old Mrs. Pawson and the chamber pot, she turned her face to him and almost laughed. It was obviously doing her so much good that he went on and told her about the Castle and Gabriel de Witt, and even managed to make that funny too. When he told her about the way he kept seeing a lion's paw, he had her in fits of laughter.

"But that's stupid of you!" she chuckled. "When there are things I can't do for Mother Proudfoot, I just pretend I can. Just say you can see his hand. He'll believe you."

"I never thought of that," Christopher confessed.

"No, you're too honest," she said, and looked at him closely. "Silver forces you to tell the truth," she said. "The Gift of Asheth tells me. So you got into the habit of never lying." Mentioning Asheth sobered her up. "Thank you for telling me about yourself," she said seriously. "I think you've had a *rotten* life, even worse than mine!" Quite suddenly she was crying again. "People only want either of us for what *use* we are to them!" she sobbed. "You for your nine lives and me for my Goddess attributes. And both of us are caught and stuck and *trapped* in a life with a future all planned out by someone else—like a long, long tunnel with no way *out*!"

Christopher was a little astonished at this way of putting things, even though his anger at being forced to be the next Chrestomanci certainly made him feel trapped most of the time. But he saw the Goddess was mostly talking about herself. "You stop being the Living Asheth when you grow up," he pointed out.

"*Oh*, I do so want to stop!" the Goddess wept. "I want to stop being her *now*! I want to go to school, like Millie in the *Millie* books. I want to do Prep and eat stodge and learn French and play hockey and write lines—"

"You wouldn't want to write lines," Christopher said, quite anxious at how emotional she was getting. "Honestly, you wouldn't."

"Yes I *do*!" screamed the Goddess. "I want to cheek the Prefects and cheat in Geography tests and sneak on my friends! I want to be *bad* as well as good! I want to go to school and be *bad*, do you hear!"

By this time she was kneeling up on her cushion, with tears pouring off her face into the white cat's fur, making more noise than Throgmorten had when Christopher ran through the Temple with him in the basket. It was not surprising that somebody in sandals came hurrying and stumbling through the rooms beyond, calling breathlessly, "Goddess *dear*! Goddess! What's wrong, love?"

Christopher spun himself round and dived through the nearest wall without bothering to get up first. He came out face down in the hot yard full of cats. There he picked himself up and sprinted for the outside wall. After that, he did not stop running until he reached the city gate. Girls! he thought. They really were a Complete Mystery. Fancy *wanting* to write lines!

Nevertheless, as he went up the valley and climbed through The Place Between, Christopher found himself thinking seriously about some of the things the Goddess had said. His life did indeed seem to be a long tunnel planned out by somebody else. And the reason he hated everyone so at the Castle was that he was just a Thing to them, a useful Thing with nine lives that was going to be molded into the next Chrestomanci some day. He thought he would tell Tacroy that. Tacroy would understand. Tomorrow was Thursday, and he could see Tacroy. He thought he had never looked forward to a Thursday more.

And he knew how to pretend he had witch sight now. The next afternoon, when Flavian held out a lion's paw to him, Christopher said, "It's your hand. I can see it now."

Flavian was delighted. "Then we'll go on a nice long hike tomorrow," he said.

Christopher was not altogether sure he was looking forward to that. But he could hardly wait to see Tacroy again. Tacroy was the only person he knew who did not treat him as a useful Thing. He scrambled out of bed almost as soon as he was in it and shot through the slit in the spells, hoping Tacroy would realize and be early.

Tacroy was there, leaning against the crag at the end of the valley with his arms folded, looking as if he was resigned to a long wait. "Hallo!" he said, and sounded quite surprised to see Christopher at all.

Christopher realized that it was not going to be as easy as he had thought to pour out his troubles to Tacroy, but he beamed at Tacroy as he started scrambling into his clothes. "It's good to see you again," he said. "There's no end of things to tell you. Where are we going tonight?"

Tacroy said in a careful sort of way, "The horseless carriage is waiting in Eight. Are you sure you want to go?"

"Of course," Christopher said, doing up his belt.

"You can tell me your news just as well here," Tacroy said.

This was off-putting. Christopher looked up and saw that Tacroy was unusually serious. His eyes were crinkled up unsmilingly. This made it too awkward to start telling Tacroy anything. "What's the matter?" he asked.

Tacroy shrugged. "Well," he said, "for a start, the last time I saw you, your head was bashed in—"

Christopher had forgotten that. "Oh, I never thanked you for getting me back here!" he said.

"Think nothing of it," said Tacroy. "Though I must say it was the hardest thing I've ever done in any line of work, keeping myself firm enough to bring the carriage through the interworld and heave you off here. I kept wondering why I was doing it too. You looked pretty thoroughly dead to me."

"I've got nine lives," Christopher explained.

"You've obviously got more than one," Tacroy agreed, grinning as if he did not really believe it. "Look, didn't that accident make you think? Your uncle's done hundreds of these experiments by now. We've fetched him a mass of results. It's all right for me—I get paid. But there's nothing in it for you that I can see, except the danger of getting hurt again."

Tacroy truly meant this, Christopher could see. "I don't mind," he protested. "Honestly. And Uncle Ralph did give me two sovereigns."

At this Tacroy threw back his curly head and laughed. "Two sovereigns! Some of the things we got him were worth hundreds of pounds—like that Asheth Temple cat, for instance."

"I know," Christopher said, "but I want to keep on with the experiments. The way things are now, it's the only pleasure I have in life." There, he thought. Now Tacroy will have to ask about my troubles.

But Tacroy only sighed. "Let's get going then."

It was not possible to talk to Tacroy in The Place Between. While Christopher climbed and slithered and panted, Tacroy was a floating nebulous ghost nearby, drifting in the wind, with rain beating through him. He did not firm up until the opening of the valley where Christopher had long ago written a large 8 in the mud of the path. The 8 was still there, as if it had been written yesterday. Beyond it the carriage floated. It had been improved again and was now painted a smart duck-egg blue.

"All set, I see," Tacroy said. They climbed down and picked up the guide ropes of the carriage. It immediately started to follow them smoothly down the valley. "How's the cricket?" Tacroy asked in a social sort of way.

Now was Christopher's chance to tell him things. "I haven't played," he said gloomily, "since Papa took me away from school. Up till yesterday, I didn't think they'd even heard of cricket at the Castle—you know I'm living at the Castle now?"

"No," said Tacroy. "Your uncle never has told me much about you. Which castle is this?"

"Chrestomanci Castle," said Christopher. "But yesterday my tutor said there was a match against the village this Saturday. Nobody dreams of asking me to play of course, but I get to work the scoreboard for it."

"Do you indeed?" said Tacroy. His eyes screwed into wrinkles.

"They don't know I'm here of course," Christopher said.

"I should just think they don't!" Tacroy said, and the way he said it seemed to stop the conversation dead. They walked on in front of the carriage without speaking, until they came to the long hillside with the farmhouse squatting in a dip halfway up it. The place looked bleaker and more lonely than ever, under a heavy gray sky that made the rolls of moor and hill seem yellowish. Before they reached the farm, Tacroy stopped and kicked the carriage out of the way when it nudged the back of his legs, trying to go on. His face was as bleak and yellowish and wrinkled as the moors. "Listen, Christopher," he said, "those folk at Chrestomanci Castle are not going to be pleased to find you've been here doing this."

Christopher laughed. "They aren't! But they're not going to find out!"

"Don't be too sure about that," Tacroy said. "They're experts in every kind of magic there."

"That's what makes it such a good revenge on them," Christopher explained. "Here I am slipping out from under their stupid stuffy boring noses, when they think they've got me. I'm just a Thing to them. They're using me."

The people at the farmhouse had seen them coming. A little group of women ran out into the yard and stood beside a heap of bundles. One waved. Christopher waved back and, since Tacroy did not seem to be as interested in his feelings as he had hoped, he set off up the hill. That started the carriage moving again.

Tacroy hurried to catch up. "Doesn't it occur to you," he said, "that your uncle may be using you too?"

"Not like the Castle people are," said Christopher. "I do these experiments of my own free will."

At this, Tacroy looked up at the low cloudy sky. "Don't say I didn't try!" he said to it.

The women breathed garlic over Christopher when they greeted him in the farmyard, just as they always did. As usual, that smell mixed with the smell from the bundles as he loaded them. The bundles always had this smell in Eight—a sharp, heady, coppery smell. Now, after the practical lessons he had had from Flavian, Christopher paused and sniffed it. He knew what the smell was. Dragons' blood! It surprised him, because this was the most dangerous and powerful ingredient of magic. He put the next bundle on the carriage much more carefully and as he gingerly picked up the next one, knowing some of the things it could do, he looked across at Tacroy to see if Tacroy knew what the bundles were. But Tacroy was leaning against the wall of the yard staring sadly up the hill. Tacroy said he never had much sense of smell when he was out of his body anyway.

As Christopher looked, Tacroy's eyes went wide and he jumped away from the wall. "I say!" he said.

One of the women yelled and pointed away up the hill. Christopher turned to see what was the matter, and stared, and went on staring in amazement, standing where he was with the bundle in his hands. A very large creature was on its way down towards the farm. It was a kind of purplish black. The moment Christopher first saw it, it was folding its great leathery wings and putting its clawed feet down to land, gliding down the hill so fast that he did not see at once how very large it was. While he was still thinking it was a house-sized animal halfway up the hill, it had landed just behind the farm, and he realized he could still see most of it towering up above the farmhouse.

"It's a dragon!" Tacroy shrieked. "Christopher, get *down*! Look *away*!"

Around Christopher, the women were running for the barns. One came running back, carrying a big heavy gun in both arms, which she tried frantically to wrestle up onto a tripod. She got it up and it fell down.

While she picked the gun up again, the dragon put its gigantic jagged black head down on the farm roof between the chimneys, crushing it in quite casually, and gazed at the farmyard with huge shining green eyes.

"It's huge!" Christopher said. He had never seen anything like it.

"*Down!*" Tacroy screamed at him.

The dragon's eyes met Christopher's, almost soulfully. Among the ruins and rafters of the farm roof, it opened its huge mouth. It was rather as if a door had opened into the heart of a sun. A white-orange prominence spouted from the sun, one strong accurate shaft of it, straight at Christopher. WHOOF. He was in a furnace. He heard his skin fry. During an instant of utter agony, he had time to think, Oh bother! Another hundred lines!

Tacroy's panting was the first thing Christopher heard, some time after that. He found Tacroy struggling to heave him off the charred bed of the horseless carriage onto the path. The carriage and Tacroy were wobbling about just beside Christopher's pajamas.

"It's all right," Christopher said, sitting up wincingly. His skin smarted all over. His clothes seemed to have been burned off him. The parts of him he could see were a raw pink and smirched with charcoal from the half-burned carriage. "Thanks," he gasped, because he could see that Tacroy had rescued him again.

"You're welcome," Tacroy panted. He was fading to a gray shadow of himself. But he put forth a great effort. His eyes closed and his mouth spread into a grin with it, all transparent, with the grass of the valley shining through his face. Then, for a second, he became clear and solid. He bent over Christopher. "This is *it*!" he said. "You're not going on these jaunts ever again. You drop it, see? You stop. You come out here again and I won't be here." By this time he was fading to gray, and then to milkiness beyond the gray. "I'll square your uncle," his voice whispered. Christopher had to guess that the last word was "uncle." Tacroy had faded out by then.

Christopher flopped off the carriage and that disappeared too, leaving nothing but the empty, peaceful valley and a strong scent of burning.

"But I don't *want* to drop it!" Christopher said. His voice sounded so dry and cracked that he could hardly hear it above the brawling of the stream in the valley. A couple of tears made smarting tracks down his face while he collected his pajamas and crawled back through the split in the spells.

CHAPTER 14

Again there was nothing wrong with Christopher when he woke up. He listened to Flavian that morning with a polite, vague look on his face while he marveled about that dragon. His marveling kept being interrupted by gusts of misery—he would never see Tacroy again!—and he had to work quite hard to keep thinking of the dragon instead. It was awesome. It was almost worth losing a life to have seen a sight like that. He wondered how long it would be before someone in the Castle noticed he had lost another life. And a small anxious part of him kept saying, But have I lost it—yet?

"I've ordered us a packed lunch," Flavian said cheerfully, "and the housekeeper's dug out an oilskin that should fit you. We'll be off on our hike just as soon as you've finished that French."

It was raining quite heavily. Christopher took his time over the French, hoping that Flavian would decide that it was too wet for walking. But when Christopher could not think of any further ways to spin out the history of the pen of his aunt, Flavian said, "A little soaking never did anyone any harm," and they set out into a strong drizzle a little after midday.

Flavian was very cheerful. Tramping in the wet, with thick socks and a knapsack, was obviously his idea of heaven. Christopher licked up the water that kept running off his nose from his hair and thought that at least he was out of the Castle. But if he had to be out in wind and wet, he would have preferred to be in The Place Between. That brought him back to Tacroy, and he had to struggle with gusts of misery again. He tried to think of the dragon, but it was too wet. While they tramped across several miles of heath, all Christopher could think of was how much he was going to miss Tacroy, and how the soaking gorse bushes looked just as desolate as he felt. He hoped they would stop for lunch soon so that he could think about something else.

They came to the edge of the heath. Flavian pointed in a breezy, open-air way to a hill that was gray with distance. "That's where we'll stop for lunch. In those woods on that hill there."

"It's miles away!" Christopher said, appalled.

"Only about five miles. We'll just drop down into the valley between and then climb up again," Flavian said, striding cheerfully down the hill.

Long before they reached that hill, Christopher had stopped thinking of Tacroy and could only think how cold and wet and tired and hungry he was. It seemed to him to be nearer teatime than lunchtime when he finally struggled after Flavian into a clearing in that far-distant wood.

"Now," said Flavian, tossing off the knapsack and rubbing his hands together. "We'll have some really practical magic. You're going to collect sticks and make a good pile of them. Then you can try your hand at conjuring fire. When you've got a good fire going, we can fry sausages on sticks and have lunch."

Christopher looked up at the boughs overhead, hung with huge transparent blobs of rain. He looked round at the soaking grass. He looked at Flavian to see if he was really meaning to be fiendish. No. Flavian just thought this way was fun. "The sticks will be wet," Christopher said. "The whole wood's dripping."

"Makes it more of a challenge," Flavian said.

Christopher saw there was no point in telling Flavian he was weak with hunger. He grimly collected sticks. He piled them in a soggy heap, which collapsed, so he built the heap again, and then knelt with cold rain soaking into his knees and trickling under his collar, to conjure fire. Ridiculous. He conjured a thin yellow spire of smoke. It lasted about a second. The sticks were not even warm from it.

"Plenty of will as you raise your hands," Flavian said.

"I *know,*" Christopher said and willed savagely. Fire! *Fire! FIRE!!*

The pile of sticks went up with a roar in a sheet of flame ten feet high. Christopher once more heard his skin fry, and his wet oilskin crackled and burst into flame too. He was part of a bonfire almost instantly. *This* is the life the dragon burned! he thought amid the agony.

When his fifth life took over, which seemed to be about ten minutes later, he heard Flavian saying hysterically, "Yes, I *know,* but it ought to have been perfectly *safe!* The wood is sopping wet. That's why I told him to try."

"Dr. Pawson rather suggested that very little is safe once Christopher gets going," a dry voice observed from further away.

Christopher rolled over. He was covered with Flavian's oilskin and, under it, his skin felt very new and soft. The ground in front of him was burned black, wet and smelly with rain. Overhead, the wet leaves on the trees were brown and curled. Gabriel de Witt was sitting on a folding stool some yards away, under a large black umbrella, looking annoyed and very much out of place. As Christopher saw him, the smoking grass beside the stool burst into little orange flames. Gabriel frowned at the flames. They shrank down into smoke again.

"Ah, you appear to have taken up the threads of life again," he said. "Kindly douse this forest fire of yours. It is uncommonly persistent and I do not wish to leave the countryside burning."

"Can I have something to eat first?" said Christopher. "I'm starving."

"Give him a sandwich," Gabriel said to Flavian. "I recall that when I lost my life, the new life required a great deal of energy as it took over." He waited until Flavian had passed Christopher a packet of egg sandwiches. While Christopher was wolfing them down, he said, "Flavian says he takes full responsibility for this latest stupidity. You may thank him that I am lenient with you. I will simply point out that you have caused me to be called away at the moment when we were about to lay hands on a member of the Wraith gang I told you of. If he slips through our fingers, it will be your fault, Christopher. Now please get up and extinguish the fire."

Christopher stood up in some relief. He had been afraid that Gabriel was going to forbid him to work the scoreboard for the cricket match tomorrow. "Dousing a fire is like conjuring in reverse," Flavian told him. So Christopher did that. It was easy, except that his relief about the cricket caused little spurts of flame to keep breaking out all round the clearing.

When even the smoke was gone, Gabriel said, "Now I warn you, Christopher—if you have one more accident, fatal or not, I shall take very severe steps indeed." Having said this, Gabriel stood up and folded his stool with a snap. With the stool tucked under his arm, he reached into the umbrella and started to take it down. As the umbrella folded, Christopher found himself, with Flavian beside him, in the middle of the pentacle in the Castle hall. Miss Rosalie was standing on the stairs.

"He got away, Gabriel," she said. "But at least we know how they're doing it now."

Gabriel turned and looked at Christopher, witheringly. "Take him to his room, Flavian," he said, "and then come back for a conference." He called out to Miss Rosalie, "Tell Frederick to prepare for a trance at once. I want the World Edge patrolled constantly from now on."

Christopher pattered off beside Flavian, shivering under the oilskin. Even his shoes had been burned. "You were a crisp!" Flavian told him. "I was terrified!" Christopher believed him. That dragon had crisped him thoroughly. He was absolutely sure now that if he lost a life in an Anywhere, it somehow did not count, and he had to lose that life properly in his own world, in a way that was as like the death in the Anywhere as possible. Moral, he thought: Be careful in the Anywheres in future. And while he was putting on more clothes he skipped about with relief that Gabriel had not forbidden him to go to the cricket match. But he was afraid the rain would stop the game anyway. It was still pouring.

The rain stopped in the night, though the weather was still gray and chilly. Christopher went down to the village green with the Castle team, which was a motley mixture of Castle sorcerers, a footman, a gardener, a stable lad, Dr. Simonson, Flavian, a young wizard who had come down from Oxford specially, and, to Christopher's great surprise, Miss Rosalie. Miss Rosalie looked pink and almost fetching in a white dress and white mittens. She tripped along in little white shoes, loudly bewailing the fact that the trap to catch the Wraith had gone wrong. "I told Gabriel all along that we'd have to patrol the World Edge," she said. "By the time they get the stuff to London there are too many places for them to hide."

Gabriel himself met them on the village green, carrying his folding stool in one hand and a telegram in the other. He was dressed for the occasion in a striped blazer that looked about a hundred years old and a wide Panama hat. "Bad news," he said. "Mordecai Roberts has dislocated his shoulder and is not coming."

"Oh no!" everyone exclaimed in the greatest dismay.

"And how typical!" Miss Rosalie added. She pounced round on Christopher. "Can you bat, dear? Enough to come in at the end if necessary?"

Christopher tried to keep a cool look on his face, but it was impossible. "I should hope so," he said.

The afternoon was pure bliss. One of the stable lads lent Christopher some rather large whites, which a sorcerer obligingly conjured down from the Castle for him, and he was sent to field on the boundary. The village batted first—and they made rather a lot of runs, because the missing Mordecai Roberts had been the Castle's best bowler. Christopher got very cold in the chilly wind, but like a dream come true, he took a catch out there to dismiss the blacksmith. All the rest of the Castle people, standing round the green in warm clothes, clapped furiously.

When the Castle began their innings, Christopher sat with the rest of the team waiting his turn—or rather, hoping that he would get a turn—and was fascinated to discover that Miss Rosalie was a fine and dashing batswoman. She hit balls all round the field in the way Christopher had always wanted to do. Unfortunately, the blacksmith turned out to be a demonically cunning spin bowler. He had all the tricks that Tacroy had so often described to Christopher. He got Dr. Simonson out for one run and the Oxford wizard out for two. After that the Castle team collapsed round Miss Rosalie. But Miss Rosalie kept at it, with her hair coming down on one shoulder and her face glowing with effort. She did so well that, when Flavian went out to bat at number ten, the Castle only needed two runs to win. Christopher buckled on his borrowed pads, fairly sure he would never get a chance to bat.

"You never know," said the Castle bootboy, who was working the scoreboard instead of Christopher. "Look at him. He's hopeless!"

Flavian *was* hopeless. Christopher had never seen anyone so bad. His bat either groped about like a blind man's stick or made wild swings in the wrong place. It was obvious he was going to be out any second. Christopher picked up his borrowed bat hopefully. And Miss Rosalie was out instead. The blacksmith clean bowled her. The village people packed round the green roared, knowing they had won. Amid the roars, Christopher stood up.

"Good luck!" said all the Castle people round him. The bootboy was the only one who said it as if he thought Christopher had a chance.

Christopher waded out to the middle of the green—the borrowed pads were two sizes too large—to the sound of shouts and catcalls. "Do your best, dear," Miss Rosalie said rather hopelessly as she passed him coming in. Christopher waded on, surprised to find that he was not in the least nervous.

As he took his guard, the village team licked its lips. They crowded in close round Christopher, crouching expectantly. Wherever he looked there were large horny hands spread out and brown faces wearing jeering grins.

"Oh, I say!" Flavian said at the other end. "He's only a boy!"

"We know," said the village captain, grinning even wider.

The blacksmith, equally contemptuous, bowled Christopher a slow, loopy ball. While Christopher was watching it arc up, he had time to remember every word of Tacroy's coaching. And since the entire village team was crowded round him in a ring, he knew he only had to get the ball past that ring to score runs. He watched the ball all the way on to the bat with perfect self-possession. It turned a little, but not much. He cracked it firmly away into the covers.

"Two!" he called crisply to Flavian.

Flavian gave him a startled look and ran. Christopher ran, with the borrowed pads going flurp, flurp, flurp at every stride. The village team turned and chased the ball frantically, but Flavian and Christopher had plenty of time to make two runs. They had time to have run three, even with the borrowed pads. The Castle had won. Christopher went warm with pride and joy.

The Castle watchers cheered. Gabriel congratulated him. The boot-boy shook his hand. Miss Rosalie, with her hair still trailing, banged him on the back. Everyone crowded round Christopher saying that they did not need Mordecai Roberts after all, and the sun came out behind the church tower for the first time that day. For that short time, Christopher felt that living in the Castle was not so bad after all.

But by Sunday lunchtime it was back to the usual ways. The talk at lunch was all about anxious schemes to catch the Wraith gang, except that Mr. Wilkinson, the elderly sorcerer who looked after the Castle library, kept saying, "Those three rare books are still missing. I cannot imagine who would wish to make away with three girls' books from World B, but I cannot detect them anywhere in the Castle." Since they were girls' books, Mr. Wilkinson obviously did not suspect Christopher. In fact, neither he nor anyone else remembered Christopher was there unless they wanted him to pass the salt.

On Monday, Christopher said acidly to Flavian, "Doesn't it occur to anyone that I could help catch the Wraith?" This was the nearest he had ever come to mentioning the Anywheres to Flavian. Sunday had driven him to it.

"For heaven's sake! People who can cut up mermaids would soon make short work of *you!*" Flavian said.

Christopher sighed. "Mermaids don't come to life again. I do," he pointed out.

"The whole Wraith thing makes me sick," Flavian said and changed the subject.

Christopher felt, more than ever, that he was in a tunnel with no way out. He was worse off than the Goddess, too, because she could stop being the Living Asheth when she grew up, while he had to go on and turn into someone like Gabriel de Witt. His feelings were not improved when, later that week, he had a letter from Papa. This one had been opened and sealed up also, but unlike the letter from Mama, it had the most interesting stamps. Papa was in Japan.

My son,

My spells assure me that a time of utmost danger is coming for you. I implore you to be careful and not to endanger your future.

Your loving
Papa

From the date on the letter, it had been written a month ago. "Bother my future!" Christopher said. "His spells probably mean the lives I've just lost." And the worst of it, he thought, going back to his misery, was that he could not look forward to seeing Tacroy any more.

All the same, that Thursday night, Christopher went out through the split in the spell, hoping Tacroy would be there. But the valley was empty. He stood there a moment feeling blank. Then he went back into his room, put on his clothes and set off through The Place Between to visit the Goddess again. She was the only other person he knew who did not try to make use of him.

CHAPTER 15

The Goddess was in her bedroom-place, sitting cross-legged on the white cushions with her chin on her fists, evidently brooding. Though she did not look ill any more, there was a new feeling about her, like thunder in the air, which Christopher rather wondered about as he came in.

The Goddess's jewelry went tunk as she looked up and saw him. "Oh good," she said. "I'd been hoping you'd come back soon. I've *got* to talk to you—you're the only person I know who'll understand."

"The same goes for me," Christopher said, and he sat down on the tiles with his back against the wall. "There's you shut up here with your Priestesses, and me shut up in the Castle with Gabriel's people. Both of us are in this tunnel—"

"But that's just my trouble," the Goddess interrupted. "I'm not sure there is a tunnel for me. Tunnels have ends, after all." Her voice filled with the new thunderous feeling as she said this. The white cat knew at once. It got up from among the cushions and climbed heavily into her lap.

"What do you mean?" Christopher asked, thinking once more that girls really were a Complete Mystery.

"Poor Bethi," the Goddess said, stroking the white cat with a rhythmic tink-tink of bracelets. "She's going to have kittens *again.* I wish she wouldn't keep *on* having them—it wears her out. What I meant is that I've been thinking of all sorts of things since I was ill. I've been thinking of you and wondering how you manage to keep coming here from another world. Isn't it difficult?"

"No, it's easy," said Christopher. "Or it is for me. I think it's because I've got several lives. What I think I do is leave one of them behind in bed and set the other ones loose to wander."

"The luck of it!" the Goddess said. "But I mean what do you do to get to this world?"

Christopher told her about the valley and The Place Between and how he always had to find a corner in the bedroom to go round.

The Goddess's eyes traveled reflectively round the dim archways of her room. "I wish *I* had more than one life," she said. "But with me—you remember how you said when you were here last that I'd stop being the Living Asheth when I grew up?"

"*You* told me that when I first came here," Christopher reminded her. "You said, 'The Living Asheth is always a little girl.' Don't you remember?"

"Yes, but nobody said it the way round that you did," the Goddess said. "It made me think. What happens to the Living Asheth when she *isn't* a little girl any longer? I'm not little now. I'm nearly the age when other people are officially women."

That must happen remarkably early in Series Ten, Christopher thought. He wished he was anything like officially a man. "Don't you get made into a Priestess?"

"No," said the Goddess. "I've listened and I've asked and read all their records—and *none* of the Priestesses were ever the Goddess." She began sticking the white cat's fur up in ridges between fingers that trembled slightly. "When I asked," she said, "Mother Proudfoot said I wasn't to bother my head because Asheth takes care of all that. What do you think that means?"

She seemed to Christopher to be getting all emotional again. "I think you just get shoved out of the Temple and go home," he said soothingly. The idea made him feel envious. "But you've got all your Asheth gifts. You must be able to use those to find out for certain."

"What do you think I've been *trying* to do?" the Goddess all but screamed. Her bracelets chanked as she tossed the unfortunate Bethi aside and bounded to her feet, glaring at Christopher. "You stupid boy! I've thought and *thought,* all this week, until my head *buzzes*!"

Christopher hurriedly got to his feet and pressed his back to the wall, ready to go through it at once if the Goddess went for him. But all she did was to jump up and down in front of him, screaming.

"Think of a way I can find out, if you're so clever! *Think of a WAY!*"

As always when the Goddess screamed, feet flapped in the rooms beyond and a breathless voice called, "I'm coming, Goddess! What is it?"

Christopher backed away into the wall, swiftly and gently. The Goddess flung him a brief look that seemed to be of triumph and went rushing into the arms of the skinny old woman who appeared in the archway. "Oh, Mother Proudfoot! I had *such* an awful dream again!"

Christopher, to his horror, found that he was stuck in the wall. He could not come out forwards and he could not push through backwards. The only thing he could seem to do was use what Flavian had taught him to make himself invisible. He did that at once. He had been moving with his face forward and his rear out, so that most of his head was outside the wall. Invisible or not, he felt like one of the stuffed animal heads on the walls of the Castle dining room. At least he could see and hear and breathe, he thought in a stunned way. He was confounded at the treachery of the Goddess.

She was led away into the further rooms, with soothing murmurs. After about ten minutes, by which time Christopher had a cricked neck and cramp in one leg, she came back again, looking perfectly calm.

"There's no point in looking invisible," she said. "Everyone here has witch sight, even if you don't. Look, I'm sorry about this, but I do terribly need help and I promise I'll let you go when you've helped me."

Christopher did not make himself visible again. He felt safer like that. "You don't need help—you need hitting over the head," he said angrily. "How can I help anyone like this? I'm dying of discomfort."

"Then get comfortable and then help me," the Goddess said.

Christopher found he could move a little. The wall round him seemed to turn jelly-like, so that he could straighten up and move his arms a little and get his legs into a proper standing position. He tried doing some rapid squirming, in hopes that the jelly would give enough to let him out, but it would not. He could tell that what was holding him there was the same thing that the Goddess had used to fasten his feet to the floor when he first met her, and that was still just as mysterious to him as it had been then. "How do you want me to help?" he asked resignedly.

"By taking me with you to your world," the Goddess said eagerly, "so that I can go to a school like the one in the *Millie* books. I thought you could hide me somewhere in your Castle while I looked round for a school."

Christopher thought of Gabriel de Witt discovering the Goddess hiding in an attic. "No," he said. "I can't. I absolutely can't. And what's more I won't. Now let me out of here!"

"You took Throgmorten," said the Goddess. "You can take me."

"Throgmorten's a cat," said Christopher. "He has nine lives like me.

I *told* you I could only get here by leaving one of my lives behind. You've only got one life, so it stands to reason that I can't get you to my world because you'd be dead if I did!"

"That's just the *point*!" the Goddess whispered at him ferociously. He could tell she was trying very hard not to scream again. Tears rolled down her face. "I *know* I've only got one life and I don't want to lose it. Take me with you."

"Just so that you can go to a school out of a book!" Christopher snarled back, feeling more than ever like an animal head on a wall. "Stop being so stupid!"

"Then you can just stay in that wall until you change your mind!" the Goddess said, and flounced away with a chank and a jingle.

Christopher stood, sagging into the jelly of the wall, and cursed the day he had brought the Goddess those *Millie* books. Then he cursed himself for thinking the Goddess was sympathetic. She was just as selfish and ruthless as everyone else he knew. He squirmed and struggled and heaved to get out of the wall, but since he had not the first idea what had gone into the spell, it held him as fast as ever.

The worst of it was that now the Temple had woken up from its midday sleep, it was a decidedly busy place. Behind him, through the wall, Christopher could hear a crowd of people in the hot yard counting the cats and feeding them. Mixed with those sounds was a female voice barking orders, and the sound of armor clashing and spear butts thumping on the ground. Christopher began to be terribly afraid that his invisible backside was sticking out of the wall into that yard. He kept imagining a spear plunging into him there, and he squirmed and squidged and pulled himself in to make sure that it was not. He was not sure which he dreaded most: the feeling of a spear driving into him, or what Gabriel would do if he lost another life.

From in front of him, beyond the archway, he could hear the Goddess talking with at least three Priestesses and then all their voices muttering prayers. Why hadn't Flavian taught him any useful magic? There were probably six hundred quiet ways of breaking this spell and sliding invisibly out of the wall, and Christopher did not know one. He wondered if he could do it by blasting loose in a combined levitation, whirlwind and fire-conjuring. Maybe—although it would be terribly hard without his hands free—and people would still come running after him with spears. He decided he would try argument and cunning first.

Before long, the Goddess came in to see if he had changed his mind.

"I'll fetch it, dear," said one of the Priestesses beyond the archway.

"No, I want to have another look at Bethi too," the Goddess said over her shoulder. For honesty's sake, she went over to look at the white cat, which was lying on her bed cushions panting and looking sorry for itself. The Goddess stroked it before she came over and put her face close to Christopher's.

"Well? Are you going to help me?"

"What happens," asked Christopher, "if one of them comes in and notices my face sticking out of the wall?"

"You'd better agree to help before they do. They'd kill you," the Goddess whispered back.

"But I wouldn't be any use to you dead," Christopher pointed out. "Let me go or I'll start yelling."

"You dare!" said the Goddess, and flounced out.

The trouble was Christopher did not dare. That line of argument only seemed to end in deadlock. Next time she came in, he tried a different line. "Look," he said, "I really am being awfully considerate. I could easily blast a huge hole in the Temple and get away this minute, but I'm not doing it because I don't want to give you away. Asheth and your Priestesses are not going to be pleased if they find out you're trying to go to another world, are they?"

Tears flooded the Goddess's eyes. "I'm not asking very much," she said, twisting a bangle miserably. "I thought you were kind."

This argument seemed to be making an impression. "I'm going to have to blow the Temple up before long, if you don't let me go," Christopher said. "If I'm not back before morning, someone in the Castle is going to come in and find only one life of me lying in bed. Then they'll tell Gabriel de Witt and we'll both be in trouble. I told you he knows how to get to other worlds. If he comes here, you won't like it."

"You're selfish!" the Goddess said. "You aren't sympathetic at all—you're just scared."

At this Christopher lost his temper. "Let me go," he said, "or I'll blow the whole place sky high!"

The Goddess simply ran from the room, mopping at her face with a piece of her robe.

"Is something wrong, dear?" asked a Priestess outside.

"No, no," Christopher heard the Goddess say. "Bethi isn't very well, that's all."

She was gone for quite a long time after that. Probably she had to distract the Priestesses from coming and looking at the white cat. But soon after that, smells of spicy food began to fill the air. Christopher grew seriously alarmed. Time was getting on and it really would be morning at the Castle soon. Then he would be in real trouble. More time passed. He could hear people in the yard behind counting the cats and feeding them again. "Bethi's missing," someone said.

"She's with the Living One still," someone else answered. "Her kittens are due soon."

Still more time passed. By the time the Goddess reappeared, desperation had forced Christopher's mind into quite a new tack. He saw that he would have to give her some kind of help, even if it was not what she wanted, or he would never get away before morning.

The Goddess in her ruthless way was obviously meaning to be kind-hearted. When she came in this time, she was carrying a spicy pancake-thing wrapped round hot meat and vegetables. She tore bits off it and popped them into Christopher's mouth. There was some searing kind of pepper in it. His eyes watered. "Listen," he choked. "What's *really* the matter with you? What made you suddenly decide to make me help you?"

"I told you!" the Goddess said impatiently. "It was what you said when I was ill—that I wasn't going to be the Living Asheth when I grow up. After that I couldn't think of anything else but what was going to happen to me then."

"So you want to know for certain?" Christopher said.

"More than anything else in this world!" the Goddess said.

"Then will you let me go if I help you find out what's really going to happen to you?" Christopher bargained. "I can't take you to my world—you know I can't—but I can help you this way."

The Goddess stood twisting the last piece of pancake about in her fingers. "Yes," she said. "All right. But I can't see how you can find out any better than I can."

"I can," said Christopher. "What you have to do is go and stand in front of that golden statue of Asheth you showed me and ask it what's going to happen to you when you stop being the Living Asheth. If it doesn't say anything, you'll know nothing much is going to happen and you'll be able to leave this Temple and go to school." This struck him as pretty cunning, since there was no way that he could see that a golden statue could talk.

"Now why didn't I think of that!" the Goddess exclaimed. "That's clever! But—" She twisted the piece of pancake about again. "But Asheth doesn't talk, you know, not exactly. She does everything by signs. Portents and omens and things. And she doesn't always give one when people ask."

This was annoying. "But she'll give *you* one," Christopher said persuasively. "You're supposed to *be* her, after all, so it only amounts to asking her to remind you of something both of you know already. Go and tell her to do you a portent—only make her put a time limit on it, so that if there isn't one, you'll know that there isn't."

"I will," said the Goddess decisively. She stuffed the piece of pancake into Christopher's mouth and dusted her hands with a determined jangle. "I'll go and ask her this minute!" And she strode out of the room, chank-chink, chank-chink, sounding rather like the soldiers at that moment marching round the yard behind Christopher's back.

He spat the pancake out, shut his eyes to squeeze the water out, and wished he was able to cross his fingers.

Five minutes later, the Goddess strode back looking much more cheerful. "Done it!" she said. "She didn't want to tell me. I had to bully her. But I told her to take her very stupid face off and stop trying to fool me, and she gave in." She looked at Christopher rather wonderingly. "I've never got the upper hand of her before!"

"Yes, but what did she *say*?" Christopher asked. He would have danced with impatience if the wall had not stopped him.

"Oh, nothing yet," said the Goddess. "But I promise faithfully I'll let you go when she does. She said she couldn't manage it at once. She wanted to wait till tomorrow, but I said that was far too long. So she said that the very earliest she could manage a portent was midnight tonight—"

"Midnight!" Christopher exclaimed.

"That's only three hours away now," the Goddess told him soothingly. "And I said she had to make it on the dot, or I'd be really angry. You must understand her point of view—she has to pull the strings of Fate and that does take time."

With his heart sinking, Christopher tried to calculate what time that would make it back at the Castle. The very earliest he could get it to was ten o'clock in the morning. But perhaps the maid who came to wake him would simply think he was tired. It would take her an hour or so to get worried enough to tell Flavian or someone, and by that time he would be back with any luck. "Midnight then," he said, sighing a bit. "And you're to let me go then, or I'll summon a whirlwind, set everything on fire and take the roof off the Temple."

During those three hours, he kept wondering why he did not do that at once. It was only partly that he did not want to lose another life. He felt a sort of duty to wait and set the Goddess's mind at rest. He had started her worrying by making that remark, and before that he had made her discontented by bringing her those school stories. He had a lot of fellow-feeling for her in her strange lonely life. And of course Papa had told him that you did not use magic against a lady. Somehow all these things combined to keep Christopher sagging in a half-sitting way in the wall, patiently waiting for midnight.

Some of the time the Goddess sat on her cushions, tensely stroking the white cat, as if she expected the portent any moment. Much of the time she was busy. She was called away to lessons, and then to prayers, and finally to have a bath. While she was away, Christopher had the rather desperate idea that he might be able to get in touch with the life he knew must be lying in bed at the Castle. He thought he might be able to get it to get up and do lessons for him. But though he had a sort of feeling of a separate piece of him quite clearly, he did not seem to be in touch with it—or if he was, he had no means of knowing. Do lessons! he thought. Get out of bed and behave like me! And he wondered for the hundredth time why he did not simply blow up the Temple and leave.

Finally the Goddess came back in a long white nightgown and only two bracelets. She kissed Mother Proudfoot good-night in the archway and got among her white cushions with her arms lovingly round her white cat. "It won't be long now," she told Christopher.

"It had better not be!" he said. "Honestly, I can't think why you grumble about your life. I'd swop your Mother Proudfoot for Flavian and Gabriel any day!"

"Yes, maybe I am being silly," the Goddess agreed, rather drowsily. "On the other hand, I can tell you don't believe in Asheth and that makes you see it quite differently from me."

Christopher could tell by her breathing that she dropped off to sleep then. He must have dozed himself in the end. The jelly-like wall was not really uncomfortable.

He was roused by a strange high cheeping noise. It was an oddly desperate sound, a little like the noise baby birds make calling and calling to be fed. Christopher jumped awake to find a big bar of white moonlight falling across the tiles of the floor.

"Oh look!" said the Goddess. "It's the portent." Her pointing arm came into the moonlight, with a bracelet dangling from it. She was pointing to Bethi the white cat. Bethi was lying stiffly stretched out in the bar of moonlight. Something tiny and very, very white was crawling and scrambling all over Bethi, filling the air with desperate high crying.

The Goddess surged off her cushions and on to her knees and picked the tiny thing up. "It's frozen," she said. "Bethi's had a kitten and—" There was a long pause. "Christopher," said the Goddess, obviously trying to sound calm, "Bethi's dead. That means I'm going to die when they get a new Living Asheth."

Kneeling by the dead cat, she screamed and screamed and screamed.

Lights went on. Feet flapped on the tiles, running. Christopher struggled to get himself as far back in the wall as he could. He knew how the Goddess felt. He had felt the same when he woke up in the mortuary.

But he wished she would stop screaming. As skinny Mother Proudfoot rushed into the room followed by two other Priestesses, he did his best to begin a levitation spell.

But the Goddess kept her promise. Still screaming, she backed away from Bethi's pathetic corpse as if it horrified her, and flung out one arm dramatically, so that her dangling bracelet flipped Christopher's invisible nose. Luckily the bracelet was silver.

Christopher landed back in his own bed in the Castle with the crash he was now used to. He was solid and visible and in his pajamas, and, by the light, it was nearly midday. He sat up hastily. Gabriel de Witt was sitting in the wooden chair across the room, staring at him even more grimly than usual.

CHAPTER 16

Gabriel had his elbows on the arms of the chair and his long, knob-knuckled hands together in a point under his eagle nose. Over them, his eyes seemed as hard to look away from as the dragon's.

"So you have been spirit traveling," he said. "I suspect you do so habitually. That would explain a great deal. Will you kindly inform me just where you have been and why it took you so long to come back."

There was nothing Christopher could do but explain. He rather wished he could have died instead. Losing a life was nothing compared with the way Gabriel looked at him.

"The Temple of Asheth!" Gabriel said. "You foolish boy! Asheth is one of the most vicious and vengeful goddesses in the Related Worlds. Her military Arm has been known to pursue people across worlds and over many years, on far slighter grounds than *you* have given her. Thank goodness you refrained from blowing a hole in her Temple. And I am relieved that you at least had the sense to leave the Living Asheth to her fate."

"Her fate? They weren't really going to kill her off, were they?" Christopher asked.

"Of course they will," Gabriel said in his calmest and driest way. "That was the meaning of the portent: the older Goddess dies when the new Living Asheth is chosen. The theory, I believe, is that the older one will enrich the power of the deity. This one must be particularly valuable to them, as she seems to be quite an enchantress in her own right."

Christopher was horrified. He saw suddenly that the Goddess had known, or at least suspected, what was going to happen to her. That was why she had tried to get him to help. "How can you be so calm about it?" he said. "She's only got one life. Can't you do something to help her?"

"My good Christopher," said Gabriel, "there are, over all the Series of all the Related Worlds, more than a hundred worlds, and in more than half of them there are practices which horrify any civilized person. If I were to expend my time and sympathy on these, I would have none left over to do what I am paid to do—which is to prevent the misuse of magic *here*. This is why I must take action over you. Do you deny that you have been misusing magic?"

"I—" said Christopher.

"You most certainly have," said Gabriel. "You must have lost at least three of your lives in some other world—and you may, for all I know, have lost all six while you were spirit traveling. But since the outer life, the life you *should* have lost, was lying here apparently asleep, natural laws have been forced to bend in order to enable you to lose it in the proper way. Much more of this, and you will set up a serious singularity throughout Series Twelve."

"I didn't lose one this time," Christopher said defensively.

"Then you must have lost it last time you went spirit traveling," Gabriel said. "You are definitely one short again. And this is not going to occur any more, Christopher. Oblige me by getting dressed at once and coming with me to my office."

"Er—" Christopher said. "I haven't had breakfast yet. Can I—?"

"No," said Gabriel.

By this Christopher knew that things were very bad indeed. He found he was shaking as he got up and went to the washroom. The door of the washroom would not shut. Christopher could tell Gabriel was holding it open with a strong spell to make sure he did not try to get away. Under Gabriel's eyes, he washed and dressed quicker than he had ever done in his life.

"Christopher," Gabriel said, while he was hurriedly brushing his hair, "you must realize that I am deeply concerned about you. Nobody should lose lives at the rate that you do. What is wrong?"

"I don't do it just to annoy you," Christopher said bitterly, "if that's what you think."

Gabriel sighed. "I may be a poor guardian, but I know my duty," he said. "Come along."

He stalked silently through the corridors with Christopher half running to keep up. What *had* become of his sixth life? Christopher wondered, with what bit of his mind was not taken up with terror. He was inclined to think that Gabriel had miscounted.

Inside the twilight office, Miss Rosalie and Dr. Simonson were waiting with one of the younger men on the Castle staff. All of them were swathed in a shimmering transparent spell. Christopher's eyes flicked anxiously from them to the leather couch in the middle of the dark floor. It reminded him of a dentist's chair. Beyond it was a stand holding two bell jars. The one on the left had a large bobbin hanging from nothing inside it, while the one on the right seemed to be empty except for a curtain ring or something lying at the bottom.

"What are you going to do?" Christopher said, and his voice came out more than a little squeaky.

Miss Rosalie stepped up to Gabriel and handed him some gloves on a glass tray. As Gabriel worked his fingers into the gloves, he said, "This is the severe step I warned you of after your fire. I intend to remove your ninth life from you without harming either it or you. Afterwards I shall put it in the Castle safe, under nine charms that only I can unlock. Since you will then only be able to have that life by coming to me and asking me to unlock those nine charms, this might induce you to be more careful with the two lives you will have left."

Miss Rosalie and Dr. Simonson began wrapping Gabriel in a sheeny spell like their own. "Taking a life out intact is something only Gabriel knows how to do," Miss Rosalie said proudly.

Dr. Simonson, to Christopher's surprise, seemed to be trying to be kind. He said, "These spells are only for hygiene. Don't look so alarmed. Lie down on this couch now. I promise you it won't hurt a bit."

Just what the dentist said! Christopher thought as he quakingly lay down.

Gabriel turned this way and that to let the spell settle round him. "The reason Frederick Parkinson is here," he said, "and not patrolling the World Edge as he should be, is to make sure that you do no spirit traveling while your life is being detached. That would put you in extreme peril, Christopher, so please try to remain in this world while we work."

Someone cast a very strong sleep spell then. Christopher went out like a light. Dr. Simonson turned out to have told the truth. He felt nothing at all for several hours. When he woke up, ravenously hungry and slightly itchy deep inside somewhere, he simply felt rather cheated. If he did have to have a life taken away, he would have liked to have watched how it was done.

Gabriel and the others were leaning against the black desk, drinking tea and looking exhausted. Frederick Parkinson said, "You *kept* trying to spirit travel. I had my work cut out to stop you."

Miss Rosalie hurried to bring Christopher a cup of tea too. "We kept you asleep until your life was all on the bobbin," she said. "It's just winding down into the gold ring now—look." She pointed to the two bell jars. The bobbin inside the left hand jar was almost full of shiny pinkish thread, and it was rotating in a slow stately way in the air. In the right hand jar, the ring was up in the air now too, spinning fast and jerkily. "How are you now, dear?" Miss Rosalie asked.

"Can you feel anything? Are you quite well?" Gabriel asked. He sounded rather anxious.

Dr. Simonson seemed just as concerned. He took Christopher's pulse and then tested his mind by asking him to do sums. "He does seem to be fine," he told the others.

"Thank goodness!" Gabriel said, rubbing his face with his hands. "Tell Flavian—no he's out on the World Edge, isn't he? Frederick, would you put Christopher to bed and tell the housekeeper that he's ready for that nourishing meal now?"

Everyone was so nervous and concerned about him that Christopher realized that no one had ever tried to take someone's spare life away before. He was not sure what he felt about that. What would they have done if it hadn't worked? he wondered, while he was sitting in bed eating almost more chicken and cream puffs than he could hold. Frederick Parkinson sat by him while he ate, and went on sitting by him all evening. Christopher did not know which irritated him most: Frederick or the itch deep down inside him. He went to sleep early in order to get rid of both.

He woke up in the middle of the night to find himself alone in the room with the gaslight still burning. He got out of bed at once and went to see if the split in the Castle spells had been mended. To his surprise, it was still there. It looked as if nobody had realized how he went to the Anywheres. He was just about to go through the split, when he happened to look back at his bed. The boy lying there among the rumpled covers had a vague unreal look, like Tacroy before he was firmed up. The sight gave Christopher a most unpleasant jolt. He really did have only two lives left now. The last life was locked away in the Castle safe and there was no way he could use it without Gabriel's permission. Hating Gabriel more than ever, he went back to bed.

Flavian brought Christopher his breakfast in the morning. "Are you all right for lessons today?" he asked anxiously. "I thought we could take it easy—I had a fairly heavy day yesterday, in and out of the World Edge to absolutely no effect, so I could do with a quiet morning too. I thought we'd go down to the library and look at some of the standard reference books—Moore's *Almanac*, Prynne's *List* and so forth."

The itch inside Christopher had gone. He felt fine, probably better than Flavian, who looked pale and tired. He was irritated at the way everyone was keeping watch on him, but he knew there was no point in complaining, so he ate his breakfast and got dressed and went along the corridors with Flavian to the pink marble staircase.

They were halfway down the stairs when the five-pointed star in the hall filled with sudden action. Frederick Parkinson sprang into being first. He waved at Flavian. "We've got some of them at last!" His jubilant shout was still ringing round the hall when Miss Rosalie appeared, struggling to keep hold of an angry old woman who was trying to hit her over the head with a violin. Two policemen materialized behind her. They were carrying someone between them, one at the man's head and one at his legs. They staggered round Miss Rosalie and the fighting old woman and laid the man carefully on the tiles, where he stayed, spread out a bit as if he was asleep, with his curly head turned peacefully towards the stairs.

Christopher found himself staring down at Tacroy.

At the same moment, Flavian said, "My God! It's Mordecai Roberts!"

"I'm afraid so," Frederick Parkinson called up to him. "He's one of the Wraith gang all right. I followed him all the way into Series Seven before I went back to trace his body. He was one of their couriers. There was quite a lot of loot with him." More policemen were appearing behind him, carrying boxes and the kind of waterproof bundles Christopher knew rather well.

Gabriel de Witt hurried past Christopher and Flavian and stood at the foot of the stairs looking down at Tacroy like a black, brooding bird. "So Roberts was their carrier, was he?" he said. "No wonder we were making no headway." By then the hall was filled with people: more policemen, the rest of the Castle staff, footmen, the butler, and a crowd of interested housemaids. "Take him to the trance room," Gabriel told Dr. Simonson, "but don't let him suspect anything. I want whatever he was fetching if possible." He turned to look up at Flavian and Christopher. "Christopher, you had better be present at the questioning when Roberts returns to his body," he said. "It will be valuable experience for you."

Christopher threaded his way across the hall beside Flavian, feeling rather as if he was out of his body too. He was empty with horror. So this was what Uncle Ralph's "experiments" really were! Oh no! he thought. Let it all be a mistake!

He found it quite impossible to concentrate in the library. He kept hearing Miss Rosalie's voice saying, "But Gabriel, they had actually butchered a whole tribe of mermaids!" and his mind kept going to those fishy bundles he had loaded on the horseless carriage in Series Five and then to the silly ladies who had thought he was something called a clistoffer. He told himself that those fishy bundles had *not* been bundles of mermaid. It *was* all some terrible mistake. But then he thought of the way Tacroy had tried to warn him off, not only the time the dragon came, but several times before that, and he knew it was no mistake. He felt sick.

Flavian was almost as bad. "Just fancy it being *Mordecai*!" he kept saying. "He's been on the Castle staff for years. I used to *like* him!"

Both of them jumped up with a sort of relief when a footman came to fetch them to the Middle Drawing Room. At least, Christopher thought, as he followed Flavian across the hall, when everything came out nobody would expect him to be the next Chrestomanci any longer. Somehow the thought was not as comforting as he had hoped.

In the enormous drawing room, Gabriel was sitting at the center of a half circle of gilded armchairs, like an old black and gray king on his throne. To one side of him sat serious and important-looking policemen with notebooks and three men carrying briefcases who all wore whiskers more imposing than Papa's. Flavian whispered that these were men from the Government. Miss Rosalie and the rest of Gabriel's staff sat on the other side of the semicircle. Christopher was beckoned to a chair about halfway along. He had an excellent view when two sturdy warlock footmen brought Tacroy in and sat him in a chair facing the others.

"Mordecai Roberts," one of the policemen said, "you are under arrest and I must warn you that anything you say will be taken down and may be used in evidence later. Do you wish to have a lawyer present with you?"

"Not particularly," said Tacroy. In his body, he was not quite the Tacroy Christopher knew. Instead of the old green suit, he was wearing a much smarter brown one, with a blue silk cravat and a handkerchief that matched it in his top pocket. His boots were handmade calf. Though his curls were exactly the same, there were lines on his face that never appeared on the face of his spirit, laugh-lines set in a rather insolent and bitter pattern. He was pretending to lounge in his chair with one handmade boot swinging in a carefree way, but Christopher could tell he was not carefree at all. "No point in a lawyer," he said. "You caught me in the act after all. I've been a double agent for years now. There's no way I could deny it."

"What made you *do* it?" Miss Rosalie cried out.

"Money," Tacroy said carelessly.

"Would you care to expand on that?" Gabriel said. "When you left the Castle in order to infiltrate the Wraith organization, the Government agreed to pay you a good salary and to provide comfortable lodgings in Baker Street. You still have both."

So much for the garret in Covent Garden! Christopher thought bitterly.

"Ah, but that was in the early days," said Tacroy, "when the Wraith only operated in Series Twelve. He couldn't offer me enough to tempt me then. As soon as he expanded into the rest of the Related Worlds, he offered me anything I cared to ask." He took the silk handkerchief out of his pocket and carefully flicked imaginary dust off his good boots. "I didn't take the offer straight away, you know," he said. "I got deeper in by degrees. Extravagance gets a hold on you."

"Who *is* the Wraith?" Gabriel asked. "You owe the Government that information at least."

Tacroy's foot swung. He folded the handkerchief neatly and his eyes went carelessly round the half circle of people facing him. Christopher kept the vaguest look on his face that he could manage, but Tacroy's eyes passed over him just as they passed over everyone else, as if Tacroy had never seen him before. "There I can't help you," he said. "The man guards his identity very carefully. I only had dealings with his underlings."

"Such as the woman Effisia Bell who owns the house in Kensington where your body was seized?" one of the policemen asked.

Tacroy shrugged. "She was one of them. Yes."

Miss Bell, the Last Governess, Christopher thought. She had to be one of them. He kept his face so vague that it felt as stiff as the golden statue of Asheth.

"Who else can you name?" someone else asked.

"Nobody much, I'm afraid," Tacroy said.

Several other people asked him the same question in different ways, but Tacroy simply swung his foot and said he couldn't remember. At length Gabriel leaned forward. "We have taken a brief look at that horseless carriage on which your spirit smuggled the plunder," he said. "It's an ingenious object, Roberts."

"Yes, isn't it?" Tacroy agreed. "It must have taken quite a while to perfect. You can see it had to be fluid enough to cross the World Edge, but solid enough so that the people in the other Series could load it when I got it there. I got the impression that the Wraith had to wait until he'd got the carriage right before he could expand into the Related Worlds."

That's not true! Christopher thought. And *I* used to load it! He's lying about everything!

"Several wizards must have worked on that thing, Mordecai," Miss Rosalie said. "Who were they?"

"Heaven knows," said Tacroy. "No—wait a minute. Effie Bell dropped a name. Phelps, was it? Felper? Felperin?"

Gabriel and the policemen exchanged glances. Flavian murmured, "The Felperin brothers! We've suspected they were crooked for years."

"Another curious thing, Roberts," Gabriel said. "Our brief inspection of the carriage shows that it seems at one time to have been almost destroyed by fire."

Christopher found that he had stopped breathing.

"Accident in the workshop, I suppose," Tacroy said.

"*Dragon* fire, Mordecai," said Dr. Simonson. "I recognized it at once."

Tacroy let his bitter, anxious, laughing eyes travel round everyone's faces. Christopher still could not breathe. But once again Tacroy's eyes passed over Christopher as if he had never seen him before. He laughed. "I was joking. The sight of you all sitting round in judgment brings out the worst in me. Yes, it was burned by a dragon objecting to a load of dragons' blood I was collecting in Series Eight. It happened about a year ago." Christopher began breathing at that. "I lost the whole load," Tacroy said, "and was nearly too scalded to get back into my body. We had to suspend operations most of last autumn until the carriage was repaired. If you remember, I reported to you that the Wraith seemed to have stopped importing then."

Christopher drew in some long relieved breaths and tried not to make them too obvious. Then one of the whiskered Government men spoke up. "Did you always go out alone?" he asked, and Christopher almost stopped breathing again.

"Of course I was alone," said Tacroy. "What use would another traveler be? Mind you, I have absolutely no way of knowing how many other carriages the Wraith was sending out. He could have hundreds."

And that's nonsense! Christopher thought. Ours was the only one, or they wouldn't have had to stop last autumn when I went to school and forgot. If he had not realized by then that Tacroy was protecting him, he would have known by the end of the morning. The questions went on and on. Tacroy's eyes slid across Christopher over and over again, without a trace of recognition. And every time Tacroy's answer should have incriminated Christopher, Tacroy lied, and followed the lie up with a smoke screen of other confessions to take people's minds off the question. Christopher's face went stiff from keeping the vague look on it. He stared at Tacroy's bitter face and felt worse and worse. At least twice, he nearly jumped up and confessed. But that seemed such a waste of all Tacroy's trouble.

The questions did not stop for lunch. The butler wheeled in a trolley of sandwiches, which everyone ate over pages of notes, while they asked more questions. Christopher was glad to see one of the footmen taking Tacroy some sandwiches too. Tacroy was pale as the milkiest coffee by then and his swinging boot was shaking. He bit into the sandwiches as if he was starving and answered the next questions with his mouth full.

Christopher bit into his own sandwich. It was salmon. He thought of mermaids and was nearly sick.

"What's the matter?" whispered Flavian.

"Nothing. I just don't like salmon," Christopher whispered back. It would be stupid to give himself away now after Tacroy had worked so hard to keep him out of it. He put the sandwich to his mouth, but he just could not bring himself to take another bite.

"It could be the effect of that life-removal," Flavian murmured anxiously.

"Yes, I expect that's it," Christopher said. He laid the sandwich down again, wondering how Tacroy could bear to eat his so ravenously.

The questions were still going on when the butler wheeled the trolley away. He came back again almost at once and whispered discreetly to Gabriel de Witt. Gabriel thought, decided something, and nodded. Then, to Christopher's surprise, the butler came and leaned over him.

"Your mother is here, Master Christopher, waiting in the Small Saloon. If you will follow me."

Christopher looked at Gabriel, but Gabriel was leaning forward to ask Tacroy who collected the packages when they arrived in London. Christopher got up to follow the butler. Tacroy's eyes flickered after him. "Sorry," Christopher heard him say. "My mind's getting like a sieve. You'll have to ask me that again."

Mermaids, Christopher thought, as he crossed the hall after the butler. Fishy packages. Bundles of dragons' blood. I knew it was dragons' blood in Series Eight, but I didn't know the dragon was objecting. What's going to happen to Tacroy now? When the butler opened the door of the Small Saloon and ushered him in, he could hardly focus his mind on the large elegant room or the two ladies sitting in it.

Two ladies?

Christopher blinked at two wide silk skirts. The pink and lavender one belonged to Mama, who looked pale and upset. The brown and gold skirt that was quite as elegant belonged to the Last Governess. Christopher's mind snapped away from mermaids and dragons' blood and he stopped short halfway across the oriental carpet.

Mama held out a lavender glove to him. "Darling boy!" she said shakily. "How *tall* you are! You remember dear Miss Bell, don't you, Christopher? She's my Companion these days. Your uncle has found us a nice house in Kensington."

"Walls have ears," remarked Miss Bell in her dullest voice. Christopher remembered how her hidden prettiness never did come out in front of Mama. He felt sorry for Mama.

"Christopher can deal with that, can't you, dear?" said Mama.

Christopher pulled himself together. He had no doubt that the Saloon was hung with listening spells, probably one to each gold-framed picture. I ought to tell the police the Last Governess is here, he thought. But if the Last Governess was living with Mama, that would get Mama into trouble too. And he knew that if he gave the Last Governess away, she would tell about him and waste all Tacroy's trouble. "How did you get in?" he said. "There's a spell round the grounds."

"Your Mama cried her eyes out at the lodge gates," the Last Governess said, and gestured meaningly round the room to tell Christopher to do something about the listening spells.

Christopher would have liked to pretend not to understand, but he knew he dared not offend the Last Governess. A blanketing spell was enchanter's magic and easy enough. He summoned one with an angry blink and, as usual, he overdid it. He thought he had gone deaf. Then he saw that Mama was tapping the side of her face with a puzzled expression and the Last Governess was shaking her head, trying to clear her ears. Hastily he scraped out the middle of the spell so that they could all hear one another inside the deafness.

"Darling," Mama said tearfully, "we've come to take you away from all this. There's a cab from the station waiting outside, and you're coming back to Kensington to live with me. Your uncle wants me to be happy and he says he knows I can't be happy until I've got you. He's quite right of course."

Only this morning, Christopher thought angrily, he would have danced with joy to hear Mama say this. Now he knew it was just another way to waste Tacroy's trouble. And another plot of Uncle Ralph's of course. Uncle Wraith! he thought. He looked at Mama, and Mama looked appealingly back. He could see she meant what she said, even though she had let Uncle Ralph rule her mind completely. Christopher could hardly blame her for that. After all, he had let Uncle Ralph fascinate him, that time when Uncle Ralph tipped him sixpence all those months ago.

He looked at the Last Governess. "Your Mama is quite well off now," she told him in her smooth, composed way. "Your uncle has already restored nearly half your Mama's fortune."

Nearly half! Christopher thought. Then what has he done with the rest of the money I earned him for nothing? He must be a millionaire several times over by now!

"And with you to help," said the Last Governess, "in the way you always used to, you can restore the rest of your Mama's money in no time."

In the way I always used to! Christopher thought. He remembered the smooth way the Last Governess had worked on him, first to find out about the Anywheres and then to get him to do exactly what Uncle Ralph wanted. He could not forgive her for that, though she was even more devoted to Uncle Ralph than Mama was. And remembering that, he looked at Mama again. Mama's love for Christopher might be perfectly real, but she had left him to nursery maids and Governesses and she would leave him to the Last Governess as soon as they got to Kensington.

"We're relying on you, darling," said Mama. "Why are you looking so vague? All you have to do is to climb out of this window and hide in the cab, and we'll drive away without anyone being the wiser."

I see, Christopher thought. Uncle Ralph knew Tacroy had been caught. So now he wanted Christopher to go on with the smuggling. He had sent Mama to fetch Christopher and the Last Governess to see that they did as Uncle Ralph wanted. Perhaps he was afraid Tacroy would give Christopher away. Well, if Tacroy could lie, so could Christopher.

"I wish I could," he said, in a sad, hesitating way, although underneath he was suddenly as smooth and composed as the Last Governess. "I'd love to get out of here—but I can't. When the dragon burned me in Series Eight, that was my last life but one. Gabriel de Witt was so angry that he took my lives and hid them. If I go outside the Castle now I'll die."

Mama burst into tears. "That horrid old man! How awkward for everyone!"

"I think," said the Last Governess, standing up, "that in that case there's nothing to detain us here."

"You're right, dear," Mama sobbed. She dried her eyes and gave Christopher a scented kiss. "How terrible not to be able to call one's lives one's own!" she said. "Perhaps your uncle can think of something."

Christopher watched the two of them hurry away, rustling expensively over the carpet as soon as they came out from the silence spell. He cancelled the spell with a dejected wave. Though he knew what both of them were like, he still felt hurt and disillusioned as he watched them through the window climbing into the cab that was waiting under the cedar trees of the drive. The only person he knew who had not tried to use him was Tacroy. And Tacroy was a criminal and a double-crosser.

And so am I! Christopher thought. Now he had finally admitted this to himself, he found he could not bear to go back to the Middle Drawing Room to listen to people asking Tacroy questions. He trudged miserably up to his room instead. He opened the door. He stared.

A small girl in a dripping wet brown robe was sitting shivering on the edge of his bed. Her hair hung in damp tails round her pale round face. In one hand she seemed to be gripping a handful of soaking white fur. Her other hand was clutching a large waxed-paper parcel of what looked like books.

This was all I needed! Christopher thought. The Goddess had somehow got here and she had clearly brought her possessions with her.

CHAPTER 17

"How did you get here?" Christopher said.

The Goddess shook with shivers. She had left all her jewelry behind, which made her look very odd and plain. "B-By remembering what you said," she answered through chattering teeth, "about having to leave a l-life b-behind. And of course there are t-two of me if you count the g-golden statue as one. B-But it wasn't easy. I w-walked into the w-wall s-six times round the corner of m-my r-room b-before I g-got it right. Y-You m-must be b-brave to keep g-going through th-that awful P-Place B-Between. It was h-horrible—I n-nearly d-dropped P-Proudfoot t-twice."

"Proudfoot?" said Christopher.

The Goddess opened her hand with the white fur in it. The white fur squeaked in protest and began shivering too. "My kitten," the Goddess explained. Christopher remembered how hot it was in Series Ten. Some time ago someone had put the scarf old Mrs. Pawson had knitted him neatly away in his chest of drawers. He began searching for it. "I c-couldn't leave her," the Goddess said pleadingly. "I brought her feeding bottle with m-me. And I *had* to g-get away as soon as they l-left me alone after the p-portent. They know I know. I heard M-Mother P-Proudfoot saying they were going to have to l-look for a new L-Living One at once."

And clothes for the Goddess too, Christopher realized, hearing the way her teeth chattered. He tossed her the scarf. "Wrap the kitten in that. It was knitted by a witch so it'll probably keep her safe. How on earth did you find the Castle?"

"B-By looking into every v-valley I c-came to," said the Goddess.

"I c-can't *think* why you s-said you didn't have w-witch sight. I n-nearly m-missed the s-split in the s-spell. It's really f-faint!"

"Is *that* witch sight?" Christopher said distractedly. He dumped an armful of his warmest clothes on the bed beside her. "Go in the washroom and get those on before you freeze."

The Goddess put the kitten down carefully wrapped in a nest of scarf. It was still so young that it looked like a white rat. Christopher wondered how it had survived at all. "B-Boy's clothes?" the Goddess said.

"They're all I've got," he said. "And be quick. Maids come in and out of here all the time. You've got to hide. Gabriel de Witt told me not to have anything to do with Asheth. I don't know what he'd do if he found you here!" At this, the Goddess jumped off the bed and snatched up the clothes. Christopher was glad to see that she looked truly alarmed. He dashed for the door. "I'll go and get a hiding place ready," he said. "Wait here."

Off he went at a run to the larger of the two old tower rooms, the one that had once been a wizard's workshop. A runaway Goddess just about put the lid on his troubles, he thought. Still it was probably very lucky that everyone was taken up with poor Tacroy. With a bit of cunning, he ought to be able to keep the Goddess hidden here while he wrote to Dr. Pawson to ask what on earth to do with her permanently.

He dashed up the spiral stair and looked round the dusty room. One way and another, he had not made much progress furnishing it as a den. It was empty apart from an old stool, worm-eaten workbenches, and a rusty iron brazier. Hopeless for a Goddess! Christopher began conjuring desperately. He fetched all the cushions from the Small Saloon. Then on second thought he knew someone would notice. He sent most of them back and conjured cushions from the Large Drawing Room, the Large Saloon, the Middle Saloon, the Small Drawing Room and anywhere else where he thought there would be nobody to see. Charcoal from the gardeners' shed next to fill the brazier. Christopher summoned fire for it, almost in too much of a hurry to notice he had got it right for once. He remembered a saucepan and an old kettle by the stables and fetched those. A bucket of water he brought from the pump by the kitchen door. What else? Milk for the kitten. It came in a whole churn and he had to tip some out into the saucepan and then send the churn back—the trouble was that he had no idea where things were kept in the Castle. Teapot, tea—he had no idea where those came from, and did the Goddess drink tea? She would have to. What then? Oh, cup, saucer, plates. He fetched the ones out of the grand cabinet in the dining room. They were quite pretty. She would like those. Then spoon, knife, fork. Of course none of the silver ones would respond. Christopher fetched what must have been the whole kitchen cutlery drawer with a crash, sorted hastily through it and sent it back like the churn. And she would need food. What was in the pantry?

The salmon sandwiches arrived, neatly wrapped in a white napkin. Christopher gagged. Mermaids. But he arranged them with the other things on the bench before taking a hasty look round. The charcoal had begun to glow red in the brazier, but it needed something else to make it look homey. Yes, a carpet. The nice round one from the library would do. When the carpet came, it turned out twice as big as he had thought. He had to move the brazier to make room. There. Perfect.

He dashed back to his room. He arrived at the exact moment when Flavian opened its door and started to walk in.

Christopher hastily cast the fiercest invisibility spell he could. Flavian opened the door on utter blankness. To Christopher's relief, he stood and stared at it.

"Er-hem!" Christopher said behind him. Flavian whirled round as if Christopher had stabbed him. Christopher said airily, and as loudly as he could, "Just practicing my practical magic, Flavian." The stumbling sounds he could hear from inside the blankness stopped. The Goddess knew Flavian was there. But he had to get her out of there.

"Oh. Were you? Good," Flavian said. "Then I'm sorry to interrupt, but Gabriel says I'm to give you a lesson now because I won't be here tomorrow. He wants a full muster of Castle staff to go after the Wraith."

While Flavian was speaking, Christopher felt inside the invisibility in his room—using a magical sixth sense which up to then he did not know he had—and located first the Goddess standing by his bed, then the kitten nestled in the scarf on the bed, and sent them both fiercely to the tower room. At least, he hoped he had. He had never transported living things before and he had no idea if it was the same. He heard a heavy *whoosh* of displaced air from among the invisibility, which was the same kind of noise the milk churn had made, and he knew the Goddess had gone somewhere. He just had to hope she would understand. She had after all shown she could look after herself.

He canceled the invisibility. The room seemed to be empty. "I like to practice in private," he told Flavian.

Flavian shot him a look. "Come to the schoolroom."

As they walked along the corridor, Christopher caught up with what Flavian had been saying. "You're all going after the Wraith tomorrow?"

"If we can get him," Flavian said. "After you left, Mordecai cracked open enough to give us a few names and addresses. We think he was telling the truth." He sighed. "I'd look forward to catching them, except that I can't get over *Mordecai* being one of them!"

What about Mama? Christopher wondered anxiously. He wished he could think of a way to warn her, but he had no idea where in Kensington she was living.

They reached the schoolroom. The moment they got there, Christopher realized that he had only canceled the invisibility on his room, not on the Goddess or the kitten. He fumbled around with his mind, trying to find her in the tower room—or wherever—and get her visible again. But wherever he had sent her, she seemed too far away for him to find. The result was that he did not hear anything Flavian said for at least twenty minutes.

"I *said,*" Flavian said heavily, "that you seem a bit vague."

He had said it several times, Christopher could tell. He said hastily, "I was wondering what was going to happen to Ta—Mordecai Roberts now."

"Prison, I suppose," Flavian answered sadly. "He'll be in clink for years."

"But they'll have to put a special clink round his spirit to stop that getting away, won't they?" Christopher said.

To his surprise, Flavian exploded. "That's just the kind of damn-fool, frivolous, unfeeling remark you *would* make!" he cried out. "Of all the hardhearted, toffee-nosed, superior little beggars I've ever met, you're the worst! Sometimes I don't think you have a soul—just a bundle of worthless lives instead!"

Christopher stared at Flavian's usually pale face all pink with passion, and tried to protest that he had not meant to be unfeeling. He had only meant that it must be quite hard to keep a spirit traveler in prison. But Flavian, now he had started, seemed quite unable to stop.

"You seem to think," he shouted, "that those nine lives give you the right to behave like the Lord of Creation! That, or there's a stone wall round you. If anyone so much as tries to be friendly, all they get is haughty stares, vague looks, or pure damn rudeness! Goodness knows, *I've* tried. Gabriel's tried. Rosalie's tried. So have all the maids, and *they* say you don't even notice *them!* And now you make jokes about poor Mordecai! I've had enough! I'm sick of you!"

Christopher had no idea that people saw him like this. He was astounded. What's gone wrong with me? he thought. I'm nice really! When he went to the Anywheres as a small boy, everyone had liked him. Everybody had smiled. Total strangers had given him things. Christopher saw that he had gone on thinking that people only had to see him to like him, and it was only too clear that nobody did. He looked at Flavian, breathing hard and glaring at him. He seemed to have hurt Flavian's feelings badly. He had not thought Flavian had feelings to hurt. And it made it worse somehow that he had *not* meant to make a joke about Tacroy—not when Tacroy had just spent the whole day lying on his behalf. He *liked* Tacroy. The trouble was, he did not dare tell Flavian he did. Nor did he dare say that his mind had mostly been on the Goddess. So what *could* he say?

"I'm sorry," he said. "Truly sorry." His voice came out wobbly with shock. "I didn't mean to hurt your feelings—not this time anyway—really."

"Well!" said Flavian. The pink in his face died away. He leaned back in his chair, staring. "That's the first time I've ever heard you say sorry—meaning it, that is. I suppose it's some kind of breakthrough." He clapped his chair back to the floor and stood up. "Sorry I lost my temper. But I don't think I can go on with this lesson today. I feel too emotional. Run away, and I'll make up for it after tomorrow."

Christopher found himself free—and with mixed feelings about it—to go and look for the Goddess. He hurried to the tower room.

To his great relief she was there, in a strong smell of boiled-over milk, sitting on the many-colored silk cushions, feeding the kitten out of a tiny doll's feeding-bottle. With the charcoal warming the air and the carpet—which now had a singed patch beside the brazier—covering the stone floor, the room seemed suddenly homey.

The Goddess greeted him with a most un-Goddesslike giggle. "You forgot to make me visible again! I've never done invisibility—it took me ages to find how to cancel it, and I had to stand still the whole time in case I trod on Proudfoot. Thanks for doing this room. Those cups are really pretty."

Christopher giggled too at the sight of the Goddess in his Norfolk jacket and knee-breeches. If you looked just at the clothes, she was a plump boy, rather like Oneir, but if you looked at her grubby bare feet and her long hair, you hardly knew what she was. "You don't look much like the Living Asheth—" he began.

"Don't!" The Goddess sprang to her knees, carefully bringing the kitten and its bottle with her. "Don't say that name! Don't even think it! She's me, you know, as much as I'm *her,* and if anyone reminds her, she'll notice where I am and send the Arm of Asheth!"

Christopher realized that this must be true or the Goddess could not have got to his world alive. "Then what am I supposed to call you?"

"Millie," said the Goddess firmly, "like the girl in the school books."

He had known she would get round to school before long. He tried to keep her off the subject by asking, "Why do you call the kitten Proudfoot? Isn't that dangerous too?"

"A bit," the Goddess agreed. "But I had to put Mother Proudfoot off the scent—she was ever so flattered—I felt mean deceiving her. Luckily there was an even better reason to call her that. Look." She laid the doll's bottle down and gently spread one of the kitten's tiny front paws out over the top of her finger. Its claws were pink. The paw looked like a very small daisy, Christopher thought, kneeling down to look. Then he realized that there were an awful lot of pink claws—at least seven of them in fact. "She has a holy foot," the Goddess said solemnly. "That means she carries the luck of a certain golden deity. When I saw it, I knew it meant I should get here and go to school."

They were back on the Goddess's favorite subject again. Fortunately, at that moment a powerful contralto voice spoke outside the door. "Wong," it said.

"Throgmorten!" Christopher said. He jumped up in great relief and went to open the door. "He won't hurt the kitten, will he?"

"He'd better *not*!" said the Goddess.

But Throgmorten was entirely glad to see all of them. He ran to the Goddess with his tail up and the Goddess, despite greeting him, "Hallo, you vile cat!" rubbed Throgmorten's ears and was obviously delighted to see him. Throgmorten gave the kitten an ownerlike sniff and then settled down between Christopher and the fire, purring like a rusty clock.

In spite of this interruption, it was only a matter of time before the Goddess got round to school again. "You got into trouble—didn't you?—when I kept you in the wall," she said, thoughtfully eating a salmon sandwich. Christopher had to look away. "I know you did, or you'd have said. What are these funny fishy things?"

"Salmon sandwiches," Christopher said with a shudder, and he told her about the way Gabriel had put his ninth life in a gold ring in order to take his mind off mermaids.

"Without even asking you first?" the Goddess said indignantly. "Now you're the one who's worst off. Just let me get settled in at school and I'll think of a way to get that life back for you."

Christopher realized that the time had come to explain the realities of life in Series Twelve to the Goddess. "Look," he said, as kindly as he could, "I don't think you *can* go to school—or not to a boarding school like the one in your books. They cost no end of money. Even the uniforms are expensive. And you haven't even brought your jewelry to sell."

To his surprise, the Goddess was quite unconcerned. "My jewelry was nearly all silver. I couldn't bring it without harming you," she pointed out. "I came prepared to earn the money." Christopher wondered how. By showing her four arms in a freak show? "I know I will," the Goddess said confidently. "I have Proudfoot's holy foot as an omen."

She really did seem to believe this. "My idea was to write to Dr. Pawson," Christopher said.

"That might help," the Goddess agreed. "When Millie's friend Cora Hope-Fforbes's father broke his neck hunting, she had to borrow her school fees. I *do* know all about these things, you see."

Christopher sighed and conjured some paper and a pen from the schoolroom to write to Dr. Pawson with. This intrigued the Goddess mightily. "How did you do that? Can I learn to do it too?" she wanted to know.

"Why not?" said Christopher. "Gabriel said you were obviously an enchantress. The main rule is to visualize the thing you want to bring on its *own.* When Flavian started me conjuring, I kept fetching bits of wall and table too."

They spent the next hour or so conjuring things the Goddess needed: more charcoal, a dirt-tray for the kitten, socks for the Goddess, a blanket and several scent-sprays to counteract the strong odor of Throgmorten. In between, they considered what to write to Dr. Pawson and the Goddess made notes about it in slanting foreign-looking handwriting. They had not made much progress with the letter when the gong sounded distantly for supper. Then Christopher had to agree that the Goddess could conjure his supper tray to the tower. "But I have to go to the schoolroom first," he warned her, "or the maid that brings it will guess. Give me five minutes."

He arrived at the schoolroom at the same time as the maid. Remembering Flavian's outburst, Christopher looked at the maid carefully and then smiled at her—at least, it was partly to keep her from suspecting about the Goddess, but he smiled at her anyway.

The maid was obviously delighted to be noticed. She leaned on the table beside the tray and started to talk. "The police carried off that old woman," she said, "about an hour ago. Kicking and shouting, she was. Sally and I sneaked into the hall to watch. It was as good as a play!"

"What about Ta—Mordecai Roberts?" Christopher asked.

"Held for further questioning," said the maid, "with spells all over him. Poor Mr. Roberts—Sally said he looked tired to death when she took him in his supper. He's in that little room next the library. I know he's done wrong, but I keep trying to make an excuse to go in and have a chat with him—cheer him up a bit. Bertha's been in. She got to make up the bed there, lucky thing!"

Christopher was interested, in spite of wishing the maid would go. "You know Mordecai Roberts then?"

"Know him!" said the maid. "When he was working at the Castle, I reckon we were all a bit sweet on him." Here Christopher noticed that his supper tray was beginning to jiggle. He slammed his hand down on it. "You must admit," the maid said, luckily not looking at the tray, "Mr. Roberts is that good-looking—and so pleasant with it. I'll name no names, but there were quite a few girls who went out of their way to bump into Mr. Roberts in corridors. Silly things! Everyone knew he only had eyes for Miss Rosalie."

"Miss Rosalie!" Christopher exclaimed, more interested than ever, and he held the tray down with all his strength. The Goddess clearly thought she had got something wrong and was summoning it mightily.

"Oh yes. It was Mr. Roberts taught Miss Rosalie to play cricket," said the maid. "But somehow they never could agree. It was said that it was because of her that Mr. Roberts got himself sent off on that job in London. She did him a bad turn, did Miss Rosalie." Then, to Christopher's relief, she added, "But I ought to get along and let you eat your supper before it's cold."

"Yes," Christopher said thankfully, leaning on the tray for all he was worth and desperately trying not to seem rude at the same time. "Er—if you do get to see Tac—Mr. Roberts, give him my regards. I met him in London once."

"Will do," the maid said cheerfully and left at last. Christopher's arms were weak by then. The tray exploded out from under his hands and vanished. A good deal of the table vanished with it. Christopher pelted back to the tower.

"You silly *fool*!" he began as he opened the door.

The Goddess just pointed to two-thirds of the schoolroom table perched on a workbench. Both of them screamed with laughter.

This was wonderfully jolly, Christopher thought, when he had recovered enough to share his supper with the Goddess and Throgmorten. It was thoroughly companionable knowing a person who had the same sort of magic. He had a feeling that this was the real reason why he had kept visiting the Temple of Asheth. All the same, now that the maid had put Tacroy into his head again, Christopher could not get him out of it. While he talked and laughed with the Goddess, he could actually *feel* Tacroy, downstairs somewhere, at the other end of the Castle, and the spells which held him, which were obviously uncomfortable. He could feel that Tacroy had no hope at all.

"Would you help me do something?" he asked the Goddess. "I know I didn't help you—"

"But you did!" said the Goddess. "You're helping me now, without even grumbling about the nuisance."

"There's a friend of mine who's a prisoner downstairs," Christopher said. "I think it's going to take two of us to break the spells and get him away safely."

"Of course," said the Goddess. She said it so readily that Christopher realized he would have to tell her why Tacroy was there. If he let her help without telling her what she was in for, he would be as bad as Uncle Ralph.

"Wait," he said. "I'm as bad as he is." And he told her about the Wraith and Uncle Ralph's experiments and even about the mermaids—all of it.

"Gosh!" said the Goddess. It was a word she must have picked up from her *Millie* books. "You *are* in a mess! Did Throgmorten really scratch your uncle? Good *cat!*"

She was all for going to rescue Tacroy at once. Christopher had to hang on to the back of the Norfolk jacket to stop her. "No, listen!" he said. "They're all going to round up the rest of the Wraith tomorrow. We can set Tacroy free while they're gone. And if they catch my uncle, Gabriel might be so pleased that he won't mind finding Tacroy gone."

The Goddess consented to wait till morning. Christopher conjured her a pair of his pajamas and left her finishing the salmon sandwiches as a bedtime snack. But, remembering her treachery over the portent, he took care to seal the door behind him with the strongest spell he knew.

He was woken up next morning by a churn of milk landing beside his bed. This was followed by the remains of the schoolroom table. Christopher sent both back to the right places and rushed to the tower, dressing as he went. It looked as if the Goddess was getting impatient.

He found her standing helplessly over a hamper of loaves and a huge ham. "I've forgotten the right way to send things back," she confessed. "And I boiled that packet of tea in the kettle, but it doesn't taste nice. What did I do wrong?"

Christopher sorted her out as well as he could and chased off to the schoolroom for his own breakfast. The maid was already there, holding the tray, looking quizzical. Christopher smiled at her nervously. She grinned and nodded towards the table. It had all four legs at one end, two of them sticking up into the air.

"Oh," he said. "I—er—"

"Come clean," she said. "It was you disappeared the antique cups in the dining room, wasn't it? I told the butler I'd tax you with it."

"Well, yes," said Christopher, knowing the Goddess was drinking freshly made tea out of one at the moment. "I'll put them back. They're not broken."

"They'd better not be," said the maid. "They're worth a fortune, those cups. Now do you mind putting this table to rights so that I can put this tray down before I drop it?" While Christopher was turning the table to its proper shape, she remarked, "Feeling your gifts all of a sudden, aren't you? Things keep popping in and out all over the Castle this morning. If you'll take my advice, you'll have everything back in its proper place before ten o'clock. After Monsignor de Witt and the others leave to catch those thieves, the butler's going to go round checking the whole Castle."

She stayed and ate some of his toast and marmalade. As she remarked, she had had her breakfast two hours ago. Her name turned out to be Erica and she was a valuable source of information as well as being nice. But Christopher knew he should not have taught the Goddess to conjure. He would never keep her a secret at this rate. Then, when Erica had gone and he was free to consider his problems, it dawned on Christopher that he could solve two of them at one go. All he had to do was to ask Tacroy to take the Goddess with him when he escaped. That made it more urgent than ever to get Tacroy free.

CHAPTER 18

Gabriel de Witt and his assistants left promptly at ten. Everyone gathered in the hall round the five-pointed star, some of them carrying leather cases, some simply in outdoor clothes. Most of the footmen and two of the stable-hands were going, too. Everyone looked sober and determined and Flavian, for one, looked outright nervous. He kept running his finger round his high starched collar. Christopher could see him sweating even from the top of the stairs.

Christopher and the Goddess watched from behind the marble balustrade near the black door of Gabriel's study. They were inside a very carefully constructed cloud of invisibility, which blotted out the two of them completely but not Throgmorten trotting at their heels. Throgmorten had refused to come near enough to be blotted out too, but nothing would stop him following them.

"Leave him," the Goddess said. "He knows what I'd do to him if he gives us away "

As the silver-voiced clock over the library struck ten, Gabriel came out of his study and stalked down the staircase, wearing a hat even taller and shinier than Papa's. Throgmorten, to Christopher's relief, ignored him. But he felt a strong wrench of worry about Mama. She was certainly going to be arrested, and all she had done was to believe the lies Uncle Ralph had told her.

Gabriel reached the hall and took a look round to see that all his troops were ready When he saw they were, he pulled on a pair of black gloves and paced into the center of the five-pointed star, where he went on pacing, growing smaller and smaller and further away as he walked. Miss Rosalie and Dr Simonson followed and began to diminish, too.

The others went after them two by two. When there was only a tiny, distant black line of them, Christopher said, "I think we can go now."

They began to creep downstairs, still in the cloud of invisibility. The distant line of Gabriel's troops disappeared before they were three stairs down. They went faster. But they were still only halfway down when things began to go wrong.

Flames burst out all over the surface of the star. They were malignant-looking green-purple flames which filled the hall with vile-smelling green smoke. "What is it?" the Goddess coughed.

"They're using dragons' blood," Christopher said. He meant to sound soothing, but he found he was staring uneasily at those flames.

All at once, the pentacle thundered up into a tall five-pointed fire, ten feet, twenty feet high. The Goddess's invisible hair frizzled. Before they could back up the stairs out of range, the flames had parted, leaning majestically to left and right. Out of the gap Miss Rosalie stumbled, pulling Flavian by one arm. Following them came Dr. Simonson dragging a screaming sorceress—Beryl, Christopher thought her name was. By this time, he was standing stock still, staring at the utter rout of Gabriel's troops. Singed and wretched and staggering, all the people who had just set off came pouring back through the gap in the flames and backed away to the sides of the hall with their arms up in front of their faces, coughing in the green smoke.

Christopher looked and looked, but he could not see Gabriel de Witt anywhere among them.

As soon as Frederick Parkinson and the last footman had staggered out into the hall, the flames dipped and died, leaving the pink marble and the dome stained green. The pentagram shimmered into little blades of fire burning over blackness. Uncle Ralph came carefully stepping out among the flames. He had a long gun under one arm and what seemed to be a bag in his hand. Christopher was reminded of nothing so much as one of his Chant uncles going shooting over a stubble field. Probably it was Uncle Ralph's freckled tweeds which put that into his mind. Rather sadly, he wished he had known more about people when he first met Uncle Ralph. He had a foxy, shoddy look. Christopher knew he would never admire someone like Uncle Ralph now.

"Would you like me to throw a marble washstand at him?" whispered the Goddess.

"Wait—I think he's an enchanter too," Christopher whispered back.

"CHRISTOPHER!" shouted Uncle Ralph. The greened dome rang with it. "Christopher, where are you hiding? I can feel you near. Come out, or you'll regret it!"

Reluctantly, Christopher parted the invisibility round himself and stepped to the middle of the staircase. "What happened to Gabriel de Witt?" he said.

Uncle Ralph laughed. "This." He threw the bag he was carrying so that it spread and skidded to a stop at the foot of the stairs. Christopher stared down—rather as he had stared down at Tacroy—at a long, limp, transparent shape that was unquestionably Gabriel de Witt's. "That's his eighth life there," said Uncle Ralph. "I did that with those weapons you brought me from Series One, Christopher. This one works a treat." He patted the gun under his arm. "I spread the rest of his lives out all over the Related Worlds. He won't trouble us again. And the other weapons you brought me work even better." He gave his mustache a sly tweak and grinned up at Christopher. "I had them all set up to meet de Witt's folk and took the magic out of them in a twinkling. None of them can cast a spell to save their lives now. So there's nothing to stop us working together just like the old days. You *are* still working for me, aren't you, Christopher?"

"No," said Christopher, and stood there expecting to have his remaining lives blasted in all directions next second.

Uncle Ralph only laughed. "Yes, you are, stupid boy. You're unmasked. All these people standing here *know* you were my main carrier now. You have to work with me or go to prison—and I'm moving into this Castle with you to make sure of you."

There was a long, warbling cry from behind Christopher. A ginger streak shot downstairs past him. Uncle Ralph stared, saw his danger, and made to raise his gun. But Throgmorten was almost on him by then. Uncle Ralph realized he had no time to shoot and prudently vanished instead, in a spiral of green steam. All Throgmorten got of him was a three-cornered piece of tweed with some blood on it. He stood in a frustrated arch on the blackened pentacle, spitting his rage.

Christopher raced down the stairs. "Shut all the doors!" he shouted to the stunned, staring Castle people. "Don't let Throgmorten out of the hall! I want him on guard to stop Uncle Ralph coming back."

"Don't be stupid!" the Goddess shouted, galloping after him, visible to everyone. "Throgmorten's a Temple cat—he understands speech. Just *ask* him."

Christopher wished he had known that before. Since it was too late to do anything much about anything else, he knelt on the greenishly charred floor and spoke to Throgmorten. "Can you guard this pentacle, please, and make sure Uncle Ralph doesn't come back? You know Uncle Ralph wanted to cut you to pieces? Well, you can cut *him* to pieces if he shows up again."

"Wong!" Throgmorten agreed with his tail lashing enthusiastically.

He sat himself down at one point of the star and stared fixedly at it, as still as if he were watching a giant mousehole. Malice oozed out of every hair of him.

It was clear Uncle Ralph would not get past Throgmorten in a hurry. Christopher stood up to find himself and the Goddess inside a ring of Gabriel's dejected helpers. Most of them were staring at the Goddess.

"This is my friend the G—Millie," he said.

"Pleased to meet you," Flavian said wanly.

Dr. Simonson swept Flavian aside. "Well what are we going to do now?" he said. "Gabriel's gone and we're left with this brat—who turns out to be the little crook I always suspected he was—and not a spell to rub together between us! What I say—"

"We must inform the Minister," said Mr. Wilkinson the librarian.

"Now wait a moment," said Miss Rosalie. "The Minister's only a minor warlock, and Christopher said he wasn't working for the Wraith any more."

"That child would say anything," said Dr. Simonson.

In their usual way, they were behaving as if Christopher was not there. He beckoned to the Goddess and backed out from among them, leaving them crowded round Miss Rosalie arguing.

"What are we doing?" the Goddess asked.

"Getting Tacroy out before they think of stopping us," said Christopher. "After that, I want to make sure Throgmorten catches Uncle Ralph, even if it's the last thing I do."

They found Tacroy sitting dejectedly by the table in an empty little room. From the tumbled look of the camp bed in the corner, Tacroy had not managed to get much sleep that night. The door of the room was half open and at first sight there seemed no reason why Tacroy did not simply walk out. But now the Goddess had made it clear to Christopher what witch sight was, all he had to do was look at the room the way he looked at The Place Between to understand why Tacroy stayed where he was. There were strands of spell across the doorway. The floor was knee-deep in more, criss-crossed all over. Tacroy himself was inside a perfect mass of other spells, intricately knotted over him, particularly round his head.

"You were right about it needing two of us," the Goddess said. "You do him, and I'll go and look for a broom and do the rest."

Christopher pushed through the spells over the door and waded through the others until he reached Tacroy. Tacroy did not look up. Perhaps he could not even see Christopher or hear him. Christopher began gently picking the spells undone, rather in the way you untie a mass of tight knots round a parcel, and because it was so boring and fiddly, he talked to Tacroy while he worked. He talked all the time the Goddess was gone. Naturally, most of what he told him was about that cricket match. "You missed that deliberately, didn't you?" he said. "Were you afraid I'd give you away?" Tacroy gave no sign of having heard, but as Christopher went on to tell him the way Miss Rosalie batted and how bad Flavian was, the hard tired lines of his face gradually smoothed out behind the strands of spell, and he grew more like the Tacroy Christopher knew from The Place Between.

"So, thanks to you teaching me, we won by two runs," Christopher was saying, when the Goddess reappeared with the broom Miss Rosalie used to chase Throgmorten with and started sweeping the room-spells into heaps as if they were cobwebs.

Tacroy almost smiled. Christopher told him who the Goddess was and then explained what had just happened in the hall. The smile clouded away from Tacroy's face. He said, a little thickly, "Then I rather wasted my time trying to keep you out of it, didn't I?"

"Not really," said Christopher, wrestling with a spell-knot above Tacroy's left ear.

The bitter lines came back to Tacroy's face. "Don't run away with the idea that I'm a knight in shining armor," he said. "I knew what was in most of those parcels."

"The mermaids?" Christopher asked. It was the most important question he had ever asked.

"Not till afterwards," Tacroy admitted. "But you notice I didn't stop when I knew. When I first met you, I would have reported you quite cheerfully to Gabriel de Witt if you hadn't been so small. And I knew Gabriel had some kind of a trap set up in Series Ten that time you lost a life. I just hadn't expected it would be that lethal. And—"

"Stow it, Tacroy," said Christopher.

"Tacroy?" said Tacroy. "Is that my spirit name?" When Christopher nodded, concentrating on the knot, Tacroy muttered, "Well, that's one less hold they have." Then as the Goddess, having dealt with the room-spells, came and leaned on her broom, watching his face as Christopher worked, he said, "You'll know me again, young lady."

The Goddess nodded. "You're like Christopher and me, aren't you? There's a part of you that's somewhere else."

Tacroy's face flushed a sudden red. Christopher could feel sweat on it under his fingers. Very surprised, he asked, "Where *is* the rest of you?"

He saw Tacroy's eyes swivel towards his, imploringly. "Series Eleven—don't ask any more! Don't *ask* me!" he said. "Under these spells I'd have to tell you and then we'd *all* catch it!"

He sounded so desperate that Christopher considerately did not ask any more—though he could not resist exchanging a look with the Goddess—and worked until he got that knot undone at last. It proved to be the key knot. The rest of the spell at once fell away in dissolving strands round Tacroy's handmade boots. Tacroy stood up stiffly and stretched.

"Thanks," he said. "What a relief! You can't imagine how vile it feels having a net bag round your spirit. What now?"

"Start running," said Christopher. "Do you want me to break the spells round the grounds for you?"

Tacroy's arms stopped in the middle of a stretch. "Now *you* stow it!" he said. "From what you said, there's no one apart from you two youngsters and me in this Castle with any magic worth speaking of, and your uncle could come back any minute. And you expect me just to walk out?"

"Well—" Christopher began.

But at that moment, Miss Rosalie came in with Dr. Simonson and most of the rest of Gabriel's staff crowding behind her. "Why, Mordecai!" she said brightly. "Do I actually hear you uttering a noble sentiment?"

Tacroy took his arms down and folded them. "Strictly practical," he said. "You know me, Rosalie. Have you come to lock me up again? I can't see you doing it without your magic, but you're welcome to try."

Miss Rosalie drew herself up to a majestic five feet. "I wasn't coming to see you at all," she said. "We were looking for Christopher. Christopher, we're going to have to ask you to take over as the next Chrestomanci, at least for the moment. The Government will probably appoint some other enchanter in the end, but this is *such* a crisis. Do you think you can do it, dear?"

They were all staring at Christopher appealingly, even Dr. Simonson. Christopher wanted to laugh. "You knew I'd have to," he said, "and I will on two conditions. I want Mordecai Roberts set free and not arrested again afterwards. And I want the G—Millie as my chief helper and she's to be paid by being sent to boarding school."

"Anything you want, dear," Miss Rosalie said hastily.

"Good," said Christopher. "Then let's go back to the hall."

In the hall, people were gathering dejectedly under the green-stained dome. The butler was there and two men in cook's hats, and the housekeeper with most of the maids and footmen. "Tell them to get the gardeners and the stable people, too," Christopher said, and went to look at the five-pointed star where Throgmorten sat watching. By screwing up his eyes and forcing his witch sight to its utmost, he could see a tiny round space in the middle of the star—a sort of ghostly mousehole—which Throgmorten never took his eyes off. Throgmorten had quite impressive magic. On the other hand, Throgmorten would be only too pleased if Uncle Ralph came back. "How do we stop someone coming through?" Christopher asked.

Tacroy ran to a cupboard under the staircase and came back with an armful of queer candles in star-shaped holders. He showed Christopher and the Goddess where to put them and what words to say. Then he had Christopher stand back and conjure all the candles to flame. Tacroy was, Christopher realized, among other things, a fully trained magician. As the candles flared up, Throgmorten's tail twitched scornfully.

"The cat's right," Tacroy said. "This would stop most people, but with the amount of dragons' blood your uncle has stored away, he could break through any time he wants."

"Then we'll catch him when he does," Christopher said. He knew what he would do himself, if he knew Throgmorten was lying in wait, and he was fairly sure Uncle Ralph would do the same. He suspected their minds worked the same way. If he was right, it would take Uncle Ralph a little time to get ready.

By this time, quite a crowd of people had come into the hall through the big front door, where they were standing clutching their caps and awkwardly brushing earth off their boots. Christopher went to stand a little way up the staircase, looking down on the long, limp remains of Gabriel de Witt and everyone's faces, anxious and depressed, lit half by greenish daylight from the stained dome and half by the flames of the strange candles. He knew just what needed saying. And he was surprised to find he was enjoying himself hugely.

He shouted, "Hands up everyone who can do magic."

Most of the gardeners' hands went up and so did a couple of the stable lads'. When he looked at the indoor people, he saw the butler's hand was up and one of the cooks'. There was the bootboy who had worked the scoreboard and three of the maids, one of whom was Erica. Tacroy's hand was up and so was the Goddess's. Everyone else was looking at the floor, dismally.

Christopher shouted, "Now hands up anyone who can do woodwork or metalwork."

Quite a number of the dismal people put their hands up, looking surprised. Dr. Simonson was one, Flavian was another. All the stable people had their hands up, and the gardeners too. Good. Now all they needed was encouragement.

"Right," said Christopher. "We've got two things to do. We've got to keep my uncle out of here until we're ready to catch him. And we've got to get Gabriel de Witt back."

The second thing made everyone murmur with surprise, and then with hope. Christopher knew he had been right to say it, even though he was not sure it could be done—and as far as his own feelings went, Gabriel could stay in eight limp pieces for the rest of both their lives. He found he was enjoying himself more than ever.

"That's what I said," he said. "My uncle didn't kill Gabriel. He just scattered all his lives. We'll have to find them and put them together. But first—" He looked at the greened glass of the dome and the chandelier that hung from it on its long chain. "I want a birdcage-thing made, big enough to cover the pentacle, and hung from there, so that it can be triggered by a spell to come down over anything that tries to get through." He pointed to Dr. Simonson. "You're in charge of making it. Collect everyone who can do woodwork and metalwork, but make sure some of them can do magic too. I want it reinforced with spells to stop anyone breaking out of it."

Dr. Simonson's beard began to jut in a proud, responsible way. He gave a slightly mocking bow. "It shall be done."

Christopher supposed he deserved that. The way he was behaving would have had the Last Governess accusing him of having a swelled head. But then he was beginning to suspect that he worked best when he was feeling bumptious. He was annoyed with the Last Governess for stopping him realizing this before.

"But before anyone starts on the birdcage," he said, "the spells round the grounds need reinforcing, or my uncle will try to bring the Wraith organization in that way. I want everyone except Ta—Mordecai and the G—Millie to go all round the fences and walls and hedges casting every spell they can think of that will keep people out."

That made a mixed murmur. Gardeners and housemaids looked at one another doubtfully. One of the gardeners' hands went up. "Mr. McLintock, Head Gardener," he announced himself. "I'm not questioning your wisdom, lad—just wishing to explain that our specialty is growing things, green fingers, and the like, and not any too much to do with defense."

"But you can grow cactuses and bushes with long spines and ten-foot nettles and so on, can't you?" Christopher said.

Mr. McLintock nodded, with a pawky sort of grin. "Aye. Thistles, too, and poison ivy."

This emboldened the cook to put his hand up. "*Je suis chef de cuisine,*" he said. "A cook only. My magic is with the good food."

"I bet you can reverse it," said Christopher. "Go and poison the walls. Or if you can't, hang rotten steaks and mouldy soufflés on them."

"Not since my student days have I—" the cook began indignantly. But this seemed to bring back memories to him. A wistful look came over his face, which was followed by a gleeful grin. "I will try," he said.

Now Erica's hand was up. "If you please," she said, "me and Sally and Bertha can only really do *little* things—charms and sendings and the like."

"Well go and do them—as many as you can," Christopher said. "A wall is built brick by brick after all." That expression pleased him. He caught the Goddess's eye. "If you can't think what charms to work, consult my assistant, Millie. She's full of ideas."

The Goddess grinned. So did the bootboy. From the look on his face, he was full of appalling notions which he could hardly wait to try. Christopher watched the bootboy troop out with the gardeners, the cook and the maids, and rather envied him.

He beckoned Flavian over. "Flavian, there's still loads of magic I don't know. Would you mind standing by to teach me things as they come up?"

"Well, I—" Flavian gave an embarrassed sideways look at Tacroy leaning on the banisters below Christopher. "Mordecai could do that just as well."

"Yes, but I'm going to need him to go into trances and look for Gabriel's lives," said Christopher.

"Are you indeed?" said Tacroy. "And Gabriel's going to burst into tears of joy when he sees me, isn't he?"

"I'll go with you," said Christopher.

"Quite like old times," said Tacroy. "Gabriel's going to burst into tears when he sees you, too. What it is to be loved!" His eyes flickered over at Miss Rosalie. "If only I had my young lady who plays the harp now—"

"Don't be absurd, Mordecai," said Miss Rosalie. "You shall have everything you need. What do you want the rest of us to do, Christopher? Mr. Wilkinson and I are no good at woodwork, and nor are Beryl and Yolande."

"You can act as advisers," said Christopher.

CHAPTER 19

The next twenty-four hours were the busiest Christopher had ever spent. They held a council-of-war in Gabriel's twilight office, where Christopher discovered that some of the dark panels rolled back to connect it with the rooms on either side. Christopher had the desks and the type-writing machines shoved to the walls and turned the whole space into one big operations room. It was much lighter like that, and became more and more crowded and busy as the various plans were set up.

There were, everyone told Christopher, many different ways of divining whether a living person was present in a world. Mr. Wilkinson had whole lists of methods. It was agreed that they try to use these to narrow down Tacroy's search for Gabriel. One of every kind was set up, but since nobody was sure if Gabriel's separated lives quite counted as alive, they all had to be set to maximum strength, and it turned out that, apart from Christopher, only the Goddess had strong enough magic to activate them and tune them from Series to Series. But anyone could watch them. The room was soon full of tense helpers staring into globes, mirrors, pools of mercury or ink, and spare sheets coated with liquid crystal, while the Goddess was kept busy adjusting the various spells and making a chart, in her foreig ı writing, of the readings from all the devices.

Miss Rosalie insisted that the council-of-war should also decide how to tell the Ministry what was goi g on, but that never did get decided, because Christopher kept getting called away. First, Dr. Simonson called him down to the hall to explain how they planned to make the birdcage. Dr. Simonson was taking it much more seriously than Christopher expected. "It's highly unorthodox," he said, "but who cares so long as it catches our man?"

Christopher was halfway upstairs again when the butler came to tell Christopher that they had done all they could think of to defend the grounds, and would Master Christopher come and see? So Christopher went—and marveled. The main gates, and the other smaller ones, were hung with curses and dripping poison. Brambles with six-inch thorns had been grown along the walls, while the hedges put Christopher in mind of Sleeping Beauty's castle, so high and thick with thorns, nettles and poison weeds were they. Ten-foot thistles and giant cactus guarded the fences, and every single weak place had been booby-trapped by the bootboy. He demonstrated, using his pet ferret, how anything that stepped here would become a caterpillar; or here would sink into bottomless sewage; or here would be seized by giant lobster claws; or here—anyway, he had made nineteen booby traps, each one nastier than the last. Christopher ran back to the Castle thinking that if they did manage to get Gabriel back, he would have to ask him to promote the bootboy. He was too good to waste on boots.

Back in the operations room, he had a set of magic mirrors set up, each focused on a different part of the defenses, so that they would know at once if anyone tried to attack. Flavian was just showing him how to activate the spells painted on the backs of the mirrors, when it was the housekeeper's turn to interrupt. "Master Christopher, this Castle isn't supplied to stand a siege. How am I to get the butcher and the baker and the milk through? There's a lot of mouths to feed here."

Christopher had to make a list of when the deliveries arrived, so that he and the Goddess could conjure them through at the right moment. The Goddess pinned it up beside the mirror-watch rota, the divining charts, the duty rota, the patrol rota—the wall was getting covered with lists.

In the midst of all this, two ladies called Yolande and Beryl (whom Christopher still could not tell apart) sat themselves down at the typewriters and started to clatter away. "We may not be sorceresses any longer," said Beryl (unless she was Yolande), "but that doesn't stop us trying to keep the usual business running. We can deal with urgent inquiries or advice at least."

Shortly they were calling Christopher away, too. "The trouble is," Yolande (unless her name was Beryl) confessed, "Gabriel usually signs all the letters. We don't think you should forge his signature, but we wondered if you simply wrote Chrestomanci—?"

"Before you conjure the mailbag down to the Post Office for us," Beryl (or maybe Yolande) added.

They showed Christopher how to set the sign of a nine-lifed enchanter on the word *Chrestomanci,* to protect it from being used against him in witchcraft. Christopher had great fun developing a dashing style of signature, sizzling with the enchanter's mark that kept it safe even from Uncle Ralph. It occurred to him then that he was enjoying himself more than he ever had done in his life. Papa had been right. He really was cut out to be the next Chrestomanci. But suppose he hadn't been? Christopher thought, making another sizzling signature. It was simply luck that he was. Well then, he thought, something could have been done about it. There had been no need at all to feel trapped.

Someone called him from the other end of the room then. "I think I've got much the most restful job," Tacroy laughed up at him from the couch in the middle, where he was preparing to go into his first trance. They had agreed that Tacroy should try a whole lot of short trances, to cover as many worlds as possible. And Miss Rosalie had agreed to play the harp for him, despite not having any magic. She was sitting on the end of the couch. As Christopher passed, Tacroy shut his eyes and Miss Rosalie struck a sweet rippling chord. Tacroy's eyes shot open. "For crying out loud, woman! Are you trying to clog my spirit in toffee or something? Don't you know any *reasonable* music?"

"As I remember, you always object to anything I play!" Miss Rosalie retorted. "So I shall play something *I* like, regardless!"

"I hate your taste in music!" Tacroy snarled.

"Calm down, or you won't go into a trance. I don't want to have sore fingers for nothing!" Miss Rosalie snapped.

They reminded Christopher of something—of someone. He looked back on his way over to the pool of ink where Flavian was beckoning. Tacroy and Miss Rosalie were staring at each other, both making sure the other knew their feelings were deeply hurt. Who have I seen look like that before? Christopher wondered. Underneath, he could tell, Tacroy and Miss Rosalie were longing to stop being rude to one another, but both too proud to make the first move. Who was that like?

As Christopher bent over the pool of ink, he got it. Papa and Mama! They had been exactly the same!

When the pool of ink was showing World C in Series Eight, Christopher went back past Miss Rosalie staring stormily ahead and playing a jig, to where Yolande and Beryl were typing. "Can I send someone an official letter of my own?" he asked.

"Just dictate," Yolande (or possibly Beryl) said, with her fingers on the keys.

Christopher gave her Dr. Pawson's address. "Dear Sir," he said, in the way all the letters he had signed went. "This office would be obliged if you would divine the whereabouts of Mr. Cosimo Chant, last heard of in Japan, and forward his address to Mrs. Miranda Chant, last heard of living in Kensington." Blushing a bit, he asked, "Will that do?"

"For Dr. Pawson," Beryl (or perhaps Yolande) said, "you have to add, 'The customary fee will be forwarded.' Dr. Pawson never works without a fee. I'll put the request through Accounts for you. Mr. Wilkinson needs you at the quicksilver bowl now."

While Christopher rushed back across the room, the Goddess remembered that Proudfoot the kitten would be starving by then. She conjured her from the tower room, scarf, bottle and all. One of the helpers ran for milk. It took a while. Proudfoot, impatient with the delay, opened eyes like two chips of sapphire and glared blearily around. "Mi-i-i-ilk!" she demanded from an astonishingly wide pink mouth.

Even when an ordinary kitten opens its eyes for the first time, it is a remarkable moment. Since Proudfoot was an Asheth Temple cat, the effect was startling. She suddenly had a personality at least as strong as Throgmorten's, except that it seemed to be just the opposite. She was passed from hand to hand for people to take turns at cooing over her and feeding her. Flavian was so besotted with her that he would not let go of her until Tacroy came out of his trance, very dejected because he had not been able to sense Gabriel in any of the three worlds he had visited. Flavian gave him Proudfoot to cheer him up. Tacroy put her under his chin and purred at her, but Miss Rosalie took her away in order to give Tacroy a strong cup of tea instead, and then spent the next half hour doting on Proudfoot herself.

All this devotion seemed to Christopher to be unfair to Throgmorten. He went out on the stairs to see if Throgmorten was all right, where he paused for a moment, struck with how different it all was. The green from the dragons' blood was fading, but there was still quite a greenish tinge in the light from the dome. Under it, Dr. Simonson, Frederick Parkinson, and a crowd of helpers were sawing, hammering, and welding in their shirt-sleeves. The hall was littered with timber, tools, and metal rods, and more helpers were constantly bringing further wood and tools in through the open front door. Various people sat on the stairs drinking cups of tea while they waited to take a turn in front of the divining spells. If someone had told Christopher a week ago that Chrestomanci Castle would look like a rather disorderly workshop, he would never have believed him, he thought.

The candles were still burning, flaring sideways in the draft from the front door, and there in the blackened pentacle Throgmorten sat like a statue, staring fiercely at his Uncle Ralph mousehole. Christopher was glad to see that he was surrounded by all that a cat could desire. An earth-tray, a bowl of milk, saucers of fish, a plate of meat and a chicken wing had been carefully pushed between the candle-holders to the edges of the star. But Throgmorten was ignoring it all.

It was clear no one had liked to disturb Gabriel's life. It was still lying on the floor where Uncle Ralph had thrown it, limp and transparent. Someone had carefully fenced it off with black rope tied round four chairs from the library. Christopher stared down at it. No wonder Tacroy couldn't find anything and none of the divining spells showed anything, if all the lives were like this, he was thinking, when one of the gardeners ran in through the front door and waved at him urgently.

"Can you come and look?" he panted. "We don't know if it's the Wraith or not. There's hundreds of them, all round the grounds in fancy-dress-like!"

"I'll look in the mirrors," Christopher called back. He raced back into the operations room to the magic mirrors. The one trained on the main gate was giving a perfect view of the peculiar soldiers staring through the bars. They wore short tunics and silver masks and they were all carrying spears. Christopher's stomach jumped nastily at the sight. He turned round and looked at the Goddess. She was white.

"It's the Arm of Asheth," she whispered. "They've found me."

"I'll go and make sure they can't get in," Christopher said. He ran back down the stairs and through the hall and then out into the grounds with the gardener. On the lawn, Mr. McLintock was lining up all the rest of the outside workers and making sure each of them had a billhook or a sharp hoe.

"I'm not letting any of those heathen bodies into *my* gardens," he said.

"Yes, but those spears are deadly. You'll have to keep everyone out of throwing-range," Christopher said. He felt a sharp stabbing pain in his chest just at the thought.

He went round the grounds with Mr. McLintock, as near as they dared to the fences and walls. The soldiers of the Arm of Asheth were just standing outside, as if the spells were keeping them out, but to be on the safe side, Christopher doubled the strength of each one as he came to it. The distant glimpses he got of silver masks and spear points made him feel ill.

As he turned and hurried back to the Castle, he realized that he was not enjoying himself any longer. He felt weak and young and anxious. Uncle Ralph was one thing, but he knew he just did not know how to deal with the Arm of Asheth. If only Gabriel was here! he found himself thinking. Gabriel knew all about the Temple of Asheth. Probably he could have sent the soldiers away with one cool, dry word. And then,

Christopher thought, he'd punish me for hiding the Goddess here when he told me not to, but even that would be worth it.

He went back through the hall, where the birdcage was only a pile of sawed wood and three bent rods. He knew it would be nothing like ready by the night, and Uncle Ralph was bound to try to come back tonight. Past Gabriel's limp fenced-off life he went, and up the stairs into the operations room, to find Tacroy coming out of another trance shaking his head dismally. The Goddess was white and trembling and everyone else was exasperated because none of the various shadows and flickers in the divining spells seemed to be anything to do with Gabriel.

"I think I'd better conjure out a telegram to the Ministry to send in the army," Christopher said dejectedly.

"You'll do no such thing!" snapped Miss Rosalie. She made Christopher and the Goddess sit beside Tacroy on the couch and made them all drink the hot, sweet tea that Erica had just brought in. "Now listen, Christopher," she said. "If you let the Ministry know what's happened to Gabriel, they'll insist on sending some adult enchanter to take over, and he won't be the slightest good because his magic won't be as strong as yours. You're the only nine-lifed enchanter left. We need you to put Gabriel back together when we find him. You're the only one who can. And it's not as if the Arm of Asheth can get into the grounds, is it?"

"No—I doubled the spells," Christopher said.

"Good," said Miss Rosalie. "Then we're no worse off than we were. I didn't argue all this through with Dr. Simonson just to have *you* let me down, Christopher! We'll find Gabriel before long and then everything will be all right, you'll see."

"Mother Proudfoot always says the darkest hour is before the dawn," the Goddess put in. But she did not say it as if she believed it.

As if to prove Mother Proudfoot right, Christopher was just finishing his tea when Flavian cried out, "Oh, I understand now!" Flavian was sitting at the big dark desk trying to make sense of all the shadows and flickers showing up on the divining spells. All the people sitting slumped around the operations room sat up and looked at him hopefully. "It's taking Gabriel's lives a long time to settle," Flavian said. "There are clear signs of one drifting about Series Nine, and another in Series Two, but neither of them have come down into a world yet. I think we may find that the rest of them are still floating about the World Edge if we retune all the spells."

Tacroy jumped up and came to look over Flavian's shoulder. "You may be right at that!" he said. "The one time I thought I caught a whiff of Gabriel was on the World Edge near Series One. Does anything show up there?"

The World Edge meant The Place Between, Christopher thought, as he hurried with the Goddess to adjust all the divining apparatus. "I can go and climb about there and bring them in," he said.

There was an instant outcry against him. "No," said Flavian. "I'm still your tutor and I forbid it."

"We need you here to deal with your uncle," Tacroy said.

"You can't leave me here with the Arm of Asheth!" said the Goddess. "Besides, what happens if you lose another life?"

"Exactly," said Miss Rosalie. "Your last life is shut in the safe under charms only Gabriel can break. You daren't risk losing another one. We'll just have to wait until the lives settle. Then we can set up a properly guarded Gate and send you through to collect them."

With even the Goddess against him, Christopher gave in for the moment. He knew he could always sneak off to The Place Between if he needed to. Just now, Uncle Ralph was more important than Gabriel and probably more of a danger even than the Arm of Asheth.

He arranged watches and patrols for the night with Tacroy and Mr. McLintock. They had supper camped about the hall and up the stairs, under the ladders and planks Dr. Simonson was using to lower the chandelier. At this stage, the birdcage was still only a collection of metal hoops and wooden rods. The cooks carried cauldrons and casseroles to Dr. Simonson's team as they worked, so that they could carry on until the daylight failed, but Christopher knew they were not going to get it finished that day. Throgmorten came off duty long enough to eat a plate of caviar to strengthen him for the night's work. Proudfoot was taken to the kitchen for safety, to be doted on there, and everyone settled down tensely for the night.

Christopher had arranged the watches so that there was always a mixture of able-bodied people with ones that still had magic. He took the first watch himself. The Goddess took the next one. Christopher was asleep in the library next to Frederick Parkinson when something happened in the middle of the Goddess's watch. The Goddess was panting and flustered and said she was sure Uncle Ralph had tried to come through the pentacle. "I conjured him away," she kept saying. There was certainly a wild hullaballoo from Throgmorten. But by the time Christopher got there all he saw was a wisp of steam rising from the invisible mousehole and Throgmorten pacing round it like a frustrated tiger.

Oddly enough, there was no smell of dragons' blood. It looked as if Uncle Ralph had either been testing their defenses or trying to deceive them about his plans. The real attack came just before dawn, when Tacroy and the bootboy were on watch. And it came from outside the

Castle grounds. Bells rang all over the Castle, showing that the spells had been breached. As Christopher pelted across the dewy lawn, he thought that the screams, yells, and clangs coming from the walls would have woken everyone even if the bells had not rung. Again he got there too late. He arrived to find Tacroy and the bootboy furiously chanting spells to fill two gaps in Mr. McLintock's vast spiny hedge. He could dimly see a few figures in silver armor milling about beyond the gaps. Christopher hastily reinforced the spells for all he was worth.

"What happened?" he panted.

"The Wraith seems to have walked into the Arm of Asheth," Tacroy said, shivering in the early mist. "It's an ill wind." While the gardeners hurried up with cactuses to fill the gaps and the bootboy booby-trapped them, he said he thought that a small army of the Wraith's men had tried to break into the grounds. But the Arm of Asheth must have thought the Wraith was attacking *them* and accidentally defended the Castle. At all events, the attackers had run for their lives.

Christopher sniffed the reek of dragons' blood in the mist and thought Tacroy was certainly right.

By the time he got back to the Castle, it was light enough for Dr. Simonson and his helpers to be hard at work again. Flavian was stumbling about the operations room, pale and yawning from having been up all night. "I was right about Gabriel's lives!" he said jubilantly. "They're all settling down into the Related Worlds. I've got six of them more or less pinpointed now—though I can't spot the seventh at all yet. I suggest you go and collect those six anyway as soon as they've finished that lobster pot of yours."

The Lobster Pot, as everyone came to call it, was hoisted triumphantly up into the air above the pentacle soon after breakfast. Christopher jumped into the star himself to test it. The spell tripped, just as it was supposed to, and the cage came crashing down around him. Throgmorten looked up irritably. Christopher grinned and tried to conjure the thing away. It would not budge. He rattled the flimsy bars with his hands and tried to heave up one edge, but he could not budge it that way either. In something of a panic, he realized that the thing was impossible to get out of, even though he had set most of the spells on it himself.

"Your face was rather a study," the Goddess said, with a weak chuckle. "You should have seen the relief on it when they hauled it up again!" The Goddess was not at all happy. She was pale and nervous in spite of trying to joke.

She has only one life, Christopher reminded himself, and the Arm of Asheth is waiting outside for her. "Why don't you come with me to collect Gabriel's lives?" he said. "It will puzzle the Arm of Asheth no end if you start hopping from world to world."

"Oh *may* I?" the Goddess said gladly. "I feel so responsible."

There had been much discussion, some of it very learned, among Flavian, Beryl, Yolande and Mr. Wilkinson about how to collect Gabriel's lives. Christopher had no idea there were so many ways to send people to different worlds. Miss Rosalie settled it by saying briskly, "We set up a Gate here in this room and send Mordecai into a trance with a spirit-trace so that we can focus the Gate on him as soon as he finds a Gabriel. Then Christopher and Millie go through and persuade the Gabriel that he's needed at the Castle. What could be simpler?"

Many things could have been simpler, Christopher thought, as he and the Goddess worked on the complex magics of the Gate to Flavian's endless, patient instructions. He felt slow and reluctant anyway. Even though only Gabriel could give him his ninth life back, even though Gabriel was desperately needed, Christopher did not want him back. All the fun would end then. Everything in the Castle would go quiet and respectable and grown-up again. Only the fact that he always liked working on magic that really did something kept Christopher working properly on the Gate.

When it was finished, the Gate looked simple indeed. It was a tall square frame of metal, with two mirrors sloping together to make a triangle at the back of it. No one would know, to look at it, how difficult it had been to do.

Christopher left Tacroy lying on the couch with the little blue blob of the spirit-trace on his forehead and went, rather moodily, to conjure the baker's cart into the Castle grounds. This is the last time they'll let me do this, he thought, as the Arm of Asheth angrily shook their spears at the baker.

When he came back, Tacroy was pale and still and covered with blankets and Miss Rosalie was gently playing her harp.

"There he is in the Gate," Flavian said.

The two mirrors had become one slightly misty picture of somewhere in Series One. Christopher could see a line of the great pylons that carried the ring trains stretching away into the distance. Tacroy was standing under the nearest one, wearing the green suit Christopher knew so well. It must be what Tacroy's spirit always wore. The spirit had its hands spread out frustratedly.

"Something seems to be wrong," Flavian said.

Everyone jumped when the body lying on the couch spoke suddenly, in a strange, husky voice. "I had him!" Tacroy's body said. "He was watching the trains. He was just telling me he could invent a better train. Then he simply vanished! What do I do?"

"Go and try for the Gabriel in Series Two," Miss Rosalie said, plucking a rippling, soothing tune.

"It'll take a moment," Tacroy's body croaked.

The picture in the Gate vanished. Christopher imagined Tacroy scrambling and wafting through The Place Between. Everyone round him wondered anxiously what had gone wrong.

"Maybe Gabriel's lives just don't trust Mordecai," Flavian suggested.

The mirrors combined into a picture again. This time they all saw Gabriel's life. It was standing on a hump-backed bridge, gazing down into the river below. It was surprisingly frail and bent and old, so old that Christopher realized that the Gabriel he knew was nothing like as elderly as he had thought. Tacroy's spirit was there too, edging gently up the hump of the bridge towards Gabriel's life, for all the world like Throgmorten stalking a big black bird. Gabriel did not seem to see Tacroy. He did not look round. But his bent black figure was suddenly not there any more. There was only Tacroy on the bridge, staring at the place where Gabriel had been.

"That one went, too," Tacroy's body uttered from the couch. "What *is* this?"

"Hold it!" Flavian whispered and ran to check the nearest divining spells.

"Stay there a moment, Mordecai," Miss Rosalie said gently.

In the mirrors, Tacroy's spirit leaned its elbows on the bridge and tried to look patient.

"I don't *believe* this!" Flavian cried out. "Everyone check, quickly! All the lives seem to be disappearing! Better call Mordecai back, Rosalie, or he'll waste his strength for nothing."

There was a rush for the crystals, bowls, mirrors and scrying pools. Miss Rosalie swept both hands across her harp and, inside the Gate, Tacroy's spirit looked up, looked surprised, and vanished as suddenly as Gabriel's life. Miss Rosalie leaned over and watched anxiously as Tacroy's body stirred. Color flooded back to his face. His eyes opened. "What's going on?" he said, pushing the blankets back.

"We've no idea," said Miss Rosalie. "All the Gabriels are disappearing—"

"No they're not!" Flavian called excitedly. "They're all collecting into a bunch, and they're coming this way, the lot of them!"

There was a tense half hour, during which everyone's hopes and fears seesawed. Since Christopher's hopes and fears on the whole went the opposite way to everyone else's, he thought he could not have borne it without Proudfoot the kitten. Erica brought Proudfoot with her when she hurried in with a tray of tea to restore Tacroy. Proudfoot became very busy taking her first long walk, all the way under Gabriel's black desk, with her string of a tail whipping about for balance. She was something much better to watch than the queer clots and whorls that Gabriel's lives made as they drifted steadily towards Series Twelve. Christopher was watching Proudfoot when Flavian said, "Oh dear!" and turned away from the scrying pool.

"What's the matter?" he asked.

Flavian's shoulders drooped. He tore off his tight, crumpled collar and threw it on the floor. "All the lives have stopped," he said. "They're faint but certain. They're in Series Eleven, I'm afraid. I think that was where the seventh life was all along. So much for our hopes!"

"Why?" said Christopher.

"Nobody can get there, dear," said Miss Rosalie. She looked as if she might cry. "At least, nobody ever comes back from there if they do."

Christopher looked at Tacroy. Tacroy had gone pale, paler even than when he went in a trance. He was the color of milk with a dash of coffee in it.

CHAPTER 20

Here was the perfect excuse to stop looking for Gabriel. Christopher expected to have a short struggle with himself. He quite took himself by surprise when he stood up straight away. He did not even have to think that the Goddess had also heard Tacroy confess that part of himself was in Series Eleven. "Tacroy," he said. He knew it was important to call Tacroy by his spirit name. "Tacroy, come to that empty office for a moment. I have to talk to you."

Slowly and reluctantly Tacroy stood up. Miss Rosalie said sharply, "Mordecai, you look ill. Do you want me to come with you?"

"No!" Tacroy and Christopher said together.

Tacroy sat on the edge of a desk in the empty office and put his face in his hands. Christopher was sorry for him. He had to remind himself that he and Tacroy were the ones who had brought Uncle Ralph the weapon which had blown Gabriel's lives apart, before he could say, "I've got to ask you."

"I know that," Tacroy said.

"So what is it about Series Eleven?" said Christopher.

Tacroy raised his head. "Put the strongest spell of silence and privacy round us that you can," he said. Christopher did so, even more fiercely than he had done for Miss Bell and Mama. It was so extreme that he went numb and could hardly feel to scrape out the center of the spell so that he and Tacroy could hear one another. When he had done it, he was fairly sure that even someone standing just beside them could not have overheard a word. But Tacroy shrugged. "They can probably hear anyway," he said. "Their magic's nothing like ours. And they have my soul, you see. They know most of what I do from that, and what they don't know I have to go and report to them in spirit. You saw me going there once—they summon me to a place near Covent Garden."

"Your soul?" said Christopher.

"Yes," Tacroy said bitterly. "The part that makes you the person you are. With you, it's the part that carries on from life to life. Mine was detached from me when I was born, as it is with all Eleven people. They kept it there when they sent me here to Twelve as a baby."

Christopher stared at Tacroy. He had always known that Tacroy did not look quite like other people, with his coffee-colored skin and curly hair, but he had not thought about it before because he had met so many stranger people in the Anywheres. "Why did they send you?"

"To be their guinea pig," said Tacroy. "The Dright puts someone in another world from time to time when he wants to study it. This time he decided he wanted to study good and evil, so he ordered me to work for Gabriel first and then for the worst villain he could find—who happened to be your uncle. They don't go by right and wrong in Eleven. They don't consider themselves human—Or no, I suppose they think they're the only real people, and they study the rest of you like something in a zoo when the Dright happens to feel interested."

Christopher could tell from Tacroy's voice that he hated the Eleven people very deeply. He well understood that. Tacroy was even worse off than the Goddess. "Who's the Dright?"

"King, priest, chief magician—" Tacroy shrugged. "No, he's not quite any of those, quite. He's called High Father of the Sept and he's thousands of years old. He's lived that long because he eats someone's soul whenever his power fails—but he's quite within his rights, doing that. All the Eleven people and their souls belong to him by Eleven law. *I* belong to him."

"What's the law about him fetching himself all Gabriel's lives?" Christopher asked. "That's what he's done, hasn't he?"

"I knew he had—as soon as Flavian said 'Series Eleven,'" Tacroy said. "I know he's always wanted to study someone with nine lives. They can't get them in Eleven, because there's only one world there, not a Series. The Dright keeps it down to one world so he won't have any rivals. And you know your nine lives came about—don't you?—because all the doubles you might have had in the other worlds in Twelve never got born for some reason."

"Yes, but what's Eleven law about pinching most of an enchanter?" Christopher insisted.

"I'm not sure," Tacroy confessed. "I'm not sure they *have* laws like we do. It's probably legal if the Dright can get away with it. They go by pride and appearance and what people *do* mostly."

Christopher at once resolved that the Dright should *not* get away with this if he could help it. "I suppose he just waited to see how many lives there were loose and then collected them," he said. "Tell me everything about Eleven that you can think of."

"Well," said Tacroy, "I haven't been there since I was born, but I know they control everything with magic. They have the weather controlled, so that they can live out in the open forest and control what trees grow and where. Food comes when they call and they don't use fire to cook it. They don't use fire at all. They think you're all savages for using it, and they're just as scornful about the kind of magic all the other worlds use. The only time they think any of you are any good is when one of you is absolutely loyal to a king or chief or someone. They admire people like that, particularly if they cheat and lie out of loyalty. . . ."

Tacroy talked for the next half hour. He talked as if it was a relief for him to tell it at last, but Christopher could see it was a strain too. Halfway through, when the lines on Tacroy's face made him look haggard, Christopher told him to wait and slipped out of the secrecy spell to the door. As he had expected, Miss Rosalie was standing outside looking more than usually fierce.

"Mordecai's worked himself to the bone for you, one way and another!" she hissed at him. "What are you *doing* to him in there?"

"Nothing, but he needs something to keep him going," Christopher said. "Could you—?"

"What do you take me for?" snapped Miss Rosalie. Erica rushed up with a tray almost at once. As well as tea, and two plates piled high with cakes, there was a tiny bottle of brandy nestling in the corner of the tray. When Christopher carried the tray back inside the spell, Tacroy looked at the brandy, grinned, and poured a good dollop of it into his cup of tea. It seemed to revive him as much as the cakes revived Christopher. While they polished off the trayful together, Tacroy thought of a whole new set of things to say.

One of the things he said was, "If you saw some Eleven people without being warned, you might take them for noble savages, but you'd be making a big mistake if you did. They're very, very civilized. As for being noble—" Tacroy paused with a cake halfway to his mouth.

"Eat your elevenses," said Christopher.

Tacroy gave a brief grin at the joke. "Your worlds know about them a bit," he said. "They're the people who gave rise to all the stories about Elves. If you think about them like that—cold, unearthly people who go by quite different rules—that will give you some idea. I don't understand them really, even though I was born one of them."

By this time Christopher knew that getting Gabriel back was going to be the toughest thing he had ever done in his lives. If it was not impossible. "Can you bear to come to Eleven with me?" he asked Tacroy. "To stop me making mistakes."

"As soon as they realize I've told you, they'll haul me back there anyway," Tacroy said. He was very pale again. "And you're in danger for knowing."

"In that case," said Christopher, "we'll tell everyone in the Castle, and get Yolande and Beryl to type a report to the Government about it. The Dright can't kill everyone."

Tacroy did not look any too sure about this, but he went back with Christopher to the operations room to explain. Naturally, it caused another outcry. "*Eleven!*" everyone exclaimed. "You can't!" People crowded in from the rest of the Castle to tell Christopher he was being a fool and that getting Gabriel back was quite impossible. Dr. Simonson left off making final adjustments to the Lobster Pot to march upstairs and forbid Christopher to go.

Christopher had expected this. "Fudge!" he said. "You can catch the Wraith without me now."

What he had not expected was that the Goddess would wait for the clamor to die down and then announce, "And I'm coming with you."

"Why?" said Christopher.

"Out of loyalty," the Goddess explained. "In the *Millie* books, Millie never let her chums down."

There was no accounting for the Goddess's obsession, Christopher thought. He suspected she was really afraid to stay where the Arm of Asheth could find her on her own, but he did not say so. And if she came along, she would almost double the amount of magic they had between them.

Then, on Tacroy's advice, he dressed for the journey. "Fur," Tacroy said. "The more you wear, the higher your rank." Christopher conjured the tigerskin rug from the Middle Saloon and the Goddess cut a hole in it for his head. Miss Rosalie found him a lordly belt with great brass studs in it to go round the middle, while the housekeeper produced a fox fur to wrap round his neck and a mink stole for the Goddess. "And it would help to have it hung all over with ornaments," said Tacroy.

"Not silver ones, remember," Christopher called as everyone rushed away to find things.

He ended up with three gold necklaces and a rope of pearls. Yolande's entire stock of earrings was pinned artfully here and there on the tigerskin, with Beryl's brooches in between. Round his head he had Miss Rosalie's gold evening belt with Erica's mother's mourning brooch pinned to the front of it over his forehead. He chinked in a stately way when he moved, rather like the Goddess in the Temple. The Goddess herself merely had a cluster of ostrich feathers at the front of her head and somebody's gold bracelets round the bottom of her Norfolk breeches. They wanted to make it clear that Christopher was the most important one. Tacroy stayed just as he was. "They know me," he said. "I have no rank in the Sept at all."

They shook hands with everyone in the operations room and turned to the Gate. It was now tuned to Eleven as far as Flavian and Tacroy knew, but Miss Rosalie warned Christopher that the spells round Eleven would probably take all their strength to break, and even that might not be enough. So Christopher paced, chinking in the lead, pushing with all his might, and the Goddess walked after with her ghostly pair of arms spread under the real pair. Behind them, Tacroy muttered an incantation.

And it was easy. Suspiciously easy, they all felt at once. There was an instant of formlessness, like one short breath of The Place Between. Then they were in a forest and a man who looked like Tacroy was staring at them.

The forest was smoothly beautiful, with a green grassy floor and no bushes of any kind. There were simply tall slender trees that all seemed to be the same kind. Among the smooth and slightly shiny trunks, the man was poised on one foot, something like a startled deer, looking over his naked brown shoulder at them. He was like Tacroy in that he had the same sort of coffee-colored skin and paler curly hair, but there the likeness ended. He was naked except for a short fur skirt, which made him look like a particularly stylish Greek statue, apart from his face. The expression on the man's face reminded Christopher of a camel. It was all haughty dislike and scorn.

"Call him. Remember what I told you," Tacroy whispered.

You had to be rude to Eleven people or they did not respect you. "Hey, you!" Christopher called out in the most lordly way he could. "You there! Take me to the Dright at once!"

The man behaved as if he had not heard. After staring a second longer, he took the step he had been in the middle of and walked away among the trees.

"Didn't he hear?" asked the Goddess.

"Probably," said Tacroy. "But he wanted to make it clear he was more important than you. He was obviously low in the Sept. Even the lowest ones like to think they're better than anyone else in the Related Worlds. Walk on, and we'll see if anything comes of it."

"Which way?" asked Christopher

"Any way," said Tacroy, with a slight smile. "They control distance and direction here."

They walked forward the way they were facing. The trees were all so much the same and so evenly spaced that, after about twenty steps, Christopher wondered if they were moving at all. He looked round and was relieved to see the square frame of the Gate among the tree-trunks about the right distance behind. He wondered if the whole of Eleven was covered with trees. If it was, it was hardly surprising that its people did not use fire. They would risk burning the whole forest down. He looked to the front again and found that, without any change in the landscape, they were somehow walking towards a fence.

The fence stretched for as far as they could see into the trees on either side. It was made of stakes of wood, nicely varnished and wickedly pointed on top, driven into the turf about a foot apart. The points at the top only came to Tacroy's waist. It did not look much of a barrier. But when they turned sideways to get between the stakes, the stakes seemed much too close together to let them through. When Tacroy took his jacket off to cover the points on top so that they could climb over, his jacket would not go anywhere that was not their side of the fence. As Tacroy picked his jacket up for the sixth time, the Goddess looked to the left and Christopher looked to the right, and they discovered that the fence was now all round them. Behind them, there was no sign of the Gate among the trees—nothing but a row of stakes blocking the way back.

"He did hear," said the Goddess.

"I think they were expecting us," said Christopher.

Tacroy spread his jacket on the grass and sat on it. "We'll just have to wait and see," he said glumly. "No, not you," he said to Christopher as Christopher started to sit down too. "The important people always stand here. I was told that the Dright hasn't sat down for years."

The Goddess sank down beside Tacroy and rubbed her bare toes in the grass. "Then I'm not going to be important," she said. "I'm sick of being important anyway. I say! Was *he* here before?"

A nervous-looking boy with a scruffy piece of sheepskin wound round his hips like a towel was standing on the other side of Tacroy. "I *was* here," he said shyly. "You just didn't seem to see me. I've been inside this fence all morning."

The fence surrounded a small grassy space no bigger than the tower room where Christopher had hidden the Goddess. Christopher could not understand how they could have missed seeing the boy, but given the queerness of everything perhaps they could. Judging by the boy's lank white body and straight fair hair, he was not one of the Eleven people.

"Did the Dright take you prisoner?" the Goddess asked.

The boy rubbed his funny little hooked nose in a puzzled way. "I'm not sure. I don't seem to remember coming here. What are you doing here?"

"Looking for someone," said Tacroy. "You don't happen to have seen a man—or several men, maybe—called Gabriel de Witt, do you?"

"Gabriel de Witt!" said the boy. "But that's *my* name!"

They stared at him. He was a timid, gangling boy with mild blue eyes. He was the kind of boy Christopher—and probably the Goddess, too—would naturally have started to boss about in the next minute or so. They would have bossed him quite kindly though, because it was easy to see that it would not take much to upset him and make him sick with nerves, rather like Fenning at school. In fact, Christopher thought, this boy reminded him of a tall, thin Fenning more than anything else. But now he knew, he saw that the boy's face had the same pointed outline as Gabriel's.

"How many lives have you?" he asked disbelievingly.

The boy seemed to look within himself. "That's odd," he said. "Usually I have nine. But I can only seem to find seven."

"Then we've got all of him," said the Goddess.

"With complications," said Tacroy. "Does the title Chrestomanci mean anything to you?" he asked the boy.

"Isn't he some boring old enchanter?" asked the boy. "I think his real name's Benjamin Allworthy, isn't it?"

Gabriel had gone right back to being a boy. Benjamin Allworthy had been the last Chrestomanci but one. "Don't you remember Mordecai Roberts or me?" Christopher asked. "I'm Christopher Chant."

"Pleased to meet you," Gabriel de Witt said, with a polite, shy smile. Christopher stared at him, wondering how Gabriel had come to grow up so forbidding.

"It's no use," Tacroy said. "Neither of us was born when he was that age."

"More people," said the Goddess.

There were four of them, three men and a woman, a little way off among the trees. The men all wore fur tunics that only covered one shoulder and the woman had a longer one that was more like a dress. The four of them stood half turned away from the fence, chatting together. Occasionally one of them looked scornfully over a bare shoulder at the fence.

Tacroy sank down into himself. His face was full of misery. "Take no notice, Christopher, definitely," he whispered. "Those are the ones I usually had to report to. I think they're important."

Christopher stood and stared haughtily over everyone's heads. His feet began to ache.

"They keep turning up like that," Gabriel said. "Rude beasts! I asked them for something to eat and they pretended not to hear."

Five minutes passed. Christopher's feet felt wider and hotter and more overused every second. He began to hate Eleven. There seemed to be no birds here, no animals, no wind. Just ranks of beautiful trees that all looked alike. The temperature never changed from just right. And the people were horrible.

"I hate this forest," Gabriel said. "It's so *samey*."

"That woman-one," said the Goddess, "reminds me of Mother Anstey. She's going to giggle about us behind her hand any moment, I know she is."

The woman put her hand up to her mouth and gave a scornful, tinkling laugh.

"What did I tell you?" the Goddess said. "And good riddance!"

The group of people was suddenly gone.

Christopher stood on one foot, then on the other. It made no difference to the ache. "You were lucky, Tacroy," he said. "If they hadn't dumped you in our world, you'd have had to *live* here." Tacroy looked up with a crinkled, unhappy smile and shrugged.

A minute or so after that, the man they had seen first was back, strolling among the trees a little way off. Tacroy nodded at Christopher. Christopher called out loudly and angrily, "Hey, you! I told you to take us to the Dright! What do you mean by disobeying me like this?"

The man gave no sign that he had heard. He came and leaned on the fence and stared at them as if they were something in a zoo. In order to put his elbows on top of the sharp stakes, he had somehow made a wooden armrest appear. Christopher could not fathom the peculiar magic he used to do that. But the Goddess always seemed a little quicker on the uptake than Christopher. She frowned at the armrest and seemed to get the hang of it. The block of wood hurtled away into the trees sending the man's arms down on to the spikes, quite hard. Gabriel laughed, an ordinary, unforbidding gurgle. The man sprang upright indignantly, went to rub his arm and then remembered that he should not show pain before inferiors. He swung round and went marching away.

Christopher was annoyed, both with the man and with the Goddess for being so much quicker than he was. The two things together made him so angry that he raised his arms and tried to hurl the man upwards, the way he had levitated all the things in Dr. Pawson's house. It was almost impossible to do. True, the man went up six feet or so. But he came down again gently and easily the next second, and looked jeeringly over his shoulder as he slipped earthwards.

This seemed to make the Goddess even angrier than Christopher. "*All* do it!" she said. "Come on, Gabriel!"

Gabriel shot her a mischievous grin and they all heaved together. Between them they only seemed to be able to raise the man three feet into the air, but they found they could keep him there. He pretended nothing was happening and kept walking as if he was still on the ground, which looked decidedly silly. "Take us to the Dright!" Christopher yelled.

"Now down," said the Goddess. And they bumped him to the ground again. He walked away, still pretending nothing was happening, which gave Gabriel a fit of the giggles.

"Did that do any good?" Christopher asked Tacroy.

"No way of knowing," said Tacroy. "They always like to keep you waiting until you're too tired and angry to think straight." He settled down in a miserable huddle, with his arms round his knees.

They waited. Christopher was wondering whether it was worth the enormous effort it would take to levitate himself in order to get the weight off his feet, when he noticed that the trees were sliding aside, to the right and left of the fence. Or perhaps the fenced enclosure was moving forward without any change to the smooth grass inside or out. It was hard to tell which. Either made Christopher feel queasy. He swallowed and kept his eyes haughtily on the trees ahead. But in less than a second those trees had wheeled away to nowhere, leaving a widening green glade. A person was in sight at the distant end of the glade, a tall, bulky person, who was sauntering slowly towards them.

Tacroy gulped a little. "That's the Dright."

Christopher narrowed his eyes to get his witch sight working and watched the trees sliding further and further apart. It reminded him of the way he had played at shunting the trees up the Trumpington Road. He could see the Dright doing it now. In order to work magic in this world, you seemed to have to work in a way that was tipped sideways from the way you did it on any other world, with a bend and a ripple to the magic, as if you were watching yourself work it in a wavy glass ball. Christopher was not sure he was going to be able to do it.

"I don't get the hang of this foreign magic," Gabriel sighed.

As the Dright sauntered slowly nearer, Christopher squeezed the corners of his mouth in, in order to stop a grin of delight at the thought that he was actually quicker at understanding it than Gabriel was. By now, the trees had sped away to leave a big circular meadow full of greenish sunlight. The Dright was near enough for them to see that he was dressed rather like Christopher in at least two lion skins hung all over with bright chinking ornaments. His curly hair and his crisp beard were white. There were rings on the toes of his smooth brown feet.

"He looks like one of those rather nasty gods—the ones that eat their own children," Gabriel said in a clear and carrying voice.

Christopher had to bite his tongue or he would have laughed. He was beginning to like this version of Gabriel. By the time he had the laugh under control, he was standing facing the Dright some yards outside the fence. He looked back incredulously. The Goddess and Gabriel were standing behind the fence, still prisoners, looking a little stupefied. Tacroy was still sitting on the ground, doing his best not to be noticed.

Christopher lifted his chin and looked up at the Dright's face. The smooth brown features did not have any expression on them at all. But Christopher stared, trying to see the person behind the blankness. What feelings the Dright had were so different from his own, and so lofty, that for a moment he felt like an insect. Then he remembered that glacier, years ago in Series Seven, which Tacroy had said reminded him of two people. Christopher knew that one of the people was the Dright. Like the glacier, the Dright was cold and high and too crusted with ancient knowledge for ordinary people to understand. On the other hand, the other person the glacier had reminded Tacroy of was Uncle Ralph. Christopher looked carefully for any signs that the Dright was like Uncle Ralph. There was not much of Uncle Ralph's shoddy look to the Dright's grand face, but his features did not seem sincere. Christopher could tell that the Dright would cheat and lie if it suited him, like Uncle Ralph, but he thought that the main way the two were alike was that they were both utterly selfish. Uncle Ralph used people. So did the Dright.

"What are you?" the Dright said. His voice was deep and scornful.

"I'm the Dright," said Christopher. "Dright for world Twelve-A. The word for it there is Chrestomanci, but it amounts to the same thing." His legs were shaking at the sheer cheek of this. But Tacroy *had* said that the one thing the Dright respected was pride. He held his knees stiff and made his face haughty.

There was no way of telling whether the Dright believed Christopher or not. He did not answer and his face was blank. But Christopher could feel the Dright putting out small tendrils of sideways, rippled Eleven magic, testing him, feeling at him to see what his powers were and what were his weak points. To himself, Christopher felt he was all weak points. But it seemed to him that, since the magic here was so peculiar, he had no idea what his own powers were, and that meant the Dright probably had no idea either.

The meadow behind the Dright became full of people. They had not been there at first, but they were there now, a pale-headed, brown-skinned crowd, wearing all possible degrees of fur, from tiny loin-wraps to long bearskin robes. It seemed that the Dright was saying, "Call yourself Dright if you like, but take a look at the power *I* have." Every one of the people was staring at Christopher with contempt and dislike. Christopher put his face into the same expression and stared back. And he realized that his face was rather used to looking this way. He had worn this expression most of the time he had lived at the Castle. It gave him an unpleasant shock to find that he had been quite as horrible as these Eleven people.

"Why are you here?" said the Dright.

Christopher pushed aside his shock. If I get out of here, I'll try to be nicer, he thought, and then concentrated carefully on what Tacroy had told him might be the best things to say. "I've come to fetch back something of my own," he said. "But first, let me introduce you to my colleague the Living Asheth. Goddess, this is the Dright of Eleven." The ostrich feather fluttered on the Goddess's head as she stepped up to the sharp stakes and bowed graciously. There was the slightest twitch to the Dright's features that suggested he was impressed that Christopher had actually brought the Living Asheth, but the Goddess was still behind the fence in spite of that. "And of course you know my man Mordecai Roberts already," Christopher said grandly, trying to slip that point past as a piece of pride.

The Dright said nothing about that either. But behind him, the people were now all sitting down. It was as if they had never been any other way. By this, the Dright seemed to be saying, "Very well. You are my equal, but I'd like to point out that my followers outnumber yours by several thousand to one—and mine are obedient to my slightest whim." Christopher was amazed that he had won even this much. He tried to squash down his amazement by watching the people. Some were talking and laughing together, though he could not hear them. Some of them were cooking food over little balls of bluish witchfire, which they seemed to use instead of fire. There were very few children. The two or three Christopher could see were sitting sedately doing nothing. I'd hate to grow up on Eleven! he thought. It must be a hundred times more boring than the Castle.

"What thing of your own have you allowed to stray into my world?" the Dright said at length.

They were getting down to business at last, even though the Dright was trying to pretend that Christopher had been careless. Christopher smiled and shook his head, to show he thought that was a joke of the

Dright's. "Two things," he said. "First, I have to thank you for retrieving the lives of Gabriel de Witt for me. It has saved me a lot of trouble. But you seem to have put the lives together in the wrong way and made Gabriel into a boy."

"I put them into the form which is easiest to deal with," said the Dright. Like everything he said, this was full of other meanings.

"If you mean that boys are easy to deal with," Christopher said, "I'm afraid this is not the case. Not boys from Twelve-A."

"And not girls either," the Goddess said loudly. "Not from anywhere."

"What is Gabriel de Witt to you?" the Dright asked.

"He is as father to son," said Christopher. Rather proud of the way he had carefully not said who was which, he glanced through the fence at Tacroy. Tacroy was still sitting wrapped into a ball, but Christopher thought his curly head nodded slightly.

"You have a claim to de Witt," the Dright said. "He can be yours, depending on what else you have to say." The fence round the other three slid and poured smoothly away sideways until it was out of sight, just as the trees had.

Gabriel looked puzzled. The Goddess stood where she was, clearly suspicious. Christopher looked warily at the Dright. This was too good to be true. "The other thing I have to say," he said, "is about this man of mine who is usually known as Mordecai Roberts. I believe he used to be yours, which means you still have his soul. Since he is my man now, perhaps you could let me have his soul?"

Tacroy's head came up and he stared at Christopher in horror and alarm. Christopher took no notice. He had known this would be pressing his luck, but he had always meant to try for Tacroy's soul. He planted his aching feet astride, folded his arms across his fur and jewelry, and tried to smile at the Dright as if what he was asking was the most ordinary and reasonable thing in any world.

The Dright gave no sign of anger or surprise. It was not simply self-control or pride. Christopher knew the Dright had been expecting him to ask and did not mind if Christopher knew. His mind began to work furiously. The Dright had made it easy for them to come to Eleven. He had pretended to accept Christopher as an equal, and he had told him he could have Gabriel's lives. That meant there was something the Dright expected to get out of this, something he must want very much indeed. But what?

"If my Septman claims to be your man, you should have his soul-name," the Dright observed. "Has he given you that name?"

"Yes," said Christopher. "It's Tacroy."

The faces of all the people sitting in the meadow behind the Dright turned his way. Every one of them was outraged. But the Dright only said, "And what has Tacroy done to make himself yours?"

"He lied for me for a whole day," Christopher said. "And he was *believed.*"

The first real sound in this place swept through the seated people. It was a long throaty murmur. Of awe? Approval? Whatever it was, Christopher knew he had said the right thing. As Tacroy had told him, these people naturally lied for their Dright. And to lie convincingly for a whole day showed the utmost loyalty.

"He could then be yours," the Dright admitted, "but on two conditions. I make two conditions because you have asked me for two things. The first one is of course that you show you know which the Septman's soul *is.*" He made a small gesture with one powerful brown hand.

A movement in the trees to one side caught Christopher's eye. He looked and found the slender trunks pouring silently aside there. When they stopped, there was a grassy lane leading to the square framework of the Gate. It was about fifty feet away. The Dright was showing him that he *could* get home, provided he did what was wanted.

"There's a huge block of their magic in the way," the Goddess whispered.

Gabriel craned over his shoulder to look longingly at the Gate. "Yes, it's just a carrot in front of the donkey," he agreed.

Tacroy simply groaned, with his head on his knees.

In front of Christopher, people were bringing things and laying them out in a wide crescent-shape. Each man or woman brought two or three, and stared derisively at Christopher as he or she thunked the things down in the growing line. He looked at the things. Some were almost black, some yellowish, and others white or shiny. He was not sure if they were statuettes or blobs of stuff that had melted and hardened into peculiar shapes. A few of them looked vaguely human. Most were no shape that meant anything. But the stuff they were made of meant a great deal. Christopher's stomach twisted and he had a hard job to go on staring haughtily as he realized that all the things were made of silver

When there were about a hundred of the objects sitting on the green turf, the Dright waved his hand again and the people stopped bringing them. "Pick out the soul of Tacroy from the souls of my people," he said.

Miserably, Christopher paced along the curving row with his hands clasped behind him to stop them trembling and Beryl's ornaments chinking. He felt like a General reviewing an army of metal goblins. He paced the entire line, from left to right, and none of the objects meant anything to him. Use witch sight, he told himself, as he wheeled on the right wing and started back again. It might just work on the silver statues provided he did not touch them.

He forced himself to look in that special way at the statues. It was a real effort to do it through the wavy sideways magic of Eleven. And, as he had feared, the things looked just the same, just as grotesque, just as meaningless. His witch sight was working, he knew. He could tell that a number of the people sitting in the meadow were not really there. They were in other parts of the forest busy with other schemes of the Dright's and projecting their images here in obedience to the Dright's command. But his witch sight would not work on silver.

So how else could he tell? He paced along the line, thinking. The people watched him jeeringly and the Dright's head turned majestically to follow him as he passed. They were all so unpleasant, he thought, that it was no wonder their souls were like little silver monsters. Tacroy was the only nice one—Ah! *There* was Tacroy's soul! It was some way round to the left. It looked no more human than any of the others, but it looked *nice,* fifty times nicer than the rest.

Christopher tried to go on pacing towards it as if he had not seen it, wondering what would happen when he picked it up and lost every scrap of his magic. He would have to rely on the Goddess. He hoped she realized.

His face must have changed. The Dright knew he had found the right soul and instantly began to cheat as Christopher had known he would. The line of twisty objects was suddenly a good mile long, with Tacroy's soul away in the far distance. And all of them were changing shape, melting into new queer blobs and fresh formless forms.

Then, with a sort of wavy jolt, everything went back to the way it was at first. Thank goodness! Christopher thought. The Goddess! He kept his eye on the soul and it was quite near. He dived forward and picked it up. As soon as he touched it, he was weak and heavy and tired. He felt like crying, but he stood up holding the soul. Sure enough, the Goddess was staring at the Dright with her arms spread. Christopher was surprised to find that, even without his magic, he could see the second pair of ghostly arms spread out underneath.

"My priestesses taught me that it was low to cheat," she said. "I'd have thought you were too proud to stoop to it."

The Dright looked down his nose at her. "I named no rules," he said. Being without magic was a little like another kind of witch sight, Christopher thought. The Dright looked smaller to him now and not nearly so magnificent. There were clear signs of the shoddiness that he had seen in Uncle Ralph. Christopher was still scared stiff, but he felt much better about things now he had seen that.

While the Goddess and the Dright stared at one another, he lumbered weakly over to Tacroy. "Here you are," he said, thrusting the strange statue at him. Tacroy scrambled on to one knee, looking as if he could not believe it. His hands shook as they closed round the soul. As soon as he had hold of it, the thing melted into his hands. The fingernails and the veins turned silvery. An instant later, Tacroy's face flushed silvery too. Then the flush faded and Tacroy looked much as usual, except that there was a glow about him which made him much more like the Tacroy Christopher knew from The Place Between.

"Now I really am your man!" Tacroy said. He was laughing in a way that was rather like sobbing. "You can see I couldn't ask Rosalie—Watch the Dright!"

Christopher spun round and found the Goddess on her knees, looking bewildered. It was not surprising. The Dright had thousands of years of experience. "Leave her alone!" he said.

The Dright looked at him and for a moment Christopher felt the strange distorted magic trying to force him to his knees too. Then it stopped. The Dright still had not got what he wanted from Christopher. "We now come to my second condition," the Dright said calmly. "I am moderate. You came here demanding seven lives and a soul. I give you them. All I ask in exchange is one life."

Gabriel laughed nervously. "I *have* got a few to spare," he said. "If it means getting out of here—"

This was what the Dright wanted, Christopher realized. He had been aiming for the life of a nine-lifed enchanter, freely handed over, all along. If Christopher had not dared to ask for Tacroy's soul, he would have asked for a life for setting Gabriel free. For just a second, Christopher thought they might as well let him have one of Gabriel's lives. He had seven, after all, and another lying on the floor back in the Castle. Then he saw it would be the most dangerous thing he could do. It would give the Dright a hold over Gabriel—the same hold he had had over Tacroy—for as long as his other lives lasted. The Dright was aiming to control the Chrestomanci, just like Uncle Ralph was aiming to control Christopher. They did not dare give him one of Gabriel's lives.

"All right," Christopher said. For the first time, he was truly grateful to Gabriel that his ninth life was safely locked in the Castle safe. "As you see, I've still got two lives left. You can have *one* of them," he said, naming conditions very carefully, because he knew the Dright would cheat if he could, "because if you take more than one it would kill me and give my world the right to punish yours. Once you have that life in your hands, your conditions are fulfilled and you must let all four of us go through the Gate back to Twelve-A."

"Agreed," said the Dright. He was keeping his face as expressionless as always, but underneath Christopher could tell he was hugging himself and chuckling. He stepped solemnly up to Christopher. Christopher braced himself and hoped it would not hurt much. In fact, it hurt so little that he was almost taken by surprise. The Dright stepped back a mere instant later with a floppy transparent shape dangling in his hands. The shape was wearing a ghostly tiger-skin and it had a dim gold band fluttering from its transparent head.

Christopher conjured fire to that shape, hard and sideways and wavily, with all the power he had. Fire was the one thing the Dright was not used to. He knew it was the one thing that might cancel out those thousand years of experience. To his relief, the Goddess had made exactly the same calculations. He had a glimpse of her, with all four arms spread, conjuring fire down as he called it up.

His seventh life leapt into flame all over at once. The Dright hung on to its shoulders as it blazed, grimly trying to quench it, but Christopher had been right. Fire magic was the Dright's weak point. His attempt to reverse the spell was slow and hesitating. But he kept trying, and hung on to the life by its shoulders, until he had to let go or lose both hands. By that time the front of his lion-skin was on fire too. Christopher glimpsed him trying to beat it out and coughing in the smoke, as he collapsed himself into a writhing heap on the turf. It was worse than being crisped by the dragon. He was in agony. He had not realized it would hurt at all, let alone this much.

Tacroy scooped him up, threw him over one shoulder in a fireman's hoist, and raced for the Gate. Every step bumped Christopher and every bump was torment. But his watering eyes caught sight of the Goddess seizing Gabriel's arm in at least three hands and dragging him to the Gate in a mixture of brute force and magic. They all reached it together and plunged through. Christopher kept just enough sense to cancel the spells and slam the Gate shut behind them.

CHAPTER 21

The pain stopped the instant the Gate shut. Tacroy lowered Christopher gently to the floor, looked at him to see if he was all right, and made for Miss Rosalie.

"Gosh—look!" said the Goddess, pointing at Gabriel.

Tacroy did not look. He was too busy hugging Miss Rosalie. Christopher sat on the floor and stared with the rest of the people in the operations room. As the Dright's magic left him, Gabriel was growing up in bursts. First he was a young man with a floral silk tie and a keen, wistful look; then he was an older keener man in a dingy suit. After that he was middle-aged and bleached and somehow hopeless and desperate, as if everything he hoped for was gone. The next instant, this man had pulled himself together into a brisk, silvery gentleman; and then the same gentleman, older and grimmer. Christopher stared, awed and rather touched. He realized that Gabriel had hated being the Chrestomanci, and they were seeing the stages by which he had come to terms with it. I'm glad I'm going to find it easier than *that!* Christopher thought, as Gabriel finally became the grim old man that Christopher knew. At which point, Gabriel tottered to Tacroy's trance-couch and folded down onto it.

Beryl and Yolande rushed forward with cups of tea. Gabriel drank Beryl's (or Yolande's) at a gulp. Then he took Yolande's (or Beryl's) and sipped it slowly with his eyes almost shut. "My heartiest thanks, Christopher," he said. "I hope the pain has gone."

"Yes, thanks," Christopher said, taking the cup of tea Erica handed him.

Gabriel glanced to where Tacroy was still wrapped round Miss Rosalie. "By the look of him, Mordecai has even more to thank you for than I have."

"Don't let him get sent to prison," Christopher said. And there was the bootboy to ask about too, he thought distractedly.

"I'll do what I can," Gabriel promised. "Now that I know the circumstances. That fearsome Dright has much to answer for—though I *may* be right in supposing that Mordecai went on working with you for your equally fearsome uncle because he knew that any other spirit traveler your uncle chose would have turned you into a hardened criminal before long. Would you agree?"

"Well," said Christopher, trying to be honest. "I think some of it was because we were both so keen on cricket."

"Really?" Gabriel said politely. He turned to the Goddess. She had found Proudfoot and was holding her lovingly in both hands. Gabriel looked from the kitten to the Goddess's bare feet. "Young lady," he said. "You *are* a young lady, are you not? Pray show me the sole of your left foot."

A little defiantly, the Goddess turned round and tipped her foot up. Gabriel looked at the purple-blue mark. He looked at Christopher.

"Yes, I am really Asheth," said the Goddess, "but you're not to look at Christopher like that! I came here of my own accord. I did it quite capably."

Gabriel's eyes narrowed. "By using the Goddess Asheth as your second life?" The Goddess looked down from his eyes and nodded. Gabriel put down his empty cup and took the full one Flavian handed him. "My dear girl," he said as he sipped it, "what a very foolish thing to have done! You are clearly a powerful enchantress in your own right. You had no need to use Asheth. You have simply given her a hold over you. The Arm of Asheth is going to haunt you for the rest of your life."

"But I thought that the magic I can do *came* from Asheth!" the Goddess protested.

"Oh no," said Gabriel. "Asheth has powers, but she never shares them. The ones you have are yours."

The Goddess's mouth dropped open. She looked as if she might cry. Flavian said apologetically, "Gabriel, I'm afraid the Arm of Asheth is all round—"

There was a violent CRASH from below as the Lobster Pot came down.

Everyone raced for the stairs, except for Gabriel. He put his cup down slowly, obviously wondering what was happening. Christopher dashed to the stairs and then, for speed, did what he had always longed to do and slid down the rosy curve of marble banister. The Goddess followed him. When they tumbled off at the bottom, Gabriel was already there, standing by the black rope gazing down at his limp transparent life. But no one else had eyes for that.

Uncle Ralph had come through the pentacle in a suit of armor, carrying a heavy mace. Christopher had thought he might. If he had brought any anti-cat spells, however, these obviously did not work on Temple cats. The Lobster Pot had come down precisely over the pentacle, trapping Throgmorten in with Uncle Ralph, and Throgmorten was doing his best to get Uncle Ralph. Through the wreathing smoke of dragons' blood, Uncle Ralph could be seen tramping slowly round and round inside the cage, smashing cat-saucers under his metal feet and taking violent swings at Throgmorten with his mace. Throgmorten could move faster than Uncle Ralph, or his mace, and he could climb the walls of the Lobster Pot, but he could not get at Uncle Ralph through his armor. All he could do was make shrill metal scratches on it. It was a standoff.

Christopher looked round to find Gabriel beside him. Gabriel's face had a most unusual big wicked smile on it—no, not unusual, Christopher thought: it was the same smile Gabriel had worn when they levitated the man in Eleven.

"Shall we give the cat his chance?" Gabriel said. "For one minute?"

Christopher nodded.

Uncle Ralph's armor vanished, leaving him in his foxy tweed suit. Throgmorten instantly became a seven-legged, three-headed, razor-clawed, flying, spitting fury. He was up and down and all over Uncle Ralph several times in the first second. So much blood got shed that Christopher was quite sorry for Uncle Ralph after fifteen such seconds. After thirty seconds, he was quite glad when Throgmorten vanished with a snarl and a jerk.

Throgmorten reappeared kicking and struggling over the Goddess's arm. "*No,* Throgmorten," she said. "I told you before you're not to go for people's eyes. That's not nice."

"Nice or not," Gabriel said regretfully, "I was enjoying it." He was busy winding something unseen into a careful skein over one hand. "Simonson," he called. "Simonson, are you in charge of the cage? I got his magic off him while his mind was elsewhere. You can move the cage now and shut him up until the police can come for him."

This produced another standoff. Throgmorten leaped for the space under the cage as soon as it started to rise. Uncle Ralph screamed. In the end, one of the stable lads had to climb up and unhook the cage from the chandelier chain. Then the cage was shoved across the floor with Uncle Ralph stumbling inside it and Throgmorten prowling after, uttering low throbbing sounds.

As soon as the cage was off the pentacle, a silver pillar rose out of the blood-spattered floor. The pillar looked human, but it was impossibly tall for a human, a good foot taller than Gabriel. Up and up it rose, a woman robed in silver, wearing a silver mask and carrying a silver spear.

The Goddess wailed with terror and tried to hide behind Christopher. "Silver," he warned her. "I can't help against silver." His teeth chattered. For the first time, he realized how naked and soft it felt to have only one life.

The Goddess dashed behind Gabriel and clutched his black frock coat. "It's Asheth! Save me!"

"Madam," Gabriel said politely to the apparition, "to what do we owe the honor of this visitation?"

The apparition looked keenly through the slits in its mask, first at Gabriel and the Goddess crouching behind him, then at Christopher, then at the Lobster Pot and the general chaos in the hall. "I had hoped to find this a more respectable establishment," she said. The voice was deep and melodious. She pushed up her mask to the top of her head, revealing a severe narrow old face. It was the kind of face that at once made Christopher feel very silly to be dressed in a tiger rug and earrings.

"Mother Proudfoot!" exclaimed the Goddess.

"I've been trying to get through this pentacle ever since I traced you, child," Mother Proudfoot said testily. "I wish you had talked to me before you bolted like that. You surely knew I would have stretched the rules for you if I could." She turned commandingly to Gabriel. "You seem respectable enough. You're that Twelve-A enchanter de Witt, aren't you?"

"At your service, madam," said Gabriel. "Do forgive our present disorder. There have been problems. We are usually a highly respectable body of people."

"That was what I thought," Mother Proudfoot said. "Would you be able to take charge of this Asheth Daughter for me? It would suit me ideally if you could, since I have to report her dead."

"In what way—Take charge?" Gabriel asked cautiously.

"See her educated at a good school and so forth—consider becoming her legal guardian," said Mother Proudfoot. She stepped majestically down from what seemed to be her pedestal. Now she was about the same height as Gabriel. They were quite alike in a gaunt, stern way. "This one was always my favorite Asheth," she explained. "I usually try to spare their lives anyway when they get too old, but most of them are such stupid little lumps that I don't bother to do much more. But as soon as I knew this one was different, I started saving from the Temple funds. I think I have enough to pay her way."

She swept her trailing skirt aside. The pedestal turned out to be a small strong chest. Mother Proudfoot threw back the lid of it with a flourish. Inside, it seemed to be full of blurred glassy quartz in little pieces, like road gravel. But Gabriel's face was awestruck. Christopher caught sight of Tacroy and Flavian mouthing a word at one another with their eyes popping. The word seemed to be "Diamonds!"

"The diamonds are uncut, I'm afraid," said Mother Proudfoot. "Do you think there will be enough of them?"

"I think less than half that number would be more than adequate," Gabriel said.

"But I had in mind a Swiss finishing school too," Mother Proudfoot said sharply. "I've studied this world and I want no skimping. Will you do this for me? Naturally I shall make sure that followers of Asheth will do any favor you care to ask them in return."

Gabriel looked from Mother Proudfoot to the Goddess. He hesitated. He looked at Christopher. "Very well," he said at last.

"Gosh, you *darling*!" said the Goddess. She scrambled to the front of Gabriel and hugged him. Then she hurled herself on Mother Proudfoot and hugged her mightily too. "I love you, Mother Proudfoot," she said, all mixed in silver drapery.

Mother Proudfoot sniffed a little as she hugged the Goddess in return. But she pulled herself together and looked sternly at Gabriel over the Goddess's head. "There is one tiresome detail," she said. "Asheth truly does require a life, you know, one for each Living Asheth." Christopher sighed. Everyone in all the Anywheres seemed to want him to give them lives. Now he would be down to the one in the Castle safe.

Gabriel drew himself up, looking his most forbidding.

"Asheth isn't very discriminating," Mother Proudfoot said, before he could speak. "I usually strip a life off one of the Temple cats." She pointed with her silver spear to where Throgmorten was stalking round the Lobster Pot making noises like a kettle boiling. "That old ginger's still got three lives or so left. I'll take one of his."

The kettle noises stopped. Throgmorten showed what he thought of this proposal by becoming a ginger streak racing upstairs.

"No matter," Gabriel said. "Now I think of it, I have a spare life, as it happens." He stepped over to the black ropes and picked his limp transparent likeness out from among the library chairs. Courteously, he draped it over the end of Mother Proudfoot's spear. "There. Will this one serve?"

"Admirably," said Mother Proudfoot. "Thank you." She gave the Goddess a kiss and descended majestically into the ground beside the chest of diamonds.

The Goddess shut the chest and sat on it. "School!" she said, smiling blissfully. "Rice pudding, prefects, dormitories, midnight feasts, playing the game—" She stopped without changing the smile, although it was not a smile any more. "Honor," she said. "Owning up. Sir de Witt, I think I'd better stay in the Castle because of all the trouble I caused Christopher. He—er—he's lonely, you know."

"I would be a fool not to have realized that," Gabriel said. "I am in the middle of arranging with the Ministry to bring a number of young enchanters here to be trained. At the moment, you know, I am only able to employ them as domestics—like young Jason the bootboy over there—but this will shortly change. There is no reason why you should not go to school—"

"But there *is*!" said the Goddess. Her face was very red and there were tears in her eyes. "I have to own up, like they do in the books. I don't *deserve* to go to school! I'm very wicked. I didn't use Asheth as my second life in order to come here. I used one of Christopher's. I didn't dare use Asheth in case she stopped me, so I took one of Christopher's lives when he was stuck in the wall and used that instead." Tears ran down her face.

"Where is it?" Christopher asked, very much astonished.

"Still in the wall," the Goddess sobbed. "I pushed it right in so that no one will find it, but I've felt bad ever since. I've tried to help and atone for it, but I haven't done much and I think I ought to be punished."

"There is absolutely no need," said Gabriel. "Now we know where the life is, we can send Mordecai Roberts to fetch it. Stop crying, young lady. You will have to go to school because I should be misusing your chest of diamonds if you do not. Regard that as your punishment. You may come and live in the Castle with the rest of the young enchanters during the holidays."

The Goddess's blissful smile came back and diverted the tears on her face round her ears and into her hair. "Hols," she corrected Gabriel. "The books always call them the hols."

That is really all, except for a letter that arrived for Christopher from Japan soon after New Year.

Darling Christopher,

Why did you not tell me that your dear Papa was settled here in Japan? It is such an elegant country, once one is used to the customs, and your Papa and I are both very happy here. Your Papa's horoscopes have had the honor to interest some people who have the ear of the Emperor. We are already moving in the highest circles and hope to move higher still before long. Your dear Papa sends love and best wishes for your future as the next Chrestomanci. My love as well.

Mama

DIANA WYNNE JONES was raised in the village of Thaxted, in Essex, England. She has been a compulsive storyteller for as long as she can remember, enjoying most ardently those tales dealing with witches, hobgoblins, and the like. She is the author of such outstanding books for young readers as *Stopping for a Spell; Aunt Maria; Castle in the Air* (an ALA Notable Children's Book and Best Book for Young Adults); *The Ogre Downstairs; Dogsbody; Howl's Moving Castle* (an ALA Notable Children's Book and Best Book for Young Adults, and winner of the *Boston Globe/Horn Book* Award); and *Archer's Goon* (an ALA Notable Children's Book and Best Book for Young Adults). She is also the editor of *Hidden Turnings: A Collection of Stories Through Time and Space.* Ms. Jones lives in Bristol, England, with her husband, a professor of English at Bristol University. They have three sons and two granddaughters.